THE TIN DRUM

Günter Grass, born in Danzig in 1927, is Germany's most celebrated contemporary writer. He is a creative artist of remarkable versatility: novelist, poet, playwright, essayist, graphic artist. Among his many works are *The Tin Drum, Cat and Mouse, Dog Years, The Flounder*, and *The Rat, From the Diary of a Snail* and *The Call of the Toad*.

Günter Grass

THE TIN DRUM

TRANSLATED FROM THE GERMAN BY
Ralph Manheim

VINTAGE

Published by Vintage 1998

6 8 10 9 7

Originally published in German
under the title *Die Blechtrommel*
First published in Great Britain by
Martin Secker & Warburg Limited 1962

Vintage
Random House, 20 Vauxhall Bridge Road,
London SW1V 2SA

Random House Australia (Pty) Limited
20 Alfred Street, Milsons Point, Sydney,
New South Wales 2061, Australia

Random House New Zealand Limited
18 Poland Road, Glenfield,
Auckland 10, New Zealand

Random House (Pty) Limited
Endulini, 5a Jubilee Road, Parktown 2193, South Africa

The Random House Group Limited Reg. No. 954009
www.randomhouse.co.uk

A CIP catalogue record for this book
is available from the British Library

ISBN 0 7493 9475 7

Papers used by Random House are natural, recyclable
products made from wood grown in sustainable forests.
The manu-facturing processes conform to the environ-
mental regulations of the country of origin.

Printed and bound in Great Britain by
Cox & Wyman Ltd, Reading, Berkshire

For Anna Grass

Contents

BOOK ONE

The Wide Skirt

Granted: I am an inmate of a mental hospital; my keeper is watching me, he never lets me out of his sight; there's a peephole in the door, and my keeper's eye is the shade of brown that can never see through a blue-eyed type like me.

So you see, my keeper can't be an enemy. I've come to be very fond of him; when he stops looking at me from behind the door and comes into the room, I tell him incidents from my life, so he can get to know me in spite of the peephole between us. He seems to treasure my stories, because every time I tell him some fairy tale, he shows his gratitude by bringing out his latest knot construction. I wouldn't swear that he's an artist. But I am certain that an exhibition of his creations would be well received by the press and attract a few purchasers. He picks up common pieces of string in the patients' rooms after visiting hours, disentangles them, and works them up into elaborate contorted spooks; then he dips them in plaster, lets them harden, and mounts them on knitting needles that he fastens to little wooden pedestals.

He often plays with the idea of coloring his works. I advise him against it, taking my white enamel bed as an example and bidding him try to imagine how this most perfect of all beds would look if painted in many colors. He raises his hands in horror, tries to give his rather expressionless face an expression of extreme disgust, and abandons his polychrome projects.

So you see, my white-enameled, metal hospital bed has become a norm and standard. To me it is still more: my bed is a goal attained at last, it is my consolation and might become my faith if the management allowed me to make a few changes: I should like, for instance, to have the bars built up higher, to prevent anyone from coming too close to me.

Once a week a visiting day breaks in on the stillness that I plait between the white metal bars. This is the time for the people who want to save me, whom it amuses to love me, who try to esteem and respect themselves, to get to know themselves, through me. How blind, how nervous and ill-bred they are! They scratch the white enamel of my bedstead with their fingernail scissors, they scribble obscene little men on it with their ballpoint pens and blue pencils. No sooner has my lawyer blasted the room with his hello than he slaps his nylon hat down over the lower left-hand bedpost – an act of violence that shatters my peace of mind for the duration of his visit, and lawyers find a good deal to talk about.

After my visitors have deposited their gifts beneath the water color of the anemones, on the little white table covered with oil-cloth, after they have submitted their current projects for my salvation, and convinced me, whom they are working indefatig-ably to save, of the high quality of their charity, they recover their relish in their own existence, and leave me. Then my keeper comes in to air the room and collect the strings from the gift packages. Often after airing he finds time to sit by my bed for a while, disentangling his strings, and spreading silence until I call the silence Bruno and Bruno silence.

Bruno Münsterberg – this time I mean my keeper, I've stopped playing with words – has bought me five hundred sheets of writing paper.

Should this supply prove insufficient, Bruno, who is unmarried and childless and hails from the Sauerland, will go to the little stationery store that also sells toys, and get me some more of the unlined space I need for the recording of my memories – I only hope they are accurate. I could never have asked such a service of my visitors, the lawyer for instance, or Klepp. The solicitous affection prescribed in my case would surely have deterred my friends from bringing me anything so dangerous as blank paper and making it available to this mind of mine which persists in excreting syllables.

'Oh, Bruno,' I said, 'would you buy me a ream of virgin paper?' And Bruno, looking up at the ceiling and pointing his index finger in the same direction by way of inviting a comparison, replied: 'You mean white paper, Herr Oskar?'

I stuck to 'virgin' and asked Bruno to say just that in the store. When he came back late in the afternoon with the package, he gave the impression of a Bruno shaken by thought. Several times he looked fixedly up at the ceiling from which he derived all his inspiration. And a little later he spoke: 'That was the right word you told me. I asked for virgin paper and the salesgirl blushed like mad before getting it.'

Fearing an interminable conversation about salesgirls in stationery stores, I regretted having spoken of virgin paper and said nothing, waiting for Bruno to leave the room. Only then did I open the package with the five hundred sheets of writing paper.

For a time I weighed the hard, flexible ream in my hands; then I counted out ten sheets and stowed the rest in my bedside table. I found my fountain pen in the drawer beside the photograph album: it's full, ink is no problem, how shall I begin?

You can begin a story in the middle and create confusion by striking out boldly, backward and forward. You can be modern, put aside all mention of time and distance and, when the whole thing is done, proclaim, or let someone else proclaim, that you have finally, at the last moment, solved the space-time problem. Or you can declare at the very start that it's impossible to write a novel nowadays, but then, behind your own back so to speak, give birth to a whopper, a novel to end all novels. I have also been told that it makes a good impression, an impression of modesty so to speak, if you begin by saying that a novel can't have a hero any more because there are no more individualists, because individuality is a thing of the past, because man – each man and all men together – is alone in his loneliness and no one is entitled to individual loneliness, and all men lumped together make up a 'lonely mass' without names and without heroes. All this may be true. But as far as I and Bruno my keeper are concerned, I beg leave to say that we are both heroes, very different heroes, he on his side of the peephole, and I on my side;

and even when he opens the door, the two of us, with all our friendship and loneliness, are still far from being a nameless, heroless mass.

I shall begin far away from me; for no one ought to tell the story of his life who hasn't the patience to say a word or two about at least half of his grandparents before plunging into his own existence. And so to you personally, dear reader, who are no doubt leading a muddled kind of life outside this institution, to you my friends and weekly visitors who suspect nothing of my paper supply, I introduce Oskar's maternal grandmother.

Late one October afternoon my grandmother Anna Bronski was sitting in her skirts at the edge of a potato field. In the morning you might have seen how expert my grandmother was at making the limp potato plants into neat piles; at noon she had eaten a chunk of bread smeared with lard and syrup; then she had dug over the field a last time, and now she sat in her skirts between two nearly full baskets. The soles of her boots rose up at right angles to the ground, converging slightly at the toes, and in front of them smoldered a fire of potato plants, flaring up asthmatically from time to time, sending a queasy film of smoke out over the scarcely inclined crust of the earth. The year was 1899; she was sitting in the heart of Kashubia, not far from Bissau but still closer to the brickworks between Ramkau and Viereck, in front of her the Brenntau highway at a point between Dirschau and Karthaus, behind her the black forest of Goldkrug; there she sat, pushing potatoes about beneath the hot ashes with the charred tip of a hazel branch.

If I have made a special point of my grandmother's skirt, leaving no doubt, I hope, that she was sitting in her skirts; if indeed I have gone so far as to call the whole chapter 'The Wide Skirt,' it is because I know how much I owe to this article of apparel. My grandmother had on not just one skirt, but four, one over the other. It should not be supposed that she wore one skirt and three petticoats; no, she wore four skirts; one supported the next, and she wore the lot of them in accordance with a definite system, that is, the order of the skirts was changed from day to day. The one that was on top yesterday was today in second place; the second became the third. The one that was third yesterday was next to her skin today. The one that was closest to her yesterday

4

clearly disclosed its pattern today, or rather its lack of pattern: all my grandmother Anna Bronski's skirts favored the same potato color. It must have been becoming to her.

Aside from the color, my grandmother's skirts were distinguished by a lavish expanse of material. They puffed and billowed when the wind came, crackled as it passed, and sagged when it was gone, and all four of them flew out ahead of her when she had the wind in her stern. When she sat down, she gathered her skirts about her.

In addition to the four skirts, billowing, sagging, hanging down in folds, or standing stiff and empty beside her bed, my grandmother possessed a fifth. It differed in no way from the other four potato-coloured garments. And actually the fifth skirt was not always fifth. Like its brothers – for skirts are masculine by nature – it was subject to change, it was worn like the other four, and like them when its time had come, took its turn in the wash trough every fifth Friday, then Saturday on the line by the kitchen window, and when dry on the ironing board.

When, after one of these Saturdays spent in housecleaning, baking, washing and ironing, after milking and feeding the cow, my grandmother immersed herself from top to toe in the tub, when after leaving a little of herself in the soapsuds and letting the water in the tub sink back to its normal level, she sat down on the edge of the bed swathed in a great flowery towel, the four worn skirts and the freshly washed skirt lay spread out before her on the floor. She pondered, propping the lower lid of her right eye with her right index finger, and since she consulted no one, not even her brother Vincent, she quickly made up her mind. She stood up and with her bare toes pushed aside the skirt whose potato color had lost the most bloom. The freshly laundered one took its place.

On Sunday morning she went to church in Ramkau and inaugurated the new order of skirts in honor of Jesus, about whom she had very set ideas. Where did my grandmother wear the laundered skirt? She was not only a cleanly woman, but also a rather vain one; she wore the best piece where it could be seen in the sunlight when the weather was good.

But now it was a Monday afternoon and my grandmother was sitting by the potato fire. Today her Sunday skirt was one layer closer to her person, while the one that had basked in the warmth of her skin on Sunday swathed her hips in Monday gloom. Whistling with no particular tune in mind, she coaxed the first cooked potato out of the ashes with her hazel branch and pushed it away from the smoldering mound to cool in the breeze. Then she spitted the charred and crusty tuber on a pointed stick and held it close to her mouth; she had stopped whistling and instead pursed her cracked, wind-parched lips to blow the earth and ashes off the potato skin.

In blowing, my grandmother closed her eyes. When she thought she had blown enough, she opened first one eye, then the other, bit into the potato with her widely spaced but otherwise perfect front teeth, removed half the potato, cradled the other half, mealy steaming, and still too hot to chew, in her open mouth, and, sniffing at the smoke and the October air, gazed wide-eyed across the field toward the nearby horizon, sectioned by telegraph poles and the upper third of the brickworks chimney.

Something was moving between the telegraph poles. My grandmother closed her mouth. Something was jumping about. Three men were darting between the poles, three men made for the chimney, then round in front, then one doubled back. Short and wide he seemed, he took a fresh start and made it across the brickyard, the other two, sort of long and thin, just behind him. They were out of the brickyard, back between the telegraph poles, but Short and Wide twisted and turned and seemed to be in more of a hurry than Long and Thin, who had to double back to the chimney, because he was already rolling over it when they, two hands' breadths away, were still taking a start, and suddenly they were gone as though they had given up, and the little one disappeared too, behind the horizon, in the middle of his jump from the chimney.

Out of sight they remained, it was intermission, they were changing their costumes, or making bricks and getting paid for it.

Taking advantage of the intermission, my grandmother tried to spit another potato, but missed it. Because the one who seemed to be short and wide, who hadn't changed his clothes after all, climbed up over the horizon as if it were a fence and he had left his pursuers behind it, in among the bricks or on the road to Brenntau. But he was still in a hurry; trying to go faster than the telegraph poles, he took long slow leaps across the field; the mud flew from his boots as he leapt over the soggy ground, but leap as he might, he seemed to be crawling. Sometimes he seemed to stick in the ground and then to stick in mid-air, short and wide, time enough to wipe his face before his foot came down again in the freshly plowed field, which bordered the five acres of potatoes and narrowed into a sunken lane.

He made it to the lane; short and wide, he had barely disappeared into the lane, when the two others, long and thin, who had probably been searching the brickyard in the meantime, climbed over the horizon and came plodding through the mud, so long and thin, but not really skinny, that my grandmother missed her potato again; because it's not every day that you see this kind of thing, three full-grown men, though they hadn't grown in exactly the same directions, hopping around telegraph poles, nearly breaking the chimney off the brickworks, and then at intervals, first short and wide, then long and thin, but all with the same difficulty, picking up more and more mud on the soles of their boots, leaping through the field that Vincent had plowed two days before, and disappearing down the sunken lane.

Then all three of them were gone and my grandmother ventured to spit another potato, which by this time was almost cold. She hastily blew the earth and ashes off the skin, popped the whole potato straight into her mouth. They must be from the brickworks, she thought if she thought anything, and she was still chewing with a circular motion when one of them jumped out of the lane, wild eyes over a black mustache, reached the fire in two jumps, stood before, behind, and beside the fire all at once, cursing, scared, not knowing which way to go, unable to turn back, for behind him Long and Thin were running down the lane. He hit his knees, the eyes in his head were like to pop out, and sweat poured from his forehead. Panting, his whole face a tremble, he ventured to crawl closer, toward the soles of my grandmother's boots, peering up at her like a squat little animal. Heaving a great sigh, which made her stop chewing on her potato, my grandmother let her feet tilt over, stopped thinking about bricks and brickmakers, and lifted high her skirt, no, all four skirts, high enough so that Short and Wide, who was not from the brickworks, could crawl underneath. Gone was his black mustache; he didn't look like an animal any more, he was neither from Ramkau nor from Viereck, at any rate he had vanished with his fright, he had ceased to be wide or short but he took up room just the same, he forgot to pant or tremble and he had stopped hitting his knees; all was as still as on the first day of Creation or the last; a bit of wind hummed in the potato fire, the telegraph poles counted themselves in silence, the chimney of the brickworks stood at attention, and my grandmother smoothed down her uppermost skirt neatly and sensibly over the second one; she scarcely felt him under her fourth skirt, and her third skirt wasn't even aware that there was anything new and unusual next to her skin. Yes, unusual it was, but the top was nicely smoothed out and the second and third layers didn't know a thing; and so she scraped two or three potatoes out of the ashes, took four raw ones from the basket beneath her right elbow, pushed the raw spuds one after another into the hot ashes, covered them over with more ashes, and poked the fire till the smoke rose in clouds – what else could she have done?

My grandmother's skirts had barely settled down; the sticky smudge of the potato fire, which had lost its direction with all the poking and thrashing about, had barely had time to adjust itself to the wind and resume its low yellow course across the field to southwestward, when Long and Thin popped out of the lane, hot in pursuit of Short and Wide, who by now had set up housekeeping beneath my grandmother's skirts; they were indeed long and thin and they wore the uniform of the rural constabulary.

They nearly ran past my grandmother. One of them even jumped over the fire. But suddenly they remembered they had heels and used them to brake with, about-faced, stood booted and uniformed in the smudge, coughed, pulled their uniforms out of the smudge, taking some of it along with them, and, still coughing, turned to my grandmother, asked her if she had seen Koljaiczek, 'cause she must have seen him 'cause she was sitting here by the lane and that was the way he had come.

My grandmother hadn't seen any Koljaiczek because she didn't know any Koljaiczek. Was he from the brickworks, she asked, 'cause the only ones she knew were the ones from the brickworks. But according to the uniforms, this Koljaiczek had nothing to do with bricks, but was short and stocky. My grandmother remembered she had seen somebody like that running and pointed her stick with the steaming potato on the end toward Bissau, which, to judge by the potato, must have been between the sixth and seventh telegraph poles if you counted westward from the chimney. But whether this fellow that was running was a Koljaiczek, my grandmother couldn't say; she'd been having enough trouble with this fire, she explained, it was burning poorly, how could she worry her head about all the people that ran by or stood in the smoke, and anyway she never worried her head about people she didn't know, she only knew the people in Bissau, Ramkau, Viereck, and the brickworks – and that was plenty for her.

After saying all this, my grandmother heaved a gentle sigh, but it was enough of a sigh to make the uniforms ask what there was to sigh about. She nodded toward the fire, meaning to say that she had sighed because the fire was doing poorly and maybe a little on account of the people standing in the smoke; then she bit off half her potato with her widely spaced incisors, and gave her undivided attention to the business of chewing, while her eyeballs rolled heavenward.

My grandmother's absent gaze told the uniforms nothing; unable to make up their minds whether to look for Bissau behind the telegraph poles, they poked their bayonets into all the piles of potato tops that hadn't been set on fire. Responding to a sudden inspiration, they upset the two baskets under my grandmother's elbows almost simultaneously and were quite bewildered when nothing but potatoes came rolling out, and no Koljaiczek. Full of suspicion, they crept round the stack of potatoes, as though Koljaiczek had somehow got into it, thrust in their bayonets as though deliberately taking aim, and were disappointed to hear no cry. Their suspicions were aroused by every bush, however abject, by every mousehole, by a colony of molehills, and most of all by my grandmother, who sat there as if rooted to the spot sighing, rolling her eyes so that the whites showed, listing the Kashubian names of all the saints – all of which seemed to have been brought on by the poor performance of the fire and the overturning of her potato baskets.

The uniforms stayed on for a good half-hour. They took up positions at varying distances from the fire, they took an azimuth on the chimney, contemplated an offensive against Bissau but postponed it, and held out their purple hands over the fire until my grandmother, though without interrupting her sighs, gave each of them a charred potato. But in the midst of chewing, the uniforms remembered their uniforms, dashed a little way out into the field along the furze bordering the lane, and scared up a hare which, however, turned out not to be Koljaiczek. Returning to the fire, they recovered the mealy, steaming spuds and then, wearied and rather mellowed by their battles, decided to pick up the raw potatoes and put them back into the baskets which they had overturned in line of duty.

Only when evening began to squeeze a fine slanting rain and an inky twilight from the October sky did they briefly and without enthusiasm attack a dark boulder at the other end of the field, but once this enemy had been disposed of they decided to let well enough alone. After flexing their legs for another moment or two and holding out their hands in blessing over the rather dampened fire, they coughed a last cough and dropped a last tear in the green and yellow smudge, and plodded off coughing and weeping in the direction of Bissau. If Koljaiczek wasn't here, he must be in Bissau. Rural constables never envisage more than two possibilities.

The smoke of the slowly dying fire enveloped my grandmother like a spacious fifth skirt, so that she too with her four skirts, her sighs, and her holy names, was under a skirt. Only when the uniforms had become staggering dots, vanishing in the dusk between the telegraph poles, did my grandmother arise, slowly and painfully as though she had struck root and now, drawing earth and fibers along with her, were tearing herself out of the ground.

Suddenly Koljaiczek found himself short, wide, and coverless in the rain, and he was cold. Quickly he buttoned his pants, which fear and a boundless need for shelter had bidden him open during his stay beneath the skirts. Hurriedly he manipulated the buttons, fearing to let his piston cool too quickly, for there was a threat of dire chills in the autumn air.

My grandmother found four more hot potatoes under the ashes. She gave Koljaiczek three of them and took one for herself; before biting into it she asked if he was from the brickworks, though she knew perfectly well that Koljaiczek came from somewhere else and had no connection with bricks. Without waiting for an answer, she lifted the lighter basket to his back, took the heavier one for herself, and still had a hand free for her rake and hoe. Then with her basket, her potatoes, her rake, and her hoe, she set off, like a sail billowing in the breeze, in the direction of Bissau Quarry.

That wasn't the same as Bissau itself. It lay more in the direction of Ramkau. Passing to the right of the brickworks, they headed for the black forest with Goldkrug in it and Brenntau behind it. But in a hollow, before you come to the forest, lay Bissau Quarry. Thither Joseph Koljaiczek, unable to tear himself away from her skirts, followed my grandmother.

Under the Raft

It is not so easy, lying here in this scrubbed hospital bed under a glass peephole with Bruno's eye in it, to give a picture of the smoke clouds that rose from Kashubian potato fires or of the slanting October rain. If I didn't have my drum, which, when handled adroitly and patiently, remembers all the incidentals that I need to get the essential down on paper, and if I didn't have the permission of the management to drum on it three or four hours a day, I'd be a poor bastard with nothing to say for my grandparents.

In any case, my drum tells me this: That afternoon in the year 1899, while in South Africa Oom Kruger was brushing his bushy anti-British eyebrows, my mother Agnes, between Dirschau and Karthaus, not far from the Bissau brickworks, amid smoke, terrors, sighs, and saints' names, under four skirts of identical color, under the slanting rain and the smoke-filled eyes of two rural constables asking uninspired questions, was begotten by the short but stocky Joseph Koljaiczek.

That very night my grandmother Anna Bronski changed her name; with the help of a priest who was generous with the sacraments, she had herself metamorphosed into Anna Koljaiczek and followed Joseph, if not into Egypt, at least to the provincial capital on the river Mottlau, where Joseph found work as a raftsman and temporary peace from the constabulary.

Just to heighten the suspense, I'm going to wait a while before telling you the name of the city at the mouth of the Mottlau, though there's ample reason for mentioning it right now because it is there that my mama first saw the light of day. At the end of July, 1900 – they were just deciding to double the imperial naval building program – my mother was born under the sign of Leo. Self-confident, romantic, generous, and vain. The first house, known also as *domus vitae*, in the sign of the ascendant: Pisces, impressionable. The constellation of the sun in opposition to Neptune, seventh house or *Domus matrimonii uxoris*, would bring confusion. Venus in opposition to Saturn, which is termed the sour planet and as everyone knows induces ailments of the liver and spleen, which is dominant in Capricorn and meets its end in Leo, to which Neptune offers eels and receives the mole in return, which loves belladonna, onions, and beets, which coughs lava and sours the wine; it lived with Venus in the eighth house, the house of death; that augured accidental death, while the fact of being begotten in the potato field gave promise of hazardous happiness under the protection of Mercury in the house of relatives.

Here I must put in a protest from my mama, for she always denied having been begotten in the potato field. It was true – this much she admitted – that her father had done his best on that memorable occasion, but neither his position nor that of Anna Bronski had been such as to favor impregnation. 'It must have happened later that night, maybe in Uncle Vincent's boxcart, or maybe still later in Troyl when the raftsmen took us in.'

My mama liked to date the beginnings of her existence with words such as these, and then my grandmother, who must have known, would nod patiently and say: 'Yes, child, it must have been in the cart or later in Troyl. It couldn't have been in the field, 'cause it was windy and raining all getout.'

Vincent was my grandmother's brother. His wife had died young and then he had gone on a pilgrimage to Częstochowa where the Matka Boska Częstochowska had enjoined him to consider her as the future queen of Poland. Since then he had spent all his time poking around in strange books, and every sentence he read was a confirmation of the Virgin Mother's claim to the

Polish throne. He had let his sister look after the house and the few acres of land. Jan, his son, then four years of age, a sickly child always on the verge of tears, tended the geese; he also collected little colored pictures and, at an ominously early age, stamps.

To this little farm dedicated to the heavenly Queen of Poland, my grandmother brought her potato baskets and Koljaiczek. Learning the lay of the land, Vincent hurried over to Ramkau and stirred up the priest, telling him to come quick with the sacraments and unite Anna and Joseph in holy wedlock. Scarcely had the reverend father, groggy with sleep, given his long yawned-out blessing and, rewarded with a good side of bacon, turned his consecrated back than Vincent harnessed the horse to the boxcart, bedded the newlyweds down in straw and empty potato sacks, propped up little Jan, shivering and wispily weeping beside him on the driver's seat, and gave the horse to understand that he was to put straight out into the night: the honeymooners were in a hurry.

The night was still dark though far advanced when the vehicle reached the timber port in the provincial capital. There Koljaiczek found friends and fellow raftsmen who sheltered the fugitive pair. Vincent turned about and headed back to Bissau; a cow, a goat, the sow with her porkers, eight geese, and the dog demanded to be fed, while little Jan had developed a slight fever and had to be put to bed.

Joseph Koljaiczek remained in hiding for three weeks. He trained his hair to take a part, shaved his mustache, provided himself with unblemished papers, and found work as a raftsman under the name of Joseph Wranka. But why did Koljaiczek have to apply for work with the papers of one Joseph Wranka, who had been knocked off a raft in a fight and, unbeknownst to the authorities, drowned in the river Bug just above Modlin? Because having given up rafting for a time and gone to work in a sawmill at Schwetz, he had had a bit of trouble with the boss over a fence which he, Koljaiczek, had painted a provocative white and red. Whereupon the boss had broken one white and one red slat out of the fence and smashed the patriotic slats into tinder over Koljaiczek's Kashubian back. To Koljaiczek this had seemed ground enough for setting red fire to the brand-new, resplendently whitewashed sawmill the very next night, a starry night no doubt, in honor of a partitioned but for this very reason united Poland.

And so Koljaiczek became a firebug, and not just once, for throughout West Prussia in the days that followed, sawmills and woodlots provided fuel for a blazing bicolored national sentiment. As always where the future of Poland is at stake, the Virgin Mary was in on the proceedings, and there were witnesses – some of them may still be alive – who claimed to have seen the Mother of God, bedecked with the crown of Poland, enthroned on the collapsing roofs of several sawmills. The crowd that always turns up at big fires is said to have struck up the hymn to the Bogarodzica, Mother of God – Koljaiczek's fires, we have every reason to believe, were solemn affairs, and solemn oaths were sworn.

And so Koljaiczek was wanted as an incendiary, whereas the raftsman Joseph Wranka, a harmless fellow with an irreproachable past and no parents, a man of limited horizon whom no one was looking for and hardly anyone even knew, had divided his chewing tobacco into daily rations, until one day he was gathered in by the river Bug, leaving behind him three daily rations of tobacco and his papers in the pocket of his jacket. And since Wranka, once drowned, could no longer report for work and no one asked embarrassing questions about him, Koljaiczek, who had the same build and the same round skull, crept first into his jacket, then into his irreproachable official skin, gave up pipe-smoking, took to chewing tobacco, and even adopted Wranka's most personal and characteristic trait, his speech defect. In the years that followed he played the part of a hard-working, thrifty raftsman with a slight stutter, rafting whole forests down the Niemen, the Bobr, the Bug, and the Vistula. He even rose to be a corporal in the Crown Prince's Leib-Hussars under Mackensen, for Wranka hadn't yet done his military service, whereas Koljaiczek, who was four years older, had left a bad record behind him in the artillery at Thorn.

In the very midst of their felonious pursuits the most desperate thieves, murderers, and incendiaries are just waiting for an opportunity to take up a more respectable trade. Whether by effort or by luck, some of them get the chance: under the identity of Wranka, Koljaiczek was a good husband, so well cured of the fiery vice that the mere sight of a match gave him the shakes. A box of matches, lying smugly on the kitchen table, was never safe from this man who might have invented matches. He threw the temptation out of the window. It was very hard for my grandmother to serve a warm meal on time. Often the family sat in the dark because there was nothing to light the lamp with.

Yet Wranka was not a tyrant. On Sunday he took his Anna Wranka to church in the lower city and allowed her, his legally wedded wife, to wear four superimposed skirts, just as she had done in the potato field. In winter when the rivers were frozen over and the raftsmen were laid off, he sat quietly at home in Troyl, where only raftsmen, longshoremen, and wharf hands lived, and supervised the upbringing of his daughter Agnes, who seemed to take after her father, for when she was not under the bed she was in the clothes cupboard, and when there were visitors, she was under the table with her rag dolls.

The essential for little Agnes was to remain hidden; in hiding she found other pleasures but the same security as Joseph had found under Anna's skirts. Koljaiczek the incendiary had been sufficiently burnt to understand his daughter's need for shelter. When it became necessary to put up a rabbit hutch on the balcony-like appendage to their one-and-a-half-room flat, he built a special little house to her measure. Here sat my mother as a child, playing with dolls and getting bigger. Later, when she went to school, she is said to have thrown away the dolls and shown her first concern with fragile beauty in the form of glass beads and colored feathers.

Perhaps, since I am burning to announce the beginning of my own existence, I may be permitted to leave the family raft of the Wrankas drifting peacefully along, until 1913, when the *Columbus* was launched in Schichau; for it was then that the police, who never forget, caught up with Wranka.

The trouble began in August, 1913 when, as every summer, Koljaiczek was to help man the big raft that floated down from Kiev to the Vistula by way of the Pripet, the canal, the Bug, and the Modlin. Twelve raftsmen in all, they boarded the tugboat *Radaune*, operated by their sawmill, and steamed from Westlich Neufähr up the Dead Vistula to Einlage, then up the Vistula past Käsemark, Letzkau, Czattkau, Dirschau, and Pieckel, and tied up for the night at Thorn. There the new manager of the sawmill, who was to supervise the timber-buying in Kiev, came on board. By the time the *Radaune* cast off at four in the morning, word got around that he had come on. Koljaiczek saw him for the first time at breakfast in the galley. They sat across from one another, chewing and slopping up barley coffee. Koljaiczek knew him right off. Broad-shouldered and bald, the boss sent for vodka and had it poured into the men's empty coffee cups. In the midst of chewing, while the vodka was still being poured at the far end, he introduced himself: 'Just so you know what's what, I'm the new boss, my name is Dückerhoff, I like order and I get it.'

At his bidding, the crew called out their names one after another in their seating order, and drained their cups so their Adam's apples jumped. Koljaiczek drank first, then he said 'Wranka,' looking Dückerhoff straight in the eye. Dückerhoff nodded as he had nodded each time and repeated 'Wranka' as he had repeated the names of the rest of the crew. Nevertheless it seemed to Koljaiczek that there was something special about Dückerhoff's way of saying the dead raftsman's name, not exactly pointed, but kind of thoughtful.

The *Radaune* pounded her way against the muddy current, deftly avoiding sandbanks with the help of changing pilots. To right and left, behind the dikes the country was always the same, hilly when it wasn't flat, but always reaped over. Hedges, sunken lanes, a hollow overgrown with broom, here and there an isolated farm, a landscape made for cavalry attacks, for a division of Uhlans wheeling in from the left across the sandbox, for hedge-leaping hussars, for the dreams of young cavalry officers, for the battles of the past and the battles to come, for heroic painting: Tartars flat against the necks of their horses, dragoons rearing, knights in armor falling, grand masters in blood-spattered mantles, not a scratch on their breastplates, all but one, who was struck down by the Duke of Mazowsze; and horses, better than a circus, bedecked with tassels, sinews delineated with precision, nostrils dilated, carmine red, sending up little clouds and the clouds are pierced by lowered lances hung with pennants, sabers part the sky and the sunset, and there in the background – for every painting has a background – pasted firmly against the horizon, a little village with peacefully smoking chimneys between the hind legs of the black stallion, little squat cottages with moss-covered walls and thatched roofs; and in the cottages the pretty little tanks, dreaming of the day to come when they too will sally forth into the picture behind the Vistula dikes, like light foals amid the heavy cavalry.

Off Wloclawek, Dückerhoff tapped Koljaiczek on the shoulder: 'Tell me, Wranka, didn't you work in the mill at Schwetz a few years back? The one that burned down?' Koljaiczek shook his head heavily, as though he had a stiff neck, and managed to make his eyes so sad and tired that Dückerhoff kept any further questions to himself.

When Koljaiczek at Modlin, where the Bug flows into the Vistula and the *Radaune* turned into the Bug, leaned over the rail as the raftsmen did in those days and spat three times, Dückerhoff was standing beside him with a cigar and asked for a light. That little word, like the word 'match,' had a strange effect on Koljaiczek. 'Man, you don't have to blush because I want a light. You're not a girl, or are you?'

It wasn't until after they left Modlin behind them that Koljaiczek lost his blush, which was not a blush of shame, but the lingering glow of the sawmills he had set on fire.

Between Modlin and Kiev, up the Bug, through the canal that joins the Bug and the Pripet, until the *Radaune*, following the Pripet, found its way to the Dniepr, nothing happened that can be classified as an exchange between Koljaiczek-Wranka and Dückerhoff. There was surely a bit of bad blood aboard the tug, among the raftsmen, between stokers and raftsmen, between helmsman, stokers, and captain, between captain and the constantly changing pilots; that's said to be the way with men, and maybe it really is. I can easily conceive of a certain amount of backbiting between the Kashubian logging crew and the helmsman, who was a native of Stettin, perhaps even the beginning of a mutiny: meeting in the galley, lots drawn, passwords given out, cutlasses sharpened. But enough of that. There were neither political disputes, nor knife battles between Germans and Poles, nor any mutiny springing from social grievances. Peacefully devouring her daily ration of coal, the *Radaune* went her way; once she ran aground on a sandbank – a little way past Plock, I think it was – but got off on her own power. A short but heated altercation between Captain Barbusch from Neufahrwasser and the Ukrainian pilot, that was all – and you wouldn't find much more in the log.

But if I had to keep a journal of Koljaiczek's thoughts or of Dückerhoff's inner life, there'd be plenty to relate: suspicion, suspicion confirmed, doubt, hesitation, suspicion laid at rest, more suspicion. They were both afraid. Dückerhoff more than Koljaiczek; for now they were in Russia. Dückerhoff could easily have fallen overboard like poor Wranka in his day, or later on in Kiev, in the timberyards that are so labyrinthine and enormous you can easily lose your guardian angel in their mazes, he could somehow have slipped under a suddenly toppling pile of logs. Or for that matter, he could have been rescued. Rescued by Koljaiczek, fished out of the Pripet or the Bug, or in the Kiev woodyard, so deplorably short of guardian angels, pulled at the last moment from the path of an avalanche of logs. How touching it would be if I could tell you how Dückerhoff, half-drowned or half-crushed, still gasping, a glimmer of death still barely discernible in his eyes, had whispered in the ostensible Wranka's ear: 'Thank you, Koljaiczek, thanks old man.' And then after the indispensable pause: 'That makes us quits. Let bygones be bygones.'

And with gruff bonhomie, smiling shamefacedly into each other's manly eyes with a twinkle that might almost have been a tear, they would have clasped one another's diffident but horny hands.

We know the scene from the movies: the reconciliation between two enemy brothers, brilliantly performed, brilliantly photographed, from this day onward comrades forever, through thick and thin; Lord, what adventures they'll live through together!

But Koljaiczek found opportunity neither to drown Dückerhoff nor to snatch him from the jaws of death. Conscientiously, intent on the best interests of the firm, Dückerhoff bought his lumber in Kiev, supervised the building of the nine rafts, distributed a substantial advance in Russian currency to see the men through the return trip, and boarded the train, which carried him by way of Warsaw, Modlin, Deutsch-Eylau, Marienburg, and Dirschau back to his company, whose sawmill was situated in the timber port between the Klawitter dockyards and the Schichau dockyards.

Before I bring the raftsmen down the rivers from Kiev, through the canal and at last, after weeks of grueling toil, into the Vistula, there is a question to be considered: was Dückerhoff sure that this Wranka was Koljaiczek the firebug? I should say that as long as the mill boss had Wranka, a good-natured sort, well liked by all despite his very medium brightness, as his traveling companion on the tug, he hoped, and preferred to believe, that the raftsman was not the desperado Koljaiczek. He did not relinquish this hope until he was comfortably settled in the train. And by the time the train had reached its destination, the Central Station in Danzig – there, now I've said it – Dückerhoff had made up his mind. He sent his bags home in a carriage and strode briskly to the nearby Police Headquarters on the Wiebenwall, leapt up the steps to the main entrance, and, after a short but cautious search, found the office he was looking for, where he submitted a brief factual report. He did not actually denounce Koljaiczek-Wranka; he merely entered a request that the police look into the case, which the police promised to do.

In the following weeks, while the logs were floating slowly downstream with their burden of reed huts and raftsmen, a great deal of paper was covered with writing in a number of offices. There was the service record of Joseph Koljaiczek, buck private in the so-and-soeth West Prussian artillery regiment. A poor soldier, he had twice spent three days in the guardhouse for shouting anarchist slogans half in Polish and half in German while under the influence of liquor. No such black marks were to be discovered in the record of Corporal Wranka, who had served in the second regiment of Leib-Hussars at Langfuhr. He had done well; as battalion dispatch runner on maneuvers, he had made a favorable impression on the Crown Prince and had been rewarded with a Crown Prince thaler by the Prince, who always carried a pocketful of them. The thaler was not noted in Corporal Wranka's military record, but reported by my loudly lamenting grandmother Anna when she and her brother Vincent were questioned.

And that was not her only argument against the allegation of arson. She was able to produce papers proving that Joseph Wranka had joined the volunteer fire department in Danzig-Niederstadt as early as 1904, during the winter months when the raftsmen are idle, and that far from lighting fires he had helped to put them out. There was also a document to show that Fireman Wranka, while fighting the big fire at the Troyl railroad works in 1909, had saved two apprentice mechanics. Fire captain Hecht spoke in similar terms when called up as a witness. 'Is a man who puts fires out likely to light them?' he cried. 'Why, I can still see him up there on the ladder when the church in Heubude was burning. A phoenix rising from flame and ashes, quenching not only the fire, but also the conflagration of this world and the thirst of our Lord Jesus! Verily I say unto you: anyone who sullies the name of the man in the fire helmet, who has the right of way, whom the insurance companies love, who always has a bit of ashes in his pocket, perhaps because they dropped into it in the course of his duties or perhaps as a talisman – anyone, I say, who dares to accuse this glorious phoenix of arson deserves to have a millstone tied round his neck and . . .'

Captain Hecht, as you may have observed, was a parson, a warrior of the word. Every Sunday, he spoke from the pulpit of his parish church of St. Barbara at Langgarten, and as long as the Koljaiczek-Wranka investigation was in progress he dinned parables about the heavenly fireman and the diabolical incendiary into the ears of his congregation.

But since the detectives who were working on the case did not go to church at St. Barbara's and since, as far as they were concerned, the word 'phoenix' sounded more like *lèse-majesté* than a disculpation of Wranka, Wranka's activity in the fire department was taken as a bad sign.

Evidence was gathered in a number of sawmills and in the town halls of both men's native places: Wranka had first seen the light of day in Tuchel, Koljaiczek in Thorn. When pieced together, the statements of older raftsmen and distant relatives revealed slight discrepancies. The pitcher, in short, kept going to the well; what could it do in the end but break? This was how things stood when the big raft entered German territory: after Thorn it was under discreet surveillance, and the men were shadowed when they went ashore.

It was only after Dirschau that my grandfather noticed his shadows. He had been expecting them. It seems to have been a profound lethargy, verging on melancholia, that deterred him from trying to make a break for it at Letzkau or Käsemark; he might well have succeeded, for he knew the region inside out and he had good friends among the raftsmen. After Einlage, where the rafts drifted slowly, tamping and thumping, into the Dead Vistula, a fishing craft with much too much of a crew ran along close by, trying rather conspicuously not to make itself conspicuous. Shortly after Plehnendorf two harbor police launches shot out of the rushes and began to race back and forth across the river, churning up the increasingly brackish waters of the estuary. Beyond the bridge leading to Heubude, the police had formed a cordon. They were everywhere, as far as the eye could see, in among the fields of logs, on the wharves and piers, on the sawmill docks, on the company dock where the men's relatives were waiting. They were everywhere except across the river by Schichau; over there it was all full of flags, something else was going on, looked like a ship was being launched, excited crowds, the very gulls were frantic with excitement, a celebration was in progress – a celebration for my grandfather?

Only when my grandfather saw the timber basin full of blue uniforms, only when the launches began crisscrossing more and more ominously, sending waves over the rafts, only when he became fully cognizant of the expensive maneuvers that had been organized all for his benefit, did Koljaiczek's old incendiary heart awaken. Then he spewed out the gentle Wranka, sloughed off the skin of Wranka the volunteer fireman, loudly and fluently disowned Wranka the stutterer, and fled, fled over the rafts, fled over the wide, teetering expanse, fled barefoot over the unplanned floor, from log to log toward Schichau, where the flags were blowing gaily in the wind, on over the timber, toward the launching ceremony, where beautiful speeches were being made, where no one was shouting 'Wranka,' let alone 'Koljaiczek,' and the words rang out: I baptize you H.M.S. *Columbus*, America, forty thousand tons, thirty thousand horsepower, His Majesty's ship, first-class dining room, second-class dining room, gymnasium, library, America, His Majesty's ship, modern stabilizers, promenade deck, *Heil dir im Siegerkranz*, ensign of the home port. There stands Prince Heinrich at the helm, and my grandfather Koljaiczek barefoot, his feet barely touching the logs, running toward the brass band, a country that has such princes, from raft to raft, the people cheering him on, *Heil dir im Siegerkranz* and the dockyard sirens, the siren of every ship in the harbor, of every tug and pleasure craft, *Columbus*, America, liberty, and two launches mad with joy running along beside him, from raft to raft, His Majesty's rafts, and they block the way, too bad, he was making good time, he stands alone on his raft and sees America, and there are the launches. There's nothing to do but take to the water, and my grandfather is seen swimming, heading for a raft that's drifting into the Mottlau. But he has to dive on account of the launches and he has to stay under on account of the launches, and the raft passes over him and it won't stop, one raft engenders another: raft of thy raft, for all eternity: raft.

The launches stopped their motors. Relentless eyes searched the surface of the water. But Koljaiczek was gone forever, gone from the band music, gone from the sirens, from the ship's bells on His Majesty's ship, from Prince Heinrich's baptismal address, and from His Majesty's frantic gulls, gone from *Heil dir im Siegerkranz* and from His Majesty's soft soap used to soap the ways for His Majesty's ship, gone from America and from the *Columbus*, from police pursuit and the endless expanse of logs.

My grandfather's body was never found. Though I have no doubt whatever that he met his death under the raft, my devotion to the truth, the whole truth, compels me to put down some of the variants in which he was miraculously rescued.

According to one version he found a chink between two logs, just wide enough on the bottom to enable him to keep his nose above water, but so narrow on top that he remained invisible to the minions of the law who continued to search the rafts and even the reed huts until nightfall. Then, under cover of darkness – so the tale went on – he let himself drift until, half-dead with exhaustion, he reached the Schichau dockyard on the opposite bank; there he hid in the scrap-iron dump and later on, probably with the help of Greek sailors, was taken aboard one of those grimy tankers that are famous for harboring fugitives.

Another version is that Koljaiczek, a strong swimmer with remarkable lungs, had not only swum under the raft but traversed the whole remaining width of the Mottlau under water and reached the shipyard in Schichau, where, without attracting attention, he had mingled with the enthusiastic populace, joined in singing *Heil dir im Siegerkranz*, joined in applauding Prince Heinrich's baptismal oration, and after the launching, his clothes half-dried by now, had drifted away with the crowd. Next day – here the two versions converge – he had stowed away on the same Greek tanker of famed ill fame.

For the sake of completeness, I must also mention a third preposterous fable, according to which my grandfather floated out to sea like a piece of driftwood and was promptly fished out of the water by some fishermen from Bohnsack who, once outside the three-mile limit, handed him over to a Swedish deep-sea fisherman. After a miraculous recovery he reached Malmö, and so on.

All that is nonsense, fishermen's fish stories. Nor would I give a bent penny for the reports of the eyewitnesses – such eyewitnesses are to be met with in every seaport the world over – who claim to have seen my grandfather shortly after the First World War in Buffalo, U.S.A. Called himself Joe Colchic, said he was importing lumber from Canada, big stockholder in a number of match factories, a founder of fire insurance companies. That was my grandfather, a lonely multimillionaire, sitting in a skyscraper behind an enormous desk, diamond rings on every finger, drilling his bodyguard, who wore firemen's uniforms, sang in Polish, and were known as the Phoenix Guard.

Moth and Light Bulb

A man left everything behind him, crossed the great water, and became rich. Well, that's enough about my grandfather regardless of whether we call him Goljaczek (Polish), Koljaiczek (Kashubian), or Joe Colchic (American).

It's not easy, with nothing better than a tin drum, the kind you can buy in the dimestore, to question a river clogged nearly to the horizon with log rafts. And yet I have managed by drumming to search the timber port, with all its driftwood lurching in the bights or caught in the rushes, and, with less difficulty, the launching ways of the Schichau shipyard and the Klawitter shipyard, and the drydocks, the scrap-metal dump, the rancid coconut stores of the margarine factory, and all the hiding places that were ever known to me in those parts. He is dead, he gives me no answer, shows no interest at all in imperial ship launchings, in the decline of a ship, which begins with its launching and sometimes goes on for as much as twenty or thirty years, in the present instance the decline of the H.M.S. *Columbus*, once termed the pride of the fleet and assigned, it goes without saying, to the North Atlantic run. Later on she was sunk or scuttled, then perhaps refloated, renamed, remodeled, or, for all I know, scrapped. Possibly the *Columbus*, imitating my grandfather, merely dived, and today, with her forty thousand tons, her dining rooms, her swimming pool, her gymnasium and massaging rooms, is knocking about a thousand fathoms down, in the Philippine Deep or the Emden Hollow; you'll find the whole story in Weyer's *Steamships* or in the shipping calendars – it seems to me that the *Columbus* was scuttled, because the captain couldn't bear to survive some sort of disgrace connected with the war.

I read Bruno part of my raft story and then, asking him to be objective, put my question to him.

'A beautiful death,' Bruno declared with enthusiasm and began at once to transform my poor drowned grandfather into one of his knotted spooks. I could only content myself with his answer and abandon all harebrained schemes of going to the U.S.A. in the hope of cadging an inheritance.

My friends Klepp and Vittlar came to see me. Klepp brought me a jazz record with King Oliver on both sides; Vittlar, with a mincing little gesture, presented me with a chocolate heart on a pink ribbon. They clowned around, parodied scenes from my trial, and to please them I put a cheerful face on it, as I always did on visiting days, and managed to laugh even at the most dismal jokes. Before Klepp could launch into his inevitable lecture about the relationship between jazz and Marxism, I told my story, the story of a man who in 1913, not long before the shooting started, was submerged under an endless raft and never came up again, so that they had never even found his body.

In answer to my questions – I asked them in a very offhand manner, with an affectation of boredom – Klepp dejectedly shook his head over an adipose neck, unbuttoned his vest and buttoned it up again, made swimming movements, and acted as if he were under a raft. In the end he dismissed my question with a shake of his head, and said it was too early in the afternoon for him to form an opinion.

Vittlar sat stiffly, crossed his legs, taking good care not to disturb the crease in his pin-striped trousers, and putting on the expression of eccentric hauteur characteristic only of himself and perhaps of the angels in heaven, said: 'I am on the raft. It's pleasant on the raft. Mosquitoes are biting me, that's bothersome. I am under the raft. It's pleasant under the raft. The mosquitoes aren't biting me any more, that is pleasant. I think I could live very nicely under the raft if not for my hankering to be on the top of the raft, being molested by mosquitoes.'

Vittlar paused as usual for effect, looked me up and down, raised his already rather lofty eyebrows, as he always did when he wished to look like an owl, and spoke in piercing theatrical tones: 'I assume that this man who was drowned, the man under the raft, was your great-uncle if not your grandfather. He went to his death because as a great-uncle, or in far greater measure as a grandfather, he felt he owed it to you, for nothing would be more burdensome to you than to have a living grandfather. That makes you the murderer not only of your great-uncle but also of your grandfather. However, like all true grandfathers, he wanted to punish you a little; he just wouldn't let you have the satisfaction of pointing with pride to a bloated, water-logged corpse and declaiming: Behold my dead grandfather. He was a hero. Rather than fall into the hands of his pursuers, he jumped in the river. Your grandfather cheated the world and his grandchild out of his corpse. Why? To make posterity and his grandchild worry their heads about him for many years to come.'

Then, with a quick transition from one brand of pathos to another, he bent slightly forward and assumed the wily countenance of a purveyor of false consolation: 'America! Take heart, Oskar. You have an aim, a mission in life. You'll be acquitted, released. Where should you go if not to America, the land where people find whatever they have lost, even missing grandfathers.'

Sardonic and offensive as Vittlar's answer was, it gave me more certainty than my friend Klepp's ill-humored refusal to decide between life and death, or the reply of Bruno, my keeper, who thought my grandfather's death had been beautiful only because it had been immediately followed by the launching of the *Columbus*. God bless Vittlar's America, preserver of grandfathers, goal and ideal by which to rehabilitate myself when, weary of Europe, I decide to lay down my drum and pen: 'Go on writing, Oskar. Do it for your grandfather, the rich but weary Koljaiczek, the lumber king of Buffalo, U.S.A., the lonely tycoon playing with matches in his skyscraper.'

When Klepp and Vittlar had finally taken their leave, Bruno drove their disturbing aroma out of the room with a thorough airing. I went back to my drum, but I no longer drummed up the logs of death-concealing rafts; no, I beat out the rapid, erratic rhythm which commanded everybody's movements for quite some time after August, 1914. This makes it impossible for me to touch more than briefly on the life, up to the hour of my birth, of the little group of mourners my grandfather left behind him in Europe.

When Koljaiczek disappeared under the raft, my grandmother, her daughter Agnes, Vincent Bronski, and his seven-year-old son Jan were standing among the raftsmen's relatives on the sawmill dock, looking on in anguish. A little to one side stood Gregor Koljaiczek, Joseph's elder brother, who had been summoned to the city for questioning. Gregor had always had the same answer ready for the police: 'I hardly know my brother. All I'm really sure of is that he was called Joseph. Last time I saw him, he couldn't have been more than ten or maybe twelve years old. He shined my shoes and went out for beer when mother and I wanted beer.'

Though it turned out that my great-grandmother actually did drink beer, Gregor Koljaiczek's answer was no help to the police. But the elder Koljaiczek's existence was a big help to my grandmother Anna. Gregor, who had spent most of his life in Stettin, Berlin, and lastly in Schneidemühl, stayed on in Danzig, found work at the gunpowder factory, and after a year's time, when all the complications, such as her marriage with the false Wranka, had been cleared up and laid at rest, married my grandmother, who was determined to stick by the Koljaiczeks and would never have married Gregor, or not so soon at least, if he had not been a Koljaiczek.

His work in the gunpowder factory kept Gregor out of the

peacetime and soon the wartime army. The three of them lived together in the same one-and-a-half-room apartment that had sheltered the incendiary for so many years. But it soon became evident that one Koljaiczek need not necessarily resemble another, for after the first year of marriage my grandmother was obliged to rent the basement shop in Troyl, which happened to be available, and to make what money she could selling miscellaneous items from pins to cabbages, because though Gregor made piles of money at the powder works, he drank it all up; what he brought home wasn't enough for the barest necessities. Unlike Joseph my grandfather, who merely took an occasional nip of brandy, Gregor was a real drinker, a quality he had probably inherited from my great-grandmother. He didn't drink because he was sad. And even when he seemed cheerful, a rare occurrence, for he was given to melancholia, he didn't drink because he was happy. He drank because he was a thorough man, who liked to get to the bottom of things, of bottles as well as everything else. As long as he lived, no one ever saw Gregor Koljaiczek leave so much as a drop in the bottom of his glass.

My mother, then a plump little girl of fifteen, made herself useful around the house and helped in the store; she pasted food stamps in the ledger, waited on customers on Saturdays, and wrote awkward but imaginative missives to those who bought on credit, admonishing them to pay up. It's a pity that I possess none of these letters. How splendid if at this point I could quote some of my mother's girlish cries of distress – remember, she was half an orphan, for Gregor Koljaiczek was far from giving full value as a stepfather. Quite the contrary, it was only with great difficulty that my grandmother and her daughter were able to conceal their cashbox, which consisted of a tin plate covered by another tin plate and contained more copper than silver, from the sad and thirsty gaze of the gunpowder-maker. Only when Gregor Koljaiczek died of influenza in 1917 did the profits of the shop increase a little. But not much; what was there to sell in 1917?

The little room which had remained empty since the powder-maker's death, because my mama was afraid of ghosts and refused to move into it, was occupied later on by Jan Bronski, my mother's cousin, then aged about twenty, who, having graduated from the high school in Karthaus and served a period of apprenticeship at the post office in the district capital, had left Bissau and his father Vincent to pursue his career at the main post office in Danzig. In addition to his suitcase, Jan brought with him a large stamp collection that he had been working on since he was a little boy. So you see, he had more than a professional interest in the post office; he had, indeed, a kind of private solicitude for that branch of the administration. He was a sickly young man who walked with a slight stoop, but he had a pretty oval face with perhaps a little too much sweetness about it, and a pair of blue eyes that made it possible for my mama, who was then seventeen, to fall in love with him. Three times Jan had been called to the colors, but each time had been deferred because of his deplorable physical condition, a circumstance which threw ample light on Jan Bronski's constitution in those days, when every male who could stand halfway erect was being shipped to Verdun to undergo a radical change of posture from the vertical to the eternal horizontal.

Their flirtation ought reasonably to have begun as they were looking at stamps together, as their two youthful heads leaned over the perforations and watermarks. Actually it began or, rather, erupted only when Jan was called up for service a fourth time. My mother, who had errands in town, accompanied him to district headquarters and waited for him outside the sentry box occupied by a militiaman. The two of them were both convinced that this time Jan would have to go, that they would surely send him off to cure his ailing chest in the air of France, famed for its iron and lead content. It is possible that my mother counted the buttons on the sentry's uniform several times with varying results. I can easily imagine that the buttons on all uniforms are so constituted that the last to be counted always means Verdun, the Hartmannsweilerkopf, or some little river, perhaps the Somme or the Marne.

When, barely an hour later, the four-times-summoned young man emerged from the portal of the district headquarters, stumbled down the steps, and, falling on the neck of Agnes, my mama, whispered the saying that was so popular in those days: 'They can't have my front, they can't have my rear. They've turned me down for another year' – my mother for the first time held Jan Bronski in her arms, and I doubt whether there was ever more happiness in their embrace.

The details of this wartime love are not known to me. Jan sold part of his stamp collection to meet the exigencies of my mama, who had a lively appreciation of everything that was pretty, becoming to her, and expensive, and is said to have kept a diary which has unfortunately been lost. Evidently my grandmother tolerated the relations between the young people – which seem to have been more than cousinly – for Jan Bronski stayed on in the tiny flat in Troyl until shortly after the war. He moved out only when the existence of a Mr. Matzerath became undeniable and undenied. My mother must have met this Mr. Matzerath in the summer of 1918, when she was working as an auxiliary nurse in the Silberhammer Hospital near Oliva. Alfred Matzerath, a native of the Rhineland, lay there wounded – the bullet had passed clear through his thigh – and soon with his merry Rhenish ways became the favorite of all the nurses, Sister Agnes not excluded. When he was able to get up, he hobbled about the corridor on the arm of one of the nurses and helped Sister Agnes in the kitchen, because her little nurse's bonnet went so well with her little round face and also because he, an impassioned cook, had a knack for metamorphosing feelings into soup.

When his wound had healed, Alfred Matzerath stayed in Danzig and immediately found work as representative of the Rhenish stationery firm where he had worked before the war. The war had spent itself. Peace treaties that would give ground for more wars were being boggled into shape: the region round the mouth of the Vistula – delimited roughly by a line running from Vogelsang on the Nehrung along the Nogat to Pieckel, down the Vistula to Czattkau, cutting across at right angles as far as Schönfliess, looping round the forest of Saskoschin to Lake Ottomin, leaving Mattern, Ramkau, and my grandmother's Bissau to one side, and returning to the Baltic at Klein-Katz – was proclaimed a free state under League of Nations control. In the city itself Poland was given a free port, the Westerplatte including the munitions depot, the railroad administration, and a post office of its own on the Heveliusplatz.

The postage stamps of the Free City were resplendent with red and gold Hanseatic heraldry, while the Poles sent out their mail marked with scenes from the lives of Casimir and Batory, all in macabre violet.

Jan Bronski opted for Poland and transferred to the Polish Post Office. The gesture seemed spontaneous and was generally interpreted as a reaction to my mother's infidelity. In 1920, when Marszalek Pilsudski defeated the Red Army at Warsaw, a miracle which Vincent Bronski and others like him attributed to the Virgin Mary and the military experts either to General Sikorski or to General Weygand – in that eminently Polish year, my mother became engaged to Matzerath, a citizen of the German Reich. I am inclined to believe that my grandmother Anna was hardly more pleased about it than Jan. Leaving the cellar shop in Troyl, which had meanwhile become rather prosperous, to her daughter, she moved to her brother Vincent's place at Bissau, which was Polish territory, took over the management of the farm with its beet and potato fields as in the pre-Koljaiczek era, left her increasingly grace-ridden brother to his dialogues with the Virgin Queen of Poland, and went back to sitting in four skirts beside autumnal potato-top fires, blinking at the horizon, which was still sectioned by telegraph poles.

Not until Jan Bronski had found and married his Hedwig, a Kashubian girl who lived in the city but still owned some fields in Ramkau, did relations between him and my mother improve. The story is that the two couples ran into each other at a dance at the Café Woyke, and that she introduced Jan and Matzerath. The two men, so different by nature despite the similarity of their feeling for Mama, took a shine to one another, although Matzerath in loud, unvarnished Rhenish qualified Jan's transfer to the Polish Post Office as sheer damn-foolishness. Jan danced with Mama, Matzerath danced with the big, rawboned Hedwig, whose inscrutable bovine gaze tended to make people think she was pregnant. After that they danced with, around, and into one another all evening, thinking always of the next dance, a little ahead of themselves in the polka, somewhat behind hand in the English waltz, but at last achieving self-confidence in the Charleston and in the slow foxtrot sensuality bordering on religion.

In 1923, when you could paper a bedroom with zeros for the price of a matchbox, Alfred Matzerath married my mamma. Jan was one witness, the other was a grocer by the name of Mühlen.

There isn't much I can tell you about Mühlen. He is worth mentioning only because, just as the Rentenmark was coming in, he sold Mama and Matzerath a languishing grocery store ruined by credit, in the suburb of Langfuhr. In a short time Mama, who in the basement shop in Troyl had learned how to deal with every variety of nonpaying customer and who in addition was favored with native business sense and ready repartee, managed to put the business back on its feet. Matzerath was soon obliged to give up his job – besides, the paper market was glutted – in order to help in the store.

The two of them complemented each other wonderfully. My mother's prowess behind the counter was equalled by Matzerath's ability to deal with salesmen and wholesalers. But what made their association really perfect was Matzerath's love of kitchen work, which even included cleaning up – all a great blessing for Mama, who was no great shakes as a cook.

The flat adjoining the store was cramped and badly constructed, but compared with the place in Troyl, which is known to me only from hearsay, it had a definite middle-class character. At least in the early years of her marriage, Mama must have felt quite comfortable.

There was a long, rather ramshackle hallway that usually had cartons of soap flakes piled up in it, and a spacious kitchen, though it too was more than half-full of merchandise: canned goods, sacks of flour, packages of rolled oats. The living room had two windows overlooking the street and a little patch of greenery decorated with sea shells in summer. The wallpaper had a good deal of wine-red in it and the couch was upholstered in an approximation of purple. An extensible table rounded at the corners, four black leather-covered chairs, a little round smoking table, which was always being moved about, stood black-legged on a blue carpet. An upright clock rose black and golden between the windows. Black against the purple couch squatted the piano, first rented then purchased in installments; and under the revolving stool lay the pelt of some yellowish-white long-haired animal. Across from the piano stood the sideboard, black with cut-glass sliding panels, enchased in black eggs-and-anchors. The lower doors enclosing the china and linen were heavily ornamented with black carvings of fruit; the legs were black claws; on the black carved top-piece there was an empty space between the crystal bowl of artificial fruit and the green loving cup won in a lottery; later on, thanks to my mama's business acumen, the gap was to be filled with a light-brown radio.

The bedroom ran to yellow and looked out on the court of the four-story apartment house. Please believe me when I tell you that the canopy over the citadel of wedlock was sky-blue and that under its bluish light a framed, repentant, and flesh-colored Mary Magdalene lay in a grotto, sighing up at the upper right-hand edge of the picture and wringing so many fingers that you couldn't help counting them for fear there would be more than ten. Opposite the bed stood a white-enameled wardrobe with mirror doors, to the left of it a dressing table, to the right a marble-covered chest of drawers; the light fixture hung on brass arms from the ceiling, not covered with satin as in the living room, but shaded by pale-pink porcelain globes beneath which the bulbs protruded.

I have just drummed away a long morning, asking my drum all sorts of questions. I wished to know, for instance, whether the light bulbs in our bedroom were forty or sixty watts. The question is of the utmost importance to me, and this is not the first time I have asked it of myself and my drum. Sometimes it takes me hours to find my way back to those light bulbs. For I have to extricate myself from a forest of light bulbs, by good solid drumming without ornamental flourishes I have to make myself forget the thousands of lighting mechanisms it has been my lot to kindle or quench by turning a switch upon entering or leaving innumerable dwellings, before I can get back to the illumination of our bedroom in Labesweg.

Mama's confinement took place at home. When her labor pains set in, she was still in the store, putting sugar into blue pound and half-pound bags. It was too late to move her to the hospital; an elderly midwife who had just about given up practicing had to be summoned from nearby Hertastrasse. In the bedroom she helped me and Mama to get away from each other.

Well, then, it was in the form of two sixty-watt bulbs that I first saw the light of this world. That is why the words of the Bible, 'Let there be light and there was light,' still strike me as an excellent publicity slogan for Osram light bulbs. My birth ran off smoothly except for the usual rupture of the perineum. I had no difficulty in freeing myself from the upside-down position so favored by mothers, embryos, and midwives.

I may as well come right out with it: I was one of those clair-audient infants whose mental development is completed at birth and after that merely needs a certain amount of filling in. The moment I was born I took a very critical attitude toward the first utterances to slip from my parents beneath the light bulbs. My ears were keenly alert. It seems pretty well established that they were small, bent over, gummed up, and in any case cute, yet they caught the words that were my first impressions and as such have preserved their importance for me. And what my ear took in my tiny brain evaluated. After meditating at some length on what I had heard, I decided to do certain things and on no account to do certain others.

'It's a boy,' said Mr. Matzerath, who presumed himself to be my father. 'He will take over the store when he grows up. At last we know why we've been working our fingers to the bone.'

Mama thought less about the store than about outfitting her son: 'Oh, well, I knew it would be a boy even if I did say once in a while that it was going to be a girl.'

Thus at an early age I made the acquaintance of feminine logic. The next words were: 'When little Oskar is three, he will have a toy drum.'

Carefully weighing and comparing these promises, maternal and paternal, I observed and listened to a moth that had flown into the room. Medium-sized and hairy, it darted between the two sixty-watt bulbs, casting shadows out of all proportion to its wing spread, which filled the room and everything in it with quivering motion. What impressed me most, however, was not the play of light and shade but the sound produced by the dialogue between moth and bulb: the moth chattered away as if in haste to unburden itself of its knowledge, as though it had no time for future colloquies with sources of light, as though this dialogue were its last confession; and as though, after the kind of absolution that light bulbs confer, there would be no further occasion for sin or folly.

Today Oskar says simply: The moth drummed. I have heard rabbits, foxes and dormice drumming. Frogs can drum up a storm.

Woodpeckers are said to drum worms out of their hiding places. And men beat on basins, tin pans, bass drums, and kettle-drums. We speak of drumfire, drumhead courts; we drum up, drum out, drum into. There are drummer boys and drum majors. There are composers who write concerti for strings and percussion. I might even mention Oskar's own efforts on the drum; but all this is nothing beside the orgy of drumming carried on by that moth in the hour of my birth, with no other instrument than two ordinary sixty-watt bulbs. Perhaps there are Negroes in darkest Africa and others in America who have not yet forgotten Africa who, with their well-known gift of rhythm, might succeed, in imitation of African moths – which are known to be larger and more beautiful than those of Eastern Europe – in drumming with such disciplined passion; I can only go by my Eastern European standards and praise that medium-sized powdery-brown moth of the hour of my birth; that moth was Oskar's master.

It was in the first days of September. The sun was in the sign of Virgo. A late-summer storm was approaching through the night, moving crates and furniture about in the distance. Mercury made me critical, Uranus ingenious, Venus made me believe in comfort and Mars in my ambition. Libra, rising up in the house of the ascendant, made me sensitive and given to exaggeration. Neptune moved into the tenth house, the house of middle life, establishing me in an attitude between faith in miracles and disillusionment. It was Saturn which, coming into opposition to Jupiter in the third house, cast doubt on my origins. But who sent the moth and allowed it, in the midst of a late-summer thunderstorm roaring like a high school principal, to make me fall in love with the drum my mother had promised me and develop my aptitude for it?

Outwardly wailing and impersonating a meat-colored baby, I made up my mind to reject my father's projects, in short everything connected with the grocery store, out of hand, but to give my mother's plan favorable consideration when the time came, to wit, on my third birthday.

Aside from all this speculation about my future, I quickly realized that Mama and this Mr. Matzerath were not equipped to understand or respect my decisions whether positive or negative. Lonely and misunderstood, Oskar lay beneath the light bulbs, and figuring that things would go on like this for some sixty or seventy years, until a final short circuit should cut off all sources of light, he lost his enthusiasm even before this life beneath the light bulbs had begun. It was only the prospect of the drum that prevented me then from expressing more forcefully my desire to return to the womb.

Besides, the midwife had already cut my umbilical cord. There was nothing more to be done.

The Photograph Album

I am guarding a treasure. Through all the bad years consisting only of calendar days, I have guarded it, hiding it when I wasn't looking at it; during the trip in the freight car I clutched it to my breast, and when I slept, Oskar slept on his treasure, his photograph album.

What should I do without this family cemetery which makes everything so perfectly clear and evident? It has a hundred and twenty pages. On each page, four or six or sometimes only two photographs are carefully mounted, sometimes symmetrically, sometimes less so, but always in an arrangement governed by the right angle. It is bound in leather and the older it grows the stronger it smells of leather. At times my album has been exposed to the wind and weather. The pictures came loose and seemed so helpless that I hastened to paste them back in their accustomed places.

What novel – or what else in the world – can have the epic scope of a photograph album? May our Father in Heaven, the untiring amateur who each Sunday snaps us from above, at an unfortunate angle that makes for hideous foreshortening, and pastes our pictures, properly exposed or not, in his album, guide me safely through this album of mine; may he deter me from dwelling too long on my favorites and discourage Oskar's penchant for the tortuous and labyrinthine; for I am only too eager to get on from the photographs to the originals.

So much for that. Shall we take a look? Uniforms of all sorts, the styles and the haircuts change, Mama gets fatter and Jan gets flabbier, some of these people I don't even know, but I can guess who they are. I wonder who took this one, the art was on the downgrade. Yes, gradually the art photo of 1900 degenerates into the utilitarian photo of our day. Take this monument of my grandfather Koljaiczek and this passport photo of my friend Klepp. One need only hold them side by side, the sepia print of my grandfather and this glossy passport photo that seems to cry out for a rubber stamp, to see what progress has brought us to in photography. And all the paraphernalia this quick photography takes. Actually I should find fault with myself even more than with Klepp, for I am the owner of the album and should have maintained certain standards. If there is a hell in wait for us, I know what one of the more fiendish torments will be: they will shut up the naked soul in a room with the framed photographs of his day: Quick, turn on the pathos: O man amid snapshots, passport photos. O man beneath the glare of flash bulbs, O man standing erect by the leaning tower of Pisa, O photomaton man who must expose his right ear if he is to be worthy of a passport! And – off with the pathos. Maybe this hell will be tolerable because the worst pictures of all are not taken but only dreamed or, if they are taken, never developed.

Klepp and I had these pictures taken and developed during our early days in Jülicher-Strasse, when we ate spaghetti together and made friends. In those days I harbored plans for travel. That is, I was so gloomy that I resolved to take a trip and, to that end, apply for a passport. But since I hadn't money enough to finance a real trip, including Rome, Naples, or at least Paris, I was glad of the lack of cash, for what could have been more dismal than to set out on a trip in a state of depression? But since we had enough money to go to the movies, Klepp and I in those days attended motion picture theaters where, in keeping with Klepp's taste, wild West films were shown, and, in response to my needs, pictures where Maria Schell was the tearful nurse and Borsche, as the surgeon, played Beethoven sonatas by the open window after a difficult operation, and displayed a lofty sense of responsibility.

We were greatly dissatisfied that the performances should take only two hours. We should have been glad to see some of the programs twice. Often we arose at the end, determined to buy tickets for the next showing. But once we had left the hall and saw the line waiting outside the box office, our courage seeped away. Not only the thought of a second encounter with the ticket-seller but also the insolent stares with which total strangers mustered our physiognomies shamed us out of lengthening the line.

The upshot was that after nearly every show we went to a photo studio not far from the Graf-Adolf-Platz and had passport pictures taken. We were well known and our entrance was greeted with a smile; however, we were paying customers and treated politely as such. As soon as the booth was free, we were pushed into it by a young lady – all I remember about her is that she was nice. She deftly set our heads at the right angle, first mine, then Klepp's, and told us to fix our eyes on a certain point, and a moment later a flash of light and a bell synchronized with it announced that six successive likenesses had been transferred to the plate.

Still stiff around the corners of the mouth, we were pressed into comfortable wicker chairs by the young lady, who nicely, but no more than nicely, and nicely dressed too, asked us to be patient for five minutes. We were glad to wait. For now we had something to wait for – our passport pictures – and we were curious to see how they would turn out. In exactly seven minutes the still nice but otherwise nondescript young lady handed us two little paper envelopes and we paid.

The triumph in Klepp's slightly protuberant eyes! As soon as we had our envelopes, we had ipso facto an excuse for repairing to the nearest beer saloon, for no one likes to look at his own passport pictures on the open, dusty street, standing amid all the noise and bustle and blocking the traffic. Just as we were faithful to the photo studio, we always went to the same saloon in Friedrichstrasse. We ordered beer, blood sausage, onions, and rye bread, and, even before our order came, spread out the slightly damp photographs over the little round table and, while partaking of our beer and blood sausage, which had arrived in the meantime, immersed ourselves in our own strained features.

We always brought along other photographs taken on the occasion of previous movie shows. This gave us a basis for comparison; and where there is a basis for comparison, there is also ground for ordering a second, third, fourth glass of beer, to create merriment, or, as they say in the Rhineland, *ambiance*.

I am not trying to say that a passport photo of himself can cure a gloomy man of a gloom for which there is no ground; for true gloom is by nature groundless; such gloom, ours at least, can be traced to no identifiable cause, and with its almost riotous gratuitousness this gloom of ours attained a pitch of intensity that would yield to nothing. If there was any way of making friends with our gloom, it was through the photos, because in these serial snapshots we found an image of ourselves which, though not exactly clear, was – and that was the essential – passive and neutralized. They gave us a kind of freedom in our dealings with ourselves; we could drink beer, torture our blood sausages, make merry, and play. We bent and folded the pictures, and cut them up with the little scissors we carried about with us for this precise purpose. We juxtaposed old and new pictures, made ourselves one-eyed or three-eyed, put noses on our ears, made our exposed right ears into organs of speech or silence, combined chins and foreheads. And it was not only each with his own likeness that we made these montages; Klepp borrowed features from me and I from him: thus we succeeded in making new and, we hoped, happier creatures. Occasionally we gave a picture away.

We – I am speaking only of Klepp and myself, setting aside all synthetic photo-personalities – got into the habit of donating a photo to the waiter, whom we called Rudi, every time we saw him, and that happened at least once a week. Rudi, a type who ought to have had twelve children and at least eight wards, appreciated our distress; he had dozens of profiles of us and still more full-faced views, and even so his eyes were full of sympathy and he said thank you when after long deliberation and a careful process of selection we handed him his photo.

Oskar never gave any pictures to the waitress at the counter or to the redheaded young thing with the cigarette tray; it's not a good idea to give women pictures, for you never know what use they may make of them. Klepp, however, who with all his easy-going corpulence was a setup for the fair sex, who was communicative to the point of folly and required only a feminine presence to make him spill his innermost guts, must have given the cigarette girl a photo unbeknownst to me, for he became engaged to the snippety little thing and married her one day, because he wanted to have his picture back.

I have gotten ahead of myself and devoted too many words to the last pages of my album. The silly snapshots don't deserve it; however, if taken as a term of comparison, they may give you an idea how sublimely grandiose, how artistic if you will, the portrait of my grandfather Koljaiczek on the first page of the album still seems to me.

Short and stocky he stands there behind a richly carved coffee table. Unfortunately he had himself photographed not as a fire-bug, but as Wranka the volunteer fireman. But the tight-fitting fireman's uniform with the rescue medal and the fireman's helmet that gives the table the aspect of an altar almost take the place of the incendiary's mustache. How solemn is his gaze, how full of all the sorrow of those sorrowful years. That proud though tragic gaze seems to have been popular and prevalent in the days of the German Empire; we find it again in Gregor Koljaiczek, the drunken gunpowder-maker, who looks rather sober in his pic-tures. Taken in Czestochowa, the picture of Vincent Bronski holding a consecrated candle is more mystical in tone. A youthful portrait of the sickly Jan Bronski is a record of self-conscious melancholy, achieved by the methods of early photography.

The women of those days were less expert at finding the expression suited to their personality. In the photographs taken shortly before the First World War even my grandmother Anna, who, believe me, was somebody, hides behind a silly glued-on smile that carries not the slightest suggestion of her four great, asylum-giving skirts.

During the war years they continued to smile at the photog-rapher as he danced about beneath his black cloth. From this period I have a picture, double postcard size on stiff cardboard, of twenty-three nurses, including my mother, clustering timidly round the reassuring solidity of an army doctor. The nurses seem somewhat more relaxed in a picture of a costume ball attended by convalescent warriors. Mama ventures a wink and a rosebud mouth which despite her angel's wings and the tinsel in her hair seem to say that even angels have a sex. Matzerath is seen kneeling at her feet in a costume that he would have been only too glad to wear every day: he has on a starched chef's hat and he is even brandishing a ladle. But when wearing his uniform adorned with the Iron Cross Second Class, he too, like Koljaiczek and Bronski, peers into the distance with a wittingly tragic look, and in all the pictures he is superior to the women.

After the war the faces changed. The men look rather demobilized; now it is the women who rise to the occasion, who have grounds for looking solemn, and who, even when smiling, make no attempt to conceal an undertone of studied sorrow. Melancholy was becoming to the women of the twenties. With their little black spit curls they managed, whether sitting, standing, or half-reclining, to suggest a harmonious blend of madonna and harlot.

The picture of my mama at the age of twenty-three – it must have been taken shortly before the inception of her pregnancy – shows a young woman with a round, tranquil face slightly tilted on a firm, substantial neck. But tilted or not, she is always looking you straight in the eye. Good solid flesh, but the effect of solidity is called into question by the melancholy smile of the day and by those eyes, more grey than blue, which seem to look upon the souls of her fellow men – and her own soul as well – as solid objects, something like teacups or cigarette holders. I should say that the look in my mama's eyes is something more than soulful.

Not more interesting, but easier to appraise and hence more revealing, are the group photos of that period. How beautiful, how nuptial the wedding dresses were in the days of the Treaty of Rapallo. In his wedding photo Matzerath is still wearing a stiff collar. A fine figure of a man, he looks distinctly elegant, almost intellectual. His right foot is thrust forward, and he rather resembles a movie actor of the day, Harry Liedtke perhaps. The dresses were short. My mama's wedding dress, white and accordion-pleated, reaches barely below the knee, showing her shapely legs and cunning little dancing feet in white buckled shoes. Other pictures show the whole bridal assemblage. Surrounded by people who dress and pose like city dwellers, my grandmother Anna and her grace-favored brother Vincent are always conspicuous for their provincial gravity and a confidence-inspiring air of unsureness. Jan Bronski, who like my mama stems from the same potato field as his father and his Aunt Anna, manages to hide his rural Kashubian origins behind the festive elegance of a Polish postal official. He is small and frail amid these robust occupiers of space, and yet the extraordinary look in his eyes, the almost feminine regularity of his features, make him the center of every picture, even when he is on the edge of it.

For some time now I have been looking at a group picture taken shortly after the marriage. I have been compelled to take up my drum and drumsticks and, gazing at the faded brownish rectangle, attempt to conjure up the dimly visible three-cornered constellation.

The picture must have been taken in the Bronski flat in Magdeburger-Strasse not far from the Polish Students' House, for in the background we perceive a sunlit balcony of a type seen only in the Polish quarter, half-concealed by the vinelike foliage of pole beans. Mama is seated, Matzerath and Jan Bronski are standing. But how she sits and how they stand! For a time I foolishly tried to plot the constellation of this triumvirate – for she gave the full value of a man – with the help of a ruler, a triangle, and a school compass that Bruno had to go out for. Starting with the angle between neck and shoulder, I drew a triangle; I spun out projections, deduced similarities, described arcs which met significantly outside the triangle, i.e., in the foliage, and provided a point, because I needed a point, a point of vantage, a point of departure, a point of contact, a point of view.

All I accomplished with my metaphysical geometry was to dig a number of small but annoying holes in the precious photo with the point of my compass. What, I cannot help wondering, is so remarkable about that print? What was it that made me seek and, if you will, actually find mathematical and, preposterously enough, cosmic references in it? Three persons: a woman sitting, two men standing. She with a dark marcel wave, Matzerath curly blond, Jan chestnut brown, combed back flat from the forehead. All three are smiling, Matzerath more than Jan Bronski; and both men a good deal more than Mama, for their smile shows their upper teeth while of her smile there is barely a trace in the corners of her mouth and not the least suggestion in her eyes. Matzerath has his left hand resting on Mama's right shoulder; Jan contents himself with leaning his right hand lightly on the back of the chair. She, her knees slightly to one side but otherwise directly facing the camera, has in her lap a portfolio which I took years ago for one of Jan's stamp albums, later reinterpreted as a fashion magazine, and more recently as a collection of movie stars out of cigarette packages. Her hands look as if she would begin to leaf through the album the moment the picture was taken. All three seem happy, as though congratulating one another on their immunity to surprises of the sort that can arise only if one member of the triumvirate should acquire a secret life – if he hasn't had one all along. In their tripartite solidarity, they have little need of the fourth person, Jan's wife Hedwig Bronski née Lemke, who may at that time have been pregnant with the future Stephan; all they needed her for was to aim the camera at them, so perpetuating their triangular felicity, photographically at least.

I have detached other rectangles from the album and held them next to this one. Scenes showing either Mama with Matzerath or Mama with Jan Bronski. In none of these pictures is the immutable, the ultimate solution so clearly discernible as in the balcony picture. Jan and Mama by themselves: this one smacks of tragedy, money-grubbing, exaltation turning to surfeit, a surfeit of exaltation. Matzerath and Mama: here we find an atmosphere of conjugal weekends at home, a sizzling of cutlets, a bit of grumbling before dinner and a bit of yawning after dinner; jokes are told before going to bed, and the tax returns are discussed: here we have the cultural background of the marriage. And yet I prefer such photographed boredom to the distasteful snapshot of later years, showing Mama seated on Jan Bronski's lap in the Forest of Oliva near Freudenthal; because this last picture with its lewdness – Jan's hand has disappeared under Mama's skirt – communicates nothing but the mad passion of this unhappy pair, steeped in adultery from the very first day of Mama's marriage; Matzerath, I presume, was the disabused photographer. Here we see none of the serenity of the balcony picture, none of the delicate, circumspect little gestures which seem to have been possible only when both men were together, standing behind or beside Mama or lying at her feet as on the bathing beech at Heubude; see photo.

There is still another picture which shows the three protagonists of my early years forming a triangle. Though it lacks the concentration of the balcony scene, it emanates the same tense peace, which can probably be concluded only among three persons. We may get pretty sick of the triangle situations in plays; but come to think of it, what can two people do if left to themselves on the stage except dialogue each other to death or secretly long for a third? In my picture the three of them are together. They are playing skat. That is, they are holding their cards like well-organized fans, but instead of looking at their trumps and plotting their strategy, they are looking into the camera. Jan's hand lies flat, except for the raised forefinger, beside a pile of change; Matzerath is digging his nails into the tablecloth; Mama is indulging in a little joke which strikes me as rather good: she has drawn a card and is showing it to the camera lens but not to her fellow players. How easy it is with a single gesture, by merely showing the queen of hearts, to conjure up a symbol that is not too blatant; for who would not swear by the queen of hearts?

Skat – as everyone should know, skat can only be played three-handed – was not just a handy game for Mama and the two men; it was their refuge, their haven, to which they always retreated when life threatened to beguile them into playing, in one combination or another, such silly two-handed games as backgammon or sixty-six.

That's enough now for those three, who brought me into the world though they wanted for nothing. Before I come to myself, a word about Gretchen Scheffler, Mama's girl friend, and her baker consort Alexander Scheffler. He bald-headed, she laughing with her great equine teeth, a good half of which were gold. He short-legged, his feet when he is sitting down dangling several inches above the carpet, she always in dresses she herself had knitted, with patterns that could not be too intricate. From later years, photos of both Schefflers in deck chairs or standing beside lifeboats belonging to the 'Strength through Joy' ship *Wilhelm Gustloff*, or on the promenade deck of the *Tannenberg* (East Prussian Steamship Lines). Year by year they took trips and brought souvenirs from Pillau, Norway, the Azores, or Italy safely home to their house in Kleinhammer-Weg, where he baked rolls and she embroidered cushion covers. When Alexander Scheffler was not talking, he never stopped moistening his upper lip with the tip of his tongue, a habit which Matzerath's friend, Greff the greengrocer who lived across the way, thought obscene and disgusting.

Although Greff was married, he was more scout leader than

husband. A photo shows him broad, healthy, and unsmiling, in a uniform with shorts, wearing a scout hat and the braid of a leader. Beside him in the same rig stands a blond lad of maybe thirteen, with rather too large eyes. Greff's arm is thrown affectionately over his shoulder. I didn't know the boy, but I was later to become acquainted with Greff through his wife Lina and to learn to understand him.

I am losing myself amid snapshots of 'Strength through Joy' tourists and records of tender boy-scout eroticism. Let me skip a few pages and come to myself, to my first photographic likeness.

I was a handsome child. The picture was taken on Pentecost, 1925. I was eight months old, two months younger than Stephan Bronski, who is shown on the next page in the same format, exuding an indescribable commonplaceness. My postcard has a wavy scalloped edge; the reverse side has lines for the address and was probably printed in a large edition for family consumption. Within the wide rectangle the photograph itself has the shape of an oversymmetrical egg. Naked and symbolizing the yolk, I am lying on my belly on a white fur, which must have been the gift of a benevolent polar bear to an Eastern European photographer specializing in baby pictures. For my first likeness, as for so many photos of the period, they selected the inimitable warm brownish tint which I should call 'human' in contrast to the inhumanly glossy black-and-white photographs of our day. Some sort of hazy greenery, probably artificial, provides a dark background, relieved only by a few spots of light. Whereas my sleek healthy body lies flat and complacent on the fur, basking in polar well-being, my billiard-ball skull strains upward and peers with glistening eyes at the beholder of my nakedness.

A baby picture, you may say, like all other baby pictures. Consider the hands, if you please. You will have to admit that my earliest likeness differs conspicuously from all the innumerable records of cunning little existences you may have seen in photograph albums the world over. You see me with clenched fists. You don't see any little sausage fingers playing with tufts of fur in self-forgetful response to some obscure haptic urge. My little claws hover in earnest concentration on a level with my head, ready to descend, to strike. To strike what? The drum!

It is still absent, the photo shows no sign of that drum which, beneath the light bulbs of my Creation, had been promised me for my third birthday; yet how simple it would be for anyone experienced in photo-montage to insert a toy drum of the appropriate size. There would be no need to change my position in any way. Only the ridiculous stuffed animal, to which I am not paying the slightest attention, would have to be removed. It is a disturbing element in this otherwise harmonious composition commemorating the astute, clear-sighted age when the first milk teeth are trying to pierce through.

After a while, they stopped putting me on polar-bear skins. I was probably about a year and a half old when they pushed me, ensconced in a high-wheeled baby carriage, close to a board fence covered by a layer of snow which faithfully follows its contours and convinces me that the picture was taken in January, 1926. When I consider it at length, the crude construction of the fence, the smell of tar it gives off, connect me with the suburb of Hochstriess, whose extensive barracks had formerly housed the Mackensen Hussars and in my time the Free City police. But since I remember no one who lived out there, I can only conclude that the picture was taken one day when my parents were paying a visit to some people whom we never, or only seldom, saw in the ensuing period.

Despite the wintry season, Mama and Matzerath, who flank the baby carriage, are without overcoats. Mama has on a long-sleeved embroidered Russian blouse: one cannot help imagining that the Tsar's family is having its picture taken in deepest, wintriest Russia, that Rasputin is holding the camera, that I am the Tsarevich, and that behind the fence Mensheviks and Bolsheviks are tinkering with homemade bombs and plotting the downfall of my autocratic family. But the illusion is shattered by Matzerath's correct, Central European, and, as we shall see, prophetic shop-keeper's exterior. We were in the quiet suburb of Hochstriess, my parents had left the house of our host just for a moment – why bother to put coats on? – just time enough to let their host snap them with little Oskar, who obliged with his cunningest look, and a moment later they would be deliciously warming themselves over coffee, cake, and whipped cream.

There are still a dozen or more snapshots aged one, two, and two and a half, lying, sitting, crawling, and running. They aren't bad; but all in all, they merely lead up to the full-length portrait they had taken of me in honor of my third birthday.

Here I've got it. I've got my drum. It is hanging in front of my tummy, brand-new with its serrated red and white fields. With a solemnly resolute expression, I hold the sticks crossed over the top of it. I have on a striped pull-over and resplendent patent leather shoes. My hair is standing up like a brush ready for action and in each of my blue eyes is reflected the determination to wield a power that would have no need of vassals or henchmen. It was in this picture that I first arrived at a decision which I have had no reason to alter. It was then that I declared, resolved, and determined that I would never under any circumstances be a politician, much less a grocer, that I would stop right there, remain as I was – and so I did; for many years I not only stayed the same size but clung to the same attire.

Little people and big people, Little Claus and Great Claus, Tiny Tim and Carolus Magnus, David and Goliath, Jack the Giant Killer and, of course, the giant; I remained the three-year-old, the gnome, the Tom Thumb, the pigmy, the Lilliputian, the midget, whom no one could persuade to grow. I did so in order to be exempted from the big and little catechism and in order not, once grown to five-foot-eight adulthood, to be driven by this man who face to face with his shaving mirror called himself my father, into a business, the grocery business, which as Matzerath saw it, would, when Oskar turned twenty-one, become his grownup world. To avoid playing the cash register I clung to my drum and from my third birthday on refused to grow by so much a finger's breadth. I remained the precocious three-year-old, towered over by grownups but superior to all grownups, who refused to measure his shadow with theirs, who was complete both inside and outside, while they, to the very brink of the grave, were condemned to worry their heads about 'development,' who had only to confirm what they were compelled to gain by hard and often painful experience, and who had no need to change his shoe and trouser size year after year just to prove that something was growing.

However, and here Oskar must confess to development of a sort, something did grow – and not always to my best advantage – ultimately taking on Messianic proportions; but what grownup in my day had eyes and ears for Oskar, the eternal three-year-old drummer?

Smash a Little Windowpane

I have just described a photograph showing Oskar full length with drum and drumsticks, and at the same time disclosed what decisions, having had three years in which to mature, were definitely taken by Oskar as he was being photographed at his birthday party, not far from a cake with three candles. But now the album lies silent beside me, and I must speak of certain events about which it has nothing to say. Even if they do not explain why I continued to be three years old, there is no doubt that they happened, and what is more, that I made them happen.

From the very beginning it was plain to me: grownups will not understand you. If you cease to offer them any discernible growth, they will say you are retarded; they will drag you and their money to dozens of doctors, looking for an explanation if not a cure for your deficiency. Consequently I myself, in order to keep the consultations within tolerable limits, felt obliged to provide a plausible ground for my failure to grow, even before the doctor should offer his explanation.

A sunny day in September, my third birthday. An atmosphere of late summer reverie; even Gretchen Scheffler's laughter was muffled. Mama at the piano intoning airs from the *Gypsy Baron*, Jan standing behind her, his hand grazing her shoulder, giving himself an air of following the music. Matzerath in the kitchen, already getting supper. Grandma Anna with Hedwig Bronski and Alexander Scheffler moving over to sit with Greff, because the greengrocer always knew stories, boy-scout stories full of loyalty and courage; and in the background, the upright clock which didn't miss a single quarter-hour of that finespun September day. And since, like the clock, they were all so busy, and since a line ran from the Gypsy Baron's Hungary by way of Greff's boy scouts (who were touring the Vosges Mountains), past Matzerath's kitchen, where Kashubian mushrooms with scrambled eggs and

47

tripe were sputtering in the frying pan, down the hallway to the shop, I, vaguely improvising on my drum, followed it. Soon I was in the shop, standing behind the counter – piano, mushrooms, and Vosges already far behind me. There I noticed that the trap door leading to the cellar was open; Matzerath, who had gone down to get a can of mixed fruit for dessert, must have forgotten to close it.

It was a moment before I realized what that trap door demanded of me. Not suicide, certainly not. That would have been too simple. The alternative, however, was difficult and painful; it demanded sacrifice, and even then, as has been the case ever since when a sacrifice has been required of me, such an idea brought the sweat to my forehead. Above all, no harm must come to my drum; I would have to carry it carefully down the sixteen worn-down steps and lodge it among the flour sacks, so motivating its unharmed condition. Then back up again as far as the eighth step, no, the seventh, no, actually the fifth would do just as well. But from that height it would be impossible to combine safety with plausible injury. Back up again, too high this time, to the tenth, then finally, from the ninth step, I flung myself down, carrying a shelf laden with bottles of raspberry syrup along with me, and landed head first on the cement floor of our cellar.

Even before the curtain passed over my consciousness, I registered the success of my experiment: the bottles of raspberry syrup which I had intentionally taken with me in my fall made clatter enough to bring Matzerath from the kitchen, Mama from the piano, and the rest of the birthday party from the Vosges, all running into the shop, to the open trap door, and down the stairs.

Before they arrived, I had time to enjoy a whiff of the raspberry syrup, to observe that my head was bleeding, and to wonder – by now they were already on the stairs – whether it was Oskar's blood or the raspberries that smelled so sweet and sleepy-making, but I was delighted that everything had gone off smoothly and that, thanks to my foresight, the drum had suffered no injury.

I think it was Greff who carried me upstairs. It was only in the living room that Oskar emerged from a cloud which consisted no doubt half of raspberry syrup and half of his juvenile blood. The doctor had not arrived yet; Mama was screaming and flailing out at Matzerath, who was trying to pacify her, striking him in the face, and not just with her palm but with her knuckles as well, calling him a murderer.

And so with a single fall, not exactly without gravity but its degree of gravity calculated by myself in advance, I not only supplied a reason – repeatedly confirmed by the doctors and in general satisfactory to the grownups who simply have to have their explanations for things – for my failure to grow, but in addition and without any real intention on my part, transformed our harmless, good-natured Matzerath into a guilty Matzerath. He had left the trap door open, my mother put all the blame on him, and for years to come he incurred Mama's merciless, though not too frequent reproaches.

My fall brought me four weeks in the hospital and after that, apart from the weekly visits to Dr. Hollatz later on, relative peace from the medical profession. On my very first day as a drummer I had succeeded in giving the world a sign; my case was explained even before the grownups so much as suspected the true nature of the condition I myself had induced. Forever after the story was: on his third birthday our little Oskar fell down the cellar stairs, no bones were broken, but he just wouldn't grow any more.

And I began to drum. Our apartment house had four stories. From the ground floor to the attic I drummed up and down stairs. From Labesweg to Max-Halbe-Platz, thence to Neuschottland, Marienstrasse, Kleinhammer Park, the Aktien Brewery, Aktien Pond, Fröbel Green, Pestalozzi School, the Neue Markt, and back again to Labesweg. The drum stood up well under the strain, the grownups around me not quite so well, they were always wanting to interrupt my drum, to cross it up, to crimp my drumsticks – but nature looked out for me.

The ability to drum the necessary distance between grownups and myself developed shortly after my fall, almost simultaneously with the emergence of a voice that enabled me to sing in so high-pitched and sustained a vibrato, to sing-scream so piercingly that no one dared to take away the drum that was destroying his eardrums; for when the drum was taken away from me, I screamed, and when I screamed, valuable articles burst into bits: I had the gift of shattering glass with my singing: my screams demolished vases, my singing made windowpanes crumple and drafts prevail; like a chaste and therefore merciless diamond, my voice cut through the doors of glass cabinets and, without losing its innocence, proceeded inside to wreak havoc on harmonious, graceful liqueur glasses, bestowed by loving hands and covered with a light film of dust.

It was not long before my talents became known the whole length of our street, from Brösener-Weg to the housing development by the airfield. Whenever I caught the attention of the neighborhood children, whose games – such as 'Pickled herring, one, two, three' or 'Where's the Witch, black as pitch?' or 'I see something you don't see' – didn't interest me in the slightest, the whole unwashed chorus of them would begin to squeal:

> Smash a little windowpane,
> Put sugar in the beer,
> Mrs. Biddle plays the fiddle,
> Dear, dear, dear.

It was a silly, meaningless jingle and troubled me very little; I took up the simple rhythm, which was not without charm, and drummed my way from start to finish, through the little pieces and through Mrs. Biddle. Thus drumming, I marched down the street and though I was not the Pied Piper, the children followed in my wake.

Even today, when Bruno is washing my windows, for instance, my drum, as often as not, will find a moment for the rhythm of that little jingle.

More irritating than the children's lyrical mockery, especially for my parents, was the costly fact that every windowpane broken in the entire neighborhood by rowdies big or little was blamed on me and my voice. At first Mama conscientiously paid for the breakage, most of which was the work of slingshots, then at last she saw what was what and, putting on her frosty businesslike look, demanded proof when damages were claimed. And indeed, I was unjustly accused. Nothing could have been more mistaken at the time than to suppose that I was possessed by a childlike passion for destruction, that I was consumed by an unreasoning hatred of glass and glassware. Only children who play are destructive out of mischief. I never played, I worked on my drum, and as for my voice, its miraculous powers were mobilized, in the beginning at least, only in self-defense. It was only when my right to drum was threatened that I made weapons of my vocal cords. If with the same tones and techniques I had been able to cut up Gretchen Scheffler's beastly, intricately embroidered tablecloths or to remove the somber polish from the piano, I should gladly have left all glassware intact. But tablecloths and varnish were impervious to my voice. It was beyond my powers to efface the pattern of the wallpaper with my screams, or by rubbing together two long-drawn-out tones as our Stone Age ancestors rubbed flints, to produce the heat that would produce the spark needed to kindle decorative flames in the tinder-dry curtains, spiced with tobacco smoke, of our living room windows. I never sang the leg off a chair in which Matzerath or Alexander Scheffler was sitting. I should gladly have defended myself in less destructive, less miraculous ways, but no other weapon was available; only glass heeded my commands, and had to pay for it.

It was shortly after my third birthday that I staged my first successful performance of this nature. I had been in possession of the drum for about four weeks and, conscientious as I was, I had pretty well worn it out. The serrated red and white cylinder still held top and bottom together, but the hole in the playing surface could not be overlooked; since I scorned to use the other side, it became larger and larger, spread out in all directions, and developed fierce jagged edges. Bits of tin worn thin by my drumming broke off, fell inside the drum, and at every beat set up a disgruntled clatter of their own; white specks of enamel, unequal to the hard life the drum had been leading, took up residence on the living room rug and the red-brown flooring of the bedroom.

It was feared that I would cut myself on the sharp edges. Particularly Matzerath, who had become exceedingly safety-minded since my fall from the cellar stairs, pleaded with me to be careful. Since, when I drummed, my violently agitated wrists were always close to the jagged edge of the crater, I must own that Matzerath's fears were not groundless, though they may have been exaggerated. Of course they could have forestalled all danger by giving me a new drum; but this was not their plan; they simply wanted to deprive me of my good old drum, which had taken the fall with me, which had gone to the hospital with me and come home with me, which accompanied me upstairs and down, over cobblestones and sidewalks, through 'Pickled herring, one two three' and past 'I see something you don't see' and 'Where's the Witch' – yes, they wanted to take it away from me and give me nothing in return. They tried to bribe me with some silly old chocolate. Mama held it out to me, pursing her lips. It was Matzerath who, with a show of severity, laid hands on my decrepit instrument. I clung to it with all my might. He pulled. My strength, which was barely enough for drumming, began to give out. Slowly, one red tongue of flame after another, the cylinder was slipping from my grasp. At this moment Oskar, who until then had passed as a quiet, almost too well-behaved child, succeeded in emitting that first annihilating scream: the polished round crystal which protected the honey-colored dial of our clock from dust and moribund flies burst and fell to the floor (for the carpet did not reach all the way to the base of the clock), where the destruction was completed. However, the inside of the precious mechanism incurred no harm; serenely the pendulum continued on its way, and so did the hands. Not even the chimes, which otherwise reacted almost hysterically to the slightest jolt, which would be thrown off kilter by the passage of a beer truck, were one bit dismayed by my scream; it was only the glass that broke, but it did a thorough job of it.

'The clock is broken!' cried Matzerath and let go of the drum. With a brief glance I convinced myself that nothing had happened to the clock proper, that only the glass was gone. But to Matzerath, as well as to Mama and Uncle Jan Bronski, who was paying his usual Sunday afternoon call, it seemed that the damage must be much more serious. They blanched, exchanged shifty, helpless glances, and reached for the nearest solid object, the tile stove, the piano, the sideboard. There they stood fast, afraid to budge. Jan Bronski's eyes were filled with supplication and I could see his parched lips move. I still believe that he was inwardly muttering a prayer, perhaps: 'O Lamb of God, Who taketh away the sins of the world, *miserere nobis*.' Three of these, followed by a 'Lord, I am not worthy that Thou shouldst enter under my roof; say but the word . . .'

Naturally the Lord didn't say a thing. Besides, the clock wasn't broken, but just the glass. However, there is something very strange and childish in the way grownups feel about their clocks

– in that respect, I was never a child. I am willing to agree that the clock is probably the most remarkable thing that grownups ever produced. Grownups have it in them to be creative, and sometimes, with the help of ambition, hard work, and a bit of luck they actually are, but being grownups, they have no sooner created some epoch-making invention than they become a slave to it.

What, after all, is a clock? Without your grownup it is nothing. It is the grownup who winds it, who sets it back or ahead, who takes it to the watchmaker to be checked, cleaned, and when necessary repaired. Just as with the cuckoo that stops calling too soon, just as with upset saltcellars, spiders seen in the morning, black cats on the left, the oil portrait of Uncle that falls off the wall because the nail has come loose in the plaster, just as in a mirror, grownups see more in and behind a clock than any clock can justify.

At length, Mama, who with all her flightiness had a cool head on her shoulders and whose very frivolity led her to put optimistic interpretations on all ostensible signs or portents, found words to save the situation.

'Shards are good luck!' she cried, snapping her fingers, brought dustpan and brush, and swept up the good luck.

If Mama's words are taken at face value, I brought my parents, relatives, friends, and even a good many total strangers plenty of good luck by screaming or singing to pieces any glassware belonging to or being used by persons who tried to take my drum away, including windowpanes, crystal bowls full of artificial fruit, full beer glasses, empty beer bottles, or those little flacons of vernal fragrance that laymen call perfume bottles, in short, any product whatever of the glass blower's art.

To limit the damage, for I have always been a lover of the glassware, I concentrated, when they tried to take my drum away at night instead of letting me take it to bed with me, on shattering one or more of the four bulbs in our living room lamp. On my fourth birthday, at the beginning of September, 1928, I threw the whole assembled company – my parents, the Bronskis, Grandma Koljaiczek, the Schefflers, and the Greffs, who had given me everything conceivable, tin soldiers, a sailboat, a fire engine, but no drum; who wanted me to play with tin soldiers and waste my time with this fool fire engine, who were planning to rob me of my battered but trusty old drum, to steal it away from me and leave me, in its place, this sailboat, useless in itself and incorrectly rigged to boot – as I was saying, I threw the whole lot of them, who had eyes for the sole purpose of overlooking me and my desires, into primeval darkness with a circular scream that demolished all four bulbs in our hanging lamp.

Ah, grownups! After the first cries of terror, after the first almost desperate demands for light, they grew accustomed to the darkness, and by the time my Grandma Koljaiczek, who aside from little Stephan Bronski was the only one who had nothing to gain by the darkness, had gone to the shop, with blubbering little Stephan hanging on her skirts, for candles and returned to the room bearing light, the rest of the company, by now in an advanced state of intoxication, had paired off strangely.

As was to be expected, Mama, with disheveled corsage, was sitting on Jan Bronski's lap. It was the opposite of appetizing to see Alexander Scheffler, the short-legged baker, almost submerged amid the billows of Mrs. Greff. Matzerath was licking Gretchen Scheffler's gold horse teeth. Only Hedwig Bronski sat alone with her hands in her lap, her cow's eyes pious in the candlelight, close but not too close to Greff the greengrocer, who, though he had had nothing to drink, was singing in a sad sweet voice, full of languor and melancholy. Turning toward Hedwig Bronski, he invited her to join him in a duet and together they sang a boyscout song about a scoutmaster named Rübezahl whose spirit haunted the mountains of Bohemia.

I had forgotten. Under the table sat Oskar with the ruins of his drum, coaxing a last vestige of rhythm from it. My feeble but regular drumbeats may well have been welcome to the ecstatically displaced persons who were sitting or lying about the room. For, like varnish, my drumming covered over the persistent sounds of smacking and sucking.

I stayed under the table when my grandmother came in like an angel of wrath with her candles, beheld Sodom and Gomorrah in the candlelight, flew into a rage that made her candles tremble, called them pigs the whole lot of them, and put an end both to the idyll and to Rübezahl's excursions in the mountains by sticking the candles on saucers, taking skat cards out of the sideboard, and throwing them down on the table, all the while comforting Stephan, who was still blubbering. Soon Matzerath put new bulbs in the old fixtures of our lamp, chairs were moved, beer bottles popped open; over my head, a game of skat began for a tenth of a pfennig a point. Mama proposed at the very start that the stakes be raised to a quarter of a pfennig, but this struck Uncle Jan as too risky and the game continued on this niggardly level except when the stakes were raised by a double count or an occasional grand with four.

I felt fine under the table, in the shelter of the tablecloth. Lightly drumming, I fell in with the sounds overhead, followed the developments of the game, and in exactly an hour announced skat: Jan Bronski had lost. He had good cards, but he lost all the same. It was no wonder; he wasn't paying attention. His mind was on very different things than his diamonds without two. Right at the start, while still talking with his aunt, trying to tell her that the little orgy in the dark was nothing to get excited about, he had slipped off one shoe, and thrust forward, past my head, a grey sock with a foot in it, searching for, and finding, my mama's knee. Thereupon Mama had moved closer to the table and Jan, who, in response to Matzerath's bid, had just passed, lifted the hem of her dress with his toe, so enabling his entire inhabited sock, which luckily he had put on fresh that same day, to wander about between her thighs. I have to hand it to my mother, who in spite of this woolen provocation beneath the table managed, up there on the crisp tablecloth, to execute the most daring games, including clubs without four, accompanied by a flow of the sprightliest talk, and won while Jan, growing more and more intrepid under the table, lost several games which even Oskar would have carried to a successful conclusion with somnambulistic certainty.

Later on poor tired little Stephan joined me under the table and, quite at a loss to know what his father's trouser leg was doing under my mama's skirt, soon fell asleep.

Clear to slightly cloudy. Light showers in the afternoon. The very next day Jan Bronski came over, took away the wretched sailboat he had given me, and exchanged it for a drum at Sigismund Markus' toystore. Slightly wilted from the rain, he came back late in the afternoon with a brand-new drum of the model with which I had grown so familiar, with the same red flames on a white field, and held it out to me, at the same time withdrawing my old wreck, which had retained only the barest vestiges of its paint. As Jan gripped the tired drum and I the new one, the eyes of Jan, Mama, and Matzerath were glued on Oskar; I almost had to smile, goodness, did they think I clung to tradition for its own sake, that I was burdened by principles?

Without emitting the cry expected by all, without so much as a note of glass-destroying song, I relinquished the relic and devoted myself with both hands to the new instrument. After two hours of attentive drumming, I had got the hang of it.

But not all the grownups around me proved as understanding as Jan Bronski. Shortly after my fifth birthday, in 1929 – there had been considerable talk about the stock market crash in New York and I had begun to wonder whether my grandfather Koljaiczek, with his lumber business in far-off Buffalo, had also suffered losses – Mama, alarmed at my by now quite obvious failure to grow, took me by the hand and inaugurated our Wednesday visits to the office of Dr. Hollatz in Brünshofer-Weg. His examinations were interminable and exasperating, but I put up with them, because even at that tender age I was very much taken with the white dress of Sister Inge, Dr. Hollatz' assistant, which reminded me of Mama's much-photographed wartime activity as a nurse. Intense concentration on the new system of pleats in her uniform enabled me to ignore the stream of words, by turns sternly authoritative and unpleasantly uncle-ish, that poured from the doctor's lips.

His spectacles reflecting the furnishings of his office – lots of chrome, nickel, and smooth enamel; shelves and glass cabinets with neatly labeled bottles containing snakes, toads, salamanders, and the embryos of humans, pigs, and monkeys – Hollatz, after each examination, shook his head thoughtfully, leafed through my case history, questioned Mama about my fall, and quieted her when she began to vilify Matzerath, guilty now and forever of leaving the trap door open.

One Wednesday, after this had been going on for months, when Dr. Hollatz, probably in order to convince himself and perhaps Sister Inge as well that his treatment was bringing results, tried to take my drum away, I destroyed the greater part of his collection of snakes, toads, and embryos.

This was the first time Oskar had tried his voice on a whole set of filled and carefully sealed glasses. The success was unique and overwhelming for all present, even for Mama, who knew all about my private relation to glassware. With my very first trim, economical scream, I cut the cabinet in which Hollatz kept his loathsome curiosities wide open, and sent an almost square pane of glass toppling to the linoleum floor where, still preserving its square shape, it cracked into a thousand pieces. Then, lending my scream greater relief and throwing economy to the winds, I shattered one test tube after another.

The tubes popped like firecrackers. The greenish, partly coagulated alcohol squirted and splashed, carrying its prepared, pale, gloomy-eyed contents to the red linoleum floor, and filling the room with so palpable a stench that Mama grew sick to her stomach and Sister Inge had to open the windows.

Dr. Hollatz managed to turn the loss of his collection to his advantage. A few weeks after my act of violence, he published an article about me, Oskar M., the child with the glass-shattering voice, in a medical journal. The theory with which Dr. Hollatz succeeded in filling more than twenty pages is said to have attracted attention in medical circles both in Germany and abroad, and led to a whole series of articles by specialists, both in agreement and disagreement. He sent Mama several copies of his article and the pride she took in it gave me food for thought. She never wearied of reading passages from it to the Greffs, the Schefflers, her Jan, and, regularly after dinner, to Matzerath. Even her customers were subjected to readings and were filled with admiration for Mama, who had a strikingly imaginative way of mispronouncing the technical terms. As for me, the first appearance of my name in periodical literature left me just about cold. My already keen skepticism led me to judge Dr. Hollatz' opusculum for what it essentially was: a long-winded, not unskillfully formulated display of irrelevancies by a physician who was angling for a professorship.

Today as he lies in his mental hospital, unable to damage even his toothbrush glass with his singing, with doctors of the same type as Hollatz coming in and out, giving him Rorschach tests, association tests, and tests of every other conceivable kind in the hope of finding a high-sounding name for the disorder that led to his confinement, Oskar likes to think back on the archaic period of his voice. In those early days he shattered glass only when necessary, but then with great thoroughness, whereas later on, in the heyday and decadence of his art, he exercised it even when not impelled by outward circumstances. Succumbing to the mannerism of a late period, he began to sing out of pure playfulness, becoming as it were a devotee of art for art's sake. He employed glass as a medium of self-expression, and grew older in the process.

The Schedule

Klepp often spends hours drawing up schedules. The fact that while doing so he regularly devours blood sausage and warmed-over lentils, confirms my thesis, which is simply that dreamers are gluttons. And the assiduity with which he fills in his hours and half-hours confirms another theory of mine, to wit, that only first-class lazybones are likely to turn out labor-saving inventions.

This year again Klepp has spent more than two weeks trying to schedule his activities. He came to see me yesterday. For a while he behaved mysteriously, then fished an elaborately folded sheet of paper out of his breast pocket and handed it to me. He was obviously very pleased with himself: another of his labor-saving schemes.

I looked through his handiwork, there was nothing very new about it: breakfast at ten; contemplation until lunchtime; after lunch a nap (one hour), then coffee, in bed if transportation was available; flute playing in bed (one hour); get up; play bagpipes while marching round the room (one hour); more bagpipes out in the courtyard (half an hour). Next came a two-hour period, spent every other day over beer and blood sausage and the alternate day at the movies; in either case, before the movies or over the beer, discreet propaganda for the illegal Communist Party of

Germany, not to exceed half an hour, musn't overdo it. Three nights a week to be spent playing dance music at the Unicorn; on Saturday, beer and progaganda transferred to the evening, afternoon reserved for a bath and massage in Grünstrasse, followed by hygiene with girl (three-quarters of an hour) at the 'U 9,' then with the same girl and her girl friend coffee and cake at Schwab's, a shave and if necessary a haircut just before the barber's closing time; quick to the Photomaton; then beer, blood sausage, Party propaganda, and relaxation.

I admired Klepp's carefully custom-made schedule, asked him for a copy, and inquired what he did to fill in occasional gaps. 'Sleep, or think of the Party,' he replied after the briefest reflection.

Naturally this led me to Oskar's first experience with a schedule.

It began quite harmlessly with Auntie Kauer's kindergarten. Hedwig Bronski called for me every morning and took me, along with her Stephan, to Auntie Kauer's place in Posadowski-Weg, where we and six to ten other little urchins – a few were always sick – were compelled to play ad nauseam. Luckily my drum passed as a toy, I was never obliged to play with building blocks, and I was constrained to mount a rocking horse only when an equestrian drummer in a paper helmet was required. My drumming score was Auntie Kauer's black silk, extraordinarily buttonsome dress. Several times a day I unbuttoned her on my drum and once her dress was open buttoned it up again. She was all wrinkles and very skinny, I don't think it was her body I had in mind.

The afternoon walks down avenues bordered with chestnut trees to Jeschkentaler Forest, past the Gutenberg Monument, and up to the Erbsberg were so pleasantly tedious and angelically silly that even today I should be very glad to go on one of those picture-book outings, guided by Auntie Kauer's papery hand.

First we were harnessed, all six, eight, or twelve of us. The shaft was a pale-blue strip of knitted wool. To each side were attached six woolen bridles with bells, room for twelve children in all. Auntie Kauer held the reins, and we trotted along ahead of her tinkling and twittering, I sluggishly drumming, through the autumnal suburban streets. Now and then Auntie Kauer struck up 'Jesus, for thee we live, Jesus, for thee we die' or 'Star of the

Sea, I greet thee.' We filled the clear October air with 'O Mary, help me' and 'Swe-e-e-t Mother of God,' and the passers-by found it very touching. When we came to the main street, the traffic had to stop for us. Street cars, automobiles, horse-drawn vehicles stood motionless as we carried the Star of the Sea across the avenue. There was a crackling as of paper when Auntie Kauer waved her hand to thank the policeman who had directed our crossing.

'Our Lord Jesus will reward you,' she promised with a rustle of her silk dress.

Actually I was sorry when Oskar, in the spring of his seventh year, had to leave Fräulein Kauer and her buttons along with and because of Stephan. Politics was at the bottom of it, and where there is politics, there is violence. We had just reached the Erbsberg. Auntie Kauer removed our woolen harness, the leaves glistened, and new life was stirring in the treetops. Auntie Kauer sat on a moss-covered road marker indicating the various spots that could be reached on foot in one, one and a half, and two hours. Like a young girl in whom the spring has awakened unidentified feelings, she began to sing tra-la-la with the spasmodic movements of the head that one would ordinarily expect of a guinea hen, knitting the while a new harness, which was to be flaming red. Unhappily, I never got to wear it, for just then cries were heard from the bushes, Fräulein Kauer fluttered to her feet and, drawing red yarn behind her, raced on stiltlike legs into the thicket. I followed her and the yarn, which was not as red as the sight that soon met my eyes: Stephan's nose was bleeding profusely and a boy named Lothar, with curly hair and fine blue veins on his temples, was kneeling on the sickly little fellow's chest, resolutely belaboring his nose.

'Polack!' he hissed between blows. 'Polack!' When, five minutes later, Auntie Kauer had us back in our light-blue harness – I alone ran free, winding up the red yarn – she uttered a prayer that is normally recited between Consecration and Communion: 'Bowed with shame, full of pain and remorse . . .'

We descended the Erbsberg and halted at the Gutenberg Monument. Pointing a long finger at Stephan, who was whimpering and holding a handkerchief to his nose, she remarked gently: 'He can't help it if he's a little Pole.'

On Auntie Kauer's advice, Stephan was taken out of kindergarten. Though Oskar was not a Pole and was no great admirer of Stephan, he made it clear that if Stephan couldn't go, he wouldn't either. Then Easter came and they resolved to give school a try. Dr. Hollatz decided behind his horn-rimmed glasses that it could do no harm, and this was also his spoken opinion: 'It can do little Oskar no harm.'

Jan Bronski, who was planning to send his Stephan to Polish public school after Easter, refused to be dissuaded. Over and over again he pointed out to my Mama and Matzerath that he was a Polish civil servant, receiving good pay for good work at the Polish Post Office. He was a Pole after all and Hedwig would be one too as soon as the papers came through. Besides, a bright little fellow like Stephan would learn German at home. As for Oskar – Jan always sighed a little when he said 'Oskar' – he was six years old just like Stephan; true, he still couldn't talk properly; in general, he was quite backward for his age, and as for his size, enough said, but they should try it just the same, schooling was compulsory after all – provided the school board raised no objection.

The school board expressed misgivings and demanded a doctor's certificate. Hollatz said I was a healthy child; my physical development, he had to admit, was that of a three-year-old and I didn't talk very well, but otherwise I was not mentally inferior to a normal child of five or six. He also said something about my thyroid.

I was subjected to all sorts of examinations and tests. But I had grown accustomed to that kind of thing and my attitude ranged from benevolent to indifferent, especially as no one tried to take my drum away. The destruction of Hollatz' collection of snakes, toads, and embryos was still remembered with awe.

It was only at home that I was compelled to unsheathe the diamond in my voice. This was on the morning of my first school day, when Matzerath, against his own better judgment, demanded that I leave my drum at home and moreover pass through the portals of the Pestalozzi School without it.

When at length he resorted to force, when he attempted to take what did not belong to him, to appropriate an instrument he did not know how to play and for which he lacked all feeling,

I shattered an empty and allegedly genuine vase. When the genuine vase lay on the carpet in the form of genuine fragments, Matzerath, who was very fond of it, raised a hand to strike me. But at this point Mama jumped up and Jan, who had dropped in for a moment with Stephan and a large ornate cornucopia, intervened.

'Alfred, please, please!' he said in his quiet unctuous way, and Matzerath, subdued by Jan's blue and Mama's grey gaze, dropped his hand and thrust it into his trousers pocket.

The Pestalozzi School was a new brick-red, three-story, flat-roofed, boxlike edifice, decorated with sgraffiti and frescoes, which had been built by the Senate of our prolific suburb at the vociferous insistence of the Social Democrats, who at the time were still exceedingly active. I rather liked the box, except for its smell and the Jugendstil athletes in the sgraffiti and frescoes.

In the expanse of gravel outside the gate stood a few trees so unnaturally diminutive that one was startled to find them beginning to turn green; they were supported by iron stakes that looked like croziers. From all directions poured mothers holding colored cornucopias and drawing screaming or model children after them. Never had Oskar seen so many mothers tending toward a single point. They seemed to be on their way to a market where their first- or second-born could be offered for sale.

In the entrance I already caught a whiff of that school smell which has been described often enough and which is more intimate than any perfume in the world. In the lobby four or five huge granite bowls, in a rather casual arrangement, were affixed to the tile floor. From deep down within them water spouted from several sources at once. Surrounded by boys, including some of my own age, they reminded me of my Uncle Vincent's sow at Bissau, who would occasionally lie down on one flank and tolerate the equally thirsty and violent assault of her piglets.

The boys bent over the bowls with their vertical geysers, allowing their hair to fall forward and the streams of water to gush into their open mouths. I am not sure whether they were playing or drinking. Sometimes two boys stood up almost simultaneously with bloated cheeks, and with a disgusting gurgle spat the mouth-warm water, mixed, you may be certain, with saliva and bread crumbs, into each other's faces. I, who on entering the lobby had unsuspectingly cast a glance through the open door of the adjoining gymnasium, caught sight of the leather horse, the climbing bars, the climbing rope, and the horrible horizontal bar, crying out as always for a giant swing. All this made me desperately thirsty and like the other boys I should gladly have taken a gulp of water. But it was hardly possible to ask Mama, who was holding me by the hand, to lift Oskar the Lilliputian up to one of the fountains. Even if I had stood on my drum, the fountain would have been beyond my reach. But when with a quick jump I managed to glance over the edge and noted that the drain was blocked with greasy remnants of bread and that the bottom of the bowl was full of a noxious sludge, the thirst I had accumulated in spirit, while my body was wandering in a desert of gymnastic apparatus, left me.

Mama led me up monumental stairs hewn for giants, through resounding corridors into a room over the door of which hung a sign bearing the inscription I-A. The room was full of boys my own age. Their mothers pressed against the wall opposite the window front, clutching in their arms the colored cornucopias covered with tissue paper that were traditional on the first day of school. The cornucopias towered above me. Mama was also carrying one of them.

As my mother led me in, the rabble laughed and the rabble's mothers as well. A pudgy little boy wanted to beat my drum. Not wishing to demolish any glass, I was obliged to give him a few good kicks in the shins, whereupon he fell down, hitting his well-combed head on a desk, for which offense Mama cuffed me on the back of my head. The little monster yelled. Not I, I only yelled when someone tried to take my drum away. Mama, to whom this public performance was very embarrassing, pushed me down behind the first desk in the section by the windows. Of course the desk was too high. But further back, where the rabble was still more freckled and uncouth, the desks were still higher.

I let well enough alone and sat calmly, because there was nothing to be uncalm about. Mama, who it seemed to me was still suffering from embarrassment, tried to disappear among the other mothers. Here in the presence of her peers she probably felt ashamed of my so-called backwardness. The peers all behaved as though their young dolts, who had grown much too quickly for my taste, were something to be proud of.

I couldn't look out the window at Fröbel's Meadow, for the level of the window sill was no more appropriate to my stature than was the size of the desk. Too bad. I would have been glad to gaze out at the meadow where, as I knew, scouts under the leadership of Greff the greengrocer were pitching tents, playing lansquenet, and, as befitted boy scouts, doing good deeds. Not that I was interested in their fulsome glorification of camp life. What appealed to me was the sight of Greff in his short pants. Such was his love of slender, wide-eyed, pale boys that he had donned the uniform of Baden-Powell, father of the boy scouts.

Cheated of the coveted view by the insidious architecture, I gazed up at the sky and was soon appeased. New clouds kept forming and drifting southwestward, as though that direction had some special attraction for clouds. I wedged my drum firmly between my knees and the desk, though it had never for so much as a beat thought of wandering off to southwestward. Oskar's head was protected in the rear by the back rest. Behind me my so-called schoolmates snarled, roared, laughed, wept, and raged. They threw spitballs at me, but I did not turn around; it seemed to me that the tranquil purposive clouds were better worth looking at than a horde of grimacing, hopelessly hysterical louts.

Class I-A calmed down at the entrance of a person who subsequently introduced herself as Miss Spollenhauer. I had no need to calm down for I was already calm, awaiting things to come in a state of almost complete self-immersion. To be perfectly truthful, Oskar gave barely a thought to what the future might hold in store, for he required no distraction. Let us say, then, that he was not waiting but just sitting at his desk, pleasantly aware that his drum was where it belonged and otherwise preoccupied with the clouds behind the paschally polished windowpanes.

Miss Spollenhauer had on an angularly cut suit that gave her a desiccated mannish look, an impression that was enhanced by the narrow stiff collar, of the kind, it seemed to me, that can be wiped clean, which closed round her Adam's apple, creating deep furrows in her neck. No sooner had she entered the classroom in her flat walking shoes than she felt the need to make herself popular and asked: 'Well, my dear children, are we up to singing a little song?'

The response was a roar which she must have taken to mean yes, for she embarked at once, in a mincing high-pitched voice, on 'This Is the Merry Month of May,' though it was only the middle of April. Her premature announcement of the month of May was all it needed to make hell break loose. Without waiting for the signal to come in, without more than the vaguest notion of the words, or the slightest feeling for the simple rhythm of the song, the rabble behind me began to shake loose the plaster from the walls with their howling.

Despite her bilious complexion, despite her bobbed hair and the man's tie peering out from behind her collar, I felt sorry for la Spollenhauer. Tearing myself away from the clouds which obviously had no school that day, I leapt to my feet, pulled my drumsticks out from under my suspenders, and loudly, emphatically, drummed out the time of the song. But the populace had neither ear nor feeling for my efforts. Only Miss Spollenhauer gave me a nod of encouragement, smiled at the line of mothers glued to the wall, with a special twinkle for Mama. Interpreting this as a go-ahead signal, I continued my drumming, first quietly and simply, then displaying all my arts and burgeoning into rhythmic complexities. The rabble behind me had long ceased their barbaric howls. I was beginning to fancy that my drum was teaching, educating my fellow pupils, making them into my pupils, when la Spollenhauer approached my desk. For a time she watched my hands and drumsticks, I wouldn't even say that her manner was inept; she smiled self-forgetfully and tried to clap her hands to my beat. For a moment she became a not unpleasant old maid, who had forgotten her prescribed occupational caricature and become human, that is, childlike, curious, complex, and immoral.

However, when she failed to catch my rhythm, she fell back into her usual rectilinear, obtuse, and to make matters worse underpaid role, pulled herself together as teachers occasionally must, and said: 'You must be little Oskar. We have heard so much about you. How beautifully you drum! Doesn't he, children? Isn't our Oskar a fine drummer?'

The children roared, the mothers huddled closer together, Miss Spollenhauer was herself again. 'But now,' she piped with a voice like a pencil sharpener, 'we shall put the drum in the locker; it must be tired and want to sleep. Then when school is out, you will have it back again.'

Even before she had finished reeling off this hypocritical nonsense, she bared her close-clipped teacher's fingernails and ten close-clipped fingers tried to seize my drum, which, so help me, was neither tired nor sleepy. I held fast, clutching the red and white casing in the sleeves of my sweater. At first I stared at her, but when she kept on looking like a stencil of a public school teacher, I preferred to look through her. In Miss Spollenhauer's interior I found enough interesting material for three scabrous chapters, but since my drum was in danger, I tore myself away from her inner life and, my gimlet eyes drilling between her shoulder blades, detected, mounted on well-preserved skin, a mole the size of a gulden with a clump of long hairs growing in it.

I can't say whether it was because she felt herself seen through or whether it was my voice with which I gave her a harmless warning scratch on the lens of her right eyeglass: in any case, she suspended the show of force that had already blanched her knuckles. It seems likely that she could not bear the scraping on the glass, probably it gave her goose flesh. With a shudder she released my drum and, casting a look of reproach at my Mama, who was preparing to sink into the earth, declared: 'Why, you are a wicked little Oskar.' Thereupon she left me my wide-awake drum, about-faced, and marched with flat heels to her desk, where she fished another pair of spectacles, probably her reading glasses, from her briefcase, briskly took off her nose those which my voice had scraped as one scrapes windowpanes with one's fingernails, with a grimace which seemed to imply that I had profaned her spectacles, put on the other pair, straightening herself up so you could hear the bones rattle, and, reaching once again into her briefcase, announced: 'I will now read you your schedule!'.

What issued from the briefcase this time was a little bundle of cards. Keeping one for herself, she passed the rest on to the mothers, including Mama, and at length communicated the schedule to the already restive class. 'Monday: religion, writing, arithmetic, play; Tuesday: arithmetic, penmanship, singing, nature study; Wednesday: arithmetic, writing, drawing, drawing; Thursday: geography, arithmetic, writing, religion; Friday: arithmetic, writing, play, penmanship; Saturday: arithmetic, singing, play, play.'

Proclaimed in a stern voice that neglected not one jot or tittle, this product of a solemn faculty meeting assumed the force of irrevocable fate. But then, remembering what she had learned at Normal School, Miss Spollenhauer became suddenly mild and mellow. 'And now, my dear children,' she cried in an outburst of progressive merriment, 'let us all repeat that in unison: Now: Monday?'

The horde shouted 'Monday.'

'Religion?' And the baptized heathen roared 'religion.' Rather than strain my voice, I for my part beat out the syllables on my drum.

Behind me, spurred on by la Spollenhauer, the heathen bellowed: 'Writing!' Boom-boom went my drum. 'A-rith-metic!' That was good for four beats.

Before me la Spollenhauer's litany, behind me the howling of the mob. Putting a good face on a sorry and ludicrous business, I beat out the syllables, with moderation I should say, and so it continued until la Spollenhauer, goaded by some inner demon, leapt up in palpable fury, but not over the Tartars behind me; no, it was I who sent the red blotches to her cheeks; Oskar's poor little drum was her stumbling block, her bone of contention; it was I she chose to rebuke.

'Oskar, you will now listen to me: Thursday, geography?' Ignoring the word Thursday, I drummed four beats for geography, four beats for arithmetic, and two for writing; to religion I devoted not four, but, in accordance with sound theological principles, three triune and only-saving drumbeats.

But la Spollenhauer had no ear for subtleties. To her all drumming was equally repugnant. Once again she bared her ten truncated fingernails and once again they tried to seize my drum.

But before she had so much as touched it, I unleashed my glass-demolishing scream, which removed the upper panes from the three oversized windows. The middle windows succumbed to a second cry. Unobstructed, the mild spring air poured into the classroom. With a third shriek I annihilated the lower window-panes, but this I admit was quite superfluous, pure exuberance as it were, for la Spollenhauer had already drawn in her claws at the discomfiture of the upper and middle panes. Instead of assaulting the last remaining windowpanes out of pure and, from an artistic standpoint, questionable malice, Oskar would have done more wisely to keep an eye on la Spollenhauer as she beat a disorderly retreat.

Lord only knows where she found that cane. In any case it was suddenly at hand, vibrant in the classroom air now mingled with springtime air. Through this atmospheric mixture she whished it, endowing it with resiliency, with hunger and thirst for bursting skin, for the whistling wind, for all the rustling curtains that a whishing cane can impersonate. And down it came on my desk so hard that a violet streak sprang from my inkwell. Then, when I wouldn't hold out my hand to be whipped, she struck my drum. She struck my darling. She, la Spollenhauer, struck my instrument. What ground had she to strike? And if she was bent on hitting something, why my drum? What about the yokels behind me? Did it have to be my drum? By what right did she, who knew nothing, nothing whatsoever, about the drummer's art, assault and batter my drum? What was that glint in her eye? That beast ready to strike? What zoo had it escaped from, what did it lust for, what prey was it after? The very same beast invaded Oskar; rising from unknown depths, it rose up through the soles of his shoes, through the soles of his feet, rose and rose, investing his vocal cords and driving him to emit a rutting cry that would have sufficed to unglass a whole Gothic cathedral resplendent with the refracted light of a hundred windows.

In other words, I composed a double cry which literally pulverized both lenses of la Spollenhauer's spectacles. Slightly bleeding at the eyebrows, squinting through the empty frames, she groped her way backward, and finally began to blubber repulsively, with a lack of self-control quite unbefitting an educator, while the rabble behind me fell into a terrified silence, some sitting there with chattering teeth, others vanishing beneath their desks. A few of them slid from desk to desk in the direction of the mothers. The mothers for their part, perceiving the extent of the damage, looked round for the culprit and were about to pounce on my mother. They would surely have torn her to pieces had I not gathered up my drum and rushed to her assistance.

Past the purblind Miss Spollenhauer, I made my way to my

mama, who was menaced by the Furies, seized her by the hand, and drew her out of the drafty headquarters of Class I-A. Resounding corridors, stone stairs for giant children. Crusts of bread in gushing granite fountains. In the open gymnasium boys were trembling beneath the horizontal bar. Mama was still holding her little card. Outside the portals of the Pestalozzi School, I took it from her and transformed a schedule into a speechless wad of paper.

However, Oskar allowed the photographer, who was waiting for the new pupils and their mothers between the doorposts, to take a picture of him and of his cornucopia, which for all the tumult had not been lost. The sun came out, classrooms buzzed overhead. The photographer placed Oskar against a blackboard on which was written: My First School Day.

Rasputin and the Alphabet

I have just been telling my friend Klepp and Bruno my keeper, who listened with only half an ear, about Oskar's first experience with a school schedule. On the blackboard (I said) which provided the photographer with the traditional background for postcard-size pictures of six-year-old boys with knapsacks and cornucopias, these words were inscribed: My First School Day.

Of course the words could only be read by the mothers who, much more excited than their children, were standing behind the photographer. The boys, who were in front of the blackboard, would at best be able to decipher the inscription a year later, either at Easter time when the next first grade would turn up at school or on their own old photographs. Then and only then would they be privileged to read that these lovely pictures had been taken on the occasion of their first school day.

This testimonial to a new stage in life was recorded in Sütterlin script that crept across the blackboard with malignant angularity. However, the loops were not right, too soft and rounded. The fact is that Sütterlin script is especially indicated for succinct, striking statements, slogans for instance. And there are also certain documents which, though I admit I have never seen them, I can only visualize in Sütterlin script. I have in mind vaccination certificates, sport scrolls, and handwritten death sentences. Even then, I knew what to make of the Sütterlin script though I couldn't read it: the double loop of the Sütterlin M, with which the inscription began, smelled of hemp in my nostrils, an insidious reminder of the hangman. Even so, I would have been glad to read it letter for letter and not just dimly guess at what is said. Let no one suppose that I drummed in revolutionary protest and shattered glass so highhandedly at my first meeting with Miss Spollenhauer because I had already mastered my ABC's. Oh, no, I was only too well aware that this intuition of mine about Sütterlin script was not enough, that I lacked the most elementary school learning. It was just unfortunate that Miss Spollenhauer's methods of inculcating knowledge did not appeal to Oskar.

Accordingly, when I left the Pestalozzi School, I was far from deciding that my first school day should be my last, that I had had my fill of pencils and books, not to mention teacher's dirty looks. Nothing of the sort. Even while the photographer was capturing my likeness for all eternity, I thought: There you are in front of a blackboard, under an inscription that is probably important and possibly portentous. You can judge the inscription by the character of the writing and call forth associations such as solitary confinement, protective custody, inspector, and hang-them-all-by-one-rope, but you can't read the words. And yet, with all your ignorance that cries out to the overcast heavens, you will never again set foot in this schedule-school. Where, oh where, Oskar, are you going to learn your big and little alphabet?

Actually a little alphabet would have been plenty for me, but I had figured out that there must be a big as well as a little one, among other things from the crushing and undeniable fact of the existence of big people, who called themselves grownups.

In the next few months, neither Matzerath nor Mama worried about my education. They had tried to send me to school, and as far as they were concerned, this one attempt, so humiliating for Mama, was quite sufficient. They behaved just like Uncle Jan Bronski, sighed as they looked down on me, and dug up old stories such as the incident on my third birthday: 'The trap door! You left it open, didn't you? You were in the kitchen and before that you'd been down in the cellar, hadn't you? You brought up a can of mixed fruit for dessert, didn't you? You left the cellar door open, didn't you?'

Everything Mama held up to Matzerath was true, and yet, as we know, it was not. But he took the blame and sometimes even wept, for he was a sensitive soul at times. Then Mama and Jan Bronski had to comfort him, and they spoke of me, Oskar, as a cross they had to bear, a cruel and no doubt irrevocable fate, a trial that had been visited on them, it was impossible to see why.

Obviously no help was to be expected from such sorely tried cross-bearers and victims of fate. Nor could Aunt Hedwig, who often took me to Steffens-Park to play in the sand pile with her two-year-old Marga, have possibly served as my preceptor. She was good-natured enough, but as dull-witted as the day is long. I also had to abandon any ideas about Dr Hollatz' Sister Inge, who was neither dull-witted nor good-natured, for she was no common door-opener but a real and indispensable doctor's assistant and consequently had no time for me.

Several times a day I tramped up and down the steps of the four-story apartment house – there were more than a hundred of them – drumming in quest of counsel at every landing. I sniffed to see what each of the nineteen tenants was having for dinner, but I did not knock at any of the doors, for I recognized my future preceptor neither in old man Heilandt nor in Laubschad the watchmaker, and definitely not in the corpulent Mrs Kater nor, much as I liked her, in Mother Truczinski.

Under the eaves dwelt Meyn the trumpet player. Mr Meyn kept four cats and was always drunk. He played dance music at 'Zinglers Höhe' and on Christmas Eve he and five fellow sots plodded through the snow-clad streets battling the frost with carols. One day I saw him in his attic: clad in black trousers and a white evening shirt, he lay on his back, rolling an empty gin bottle about with his unshod feet and playing the trumpet just wonderfully. He did not remove his instrument from his lips, but merely squinted vaguely round at me for a moment. He acknowledged me as his drummer accompanist. His instrument was no more precious to him than mine to me. Our duet drove his four cats out on the roof and set up a slight vibration in the gutter tiles.

When the music was finished and we lowered our instruments, I drew an old copy of the *Neueste Nachrichten* from under my sweater, smoothed out the paper, sat down beside the trumpeter, held out my reading matter, and asked him to instruct me in the big and little alphabets.

But Mr. Meyn had fallen directly from his trumpeting into a deep sleep. His spirit recognized only three repositories: his bottle of gin, his trumpet, and his slumber. It is true that for quite some time after that – to be exact, until he joined the band of the Mounted SA and temporarily gave up gin – we would quite frequently play unrehearsed duets in the attic for the benefit of the roof tiles, the chimneys, the pigeons, and the cats; but I could never get anything out of him as a teacher.

I tried Greff the greengrocer. Without my drum, for Greff didn't appreciate it, I paid several visits to the basement shop across the way. The wherewithal for thorough and many-sided study seemed to be at hand. In every corner of the two-room flat, all over the shop, under and behind the counter, even in the relatively dry potato cellar, lay books, adventure stories, song books, *Der Cherubinische Wandersmann*, the works of Walter Flex, Wiechert's *Simple Life*, *Daphnis and Chloë*, monographs about artists, piles of sport magazines and illustrated volumes full of half-naked youths, most of whom, for some unfathomable reason, were chasing after a ball amid sand dunes, exhibiting oiled and glistening muscles.

Even then Greff was having a good deal of trouble in the shop. The inspectors from the Bureau of Weights and Measures had not been quite satisfied with his weights. There was talk of fraud. Greff had to pay a fine and buy new weights. He was bowed down with cares; his books and scout meetings and weekend excursions were his only cheer.

He was making out price tabs when I came in and hardly noticed me. Taking advantage of his occupation, I picked up three or four white squares of cardboard and a red pencil and, in the hope of attracting his attention, made a great show of zeal copying his handiwork in my own version of Sütterlin script.

But Oskar was clearly too little for him, not pale and wide-eyed enough. I dropped the red pencil, picked out a book full of the nudities that so appealed to Greff, and pretended to be very busy, inspecting photographs of boys bending and boys stretching and twisting them about so he could see them.

But when there were no customers in the shop asking for beets or cabbages, the greengrocer had eyes only for his price tabs. I tried to arouse his interest in my unlettered presence by clapping book covers or making the pages crackle as I turned them.

To put it very simply: Greff did not understand me. When scouts were in the shop – and in the afternoon there were always two or three of his lieutenants around him – Greff didn't notice Oskar at all. And when Greff was alone, he was quite capable of jumping up in nervous irritation and dealing out commands: 'Oskar, will you leave that book alone. You can't make head or tail of it anyway. You're too dumb and you're too little. You'll ruin it. That book costs more than six gulden. If you want to play, there's plenty of potatoes and cabbages.'

He took his nasty old book away and leafed expressionlessly through the pages, leaving me standing amid potatoes and several representatives of the cabbage family, white cabbage, red cabbage, savoy cabbage, Brussels sprouts, and kohlrabi, wretchedly lonely, for I had left my drum at home.

There was still Mrs. Greff, and after her husband's brush-off, I usually made my way to the matrimonial bedroom. Even then Mrs. Lina Greff would lie in bed for whole weeks, vaguely ailing; she smelled of decaying nightgown and though her hands were very active, one thing she never touched was a book that might have taught me anything.

It was not without a suspicion of envy that Oskar, in the weeks that followed, looked upon his contemporaries and their school-bags from which dangled importantly the little sponges or cloths used for wiping off slates. Even so, he cannot remember having harbored such thoughts as: you've made your own bed, Oskar, you should have put a good face on the school routine; you shouldn't have made an everlasting enemy of la Spollenhauer. Those yokels are getting ahead of you. They have mastered the big or at least the little alphabet, whereas you don't even know how to hold the *Neueste Nachrichten* properly.

A suspicion of envy, I have said, and that is all it was. A little smell test is all that was needed to disgust me with school for all time. Have you ever taken a sniff of those inadequately washed, worm-eaten sponges appended to pealing, yellow-rimmed slates, those sponges which somehow manage to store up all the effluvia of writing and 'rithmetic, all the sweat of squeaking, halting, slipping slate pencils moistened with saliva? Now and then, when children on their way home from school laid down their bags to play football or Völkerball, I would bend down over those sponges steaming in the sun, and the thought came to me that if Satan existed, such would be the acrid stench of his armpits.

Certainly I had no yearning for the school of slates and sponges. But, on the other hand, it would be an exaggeration to say that Gretchen Scheffler, who soon took his education in hand, was the precise answer to Oskar's dreams.

Everything about the Scheffler dwelling behind the bakery in Kleinhammer-Weg set my teeth on edge. Those ornamental coverlets, those cushions embroidered with coats-of-arms, those Käthe Kruse dolls lurking in sofa corners, those plush animals wheresoever one turned, that china crying out for a bull, those ubiquitous travel souvenirs, those beginnings of knitting, crocheting, and embroidery, of plaiting, knotting, and lacework. The place was too sweet for words, so cunning and coy, stiflingly tiny, overheated in winter and poisoned with flowers in summer. I can think of only one explanation: Gretchen Scheffler was childless; oh, if she had had some little creature to knit for, who can say whether she or Scheffler was to blame, oh, how happy she would have been with a little sugarplum baby, something she could love to pieces and swathe in crocheted blankets and cover with lace and ribbons and little kisses in cross-stitch.

This is where I went to learn my big and little alphabets. I made a heroic effort to spare the china and the souvenirs. I left my glass-destroying voice at home and bore it meekly when Gretchen expressed the opinion that I had drummed enough for now and, baring her equine gold teeth in a smile, removed my drum from my knees and laid it among the teddy bears.

I made friends with two of the Käthe Kruse dolls, clutched the little dears to my bosom, and manipulated the lashes of their permanently startled eyes as though I were madly in love with them. My purpose in this display of affection for dolls, which seemed sincere just because it was so completely false, was to knit a snare round Gretchen's knitted, knit two purl two, heart.

My plan was not bad. It took only two visits before Gretchen opened her heart; that is, she unraveled it as one unravels a stocking, disclosing a long crinkly thread worn thin in places. She opened all her cupboards, chests, and boxes and spread out all her beaded rubbish, enough baby jackets, baby pants, and bibs to clothe a set of quintuplets, held them up against me, tried them on, and took them off again.

Then she showed me the marksman's medals won by Scheffler at the veterans' club and photographs to go with them, some of which were identical with ours. Then she went back to the baby clothes and at long last, while searching for heaven knows what cute little object, she unearthed some books. That was what Oskar had been building up to. He fully expected her to find books under the baby things; he had heard her talk about books with Mama; he knew how feverishly the two of them, while still engaged and after their early and almost simultaneous marriages, had exchanged books and borrowed books from the lending library by the Film-Palast, in the hope of imparting wider horizons and greater luster to their grocery store and bakery marriages.

Gretchen had little enough to offer me. Like Mama, who had given up reading in favor of Jan Bronski, she who no longer read, now that she spent all her time knitting, had evidently given away the sumptuous volumes of the book club, to which both had belonged for years, to people who still read because they did not knit and had no Jan Bronski.

Even bad books are books and therefore sacred. What I found there can only be described as miscellaneous; most of it came, no doubt, from the book chest of Gretchen's brother Theo, who had met a seaman's death on the Dogger-Bank. Seven or eight volumes of Köhler's *Naval Calendar*, full of ships that had long since sunk, the *Service Ranks of the Imperial Navy, Paul Beneke, the Naval Hero* – these could scarcely have been the nourishment for which Gretchen's heart had yearned. It seemed equally certain that Erich Keyser's *History of the City of Danzig* and *A Struggle for Rome*, which a man by the name of Felix Dahn seems to have fought with the help of Totila and Teja, Belisarius and Narses, had arrived at their present state of dilapidation beneath the hands of the seafaring brother. To Gretchen's own collection I attributed a book by Gustav Freytag about *Debit and Credit*, something by Goethe about *Elective Affinities*, and a copiously illustrated thick volume entitled: *Rasputin and Women*.

After long hesitation – the selection was too small to permit me to make up my mind quickly – I picked out first Rasputin and then Goethe. I had no idea what I was taking, I was just following the well-known inner voice.

The conflicting harmony between these two was to shape or influence my whole life, at least what life I have tried to live apart from my drum. To this very day – and even now that Oskar in his eagerness for learning is gradually plowing his way through the whole hospital library – I snap my fingers at Schiller and company and fluctuate between Rasputin and Goethe, between the faith healer and the man of the Enlightenment, between the dark spirit who cast a spell on women and the luminous poet prince who was so fond of letting women cast a spell on him. If for a time I inclined more toward Rasputin and feared Goethe's intolerance, it was because of a faint suspicion that if you, Oskar, had lived and drummed at his time, Goethe would have thought you unnatural, would have condemned you as an incarnation of anti-nature, that while feeding his own precious nature – which essentially you have always admired and striven for even when it gave itself the most unnatural airs – on honeybuns, he would have taken notice of you, poor devil, only to hit you over the head with *Faust* or a big heavy volume of his *Theory of Colors*.

But back to Rasputin. With the help of Gretchen Scheffler he taught me the big and little alphabets, taught me to be attentive to women, and comforted me when Goethe hurt my feelings.

It was not so easy to learn how to read while playing the ignoramus. It proved even more difficult than impersonating a bed-wetter, as I did for many years. In wetting my bed, after all, I merely had to offer purely material proof each morning of a disorder that I did not really need in the first place. But to play the ignoramus meant to conceal my rapid progress, to carry on a constant struggle with my nascent intellectual pride. If grown-ups wished to regard me as a bed-wetter, that I could accept with an inner shrug of the shoulders, but that I should have to behave

like a simpleton year in year out was a source of chagrin to Oskar
and to his teacher as well.

The moment I had salvaged the books from the baby clothes,
Gretchen cried out for joy; she had sensed her vocation as a
teacher. I succeeded in disentangling the poor childless woman
from her wool and in making her almost happy. Actually she
would have preferred for me to choose *Debit and Credit* as my
reader; but I insisted on Rasputin, demanded Rasputin when she
produced a common primer for our second lesson, and finally
resolved to speak when she kept coming up with fairy tales such
as *Dwarf Longnose* and *Tom Thumb*. 'Rasputin!' I would cry, or
occasionally: 'Rashushin!' Sometimes Oskar would lay it on really
thick with 'Rashu, Rashu!' The idea was to make it perfectly clear
what reading matter I desired but at the same time to leave her
in ignorance of my awakening literary genius.

I learned quickly and regularly without much effort. A year
later I had the impression of living in St. Petersburg, in the
apartments of the Tsar of all the Russias, in the nursery of
the ailing Tsarevich, amid conspirators and popes, an eyewitness
to Rasputin's orgies. The tone of the thing appealed to me; here,
I soon saw, was a dominant figure. How dominant was also made
evident by the contemporary engravings scattered through the
book, showing the bearded Rasputin with the coal-black eyes,
surrounded by ladies wearing black stockings and nothing else.
His death made a deep impression on me: they poisoned him
with poisoned cake and poisoned wine; then, when he wanted
more cake, they shot him with pistols, and when the lead in his
chest made him feel like dancing, they bound him and lowered
him into the Neva, through a hole in the ice. All this was done
by officers of the male sex. The ladies of St. Peterburg would
never have given their little father Rasputin poisoned cake, though
they would have given him anything else he wanted. The women
believed in him, whereas the officers had to get rid of him if they
were ever again to believe in themselves.

Is it any wonder that I was not the only one to delight in the
life and death of the athletic faith healer? Little by little Gretchen
recovered her old pleasure in reading. Sometimes, as she read
aloud, she would break down completely; she would tremble at
the word 'orgy' and utter it with a special sort of gasp; when she

said 'orgy' she was ready and willing for an orgy, though she certainly had very little idea of what an orgy might be.

Things took a salty turn when Mama came with me and attended my lesson in the flat over the bakery. Sometimes the reading degenerated into an orgy and became an end in itself; little Oskar's lesson was quite forgotten. Every third sentence produced a duet of giggles, which left the ladies with parched lips. Beneath Rasputin's spell the two of them moved closer and closer to one another; they would begin to fidget on the sofa cushions and press their thighs together. In the end, the giggling turned to moaning. Twelve pages of Rasputin produced results that they had hardly expected in mid-afternoon but were perfectly glad to accept. In any case Rasputin would not have minded; on the contrary, he may be counted on to distribute such blessings free of charge for all eternity.

At length, when both ladies had said 'goodness, goodness' and sat back in embarrassment, Mama expressed some misgiving: 'Are you sure little Oskar doesn't understand?' 'Don't be silly,' Gretchen reassured her, 'you can't imagine how hard I work over him, but he just doesn't learn. My honest opinion is that he'll never be able to read.'

As an indication of my incorrigible ignorance, she added: 'Just imagine, Agnes, he tears the pages out of our Rasputin and crumples them up. They just disappear. Sometimes I feel like giving up. But when I see how happy he is with the book, I let him tear and destroy. I've already told Alex to get us a new Rasputin for Christmas.'

As you have no doubt suspected, I succeeded very gradually, over a period of three or four years – Gretchen Scheffler went on teaching me that long and a bit longer – in carrying away over half the pages of Rasputin. I tore them out very carefully while putting on a wanton destructiveness act, crumpled them up, and hid them under my sweater. Then at home in my drummer's corner, I would smooth them out, pile them up, and read them in secret, undisturbed by any feminine presence. I did the same with Goethe, whom I would demand of Gretchen every fourth lesson with a cry of 'Doethe.' I didn't want to stake everything on Rasputin, for only too soon it became clear to me that in this world of ours every Rasputin has his Goethe, that every Rasputin draws a Goethe or if you prefer every Goethe a Rasputin in his wake, or even makes one if need be, in order to be able to condemn him later on.

With his unbound book Oskar would repair to the attic or hide behind the bicycle frames in old Mr. Heilandt's shed, where he would shuffle the loose leaves of *Rasputin* and *The Elective Affinities* like playing cards, so creating a new book. He would settle down to read this remarkable work and look on with intense though smiling wonderment as Ottilie strolled demurely through the gardens of Central Germany on Rasputin's arm while Goethe, seated beside a dissolutely aristocratic? Olga, went sleighing through wintry St. Petersburg from orgy to orgy.

But let us get back to my schoolroom in Kleinhammer-Weg. Even if I seemed to be making no progress, Gretchen took the most maidenly pleasure in me. Thanks to me, though the invisible but hairy hand of the Russian faith healer also had something to do with it, she blossomed mightily and even imparted some of her newfound vitality to her potted trees and cactuses. If Scheffler in those years had only seen fit once in a while to take his fingers out of his dough, to relinquish his bakery rolls for a human roll! Gretchen would gladly have let him knead her and roll her, brush her with egg white and bake her. Who knows what might have come out of the oven. Perhaps, in the end, a baby. Too bad. It was a pleasure she had coming to her.

As it was, she sat there after an impassioned reading of Rasputin with fiery eyes and slightly tousled hair; her gold horse teeth moved but she had nothing to bite on, and she sighed mercy me, thinking of flour and dough, flour and dough. Since Mama, who had her Jan, had no way of helping Gretchen, this part of my education might have ended in grief if Gretchen had not been so buoyant of heart.

She would leap into the kitchen and come back with the coffee mill; embracing it like a lover, she would sing with melancholy passion while grinding, 'Dark Eyes' or 'Red Sarafan,' and Mama would join in. Taking the Dark Eyes into the kitchen with her, she would put water on to boil; then as the water was heating over the gas flame, she would run down to the bakery and, often over Scheffler's opposition, bring back cakes and pastries, set the table with flowered cups, cream pitchers, sugar bowls, and cake forks, and strew pansies in the interstices. She would pour the coffee, hum airs from *The Tsarevich*, pass around the sand tarts and chocolate dewdrops. A soldier stands on the Volga shore, coffee ring garnished with splintered almonds, Have you many angels with you up there?, topped off with meringues filled with whipped cream, so sweet, so sweet. As they chewed, the conversation would come back to Rasputin, but now things appeared to them in their proper perspective, and once glutted with cake, they were even able to deplore, in all sincerity, the abysmal corruption of court life under the tsars.

I ate much too much cake in those years. As the photographs show, I grew no taller, just fat and lumpy. After the cloying sweetness of those lessons in Kleinhammer-Weg I would often sneak into our shop and await my opportunity. As soon as Matzerath had his back turned, I would tie a string around a piece of dry bread, dip the bread in the pickled herring barrel, and remove it only when the bread was saturated with brine. You can't imagine what a blissful emetic that was for one who had eaten too much cake. In the hope of reducing, Oskar would often vomit up a whole Danzig gulden's worth of Scheffler's cake in our toilet. That was a lot of money in those days.

I paid for Gretchen's lessons in still another way. With her passion for sewing, knitting, or crocheting baby clothes, she used me as a dressmaker's dummy. I was compelled to try on little frocks and little bonnets, little pants and little coats with and without hoods, in all styles, colors, and materials.

I do not know whether it was Mama or Gretchen who transformed me, on the occasion of my eighth birthday, into a little tsarevich who fully deserved to be shot. Their Rasputin cult was then at its height. A photo taken that day shows me standing beside a birthday cake hedged about by eight dripless candles; I am wearing an embroidered Russian smock, a Cossack's cap perched at a jaunty angle, two crossed cartridge belts, baggy white breeches, and low boots.

Luckily my drum was allowed to be in the picture. Another bit of luck was that Gretchen Scheffler – possibly I had asked her to do so – tailored me a suit which, cut in the unassuming, electively affinitive style of the early nineteenth century, still conjures up the spirit of Goethe in my album, bearing witness to the two souls in my breast, and enables me, with but a single drum, to be in St. Petersburg and in Weimar at once, descending to the realm of the Mothers and celebrating orgies with ladies.

The Stockturm. Long-Distance Song Effects

DR. Hornstetter, the lady doctor who drops in on me almost every day just long enough to smoke a cigarette, who is supposed to be taking care of me but who, thanks to my treatment, leaves the room after every visit a little less nervous than she was when she came, a retiring sort who is intimate only with her cigarettes, keeps insisting that I suffered from isolation in my childhood, that I didn't play enough with other children.

Well, as far as other children are concerned, she may be right. It is true that I was so busy with Gretchen Scheffler's lessons, so torn between Goethe and Rasputin, that even with the best of intentions I could have found no time for ring-around-a-rosy or post office. But whenever, as scholars sometimes do, I turned my back on books, declaring them to be the graveyards of the language, and sought contact with the simple folk, I encountered the little cannibals who lived in our building, and after brief association with them, felt very glad to get back to my reading in one piece.

Oskar had the possibility of leaving his parents' flat through the shop, then he came out on Labesweg, or else through the front door that led to the stairwell. From here he could either continue straight ahead to the street, or climb four flights of stairs to the attic where Meyn the musician was blowing his trumpet, or, lastly, go out into the court. The street was paved with cobblestones. The packed sand of the court was a place where rabbits multiplied and carpets were beaten. Aside from occasional duets with the intoxicated Mr. Meyn, the attic offered a view and that pleasant but deceptive feeling of freedom which is sought by all climbers of towers and which makes dreamers of those who live in attics.

While the court was fraught with peril for Oskar, the attic

offered him security until Axel Mischke and his gang drove him out of it. The court was as wide as the building, but only seven paces deep; in the rear it was separated from other courts by a tarred board fence topped with barbed wire. The attic offered a good view of this maze which occupied the inside of the block bordered by Labesweg, by Hertastrasse and Luisenstrasse on either side, and Marienstrasse in the distance. In among the irregularly shaped courts that made up the sizable rectangle there was also a cough-drop factory and several run-down repair shops. Here and there in the yards one could discern some tree or shrub indicative of the time of year. The courts varied in size and shape, but all contained rabbits and carpet-beating installations. The rabbits were present and active every day; carpets, however, as the house regulations decreed, were beaten only on Tuesdays and Fridays. On Tuesdays and Fridays it became evident how large the block really was. Oskar looked and listened from the attic as more than a hundred carpets, runners, and bedside rugs were rubbed with sauerkraut, brushed, beaten, and bullied into showing the patterns that had been woven into them. With a great display of bare arms a hundred housewives, their hair tied up in kerchiefs, emerged from the houses carrying mounds of carpets, threw the victims over the rack supplied for that very purpose, seized their plaited carpet beaters, and filled the air with thunder.

Oskar abhorred this hymn to cleanliness. He battled the noise with his drum and yet, even in the attic, far away from the source of the thunder, he had to admit defeat. A hundred carpet-beating females can storm the heavens and blunt the wings of young swallows; with half a dozen strokes they tumbled down the little temple that Oskar's drumming had erected in the April air.

On days when no carpets were being beaten, the children of our building did gymnastics on the wooden carpet rack. I was seldom in the court. The only part of it where I felt relatively secure was Mr. Heilandt's shed. The old man kept the other children out but admitted me to his collection of vises, pulleys, and broken-down sewing machines, incomplete bicycles, and cigar boxes full of bent or straightened nails. This was one of his principal occupations: when he was not pulling nails out of old crates, he was straightening those recovered the day before on an anvil. Apart from his salvaging of nails, he was the man who helped on moving day, who slaughtered rabbits for holidays, and who spat tobacco juice all over the court, stairs, and attic.

One day when the children, as children do, were cooking soup not far from his shed, Nuchi Eyke asked old man Heilandt to spit in it three times. The old man obliged, each time with a cavernous clearing of the throat, and then disappeared into his shanty, where he went on hammering the crimps out of nails. Axel Mischke added some pulverized brick to the soup. Oskar stood to one side, but looked on with curiosity. Axel Mischke and Harry Schlager had built a kind of tent out of blankets and old rags to prevent grownups from looking into their soup. When the brick gruel had come to a boil, Hänschen Kollin emptied his pockets and contributed two live frogs he had caught in Aktien Pond. Susi Kater, the only girl in the tent, puckered up her mouth with disappointment and bitterness when the frogs vanished ingloriously into the soup without the slightest attempt at a swan song or a last jump. Undeterred by Susi's presence, Nuchi Eyke unbuttoned his fly and peed into the one-dish meal. Axel, Harry, and Hänschen Kollin followed suit. Shorty tried to show the ten-year-olds what he could do, but nothing came. All eyes turned toward Susi, and Axel Mischke handed her a sky-blue enamel cook pot. Oskar was already on the point of leaving. But he waited until Susi, who apparently had no panties on under her dress, had squatted down on the pot, clasping her knees, looking off expressionlessly into space, and finally crinkling her nose as the pot emitted a tinny tinkle, showing that Susi had done her bit for the soup.

At this point I ran away. I should not have run; I should have walked with quiet dignity. Their eyes were all fishing in the cook pot, but because I ran, they looked after me. I heard Susi Kater's voice: 'What's he running for, he's going to snitch on us.' It struck me in the back, and I could still feel it piercing me as I was catching my breath in the loft after hobbling up the four flights of steps.

I was seven and a half. Susi may have been nine. Shorty was just eight. Axel, Nuchi, Hänschen, and Harry were ten or eleven. There was still Maria Truczinski. She was a little older than I, but she never played in the court; she played with dolls in Mother

Truczinski's kitchen or with her grown-up sister Guste who helped at the Lutheran kindergarten.

Is it any wonder if to this day I can't abide the sound of women urinating in chamberpots? Up in the attic Oskar appeased his ears with drumming. Just as he was beginning to feel that the bubbling soup was far behind him, the whole lot of them, all those who had contributed to the soup, turned up in their bare feet or sneakers. Nuchi was carrying the pot. They formed a ring around Oskar, Shorty arrived a moment later. They poked each other, hissing: 'Go on, I dare you.' Finally, Axel seized Oskar from behind and pinned his arms. Susi laughed, showing moist regular teeth with her tongue between them, and said why not, why shouldn't they. She took the tin spoon from Nuchi, wiped it silvery on her behind, and plunged it into the steaming brew. Like a good housewife, she stirred slowly, testing the resistance of the mash, blew on the full spoon to cool it, and at length forced it into Oskar's mouth, yes, she forced it into my mouth. Never in all these years have I eaten anything like it, the taste will stay with me.

Only when my friends who had been so concerned over my diet had left me, because Nuchi had been sick in the soup, did I crawl into a corner of the drying loft where only a few sheets were hanging at the time, and throw up the few spoonfuls of reddish brew, in which I was surprised to find no vestiges of frogs. I climbed up on a chest placed beneath the open attic window. Crunching powdered brick, I looked out at distant courts and felt an urge for action. Looking toward the distant windows of the houses in Marienstrasse, I screamed and sang in that direction. I could see no results and yet I was so convinced of the possibilities of long-distance action by singing that from then on the court and all the many courts became too small for me. Thirsting for distance, space, panorama, I resolved to take advantage of every opportunity to leave our suburban Labesweg, whether alone or with Mama, to escape from the pursuits of the soup-makers in the court that had grown too small.

Every Thursday Mama went into the city to shop. Usually she took me with her. She always took me along when it became necessary to buy a new drum at Sigismund Markus' in Arsenal Passage off the Kohlenmarkt. In that period, roughly between the ages of seven and ten, I went through a drum in two weeks flat. From ten to fourteen I demolished an instrument in less than a week. Later, I became more unpredictable in my ways; I could turn a new drum into scrap in a single day, but then a period of mental balance might set in, and for as much as three or four months I would drum forcefully but with a moderation and control that left my instrument intact except for an occasional crack in the enamel.

But let us get back to the days when I escaped periodically from our court with its carpet beating and its soup chefs, thanks to my mama, who took me every two weeks to Sigismund Markus' store, where I was permitted to select a new drum. Sometimes Mama let me come even when my old drum was in relatively good condition. How I relished those afternoons in the multi-colored old city; there was always something of the museum about it and there was always a pealing of bells from one church or another.

Usually our excursions were pleasantly monotonous. There were always a few purchases to be made at Leiser's, Sternfeld's, or Machwitz'; then we went to Markus'. It had got to be a habit with Markus to pay Mama an assortment of the most flattering compliments. He was obviously in love with her, but as far as I know, he never went any further than to clutch my mother's hand, ardently described as worth its weight in gold, and to impress a silent kiss upon it – except for the time I shall speak of in a moment, when he fell on his knees.

Mama, who had inherited Grandma Koljaiczek's sturdy, imposing figure and her lovable vanity tempered with good nature, put up with Markus' attentions. To some extent, no doubt, she was influenced by the silk stockings – he bought them up in job lots but they were of excellent quality – which he sold her so cheap that they were practically gifts. Not to mention the drums he passed over the counter every two weeks, also at bargain prices.

Regularly at half-past four Mama would ask Sigismund if she might leave me, Oskar, in his care, for it was getting late and she still had a few important errands. Strangely smiling, Markus would bow and promise with an ornate turn of phrase to guard me, Oskar, like the apple of his eye, while she attended to her important affairs. The mockery in his tone was too faint to give

85

offense, but sometimes it brought a blush to Mama's cheeks and led her to suspect that Markus knew what was what.

As for me, I knew all about the errands that Mama characterized as important and attended to so zealously. For a time she had let me accompany her to a cheap hotel in Tischlergasse, where she left me with the landlady and vanished up the stairs for exactly three-quarters of an hour. Without a word the landlady, who as a rule was sipping half-and-half, set a glass of some foul-tasting soda pop before me, and there I waited until Mama, in whom no particular change was discernible, returned. With a word of good-by to the landlady, who didn't bother to look up from her half-and-half, she would take me by the hand. It never occurred to her that the temperature of her hand might give me ideas. Hand in overheated hand, we went next to the Café Weitzke in Wollwebergasse. Mama would order mocha, Oskar lemon ice, and they would wait, but not for long, until Jan Bronski should happen by, and a second cup of mocha should be set down on the soothingly cool marble table top.

They spoke in my presence almost as though I were not there, and their conversation corroborated what I had long known: that Mama and Uncle Jan met nearly every Thursday to spend three-quarters of an hour in a hotel room in Tischlergasse, which Jan paid for. It must have been Jan who objected to these visits of mine to Tischlergasse and the Café Weitzke. Sometimes he was very modest, more so than Mama, who saw no reason why I should not witness the epilogue to their hour of love, of whose legitimacy she always, even afterward, seemed to be convinced.

At Jan's request, then, I spent almost every Thursday afternoon, from half-past four to shortly before six o'clock, with Sigismund Markus. I was allowed to look through his assortment of drums, and even to use them – where else could Oskar have played several drums at once? Meanwhile, I would contemplate Markus' hangdog features. I didn't know where his thoughts came from, but I had a pretty fair idea where they went; they were in Tischlergasse, scratching on numbered room doors, or huddling like poor Lazarus under the marble-topped table at the Café Weitzke. Waiting for what? For crumbs?

Mama and Jan Bronski left no crumbs. Not a one. They ate everything themselves. They had the ravenous appetite that never dies down, that bites its own tail. They were so busy that at most they might have interpreted Markus' thoughts beneath the table as the importunate attentions of a draft.

On one of those afternoons – it must have been in September, for Mama left Markus' shop in her rust-colored autumn suit – I saw that Markus was lost in thought behind his counter. I don't know what got into me. Taking my newly acquired drum, I drifted out into Arsenal Passage. The sides of the cool dark tunnel were lined with sumptuous window displays: jewelry, books, fancy delicatessen. But desirable as these articles may have been, they were clearly beyond my reach. They did not hold me; I kept on going, through the passage and out to the Kohlenmarkt. Emerging in the dusty light, I stood facing the Arsenal. The basalt grey façade was larded with cannon balls dating back to various sieges, which recorded the history of the city of Danzig for the benefit of all who should pass by. The cannon balls were of no interest to me, particularly as I knew that they had not stuck in the wall of their own accord, that there lived in the city of Danzig a mason employed and paid conjointly by the Public Building Office and the Office for the Conservation of Monuments, whose function it was to immure the ammunition of past centuries in the façades of various churches and town halls, and specifically in the front and rear walls of the Arsenal.

I decided to head for the Stadt-Theater, whose portico I could see on the right, separated from the Arsenal only by a short unlighted alley. Just as I had expected, the theater was closed – the box office for the evening performance opened only at seven. Envisaging a retreat, I drummed my way irresolutely to leftward. But then Oskar found himself between the Stockturm and the Langgasser Gate. I didn't dare to pass through the gate into Langgasse and turn left into Grosse Wollwebergasse, for Mama and Jan Bronski would be sitting there; and if they were not there yet, it seemed likely that they had just completed their errand in Tischlergasse and were on their way to take their refreshing mochas on the little marble table.

I have no idea how I managed to cross the Kohlenmarkt, to thread my way between the streetcars hastening to squeeze through the arch or popping out of it with a great clanging of bells and screeching round the curve as they headed for the

Holzmarkt and the Central Station. Probably a grownup, perhaps a policeman, took me by the hand and guided me through the perils of the traffic.

I stood facing the Stockturm, steep brick wall pinned against the sky, and it was only by chance, in response to a faint stirring of boredom, that I wedged my drumsticks in between the masonry and the iron mounting of the door. I looked upward along the brickwork, but it was hard to follow the line of the façade, for pigeons kept flying out of niches and windows, to rest on the oriels and waterspouts for the brief time it takes a pigeon to rest before darting downward and forcing my gaze to follow.

Those pigeons really got on my nerves with their activity. There was no point in looking up if I couldn't follow the wall to its end in the sky, so I called back my gaze and, to dispel my irritation, began in earnest to use my drumsticks as levers. The door gave way. It had no need to open very far, already Oskar was inside the tower, climbing the spiral staircase, advancing his right foot and pulling the left one after it. He came to the first dungeons and still he climbed, on past the torture chamber with its carefully preserved and instructively labeled instruments. At this point he began to advance his left foot and draw the right one after it. A little higher he glanced through a barred window, estimated the height, studied the thickness of the masonry, and shooed the pigeons away. At the next turn of the staircase he met the same pigeons. Now he shifted back to his right foot and after one more change reached the top. He felt a heaviness in his legs, but it seemed to him that he could have kept on climbing for ages. The staircase had given up first. In a flash Oskar understood the absurdity, the futility of building towers.

I do not know how high the Stockturm was (and still is; for it survived the war). Nor have I any desire to ask Bruno my keeper for a reference work on East German brick Gothic. My guess is that it must measure a good 150 feet from top to toe.

I was obliged – because of that staircase that lacked the courage of its convictions – to stop on the gallery that ran around the spire. I sat down, thrust my legs between the supports of the balustrade, and leaned forward. I clasped one of the supports in my right arm and looked past it, down toward the Kohlenmarkt, while with my left hand I made sure that my drum, which had participated in the whole climb, was all right.

I have no intention of boring you with a bird's-eye view of Danzig – venerable city of many towers, city of belfries and bells, allegedly still pervaded by the breath of the Middle Ages – in any case you can see the whole panorama in dozens of excellent prints. Nor shall I waste my time on pigeons, or doves as they are sometimes called, though some people seem to regard them as a fit subject for literature. To me pigeons mean just about nothing, even gulls are a little higher in the scale. Your 'dove of peace' makes sense only as a paradox. I would sooner entrust a message of peace to a hawk or a vulture than to a dove, which is just about the most quarrelsome animal under God's heaven. To make a long story short: there were pigeons on the Stockturm. But after all, there are pigeons on every self-respecting tower.

At all events it was not pigeons that held my eyes but something different: the Stadt-Theater, which I had found closed on my way from the Arsenal. This box with a dome on it looked very much like a monstrously blown-up neoclassical coffee mill. All the Temple of the Muses lacked was a crank with which to grind up its contents, actors and public, sets and props, Goethe and Schiller, slowly but exceeding small. The building annoyed me, especially the column-flanked windows of the lobby, sparkling in the rays of a sagging afternoon sun which kept mixing more and more red in its palette.

Up there on the tower, a good hundred feet above the Kohlenmarkt with its streetcars and throngs of homeward-bound office workers, high above Markus' sweet-smelling shop and the Café Weitzke with its cool marble table tops, two cups of mocha, far above Mama and Jan Bronski, above all courtyards, all bent and straightened nails, all juvenile soup-makers – up there on the tower, I who had hitherto screamed only for good and sufficient reason, became a gratuitous screamer. Until the day when I took it into my head to climb the Stockturm I had projected my cutting notes upon glasses, light bulbs, beer bottles, but only when someone wanted to take away my drum; now on the tower I screamed though my drum was not even remotely threatened.

No one was trying to take Oskar's drum away, and still he screamed. No pigeon had sullied his drum with its droppings.

Near me there was verdegris on copper plates, but no glass. And nevertheless Oskar screamed. The eyes of the pigeons had a reddish glitter, but no one was eying him out of a glass eye; yet he screamed. What did he scream at? What distant object? Did he wish to apply scientific method to the experiment he had attempted for the hell of it in the loft after his meal of brick soup? What glass had Oskar in mind? What glass – and it had to be glass – did Oskar wish to experiment with?

It was the Stadt-Theater, the dramatic coffee mill, whose windowpanes gleaming in the evening sun attracted the modernistic tones, bordering on mannerism, that I had first tried out in our loft. After a few minutes of variously pitched screams which accomplished nothing, I succeeded in producing an almost soundless tone, and a moment later Oskar noted with joy and a blush of telltale pride that two of the middle panes in the end window of the lobby had been obliged to relinquish their share of the sunset, leaving two black rectangles that would soon require attention from the glazier.

Still, the effect had to be verified. Like a modern painter who, having at last found the style he has been seeking for years, perfects it and discloses his full maturity by turning out one after another dozens of examples of his new manner, all equally daring and magnificent, I too embarked on a productive period.

In barely a quarter of an hour I succeeded in unglassing all the lobby windows and some of the doors. A crowd, from where I was standing one would have said an excited crowd, gathered outside the theater. But the stupidest incident draws a crowd. The admirers of my art made no particular impression on me. At most they led Oskar to discipline his art, to strive for greater formal purity. I was just getting ready to lay bare the very heart of things with a still more daring experiment, to send a very special cry through the open lobby, through the keyhole of one of the loge doors into the still darkened theater, a cry that should strike the pride of all subscribers, the chandelier with all its polished, facetted, light-reflecting and refracting hardware, when my eye lit on a bit of rust-brown material in the crowd outside of the theater: Mama was on her way back from the Café Weitzke, she had had her mocha and left Jan Bronski.

Even so, it must be admitted that Oskar aimed a cry at the

chandelier. But apparently it had no effect, for the newspapers next day spoke only of the windows and doors that had burst asunder for unknown, mysterious reasons. For several weeks purveyors of scientific and semiscientific theories were to fill the back pages of the daily press with columns of fantastic nonsense. The *Neueste Nachrichten* spoke of cosmic rays. The unquestionably well-informed staff of the local observatory spoke of sunspots.

I for my part descended the spiral staircase as quickly as my short legs would carry me and, rather out of breath, joined the crowd outside the theater. Mama's rust-brown autumn suit was nowhere to be seen, no doubt she was in Markus' shop, telling about the destruction wrought by my voice. And Markus, who took my so-called backwardness and my diamond-like voice perfectly for granted, would be wagging the tip of his tongue and rubbing his yellowed white hands.

As I entered the shop the sight that met my eyes made me forget all about my success as a singer. Sigismund Markus was kneeling at Mama's feet, and all the plush animals, bears, monkeys, dogs, the dolls with eyes that opened and shut, the fire engines, rocking horses, and even the jumping jacks that guarded the shop, seemed on the point of kneeling with him. He held Mama's two hands in his, there were brownish fuzzy blotches on the backs of his hands, and he wept.

Mama also looked very solemn, as though she were giving the situation the attention it deserved. 'No, Markus,' she said, 'please, Markus. Not here in the store.'

But Markus went on interminably. He seemed to be overdoing it a little, but still I shall never forget the note of supplication in his voice. 'Don't do it no more with Bronski, seeing he's in the Polish Post Office. He's with the Poles, that's no good. Don't bet on the Poles; if you gotta bet on somebody, bet on the Germans, they're coming up, maybe sooner maybe later. And suppose they're on top and Mrs. Matzerath is still betting on Bronski. All right if you want to bet on Matzerath, what you got him already. Or do me a favor, bet on Markus seeing he's just fresh baptized. We'll go to London, I got friends there and plenty stocks and bonds if you just decide to come, or all right if you won't come with Markus because you despise me, so despise me. But I beg you down on my knees, don't bet no more on Bronski that's meshugge enough to stick by the Polish Post Office when the Poles are pretty soon all washed up when the Germans come.'

Just as Mama, confused by so many possibilities and impossibilities, was about to burst into tears, Markus saw me in the doorway and pointing five eloquent fingers in my direction: 'Please, Mrs. Matzerath. We'll take him with us to London. Like a little prince he'll live.'

Mama turned toward me and managed a bit of a smile. Maybe she was thinking of the paneless windows in the theater lobby or maybe it was the thought of London Town that cheered her. But to my surprise she shook her head and said lightly, as though declining a dance: 'Thank you, Markus, but it's not possible. Really it's impossible – on account of Bronski.'

Taking my uncle's name as a cue, Markus rose to his feet and bowed like a jackknife. 'I beg your pardon,' he said. 'That's what I was thinking all along. On account of him you couldn't do it.'

It was not yet closing time when we left the shop, but Markus locked up from outside and escorted us to the streetcar stop. Passers-by and a few policemen were still standing outside the theater. But I wasn't the least bit scared, I had almost forgotten my triumph. Markus bent down close to me and whispered, more to himself than to us: 'That little Oskar! He knocks on the drum and hell is breaking loose by the theater.'

The broken glass had Mama worried and he made gestures that were intended to set her mind at rest. Then the car came and he uttered a last plea as we were climbing into the trailer, in an undertone for fear of being overheard: 'Well, if that's the case, do me a favor and stay by Matzerath what you got him already, don't bet no more on that Polisher.'

When today Oskar, lying or sitting in his hospital bed but in either case drumming, revisits Arsenal Passage and the Stockturm with the scribbles on its dungeon walls and its well-oiled instruments of torture, when once again he looks down on those three windows outside the lobby of the Stadt-Theater and thereafter returns to Arsenal Passage and Sigismund Markus' store, searching for the particulars of a day in September, he cannot help looking for Poland at the same time. How does he look for it? With his drumsticks. Does he also look for Poland with his soul?

He looks for it with every organ of his being, but the soul is not an organ.

I look for the land of the Poles that is lost to the Germans, for the moment at least. Nowadays the Germans have started searching for Poland with credits, Leicas, and compasses, with radar, divining rods, delegations, and moth-eaten provincial students' associations in costume. Some carry Chopin in their hearts, others thoughts of revenge. Condemning the first four partitions of Poland, they are busily planning a fifth; in the meantime flying to Warsaw via Air France in order to deposit, with appropriate remorse, a wreath on the spot that was once the ghetto. One of these days they will go searching for Poland with rockets. I, meanwhile, conjure up Poland on my drum. And this is what I drum: Poland's lost, but not forever, all's lost, but not forever, Poland's not lost forever.

The Rostrum

It was in singing away the lobby windows of our Stadt-Theater that I sought and found my first contact with the Thespian art. Despite Markus' attentions Mama must have observed my direct tie with the theater that afternoon, for when the Christmas holidays came, she bought four theater tickets, for herself, for Stephan and Marga Bronski, and for Oskar, and the last Sunday of Advent she took us to see the Christmas play. The fancy chandelier over the orchestra did its best to please, and I was glad I hadn't sung it to pieces.

Even in those days there were far too many children. In the balcony there were more children than mothers, while the balance was about even in the orchestra frequented by the more prosperous citizens, who were more cautious in their begetting and conceiving. Why can't children sit still? Marga Bronski, who was sitting between me and the relatively well-behaved Stephan, slid off her seat that promptly folded up, made a stab at climbing back again, but found it more interesting to do gymnastics on the balcony rail, got stuck in her folding seat, and started to scream, though no louder than the other little demons around us and only briefly, because Mama wisely poured candy into her open mouth. Sucking candy and tuckered out by her struggles with her seat, Marga fell asleep soon after the performance began, but had to be awakened after each act to clap, which she did with enthusiasm.

The play was *Tom Thumb*, which obviously had a special appeal for me and gripped me from the start. They did it very cleverly. They didn't show Tom Thumb at all, you only heard his voice and saw the grownups chasing around after him. He was invisible but very active. Here he is sitting in the horse's ear. Now his father is selling him to two tramps for good money, now he is taking a walk, very high and mighty, on the brim of one of the tramps' hats. Later he crawls into a mousehole and then into a snail shell. He joins a band of robbers, lies down with them, and along with a mouthful of hay makes his way into the cow's stomach. But the cow is slaughtered because she speaks with Tom Thumb's voice. The cow's stomach, however, with Tom inside it, is thrown out on the dump heap, and gobbled up by the wolf. Tom cleverly persuades the wolf to pillage his father's storeroom and starts to scream just as the wolf's is getting to work. The end was like the fairy tale: The father kills the wicked wolf, the mother cuts open the wolf's stomach with her scissors, and out comes Tom Thumb, that is, you hear his voice crying: 'Oh, father, I've been in a mousehole, a cow's stomach, and a wolf's stomach: now I'm going to stay home with you.'

The end touched me, and when I looked up at Mama, I saw that she was hiding her nose in her handkerchief; like me, she had identified herself with the action on the stage. Mama's feelings were easily stirred, and for the next few weeks, especially for the remainder of the Christmas holidays, she kept hugging and kissing me and, laughing or wistful, calling me Tom Thumb. Or: My little Tom Thumb. Or: My poor, poor Tom Thumb.

It was not until the summer of '33 that I went to the theater again. Because of a misunderstanding on my part, the venture turned out badly, but it was a profound experience that stayed with me. The thundering surge still rings in my ears. No, I am not exaggerating, all this took place at the Zoppot Opera-in-the-

Woods, where summer after summer Wagner was poured forth upon nature beneath the night sky.

It was only Mama who actually cared anything about opera. Even operettas were too much for Matzerath. Jan took his lead from Mama and raved about arias, though despite his musical appearance he was completely tone deaf. However, he was friends with the Formella brothers, former schoolmates at Karthaus High School, who lived at Zoppot, had charge of the floodlights illuminating the lakeside path and the fountain outside the Casino, and also attended to the lighting effects at the Opera-in-the-Woods.

The way to Zoppot led through Oliva. A morning in the Castle Park. Goldfish and swans, Mama and Jan Bronski in the famous Whispering Grotto. Afterward more goldfish and swans, obviously working hand in glove with a photographer. While the picture was being taken, Matzerath let me ride on his shoulders. I rested my drum on the top of his head, that was always good for a laugh, even later after the picture had been pasted in the album. And then good-by goldfish, good-by swans, good-by Whispering Grotto. Not only in the Castle Park was it Sunday but also outside the gate and in the streetcar bound for Glettkau, and in the Glettkau Casino, where we had lunch, while the Baltic, as though it had nothing else to do, held out an invitation to bathe; everywhere it was Sunday. As we approached Zoppot along the beach promenade, Sunday came out to meet us and Matzerath had to pay admission for the lot of us.

We bathed at South Beach because it was supposedly less crowded than North Beach. The men undressed in the men's cabins, Mama took me to a ladies' cabin where she, who was already beginning to overflow her banks, poured her flesh into a straw-colored bathing suit. I was expected to go naked. To put off my encounter with the thousands of eyes on the beach, I shielded my private parts with my drum and later lay down on my belly in the sand. The waters of the Baltic were inviting but I had no desire to go in, preferring to play the ostrich and shelter my modesty in the sand. Both Matzerath and Jan Bronski looked so ridiculous verging on pathetic with their incipient potbellies that I was glad when, late in the afternoon, we returned to the bath houses and, having anointed our sunburns, slipped back into Sunday civilian dress.

Coffee and cake at the Seestern. Mama wanted a third helping of the five-story cake. Matzerath was against, Jan was for and against. Mama ordered her cake, gave Matzerath a bite, fed Jan a spoonful, and, having provided for the well-being of her men, crammed the rest of the buttery-sweet wedge into her stomach, spoonful by spoonful.

O sacred butter cream, O clear to slightly cloudy Sunday afternoon dusted with powdered sugar! Polish nobles sat behind blue sunglasses and intense soft drinks that they did not touch. The ladies played with their violet fingernails and the sea breeze wafted over to us the mothflake smell of the fur capes they rented for the season. Matzerath thought the fur capes were idiotic. Mama would have loved to rent one, if only for a single afternoon. Jan maintained that the boredom of the Polish nobility had risen to such heights that despite mounting debts they had stopped speaking French and out of sheer snobbery taken to conversing in the most ordinary Polish.

We couldn't sit forever at the Seestern, studying the blue sunglasses and violet fingernails of the Polish nobility. Replete with cake, my mama needed exercise. We repaired to the Casino Park, where I had to ride a donkey and pose for another picture. Goldfish and swans – what nature won't think of next – and more goldfish and swans, what else is fresh water good for?

Amid clipped yew trees which, however, did not whisper as they are supposed to, we met the Formella Brothers, illuminators of the casino grounds and of the Opera-in-the-Woods. First the younger Formella had to reel off all the jokes that came his way in the course of his illuminating professional activities. The elder Formella brother knew all the jokes by heart but brotherly love made him laugh contagiously at the right places, showing one more gold tooth than his younger brother, who had only three. We went to Springer's for a drop of gin, though Mama would have preferred the Kurfürst. Then, still dealing out jokes from an inexhaustible stock, the generous younger brother invited us all to dinner at the Papagei. At the Papagei we met Tuschel, who owned half of Zoppot, a share in the Opera-in-the-Woods, and five movie theaters. He was also the Formella brothers' boss and was glad to make our acquaintance, just as we were glad to make his. Tuschel kept twisting a ring on his finger, but it couldn't have been a wishing ring or a magic ring, for nothing happened at all, except that Tuschel in turn began telling jokes, the same Formella jokes we had heard before, though he made them more complicated because he had fewer gold teeth. Even so, the whole table laughed, because Tuschel was doing the telling. I alone remained solemn, trying to puncture his punch lines with the straightness of my face. Ah, how those salvos of laughter, like the bull's-eye panes in the partition of our dining corner, fostered well-being, even if they were not genuine. Tuschel was visibly grateful, told a few more, ordered Goldwasser, and suddenly, floating in laughter and Goldwasser, turned his ring around a different way. This time something happened. Tuschel invited us all to the Opera-in-the-Woods; unfortunately he couldn't attend, an appointment and that kind of thing, but would we kindly accept his seats, they were in a loge with upholstered seats, the little fellow could sleep if he was tired; and with a silver mechanical pencil he wrote a few words in Tuschel's hand on Tuschel's visiting card; it would open all doors, he said – and so it did.

What happened next can be related in a few words: A balmy summer evening, the Opera-in-the-Woods was sold out, full of foreigners. Even before it started, the mosquitoes were on hand. And only when the last mosquito, which always comes a little late, just to be chic, announced its arrival with a bloodthirsty buzzing, did the performance really get under way. It was *The Flying Dutchman*. A ship, looking more like a poacher than a pirate, drifted in from the woods that had given the Opera-in-the-Woods its name. Sailors began to sing at the trees. I fell asleep on Tuschel's upholstery, and when I woke up, the sailors were still singing, or maybe they were different sailors: Helmsman, keep watch . . . but Oskar fell asleep once more, happy even in dozing off that Mama, gliding with the waves and heaving in the true Wagnerian spirit, was taking so much interest in the *Dutchman*. She failed to notice that Matzerath and her Jan had covered their faces with their hands and were sawing logs of different thicknesses and that I too kept slipping through Wagner's fingers. Then suddenly Oskar awoke for good, because a woman was standing all alone in the forest, screaming for all she was worth. She had yellow hair and she was yelling because a spotlight, probably manipulated by the younger Formella, was blinding her. 'No!' she cried. 'Woe's me!' and: 'Who hath made me suffer so?' But Formella, who was making her suffer, didn't divert the spotlight. The screams of the solitary woman – Mama referred to her afterward as a soloist – subsided to a muffled whimper, but only to rise again in a silvery bubbling fountain of high notes which blighted the leaves of the trees before their time but had no effect at all on Formella's spotlight. A brilliant voice, but its efforts were of no avail. It was time for Oskar to intervene, to locate that importunate source of light and, with a single long-distance cry, lower-pitched than the persistent buzzing of the mosquitoes, destroy it.

It was not my plan to create a short circuit, darkness, flying sparks, or a forest fire which, though quickly put out, provoked a panic. I had nothing to gain. Not only did I lose my mama and the two roughly awakened gentlemen in the confusion; even my drum got lost.

This third of my encounters with the theater gave my mama, who had begun, after that evening at the Opera-in-the-Woods, to domesticate Wagner in easy arrangements on our piano, the idea of taking me to the circus. It was put into effect in the spring of '34.

Oskar has no intention of chewing your ear off about trapeze artists darting through the air like streaks of silver, about ferocious tigers or the incredible dexterity of the seals. No one fell headlong from the dome. Nothing was bitten off any of the animal-tamers. And the seals did just what they had been taught: they juggled with balls and were rewarded with live herring which they caught in mid-air. I am indebted to the circus for many happy hours and for my meeting, which was to prove so important in my life, with Bebra, the musical clown, who played 'Jimmy the Tiger' on bottles and directed a group of Lilliputians.

We met in the menagerie. Mama and her two cavaliers were letting the monkeys make monkeys of them. Hedwig Bronski, who for once had come along, was showing her children the ponies. After a lion had yawned at me, I foolishly became involved with an owl. I tried to stare him down, but it was the owl that stared me down. Oskar crept away dismayed, with burning ears and a feeling of inner hurt, taking refuge between two blue and white trailers, because apart from a few tied-up dwarf goats, there were no animals here.

He was in braces and slippers, carrying a pail of water. Our eyes met as he was passing and there was instant recognition. He set down his pail, leaned his great head to one side, and came toward me. I guessed that he must be about four inches taller than I.

'Will you take a look at that!' There was a note of envy in his rasping voice. 'Nowadays it's the three-year-olds that decide to stop growing.' When I failed to answer, he tried again: 'My name is Bebra, directly descended from Prince Eugene, whose father was Louis XIV and not some Savoyard as they claim.' Still I said nothing, but he continued: 'On my tenth birthday I made myself stop growing. Better late than never.'

Since he had spoken so frankly, I too introduced myself, but without any nonsense about my family tree. I was just Oskar.

'Well, my dear Oskar, you must be fourteen or fifteen. Maybe as much as sixteen. What, only nine and a half? You don't mean it?'

It was my turn to guess his age. I purposely aimed too low.

'You're a flatterer, my young friend. Thirty-five, that was once upon a time. In August I shall be celebrating my fifty-third birthday. I could be your grandfather.'

Oskar said a few nice things about his acrobatic clown act and complimented him on his gift for music. That aroused my ambition and I performed a little trick of my own. Three light bulbs were the first to be taken in. Bravo, bravissimo, Mr. Bebra cried, and wanted to hire Oskar on the spot.

Even today I am occasionally sorry that I declined. I talked myself out of it, saying: 'You know, Mr. Bebra, I prefer to regard myself as a member of the audience. I cultivate my little art in secret, far from all applause. But it gives me pleasure to applaud your accomplishments.' Mr. Bebra raised a wrinkled forefinger and admonished me: 'My dear Oskar, believe an experienced colleague. Our kind has no place in the audience. We must perform, we must run the show. If we don't, it's the others that run us. And they don't do it with kid gloves.'

His eyes became as old as the hills and he almost crawled into my ear. 'They are coming,' he whispered. 'They will take over the meadows where we pitch our tents. They will organize torchlight parades. They will build rostrums and fill them, and down from the rostrums they will preach our destruction. Take care, young man. Always take care to be sitting on the rostrum and never to be standing out in front of it.'

Hearing my name called, Mr. Bebra took up his pail. 'They are looking for you, my friend. We shall meet again. We are too little to lose each other. Bebra always says: Little people like us can always find a place even on the most crowded rostrum. And if not on it, then under it, but never out in front. So says Bebra, who is descended in a straight line from Prince Eugene.'

Calling Oskar, Mama stepped out from behind a trailer just in time to see Mr. Bebra kiss me on the forehead. Then he picked up his pail of water and, swaying his shoulders, headed for his trailer.

Mama was furious. 'Can you imagine,' she said to Matzerath and the Bronskis. 'He was with the midgets. And a gnome kissed him on the forehead. I hope it doesn't mean anything.'

To me that kiss on the forehead was to mean a good deal. The political events of the ensuing years bore him out: the era of torchlight processions and parades past rostrums and reviewing stands had begun.

I took Mr. Bebra's advice, and Mama, for her part, followed a part of the advice Sigismund Markus had given her in Arsenal Passage and continued to repeat every Thursday. Though she did not go to London with Markus – I should not have had much objection to the move – she stayed with Matzerath and saw Bronski only in moderation, that is, in Tischlergasse at Jan's expense and over the family skat games, which became more and more costly for Jan, because he always lost. Matzerath, however, on whom Mama had bet, on whom, following Markus' advice, she let her stakes lie though she did not double them, joined the Party in '34. But though he espoused the forces of order at a relatively early date, he never attained any higher position than unit leader. Like all unusual happenings, his promotion was the occasion for a family skat game. It was then that Matzerath introduced a new note of severity mingled with alarm into the warnings he had long been meting out to Jan Bronski on the subject of his activity in the Polish Post Office.

Otherwise there was no great change. The picture of the gloomy Beethoven, a present from Greff, was removed from its nail over the piano, and Hitler's equally gloomy countenance was hung up on the same nail. Matzerath, who didn't care for serious music, wanted to banish the nearly deaf musician entirely. But Mama, who loved Beethoven's slow movements, who had learned to play two or three of them even more slowly than indicated and decanted them from time to time, insisted that is Beethoven were not over the sofa, he would have to be over the sideboard. So began the most sinister of all confrontations: Hitler and the genius, face to face and eye to eye. Neither of them was very happy about it.

Little by little Matzerath pieced together the uniform. If I remember right, he began with the cap, which he liked to wear even in fine weather with the 'storm strap' in place, scraping his chin. For a time he wore a white shirt and black tie with the cap, or else a leather jacket with black armband. Then he bought his first brown shirt and only a week later he wanted the shit-brown riding breeches and high boots. Mama was opposed to these acquisitions and several weeks passed before the uniform was complete.

Each week there were several occasions to wear the uniform but Matzerath contented himself with the Sunday demonstrations on the Maiwiese near the Sports Palace. But about these he was uncompromising even in the worst weather and refused to carry an umbrella when in uniform. 'Duty is duty and schnaps is schnaps,' he said. That became a stock phrase with him and we were to hear it very often. He went out every Sunday morning after preparing the roast for dinner. This put me in an embarrassing situation, for Jan Bronski quickly grasped the new Sunday political situation and, incorrigible civilian that he was, took to calling on my poor forsaken mama while Matzerath was drilling and parading.

What could I do but make myself scarce? I had no desire to disturb the two of them on the sofa, or to spy on them. As soon as my uniformed father was out of sight and before the civilian, whom I already looked upon as my presumptive father, should arrive, I consequently slipped out of the house and drummed my way toward the Maiwiese.

Did it have to be the Maiwiese? you may ask. Take my word for it that nothing was doing on the waterfront on Sundays, that I had no inclination to go walking in the woods, and that in those days the interior of the Church of the Sacred Heart still had no appeal for me. There were still Mr. Greff's scouts, to be sure, but even at the risk of being thought a fellow traveler I must admit that I preferred the doings on the Maiwiese to the repressed eroticism of the scout meetings.

There was always a speech either by Greiser or by Löbsack, the district chief of training. Greiser never made much of an impression on me. He was too moderate and was later replaced as Gauleiter by a Bavarian named Forster, who was more forceful. But for Löbsack's humpback, it would have been hard for the Bavarian to get ahead in our northern seaport. Recognizing Löbsack's worth, regarding his hump as a sign of keen intelligence, the Party made him district chief of training. He knew his business. All Forster knew how to do was to shout 'Home to the Reich' in his soul Bavarian accent, but Löbsack had a head for particulars. He spoke every variety of Danzig Plattdeutsch, told jokes about Bollermann and Wullsutzki, and knew how to talk to the longshoremen in Schichau, the proletariat in Ohra, the middle class of Emmaus, Schidlitz, Bürgerwiesen, and Praust. It was a pleasure to hear the little man, whose brown uniform lent a special prominence to his hump, stand up to the feeble heckling of the Socialists and the sullen beer-drinker's aggressiveness of the Communists.

Löbsack had wit. He derived all his wit from his hump, which he called by its name; the crowd always likes that. Before the Communists would be allowed to take over he would lose his hump. It was easy to see that he was not going to lose his hump, that his hump was there to stay. It followed that the hump was right and with it the Party – whence it can be inferred that a hump is an ideal basis for an idea.

When Greiser, Löbsack, or later Forster spoke, they spoke from the rostrum. This was one of the rostrums that little Mr. Bebra had commended. Consequently I long regarded Löbsack, who was humpbacked and gifted and spoke from a rostrum, as an emissary from Bebra, one who stood brown-clad on the rostrum fighting for Bebra's cause and mine.

What is a rostrum? Regardless of whom it is built for, a rostrum must be symmetrical. And that rostrum on our Maiwiese was indeed striking in its symmetry. From back to front: six swastika banners side by side; then a row of flags, pennants, standards; then a row of black-uniformed SS men who clutched their belt buckles during the singing and the speeches; then, seated, several rows of uniformed Party comrades; behind the speaker's stand more Party comrades, leaders of women's associations with motherly looks on their faces, representatives of the Senate in civilian garb, guests from the Reich, and the police chief or his representative.

The front of the rostrum was rejuvenated by the Hitler Youth or, more precisely, by the Regional Bands of the Hitler Young Folk and the Hitler Youth. At some of the demonstrations a mixed chorus, also symmetrically arranged, would recite slogans or sing the praises of the east wind, which, according to the text, was better than any other wind at unfurling banners.

Bebra, who kissed me on the forehead, had also said: 'Oskar, never be a member of the audience. Never be standing out in front. The place for our kind is on the rostrum.'

Usually I was able to find a place among the leaders of the women's associations. Unfortunately the ladies never failed to caress me for propaganda purposes during the rally. I couldn't slip in between the drums and trumpets at the foot of the platform because of my own drum, which the trooper musicians rejected. An attempt to enter into relations with Löbsack, the district chief of training, ended in failure. I had been sorrily mistaken in the man. Neither was he, as I had hoped, an emissary from Bebra, nor, despite his promising hump, had he the slightest understanding of my true stature.

On one of those rostrum Sundays I went up to him as he stood near the pulpit, gave him the party salute, looked brightly up at him for a moment, and then whispered with a wink: 'Bebra is our leader!' But no light dawned. No, he patted me just like the ladies of the National Socialist women's associations and finally had Oskar removed from the platform – after all he had a speech to make. I was taken in hand by two representatives of the League of German Girls, who questioned me about my papa and mama all through the speech.

Thus it will come as no surprise when I tell you that by the summer of '34 I began to be disillusioned with the Party – the Roehm putsch had nothing to do with it. The longer I contemplated the rostrum from out in front, the more suspicious I became of its symmetry, which was not sufficiently relieved by Löbsack's hump. Of course Oskar's criticism was leveled first of all at the drummers and horn-blowers; and one sultry demonstration Sunday in '35, I tangled with the young drummers and trumpet-players at the foot of the reviewing stand.

Matzerath left home at nine o'clock. To get him out of the house on time, I had helped him shine his brown leather puttees. Even at that early hour it was intolerably hot, and even before he went out in the sun, there were dark and spreading spots of sweat under the arms of his Party shirt. At half past nine on the dot Jan Bronski arrived in an airy, light-colored summer suit, tender-grey, pierced oxfords, and a straw hat. Jan played with me for a while, but even as he played, he could not take his eyes off Mama, who had washed her hair the night before. I soon realized that my presence inhibited their conversation; there was a stiffness in her bearing and an air of embarrassment in Jan's movements. It was plain that he felt cramped in those summer trousers of his. And so I made off, following in the footsteps of Matzerath, though I did not take him as my model. Carefully I avoided streets that were full of uniformed folk on their way to the Maiwiese and for the first time approached the drill ground from the direction of the tennis courts which were beside the Sports Palace. Thanks to this indirect route, I obtained a rear view of the rostrum.

Have you ever seen a rostrum from behind? All men and women – if I may make a suggestion – should be familiarized with the rear view of a rostrum before being called upon to gather in front of one. Everyone who has ever taken a good look at a rostrum from behind will be immunized ipso facto against any magic practiced in any form whatsoever on rostrums. Pretty much the same applies to rear views of church altars; but that is another subject.

Oskar was already inclined to thoroughness; he did not content himself with viewing the naked ugliness of the scaffolding. Remembering the words of Bebra his mentor, he made his way to the rostrum. This rostrum was meant to be viewed only from the front, but he approached its uncouth rear. Clutching his drum, without which he never went out, he squeezed between uprights, bumped his head on a projecting beam, and gashed his knee on a protruding nail. He heard the boots of the party comrades overhead, and a moment later the little shoes of the women's associations. Finally he reached the place where the August heat was most stifling. At the foot of the stand he found a nook where, hidden behind a slat of plywood, he was able to enjoy the accoustical delights of the political rally at his ease, free from the optical irritation of banners and uniforms.

And so I huddled under the speaker's stand. To the left and right of me and above me stood the younger drummers of the Young Folk and the older drummers of the Hitler Youth, squinting, as I knew, beneath the blinding sunlight. And then the crowd. I smelled them through the cracks in the planking. They stood there rubbing elbows and Sunday clothes. They had come on foot or by streetcar; some had brought their fiancées, to give them a treat; all these people wanted to be present while history was being made, even if it took up the whole morning.

No, said Oskar to himself. It wouldn't be right if they had come for nothing. He set an eye to a knothole in the planking and watched the hubbub approaching from the Hindenburg-Allee. *They* were coming! Commands rang out over his head, the band leader fiddled with his baton, the musicians set their polished and gleaming trumpets to their lips and adjusted their mouthpieces. And then the grim trumpeting of the young troopers began. 'Poor SA Man Brand,' said Oskar to himself in bitter pain, 'and poor Hitler Youth Quex, you have died in vain.'

As though to confirm Oskar's sorrowful obituary for the martyrs of the movement, a massive pounding on taut calfskin mingled with the trumpets. Down the lane leading through the crowd to the rostrum, I dimly saw uniforms approaching in the distance. 'Now, my people,' Oskar cried out. 'Now, my people. Hearken unto me!'

The drum was already in place. Supplely and tenderly I manipulated the sticks, imprinting an artful and joyous waltz rhythm upon it. Conjuring up Vienna and the Danube, I beat more and more loudly until the first and second bass drums of the troopers were drawn to my waltz and the kettledrums of the older boys took up my prelude with varying skill. Here and there, of course, there was a diehard, hard also of hearing no doubt, who went on playing boom-boom, whereas what I had in mind was the three-four time so beloved of the simple folk. Oskar was on the point of giving up when the trumpets saw the light and the fifes, oh, Danube, oh, how blue they blew! Only the leaders of the trumpeters' and the drummers' corps refused to bow to the waltz king and kept shouting their exasperating commands. But I had deposed them, the music was mine. The simple folk were full of gratitude. Laughter rang out close to the rostrum, here and there I heard singing, oh, Danube, and across the whole field so blue, as far as the Hindenburg-Allee so blue and the Steffens-Park so blue, my rhythm went hopping, amplified by the wide-open microphone above me. And when, still energetically drumming, I looked out into the open through my knothole, I saw that the people were enjoying my waltz, they were hopping about merrily, they had it in their legs: already nine couples and yet another couple were dancing, brought together by the waltz king. Only Löbsack, who appeared on the meadow followed by a long brown train of party dignitaries, Forster, Greiser, Rauschning, and others, whose passage to the rostrum was blocked by the crowd, stood there fuming and surprisingly disgruntled by my three-quarter time. He was used to being escorted to the rostrum by rectilinear march music. These frivolous sounds shook his faith in the people. Through the knothole I observed his sufferings. A draft was blowing through the hole. Though threatened with an inflammation of the eye, I felt sorry for him and changed over to a Charleston: 'Jimmy the Tiger.' I took up the rhythm that Bebra the clown had drummed in the circus on empty seltzer siphons; but the young troopers out in front didn't dig the Charleston. They belonged to a different generation. What could they know of the Charleston and 'Jimmy the Tiger'? What those drums were pounding – oh, Bebra, my dear friend – wasn't Jimmy the Tiger, it was pure chaos, and the trumpets blew Sodom and Gomorrah. It's all one to us, thought the fifes. The trumpet leader cursed in all directions. And nevertheless the troopers drummed, piped, and trumpeted for all they were worth, bringing joy to Jimmy's heart in the sweltering tigery August heat, and at last the national comrades who were crowding round the stand by the thousands caught on: it's Jimmy the Tiger, summoning the people to the Charleston.

All those who were not yet dancing hastened to snatch up the last available partners. But Löbsack had to dance with his hump, for near him there was not a single member of the fair sex to be had, and the NS ladies who might have come to his help were far away, fidgeting on the hard wooden benches of the rostrum. Nevertheless – as his hump advised him – he danced, trying to put a good face on the horrible Jimmy music and to save what could still be saved.

But the situation was beyond saving. The national comrades danced away from the Maiwiese and soon the grassy field, though badly trampled, was quite deserted. The national comrades had vanished with Jimmy the Tiger in the spacious grounds of the nearby Steffens-Park. There they found the jungle that Jimmy promised; there tigers moved on velvet paws, an ersatz jungle for the sons and daughters of the German nation, who only a short while before had been crowding round the rostrum. Gone were law and order. The more culture-minded element repaired to the Hindenburg-Allee, where trees had first been planted in the eighteenth century, where these same trees had been cut down in 1807 when the city was being besieged by Napoleon's troops, and a fresh set had been planted in 1810 in honor of Napoleon. On this historic ground, the dancers were still able to benefit by my music, because no one turned off the microphone above me. I could be heard as far as Oliva Gate. In the end the excellent lads at the foot of the rostrum succeeded, with the help of Jimmy's unleashed tiger, in clearing the Maiwiese of everything but daisies.

Even when I gave my instrument a well-deserved rest, the drummer boys kept right on. It was quite some time before my musical influence wore off.

Oskar was not able to leave his hiding place at once, SA men and SS men spent more than an hour kicking at the planks, poking into crannies, tearing holes in their brown and black uniforms. They seemed to be looking for something under the rostrum, perhaps a Socialist or a team of Communist saboteurs. I shall not describe my dodges and maneuvers. Suffice it to say that they did not find Oskar, because they were no match for him.

At least it was quiet in my wooden labyrinth, which was about the size of the whale's belly where Jonah sat staining his prophet's robes with blubber. But Oskar was no prophet, he was beginning to feel hungry. There was no Lord to say: 'Arise, go unto Nineveh, that great city, and preach unto it.' For me the Lord saw no need to make a gourd grow and send a worm to destroy it. I lamented neither for a biblical gourd nor for Nineveh, even if its name was Danzig. I tucked my very unbiblical drum under my sweater and concentrated on my own troubles. Carefully avoiding overhanging beams and protruding nails, I emerged by my own resources from the bowels of a rostrum intended for meetings and rallies of all sorts and which happened only by the merest accident to have the proportions of a prophet-swallowing whale.

Who would have noticed a wee mite of a three-year-old, whistling as he skirted the Maiwiese in the direction of the Sports Palace. Behind the tennis courts my boys from the rostrum were hopping about with their bass drums and kettledrums, their fifes and trumpets. Punitive drill, I observed, as they hopped about in response to their leader's whistle. I felt only moderately sorry for them. Aloof from his assembled staff, Löbsack was walking up and down, alone with his hump. About-facing on the heels of his boots, he had managed to eradicate all the grass and daisies at the extremities of his course

Dinner was on the table when Oskar reached home. There was meat loaf with boiled potatoes, red cabbage, and for dessert chocolate pudding with vanilla sauce. Matzerath didn't say a word. Mama's thoughts were somewhere else. But that afternoon there was a family quarrel hinging on jealousy and the Polish Post Office. Toward evening came a refreshing storm, a cloudburst accompanied by a fine drum solo of hail. Oskar's weary instrument was able to rest and listen.

Shopwindows

For several years, until November, '38, to be exact, my drum and I spent a good bit of our time huddling under rostrums, observing successful or not so successful demonstrations, breaking up rallies, driving orators to distraction, transforming marches and hymns into waltzes and fox trots.

Today I am private patient in a mental hospital, and all that has become historical, old stuff, dead as a doornail, though still much debated and discussed. It has become possible for me to see my drumming under rostrums in proper perspective, and it would never occur to me to set myself up as a resistance fighter because I disrupted six or seven rallies and threw three or four parades out of step with my drumming. That word 'resistance' has become very fashionable. We hear of the 'spirit of resistance,' of 'resistance circles.' There is even talk of an 'inward resistance,' a 'psychic emigration.' Not to mention those courageous and uncompromising souls who call themselves Resistance Fighters, men of the Resistance, because they were fined during the war for not blacking out their bedroom windows properly.

Let us cast one more glance beneath Oskar's rostrums. Did Oskar drum for the people? Did he, following the advice of Bebra his mentor, take the action in hand and provoke the people out in front of the rostrum to dance? Did he confound and perplex Löbsack, the shrewd and able chief of training? Did he, on a one-dish Sunday in August, 1935 and on several occasions thereafter, break up brown rallies on a drum which though red and white was not Polish?

Yes, I did all that. But does that make me, as I lie in this mental hospital, a Resistance Fighter? I must answer in the negative, and I hope that you too, you who are not inmates of mental hospitals, will regard me as nothing more than an eccentric who, for private and what is more esthetic reasons, though to be sure the advice of Bebra my mentor had something to do with it, rejected the cut and color of the uniforms, the rhythm and tone of the music normally played on rostrums, and therefore drummed up a bit of protest on an instrument that was a mere toy.

In those days it was possible to reach the people on and in front of a rostrum with a wretched toy drum, and I must admit that I perfected this little trick, as I had my long-distance, glass-shattering song, for its own sake. For it was not only demonstrations of a brown hue that I attacked with my drumming. Oskar huddled under the rostrum for Reds and Blacks, for Boy Scouts and Spinach Shirts, for Jehovah's Witnesses, the Kyffhäuser Bund, the Vegetarians, and the Young Polish Fresh Air Movement. Whatever they might have to sing, trumpet, or proclaim, my drum knew better.

Yes, my work was destructive. And what I did not defeat with my drum, I killed with my voice. In the daytime I assaulted the symmetry of rostrums; at night – this was in the winter of '36 to '37 – I played the tempter. My earliest instruction in the tempting of my fellow men was provided by my grandmother Koljaiczek, who in that hard winter opened a stand at the weekly market in Langfuhr: there she sat in her four skirts, crying plaintively: 'Fresh eggs, golden creamy butter, geese not too fat, not too thin.' Every Tuesday was market day. She took the narrow-gauge railway from Viereck; shortly before Langfuhr she removed the felt slippers she wore in the train, donned a pair of shapeless galoshes, took up her two baskets, and made her way to the stall in Bahnhofstrasse. Over it hung a sign: Anna Koljaiczek, Bissau. How cheap eggs were in those days! You could get two and a half dozen of them for one gulden, and Kashubian butter cost less than margarine. My grandmother's place was between two fish vendors who called: 'Fresh flounder and cod!' The cold made the butter hard as stone, kept the eggs fresh, turned fish scales into extra-thin razor blades, and provided work for a one-eyed man named Schwerdtfeger who heated bricks over a charcoal fire, wrapped them in newspaper, and rented them out to the market women.

Every hour on the dot Schwerdtfeger pushed a hot brick under my grandmother's four skirts with an iron rake. He pushed the steaming package under the scarcely lifted hems, discharged it, caught hold of the brick of the preceding hour, which was almost cold by now, and pulled it out.

How I envied those bricks wrapped in newspaper, those storehouses and bestowers of warmth! To this day I wish I could be a toasty warm brick, constantly exchanged for myself, lying beneath my grandmother's skirts. What, you will ask, can Oskar be after beneath his grandmother's skirts? Does he wish to imitate his grandfather Koljaiczek and take liberties with an old woman? Is he searching for oblivion, a home, the ultimate Nirvana?

Oskar replies: I was looking for Africa under the skirts, or perhaps Naples, which, as we all know, one must have seen before dying. This was the watershed, the union of all streams; here special winds blew, or else there was no wind at all; dry and warm, you could listen to the whishing of the rain; here ships made fast or weighed anchors; here our Heavenly Father, who has always been a lover of warmth, sat beside Oskar; the Devil cleaned his spyglass, and the angels played blindman's buff; beneath my grandmother's skirts it was always summer, even when it was time to light the candles on the Chrismas tree or to hunt for Easter eggs; even on All Saints' Day. Nowhere could I have been more at peace with the calendar than beneath my grandmother's skirts.

But she seldom let me take shelter under her tent, and never at market. I sat beside her on a crate, receiving a kind of warmth from her arm, and looked on as the bricks came and went. Here it was that I learned my grandmother's trick of tempting people. Her equipment consisted of Vincent Bronski's old pocketbook with a string tied to it. She would toss the pocketbook out on the hard-packed snow of the sidewalk. Against the grey sand strewn over the slipperiness no one but my grandmother and I could see the string.

Housewives came and went. Cheap as her wares were, they were not in the mood to buy; they wanted the merchandise for nothing, if possible with a little premium thrown in. In this state of mind, a lady would bend down to pick up Vincent's pocketbook, her fingers were already touching it. And then my grandmother would pull in the hook, drawing a well-dressed, slightly embarrassed fish over to her stall: 'Well, my dear lady, would you like a little butter, golden creamy, or a few eggs, two and a half dozen for a gulden?'

This was how Anna Koljaiczek sold her produce. I for my part learned the magic of temptation, not the kind of temptation that lured the fourteen-year-olds on our block down to the cellar with

Susi Kater to play doctor and patient. That tempted me not at all, I avoided it like the plague after the little monsters, Axel Mischke and Nuchi Eyke, in the role of serum donors, and Susi Kater playing the doctor, had used me as a patient, making me swallow medicines that were not so sandy as the brick soup but had an aftertaste of putrid fish. My temptation was almost disembodied and kept its distance from its victims.

Long after nightfall, an hour or two after the shops closed, I slipped away from Mama and Matzerath and went out into the winter night. Standing in a doorway sheltered from the wind, I would peer across the silent, almost deserted streets at the nearby shopwindows, displays of delicatessen, haberdashery, shoes, watches, jewelry, all articles both desirable and easy to carry. All the windows were not illuminated. Indeed, I preferred those that were half in darkness, beyond the beam of the street lamps, because light attracts everyone, even the most commonplace people, while only the elect choose to linger in the penumbra.

I was not interested in the kind of people who in strolling by cast a glance into brightly lit shopwindows, more concerned with the price tags than the merchandise; nor did I concern myself with those who looked at themselves in the plate-glass panes to see if their hats were on right. The kind for whom I lurked in wait on crisp dry nights, on nights when the air was full of great silent snowflakes, or beneath the waxing wintry moon, were the kind who stopped to look in a shopwindow as though in answer to a call; their eyes did not wander about aimlessly, but quickly came to rest on a single object.

I was the hunter, they were my game. My work required patience, coolness, and a sure eye. It was my voice which felled the victim, painlessly and without bloodshed. By temptation. What sort of temptation?

The temptation to steal. With my most inaudible cry I made a circular incision in the shopwindow on a level with the bottom-most displays, close to the coveted article. And then, with a last vocal effort, I toppled the cut-out disk into the interior of the showcase. It fell with a quickly muffled tinkle, which however was not the tinkle of breaking glass. I did not hear it, Oskar was too far away; but the young woman in the threadbare brown coat with the rabbit collar heard the sound and saw the circular aperture, gave a start that sent a quiver through her rabbit fur, and prepared to set off through the snow, but stood still, perhaps because it was snowing and everything is permitted when it is snowing, provided it is snowing hard enough. Yet she looked round, suspicious of the snowflakes, looked round as though behind the snowflakes there were something else beside more snowflakes, and she was still looking round when her right hand slipped out of her muff, which was also made of bunny fur. Then she stopped looking round and reached through the circular hole, pushed aside the glass disk which had fallen on top of the desired object, and pulled out first one then the other black suede pump through the hole without scratching the heels, without cutting her hand on the sharp edge of the aperture. One to the left, one to the right, the shoes vanished into her coat pockets. For a moment, for the time it takes five snowflakes to fall, Oskar saw a pretty but insignificant profile; perhaps, the thought flashed through his mind, she was a model at Sternfeld's; and then she had vanished into the falling snow. She was once more briefly visible in the yellow glow of the next street lamp and then, emancipated model or newly wedded wife, she was gone for good.

My work done – and believe me it was hard work to lurk undrummingly in wait and to sing so neat a hole into the icy glass – I too made my way home, without spoils but with a hot flame and a cold chill in my heart.

My arts of seduction were not always crowned with such unequivocal success. One of my ambitions was to turn a couple into a couple of thieves. Either both were unwilling, or even as he stretched out his hand, she pulled it back; or it was she who had the courage while he went down on his knees and pleaded, with the result that she obeyed and despisd him forever after. Once I seduced a young couple who in the falling snow seemed particularly young. This time it was a perfumer's shop. He played the hero and seized a bottle of cologne. She whimpered and said she didn't want it. However, he wanted her to be fragrant and had his way up to the first street lamp. But there in the lamplight the young thing stood up on tiptoe and kissed him – her gestures were as blatantly demonstrative as if her purpose had been to annoy me – until he retraced his steps and put the bottle back in the window.

I had several similar experiences with elderly gentlemen, of whom I expected more than their brisk step in the wintry night promised. An old fellow would stand gazing devoutly into the window of a cigar store; his thoughts were in Havana, Brazil, or the Brissago Islands, and when my voice produced its custom-made incision and an aperture appeared directly opposite a box of 'Black Wisdom,' a jackknife folded up in his heart. He turned about, crossed the street waving his cane, and hurried past me and my doorway without noticing me, giving Oskar an opportunity to smile at his stricken countenance, yes, he looked as if the Devil had been giving him a good shaking. But there was a tinge of anxiety in my smile, for the poor old gentleman – and most of these veteran cigar-smokers were very very old – was visibly in a cold sweat and especially in changing weather I was afraid he might catch his death of cold.

Most of the stores in our suburb were insured against theft, and that winter the insurance companies had to pay out considerable indemnities. Though I never engineered any depredations on a large scale and purposely made my apertures so small that only one or two objects could be removed from the displays at a time, so many burglaries were reported that the police scarcely had a moment's rest and were nevertheless treated very harshly by the press. From November, '36 to March, '37, when Colonel Koc formed a National Front government in Warsaw, sixty-four attempted and twenty-eight successful burglaries of the same type were listed. Of course the majority of those salesmen, housemaids, old ladies, and pensioned high school principals had no vocation for theft and the police were usually able to recover the stolen articles next day; or else the amateur shoplifter, after the object of his desires had given him a sleepless night, could think of nothing better than to go to the police and say: 'Mm, I beg your pardon. It will never happen again. Suddenly there was a hole in the glass and by the time I had halfway recovered from my fright and was three blocks away, I discovered to my consternation that I was illegally harboring a pair of wonderful calfskin gloves, very expensive I'm sure, in my coat pocket.'

Since the police did not believe in miracles, all who were caught and all who went to the police of their own free will were given jail sentences ranging from four to eight weeks.

I myself was punished occasionally with house arrest, for of course Mama suspected, although she did not admit it to herself and – very wisely – refrained from communicating with the police, that my glass-cutting voice had something to do with the crime wave.

Now and then Matzerath would put on his stern, law-abiding face and try to question me. I refused to reply, taking refuge more and more astutely behind my drum and the undersized backwardness of the eternal three-year-old. After these hearings Mama would always cry out: 'It's the fault of that midget that kissed him on the forehead. Oskar never used to be that way. The moment I saw it I knew something would go wrong.'

I own that Mr. Bebra exerted a lasting influence on me. Even those terms of house arrest could not deter me from going AWOL for an hour or so whenever possible, time enough to sing the notorious circular aperture in a shopwindow and turn a hopeful young man, who happened to be drawn to a certain window display, into the possessor of a pure silk, burgundy necktie.

If you ask me: Was it evil that commanded Oskar to enhance the already considerable temptation offered by a well-polished plate-glass window by opening a passage through it? – I must reply: Yes, it was evil. If only because I stood in dark doorways. For as everyone should know, a doorway is the favorite dwelling place of evil. On the other hand, without wishing to minimize the wickedness of my acts, I am compelled, now that I have lost all opportunity or inclination to tempt anyone, to say to myself and to Bruno my keeper: Oskar, you not only contented the small and medium-sized desires of all those silent walkers in the snow, those men and women in love with some object of their dreams; no, you helped them to know themselves. Many a respectably well-dressed lady, many a fine old gentleman, many an elderly spinster whose religion had kept her young would never have come to know the thief in their hearts if your voice had not tempted them to steal, not to mention the changes it wrought in self-righteous citizens who until that hour had looked upon the pettiest and most incompetent of pickpockets as a dangerous criminal.

After I had lurked in wait for him several evenings in a row and he had thrice refused to steal but turned thief the fourth time though the police never found him out, Dr. Erwin Scholtis, the dreaded prosecuting attorney, is said to have become a mild, indulgent jurist, a hander-down of almost humane sentences, all because he sacrificed to me, the little demigod of thieves, and stole a genuine badger-hair shaving brush.

One night in January, '37 I stood for a long while shivering, across the way from a jeweler's shop which, despite its situation in this quiet suburban street bordered with maple trees, was regarded as one of the best in town. The showcase with its jewelry and watches attracted a number of possible victims whom I should have shot down without hesitation if they had been looking at the other displays, at silk stockings, velour hats, or liqueurs.

That is what jewelry does to you. You become slow and exacting, adapting your rhythm to endless circuits of beads. I no longer measured the time in minutes but in pearl years, figuring that the pearl outlasts the neck, that the wrist withers but not the bracelet, that rings but not fingers are found in ancient tombs; in short, one window-shopper struck me as too pretentious, another as too insignificant to bestow jewels on.

The showcase of Bansemer's jewelry store was not overcrowded. A few choice watches, Swiss quality articles, an assortment of wedding rings on sky-blue velvet, and in the center six or seven of the choicest pieces. There was a snake in three coils, fashioned in multicolored gold, its finely chiseled head adorned and made valuable by a topaz and two diamonds, with two sapphires for eyes. I am not ordinarily a lover of black velvet, but the black velvet on which Bansemer's snake lay was most appropriate, and so was the grey velvet which created a provocative quietness beneath certain strikingly harmonious articles of hammered silver. There was a ring with a gem so lovely that you knew it would wear out the hands of equally lovely ladies, growing more and more beautiful in the process until it attained the degree of immortality which is no doubt the exclusive right of jewels. There were necklaces such as no one can put on with impunity, necklaces that wear out their wearers; and finally, on a pale yellow velvet cushion shaped like a simplified neck base, a necklace of infinite lightness. Subtly, playfully woven, a web perpetually broken off. What spider can have secreted gold to catch six small rubies and one large one in this net? Where was the spider sitting, for what was it lurking in wait? Certainly not for more rubies; more likely for someone whose eye would be caught by the ensnared rubies which sat there like modeled blood – in other words: To whom should I, in conformity with my plan or the plan of the gold-secreting spider, give this necklace?

On the eighteenth of January, 1937, on crunching hard-trodden snow, in a night that smelled like more snow, the kind of night that is made to order for one who wishes to hold the snow responsible for anything that may happen, I saw Jan Bronski crossing the street not far from my observation post; I saw him pass the jeweler's shop without looking up and then hesitate or rather stop still as though in answer to a summons. He turned or was turned – and there stood Jan before the showcase amid the quiet maple trees topped with white.

The handsome, too handsome Jan Bronski, always rather sickly, submissive in his work and ambitious in love, a dull man enamored of beauty; Jan Bronski, who lived by my mother's flesh, who, as to this day I believe and doubt, begot me in Matzerath's name – there he stood in his fashionable overcoat that might have been cut by a Warsaw tailor, and became a statue of himself, a petrified symbol. Like Parsifal he stood in the snow, but whereas Parsifal's attention had been captured by drops of blood on the snow, Jan's gaze was riveted to the rubies in the golden necklace.

I could have called or drummed him away. My drum was right there with me. I could feel it under my coat. I had only to undo a button and it would have swung out into the frosty night. I had only to reach into my coat pockets and the sticks would have been ready for action. Hubert the huntsman withheld his arrow when that very special stag entered his field of vision. Saul became Paul. Attila turned back when Pope Leo raised his finger with the ring on it. But I released my arrow, I was not converted, I did not turn back, I, Oskar, remained a hunter intent on my game; I did not unbutton my coat, I did not let my drum swing out into the frosty night, I did not cross my drumsticks over the wintry white drumhead, I did not turn that January night into a drummer's night, but screamed silently, screamed as perhaps a star screams or a fish deep down in the sea. I screamed first into the frosty night that new snow might fall at last, and then into the glass, the dense glass, the precious glass, the cheap glass, the transparent glass, the partitioning glass, the glass between worlds, the virginal, mystical glass that separated Jan Bronski from the ruby necklace, cutting a hole just right for Jan's glove size, which was well known to me. I made the cutout fall inward like a trap door, like the gate of heaven or the gate of hell: and Jan did not flinch, his fine leather hand emerged from his coat pocket and moved heavenward; from heaven or hell it removed a necklace whose rubies would have satisfied all the angels in the world, including the fallen. Full of rubies and gold, his hand returned to his pocket, and still he stood by the gaping window although to keep standing there was dangerous, although there were no more bleeding rubies to tell him, or Parsifal, which way to look.

O Father, Son, and Holy Spirit. It was high time the spirit moved, or it would be all up with Jan, the father. Oskar the son unbuttoned his coat, reached quickly for his drumsticks, and made his drum cry out: Father, father, until Jan Bronski turned and slowly, much too slowly, crossed the street, and found me, Oskar, in the doorway.

How wonderful it was that just as Jan, still frozen in his trance but about to thaw, turned to look at me, snow began to fall. He held out a hand, but not the glove that had touched the rubies, to me and led me silent but undismayed home, where Mama was worrying about me, and Matzerath, not quite seriously but with his usual show of severity, was threatening to call the police. Jan offered no explanation; he did not stay long and was disinclined to play skat, though Matzerath put beer on the table and invited him. In leaving, he caressed Oskar and Oskar was at a loss to know whether it was discretion or friendship he was asking for.

A few days later Bronski gave my mother the necklace. Surely knowing where it came from, she wore it only when Matzerath was absent, either for herself alone or for Jan Bronski, and possibly for me.

Shortly after the war I exchanged it on the black market in Düsseldorf for twelve cartons of Lucky Strikes and a leather briefcase.

No Wonder

Today as I lie here in my mental hospital, I often regret the power I had in those days to project my voice through the wintry night to thaw frost flowers on glass, cut holes in shopwindows, and show thieves the way.

How happy I should be, for example, to unglass the peephole in my door so that Bruno my keeper might observe me more directly.

How I suffered from the loss of this power during the year before my commitment to the hospital! From time to time I would dispatch a cry into the wretched Düsseldorf suburb where I was living. When despite my eagerness for success nothing happened, I, who abhor violence, was quite capable of picking up a stone and flinging it at a kitchen window. I would have been so glad to put on a show, especially for the benefit of Vittlar the window dresser. It was past midnight when I saw him behind the plate-glass window of a men's fashions store or perhaps of a perfumer's shop. From the waist up he would be hidden by curtain, but I recognized him by his green and red socks. And though he is or might be my disciple, I desired passionately to sang his window to pieces, because I did not know then and still do not know whether to call him John or Judas.

Vittlar is noble and his first name is Gottfried. When after my humiliating vain vocal effort I called his attention to myself by drumming lightly on the unharmed plate glass and he stepped outside for a few minutes to chat with me and make light of his decorative abilities, I was reduced to calling him Gottfried because my voice could not perform the miracle that would have entitled me to call him John or Judas.

The exploit of the jewelry store, which made Jan Bronski a thief and my mama the possessor of a ruby necklace, put a temporary end to my singing outside of shopwindows with desirable displays. Mama got religion. How so? No doubt it was her association with Jan Bronski, the stolen necklace, the delicious misery of an adulterous woman's life, that made her lust after sacraments. How easily the routine of sin establishes itself. Ah, those Thursdays: rendezvous in town, deposit little Oskar with Markus, strenuous exercise, usually satisfactory, in Tischlergasse, mocha and pastry at the Café Weitzke, pick up the boy along with a few of Markus' compliments and a package of sewing silk, sold at a price which made it more a present than a purchase, and back again to the Number 5 streetcar. Smiling and far away in her thoughts, my mama enjoyed the ride past Oliva Gate through Hindenburg-Allee, scarcely noticing the Maiwiese where Matzerath spent his Sunday mornings. She gritted her teeth on the curve round the Sports Palace – how ugly that boxlike structure could be immediately after a beautiful experience! – another curve and there behind dusty trees stood the Conradinum with its red-capped schoolboys – how lovely if little Oskar could have been there in a red cap with a golden C; he would be twelve and a half, in the first year of high school, just starting in on Latin, cutting the figure of a regular little Conradinian, a good student, though perhaps a bit cocky.

After the underpass, as the car moved on toward Reichskolonie and the Helene Lange School, Mrs. Matzerath's thoughts of the Conradinum and her son Oskar's lost opportunities seeped away. Another curve to leftward, past Christ Church with its bulbiform steeple. Then at Max-Halbe-Platz, we would get out, just in front of Kaiser's grocery store. After a glance into the competitor's window, my mama turned into Labesweg, her calvary: what with her nascent ill humor, this freak of a child, her troubled conscience, and her impatience to begin all over again, my mama, torn between not enough and too much, between aversion and good-natured affection for Matzerath, plodded wearily down Labesweg with me and my drum and her package of dirt-cheap silk thread, toward the store, toward the rolled oats, the kerosene by the herring barrel, the currants, raisins, almonds, and spices, toward Dr. Oetker's Baking Powder, toward Persil Washes White, Maggi and Knorr, Kaffee Hag, Kühne's Vinegar, and four-fruit jam, toward the two strips of flypaper, buzzing in different keys, which hung honeysweet over our counter and had to be changed every other day in the summer, whereas Mama, always with the same honeysweet soul, which summer and winter, all year long, attracted sins buzzing high and buzzing low, repaired each Saturday to the Church of the Sacred Heart, where she confessed to the Right Reverend Father Wiehnke.

Just as Mama took me with her to the city on Thursday to share as it were in her guilt, she led me on Saturday over cool and Catholic flagstones through the church door, having previously stuffed my drum under my sweater or overcoat, for without my drum I would not budge, and without my drum I should never have touched my forehead, chest, and shoulders, making the Catholic cross, nor should I ever have bent my knees as though to put on my shoes and, with holy water slowly drying on the bridge of my nose, sat still and behaved on the polished wooden bench.

I could still remember this church from my baptism: there had been trouble over the heathen name they were giving me, but my parents insisted on Oskar, and Jan, as godfather, took the same position. Then Father Wiehnke blew into my face three times – that was supposed to drive Satan out of me. The sign of the cross was made, a hand was imposed, salt was sprinkled, and various other measures were taken against Satan. At the baptismal chapel the party stopped again. I kept still while the Credo and the Lord's Prayer were dished out to me. Afterward Father Wiehnke saw fit to say another 'Satan depart', and touched my nose and ears, fancying that by so doing he was opening up the senses of this child, Oskar, who had known what was what from the very first. Then he wanted one last time to hear it loud and plain and asked: 'Dost thou renounce Satan? And all his works? And all his pomp?'

Before I could shake my head – for I had no intention whatsoever of renouncing – Jan, acting as my proxy, said three times: 'I do renounce.'

Without my having said anything to spoil my relations with Satan, Father Wiehnke anointed me on the breast and between the shoulder blades. By the baptismal font another Credo, then at last I was dipped thrice in the water, my scalp was anointed with chrism, they clothed me in a white dress to make spots on, the candle for dark days was bestowed on Uncle Jan, and we were dismissed. Matzerath paid, Jan carried me outside the Church, where the taxi was waiting in fair to cloudy weather, and I asked the Satan within me: 'Did you get through it all right?'

Satan jumped up and down and whispered: 'Did you see those church windows? All glass, all glass!'

The Church of the Sacred Heart was built during the early years of the German Empire and its style could consequently be identified as Neo-Gothic. Since the brickwork had quickly darkened and the copper covering of the steeple had promptly taken on the traditional verdegris, the differences between medieval and modern brick Gothic were embarrassingly evident only to connoisseurs. Confession was heard in the same way in churches old and new. Just like the Right Reverend Father Wiehkne, a hundred other Right Reverend Fathers sat down in their confessionals on Saturdays after business hours, pressing their hairy sacerdotal ears to the shiny black grating, and the members of the congregation did their best to slip their strings of sins, bead after bead of tawdry sinfulness, through the wire meshes into the priest's ear.

While Mama, by way of Father Wiehnke's auditory canal, was communicating her commissions and omissions, her thoughts, words, and works, to the supreme authorities of the only-saving Church, I, who had nothing to confess, slipped off the wooden bench, which was too smooth for my liking, and stood waiting on the stone floor.

I must admit that the floors of Catholic churches, the smell of a Catholic church, in fact everything about Catholicism still fascinates me in some inexplicable way, just as redheaded girls fascinate me though I should like to change the color of their hair, and that Catholicism never ceases to inspire me with blasphemies which make it perfectly clear that I was irrevocably though to no good purpose baptized a Catholic. Often I surprise myself in the course of the most commonplace acts, while brushing my teeth, for instance, or even while moving my bowels, muttering commentaries on the Mass: In Holy Mass Christ's blood sacrifice is renewed, his blood is shed again for the remission of your sins. The chalice of Christ's blood, the wine is transformed whenever Christ's blood is shed, the true blood of Christ is present, through the vision of his most sacred blood the soul is sprinkled with the blood of Christ, the precious blood, washed in the blood, in the consecration the blood flows, the blood-stained flesh, the voice of Christ's blood rings through all the heavens, the blood of Christ diffuses fragrance before the face of God.

You will admit that I have maintained a certain Catholic tone. There was a time when I couldn't wait for the streetcar without thinking of the Virgin Mary. I called her blessed, full of grace, virgin of virgins, mother of divine grace, Thou blessed among women, Thou who are worthy of all veneration, Thou who hast borne the . . ., mother most amiable, mother inviolate, virgin most renowned, let me savor the sweetness of the name of Jesus as Thou savoredst it in thy heart, for it is just and meet, right and for our salvation, Queen of Heaven, thrice-blessed . . .

Sometimes, and especially on those Saturdays when Mama and I went to the Church of the Sacred Heart, that little word 'blessed' was so poisonously sweet in my heart that I thanked Satan for living through my baptism within me, for providing me with an antidote which enabled me to stride, blaspheming like a Catholic but still erect, over the flagstones of Sacred Heart.

Jesus, after whose heart the church was named, was manifested not only in the sacraments and in the bright-colored little pictures of the Calvary; there were also three colored sculptures showing him in different poses.

One was of painted plaster. He stood there, long-haired, on a golden pedestal in a Prussian blue robe and sandals. He opened his robe over his chest and, in defiance of all physiology, disclosed in the middle of his thorax a tomato-red, glorified, and stylized bleeding heart, so enabling the church to be named after this organ.

The very first time I examined this open-hearted Jesus, I couldn't help noticing an embarrassing resemblance between the Saviour and my godfather, uncle, and presumptive father Jan Bronski. The same dreamy blue eyes full of naive self-confidence. That blossoming rosebud mouth, always on the point of tears. The manly suffering in the line of the eyebrows. The full sanguine cheeks demanding to be chastised. Both had that face which men feel rather inclined to punch in the nose but which wrings caresses from women. And then there were the tired effeminate hands, well manicured and averse to manual labor, with their stigmata displayed like the prize pieces of a court jeweler. I was deeply troubled by those Bronski eyes, those eyes that misunderstood me like a father, which had been painted into Jesus' face. For my own eyes had that same blue look which can arouse enthusiasm but not convince.

Oskar turned away from the bleeding heart in the nave, hastened from the first station of the Cross, where Jesus takes up the Cross, to the seventh station where he falls for the second time beneath its weight, and on to the high altar over which hung the second sculptured image of Jesus. Perhaps he was tired or perhaps he was just trying to concentrate – in any case, this Jesus had his eyes closed. What muscles the man had! At the sight of this decathlon-winner I forgot all about Sacred-Heart Bronski. There I stood, as often as Mama confessed to Father Wiehnke, gazing devoutly at the athlete over the high altar. You can believe me that I prayed. Athlete most amiable, I called him, athlete of athletes, world's champion hanger on the Cross by regulation nails. And never a twitch or a quiver. The perpetual light quivered, but he displayed perfect discipline and took the highest possible number of points. The stop watches ticked. His time was computed. In the sacristy the sexton's none-too-clean fingers were already polishing his gold medal. But Jesus didn't compete for the sake of honors. Faith came to me. I knelt down as best I could, made the sign of the Cross on my drum, and tried to associate words like 'blessed' or 'afflicted' with Jesse Owens and Rudolf Harbig and last year's Olympic Games in Berlin; but I was not always successful, for I had to admit that Jesus had not played fair with the two thieves. Forced to disqualify him, I turned my head to the left, where, taking new hope, I saw the third statue of the divine athlete in the interior of the church.

'Let me not pray until I have seen thrice,' I stammered, then set my feet down on the flags and followed the checkerboard pattern to the left-side altar. At every step I had the feeling: he is looking after you, the saints are looking after you, Peter, whom they nailed to a cross with his head down, Andrew whom they nailed to a slanting cross – hence the St. Andrew's cross. There is a Greek cross, not to mention the Latin, or Passion, cross. Double crosses, Teutonic crosses, and Calvary crosses are reproduced on textiles, in books and pictures. I have seen the patty cross, the anchor cross, and the cloverleaf cross overlapping in relief. The Moline cross is handsome, the Maltese cross is coveted, the hooked cross, or swastika, is forbidden, while de Gaulle's cross, the cross of Lorraine, is called the cross of St. Anthony in naval battles. This same cross of St. Anthony is worn on a chain, the thieves' cross is ugly, the Pope's cross is papal, and the Russian cross is also known as the cross of Lazarus. In addition there is the Red Cross. And the anti-alcoholic Blue Cross. Yellow cross is poison, cross spiders eat one another. At the crossroads you crossed me up, crisscross, cross-examination, cross purposes, crossword puzzles. And so I turned round, leaving the Cross behind me; turned my back on the crucified athlete, and approached the child Jesus who was propped up on the Virgin Mary's right thigh.

Oskar stood by the left side-altar of the left aisle of the nave. Mary had the expression that his mama must have worn when as a seventeen-year-old shopgirl in Troyl she had no money for the movies, but made up for it by gazing spellbound at posters of Asta Nielsen.

She took no interest in Jesus but was looking at the other boy on her right knee, whom, to avert misunderstandings, I shall identify at once as John the Baptist. Both boys were my size. Actually Jesus seemed perhaps an inch taller, though according to the texts he was even younger than the little Baptist. It had amused the sculptor to make the three-year-old Saviour pink and naked. John, because he would later go out into the desert, was wearing a shaggy, chocolate-colored pelt, which covered half his chest, his belly, and his watering can.

Oskar would have done better to stay by the high altar or to mind his business in the vicinity of the confessional than to venture into the company of these two boys with that precocious look in their eyes which bore a terrifying resemblance to his own. Naturally they had blue eyes and his chestnut-brown hair. The likeness would have been complete if only the barber-sculptor had given his two little Oskars a crew cut and chopped off those preposterous corkscrew curls.

I shall not dwell too long on the boy Baptist, who pointed his left forefinger at Jesus as though counting off to see who should play first: 'Eeny meeny miny mo . . .' Ignoring such childish pastimes, I take a good look at Jesus and recognize my spit and image. He might have been my twin brother. He had my stature and exactly my watering can, in those days employed exclusively as a watering can. He looked out into the world with my cobalt blue Bronski eyes and – this was what I resented most – he had my very own gestures.

My double raised both arms and clenched his fists in such a way that one wanted desperately to thrust something into them, my drumsticks for example. If the sculptor had done that and put a red and white plaster drum on his pink little thighs, it would have been I, Oskar's very own self, who sat there on the Virgin's knee, drumming the congregation together. There are things in this world which – sacred as they may be – cannot be left as they are.

Three carpeted steps led up to the Virgin clad in green and silver, to John's shaggy, chocolate-colored pelt, and to the boy Jesus whose coloring suggested boiled ham. In front of them there was an altar outfitted with anemic candles and flowers at all prices. All three of them – the green Virgin, the brown John, and the pink Jesus – had halos the size of dinnerplates stuck to the backs of their heads – expensive plates adorned with gold leaf.

If not for the steps before the altar, I should never have climbed up. Steps, door handles, and shopwindows had a power of seduction for Oskar in those days, and though today he has no need of anything but his hospital bed, they still do not leave him indifferent. He let himself be seduced from one step to the next, though always on the same carpet. He came close enough to tap the group, at once disparagingly and respectfully with his knuckles. He was able to scratch it with his fingernails in the way that discloses the plaster under the paint. The folds in the Virgin's drapery could be followed along their devious course to the toes resting on the cloud bank. A succinct intimation of the Virgin's shin suggested that the sculptor had first created flesh and then submerged it in draperies. When Oskar felt the boy Jesus' watering can, which should have been circumcised but wasn't, when he stroked it and cautiously pressed it as though to move it, he felt a pleasant but strangely new and disturbing sensation in his own watering can, whereupon he left Jesus' alone in the hope that Jesus would let his alone.

Circumcised or uncircumcised, I let matters rest there, pulled out my drum from under my sweater, removed it from my neck, and, taking care not to nick Jesus' halo, hung the drum round his neck. In view of my size, this took a bit of doing. I had to climb up on the sculpture and stand on the cloud bank that served as a pedestal.

This did not happen in January, '36, on Oskar's first visit to church after baptism, but during Holy Week of the same year. All that winter his mama had been hard put to it to keep abreast of her dealings with Jan Bronski in the confessional. Consequently Oskar had plenty of Saturdays in which to mature his plan, to reject, justify, and revise it, to examine it from all sides, and finally, with the help of the stations of the Cross on the Monday of Holy Week, to discard all previous variants, formulate a new one, and carry it out with the utmost simplicity and directness.

Since Mama felt the need to confess before the Easter to-do should reach its climax, she took me by the hand on the afternoon of Passion Monday and led me down Labesweg to the Neue Markt and Elsenstrasse, down Marienstrasse past Wohlgemuth's butcher shop, turning left at Kleinhammer-Park, through the underpass always dripping with some disgusting yellow ooze, to the Church of the Sacred Heart across from the railway embankment.

It was late when we arrived. There were only two old women and a frightened young man waiting outside the confessional. While Mama was examining her conscience – leafing through her missal with a moistered thumb as though searching a ledger for the figures she would need in preparing her tax returns – I slipped out of the pew and, managing to avoid the eyes of the open-hearted Jesus and the Athlete on the Cross – made my way to the left side-altar.

Although I had to move quickly, I did not omit the Introit. Three steps: *Introibo ad altare Dei*. To God who giveth joy to my youth. Dragging out the Kyrie, I removed the drum from my neck and climbed up on the cloud bank; no dawdling by the watering can, no, just before the Gloria, I hung the drum on Jesus, taking care not to injure the halo. Down from the cloud bank – remission of sins, pardon, and forgiveness – but first I thrust the drumsticks into Jesus' hands that were just the right size to receive them, and one, two, three steps, I lift my eyes unto the hills, a little more carpet, then at last the flags and a prayer stool for Oskar, who knelt down on the cushion, and folded his drummer's hands before his face – *Gloria in Excelsis Deo* – squinted past the folded hands at Jesus and his drum and awaited the miracle: will he drum now, or can't he drum, or isn't he allowed to drum? Either he drums or he is not a real Jesus; if he doesn't drum now, Oskar is a realer Jesus than he is.

If it is miracles you are after, you must know how to wait. And so I waited. In the beginning at least I waited patiently, though perhaps not patiently enough, for the longer I repeated the words 'All eyes attend thee, O Lord' – substituting ears for eyes as the occasion demanded – the more disappointed Oskar became as he knelt on his prayer stool. He gave the Lord all sorts of opportunities, closed his eyes on the supposition that Little Lord Jesus, afraid that his first movements might be awkward, would be more likely to begin if no one were looking, but finally, after the third Credo, after Father, Creator of Heaven and Earth of things visible and invisible, and the only begotten Son, begotten not made by Him, true Son of true Father, consubstantial with Him, through Him, who for us men and our salvation, descended from Heaven, became incarnate, was made man, was buried, rose again, sitteth at the hand of the Father, the dead, no end, I believe in, together with the Father, spoke by, believe in the one Holy, Catholic, and ...

Well, my Catholicism survived only in my nostrils. My faith was just about washed up. But it wasn't the smell I was interested in. I wanted something else: I wanted to hear my drum, I wanted Jesus to play something for my benefit, I wanted a modest little miracle. I wasn't asking for thunder that would send Vicar Rasczeia running to the spot and Father Wiehnke painfully dragging his fat to witness the miracle; I wasn't asking for a major miracle that would demand reports to the Diocese at Oliva and impel the bishop to submit a testimonial to the Vatican. No, I was not ambitious. Oskar had no desire to be canonized. All he wanted was a little private miracle, something he could hear and see, something that would make it clear to him once and for all whether he should drum for or against; all he wanted was a sign to tell him which of the two blue-eyed identical twins was entitled and would be entitled in future to call himself Jesus.

I sat and waited. I also began to worry: Mama must be in the confessional; by now she must have the sixth commandment behind her. The old man who is always limping about churches limped past the main altar and then past the left side-altar, saluting the Virgin with the boys. Perhaps he saw the drum but without understanding. He shuffled on, growing older in the process.

Time passed, but Jesus did not beat the drum. I heard voices from the choir. If only no one starts playing the organ, I thought anxiously. If they start practicing for Easter, the organ will drown out the first feeble, hesitant drumbeats.

But no one touched the organ. Nor did Jesus drum. There was no miracle. I rose from my cushion with a cracking in my knee joints. Desolate and morose, I moved over the carpet, pulled myself up from step to step, but neglected all the gradual prayers I knew. I climbed up on the plaster cloud, upsetting some medium-priced flowers. All I wanted was to get my drum back from that preposterous naked kid.

I admit it and I always will: it was a mistake to try to teach him anything. I can't imagine what gave me the idea. Be that as it may, I took the sticks but left the drum. Softly at first, but then with the impatience of an impatient teacher, I showed little pseudo-Jesus how to do it. And finally, putting the drumsticks back into his hands, I gave him his chance to show what he had learned from Oskar.

Before I had time to wrench drum and drumsticks away from this most obstinate of all pupils without concern for his halo, Father Wiehnke was behind me – my drumming had made itself heard throughout the length and breadth of the church – Vicar Rasczeia was behind me, Mama was behind me, the old man was behind me. The Vicar pulled me down, Father Wiehnke cuffed me, Mama wept at me, Father Wiehnke whispered at me, the Vicar genuflected and bobbed up and took the drumsticks away from Jesus, genuflected again with the drumsticks and bobbed up again for the drum, took the drum away from Little Lord Jesus, cracked his halo, jostled his watering can, broke off a bit of cloud, tumbled down the steps, and genuflected once more. He didn't want to give me the drum and that made me angrier than I was before, compelling me to kick Father Wiehnke and shame my mama, who indeed had plenty to be ashamed about by the time I had finished kicking, biting, and scratching and torn myself free from Father Wiehnke, the Vicar, the old man, and Mama. Thereupon I ran out in front of the high altar with Satan hopping up and down in me, whispering as he had at my baptism: 'Oskar, look around. Windows everywhere. All glass, all glass.'

And past the Athlete on the Cross, who kept his peace and did not so much as twitch a muscle, I sang at the three high windows of the apse, red, yellow and green on a blue ground, representing the twelve apostles. But I aimed neither at Mark nor Matthew. I aimed at the dove above them, which stood on its head celebrating the Pentecost; I aimed at the Holy Ghost. My vocal chords vibrated, I battled the bird with my diamond. Was it my fault? Was it the dauntless Athlete who intervened? Was that the miracle, unknown to all? They saw me trembling and silently pouring out my powers against the apse, and all save Mama thought I was praying, though I was praying for nothing but broken glass. But Oskar failed, his time had not yet come. I sank down on the flagstones and wept bitterly because Jesus had failed, because Oskar had failed, because Wiehnke and Rasczeia misunderstood me, and were already spouting absurdities about repentance. Only Mama did not fail. She understood my tears, though she couldn't help feeling glad that there had been no broken glass.

Then Mama picked me up in her arms, recovered the drum and drumsticks from the Vicar, and promised Father Wiehnke to pay for the damage, whereupon he accorded her a belated absolution, for I had interrupted her confession: even Oskar got a little of the blessing, though I could have done without it.

While Mama was carrying me out of the Sacred Heart, I counted on my fingers: Today is Monday, tomorrow is Tuesday, then Wednesday, Holy Thursday, Good Friday, and then it will be all up with that character who can't even drum, who won't even give me the pleasure of a little broken glass, who resembles me but is false. He will go down into the grave while I shall keep on drumming and drumming, but never again experience any desire for a miracle.

Good Friday Fare

Paradoxical: that might be the word for my feelings between Passion Monday and Good Friday. On the one hand I was irritated over that plaster Boy Jesus who wouldn't drum; on the other, I was pleased that the drum was now all my own. Though on the one hand my voice failed in its assault on the church windows, on the other hand that intact multicolored glass preserved in Oskar the vestige of Catholic faith which was yet to inspire any number of desperate blasphemies.

And there was more to the paradox than that: On the one hand I managed to sing an attic window to pieces on my way home from the Church of the Sacred Heart just to see if it was still within my powers, but from that time on, on the other hand, the triumph of my voice over profane targets made me painfully aware of my failures in the sacred sector. Paradox, I have said. The cleavage was lasting; I have never been able to heal it, and it is still with me today, though today I am at home neither in the sacred nor the profane but dwell on the fringes, in a mental hospital.

Mama paid for the damage to the left side-altar. Business was good at Easter although the shop, on the insistence of Matzerath, who was a Protestant, had to be closed on Good Friday. Mama, who usually had her way, gave in on Good Fridays and closed up, demanding in return the right to close on Catholic grounds for Corpus Christi, to replace the gingerbread in the window by a gingerbread Virgin with electric lights and to march in the procession at Oliva.

We had a cardboard sign with 'Closed for Good Friday' on one side and 'Closed for Corpus Christi' on the other. On the Good Friday following that drumless and voiceless Monday of Holy Week, Matzerath hung out the sign saying 'Closed for Good Friday', and immediately after breakfast we started for Brösen on the streetcar. To run our word into the ground, the scene in Labesweg was also paradoxical. The Protestants went to church, the Catholics washed windows and beat everything vaguely resembling a carpet so vigorously and resoundingly in the courtyards that one had the impression thousands of Saviours were being nailed to thousands of Crosses all at once.

Our Holy Family however – Mama, Matzerath, Jan Bronski, and Oskar – left the Passiontide carpet-beating behind us, settled ourselves in the Number 9 streetcar, and rode down Brösener-Weg, past the airfield, the old drill ground and the new drill ground, and waited on a siding near Saspe Cemetery for the car coming in the opposite direction, from Neufahrwasser-Brösen, to pass. Mama took the wait as an occasion for gloomy, though lightly uttered observations. The abandoned little graveyard with its slanting overgrown tombstones and stunted scrub pines was pretty, romantic, enchanting, she thought.

'I'd be glad to lie there if it was still operating,' she said with enthusiasm. But Matzerath thought the soil was too sandy, found fault with the thistles and wild oats. Jan Bronski suggested that the noise from the airfield and the nearby streetcar switches might disturb the tranquility of an otherwise idyllic spot.

The car coming from Neufahrwasser-Brösen passed round us, the conductor rang twice, and we rode on, leaving Saspe and its cemetery behind us, toward Brösen, a beach resort which at that time, toward the end of April, looked mighty dismal: the refreshment stands boarded over, the casino shut tight, the seaside walk bereft of flags, long lines of empty bathhouses. On the weather table there were still chalk marks from the previous year: Air: 65; water 60; wind: northeast; prospects: clear to cloudy.

At first we all decided to walk to Glettkau, but then, though nothing was said, we took the opposite direction to the breakwater. Broad and lazy, the Baltic lapped at the beach. As far as the harbor mouth, from the white lighthouse to the beacon light on the breakwater, not a soul to be seen. A recent rainfall had imprinted its regular pattern on the sand; it was fun to break it up with our footprints; Mama and I had taken off our shoes and stockings. Matzerath picked up smooth little disks of brick the size of gulden pieces and skipped them eagerly, ambitiously over the greenish water. Less skillful, Jan Bronski looked for amber between his attempts to skip stones, and actually found a few splinters and a nugget the size of a cherry pit, which he gave

Mama, who kept looking back, as though in love with her footprints. The sun shone cautiously. The day was cool, still and clear; on the horizon you could make out a stripe that meant the Hela Peninsula and two or three vanishing smoke trails; from time to time the superstructure of a merchant ship would bob up over the horizon.

In dispersed order we reached the first granite boulders of the breakwater. Mama and I put our shoes and stockings back on. Matzerath and Jan started off into the open sea, hopping from stone to stone, while she was still helping me to lace my shoes. Scraggly clumps of seaweed grew from the interstices at the base of the wall. Oskar would have liked to comb them. But Mama took me by the hand and we followed the men, who were gamboling like schoolboys. At every step my drum beat against my knee; even here, I wouldn't let them take it away from me. Mama had on a light-blue spring coat with raspberry-colored facings. She had difficulty in negotiating the granite boulders in her high-heeled shoes. As always on Sundays and holidays, I was wearing my sailor coat with the gold anchor buttons. The band on my sailor hat came from Gretchen Scheffler's grab bag; S.M.S. *Seydlitz*, it said, and it would have fluttered if there had been any breeze. Matzerath unbuttoned his brown overcoat. Jan, always the soul of fashion, sported an ulster with a resplendent velvet collar.

We hopped and hobbled as far as the beacon at the end of the breakwater. At the base of the little tower sat an elderly man in a longshoreman's cap and a quilted jacket. Beside him there was a potato sack with something wriggling and writhing in it. The man – I figured he must be from Brösen or Neufahrwasser – was holding one end of a clothesline. The other end, caked with seaweed, vanished in the brackish Mottlau water which, still unmixed with the clear open sea, splashed against the stones of the breakwater.

We were all curious to know why the man in the longshoreman's cap was fishing with a common clothesline and obviously without a float. Mama asked him in tones of good-natured mockery, calling him 'Uncle'. Uncle grinned, showing tobacco-stained stumps; offering no explanation, he spat out a long, viscous train of tobacco juice which landed in the sludge amid the granite boulders, coated with tar and oil, at the base of the sea wall. There his spittle bobbed up and down so long that a gull circled down and, deftly avoiding the boulders, caught it up and flew off, drawing other screaming gulls in its wake.

We were soon ready to go, for it was cold out there and the sun was no help, but just then the man in the longshoreman's cap began to pull in his line hand over hand. Mama still wanted to leave. But Matzerath couldn't be moved, and Jan, who as a rule acceded to Mama's every wish, gave her no support on this occasion. Oskar didn't care whether we stayed or went. But as long as we were staying, he watched. While the longshoreman, pulling evenly hand over hand and stripping off the seaweed at every stroke, gathered the line between his legs, I noted that the merchantman which only half an hour before had barely shown its superstructure above the horizon, had changed its course; lying low in the water, she was heading for the harbor. Must be a Swede carrying iron ore to draw that much water, Oskar reflected.

I turned away from the Swede when the longshoreman slowly stood up. 'Well, s'pose we take a look.' His words were addressed to Matzerath, who had no idea what it was all about but nodded knowingly. 'Spose we take a look,' the longshoreman said over and over as he continued to haul in the line, now with increasing effort. He clambered down the stones toward the end of the line and stretched out both arms into the foaming pond between the granite blocks, clutched something – Mama turned away but not soon enough – he clutched something, changed his hold, tugged and heaved, shouted at them to make way, and flung something heavy and dripping, a great living lump of something down in our midst: it was a horse's head, a fresh and genuine horse's head, the head of a black horse with a black mane, which only yesterday or the day before had no doubt been neighing; for the head was not putrid, it didn't stink, or if it did, then only of Mottlau water; but everything on the breakwater stank of that.

The man in the longshoreman's cap – which had slipped down over the back of his neck – stood firmly planted over the lump of horsemeat, from which small light-green eels were darting furiously. The man had trouble in catching them, for eels move quickly and deftly, especially over smooth wet stones. Already the gulls were screaming overhead. They wheeled down, three or four of them would seize a small or medium-sized eel, and they refused to be driven away, for the breakwater was their domain. Nevertheless the longshoreman, thrashing and snatching among the gulls, managed to cram a couple of dozen small eels into the sack which Matzerath, who liked to be helpful, held ready for him. Matzerath was too busy to see Mama turn green and support first her hand, then her head, on Jan's shoulder and velvet collar.

But when the small and medium-sized eels were in the sack and the longshoreman, whose cap had fallen off in the course of his work, began to squeeze thicker, dark-colored eels out of the cadaver, Mama had to sit down. Jan tried to turn her head away but Mama would not allow it; she kept staring with great cow's eyes into the very middle of the longshoreman's activity.

'Take a look,' he groaned intermittently. And 'S'pose we!' With the help of his rubber boot he wrenched the horse's mouth open and forced a club between the jaws, so that the great yellow horse teeth seemed to be laughing. And when the longshoreman – only now did I see that he was bald as an egg – reached both hands into the horse's gullet and pulled out two at once, both of them as thick and long as a man's arm, my mother's jaws were also torn asunder: she disgorged her whole breakfast, pouring out lumpy egg white and threads of egg yolk mingled with lumps of bread soaked in *café au lait* over the stones of the breakwater. After that she retched but there was nothing more to come out, for that was all she had had for breakfast, because she was overweight and wanted to reduce at any price and tried all sorts of diets which, however, she seldom stuck to. She ate in secret. She was conscientious only about her Tuesday gymnastics at the Women's Association, but on this score she stood firm as a rock though Jan and even Matzerath laughed at her when, carrying her togs in a drawstring bag, she went out to join those comical old biddies, to swing Indian clubs in a shiny blue gym suit, and still failed to reduce.

Even now Mama couldn't have vomited up more than half a pound and retch as she might, that was all the weight she succeeded in taking off. Nothing came but greenish mucus, but the gulls came. They were already on their way when she began to vomit, they circled lower, they dropped down sleek and smooth; untroubled by any fear of growing fat, they fought over my

Mama's breakfast, and were not to be driven away – and who was there to drive them away in view of the fact that Jan Bronski was afraid of gulls and shielded his beautiful blue eyes with his hands.

Nor would they pay attention to Oskar, not even when he enlisted his drum against them, not even when he tried to fight off their whiteness with a roll of his drumsticks on white lacquer. His drumming was no help; if anything it made the gulls whiter than ever. As for Matzerath, he was not in the least concerned over Mama. He laughed and aped the longshoreman; ho-ho, steady nerves, that was him. The longshoreman was almost finished. When in conclusion he extracted an enormous eel from the horse's ear, followed by a mess of white porridge from the horse's brain, Matzerath himself was green about the gills but went right on with his act. He bought two large and two medium-sized eels from the longshoreman for a song and tried to bargain even after he had paid up.

My heart was full of praise for Jan Bronski. He looked as if he were going to cry and nevertheless he helped my mama to her feet, threw one arm round her waist, and led her away, steering with his other arm, which he held out in front of her. It was pretty comical to see her hobbling from stone to stone in her high-heeled shoes. Her knees buckled under her at every step, but somehow she managed to reach the shore without spraining an ankle.

Oskar remained with Matzerath and the longshoreman. The longshoreman, who had put his cap on again, had begun to explain why the potato sack was full of rock salt. There was salt in the sack so the eels would wriggle themselves to death in the salt and the salt would draw the slime from their skin and innards. For when eels are in salt, they can't help wriggling and they wriggle until they are dead, leaving their slime in the salt. That's what you do if you want to smoke the eels afterward. It's forbidden by the police and the SPCA but that changes nothing. How else are you going to get the slime out of your eels? Afterward the dead eels are carefully rubbed off with dry peat moss and hung up in a smoking barrel over beechwood to smoke.

Matzerath thought it was only fair to let the eels wriggle in salt. They crawl into the horse's head, don't they? And into human corpses, too, said the longshoreman. They say the eels were mighty fat after the Battle of the Skagerrak. And a few days ago one of the doctors here in the hospital told me about a married woman who tried to take her pleasure with a live eel. But the eel bit into her and wouldn't let go; she had to be taken to the hospital and after that they say she couldn't have any more babies.

The longshoreman, however, tied up the sack with the salted eels and tossed it nimbly over his shoulder. He hung the coiled clothesline round his neck and, as the merchantman put into port, plodded off in the direction of Neufahrwasser. The ship was about eighteen hundred tons and wasn't a Swede but a Finn, carrying not iron ore but timber. The longshoreman with the sack seemed to have friends on board, for he waved across at the rusty hull and shouted something. On board the Finn they waved back and also shouted something. But it was a mystery to me why Matzerath waved too and shouted 'Ship ahoy!' or some such nonsense. As a native of the Rhineland he knew nothing about ships and there was certainly not one single Finn among his acquaintances. But that was the way he was; he always had to wave when other people were waving, to shout, laugh, and clap when other people were shouting, laughing, and clapping. That explains why he joined the Party at a relatively early date, when it was quite unnecessary, brought no benefits, and just wasted his Sunday mornings.

Oskar walked along slowly behind Matzerath, the man from Neufahrwasser, and the overloaded Finn. Now and then I turned around, for the longshoreman had abandoned the horse's head at the foot of the beacon. Of the head there was nothing to be seen, the gulls had covered it over. A glittering white hole in the bottle-green sea, a freshly washed cloud that might rise neatly into the air at any moment, veiling with its cries this horse's head that screamed instead of whinnying.

When I had had enough, I ran away from the gulls and Matzerath, beating my fist on my drum as I ran, passed the longshoreman, who was now smoking a short-stemmed pipe, and reached Mama and Jan Bronski at the shore end of the breakwater. Jan was still holding Mama as before, but now one hand had disappeared under her coat collar. Matzerath could not see this, however, nor could he see that Mama had one hand in Jan's trouser pocket, for he was still far behind us, wrapping the four eels, which the longshoreman had knocked unconscious with a stone, in a piece of newspaper he had found between the stones of the breakwater.

When Matzerath caught up with us, he swung his bundle of eels and boasted: 'He wanted one fifty. But I gave him a gulden and that was that.'

Mama was looking better and both her hands were visible again. 'I hope you don't expect me to eat your eel,' she said. 'I'll never touch fish again as long as I live and certainly not an eel.'

Matzerath laughed: 'Don't carry on so, pussycat. You've always known how they catch eels and you've always eaten them just the same. Even fresh ones. We'll see how you feel about it when your humble servant does them up with all the trimmings and a little salad on the side.'

Jan Bronski, who had withdrawn his hand from Mama's coat in plenty of time, said nothing. I drummed all the way to Brösen so they wouldn't start in again about eels. At the streetcar stop and in the car I went right on drumming to prevent the three grownups from talking. The eels kept relatively quiet. The car didn't stop in Saspe because the other car was already there. A little after the airfield Matzerath, despite my drumming, began to tell us how hungry he was. Mama did not react, she looked past us and through us until Jan offered her one of his Regattas. While he was giving her a light and she was adjusting the gold tip to her lips, she smiled at Matzerath, for she knew he didn't like her to smoke in public.

At Max-Halbe-Platz we got out, and in spite of everything Mama took Matzerath's arm and not Jan's as I had expected. While Matzerath was opening up the apartment, Mrs. Kater, who lived on the fourth floor next door to Meyn the trumpeter, passed us on the stairs. A rolled brownish carpet was slung over her shoulder, and she was supporting it with her upraised arms, enormous and meat-red. Her armpits displayed flaming bundles of blond hair, knotted and caked with sweat. The carpet hung down in front of her and behind her. She might just as well have been carrying a drunken man over her shoulder, but her husband was no longer alive. As this mass of fat moved past us in a shiny black house smock, her effluvia struck me: ammonia, pickles, carbide – she must have had the monthlies.

Shortly thereafter the rhythmic reports of carpet-beating rose from the yard. It drove me through the apartment, it pursued me, until at last I escaped into our bedroom clothes cupboard where the worst of the pre-paschal uproar was damped out by the winter overcoats.

But it wasn't just Mrs. Kater and her carpet-beating that sent me scurrying to the clothes cupboard. Before Mama, Jan, and Matzerath had even taken their coats off, they began to argue about the Good Friday dinner. But they didn't stick to eels. As usual when they needed something to argue about, they remembered me and my famous fall from the cellar stairs: 'You're to blame, it's all your fault, now I am going to make that eel soup, don't be so squeamish, make anything you like but not eels, there's plenty of canned goods in the cellar, bring up some mushrooms but shut the trap door so it doesn't happen again or something like it. I've heard enough of that song and dance, we're having eels and that's that, with milk, mustard, parsley, and boiled potatoes, a bay leaf goes in and a clove, no, no, please Alfred, don't make eels if she doesn't want them, you keep out of this, I didn't buy eels to throw them away, they'll be nicely cleaned and washed, no, no, we'll see when they're on the table, we'll see who eats and who don't eat.'

Matzerath slammed the living room door and vanished into the kitchen. We heard him officiating with a demonstrative clatter. He killed the eels with a crosswise incision in the backs of their necks and Mama, who had an over-lively imagination, had to sit down on the sofa, promptly followed by Jan Bronski. A moment later they were holding hands and whispering in Kashubian. I hadn't gone to the cupboard yet. While the three grownups were thus distributing themselves about the apartment, I was still in the living room. There was a `baby chair beside the tile stove. There I sat, dangling my legs while Jan stared at me; I knew I was in their way, though they couldn't have done much, because Matzerath was right next door, threatening them invisibly but palpably with moribund eels that he brandished like a whip. And so they exchanged hands, pressed and tugged at twenty fingers, and cracked knuckles. For me that was the last straw. Wasn't Mrs.

Kater's carpet-beating enough? Didn't it pierce the walls, growing no louder but moving closer and closer?

Oskar slipped off his chair, sat for a moment on the floor beside the stove lest his departure be too conspicuous, and then, wholly preoccupied with his drum, slid across the threshold into the bedroom.

I left the bedroom door half-open and noted to my satisfaction that no one called me back. I hesitated for a moment whether to take refuge under the bed or in the clothes cupboard. I preferred the cupboard because under the bed I would have soiled my fastidious navy-blue sailor suit. I was just able to reach the key to the cupboard. I turned it once, pulled open the mirror doors, and with my drumsticks pushed aside the hangers bearing the coats and other winter things. In order to reach and move the heavy coats, I had to stand on my drum. At last I had made a cranny in the middle of the cupboard; though it was not exactly spacious, there was room enough for Oskar, who climbed in and huddled on the floor. I even succeeded, with some difficulty, in drawing the mirror doors to and in jamming them closed with a shawl that I found on the cupboard floor, in such a way that a finger's-breadth opening let in a certain amount of air and enabled me to look out in case of emergency. I laid my drum on my knees but drummed nothing, not even ever so softly; I just sat there in utter passivity, letting myself be enveloped and penetrated by the vapors arising from winter overcoats.

How wonderful that this cupboard should be there with its heavy, scarcely breathing woolens which enabled me to gather together nearly all my thoughts, to tie them into a bundle and give them away to a dream princess who was rich enough to accept my gift with a dignified, scarcely perceptible pleasure.

As usual when I concentrated and took advantage of my psychic gift, I transported myself to the office of Dr. Hollatz in Brunshö-fer-Weg and savored the one part of my regular Wednesday visits that I cared about. My thoughts were concerned far less with the doctor, whose examinations were becoming more and more finicky, than with Sister Inge, his assistant. She alone was permitted to undress me and dress me; she alone was allowed to measure and weigh me and administer the various tests; in short, it was Sister Inge who conscientiously though rather grumpily carried out all the experiments to which Dr. Hollatz subjected me. Each time Sister Inge, not without a certain irony, reported failure which Hollatz metamorphosed into 'partial success.' I seldom looked at Sister Inge's face. My eyes and my sometimes racing drummer's heart rested on the clean starched whiteness of her nurse's uniform, on the weightless construction that she wore as a cap, on a simple brooch adorned with a red cross. How pleasant it was to follow the folds, forever fresh, of her uniform! Had she a body under it? Her steadily aging face and rawboned though well-kept hands suggested that Sister Inge was a woman after all. To be sure, there was no such womanish smell as my mama gave off when Jan, or even Matzerath, uncovered her before my eyes. She smelled of soap and drowsy medicines. How often I was overcome by sleep as she auscultated my small, supposedly sick body: a light sleep born of the folds of white fabrics, a sleep shrouded in carbolic acid, a dreamless sleep except that sometimes in the distance her brooch expanded into heaven knows what: a sea of banners, the Alpine glow, a field of poppies, ready to revolt, against whom, Lord knows: against Indians, cherries, nosebleed, cocks' crests, red corpuscles, until a red occupying my entire field of vision provided the background for a passion which then as now was self-evident but not to be named, because the little word 'red' says nothing, and nosebleed won't do it, and flag cloth fades, and if I nonetheless say 'red,' red spurns me, turns its coat to black. Black is the Witch, black scares me green, green grow the lilacs but lavender's blue, blue is true blue but I don't trust it, do you? Green is for hope, green is the coffin I graze in, green covers me, green blanches me white, white stains yellow and yellow strikes me blue, blue me no green, green flowers red, and red was Sister Inge's brooch: she wore a red cross, to be exact, she wore it on the collar of her nurse's uniform; but seldom, in the clothes cupboard or anywhere else, could I keep my mind on this most monochrome of all symbols.

Bursting in from the living room, a furious uproar crashed against the doors of my cupboard, waked me from my scarcely begun half-slumber dedicated to Sister Inge. Sobered and with my heart in my mouth I sat, holding my drum on my knees, among winter coats of varying length and cut, breathed in the aroma of Matzerath's Party uniform, felt the presence of sword belt and shoulder straps, and was unable to find my way back to the white folds of the nurse's uniform: flannel and worsted hung down beside me, above me stood the hat fashions of the last four years, at my feet lay big shoes and little shoes, waxed puttees, heels with and without hobnails. A faint beam of light suggested the whole scene; Oskar was sorry he had left a crack open between the mirror doors.

What could those people in the living room have to offer me? Perhaps Matzerath had surprised the two of them on the couch, but that was very unlikely for Jan always preserved a vestige of caution and not just when he was playing skat. Probably, I figured, and so indeed it turned out, Matzerath, having slaughtered, cleaned, washed, cooked, seasoned, and tasted his eels, had put them down on the living room table in the form of eel soup with boiled potatoes, and when the others showed no sign of sitting down, had gone so far as to sing the praises of his dish, listing all the ingredients and intoning the recipe like a litany. Whereupon Mama began to scream. She screamed in Kashubian. This Matzerath could neither understand nor bear, but he was compelled to listen just the same and had a pretty good idea of what she was getting at. What, after all, could she be screaming about but eels, leading up, as everything led up once my Mama started screaming, to my fall down the cellar stairs. Matzerath answered back. They knew their parts. Jan intervened. Without him there could have been no show. Act Two: bang, that was the piano lid being thrown back; without notes, by heart, the three of them all at once but not together howled out the 'Huntsmen's Chorus' from *Freischütz*: 'What thing on earth resembles . . .' And in the midst of the uproar, bang shut went the piano lid, bang went the overturned piano stool, and there was Mama coming into the bedroom. A quick glance in the mirror of my mirror doors, and she flung herself, I could see it all through the cleft, on the marriage bed beneath the blue canopy and wrung her hands with as many fingers as the repentant gold-framed Mary Magdalene in the color print at the head end of the matrimonial fortress.

For a long time all I could hear was Mama's whimpering, the soft creaking of the bed, and faint murmurs from the living room. Jan was pacifying Matzerath. Then Matzerath asked Jan to go and pacify Mama. The murmuring thinned down, Jan entered the bedroom. Act Three: He stood by the bed, looking back and forth between Mama and the repentant Mary Magdalene, sat down cautiously on the edge of the bed, stroked Mama's back and rear end – she was lying face down – spoke to her soothingly in Kashubian – and finally, when words were no help, inserted his hand beneath her skirt until she stopped whimpering and he was able to remove his eyes from the many-fingered Mary Magdalene. It was a scene worth seeing. His work done, Jan arose, dabbed his fingers with his handkerchief, and finally addressed Mama loudly, no longer speaking Kashubian and stressing every word for the benefit of Matzerath in the kitchen or living room: 'Now come along, Agnes. Let's forget the whole business. Alfred dumped the eels in the toilet long ago. Now we'll play a nice game of skat, for a quarter of a pfennig if you like, and once we've all forgotten and made up, Alfred will make us mushrooms with scrambled eggs and fried potatoes.'

To this Mama said nothing, stood up from the bed, smoothed out the yellow bedspread, tossed her hair into shape in front of my mirror doors, and left the bedroom behind Jan. I removed my eye from the slit and soon heard them shuffling cards. I think Jan was bidding against Matzerath, who passed at twenty-three. Whereupon Mama bid Jan up to thirty-six; at this point he backed down, and Mama played a grand which she just barely lost. Next Jan bid diamond single and won hands down, and Mama won the third game, a heart hand without two, though it was close.

Certain that this family skat game, briefly interrupted by scrambled eggs, mushrooms, and fried potatoes, would go on far into the night, I scarcely listened to the hands that followed, but tried to find my way back to Sister Inge and her white, sleepy-making uniforms. But I was not to find the happiness I sought in Dr. Hollatz' office. Not only did green, blue, yellow, and black persist in breaking into the redness of the Red Cross pin, but the events of the morning kept crowding in as well: whenever the door leading to the consultation room and Sister Inge opened, it was not the pure and airy vision of the nurse's uniform that presented itself to my eyes, but the longshoreman at the foot of the beacon on the Neufahrwasser breakwater, pulling eels from the dripping, crawling horse's head, and what set itself up to be white, so that I tried to connect it with Sister Inge, was the gulls' wings which for barely a moment covered the horse's head and the eels in it, until the wound broke open again but did not bleed red, but was black like the black horse, and bottle-green the sea, while the Finnish timber ship contributed a bit of rust color to the picture and the gulls – don't talk to me of doves – descended like a cloud on the sacrifice, dipped in their wingtips and tossed the eel to Sister Inge, who caught it, celebrated it, and turned into a gull, not a dove, but in any case into the Holy Ghost, let it take the form of a gull, descending cloudlike upon the flesh to feast the Pentecost.

Giving up the struggle, I left the cupboard. Angrily pushing the doors open, I stepped out and found myself unchanged in front of the mirrors, but even so I was glad Mrs. Kater had stopped beating carpets. Good Friday was over for Oskar, but it was only after Easter that his Passion began.

Tapered at the Foot End

And mama's as well. On Easter Sunday we went with the Bronskis to visit Grandma and Uncle Vincent in Bissau. It was after that that her sufferings began – sufferings that the smiling spring weather was powerless to attenuate.

It is not true that Matzerath forced Mama to start eating fish again. Quite of her own accord, possessed by some mysterious demon, she began, exactly two weeks after Easter, to devour fish in such quantities, without regard for her figure, that Matzerath said: 'For the Lord's sake stop eating so much fish like somebody was making you.'

She started in at breakfast on canned sardines, two hours later, unless there happened to be customers in the shop, she would dig into a case of Bohnsack sprats, for lunch she would demand fried flounder or codfish with mustard sauce, and in the afternoon there she was again with her can opener: eels in jelly, rollmops, baked herring, and if Matzerath refused to fry or boil more fish for supper, she would waste no breath in arguing, but would quietly leave the table and come back from the shop with a chunk of smoked eel. For the rest of us it was the end of our appetites, because she would scrape the last particle of fat from the inside and outside of the eel's skin with a knife, and in general she took to eating her fish with a knife. She would have to vomit at intervals throughout the day. Helplessly anxious, Matzerath would ask: 'Maybe you're pregnant, or what's the matter with you?'

'Don't talk nonsense,' said Mama if she said anything at all. One Sunday when green eels with new potatoes swimming in cream sauce were set on the table, Grandma Koljaiczek smacked the table with the flat of her hand and cried out: 'What's the matter, Agnes? Tell us what's the matter? Why do you eat fish when it don't agree with you and you don't say why and you act like a lunatic?' Mama only shook her head, pushed the potatoes aside, pulled out an eel through the sauce, and set to with relentless determination. Jan Bronski said nothing. Once when I surprised the two of them on the couch, they were holding hands as usual and their clothing was normally disarranged, but I was struck by Jan's tear-stained eyes and by Mama's apathy, which, however, suddenly shifted into its opposite. She jumped up, clutched me, lifted me up and squeezed me, revealing an abyss of emptiness which apparently nothing could fill but enormous quantities of fried, boiled, preserved, and smoked fish.

A few days later I saw her in the kitchen as she not only fell upon the usual accursed sardines, but poured out the oil from several cans she had been saving up into a little saucepan, heated it over the gas, and drank it down. Standing in the doorway, I was so upset that I dropped my drum.

That same evening Mama was taken to the City Hospital. Matzerath wept and lamented as we were waiting for the ambulance: 'Why don't you want the child? What does it matter whose it is? Or is it still on account of that damn fool horse's head? If only we'd never gone out there. Can't you forget it, Agnes? I didn't do it on purpose.'

The ambulance came, Mama was carried out. Children and grownups gathered on the sidewalk; they drove her away and it soon turned out that Mama had forgotten neither the breakwater nor the horse's head, that she had carried the memory of that horse – regardless of whether his name was Hans or Fritz – along with her. Every organ in her body stored up the bitter memory of that Good Friday excursion and for fear that it be repeated, her organs saw to it that my mama, who was quite in agreement with them, should die.

Dr. Hollatz spoke of jaundice and fish poisoning. In the hospital they found Mama to be in her third month of pregnancy and gave her a private room. For four days she showed those of us who were allowed to visit her a face devastated by pain and nausea; sometimes she smiled at me through her nausea.

Although she tried hard to make her visitors happy, just as today I do my best to seem pleased when visitors come, she could not prevent a periodic retching from seizing hold of her slowly wasting body, though there was nothing more to come out of it except, at last, on the fourth day of that strenuous dying, the bit of breath which each of us must give up if he is to be honored with a death certificate.

We all sighed with relief when there was nothing more within her to provoke that retching which so marred her beauty. Once she had been washed and lay there in her shroud, she had her familiar, round, shrewdly naive face again. The head nurse closed Mama's eyes because Matzerath and Bronski were blind with tears.

I could not weep, because the others, the men and Grandma, Hedwig Bronski and the fourteen-year-old Stephan, were all weeping. Besides, my mama's death was no surprise to me. To Oskar, who went to the city with her on Thursdays and to the Church of the Sacred Heart on Saturdays, it seemed as though she had been searching for years for a way of breaking up the triangle that would leave Matzerath, whom perhaps she hated, with the guilt and enable Jan Bronski, her Jan, to continue his work at the Polish Post Office fortified by thoughts such as: she died for me, she didn't want to stand in my way, she sacrificed herself.

With all the cool calculation the two of them, Mama and Jan, were capable of when it was a question of finding an undisturbed bed for their love, they nevertheless revealed quite a talent for romance: it requires no great stretch of the imagination to identify them with Romeo and Juliet or with the prince and princess who allegedly were unable to get together because the water was too deep.

146

While Mama, who had received the last sacraments in plenty of time, lay submissive to the priest's prayers, cold and impervious to anything that could be said or done, I found it in me to watch the nurses, who were mostly of the Protestant faith. They folded their hands differently from the Catholics, more self-reliantly I should say, they said the Our Father with a wording that deviates from the original Catholic text, and they did not cross themselves like Grandma Koljaiczek, the Bronskis, and myself for that matter. My father Matzerath – I sometimes call him so even though his begetting of me was purely presumptive – prayed differently from the other Protestants; instead of clasping his hands over his chest, he let his fingers pass hysterically from one religion to another somewhere in the vicinity of his private parts, and was obviously ashamed to be seen praying. My grandmother knelt by the death-bed beside her brother Vincent; she prayed loudly and vehemently in Kashubian, while Vincent only moved his lips, presumably in Polish, though his eyes were wide with spiritual experience. I should have liked to drum. After all I had my mother to thank for all those red and white drums. As a counterweight to Matzerath's desires, she had promised me a drum while I lay in my cradle; and from time to time Mama's beauty, particularly when she was still slender and had no need for gymnastics, had served as the model and subject matter for my drumming. At length I was unable to control myself; once again, by my mother's deathbed, I re-created the ideal image of her grey-eyed beauty on my drum. The head nurse protested at once, and I was very much surprised when it was Matzerath who mollified her and took my part, whispering: 'Let him be, sister. They were so fond of each other.'

Mama could be very gay, she could also be very anxious. Mama could forget quickly, yet she had a good memory. Mama would throw me out with the bath water, and yet she would share my bath. When I sang windowpanes to pieces, Mama was on hand with putty. Sometimes she put her foot in it even when there were plenty of safe places to step. Sometimes Mama was lost to me, but her finder went with her. Even when Mama buttoned up, she was an open book to me. Mama feared drafts but was always stirring up a storm. She lived on an expense account and disliked to pay taxes. I was the reverse of her coin. When Mama played a heart hand, she always won. When Mama died, the red flames on my drum casing paled a little; but the white lacquer became whiter than ever and so dazzling that Oskar was sometimes obliged to close his eyes.

My mama was not buried at Saspe as she had occasionally said she would like to be, but in the peaceful little cemetery at Brenntau. There lay her stepfather Gregor Koljaiczek the powdermaker, who had died of influenza in '17. The mourners were numerous, as was only natural in view of my mama's popularity as a purveyor of groceries; in addition to the regular customers, there were salesmen from some of the wholesale houses, and even a few competitors turned up, such as Weinreich Fancy Groceries, and Mrs. Probst from Hertastrasse. The cemetery chapel was too small to hold the crowd. It smelled of flowers and black clothing seasoned with mothballs. My mother's face, in the open coffin, was yellow and ravaged. During the interminable ceremony I couldn't help feeling that her head would bob up again any minute and that she would have to vomit some more, that there was something more inside her that wanted to come out: not only that fetus aged three months who like me didn't know which father he had to thank for his existence; no, I thought, it's not just he who wants to come out and, like Oskar, demand a drum, no, there's more fish, not sardines, and not flounder, no, it's a little chunk of eel, a few whitish-green threads of eel flesh, eel from the battle of the Skagerrak, eel from the Neufahrwasser breakwater, Good Friday eel, eel from that horse's head, possibly eel from her father Joseph Koljaiczek who ended under the raft, a prey to the eels, eel of thine eel, for eel thou art, to eel returnest . . .

But my mama didn't retch. She kept it down and it was evidently her intention to take it with her into the ground, that at last there might be peace.

When the men picked up the coffin lid with a view to shutting in my mama's nauseated yet resolute face, Anna Koljaiczek barred the way. Trampling the flowers round the coffin, she threw herself upon her daughter and wept, tore at the expensive white shroud, and wailed in Kashubian.

There were many who said later that she had cursed my presumptive father Matzerath, calling him her daughter's murderer. She is also said to have spoken of my fall down the cellar stairs. She

148

took over the story from Mama and never allowed Matzerath to forget his ostensible responsibility for my ostensible misfortune. These accusations never ceased although Matzerath, in defiance of all political considerations and almost against his will, treated her with a respect bordering on reverence and during the war years supplied her with sugar and synthetic honey, coffee and kerosene.

Greff the vegetable dealer and Jan Bronski, who was weeping in a high feminine register, led my grandmother away from the coffin. The men were able to fasten the lid and at last to put on the faces that pallbearers always put on when they lift up a coffin.

In Brenntau Cemetery with its two fields on either side of the avenue bordered by elm trees, with its little chapel that looked like a set for a Nativity play, with its well and its sprightly little birds, Matzerath led the procession and I followed. It was then for the first time that I took a liking to the shape of a coffin. Since then I have often had occasion to gaze upon dark-colored wood employed for ultimate ends. My mama's coffin was black. It tapered in the most wonderfully harmonious way, toward the foot end. Is there any other form in this world so admirably suited to the proportions of the human body?

If beds only had that narrowing at the foot end! If only all our habitual and occasional lying could taper off so unmistakably toward the foot end. For with all the airs we give ourselves, the ostentatious bulk of our head, shoulders, and torso tapers off toward the feet, and on this narrow base the whole edifice must rest.

Matzerath went directly behind the coffin. He carried his top hat in his hand and, despite his grief and the slow pace, made every effort to keep his knees stiff. I always felt sorry for him when I saw him from the rear; that protuberant occiput and those two throbbing arteries that grew out of his collar and mounted to his hairline.

Why was it Mother Truczinski rather than Gretchen Scheffler or Hedwig Bronski who took me by the hand? She lived on the second floor of our house and apparently had no first name, for everyone called her Mother Truczinski.

Before the coffin went Father Wiehnke with a sexton bearing incense. My eyes slipped from the back of Matzerath's neck to the furrowed necks of the pallbearers. I had to fight down a passionate desire: Oskar wanted to climb up on the coffin. He wanted to sit up there and drum. However, it was not his tin instrument but the coffin lid that he wished to assail with his drumsticks. He wanted to ride aloft, swaying in the rhythm of the pallbearers' weary gait. He wanted to drum for the mourners who were repeating their prayers after Father Wiehnke. And as they lowered the casket into the ground, he wished to stand firm on the lid. During the sermon, the bell-ringing, the dispensing of incense and holy water, he wished to beat out his Latin on the wood as they lowered him into the grave with the coffin. He wished to go down into the pit with Mama and the fetus. And there he wished to remain while the survivors tossed in their handfuls of earth, no, Oskar didn't wish to come up, he wished to sit on the tapering foot end of the coffin, drumming if possible, drumming under the earth, until the sticks rotted out of his hands, until his mama for his sake and he for her sake should rot away, giving their flesh to the earth and its inhabitants; with his very knuckles Oskar would have wished to drum for the fetus, if it had only been possible and allowed.

No one sat on the coffin. Unoccupied, it swayed beneath the elms and weeping willows of Brenntau Cemetery. In among the graves the sexton's spotted chickens, picking for worm, reaping what they had not sowed. Then through the birches. Hand in hand with Mother Truczinski. Ahead of me Matzerath, and directly behind me my grandmother on the arms of Greff and Jan; then Vincent Bronski on Hedwig's arm, then little Marga and Stephan hand in hand, then the Schefflers. Then Laubschad the watchmaker, old Mr. Heilandt, and Meyn the trumpeter, but without his instrument and relatively sober.

Only when it was all over and the condolences started, did I notice Sigismund Markus. Black-clad and embarrassed, he joined the crowd of those who wished to shake hands with me, my grandmother, and the Bronskis and mumble something. At first I failed to understand what Alexander Scheffler wanted of Markus. They hardly knew each other, perhaps they had never spoken to one another before. Then Meyn the musician joined forces with Scheffler. They stood beside a waist-high hedge made of that green stuff that discolors and tastes bitter when you rub it between your fingers. Mrs. Kater and her daughter Susi, who was grinning behind her handkerchief and had grown rather too quickly, were just tendering their sympathies to Matzerath, naturally – how could they help it? – patting my head in the process. The altercation behind the hedge grew louder but was still unintelligible. Meyn the trumpeter thrust his index finger at Markus' black façade and pushed; then he seized one of Sigismund's arms while Scheffler took the other. Both were very careful that Markus, who was walking backward, should not stumble over the borders of the tombs; thus they pushed him as far as the main avenue, where they showed him where the gate was. Markus seemed to thank them for the information and started for the exit; he put on his silk hat and never looked around at Meyn and the baker, though they looked after him.

Neither Matzerath nor Mother Truczinski saw me wander away from them and the condolences. Assuming the manner of a little boy who has to go, Oskar slipped back past the grave-digger and his assistant. Then, without regard for the ivy, he ran to the elms, catching up with Sigismund Markus before the exit.

'If it ain't little Oskar,' said Markus with surprise. 'Say, what are they doing to Markus? What did Markus ever do to them they should treat him so?'

I didn't know what Markus had done. I took him by his hand, it was clammy with sweat, and led him through the open wrought-iron gate, and there in the gateway the two of us, the keeper of my drums and I, the drummer, possibly his drummer, ran into Leo Schugger, who like us believed in paradise.

Markus knew Leo, everyone in town knew him. I had heard of him, I knew that one sunny day while he was still at the seminary, the world, the sacraments, the religions, heaven and earth, life and death had been so shaken up in his mind that forever after his vision of the world, though mad, had been radiant and perfect.

Leo Schugger's occupation was to turn up after funerals – and no one could pass away without his getting wind of it – wearing a shiny black suit several sizes too big for him and white gloves, and wait for the mourners. Markus and I were both aware that it was in his professional capacity that he was standing there at the gate of Brenntau Cemetery, waiting with slavering mouth, compassionate gloves, and watery blue eyes for the mourners to come out.

It was bright and sunny, mid-May. Plenty of birds in the hedges and trees. Cackling hens, symbolizing immortality with and through their eggs. Buzzing in the air. Fresh coat of green, no dust. Bearing a tired topper in his left gloved hand, Leo Schugger, moving with the lightness of a dancer, for grace had touched him, stepped up to Markus and myself, advancing five mildewed gloved fingers. Standing aslant as if to brace himself against the wind, though there was none, he tilted his head and blubbered, spinning threads of saliva. Hesitantly at first, then with resolution, Markus inserted his bare hand in the animated glove. 'What a beautiful day!' Leo blubbered. 'She has already arrived where everything is so cheap. Did you see the Lord? *Habemus ad Dominum*. He just passed by in a hurry. Amen.'

We said amen. Markus agreed about the beautiful day and even said yes he had seen the Lord.

Behind us we heard the mourners buzzing closer. Markus let his hand fall from Leo's glove, found time to give him a tip, gave me a Markus kind of look, and rushed away toward the taxi that was waiting for him outside the Brenntau post office.

I was still looking after the cloud of dust that obscured the receding Markus when Mother Truczinski took my hand. They came in groups and grouplets. Leo Schugger had sympathies for all; he called attention to the fine day, asked everyone if he had seen the Lord, and as usual received tips of varying magnitude. Matzerath and Jan Bronski paid the pallbearers, the gravedigger, the sexton, and Father Wiehnke, who with a sigh of embarrassment let Leo Schugger kiss his hand and then proceeded, with his kissed hand, to toss wisps of benediction after the slowly dispersing funeral company.

Meanwhile we – my grandmother, her brother Vincent, the Bronskis with their children, Greff without wife, and Gretchen Scheffler – took our seats in two common farm wagons. We were driven past Goldkrug through the woods across the nearby Polish border to the funeral supper at Bissau Quarry.

Vincent Bronski's farm lay in a hollow. There were poplars in front of it that were supposed to divert the lightning. The barn door was removed from its hinges, laid on saw horses, and covered with tablecloths. More people came from the vicinity. It was some time before the meal was ready. It was served in the barn doorway. Gretchen Scheffler held me on her lap. First there was something fatty, then something sweet, then more fat. There was potato schnaps, beer, a roast goose and a roast pig, cake with sausage, sweet and sour squash, fruit pudding with sour cream. Toward evening a slight breeze came blowing through the open barn, there was a scurrying of mice and of Bronski children, who, in league with the neighborhood urchins, took possession of the barnyard.

Oil lamps were brought out, and skat cards. The potato schnaps stayed where it was. There was also homemade egg liqueur that made for good cheer. Greff did not drink but he sang songs. The Kashubians sang too, and Matzerath had first deal. Jan was the second hand and the foreman from the brickworks the third. Only then did it strike me that my poor mama was missing. They played until well into the night, but none of the men succeeded in winning a heart hand. After Jan Bronski for no apparent reason had lost a heart hand without four, I heard him say to Matzerath in an undertone: 'Agnes would surely have won that hand.'

Then I slipped off Gretchen Scheffler's lap and found my grandmother and her brother Vincent outside. They were sitting on a wagon shaft. Vincent was muttering to the stars in Polish. My grandmother couldn't cry any more but she let me crawl under her skirts.

Who will take me under her skirts today? Who will shelter me from the daylight and the lamplight? Who will give me the smell of melted yellow, slightly rancid butter that my grandmother used to stock for me beneath her skirts and feed me to make me put on weight?

I fell asleep beneath her four skirts, close to my poor mama's beginnings and as still as she, though not so short of air as she in her box tapered at the foot end.

Herbert Truczinski's Back

Nothing, so they say, can take the place of a mother. Soon after her funeral I began to miss my poor mama. There were no more Thursday visits to Sigismund Markus' shop, no one led me to Sister Inge's white uniforms, and most of all the Saturdays made me painfully aware of Mama's death: Mama didn't go to confession any more.

And so there was no more old city for me, no more Dr. Hollatz' office, and no more Church of the Sacred Heart. I had lost interest in demonstrations. And how was I to lure passers-by to shop-windows when even the tempter's trade had lost its charm for Oskar? There was no more Mama to take me to the Christmas play at the Stadt-Theater or to the Krone or Busch circus. Conscientious but morose, I went about my studies, strode dismally through the rectilinear suburban streets to the Kleinhammer-Weg, visited Gretchen Scheffler, who told me about Strength through Joy trips to the land of the midnight sun, while I went right on comparing Goethe with Rasputin or, when I had enough of the cyclic and endless alternation of dark and radiant, took refuge in historical studies. My old standard works, *A Struggle for Rome*, Keyser's *History of the City of Danzig*, and Köhler's *Naval Calendar*, gave me an encyclopedic half-knowledge. To this day I am capable of giving you exact figures about the building, launching, armor, firepower, and crew strength of all the ships that took part in the battle of the Skagerrak, that sank or were damaged on that occasion.

I was almost fourteen, I loved solitude and took many walks. My drum went with me but I was sparing in my use of it, because with Mama's departure a punctual delivery of tin drums became problematic.

Was it in the autumn of '37 or the spring of '38? In any case, I was making my way up the Hindenburg-Allee toward the city, I was not far from the Café of the Four Seasons, the leaves were falling or the buds were bursting, in any event something was going on in nature, when whom should I meet but my friend and master Bebra, who was descended in a straight line from Prince Eugene and consequently from Louis XIV.

We had not seen each other for three or four years and nevertheless we recognized one another at twenty paces' distance. He was not alone, on his arm hung a dainty southern beauty, perhaps an inch shorter than Bebra and three fingers' breadths taller than I, whom he introduced as Roswitha Raguna, the most celebrated somnambulist in all Italy.

Bebra asked me to join them in a cup of coffee at the Four Seasons. We sat in the aquarium and the coffee-time biddies hissed: 'Look at the midgets, Lisbeth, did you see them? They must be in Krone's circus. Let's try to go.'

Bebra smiled at me, showing a thousand barely visible little wrinkles.

The waiter who brought us the coffee was very tall. As Signora Roswitha ordered a piece of pastry, he stood there beside her, like a tower in evening clothes.

Bebra examined me: 'Our glass-killer doesn't seem happy. What's wrong, my friend? Is the glass unwilling or has the voice grown weak?'

Young and impulsive as I was, Oskar wanted to give a sample of his art that was still in its prime. I looked round in search of material and was already concentrating on the great glass façade of the aquarium with its ornamental fish and aquatic plants. But before I could begin to sing, Bebra said: 'No, no, my friend. We believe you. Let us have no destruction, no floods, no expiring fishes.'

Shamefacedly I apologized, particularly to Signora Roswitha, who had produced a miniature fan and was excitedly stirring up wind.

'My mama has died,' I tried to explain. 'She shouldn't have done that. I can't forgive her. People are always saying: a mother sees everything, a mother forgives everything. That's nonsense for Mother's Day. To her I was never anything but a gnome. She would have got rid of the gnome if she had been able to. But she couldn't get rid of me, because children, even gnomes, are marked in your papers and you can't just do away with them. Also because I was *her* gnome and because to do away with me would have been to destroy a part of herself. It's either I or the gnome, she said to herself, and finally she put an end to herself; she began to eat nothing but fish and not even fresh fish, she sent away her lovers and now that she's lying in Brenntau, they all say, the lovers say it and our customers say so too: The gnome drummed her into her grave. Because of Oskar she didn't want to live any more; he killed her.'

I was exaggerating quite a bit, I wanted to impress Signora Roswitha. Most people blamed Matzerath and especially Jan Bronski for Mama's death. Bebra saw through me.

'You are exaggerating, my good friend. Out of sheer jealousy you are angry with your dead mama. You feel humiliated because it wasn't you but those wearisome lovers that sent her to her grave. You are vain and wicked – as a genius should be.'

Then with a sigh and a sidelong glance at Signora Roswitha: 'It is not easy for people our size to get through life. To remain human without external growth, what a task, what a vocation!'

Roswitha Raguna, the Neapolitan somnambulist with the smooth yet wrinkled skin, she whose age I estimated at eighteen summers but an instant later revered as an old lady of eighty or ninety, Signora Roswitha stroked Mr. Bebra's fashionable English tailor-made suit, projected her cherry-black Mediterranean eyes in my direction, and spoke with a dark voice, bearing promise of fruit, a voice that moved me and turned me to ice: '*Carissimo*, Oskarnello! How well I understand your grief. *Andiamo*, come with us: Milano, Parigi, Toledo, Guatemala!'

My head reeled. I grasped la Raguna's girlish age-old hand. The Mediterranean beat against my coast, olive trees whispered in my ear: 'Roswitha will be your mama, Roswitha will understand. Roswitha, the great somnambulist, who sees through everyone, who knows everyone's innermost soul, only not her own, *mamma mia*, only not her own, *Dio!*'

Oddly enough, la Raguna had no sooner begun to see through me, to X-ray my soul with her somnambulist gaze, than she suddenly withdrew her hand. Had my hungry fourteen-year-old heart filled her with horror? Had it dawned on her that to me Roswitha, whether maiden or hag, meant Roswitha? She whispered in Neapolitan, trembled, crossed herself over and over again as though there were no end to the horrors she found within me, and disappeared without a word behind her fan.

I demanded an explanation, I asked Mr. Bebra to say something. But even Bebra, despite his direct descent from Prince Eugene, had lost his countenance. He began to stammer and this is what I was finally able to make out: 'Your genius, my young friend, the divine, but also no doubt the diabolical elements in your genius have rather confused my good Roswitha, and I too must own that you have in you a certain immoderation, a certain explosiveness, which to me is alien though not entirely incomprehensible. But regardless of your character,' said Bebra, bracing himself, 'come with us, join Bebra's troupe of magicians. With a little self-discipline you should be able to find a public even under the present political conditions.'

I understand at once. Bebra, who had advised me to be always on the rostrum and never in front of it, had himself been reduced to a pedestrian role even though he was still in the circus. And indeed he was not at all disappointed when I politely and regretfully declined his offer. Signora Roswitha heaved an audible sigh of relief behind her fan and once again showed me her Mediterranean eyes.

We went on chatting for a while. I asked the waiter to bring us an empty water glass and sang a heart-shaped opening in it. Underneath the cutout my voice engraved an inscription ornate with loops and flourishes: 'Oskar for Roswitha.' I gave her the glass and she was pleased. Bebra paid, leaving a large tip, and then we arose.

They accompanied me as far as the Sports Palace. I pointed a drumstick at the naked rostrum at the far end of the Maiwiese and – now I remember, it was in the spring of '38 – told my master Bebra of my career as a drummer beneath rostrums.

Bebra had an embarrassed smile, la Raguna's face was severe. The Signora drifted a few steps away from us, and Bebra, in leave-taking, whispered in my ear: 'I have failed, my friend. How can I be your teacher now? Politics, politics, how filthy it is!'

Then he kissed me on the forehead as he had done years before when I met him among the circus trailers, Lady Roswitha held out her hand like porcelain, and I bent over it politely, almost too expertly for a fourteen-year-old.

'We shall meet again, my son,' said Mr. Bebra. 'Whatever the times may be, people like us don't lose each other.'

'Forgive your fathers,' the Signora admonished me. 'Accustom yourself to your own existence that your heart may find peace and Satan be discomfited!'

It seemed to me as though the Signora had baptized me a second time, again in vain. Satan, depart – but Satan would not depart. I looked after them sadly and with an empty heart, waved at them as they entered a taxi and completely vanished inside it – for the Ford was made for grownups, it looked empty as though cruising for customers as it drove off with my friends.

I tried to persuade Matzerath to take me to the Krone circus, but Matzerath was not to be moved; he gave himself entirely to his grief for my poor mama, whom he had never possessed entirely. But who had? Not even Jan Bronski; if anyone, myself, for it was Oskar who suffered most from her absence, which upset, and threatened the very existence of, his daily life. Mama had let me down. There was nothing to be expected of my fathers. Bebra my master had found his master in Propaganda Minister Goebbels. Gretchen Scheffler was entirely taken up with her Winter Relief work. Let no one go hungry, let no one suffer cold. I had only my drum to turn to, I beat out my loneliness on its once white surface, now drummed thin. In the evening Matzerath and I sat facing one another. He leafed through his cookbooks, I lamented on my drum. Sometimes Matzerath wept and hid his head in the cookbooks. Jan Bronski's visits became more and more infrequent. In view of the political situation, both men thought they had better be careful, there was no way of knowing which way the wind would blow. The skat games with changing thirds became fewer and farther between; when there was a game, it was late at night under the hanging lamp in our living room, and all political discussion was avoided. My grandmother Anna seemed to have forgotten the way from Bissau to our place in Labesweg. She had it in for Matzerath and maybe for me too; once I had heard her say: 'My Agnes died because she couldn't stand the drumming any more.'

Despite any guilt I may have felt for my poor mama's death, I clung all the more desperately to my despised drum; for it did not die as a mother dies, you could buy a new one, or you could have it repaired by old man Heilandt or Laubschad the watchmaker, it understood me, it always gave the right answer, it stuck to me as I stuck to it.

In those days the apartment became too small for me, the streets too long or too short for my fourteen years; in the daytime there was no occasion to play the tempter outside of shopwindows and the temptation to tempt was not urgent enough to make me lurk in dark doorways at night. I was reduced to tramping up and down the four staircases of our apartment house in time to my drum; I counted a hundred and sixteen steps, stopped at every landing, breathed in the smells, which, because they too felt cramped in those two-room flats, seeped through the five doors on each landing.

At first I had occasional luck with Meyn the trumpeter. I found him lying dead-drunk among the bed sheets hung out in the attic to dry, and sometimes he would blow his trumpet with such musical feeling that it was a real joy for my drum. In May, '38 he gave up gin and told everyone he met: 'I am starting a new life.' He became a member of the band corps of the Mounted SA. Stone sober, in boots and breeches with a leather seat, he would take the steps five at a time. He still kept his four cats, one of whom was named Bismarck, because, as might have been expected, the gin gained the upper hand now and then and gave him a hankering for music.

I seldom knocked at the door of Laubschad the watchmaker, a silent man amid a hundred clocks. That seemed like wasting time on too grand a scale and I couldn't face it more than once a month.

Old man Heilandt still had his shop in the court. He still hammered crooked nails straight. There were still rabbits about and the offspring of rabbits as in the old days. But the children had changed. Now they wore uniforms and black ties and they no longer made soup out of brick flour. They were already twice my size and were barely known to me by name. That was the new generation; my generation had school behind them and were learning a trade: Nuchi Eyke was an apprentice barber, Axel Mischke was preparing to be a welder at the Schichau shipyards, Susi was learning to be a salesgirl at Sternfeld's department store and was already going steady. How everything can change in three, four years! The carpet rack was still there and the house regulations still permitted carpet-beating on Tuesdays and Fridays, but by now there was little pounding to be heard and the occasional explosions carried an overtone of embarrassment: since Hitler's coming to power the vacuum cleaner was taking over; the carpet racks were abandoned to the sparrows.

All that was left me was the stairwell and the attic. Under the roof tiles I devoted myself to my usual reading matter; on the staircase I would knock at the first door left on the second floor whenever I felt the need for human company, and Mother Truczinski always opened. Since she had held my hand at Brenntau Cemetery and led me to my poor mother's grave, she always opened when Oskar plied the door with his drumsticks.

'Don't drum so loud, Oskar. Herbert's still sleeping, he's had a rough night again, they had to bring him home in an ambulance.' She pulled me into the flat, poured me imitation coffee with milk, and gave me a piece of brown rock candy on a string to dip into the coffee and lick. I drank, sucked the rock candy, and let my drum rest.

Mother Truczinski had a little round head, covered so transparently with thin, ash-grey hair that her pink scalp shone through. The sparse threads converged at the back of her head to form a bun which despite its small size – it was smaller than a billiard ball – could be seen from all sides however she twisted and turned. It was held together with knitting needles. Every morning Mother Truczinski rubbed her round cheeks, which when she laughed looked as if they had been pasted on, with the paper from chicory packages, which was red and discolored. Her expression was that of a mouse. Her four children were named Herbert, Guste, Fritz, and Maria.

Maria was my age. She had just finished grade school and was living with a family of civil servants in Schidlitz, learning to do housework. Fritz, who was working at the railway coach factory, was seldom seen. He had two or three girl friends who received him by turns in their beds and went dancing with him at the 'Race Track' in Ohra. He kept rabbits in the court, 'Vienna blues,' but it was Mother Truczinski who had to take care of them, for Fritz had his hands full with his girl friends. Guste, a quiet soul of about thirty, was a waitress at the Hotel Eden by the Central

Station. Still unwed, she lived on the top floor of the Eden with the rest of the staff. Apart from Monsieur Fritz' occasional overnight visits, that left only Herbert, the eldest, at home with his mother. Herbert worked as a waiter in the harbor suburb of Neufahrwasser. For a brief happy period after the death of my poor mama, Herbert Truczinski was my purpose in life; to this day I call him my friend.

Herbert worked for Starbusch. Starbusch was the owner of the Sweden Bar, which was situated across the street from the Protestant Seamen's Church; the customers, as the name might lead one to surmise, were mostly Scandinavians. But there were also Russians, Poles from the Free Port, longshoremen from Holm, and sailors from the German warships that happened to be in the harbor. It was not without its perils to be a waiter in this very international spot. Only the experience he had amassed at the Ohra 'Race Track' – the third-class dance hall where Herbert had worked before going to Neufahrwasser – enabled him to dominate the linguistic volcano of the Sweden Bar with his suburban Plattdeutsch interspersed with crumbs of English and Polish. Even so, he would come home in an ambulance once or twice a month, involuntarily but free of charge.

Then Herbert would have to lie in bed for a few days, face down and breathing hard, for he weighed well over two hundred pounds. On these days Mother Truczinski complained steadily while taking care of him with equal perseverance. After changing his bandages, she would extract a knitting needle from her bun and tap it on the glass of a picture that hung across from Herbert's bed. It was a retouched photograph of a man with a mustache and a solemn steadfast look, who closely resembled some of the mustachioed individuals on the first pages of my own photograph album.

This gentleman, however, at whom Mother Truczinski pointed her knitting needle, was no member of my family, it was Herbert's, Guste's, Fritz', and Maria's father.

'One of these days you're going to end up like your father,' she would chide the moaning, groaning Herbert. But she never stated clearly how and where this man in the black lacquer frame had gone looking for and met his end.

'What happened this time?' inquired the grey-haired mouse over her folded arms.

'Same as usual. Swedes and Norwegians.' The bed groaned as Herbert shifted his position.

'Same as usual, he says. Don't make out like it was always them. Last time it was those fellows from the training ship, what's it called, well, speak up, that's it, the *Schlageter*, that's just what I've been saying, and you try to tell me it's the Swedes and Norskes.'

Herbert's ear – I couldn't see his face – turned red to the brim: 'God-damn Heinies, always shooting their yap and throwing their weight around.'

'Leave them be. What business is it of yours? They always look respectable when I see them in town on their time off. You been lecturing them about Lenin again, or starting up on the Spanish Civil War?'

Herbert suspended his answers and Mother Truczinski shuffled off to her imitation coffee in the kitchen.

As soon as Herbert's back was healed, I was allowed to look at it. He would be sitting in the kitchen chair with his braces hanging down over his blue-clad thighs, and slowly, as though hindered by grave thoughts, he would strip off his woolen shirt.

His back was round, always in motion. Muscles kept moving up and down. A rosy landscape strewn with freckles. The spinal column was embedded in fat. On either side of it a luxuriant growth of hair descended from below the shoulder blades to disappear beneath the wooden underdrawers that Herbert wore even in the summer. From his neck muscles down to the edge of the underdrawers Herbert's back was covered with thick scars which interrupted the vegetation, effaced the freckles. Multi-colored, ranging from blue-black to greenish-white, they formed creases and itched when the weather changed. These scars I was permitted to touch.

What, I should like to know, have I, who lie here in bed, looking out of the window, I who for months have been gazing at and through the outbuildings of this mental hospital and the Oberrath Forest behind them, what to this day have I been privileged to touch that felt as hard, as sensitive, and as disconcerting as the scars on Herbert Truczinski's back? In the same class I should put the secret parts of a few women and young girls, my own pecker, the plaster watering can of the boy Jesus, and the ring finger which scarcely two years ago that dog found in a rye field and brought to me, which a year ago I was still allowed to keep, in a preserving jar to be sure where I couldn't get at it, yet so distinct and complete that to this day I can still feel and count each one of its joints with the help of my drumsticks. Whenever I wanted to recall Herbert Truczinski's back, I would sit drumming with that preserved finger in front of me, helping my memory with my drum. Whenever I wished – which was not very often – to reconstitute a woman's body, Oskar, not sufficiently convinced by a woman's scarlike parts, would invent Herbert Truczinski's scars. But I might just as well put it the other way around and say that my first contact with those welts on my friend's broad back gave promise even then of acquaintance with, and temporary possession of, those short-lived indurations characteristic of women ready for love. Similarly the symbols on Herbert's back gave early promise of the ring finger, and before Herbert's scars made promises, it was my drumsticks, from my third birthday on, which promised scars, reproductive organs, and finally the ring finger. But I must go back still farther: when I was still an embryo, before Oskar was even called Oskar, my umbilical cord, as I sat playing with it, promised me successively drumsticks, Herbert's scars, the occasionally erupting craters of young and not so young women, and finally the ring finger, and at the same time in a parallel development beginning with the boy Jesus' watering can, it promised me my own sex which I always and invariably carry about with me – capricious monument to my own inadequacy and limited possibilities.

Today I have gone back to my drumsticks. As for scars, tender parts, my own equipment which seldom raises its head in pride nowadays, I remember them only indirectly, by way of my drum. I shall have to be thirty before I succeed in celebrating my third birthday again. You've guessed it no doubt: Oskar's aim is to get back to the umbilical cord; that is the sole purpose behind this whole vast verbal effort and my only reason for dwelling on Herbert Truczinski's scars.

Before I go on describing and interpreting my friend's back, an introductory remark is in order: except for a bite in the left shin inflicted by a prostitute from Ohra, there were no scars on the front of his powerful body, magnificent target that it was. It was only from behind that they could get at him. His back alone bore the marks of Finnish and Polish knives, of the snickersnees of the longshoremen from the Speicherinsel, and the sailor's knives of the cadets from the training ships.

When Herbert had had his lunch – three times a week there were potato pancakes, which no one could make so thin, so greaseless, and yet so crisp as Mother Truczinski – when Herbert had pushed his plate aside, I handed him the *Neueste Nachrichten*. He let down his braces, peeled off his shirt, and as he read let me question his back. During these question periods Mother Truczinski usually remained with us at table: she unraveled the wool from old stockings, made approving or disapproving remarks, and never failed to put in a word or two about the – it is safe to assume – horrible death of the man who hung, photographed and retouched, behind glass on the wall across from Herbert's bed.

I began my questioning by touching one of the scars with my finger. Or sometimes I would touch it with one of my drumsticks.

'Press it again, boy. I don't know which one. It seems to be asleep.' And I would press it again, a little harder.

'Oh, that one! That was a Ukrainian. He was having a row with a character from Gdingen. First they were sitting at the same table like brothers. And then the character from Gdingen says: Russki. The Ukrainian wasn't going to take that lying down; if there was one thing he didn't want to be, it was a Russki. He'd been floating logs down the Vistula and various other rivers before that, and he had a pile of dough in his shoe. He'd already spent half his shoeful buying rounds of drinks when the character from Gdingen called him a Russki, and I had to separate the two of them, soft and gentle the way I always do. Well, Herbert has his hands full. At this point the Ukrainian calls me a Water Polack, and the Polack, who spends his time hauling up muck on a dredger, calls me something that sounds like Nazi. Well, my boy, you know Herbert Truczinski: a minute later the guy from the dredger, pasty-faced guy, looks like a stoker, is lying doubled-up by the coatroom. I'm just beginning to tell the Ukrainian what the difference is between a Water Polack and a citizen of Danzig when he gives it to me from behind – and that's the scar.'

When Herbert said 'and that's the scar,' he always lent emphasis to his words by turning the pages of his paper and taking a gulp of coffee. Then I was allowed to press the next scar, sometimes once, sometimes twice.

'Oh, that one! It don't amount to much. That was two years ago when the torpedo boat flotilla from Pillau tied up here. Christ, the way they swaggered around, playing the sailor boy and driving the little chickadees nuts. How Schwiemel ever got into the Navy is a mystery to me. He was from Dresden, try to get that through your head, Oskar my boy, from Dresden. But you don't know, you don't even suspect what it means for a sailor to come from Dresden.'

Herbert's thoughts were lingering much too long for my liking in the fair city on the Elbe. To lure them back to Neufahrwasser, I once again pressed the scar which in his opinion didn't amount to much.

'Well, as I was saying. He was a signalman second class on a torpedo boat. Talked big. He thought he'd start up with a quiet kind of Scotsman while his tub was in drydock. Starts talking about Chamberlain, umbrellas and such. I advised him, very quietly the way I do, to stow that kind of talk, especially cause the Scotsman didn't understand a word and was just painting pictures with schnaps on the table top. So I tell him to leave the guy alone, you're not home now, I tell him, you're a guest of the League of Nations. At this point, the torpedo fritz calls me a 'pocketbook German', he says it in Saxon what's more. Quick I bop him one or two, and that calms him down. Half an hour later, I'm bending down to pick up a coin that had rolled under the table and I can't see 'cause it's dark under the table, so the Saxon pulls out his pickpick and sticks it into me.'

Laughing, Herbert turned over the pages of the *Neueste Nachrichten*, added 'And that's the scar,' pushed the newspaper over to the grumbling Mother Truczinski, and prepared to get up. Quickly, before Herbert could leave for the can – he was pulling himself up by the table edge and I could see from the look on his face where he was headed for – I pressed a black and violet scar that was as wide as a skat card is long. You could still see where the stitches had been.

'Herbert's got to go, boy. I'll tell you afterwards.' But I pressed again and began to fuss and play the three-year-old, that always helped.

'All right, just to keep you quiet. But I'll make it short.' Herbert sat down again. 'That was on Christmas, 1930. There was nothing doing in the port. The longshoremen were hanging around the streetcorners, betting who could spit farthest. After midnight Mass – we'd just finished mixing the punch – the Swedes and Finns came pouring out of the Seamen's Church across the street. I saw they were up to no good, I'm standing in the doorway, looking at those pious faces, wondering why they're playing that way with their anchor buttons. And already she breaks loose: long are the knives and short is the night. Oh, well, Finns and Swedes always did have it in for each other. By why Herbert Truczinski should get mixed up with those characters, God only knows. He must have a screw loose, because when something's going on, Herbert's sure to be in on it. Well, that's the moment I pick to go outside. Starbusch sees me and shouts: "Herbert, watch out!" But I had my good deed to do. My idea was to save the pastor, poor little fellow, he'd just come down from Malmö fresh out of the seminary, and this was his first Christmas with Finns and Swedes in the same church. So my idea is to take him under my wing and see to it that he gets home with a whole skin. I just had my hand on his coat when I feel something cold in my back and Happy New Year I say to myself though it was only Christmas Eve. When I come to, I'm lying on the bar, and my good red blood is running into the beer glasses free of charge, and Starbusch is there with his Red Cross medicine kit, trying to give me so-called first aid.'

'What,' said Mother Truczinski, furiously pulling her knitting needle out of her bun, 'makes you interested in a pastor all of a sudden when you haven't set foot in a church since you was little?'

Herbert waved away her disapproval and, trailing his shirt and braces after him, repaired to the can. His gait was somber and somber was the voice in which he said: 'And that's the scar.' He walked as if he wished once and for all to get away from that church and the knife battles connected with it, as though the can were the place where a man is, becomes, or remains a free-thinker.

A few weeks later I found Herbert speechless and in no mood to have his scars questioned. He seemed dispirited, but he hadn't the usual bandage on his back. Actually I found him lying back down on the living-room couch, rather than nursing his wounds in his bed, and yet he seemed seriously hurt. I heard him sigh, appealing to God, Marx, and Engels and cursing them in the same breath. Now and then he would shake his fist in the air, and then let it fall on his chest; a moment later his other fist would join in, and he would pound his chest like a Catholic crying *mea culpa, mea maxima culpa*.

Herbert had knocked a Latvian sea captain dead. The court acquitted him – he had struck, a frequent occurrence in his trade, in self-defense. But despite his acquittal the Latvian remained a dead Latvian and weighed on his mind like a ton of bricks, although he was said to have been a frail little man, afflicted with a stomach ailment to boot.

Herbert didn't go back to work. He had given notice. Starbusch, his boss, came to see him a number of times. He would sit by Herbert's couch or with Mother Truczinski at the kitchen table. From his briefcase he would produce a bottle of Stobbe's 100 proof gin for Herbert and for Mother Truczinski half a pound of unroasted real coffee from the Free Port. He was always either trying to persuade Herbert to come back to work or trying to persuade Mother Truczinski to persuade her son. But Herbert was adamant – he didn't want to be a waiter any more, and certainly not in Neufahrwasser across the street from the Seamen's Church. Actually he didn't want to be a waiter altogether, for to be a waiter means having knives stuck into you and to have knives stuck into you means knocking a Latvian sea captain dead one fine day, just because you're trying to keep him at a distance, trying to prevent a Latvian knife from adding a Latvian scar to all the Finnish, Swedish, Polish, Free-City, and German scars on Herbert Truczinski's lengthwise and crosswise belabored back.

'I'd sooner go to work for the customs than be a waiter any more in Neufahrwasser,' said Herbert. But he didn't go to work for the customs.

Niobe

In '38 the customs duties were raised and the borders between Poland and the Free City were temporarily closed. My grandmother was unable to take the narrow-gauge railway to the market in Langfuhr and had to close her stand. She was left sitting on her eggs so to speak, though with little desire to hatch them. In the port the herring stank to high heaven, the goods piled up, and statesmen met and came to an agreement. Meanwhile my friend Herbert lay on the couch, unemployed and divided against himself, mulling over his troubles.

And yet the customs service offered wages and bread. It offered green uniforms and a border that was worth guarding. Herbert didn't go to the customs and he didn't want to be a waiter any more; he only wanted to lie on the couch and mull.

But a man must work. And not only Mother Truczinski was of that opinion. Although she resisted Starbusch's pleas that she persuade Herbert to go back to waiting on tables in Neufahrwasser, she definitely wanted to get Herbert off that couch. He himself was soon sick of the two-room flat, his mulling had become purely superficial, and he began one fine day to look through the Help Wanted ads in the *Neueste Nachrichten* and, reluctantly, in the Nazi paper, the *Vorposten*.

I wanted to help him. Should a man like Herbert have to look for work other than his proper occupation in the harbor suburb? Should he be reduced to stevedoring, to odd jobs, to burying rotten herring? I couldn't see Herbert standing on the Mottlau bridges, spitting at the gulls and degenerating into a tobacco chewer. It occurred to me that Herbert and I might start up a partnership: two hours of concentrated work once a week and we would be made men. Aided by his still diamond-like voice, Oskar, his wits sharpened by long experience in this field, would open up shopwindows with worthwhile displays and stand guard at the same time, while Herbert would be quick with his fingers. We needed no blowtorch, no passkeys, no tool kit. We needed no brass knuckles or shootin' irons. The Black Maria and our partnership – two worlds that had no need to meet. And Mercury, god of thieves and commerce, would bless us because I, born in the sign of Virgo, possessed his seal, which I occasionally imprinted on hard objects.

There would be no point in passing over this episode. I shall record it briefly but my words should not be taken as a confession. During Herbert's period of unemployment the two of us committed two medium-sized burglaries of delicatessen stores and one big juicy one – a furrier's: the spoils were three blue foxes, a sealskin, a Persian lamb muff, and a pretty, though not enormously valuable, pony coat.

What made us give up the burglar's trade was not so much the misplaced feelings of guilt which troubled us from time to time, as the increasing difficulty of disposing of the goods. To unload the stuff profitably Herbert had to go back to Neufahrwasser, for that was where all the better fences hung out. But since this locality inevitably reminded him of the Latvian sea captain with the stomach trouble, he tried to get rid of the goods everywhere else, along Schichaugasse, on the Bürgerwiesen, in short everywhere else but in Neufahrwasser, where the furs would have sold like butter. The unloading process was so slow that the delicatessen finally ended up in Mother Truczinski's kitchen and he even gave her, or tried to give her, the Persian lamb muff.

When Mother Truczinski saw the muff, there was no more joking. She had accepted the edibles in silence, sharing perhaps the folk belief that the theft of food is legitimate. But the muff meant luxury and luxury meant frivolity and frivolity meant prison. Such were Mother Truczinski's sound and simple thoughts; she made mouse eyes, pulled a knitting needle out of her bun, and said with a shake of the needle: 'You'll end up like your father,' simultaneously handing her Herbert the *Neueste Nachrichten* or the *Vorposten*, which meant, Now go and get yourself a job and I mean a regular job, or I won't cook for you any more.

Herbert lay for another week on his mulling couch, he was insufferable, available neither for an interrogation of his scars nor for a visit to promising shopwindows. I was very understanding, I let him savor his torment to the dregs and spent most of my

169

time with Laubschad the watchmaker and his time-devouring clocks. I even gave Meyn the musician another try, but he had given up drinking and devoted his trumpet exclusively to the tunes favored by the Mounted SA, dressed neatly and went briskly about his business while, miserably underfed, his four cats, relics of a drunken but splendidly musical era, went slowly to the dogs. On the other hand, I often, coming home late at night, found Matzerath, who in Mama's lifetime had drunk only in company, sitting glassy-eyed behind a row of schnaps glasses. He would be leafing through the photograph album, trying, as I am now, to bring Mama to life in the little, none too successfully exposed rectangles; toward midnight he would weep himself into an elegiac mood, and begin to apostrophize Hitler or Beethoven, who still hung there looking each other gloomily in the eye. From the genius, who, it must be remembered, was deaf, he seemed to receive an answer, while the teetotaling Führer was silent, because Matzerath, a drunken little unit leader, was unworthy of Providence.

One Tuesday – so accurate is my memory thanks to my drum – Herbert finally made up his mind. He threw on his duds, that is, he had Mother Truczinski brush his blue bell-bottom trousers with cold coffee, squeezed into his sport shoes, poured himself into his jacket with the anchor buttons, sprinkled the white silk scarf from the Free Port with cologne which had also ripened on the duty-free dungheap of the Free Port, and soon stood there ready to go, stiff and square in his blue visor cap.

'Guess I'll have a look around for a job,' said Herbert, giving a faintly audacious tilt to his cap. Mother Truczinski let her newspaper sink to the table.

Next day Herbert had a job and a uniform. It was not customs-green but dark grey; he had become a guard in the Maritime Museum.

Like everything that was worth preserving in this city so altogether deserving to be preserved, the treasures of the Maritime Museum occupied an old patrician mansion with a raised stone porch and a playfully but substantially ornamented façade. The inside, full of carved dark oak and winding staircases, was devoted to records of the carefully catalogued history of our seaport town, which had always prided itself on its ability to grow or remain stinking rich in the midst of its powerful but for the most part poor neighbors. Ah, those privileges, purchased from the Teutonic Knights or from the kings of Poland and elaborately defined in elaborate documents! Those color engravings of the innumerable sieges incurred by the fortress at the mouth of the Vistula! There within the walls of the city stands Stanislaw Leszczynski, who has just fled from the Saxon anti-king. The oil painting shows exactly how scared he is. Primate Potocki and de Monti the French ambassador are also scared out of their wits, because the Russians under General Lascy are besieging the city. All these scenes are accurately labeled, and the names of the French ships are legible beneath the fleur-de-lys banner. A legend with an arrow informs us that on this ship King Stanislaw Leszczynski fled to Lorraine when the city was surrendered on the third of August. But most of the exhibits consisted of trophies acquired in wars that had been won, for the simple reason that lost wars seldom or never provide museums with trophies.

The pride of the collection was the figurehead from a large Florentine galleon which, though its home port was Bruges, belonged to the Florentine merchants Portinari and Tani. In April, 1473, the Danzig city-captains and pirates Paul Beneke and Martin Bardewiek succeeded, while cruising off the coast of Zeeland not far from Sluys, in capturing the galleon. The captain, the officers, and a considerable crew were put to the sword, while the ship with its cargo were taken to Danzig. A folding 'Last Judgment' by Memling and a golden baptismal font – both commissioned by Tani for a church in Florence – found a home in the Marienkirche; today, as far as I know, the 'Last Judgment' gladdens the Catholic eyes of Poland. It is not known what became of the figurehead after the war. But in my time it was in the Maritime Museum.

A luxuriant wooden woman, green and naked, arms upraised and hands indolently clasped in such a way as to reveal every single one of her fingers; sunken amber eyes gazing out over resolute, forward-looking breasts. This woman, this figurehead, was a bringer of disaster. She had been commissioned by Portinari the merchant from a sculptor with a reputation for carving figureheads: the model was a Flemish girl close to Portinari. Scarcely had the green figure taken its place beneath the bowsprit of a galleon than the girl, as was then customary, was put on trial for witchcraft. Put to the question before going up in flames, she had implicated her patron, the Florentine merchant, as well as the sculptor who had taken her measurements so expertly. Portinari is said to have hanged himself for fear of the fire. As to the sculptor, they chopped off both his gifted hands to prevent him from ever again transforming witches into figureheads. While the trials were still going on in Bruges, creating quite a stir because Portinari was a rich man, the ship bearing the figurehead fell into the piratical hands of Paul Beneke. Signor Tani, the second merchant, fell beneath a pirate's poleax. Paul Beneke was the next victim; a few years later he incurred the disfavor of the patricians of his native city and was drowned in the courtyard of the Stock-turm. Ships to whose bows the figurehead was affixed after Beneke's death had a habit of bursting into flames before they had even put out of the harbor, and the fire would spread to other vessels; everything burned but the figurehead, which was fireproof and, what with her alluring curves, always found admirers among shipowners. But no sooner had this woman taken her place on a vessel than mutiny broke out and the crew, who had always been a peaceful lot until then, decimated each other. The unsuccessful Danish expedition of the Danzig fleet under the highly gifted Eberhard Ferber in the year 1522 led to Ferber's downfall and bloody insurrection in the city. The history books, it is true, speak of religious disorders – in 1523, a Protestant pastor named Hegge led a mob in an iconoclastic assault on the city's seven parish churches – but we prefer to blame the figurehead for this catas-trophe whose effects were felt for many years to come; it is known at all events that the green woman graced the prow of Ferber's ship.

When Stefan Batory vainly besieged the city fifty years later, Kaspar Jeschke, abbot of the Oliva Monastery, put the blame on the sinful woman in his penitential sermons. The king of the Poles, to whom the city had made a present of her, took her with him in his encampments, and she gave him bad advice. To what extent the wooden lady affected the Swedish campaigns against the city and how much she had to do with the long incarceration of Dr. Aegidius Strauch, the religious zealot who had conspired with the Swedes and also demanded that the green woman, who had meanwhile found her way back into the city, be burned, we do not know. There is a rather obscure report to the effect that a poet by the name of Opitz, a fugitive from Silesia, was granted asylum in the city for some years but died before his time, having found the ruinous wood carving in an attic and having attempted to write poems in her honor.

Only toward the end of the eighteenth century, at the time of the partitions of Poland, were effective measures taken against her. The Prussians, who had taken the city by force of arms, issued a Royal Prussian edict prohibiting 'the wooden figure Niobe'. For the first time she was mentioned by name in an official document and at the same time evacuated or rather incarcerated in that Stockturm in whose courtyard Paul Beneke had been drowned and from whose gallery I had first tried out my long-distance song effects. Intimidated perhaps by the presence of the choice products of human ingenuity of which I have spoken (for she was lodged in the torture chamber), she minded her business throughout the nineteenth century.

When in '25 I climbed to the top of the Stockturm and haunted the windows of the Stadt-Theater with my voice, Niobe, popularly known as 'the Green Kitten', had long since and thank goodness been removed from the torture chamber of the tower. Who knows whether my attack on the neoclassical edifice would otherwise have succeeded?

It must have been an ignorant museum director, a foreigner to the city, who took Niobe from the torture chamber where her malice was held in check and, shortly after the founding of the Free City, settled her in the newly installed Maritime Museum. Shortly thereafter he died of blood poisoning, which this over-zealous official had brought on himself while putting up a sign saying that the lady on exhibition above it was a figurehead answering to the name of Niobe. His successor, a cautious man familiar with the history of the city, wanted to have Niobe removed. His idea was to make the city of Lübeck a present of the dangerous wooden maiden, and it is only because the people of Lübeck declined the gift that the little city on the Trave, with the exception of its brick churches, came through the war and its air raids relatively unscathed.

And so Niobe, or 'the Green Kitten', remained in the Maritime

Museum and was responsible in the short space of fourteen years for the death of three directors – not the cautious one, he had got himself transferred – for the demise of an elderly priest at her feet, the violent ends of a student at the Engineering School, of two graduates of St. Peter's Secondary School who had just passed their final examinations, and the end of four conscientious museum attendants, three of whom were married. All, even the student of engineering, were found with transfigured countenances and in their breasts sharp objects of a kind to be found only in maritime museums: sailor's knives, boarding hooks, harpoons, finely chiseled spearheads from the Gold Coast, sailmakers' needles; only the last of the students had been obliged to resort first to his pocketknife and then to his school compass, because shortly before his death all the sharp objects in the museum had been attached to chains or placed behind glass.

Although in every case the police as well as the coroner spoke of tragic suicide, a rumor which was current in the city and echoed in the newspapers had it that 'The Green Kitten does it with her own hands'. Niobe was seriously suspected of having dispatched men and boys from life to death. There was no end of discussion. The newspapers devoted special columns to their readers' opinions on the 'Niobe case'. The city government spoke of untimely superstition and said it had no intention whatsoever of taking precipitate action before definite proof was provided that something sinister and supernatural had actually occurred.

Thus the green statue remained the prize piece of the Maritime Museum, for the District Museum in Oliva, the Municipal Museum in Fleischergasse, and the management of the Artushof refused to accept the man-crazy individual within their walls.

There was a shortage of museum attendants. And the attendants were not alone in refusing to have anything to do with the wooden maiden. Visitors to the museum also avoided the room with the amber-eyed lady. For quite some time utter silence prevailed behind the Renaissance windows which provided the sculpture with the necessary lateral lighting. Dust piled up. The cleaning women stopped coming. As to the photographers, formerly so irrepressible, one of them died soon after taking Niobe's picture; a natural death, to be sure, but the man's colleagues had put two and two together. They ceased to furnish the press of the Free

City, Poland, Germany, and even France with likenesses of the murderous figurehead, and even went so far as to expunge Niobe from their files. From then on their photographic efforts were devoted exclusively to the arrivals and departures of presidents, prime ministers, and exiled kings, to poultry shows, National Party Congresses, automobile races, and spring floods.

Such was the state of affairs when Herbert Truczinski, who no longer wished to be a waiter and was dead set against going into the customs service, donned the mouse-grey uniform of a museum attendant and took his place on a leather chair beside the door of the room popularly referred to as 'the Kitten's parlor'.

On the very first day of his job I followed Herbert to the streetcar stop on Max-Halbe-Platz. I was worried about him.

'Go home, Oskar, my boy. I can't take you with me.' But I stood there so steadfast with my drum and drumsticks that Herbert relented: 'Oh. all right. Come as far as the High Gate. And then you'll ride back again and be a good boy.' At the High Gate I refused to take the Number 5 car that would have brought me home. Again Herbert relented; I could come as far as Heilige-Geist-Gasse. On the museum steps he tried again to get rid of me. Then with a sigh he bought a child's admission ticket. It is true that I was already fourteen and should have paid full admission, but what people don't know won't hurt them.

We had a pleasant, quiet day. No visitors, no inspectors. Now and then I would drum a little while; now and then Herbert would sleep for an hour or so. Niobe gazed out into the world through amber eyes and strove double-breasted toward a goal that was not our goal. We paid no attention to her. 'She's not my type,' said Herbert disparagingly. 'Look at those rolls of fat, look at that double chin she's got.'

He tilted his head and began to muse: 'And look at the ass on her, like a family-size clothes cupboard. Herbert's taste runs more to dainty little ladies, cute and delicate like.'

I listened to Herbert's detailed description of his type and looked on as his great shovel-like hands kneaded and modeled the contours of a lithe and lovely person of the fair sex, who was to remain for many years, to this very day as a matter of fact and even beneath the disguise of a nurse's uniform, my ideal of womanhood.

By the third day of our life in the museum we ventured to move away from the chair beside the door. On pretext of cleaning – the room really was in pretty bad shape – we made our way, dusting, sweeping away spiderwebs from the oak paneling, toward the sunlit and shadow-casting green wooden body. It would not be accurate to say that Niobe left us entirely cold. Her lures were heavy but not unshapely and she wasn't backward about putting them forward. But we did not look upon her with eyes of covetousness. Rather, we looked her over in the manner of shrewd connoisseurs who take every detail into account. Herbert and I were two esthetes soberly drunk on beauty, abstract beauty. There we were, studying feminine proportions with our thumbnails. Niobe's thighs were a bit too short; aside from that we found that her lengthwise measurements – eight head lengths – lived up to the classical ideal; beamwise, however, pelvis, shoulders, and chest demanded to be judged by Dutch rather than Greek standards.

Herbert tilted his thumb: 'She'd be a damn sight too active in bed for me. Herbert's had plenty of wrestling matches in Ohra and Fahrwasser. He don't need no woman for that.' Herbert's fingers had been burnt. 'Oh, if she was a little handful, a frail little thing that you've got to be careful not to break her in two, Herbert would have no objection.'

Actually, if it had come to brass tacks, we should have had no objection either to Niobe and her wrestler's frame. Herbert was perfectly well aware that the degree of passivity or activity he liked or disliked in naked or half-clad women is not limited to the slender type to the exclusion of the buxom or stout; there are slim young things who can't lie still for a minute and women built like barrels who show no more current than a sleepy inland waterway. We purposely simplified, reducing the whole problem to two terms and insulting Niobe on principle. We were unforgivably rude to her. Herbert picked me up so I could beat her breasts with my drumsticks, driving absurd clouds of sawdust from her sprayed and therefore uninhabited wormholes. While I drummed, we looked into her amber eyes. Not a quiver or twinge, no sign of a tear. Her eyes did not narrow into menacing, hate-spewing slits. The whole room with everything in it was reflected perfectly though in convex distortion in those two polished, more yellowish than reddish drops of amber. Amber is deceptive, everyone knows that. We too were aware of the treacherous ways of this ennobled, ornamental wood gum. Nevertheless, obstinately classifying all things womanly as active and passive in our mechanical masculine way, we interpreted Niobe's apparent indifference in a manner favorable to ourselves. We felt safe. With a malignant cackle, Herbert drove a nail into her kneecap: my knee hurt at every stroke, she didn't even flick an eyelash. Right under her eyes, we engaged in all sorts of silly horseplay. Herbert put on the overcoat of a British admiral, took up a spyglass, and donned the admiral's hat that went with it. With a little red jacket and a full-bottomed wig I transformed myself into the admiral's pageboy. We played Trafalgar, bombarded Copenhagen, dispersed Napoleon's fleet at Aboukir, rounded this cape and that cape, took historical poses, and then again contemporary poses. All this beneath the eyes of Niobe, the figurehead carved after the proportions of a Dutch witch. We were convinced that she looked on with indifference if she noticed us at all.

Today I know that everything watches, that nothing goes unseen, and that even wallpaper has a better memory than ours. It isn't God in His heaven that sees all. A kitchen chair, a coat-hanger, a half-filled ash tray, or the wooden replica of a woman named Niobe, can perfectly well serve as an unforgetting witness to every one of our acts.

We came to work in the Maritime Museum for two weeks or more. Herbert made me a present of a drum and twice brought Mother Truczinski home his weekly wages, which included a danger bonus. One Tuesday, for the museum was closed on Monday, the cashier refused to sell us a child's ticket; he refused to admit me altogether. Herbert asked why. Grumpily but not without benevolence, the cashier told us that a complaint had been made, that children could no longer be admitted; the little boy's father was against it; he didn't mind if I waited down by the ticket window, since he, as a businessman and widower, had no time to look after me, but he didn't want me in the Kitten's Parlor any more, because I was irresponsible.

Herbert was ready to give in, but I pushed him and prodded him. On the one hand he agreed that the cashier was right, on the other hand, he said I was his mascot, his guardian angel; my childlike innocence would protect him. In short, Herbert almost made friends with the cashier and succeeded in having me admitted 'one last time', those were the cashier's words, to the Maritime Museum.

Once again my big friend took me by the hand and led me up the ornate, freshly oiled winding staircase to the second floor where Niobe lived. The morning was quiet and the afternoon still more so. Herbert sat with half-closed eyes on his leather chair with the yellow studs. I sat at his feet. My drum remained silent. We blinked up at the schooners, frigates, and corvettes, the fivemasters, galleons, and sloops, the coastal sailing vessels and clippers, all of them hanging from the oak paneling, waiting for a favorable wind. We mustered the model fleet, with it we waited for a fresh breeze and dreaded the calm prevailing in the parlor. All this we did to avoid having to look at and dread Niobe. What would we not have given for the work sounds of a wood worm, proof that the inside of the green wood was being slowly but surely eaten away and hollowed out, that Niobe was perishable! But there wasn't a worm to be heard. The wooden body had been made immune to worms, immortal. Our only resource was the model fleet, the absurd hope for a favorable wind. We made a game out of our fear of Niobe, we did our very best to ignore it, to forget it, and we might even have succeeded if suddenly the afternoon sun had not struck her full in the left amber eye and set it aflame.

Yet this inflammation need not have surprised us. We were quite familiar with sunny afternoons on the second floor of the Maritime Museum, we knew what hour had struck or was about to strike when the light fell beneath the cornice and lit up the ships. The churches round about did their bit toward providing the dust-stirring movements of the sun's beam with a clock-time index, sending the sound of their historical bells to keep our historical objects company. Small wonder that the sun took on a historical character; it became an item in our museum and we began to suspect it of plotting with Niobe's amber eyes.

But that afternoon, disinclined as we were to games or provocative nonsense, Niobe's flaming eye struck us with redoubled force. Dejected and oppressed, we waited out the half-hour till closing time. The museum closed on the stroke of five.

Next day Herbert took up his post alone. I accompanied him

to the museum, but I didn't feel like waiting by the ticket window; instead I found a place across the street. With my drum I sat on a granite sphere which had grown a tail that grownups used as a banister. Small need to say that the other side of the staircase was guarded by a similar sphere with a similar cast-iron tail. I drummed infrequently but then hideously loud, protesting against the passers-by, female for the most part, who seemed to take pleasure in stopping to talk with me, asking me my name, and running their sweaty hands through my hair, which though short was slightly wavy and already looked upon as attractive. The morning passed. At the end of Heilige-Geist-Gasse the red and black brick hen of green-steepled St. Mary's brooded beneath its great overgrown bell tower. Pigeons kept pushing one another out of nooks in the tower walls; alighting not far away from me, they would chatter together; what nonsense they talked; they hadn't the faintest idea how long the hen would go on brooding or what was going to hatch, or whether, after all these centuries, the brooding wasn't getting to be an end in itself.

At noon Herbert came out. From his lunchbox, which Mother Truczinski crammed so full that it couldn't be closed, he fished out a sandwich with a finger-thick slice of blood sausage and handed it to me. I didn't feel like eating. Herbert gave me a rather mechanical nod of encouragement. In the end I ate and Herbert, who did not, smoked a cigarette. Before returning to the museum, he went, with me tagging after him, to a bar in Brotbänken-Gasse for two or three drinks of gin. I watched his Adam's apple as he tipped up the glasses. I didn't like the way he was pouring it down. Long after he had mounted his winding staircase, long after I had returned to my granite sphere, Oskar could still see his friend Herbert's Adam's apple jumping up and down.

The afternoon crept across the pale polychrome façade of the museum. It sprang from cornice to cornice, rode nymphs and horns of plenty, devoured plump angels reaching for flowers, burst into the midst of a country carnival, played blindman's buff, mounted a swing festooned with roses, ennobled a group of burghers talking business in baggy breeches, lit upon a stag pursued by hounds, and finally reached the second-story window which allowed the sun, briefly and yet forever, to illuminate an amber eye.

Slowly I slid off my granite ball. My drum struck hard against the stone. Some bits of lacquer from the white casing and the red flames broke off and lay white and red on the stone steps.

Possibly I recited something, perhaps I mumbled a prayer, or a list: a little while later the ambulance drew up in front of the museum. Passers-by gathered round the entrance. Oskar managed to slip in with the men from the emergency squad. I found my way up the stairs quicker than they, though by that time they must have begun to know their way around the museum.

It was all I could do to keep from laughing when I saw Herbert. He was hanging from Niobe's façade, he had tried to jump her. His head covered hers. His arms clung to her upraised, folded arms. He was bare to the waist. His shirt was found later, neatly folded on the leather chair beside the door. His back disclosed all its scars. I read the script, counted the letters. Not a one was missing. But not so much as the beginning of a new inscription was discernible.

The emergency squad who came rushing in not far behind me had difficulty in getting Herbert away from Niobe. In a frenzy of lust he had torn a double-edged ship's ax from its safety chain; one edge he had driven into Niobe and the other, in the course of his frantic assault, into himself. Up top, then, they were perfectly united, but down below, alas, he had found no ground for his anchor and his member still emerged, stiff and perplexed, from his open trousers.

When they spread the blanket with the inscription 'Municipal Emergency Service' over Herbert, Oskar, as always when he incurred a loss, found his way back to his drum. He was still beating it with his fists when the museum guards led him out of 'the Kitten's Parlor', down the stairs, and ultimately stowed him in a police car that took him home.

Even now, in the mental hospital, when he recalls this attempted love affair between flesh and wood, he is constrained to work with his fists in order to explore once more Herbert's swollen, multicolored back, that hard and sensitive labyrinth of scars which was to foreshadow, to anticipate everything to come, which was harder and more sensitive than anything that followed. Like a blind man he read the raised script of that back.

It is only now, now that they have taken Herbert away from

his unfeeling carving, that Bruno my keeper turns up with that awful pear-shaped head of his. Gently he removes my fists from the drum, hangs the drum over the left-hand bedpost at the foot end of my iron bed, and smoothes out my blanket.

'Why, Mr Matzerath,' he reproves me gently, 'if you go on drumming so loud, somebody's bound to hear that somebody's drumming much too loud. Wouldn't you like to take a rest or drum a little softer?'

Yes, Bruno, I shall try to dictate a quieter chapter to my drum, even though the subject of my next chapter calls for an orchestra of ravenous wild men.

Faith, Hope, Love

There was once a musician; his name was Meyn and he played the trumpet too beautifully for words. He lived on the fifth floor of an apartment house, just under the roof, he kept four cats, one of which was called Bismarck, and from morning to night he drank out of a gin bottle. This he did until sobered by disaster.

Even today Oskar doesn't like to believe in omens. But I have to admit that in those days there were plenty of omens of disaster. It was approaching with longer and longer steps and larger and larger boots. It was then that my friend Herbert Truczinski died of a wound in the chest inflicted by a wooden woman. The woman did not die. She was sealed up in the cellar of the museum, allegedly to be restored, preserved in any case. But you can't lock up disaster in a cellar. It drains into the sewer pipes, spreads to the gas pipes, and gets into every household with the gas. And no one who sets his soup kettle on the bluish flames suspects that disaster is bringing his supper to a boil.

When Herbert was buried in Langfuhr Cemetery, I once again saw Leo Schugger, whose acquaintance I had made at Brenntau. Slavering and holding out his white mildewed gloves, he tendered his sympathies, those sympathies of his which made little distinction between joy and sorrow, to all the assembled company, to

Mother Truczinski, to Guste, Fritz, and Maria Truczinski, to the corpulent Mrs. Kater, to old man Heilandt, who slaughtered Fritz' rabbits for Mother Truczinski on holidays, to my presumptive father Matzerath, who, generous as he could be at times, defrayed a good half of the funeral expenses, even to Jan Bronski, who hardly knew Herbert and had only come to see Matzerath and perhaps myself on neutral cemetery ground.

When Leo Schugger's gloves fluttered out toward Meyn the musician, who had come half in civilian dress, half in SA uniform, another omen of disaster befell.

Suddenly frightened, Leo's pale glove darted upward and flew off, drawing Leo with it over the tombs. He could be heard screaming and the tatters of words that hovered in the cemetery air had no connection with condolences.

No one moved away from Meyn the musician. And yet, recognized and singled out by Leo Schugger, he stood alone amid the funeral company. He fiddled embarrassedly with his trumpet, which he had brought along by design and had played beautifully over Herbert's grave. Beautifully, because Meyn had done what he hadn't done for a long time, he had gone back to his gin bottle, because he was the same age as Herbert and Herbert's death, which reduced me and my drum to silence, had moved him.

There was once a musician; his name was Meyn, and he played the trumpet too beautifully for words. He live on the fifth floor of an apartment house, just under the roof; he kept four cats, one of which was called Bismarck, and from morning to night he drank out of a gin bottle until, late in '36 or early in '37 I think it was, he joined the Mounted SA. As a trumpeter in the band, he made far fewer mistakes but his playing was no longer too beautiful for words, because, when he slipped on those riding breeches with the leather seat, he gave up the gin bottle and from then on his playing was loud and sober, nothing more.

When SA Man Meyn lost his long-time friend Herbert Truczinski, along with whom during the twenties he had paid dues first to a communist youth group, then to the socialist Red Falcons; when it came time for his friend to be laid in the ground, Meyn reached for his trumpet and his gin bottle. For he wanted to play beautifully and not soberly; his days in the equestrian band hadn't destroyed his ear for music. Arrived at the cemetery, he took a last swig, and while playing he kept his civilian coat on over his uniform, although he had planned to play in Brown, minus the cap, of course.

There was once an SA man who, while playing the trumpet too beautifully for words after drinking plenty of gin, kept his overcoat on over his Mounted SA uniform. When Leo Schugger, a type met with in all cemeteries, came forward to offer condolences, everyone else came in for his share of sympathy. Only the SA man was not privileged to grasp Leo's white glove, because Leo, recognizing the SA man, gave a loud cry of fear and withheld both his glove and his sympathies. The SA man went home with a cold trumpet and no sympathy. In his flat under the roof of our apartment house he found his four cats.

There was once an SA man, his name was Meyn. As a relic of the days when he drank gin all day and played the trumpet too beautifully for words, Meyn still kept four cats, one of which was called Bismarck. One day when SA Man Meyn came home from the funeral of his old friend Herbert Truczinski, sad and sobered, because someone had withheld his sympathies, he found himself all alone in the flat with his four cats. The cats rubbed against his riding boots, and Meyn gave them a newspaper full of herring heads. That got them away from his boots. That day the flat stank worse than usual of the four cats who were all toms, one of which was called Bismarck and was black with white paws. But Meyn had no gin on hand and that made the stench of the cats more unacceptable. He might have bought some gin in our store if his flat hadn't been on the fifth floor, right under the roof. But as it was, he dreaded the stairs and still more he dreaded the neighbors in whose presence and hearing he had sworn on numerous occasions that never again would a drop of gin cross his musician's lips, that he had embarked on a new life of rigorous sobriety, that from now on his motto was order and purpose, away with the vapors of a botched and aimless youth.

There was once a man, his name was Meyn. One day when he found himself all alone in his flat under the roof with his four tomcats, one of which was called Bismarck, the smell was most particularly distasteful to him, because he had had an unpleasant experience earlier in the day and also because there was no gin on hand. When his thirst and displeasure and with them the cat smell had reached a certain point, Meyn, a musician by trade and a member of the Mounted SA band, reached for the poker that was leaning against the cold stove and flailed out at the cats until it seemed safe to assume that though the cat smell in the flat had lost none of its pungency, all of them, including the one named Bismarck, were dead and done for.

Once there was a watchmaker named Laubschad who lived on the second floor of our apartment house in a two-room flat, with windows overlooking the court. Laubschad the watchmaker was unmarried, a member of the National Socialist Welfare Organization and of the SPCA. He was a kindly man who liked to help all tired humans, sick animals, and broken clocks back on their feet. One afternoon as the watchmaker sat pensively at his window, thinking about the neighbor's funeral he had attended that morning, he saw Meyn the musician, who lived on the fifth floor of the same building, carry a half-filled potato sack, which was dripping and seemed wet at the bottom, out into the court and plunge it into one of the garbage cans. But since the garbage can was already three-quarters full, the musician had trouble getting the lid back on.

There were once four tomcats, one of which was called Bismarck. These tomcats belonged to a musician by the name of Meyn. Since the tomcats, which had not been fixed, emitted a fierce, uncompromising smell, the musician clouted them with a fire poker one day when for particular reasons he found the smell particularly distasteful, stuffed their remains in a potato sack, carried the sack down four flights of stairs, and was in a great hurry to stow the bundle in the garbage can in the court beside the carpet rack, because the burlap was not water- nor bloodproof and began to drip before he was even half down the stairs. But since the garbage can was a bit full, the musician had to compress the garbage and his sack in order to close the lid. No sooner had he left the court in the direction of the street – for he had no desire to go back to his flat which though catless still stank of cats – than the compressed garbage began to expand, raised the sack, and with it the lid of the garbage can.

Once there was a musician, he slew his four cats, buried them in a garbage can, left the house, and went out to visit friends.

There was once a watchmaker who sat pensively by his window, looking on as Meyn the musician stuffed a half-filled sack in the garbage can and quickly left the court. A few moments after Meyn's departure, he saw the lid of the garbage can beginning to rise and slowly go on rising.

There were once four tomcats; because they smelled particularly strong on a certain particular day, they were knocked dead, stuffed into a sack, and buried in a garbage can. But the cats, one of which was called Bismarck, were not quite dead; they were tough customers, as cats tend to be. They moved in the sack, set the lid of the garbage can in motion, and confronted Laubschad the watchmaker, who still sat pensively at the window, with the question: what can there be in the sack that Meyn the musician threw in the garbage can?

There was once a watchmaker who could not look on with indifference while something was moving in a garbage can. He left his flat on the second floor, went down into the court, lifted up the lid of the garbage can, opened the sack, took the four badly damaged but still living tomcats home with him, and cared for them. But they died the following night under his watchmaker's fingers. This left him no other course than to enter a complaint with the SPCA, of which he was a member, and to inform the local party headquarters of a case of cruelty to animals which could only impair the party's reputation.

There was once an SA man who did four cats in with a poker. But because the cats were not all-the-way dead, they gave him away and a watchmaker reported him. The case came up for trial and the SA man had to pay a fine. But the matter was also discussed in the SA and the SA man was expelled from the SA for conduct unbecoming a storm trooper. Even his conspicuous bravery on the night of November 8, which later became known as Crystal Night, when he helped set fire to the Langfuhr synagogue in Michaelisweg, even his meritorious activity the following morning when a number of stores, carefully designated in advance, were closed down for the good of the nation, could not halt his expulsion from the Mounted SA. For inhuman cruelty to animals he was stricken from the membership list. It was not until a year later that he gained admittance to the Home Guard, which was later incorporated in the Waffen SS.

There was once a grocer who closed his store one day in

November, because something was doing in town; taking his son Oskar by the hand, he boarded a Number 5 streetcar and rode to the Langasser Gate, because there as in Zoppot and Langfuhr the synagogue was on fire. The synagogue had almost burned down and the firemen were looking on, taking care that the flames should not spread to other buildings. Outside the wrecked synagogue, men in uniform and others in civilian clothes piled up books, ritual objects, and strange kinds of cloth. The mound was set on fire and the grocer took advantage of the opportunity to warm his fingers and his feelings over the public blaze. But his son Oskar, seeing his father so occupied and inflamed, slipped away unobserved and hurried off in the direction of Arsenal Passage, because he was worried about his tin drums with their red and white lacquer.

There was once a toystore owner; his name was Sigismund Markus and among other things he sold tin drums lacquered red and white. Oskar, above-mentioned, was the principal taker of these drums, because he was a drummer by profession and was neither able nor willing to live without a drum. For this reason he hurried away from the burning synagogue in the direction of Arsenal Passage, for there dwelt the keeper of his drums; but he found him in a state which forever after made it impossible for him to sell tin drums in this world.

They, the same firemen whom I, Oskar, thought I had escaped, had visited Markus before me; dipping a brush in paint, they had written 'Jewish Sow' obliquely across his window in Sütterlin script; then, perhaps disgusted with their own handwriting, they had kicked in the window with the heels of their boots, so that the epithet they had fastened on Markus could only be guessed at. Scorning the door, they had entered the shop through the broken window and there, in their characteristic way, they were playing with the toys.

I found them still at play when I, also through the window, entered the shop. Some had taken their pants down and had deposited brown sausages, in which half-digested peas were still discernible, on sailing vessels, fiddling monkeys, and on my drums. They all looked like Meyn the musician, they wore Meyn's SA uniform, but Meyn was not there; just as the ones who were there were not somewhere else. One had drawn his dagger. He was cutting dolls open and he seemed disappointed each time that nothing but sawdust flowed from their limbs and bodies.

I was worried about my drums. They didn't like my drums. My own drum couldn't stand up to their rage; there was nothing it could do but bow down and keep quiet. But Markus had escaped from their rage. When they went to see him in his office, they did not knock, they broke the door open, although it was not locked.

The toy merchant sat behind his desk. As usual he had on sleeve protectors over his dark-grey everyday jacket. Dandruff on his shoulders showed that his scalp was in bad shape. One of the SA men with puppets on his fingers poked him with Kasperl's wooden grandmother, but Markus was beyond being spoken to, beyond being hurt or humiliated. Before him on the desk stood an empty water glass; the sound of his crashing shopwindow had made him thirsty no doubt.

There was once a drummer, his name was Oskar. When they took away his toy merchant and ransacked the shop, he suspected that hard times were in the offing for gnomelike drummers like himself. And so, in leaving the store, he picked out of the ruins a whole drum and two that were not so badly injured, hung them round his neck, and so left Arsenal Passage for the Kohlenmarkt to look for his father, who was probably looking for him. Outside, it was a November morning. Beside the Stadt-Theater, near the streetcar stop, some pious ladies and strikingly ugly young girls were handing out religious tracts, collecting money in collection boxes, and holding up, between two poles, a banner with an inscription quoted from the thirteenth chapter of the First Epistle to the Corinthians. 'Faith ... hope ... love,' Oskar read and played with the three words as a juggler plays with bottles: faith healer, Old Faithful, faithless hope, hope chest, Cape of Good Hope, hopeless love, Love's Labour's Lost, six love. An entire credulous nation believed, there's faith for you, in Santa Claus. But Santa Claus was really the gasman. I believe – such is my faith – that it smells of walnuts and almonds. But it smelled of gas. Soon, so they said, 'twill be the first Sunday of Advent. And the first, second, third, and fourth Sundays of Advent were turned on like gas cocks, to produce a credible smell of walnuts and almonds, so that all those who liked to crack nuts could take comfort and believe:

He's coming, He's coming. Who is coming? The Christ child, the Saviour? Or is it the heavenly gasman with the gas meter under his arm, that always goes ticktock? And he said: I am the Saviour of this world, without me you can't cook. And he was not too demanding, he offered special rates, turned on the freshly polished gas cocks, and let the Holy Ghost pour forth, so the dove, or squab, might be cooked. And handed out walnuts and almonds which were promptly cracked, and they too poured forth spirit and gas. Thus it was not hard, amid the dense blue air, for credulous souls to look upon all those gasmen outside department stores as Santa Clauses and Christ children in all sizes and at all prices. They believed in the only-saving gas company which symbolizes destiny with its rising and falling gas meters and staged an Advent at bargain prices. Many, to be sure, believed in the Christmas this Advent seemed to announce, but the sole survivors of these strenuous holidays were those for whom no almonds or walnuts were left – although everyone had supposed there would be plenty for all.

But after faith in Santa Claus had turned out to be faith in the gasman, an attempt was made, in disregard of the order set forth in Corinthians, to do it with love: I love you, they said, oh, I love you. Do you, too, love yourself? Do you love me, say, do you really love me? I love myself too. And from sheer love they called each other radishes, they loved radishes, they bit into each other, out of sheer love one radish bit off another's radish. And they told one another stories about wonderful heavenly love, and earthly love too, between radishes, and just before biting, they whispered to one another, whispered with all the sharp freshness of hunger: Radish, say, do you love me? I love myself too.

But after they had bitten off each other's radishes out of love, and faith in the gasman had been proclaimed the state religion, there remained, after faith and anticipated love, only the third white elephant of the Epistle to the Corinthians: hope. And even while they still had radishes, walnuts, and almonds to nibble on, they began to hope that soon it would be over, so they might begin afresh or continue, hoping after or even during the finale that the end would soon be over. The end of what? They still did not know. They only hoped that it would soon be over, over tomorrow, but not today; for what were they to do if the end came so suddenly? And then when the end came, they quickly turned it into a hopeful beginning; for in our country the end is always the beginning and there is hope in every, even the most final, end. And so too is it written: As long as man hopes, he will go on turning out hopeful finales.

For my part, I don't know. I don't know, for example, who it is nowadays that hides under the beards of the Santa Clauses, nor what Santa Claus has in his sack; I don't know how gas cocks are throttled and shut off; for Advent, the time of longing for a Redeemer, is flowing again, or flowing still, I do not know. Another thing I don't know is whether I can believe that, as I hope, they are polishing the gas cocks lovingly, so as to make them crow, what morning, what evening, I don't know, nor know I whether the time of day matters; for love knows no time of day, and hope is without end, and faith knows no limits, only knowing and not knowing are subject to times and limits and usually end before their time with beards, knapsacks, almonds, so that once again I must say: I know not, oh, I know not, for example, what they fill sausage casings with, whose guts are fit to be filled, nor do I know with what, though the prices for every filling, fine or coarse, are legibly displayed, still, I know not what is included in the price, I know not in what dictionaries they find the names for fillings. I know not wherewith they fill the dictionaries or sausage casings, I know not whose meat, I know not whose language: words communicate, butchers won't tell, I cut off slices, you open books, I read what tastes good to me, but what tastes good to you? Slices of sausage and quotations from sausage casings and books – and never will we learn who had to be reduced to silence before sausage casings could be filled, before books could speak, stuffed full of print, I know not, but I surmise: It is the same butchers who fill dictionaries and sausage casings with language and sausage, there is no Paul, the man's name was Saul and a Saul he was, and it was Saul who told the people of Corinth something about some priceless sausages that he called faith, hope, and love, which he advertised as easily digestible and which to this very day, still Saul though forever changing in form, he palms off on mankind.

189

As for me, they took away my toy merchant, wishing with him to banish all toys from the world.

There was once a musician, his name was Meyn, and he played the trumpet too beautifully for words.

There was once a toy merchant, his name was Markus and he sold tin drums, lacquered red and white.

There was once a musician, his name was Meyn and he had four cats, one of which was called Bismarck.

There was once a drummer, his name was Oskar, and he needed the toy merchant.

There was once a musician, his name was Meyn, and he did his four cats in with a fire poker.

There was once a watchmaker, his name was Laubschad, and he was a member of the SPCA.

There was once a drummer, his name was Oskar, and they took away his toy merchant.

There was once a toy merchant, his name was Markus, and he took all the toys in the world away with him out of this world.

There was once a musician, his name was Meyn, and if he isn't dead he is still alive, once again playing the trumpet too beautifully for words.

BOOK TWO

Scrap Metal

Visiting day: Maria has brought me a new drum. After passing it over the bars enclosing my bed, she wished to give me the sales slip from the store, but I waved it away and pressed the bell button at the head end of the bed until Bruno my keeper came in and did what he always does when Maria brings me a new drum. He undid the string, let the blue wrapping paper open of its own accord, solemnly lifted out the drum, and carefully folded the paper. Only then did he stride – and when I say stride, I mean stride – to the washbasin with the new drum, turn on the hot water, and, taking care not to scratch the red and white lacquer, remove the price tag.

When, after a brief, not too fatiguing visit, Maria prepared to go, she picked up the old drum, which I had pretty well wrecked during my saga of Herbert Truczinski's back, my stories about the figurehead, and my perhaps rather arbitrary interpretation of the first Epistle to the Corinthians. She was going to take it home to store in our cellar, side by side with all the other worn-out instruments that had served my professional or private purposes. 'There's not much room left in the cellar,' she said with a sigh. 'I'd like to know where I'm going to put the winter potatoes.'

I smiled, pretending not to hear this plaint of the housekeeper in Maria, and gave her my instructions: the retired drum must be numbered in black ink and the brief notes I had made on a slip of paper about the drum's career must be transferred to the diary which has been hanging for years on the inside of the cellar door and knows all about my drums since 1949.

Maria nodded in resignation and kissed me goodbye. She never did understand this passion of mine for order; in fact it strikes her as almost insane. Oskar can see how she feels, for he himself is at a loss to account for the pedantry he puts into collecting battered tin drums. The strangest part of it is that he never wants to lay eyes on that pile of scrap metal in the potato cellar again as long as he lives. For he knows from experience that children despise their father's collections and that his son Kurt will look with indifference at best on all those pitiful drums he will one day inherit.

What is it then that makes me, every three weeks, give Maria instructions which, if regularly followed, will one day take up all the room in our cellar and expel the potatoes?

The idea which lights up in my mind now and then, though more and more infrequently, that a museum might one day take an interest in my weary instruments, came to me only after several dozen of them had found their way to the cellar; hence it cannot have been at the root of my collector's passion. The more I think of it, the more I veer toward a very simple motive: fear, fear of a shortage, fear that tin drums might be prohibited, that existing stocks might be destroyed. One day Oskar might be obliged to unearth a few of the less damaged ones and have them repaired as a stopgap to carry him through a period of bleak and terrible drumlessness.

The doctors at the mental hospital offer a similar explanation, though they put it differently. Dr. (Miss) Hornstetter was even curious to know the exact date when my complex was born. I told her at once: November 9, 1938, for that was the day when I lost Sigismund Markus, who had kept me supplied with drums. After my mother's death, it had already become difficult to obtain a new drum when I needed one; there were no more Thursday visits to Arsenal Passage, Matzerath's interest in my drum supply was very halfhearted, and Jan Bronski came to see us more and more infrequently. Now that the toystore was smashed to bits, my situation became truly desperate. The sight of Markus sitting at his empty desk made it very clear to me: Markus won't give you any more drums, Markus won't be selling any more toys,

Markus has broken off business relations with the makers of your beautiful red and white drums.

At the time, however, I was not yet prepared to believe that the relatively serene and playful days of my childhood had ended with Markus' death. From the ruins of the toystore I selected a whole drum and two that were dented only at the edges and, running home with my treasures, imagined that I was secure against hard times.

I was very careful with my drums, I drummed seldom and only in cases of absolute necessity; I denied myself whole afternoons of drumming and, very reluctantly, the drumming at breakfast time that had hitherto made my days bearable. Oskar had turned ascetic; he lost weight and was taken to see Dr. Hollatz and Sister Inge, his assistant, who was getting steadily bonier. They gave me sweet, sour, bitter, and tasteless medicine and put the blame on my glands, which in Dr. Hollatz' opinion had upset my constitution by alternating between hyperfunction and hypofunction.

To escape from Dr. Hollatz' clutches, Oskar moderated his asceticism and put on weight. By the summer of '39, he was his old three-year-old self again, but in filling out his cheeks he had irrevocably demolished the last of Markus' drums. The object that hung on my belly was a pitiful wreck, rusty and full of gaping holes; the red and white lacquer was nearly gone and the sound was utterly lugubrious.

There was no point in appealing to Matzerath for help, though he was a helpful soul and even kindly in his way. Since my poor mother's death, he thought of nothing but his Party occupations; when in need of distraction, he would confer with other unit leaders. Or toward midnight, after ample consumption of spirits, he would carry on loud though confidential conversations with the black-framed likenesses of Hitler and Beethoven in our living room, the genius speaking to him of destiny and the Führer of providence. When he was sober he looked upon the collecting of Winter Aid as the destiny allotted him by providence.

I don't like to think about those collection Sundays. It was on one of them that I made a futile attempt to possess myself of a new drum. Matzerath, who had spent the morning collecting outside the Art Cinema in Hauptstrasse and Sternfeld's Department Store, came home at noon and warmed up some meatballs for our lunch. After the meal – I can still remember that it was very tasty – the weary collector lay down on the couch for a nap. No sooner did his breathing suggest sleep than I took the half-full collection box from the piano and disappeared into the store. Huddled under the counter, I turned my attention to this most preposterous of all tin cans. Not that I intended to filch so much as a penny. My absurd idea was to try the thing out as a drum. But however I beat, however I manipulated the sticks it gave but one answer: Winter Aid, please contribute. Let no one be cold or hungry. Winter Aid, please contribute.

After half an hour I gave up; I took five pfennigs from the cash drawer, contributed them to the Winter Aid, and returned the collection box thus enriched to the piano, so that Matzerath might find it and kill the rest of his Sunday shaking it for the cold and hungry.

This unsuccessful attempt cured me forever. Never again did I seriously attempt to use a tin can, an overturned bucket, or the bottom of a washbasin for a drum. If I nevertheless did so from time to time, I try my best to forget these inglorious episodes, and give them as little space as possible on this paper. A tin can is simply not a drum, a bucket is a bucket, and a washbasin is good for washing yourself or your socks. There was no more substitute then than there is now; a tin drum adorned with red flames on a white field speaks for itself and no one can speak for it.

Oskar was alone, betrayed and sold down the river. How was he to preserve his three-year-old countenance if he lacked what was most necessary to his well-being, his drum? All the deceptions I had been practicing for years: my occasional bed-wetting, my childlike babbling of evening prayers, my fear of Santa Claus, whose real name was Greff, my indefatigable asking of droll, typically three-year-old questions such as: Why have cars got wheels? – all this nonsense that grownups expected of me I now had to provide without my drum. I was soon tempted to give up. In my despair I began to look for the man who was not my father but had very probably begotten me. Not far from the Polish settlement on Ringstrasse, Oskar waited for Jan Bronski.

My poor mama's death had put an end to the relations, some-times verging on friendship, between Matzerath and my uncle, who had meanwhile been promoted to the position of postal secretary. There was no sudden break, but despite the memories they shared, they had gradually moved apart as the political crisis deepened. The disintegration of my mama's slender soul and ample body brought with it the disintegration of the friendship between these two men, both of whom had mirrored themselves in her soul and fed on her body. Deprived of this nourishment and convex mirror, they found no substitute but their meetings with men who were dedicated to opposing political ideas though they smoked the same tobacco. But neither a Polish Post Office nor meetings with unit leaders in shirtsleeves can take the place of a beautiful, tender-hearted woman. Despite the need for caution – Matzerath had to think of his customers and the Party and Jan had the postal administration to consider – my two presumptive fathers met several times between my poor mama's death and the end of Sigismund Markus.

Two or three times a month, toward midnight, we would hear Jan's knuckles tapping on our living room window. Matzerath would push the curtain aside and open the window a crack; both of them would be thoroughly embarrassed until one or the other found the saving word and suggested a game of midnight skat. They would summon Greff from his vegetable store or, if he was disinclined, which he often was on Jan's account, because as a former scout leader – he had meanwhile disbanded his troop – he had to be careful and besides he was a poor player and didn't care much about skat in the first place, they usually called in Alexander Scheffler, the baker, as third. Scheffler himself was none too enthusiastic about sitting at the same table with Jan, but a certain affection for my poor mama, which had transferred itself like a kind of legacy to Matzerath, and a firm conviction that retailers should stick together, induced the short-legged baker to hurry over from Kleinhammer-Weg in response to Matzerath's call, to take his place at our living room table, to shuffle the cards with his pale, worm-eaten, floury fingers and distribute them like rolls to the hungry multitude.

Since these forbidden games did not as a rule begin until midnight, to break off at three in the morning when Scheffler was needed in the bakery, it was only on rare occasions that I managed to rise from my bed unseen, unheard, and drumless, and slip into the shady corner beneath the table.

As you have doubtless noticed by now, I had always, under tables, been given to the easiest kind of meditation: I made comparisons. How things had changed since my poor mama's death. No longer did Jan Bronski, cautious up top and yet losing game after game, but intrepid below, send out his shoeless sock on expeditions between my mother's thighs. Sex, not to say love, had vanished from the skat table. Six trouser legs in various fishbone patterns draped six masculine legs, some bare and more or less hairy at the ankles, others affecting long underwear. Down below, all six made every effort to avoid the slightest contact, however fortuitous, while up above their extensions – trunks, heads, arms – busied themselves with a game which should have been forbidden on political grounds, for every hand lost or won admitted of such baleful or triumphant reflections as: Poland has lost a grand hand, or, the Free City of Danzig has taken a diamond single for the German Reich.

It was not hard to foresee a day when these war games would come to an end, transformed, as is the way with war games, into hard realities.

Early in the summer of '39 it became clear that Matzerath, in the course of his weekly Party conferences, had found skat partners less compromising than Polish postal officials and former scout leaders. Jan Bronski remembered – he was forced to remember – the camp to which fate had assigned him; he began to stick to his post-office friends, such as Kobyella, the crippled janitor who, since his service in Marszalek Pilsudski's legendary legion, had one leg an inch or more shorter than the other. Despite his limp, Kobyella was an excellent janitor, hence a skillful repair man who might, it seemed to me, be kind enough to make my sick drum well again. The path to Kobyella led through Jan Bronski. That was the only reason why I took to waiting for Jan near the Polish settlement toward six in the evening. Even in the most stifling August heat I waited, but Jan, who normally started punctually for home at closing time, did not appear. Without explicitly asking myself what does your presumptive father do after work? I often waited until seven or half-past. And still he did not come. I could have gone to Aunt Hedwig's. Possibly Jan was sick; maybe he had fever or he had broken a leg and had it in plaster. Oskar stayed right where he was and contented himself with staring from time to time at the windows and curtains of the postal secretary's flat. Oskar felt a strange reluctance about visiting his Aunt Hedwig, whose motherly cow's eyes made him sad. Besides, he was not especially fond of the Bronski children, his presumptive half brother and sister. They treated him like a doll. They wanted to play with him, to use him for a toy. What right had Stephan, who was just fifteen, scarcely older than himself, to treat him with the condescension of a father or schoolmaster? And ten-year-old Marga with those braids and that face that rose like a fat full moon, what gave her the right to look upon Oskar as a dummy to be dressed, combed, brushed, adjusted, and lectured at by the hour? To both of them I was nothing but a freak, a pathetic midget, while they were normal and full of promise. They were also my grandma Koljaiczek's favorites, but then I have to own that I made things pretty hard for her. I showed little interest in fairy tales and picture books. What I expected of my grandmother, what even today I dream of in the most pleasurable detail, was very clear and simple, and for that reason hard to obtain: the moment he saw her, Oskar wanted to emulate his grandfather Koljaiczek, to take refuge beneath her skirts and, if possible, never again draw a breath outside of their sheltering stillness.

What lengths I went to to gain admittance to that tent! I don't believe that she actually disliked to have Oskar sitting there. But she hesitated and usually refused me; I think she would gladly have granted refuge to anyone who halfway resembled Koljaiczek; it was only I who, having neither his build nor his ready hand with matches, was constrained to think up stratagems.

I can see Oskar playing with a rubber ball like a real three-year-old; by pure chance the ball rolls under her skirts and Oskar, in pursuit of the spherical pretext, slips in before his grandmother can see through his ruse and give back the ball.

When the grownups were present, my grandmother never tolerated me under her skirts for very long. The grownups would make fun of her, reminding her, often in rather crude terms, of her betrothal in the autumnal potato fields, until my grandmother, who was not pale by nature, would blush loud and long, which was not unbecoming to her with her hair which by then – she was past sixty – was almost white.

But when my grandmother Anna was alone – as she seldom was, and I saw her more and more rarely after my poor mama's death, and scarcely ever since she had been obliged to give up her stall at the weekly market in Langfuhr – she was more willing to let me take shelter beneath her potato-colored skirts and let me stay longer. I didn't even need the silly trick with the rubber ball. Sliding across the floor with my drum, doubling up one leg and bracing the other against the furniture, I made my way toward the grandmotherly mountain; arrived at the foot, I would raise the fourfold veils with my drumsticks and, once underneath, let them fall, all four at once. For a moment I remained perfectly still, breathing in with my whole soul the acrid smell of slightly rancid butter, which, unaffected by the changing of the seasons, pervaded this chosen habitat. Only then did Oskar begin to drum. Knowing what his grandmother liked to hear, I called forth sounds of October rain, similar to what she must have heard by the smouldering potato plants, when Koljaiczek, smelling like a hotly pursued firebug, came to her for shelter. I would make a fine slanting rain fall on the drum, until above me I could hear sighs and saints' names, and it is up to you to recognize the sighs and saints' names that were uttered in '99 when my grandmother sat in the rain and Koljaiczek sat dry in the tent.

As I waited for Jan Bronski outside the Polish settlement in August, '39, I often thought of my grandmother. Possibly she was visiting with Aunt Hedwig. But alluring as the thought may have been to sit beneath her skirts, breathing in the smell of rancid butter, I did not climb the two flights of stairs, I did not ring the bell under the name plate marked 'Jan Bronski'. What had Oskar to offer his grandmother? His drum was broken, it made no music, it had forgotten the sound of the rain, the fine rain that falls aslant on a fire of potato plants. And since these autumnal sound effects were his only way of appealing to his grandmother, he stayed out on Ringstrasse, gazing at the Number 5 cars as they approached or receded, clanging their bells in their course along the Heeresanger.

Was I still waiting for Jan? Had I not already given up? If I was still standing on the same spot, was it not simply that I had not yet thought up an acceptable way of leaving? Long waiting can be quite educational. But a long wait can also make one conjure up the awaited encounter in such detail as to destroy all possibility of a happy surprise. Nevertheless Jan surprised me. Resolved to take him unawares, to serenade him with the remains of my drum, I stood there tense, with my sticks at the ready. If only the groans and outcries of my drum could make my desperate situation clear to him, there would be no need of any long-winded explanations. Five more streetcars, I said to myself, three more, just this one; giving shape to my anxieties, I imagined that the Bronskis, at Jan's request, had been transferred to Modlin or Warsaw; I saw him as postmaster in Bromberg or Thorn. Then, in disregard of all my promises to myself, I waited for one more streetcar, and had already turned to start for home when Oskar was seized from behind. A grownup had put his hands over Oskar's eyes.

I felt soft hands that smelled of expensive soap, pleasantly dry, men's hands; I felt Jan Bronski.

When he let me loose and spun me round toward him with an overloud laugh, it was too late to demonstrate my disastrous situation on the drum. Consequently I inserted both drumsticks under the linen braces of my filthy knickers, filthy and frayed around the pockets because in those days there was no one to take care of me. That left my hands free to lift up my drum, to raise it high in accusation, as Father Wiehnke raised the host during Mass, I too might have said: this is my body and blood, but I said not a word; I just held up the battered metal. I desired no fundamental or miraculous transubstantiation; all I wanted for my drum was a repair job, nothing more.

Jan's laughter was plainly hysterical. He must have felt it to be out of place for he stopped it at once. He saw my drum, he couldn't very well help it, but soon turned away from it to seek my bright, three-year-old eyes, which at that time still had a look of candor. At first he saw nothing but two expressionless blue irises full of glints and reflections, everything in short that eyes are said to be full of, and then, forced to admit that the reflections in my eyes were no better or worse than those that can be seen in any first-class puddle, summoned up all his good will, concentrated his memory, and forced himself to find in my orbits my mama's grey, but similarly shaped eyes which for quite a few years had reflected sentiments ranging from benevolence to passion for his benefit. Perhaps he was disconcerted to find a shadow of himself, though this would not necessarily mean that Jan was my father or, more accurately, my begetter. For his eyes, Mama's, and my own were distinguished by the same naively shrewd, sparkling, inept beauty as those of nearly all the Bronskis, of Stephan, of Marga, though in lesser degree, but above all of my grandmother and her brother Vincent. Yet despite my blue eyes and black lashes, there was no overlooking a dash of incendiary Koljaiczek blood in me – how else account for my delight in shattering glass with song? – whereas it would have been hard to discern any Rhenish, Matzerath traits in me.

At that moment, when I lifted my drum and put my eyes to work, Jan himself, who preferred to sidestep such questions, would, if asked directly, have had to confess: it is his mother Agnes who is looking at me. Or perhaps I am looking at myself. His mother and I had far too much in common. But then again it might be my uncle Koljaiczek, who is in America or on the bottom of the sea. In any case it is not Matzerath who is looking at me, and that is just as well.

Jan took my drum, turned it about, tapped it. He, the impractical butterfingers, who couldn't even sharpen a pencil properly, assumed the air of a man who knows something about repairing tin drums. Visibly making a decision, which was rare with him, he took me by the hand, quite to my surprise because I had never expected things to move that quickly, and led me across Ringstrasse to the Heeresanger streetcar stop. When the car came, he pulled me after him into the trailer where smoking was permitted.

As Oskar suspected, we were going into the city, to the Hevelius-Platz, to the Polish Post Office, to see Janitor Kobyella, who possessed the tools and the skill that Oskar's drum was so sorely in need of.

That streetcar ride in the jingling, jangling Number 5 might have been a quiet pleasure jaunt if it had not taken place on the day before September 1, 1993. At Max-Halbe-Platz, the car filled up with weary but vociferous bathers from the beach at Brösen. What a pleasant summer evening would have awaited us, drinking soda pop through a straw at the Café Weitzke after depositing the drum, if the battleships *Schleswig* and *Schleswig-Holstein* had not been riding at anchor in the harbor mouth across from the Westerplatte, displaying their grim steel flanks, their double revolving turrets, and casemate guns. How lovely it would have been to ring at the porter's lodge of the Polish Post Office and leave an innocent child's drum for Janitor Kobyella to repair, if only the post office had not, in the course of the last few months, been fitted out with armor plate and turned into a fortress garrisoned by the hitherto peace-loving post-office personnel, officials, clerks, and mail carriers, who had been devoting their weekends to military training at Gdingen and Oxhöft.

We were approaching Oliva Gate. Jan Bronski was sweating profusely, staring at the dusty green trees of Hindenburg-Allee and smoking more of his gold-tipped cigarettes than his economical nature would ordinarily have permitted. Oskar had never seen his presumptive father sweat so, except for two or three times when he had watched him on the sofa with his mama.

But my poor mama had long been dead. Why was Jan Bronski sweating? When I saw how he prepared to leave the car at every approaching stop but each time remembered my presence at the last moment, when I realized that if he resumed his seat it was because of me and my drum, I knew why he was sweating. It was because Jan, as an official, was expected to help defend the Polish Post Office. He had already made his getaway, but then he had run into me and my scrap metal on the corner of Ringstrasse and the Heeresanger, and resolved to follow the call of duty. Pulling me, who was neither an official nor fit to defend a post office, after him, he had boarded the car and here he sat smoking and sweating. Why didn't he get out? I certainly would not have stopped him. He was still in the prime of life, not yet forty-five, blue of eye and brown of hair. His trembling hands were well manicured, and if he hadn't been perspiring so pitifully, the smell that came to Oskar's nostrils as he sat beside his presumptive father would have been cologne and not cold sweat.

At the Holzmarkt we got out and walked down the Altstädtischer Graben. It was a still summer night. The bells pealed heavenward as they always did toward eight o'clock, sending up clouds of pigeons. 'Be True and Upright to the Grave', sang the chimes. It was beautiful and made you want to cry. But all about us there was laughter. Women with sunburned children, terry-cloth beach robes, bright-colored balls and sailboats alit from the streetcars bearing their freshly bathed multitudes from the beaches of Glettkau and Heubude. Girls still drowsy from the sun nibbled raspberry ice. A fifteen-year-old dropped her ice cream cone and was about to pick it up, but then she hesitated and finally abandoned the rapidly melting delicacy to the paving stones and the shoe soles of future passers-by; soon she would be a grownup and stop eating ice cream in the street.

At Schneidermühlen-Gasse we turned left. The Hevelius-Platz, to which the little street led, was blocked off by SS Home Guards standing about in groups: youngsters and grown men with the armbands and rifles of the security police. It would have been easy to make a detour around the cordon and get to the post office from the Rähm. Jan Bronski went straight up to the SS men. His purpose was clear: he wanted to be stopped under the eyes of his superiors, who were certainly having the Hevelius-Platz watched from the post office, and sent back. He hoped to cut a relatively dignified figure as a thwarted hero and return home by the same Number 5 streetcar that had brought him.

The Home Guards let us through; it probably never occurred to them that this well-dressed gentleman leading a three-year-old child by the hand meant to go to the post office. They politely advised us to be careful and did not shout 'Halt' until we were through the outside gate and approaching the main entrance. Jan turned irresolutely. The heavy door was opened a crack and we were pulled inside: there we were in the pleasantly cool half-light of the main hall.

The greeting Jan Bronski received from his colleagues was not exactly friendly. They distrusted him, they had probably given him up. Some, as they declared quite frankly, had even begun to suspect that he, Postal Secretary Bronski, was going to shirk his duties. Jan had difficulty in clearing himself. No one listened. He was pushed into a line of men who were busy hauling sandbags up from the cellar. These sandbags and other incongruous objects were piled up behind the plate-glass windows; filing cabinets and other items of heavy furniture were moved close to the main entrance with a view to barricading it in case of emergency.

Someone asked who I was but had no time to wait for Jan's answer. The men were nervous; they would shout at one another and then suddenly, grown overcautious, start whispering. My drum and its distress seemed forgotten. Kobyella the janitor, on whom I had counted, whom I expected to rehabilitate the mass of scrap metal hanging from my neck, was not to be seen; he was probably on the second or third floor of the building, feverishly at work like the clerks and postmen around me, piling up sandbags that were supposed to resist bullets. Oskar's presence was obviously embarrassing to Bronski. The moment a man, whom the others called Dr. Michon, came up to give Jan instructions I slipped away. After cautiously circumnavigating this Dr. Michon, who wore a Polish steel helmet and was obviously the postmaster, I looked about and finally found the stairs leading to the second floor. Toward the end of the second-floor corridor, I discovered a medium-sized, windowless room, where no one was hauling crates of ammunition or piling sandbags. In fact, the room was deserted.

A number of baskets on rollers had been pushed close together; they were full of letters bearing stamps of all colors. It was a low-ceilinged room with ocher-red wallpaper. I detected a slight smell of rubber. An unshaded light bulb hung from the ceiling. Oskar was too tired to look for the switch. Far in the distance the bells of St. Mary's, St. Catherine's, St. John's, St. Bridget's, St. Barbara's, Trinity, and Corpus Christi announced: It is nine o'clock. You must go to sleep now, Oskar. And so I lay down in one of the mail baskets, bedded down my drum that was as tired as I was by my side, and fell asleep.

The Polish Post Office

I slept in a laundry basket full of letters mailed in Lodz, Lublin, Lemberg, Thorn, Krakau, and Tschenstochau or addressed to people in Lodz, Lublin, Lwow, Toruń, Krakow, and Czestochowa. But I dreamed neither of the Matka Boska Czestochowska nor of the Black Madonna. In my dreams I nibbled neither on Marszalek Pilsudski's heart, preserved in Cracow, nor on the gingerbread that has made the city of Thorn so famous. I did not even dream of my still unrepaired drum. Lying dreamless in a laundry basket on rollers, Oskar heard none of the whispering, twittering, and chattering that allegedly fill the air when many letters lie in a heap. To me those letters didn't breathe a word, I wasn't expecting any mail, and no one could have had the slightest ground for regarding me as an addressee, let alone a sender. Lordly and self-sufficient, I slept with retracted antennae on a mountain of mail gravid with news, a mountain which might have been the world.

Consequently I was not awakened by the letter which a certain Lech Milewczyk in Warsaw had written his niece in Danzig-Schidlitz, a letter alarming enough to have awakened a millenarian turtle; what woke me up was either the nearby machine-gun fire or the distant roar of the salvos from the double turrets of the battleships in the Free Port.

All that is so easily written: machine guns, double turrets. Might it not just as well have been a shower, a hailstorm, the approach of a late summer storm similar to the storm that had accompanied my birth? I was too sleepy and speculation of this sort was not in my repertory. With the sounds still fresh in my ears, I guessed right and like all sleepyheads called a spade a spade: They are shooting, I said to myself.

Oskar climbed out of the laundry basket and stood there wobbling on his pins. His first thought was for the fate of his sensitive drum. With both hands he scooped out a hole in the letters that had sheltered his slumbers, but he was not brutal about it; though loosely piled, the letters were often dovetailed, but he did not tear, bend, or deface, no, cautiously I picked out the scrambled letters, giving individual attention to each single envelope with its 'Poczta Polska' postmark – most of them were violet – and even to the postcards. I took care that none of the envelopes should come open, for even in the presence of events so momentous as to change the face of the world, the secrecy of the mails must remain sacred.

As the machine-gun fire increased, the crater in the laundry basket deepened. Finally I let well enough alone, laid my mortally wounded drum to rest in its freshly dug bed, and covered it well, with ten, perhaps twenty layers of envelopes fitted together in overlapping tiers, as masons fit bricks together to build a solid wall.

I had no sooner completed my precautionary measures, with which I hoped to protect my drum from bullets and shell fragments, when the first antitank shell burst against the post office façade, on the Hevelius-Platz side.

The Polish Post Office, a massive brick building, could be counted on to absorb a good many such hits. There seemed to be no danger that the Home Guard would quickly open up a breach wide enough to permit the frontal attack they had often rehearsed.

I left my safe, windowless storeroom enclosed by three offices and the corridor, to go looking for Jan Bronski. In searching for Jan, my presumptive father, there is no doubt that I was also looking, perhaps with still greater eagerness, for Kobyella, the crippled janitor. For, after all, had I not gone without supper the evening before, had I not taken the streetcar to the Hevelius-Platz and braved the soldiery to enter this post office building which under normal conditions left me cold, in order to have my drum repaired? If I should not find Kobyella on time, that is, before the all-out attack that was surely coming, it seemed scarcely possible that my ailing drum would ever get the expert treatment it needed.

And so Oskar thought of Kobyella and looked for Jan. His arms folded across his chest, he paced the long, tiled corridor and found nothing but solitude. Amid the steady not to say lavish gunfire of the Home Guard, he could make out single shots that must have been fired from inside the building, but the economy-minded defenders had no doubt stayed right in their offices, having merely exchanged their rubber stamps for other implements that could also do a stamp job of sorts. There was no one sitting, standing, or lying in the corridor in readiness for a possible counterattack. Oskar patrolled alone; drumless and defenseless he faced the history-making introitus of the early, far too early hour, which carried plenty of lead but, alas, no gold in its mouth.

The offices on the court side were equally empty. Very careless, I thought. The building should have been guarded there too, for there was only a wooden fence separating the Police Building on

Schneidermühlen-Gasse from the post office court and the package ramp – for the attackers, indeed, the layout was almost too good to be true. I pattered through the offices, the registered letter room, the money order room, the payroll room, the telegraph office. And there they lay. Behind sandbags and sheets of armor plate, behind overturned office furniture, there they lay, firing very intermittently.

In most of the rooms the windows had already made contact with the Home Guard's machine-gun fire. I took a quick look at the damage, making comparisons with the windowpanes that had collapsed in quiet, deep-breathing times of peace, under the influence of my diamond voice. Well, I said to myself, if they ask me to do my bit for the defense of the Polish Post Office, if this wiry little Dr. Michon approaches me not as postmaster but as military commander of the post office building, if he tries to enlist me in the service of Poland, my voice will do its duty. For Poland and for Poland's untilled but perpetually fruitful economy, I would gladly have shattered the windows of all the houses on the other side of the Hevelius-Platz, the transparent house fronts on the Rähm, the windows of Schneidermühlen-Gasse, including Police Headquarters; carrying my long-distance technique to new heights and lengths, I should gladly have transformed every sparkling windowpane on the Altstädtischer Graben and Rittergasse into a black, draft-fomenting hole. That would have created confusion among the Home Guard and the onlookers as well. It would have had the effect of several machine guns and, at the very outset of the war, given rise to talk of secret weapons. But it would not have saved the Polish Post Office.

Oskar's abilities were not put to the test. This Dr. Michon with the Polish steel helmet and the directorial countenance did not enlist me; instead, when, having run down the stairs to the main hall, I got tangled up in his legs, he gave me a painful box on the ear and immediately afterwards, cursing loudly in Polish, resumed his military duties. I could only swallow my chagrin. Obviously all these people, and most of all Dr. Michon, who bore the responsibility, were very excited and scared; I had to forgive them.

The clock in the main hall told me that it was 4:20. When it was 4:21, I inferred that the first hostilities had left the clockwork unharmed. The clock was running, and I was at a loss to know whether this equanimity on the part of time should be taken as a good or bad omen.

In any case, I remained for the present in the main hall, looking for Jan and Kobyella and keeping out of Dr. Michon's way. I found neither my uncle nor the janitor. I noted damage to the glass windows and also cracks and ugly holes in the plaster beside the main entrance, and I had the honor of being present when the first two wounded were carried in. One of them, an elderly gentleman, his grey hair still neatly parted, spoke excitedly and without interruption as his wound – a bullet had grazed his forearm – was being bandaged. No sooner had his arm been swathed in white than he jumped up, seized his rifle, and started back to the rampart of sandbags, which was not, I think, quite bullet-proof. How fortunate that a slight faintness brought on by loss of blood forced him to lie down again and take the rest indispensable to an elderly gentleman who has just been wounded. Moreover, the wiry little quinquagenarian, who wore a steel helmet but from whose breast pocket peered the tip of a silk handkerchief, this gentleman with the elegant movements of a knight in government office, the very same Dr. Michon who had sternly questioned Jan Bronski the previous evening, commanded the wounded elderly gentleman to keep quiet in the name of Poland.

The second wounded man lay breathing heavily on a straw tick and showed no further desire for sandbags. At regular intervals he screamed loudly and without shame; he had been shot in the belly.

Still searching, Oskar was about to give the row of men behind the sandbags another inspection when two shells, striking almost simultaneously above and beside the main entrance, set the hail to rattling. The chests that had been moved against the door burst open, releasing piles of bound records, which fluttered aloft, scattered, and landed on the tile floor where they came into contact with slips and tags whose acquaintance they were never intended to make. Needless to say, the rest of the window glass burst asunder, while great chunks and smaller chunks of plaster fell from the walls and ceiling. Another wounded man was carried into the middle of the hall through clouds of plaster and calcimine, but then, by order of the steel-helmeted Dr. Michon, taken upstairs to the first floor.

The wounded postal clerk moaned at every step. Oskar followed him and his carriers. No one called him back, no one asked him where he was going or, as Michon had done a short while before, boxed his ears. It is true that he did his best to keep out of the grown-up post-office defenders' way.

When I reached the second floor behind the slow-moving carriers, my suspicion was confirmed: the wounded man was being taken to the windowless and therefore safe storeroom that I had reserved for myself. No mattresses being available, it was decided that the mail baskets, though rather too short, would provide relatively comfortable resting places for the wounded. Already I regretted having put my drum to bed in one of these movable laundry baskets full of undeliverable mail. Would the blood of these torn and punctured postmen and postal clerks not seep through ten or twenty layers of paper and give my drum a color it had hitherto known only in the form of enamel? What had my drum in common with the blood of Poland? Let them color their records and blotting paper with their life sap! Let them pour the blue out of their inkwells and fill them up again with red! Let them dye their handkerchiefs and starched white shirts half-red and make Polish flags out of them! After all, it was Poland they were concerned with, not my drum! If they insisted that Poland, though lost, must remain white and red, was that any reason why my drum, rendered suspect by the fresh paint job, should be lost too?

Slowly the thought took root in me: it's not Poland they're worried about, it's my drum. Jan had lured me to the post office in order to give his colleagues, for whom Poland wasn't a good enough rallying signal, an inflammatory standard and watchword. That night, as I slept in a laundry basket on rollers, though neither rolling nor dreaming, the waking post office clerks had whispered to one another: A dying toy drum has sought refuge with us. We are Poles, we must protect it, especially since England and France are bound by treaty to defend us.

While these useless and abstract meditations hampered my freedom of movement outside the half-open door of the storeroom for undeliverable mail, machine-gun fire rose up for the first time from the court. As I had foreseen, the Home Guards were making their first attack from the Police Headquarters Building on Schneidermühlen-Gasse. A little later we were all sent sprawling. The Home Guard had managed to blast the door into the package room above the loading ramp. In another minute they were in the package room, and soon the door to the corridor leading to the main hall was open.

The men who had carried up the wounded man and bedded him in the mail basket where my drum lay rushed off; others followed them. By the noise I judged that they were fighting in the main-floor corridor, then in the package room. The Home Guards were forced to withdraw.

First hesitantly, then with assurance, Oskar entered the storeroom. The wounded man's face was greyish-yellow; he showed his teeth and his eyeballs were working behind closed lids. He spat threads of blood. But since his head hung out over the edge of the mail basket, there was little danger of his soiling the letters. Oskar had to stand on tiptoe to reach into the basket. The man's seat was resting, and resting heavily, exactly where Oskar's drum lay buried. At first Oskar pulled gingerly, taking care not to hurt either the wounded postal clerk or the letters; then he tugged more violently. At length, with a furious ripping and tearing, he managed to remove several dozen envelopes from beneath the groaning man.

Today, it pleases me to relate that my fingers were already touching the rim of my drum when men came storming up the stairs and down the corridor. They were coming back, they had driven the Home Guards from the package room; for the time being they were victorious. I heard them laughing.

Hidden behind one of the mail baskets, I waited near the door until they crowded round the wounded man. At first shouting and gesticulating, then cursing softly, they bandaged him.

Two antitank shells struck the wall of the façade on the level of the ground floor, then two more, then silence. The salvos from the battleships in the Free Port, across from the Westerplatte, rolled along in the distance, an even, good-natured grumbling – you got used to it.

Unnoticed by the bandagers, I slipped out of the storeroom,

leaving my drum in the lurch, to resume my search for Jan, my presumptive father and uncle, and also for Kobyella the janitor.

On the third floor was the apartment of Chief Postal Secretary Naczalnik, who had apparently sent his family off to Bromberg or Warsaw in time. First I searched a few storerooms on the court side, and then I found Jan and Kobyella in the nursery of the Naczalnik flat.

It was a light, friendly room with amusing wallpaper, which unfortunately had been gashed here and there by stray bullets. In peaceful times, it must have been pretty nice to look out the windows at the Hevelius-Platz. An unharmed rocking horse, balls of various sizes, a medieval castle full of upset tin soldiers mounted and on foot, an open cardboard box full of rails and miniature freight cars, several more or less tattered dolls, doll's houses with disorderly interiors, in short a superabundance of toys showed that Chief Postal Secretary Naczalnik must have been the father of two very spoiled children, a boy and a girl. How lucky that the brats had been evacuated to Warsaw and that I was spared a meeting with such a pair, the like of which was well known to me from the Bronskis. With a slight sadistic pleasure I reflected how sorry the little boy must have been to leave his tin soldiers. Maybe he had put a few Uhlans in his pants pocket to reinforce the Polish cavalry later on at the battle for the fortress of Modlin.

Oskar has been going on too much about tin soldiers; the truth is that there's a confession he has to make and he may as well get on with it. In this nursery there was a kind of bookcase full of toys, picture books, and games; the top shelf was taken up with miniature musical instruments. A honey-yellow trumpet lay silent beside a set of chimes which followed the hostilities with enthusiasm, that is to say, whenever a shell struck, they went bim-bim. A brightly painted accordion hung down on one side. The parents had been insane enough to give their offspring a real little fiddle with four real strings. And next to the fiddle, showing its white, undamaged roundness, propped on some building blocks to keep it from rolling off the shelf, stood – you'll never believe it! – a toy drum encased in red and white lacquer.

I made no attempt to pull the drum down from the rack by my own resources. Oskar was quite conscious of his limited reach and was not beyond asking grownups for favors in cases where his gnomelike stature resulted in helplessness.

Jan Bronski and Kobyella lay behind a rampart of sandbags filling the lower third of the windows that started at the floor. Jan had the left-hand window. Kobyella's place was on the right. I realized at once that the janitor was not likely to find the time to recover my drum from its hiding place beneath the wounded, blood-spitting post-office defender who was surely crushing it, and repair it. Kobyella was very busy; at regular intervals he fired his rifle through an embrasure in the sandbag rampart at an antitank gun that had been set up on the other side of the Hevelius-Platz, not far from Schneidermühlen-Gasse and the Radaune Bridge.

Jan lay huddled up, hiding his head and trembling. I recognized him only by his fashionable dark-grey suit, though by now it was pretty well covered with plaster and sand. The lace of his right, likewise grey shoe had come open. I bent down and tied it into a bow. As I drew the bow tight, Jan quivered, raised his disconcertingly blue eyes above his sleeve, and gave me an unconscionably blue, watery stare. Although, as Oskar quickly determined, he was not wounded, he was weeping silently. He was afraid. I ignored his whimpering, pointed to young Naczalnik's drum, and asked Jan with transparent gestures to step over to the bookcase, with the utmost caution of course and taking advantage of the dead corner of the nursery, and hand me down the drum. My uncle did not understand me. My presumptive father did not see what I was driving at. My mama's lover was busy with his fear, so full of it that my pleading gestures had no other effect than to add to his fear. Oskar would have liked to scream at him, but was afraid of distracting Kobyella, who seemed to have ears only for his rifle.

And so I lay down beside Jan on the sandbags and pressed close to him, in the hope of communicating a part of my accustomed equanimity to my unfortunate uncle and presumptive father. In a short while he seemed rather calmer. By breathing with exaggerated regularity, I persuaded his pulse to become approximately regular. But when, far too soon I must admit, I tried once more to call Jan's attention to Naczalnik Junior's drum by turning his head slowly and gently but firmly in the direction of the bookcase, he still failed to see what I wanted. Terror invaded him by way of his feet, surged up through him and filled him entirely; then it flowed back down again, but was unable to escape, perhaps because of the inner soles he always wore, and rebounded invading his stomach, his spleen, his liver, rising to his head and expanding so mightily that his blue eyes stood out from their sockets and the whites disclosed a network of blood vessels which Oskar had never before had occasion to observe in his uncle's eyes.

It cost me time and effort to drive my uncle's eyeballs back into place, to make his heart behave a little. But all my esthetic efforts were frustrated when the Home Guards began to fire that field howitzer of theirs and, with an accuracy bearing witness to the high quality of their training, flattened out the iron fence in front of the building by demolishing, one by one, the brick posts to which it was anchored. There must have been from fifteen to twenty of those posts and Jan suffered heart and soul at the demise of each one, as though it were no mere pedestals that were being pounded into dust but with them imaginary statues of imaginary gods, well known to my uncle and necessary to his very existence.

It is only by some such thought that I can account for the scream with which Jan registered each hit of the howitzer, a scream so shrill and piercing that, had it been consciously shaped and aimed, it would, like my own glass-killing creations, have had the virtue of a glass-cutting diamond. There was fervor in Jan's screaming but no plan or system; all it accomplished was at long last to attract Kobyella's attention; slowly the bony, crippled janitor crept toward us, raised his cadaverous, eyelashless bird's head, and surveyed our distress society out of watery grey eyeballs. He shook Jan. Jan whimpered. He opened Jan's shirt and passed his hand quickly over Jan's body, looking for a wound – I could hardly keep from laughing. Failing to detect the slightest scratch, he turned him over on his back, seized him by the jaw, and shook it till the joints cracked, looked him grimly in the eye, swore at him in Polish, spraying his face with saliva in the process, and finally tossed him the rifle which Jan, though provided with his own private embrasure, had thus far left untouched; in fact it was still on safety. The stock struck his kneecap with a dull thud. The brief pain, his first physical pain after so much mental torment, seemed to do him good, for he seized the rifle, took fright when he felt the coldness of the metal parts in his fingers and a moment later in his blood, but then, encouraged by Kobyella, alternately cursing and coaxing, crept to his post.

For all the effeminate lushness of his imagination, my presumptive father took so realistic a view of war that it was hard, in fact impossible, for him to be brave. Instead of surveying his field of vision through his embrasure and picking out a worth-while target, he tilted his rifle so that it pointed upward, over the roofs of the houses on the Hevelius-Platz; quickly and blindly he emptied his magazine and, again empty-handed, crawled back behind the sandbags. The sheepish look with which he implored the janitor's forgiveness made me think of a schoolboy trying to confess that he has not done his homework. Kobyella gnashed his teeth in rage; when he had had enough of that, he burst out laughing as though he never would stop. Then with terrifying suddenness, his laughter broke off, and he gave Bronski, who as postal secretary was supposed to be his superior officer, a furious kick in the shins. His ungainly foot was drawn back for a kick in the ribs, but just then a burst of machine-gun fire shattered what was left of the upper windowpanes and scored the ceiling. The orthopedic shoe fell back into place; he threw himself behind his rifle and began to fire with morose haste, as though to make up for the time he had wasted on Jan. At all events, he accounted for a fraction, however infinitesimal, of the ammunition consumed during the Second World War.

Had the janitor failed to notice me? He was ordinarily a gruff kind of man; like many war invalids, he had a way of keeping you at a respectful distance. Why, I wondered, did he tolerate my presence in this drafty room? Could Kobyella have thought: it's a nursery after all, so why shouldn't Oskar stay here and play during lulls in the battle?

I don't know how long we lay flat, I between Jan and the left-hand wall of the room, both of us behind the sandbags, Kobyella behind his rifle, shooting for two. It must have been about ten o'clock when the shooting died down. It grew so still that I could hear the buzzing of flies; I heard voices and shouts of command from the Hevelius-Platz, and occasionally turned an ear to the dull drone of the naval guns in the harbor. A fair to cloudy day in September, the sun spread a coating of old gold, the air was thin, sensitive, and yet hard of hearing. My fifteenth birthday was coming up in the next few days. And as every year in September, I wished for a drum, nothing less than a drum; renouncing all the treasures of the world, my mind was set unswervingly on a tin drum, lacquered red and white.

Jan didn't stir. Kobyella's breathing was so even that Oskar began to think he was asleep, that he was taking advantage of the brief lull in the battle to take a little nap, for do not all men, even heroes, need a refreshing little nap now and then? I alone was wide awake and, with all the uncompromising concentration of my years, intent on that drum. It should not be supposed that I *remembered* young Naczalnik's drum in this moment, as the silence gathered and the buzzing of a fly tuckered out from the summer heat died away. Oh, no. Even during the battle, even amid the tumult, Oskar hadn't taken his eyes off that drum. But it was only now that I saw the golden opportunity which every fiber of my being commanded me to seize.

Slowly Oskar arose, moved slowly, steering clear of the broken glass, but unswerving in purpose and direction, toward the bookcase with the toys; he was already figuring how, by putting the box of building blocks on one of the little nursery chairs, he would build a stand high and solid enough to make him the possessor of a brand-new drum, when Kobyella's voice and immediately thereafter his horny hand held me back. Desperately I pointed at the drum. It was so near. Kobyella pulled me back. With both arms I reached out for the drum. The janitor was weakening; he was just about to reach up and hand me happiness when a burst of machine-gun fire invaded the nursery and several antitank shells exploded in front of the entrance; Kobyella flung me in the corner beside Jan Bronski and resumed his position behind his rifle. I was still looking up at the drum when he started on his second magazine.

There lay Oskar, and Jan Bronski, my sweet blue-eyed uncle, didn't even lift up his nose when the clubfoot with the bird's head and the watery lashless eyes caught me, hard before my goal, and thrust me into the corner behind the sandbags.

Fat, bluish-white, eyeless maggots wriggled and multiplied, looking for a worthwhile corpse. What was Poland to me? Or the Poles for that matter? Didn't they have their cavalry? Let them ride. They were always kissing ladies' hands and never till it was too late did they notice that what they were kissing was not a lady's languid fingers but the unrouged muzzle of a field howitzer. And the daughter of the Krupps proceeded to vent her feelings. She smacked her lips, gave a corny yet convincing imitation of battle noises, the kind you hear in newsreels. She peppered the front door of the post office, burst into the main hall, and tried to take a bite out of the staircase, so that no one would be able to move up or down. Then came her retinue: machine guns and two trim little armored reconnaissance cars with their names painted on them. And what pretty names: *Ostmark* and *Sudetenland*. What fun they were having! Back and forth they drove, rat-tat-tatting from behind their armor and looking things over: two young ladies intent on culture and so eager to visit the castle, but the castle was still closed. Spoiled young things they were, just couldn't wait to get in. Bursting with impatience, they cast penetrating, lead-grey glances, all of the same caliber, into every visible room in the castle, making things hot, cold, and uncomfortable for the castellans.

One of the reconnaissance cars – I think it was the *Ostmark* – was just rolling back toward us from Rittergasse when Jan, my uncle, who for some time now had seemed totally inanimate, moved his right leg toward the embrasure he was supposed to be shooting through and raised it high in the air, hoping no doubt that somebody would see it and take a shot at it, or that a stray bullet would take pity on him and graze his calf or heel, inflicting the blessed injury that permits a soldier to limp – and what a limp! – off the battlefield.

A difficult position to hold for very long. From time to time Jan was obliged to relax. But then he changed his position. By lying on his back and propping up his leg with both hands, he was able to expose his calf and heel for a very considerable period and vastly improve their prospects of being hit by an aimed or errant bullet.

Great as my sympathy for Jan was and still is, I could easily understand the temper it put Kobyella in to see Postal Secretary Bronski, his superior, in this desperate, not to say ludicrous posture. The janitor leapt to his feet and with a second leap was standing over us. He seized Jan's jacket and Jan with it, lifted the bundle and dashed it down, up down, up down; dropping it for good, he hauled off with his left, hauled off with his right; then, still not satisfied, his two hands met in mid-air and clenched into one great fist that was going to crush my presumptive father when – there came a whirring as of angels' wings, a singing as of the ether singing over the radio. It didn't hit Bronski, no, it hit Kobyella, Lord, what a sense of humor that projectile had: bricks laughed themselves into splinters and splinters into dust, plaster turned to flour, wood found its ax, the whole silly nursery hopped on one foot, Käthe Kruse dolls burst open, the rocking horse ran away – how happy it would have been to have a rider to throw off! – Polish Uhlans occupied all four corners of the room at once, and at last, the toy rack toppled over: the chimes rang in Easter, the accordion screamed, the trumpet blew something or other, the whole orchestra sounded the keynote at once, as though tuning up: screaming, bursting, whinnying, ringing, scraping, chirping, high and shrill but digging down into cavernous foundations. I myself, as befits a three-year-old child, was in the safest spot, directly under the window, as the shell struck, and into my lap, as it were, fell the drum. No holes at all and hardly a crack in the lacquer. Oskar's new drum.

When I looked up from my new possession, I saw that I would have to help my uncle, who was unable by his own resources to get out from under the heavy janitor. At first I supposed that Jan too had been hit, for he was whimpering very realistically. Finally, when we had rolled Kobyella, who was groaning just as realistically, to one side, Jan's injuries proved to be negligible. His right cheek and the back of one hand had been scratched by broken glass, and that was all. A quick comparison showed me that my presumptive father's blood was lighter in color than the janitor's, which was seeping, dark and sticky, through the tops of his trouser legs.

I wondered whether it was Kobyella or the explosion that had ripped and twisted Jan's pretty grey jacket. It hung down in tatters from his shoulders, the lining had come loose, the buttons had fled, the seams had split, and the pockets had been turned inside out.

Don't be too hard on my poor Jan Bronski, who insisted on scraping his belongings together before dragging Kobyella out of the nursery with my help. He found his comb, the photographs of his loved ones – including one of my poor mama; his purse hadn't even come open. He had a hard and not undangerous time of it, for the bulwark of sandbags had been partly swept away, collecting the skat cards that had been scattered all over the room; he wanted all thirty-two of them, and he was downright unhappy when he couldn't find the thirty-second. When Oskar found it between two devastated doll's houses, and handed it to him, Jan smiled, even though it was the seven of spades.

We dragged Kobyella out of the nursery. When we finally had him in the corridor, the janitor found the strength to utter a few words that Jan Bronski was able to make out: 'Is it all there?' he asked. Jan reached into Kobyella's trousers, between his old man's legs, found a handful and nodded.

We were all happy: Kobyella had kept his pride, Jan Bronski had found all his skat cards including the seven of spades, and Oskar had a new drum which beat against his knee at every step while Jan and a man whom Jan called Victor carried the janitor, weak from loss of blood, downstairs to the storeroom for undeliverable mail.

The Card House

Though losing more and more blood, the janitor was becoming steadily heavier. Victor Weluhn helped us to carry him. Victor was very nearsighted, but at the time he still had his glasses and was able to negotiate the stone steps without stumbling. Victor's occupation, strange as it may seem for one so nearsighted, was delivering funds sent by money order. Nowadays, as often as Victor's name comes up, I refer to him as poor Victor. Just as my mama became my poor mama as a result of a family excursion to the harbor breakwater, Victor, who carried money for the post office, was transformed into poor Victor by the loss of his glasses, though other considerations played a part.

'Have you ever run into poor Victor?' I ask my friend Vittlar on visiting days. But since that streetcar ride from Flingern to

Gerresheim – I shall speak of it later on – Victor Weluhn has been lost to us. It can only be hoped that his persecutors have also been unable to locate him, that he has found his glasses or another suitable pair, and if it isn't too much to ask, that he is carrying money again, if not for the Polish Post Office – that cannot be – then for the Post Office of the Federal Republic, and that, nearsighted but bespectacled, he is once more delivering happiness in the form of multicolored banknotes and hard coins.

'Isn't it awful,' said Jan, supporting Kobyella on one side and panting under the weight.

'And the Lord knows how it will end,' said Victor, who was holding up the other side, 'if the English and the French don't come.'

'Oh, they'll come all right. Only yesterday Rydt-Smigly said on the radio: "We have their pledge," he said. "If it comes to war, all France will rise as one man." ' Jan had difficulty in maintaining his assurance until the end of the sentence, for though the sight of his own blood on the back of his hand cast no doubt on the Franco-Polish treaty of mutual defense, it did lead him to fear that he might bleed to death before all France should rise as one man and, faithful to its pledge, overrun the Siegfried Line.

'They must be on their way right now. And this very minute the British fleet must be plowing through the Baltic.' Victor Weluhn loved strong, resounding locutions. He paused on the stairs, his right hand was immobilized by the wounded janitor, but he flung its left counterpart aloft to welcome the saviors with all five fingers: 'Come, proud Britons!'

While the two of them, slowly, earnestly weighing the relations between Poland and her Western allies, conveyed Kobyella to the emergency hospital, Oskar's thoughts leafed through Gretchen Scheffler's books, looking for relevant passages. Keyser's *History of the City of Danzig*: 'During the war of 1870 between Germany and France, on the afternoon of August 21, 1870, four French warships entered Danzig Bay, cruised in the roadstead and were already directing their guns at the harbor and city. The following night, however, the screw corvette *Nymph*, commanded by Corvette Captain Weickhmann, obliged the formation to withdraw.'

Shortly before we reached the storeroom for undeliverable mail on the second floor, I formed the opinion, which was later to be confirmed, that in this desperate hour for the Polish Post Office and the whole of Poland, the Home Fleet was lying, nicely sheltered, in some firth in northern Scotland, and, as for the large French Army, that it was still at luncheon, confident that a few reconnaissance patrols in the vicinity of the Maginot Line had squared it with Poland and the Franco-Polish treaty of mutual defense.

Outside the storeroom and emergency hospital, we ran into Dr. Michon; he still had on his steel helmet and his silk handkerchief still peered from his breast pocket; he was talking with one Konrad, the liaison officer sent from Warsaw. Seized with fifty-seven varieties of terror, Jan made it plain that he was seriously wounded. Victor Weluhn, who was unhurt and as long as he had his glasses could reasonably be expected to do his bit with a rifle, was sent down to the main hall. Jan and I were admitted to the windowless room, scantily lit by tallow candles, the municipal power plant having declared and implemented its unwillingness to supply the Polish Post Office with current.

Dr. Michon wasn't exactly taken in by Jan's wounds but on the other hand he had little faith in my uncle's military prowess. Converting the postal secretary and former rifleman into a medic, he commissioned him to care for the wounded and also – at this point the postmaster and commander honored me with a brief and, it seemed to me, despairing pat on the head – to keep an eye on me, lest the poor child get mixed up in the fighting.

The field howitzer scored a hit down below. We took quite a shaking. Michon in his helmet, Konrad, the liaison officer from Warsaw, and Weluhn dashed down to their battle stations. Jan and I found ourselves with seven or eight casualties in a sealed-off room where the sounds of battle were muffled. The candles hardly flickered when the howitzer struck home. It was quiet in spite, or perhaps because, of the moaning around us. With awkward haste Jan wrapped some strips of bed sheet around Kobyella's thighs; then he prepared to treat his own wounds. But his cheek and the back of his hand had stopped bleeding. His cuts had nothing to say for themselves, yet they must have hurt and the pain fed his terror, which had no outlet in the low-ceilinged, stuffy room. Frantically he looked through his pockets and found the complete deck of cards. From then till the bitter end we played skat.

Thirty-two cards were shuffled, cut, dealt, and played. Since all the mail baskets were occupied by wounded men, we sat Kobyella down against a basket. When he kept threatening to keel over, we tied him into position with a pair of braces taken from one of the wounded men. We made him sit up straight, we forbade him to drop his cards, for we needed Kobyella. What could we have done without a third? Those fellows in the mail baskets could hardly tell black from red; they had lost all desire to play skat. Actually Kobyella didn't much feel like it either. He would have liked to lie down. Just let things take their course, that was all Kobyella wanted. He just wanted to look on, his janitor's hands inactive for once in his life, to look on through lowered lashless eyelids as the demolition work was completed. But we wouldn't stand for such fatalism, we tied him fast and forced him to play the third hand, while Oskar played the second – and no one was the least bit surprised that Tom Thumb could play skat.

When for the first time I lent my voice to adult speech and bid 'Eighteen,' Jan, it is true, emerged from his cards, gave me a brief and inconceivably blue look, and nodded. 'Twenty?' I asked him. And Jan without hesitation: 'Yes, yes.' And I: 'Two? Three? Twenty-four?' No, Jan couldn't go along. 'Pass.' And Kobyella? Despite the braces, he was sagging again. But we pulled him up and waited for the noise of a shell that had struck somewhere far from our gaming room to die down. Then Jan hissed into the erupting silence: 'Twenty-four, Kobyella. Didn't you hear the boy's bid?'

Who knows from what cavernous depths the janitor awoke. Ever so slowly he jacked up his eyelids. Finally his watery gaze took in the ten cards which Jan had pressed discreetly, conscientiously refraining from looking at them, into his hand.

'Pass,' said Kobyella, or rather we read it from his lips, which were too parched for speech.

I played a club single. On the first tricks Jan, who was playing contra, had to roar at Kobyella and poke him good-naturedly in the ribs, before he would pull himself together and remember to play. I started by drawing off all their trumps. I sacrificed the king of clubs, which Jan took with the jack of spades, but having no diamonds, I recovered the lead by trumping Jan's ace of diamonds and drew his ten of hearts with my jack. Kobyella discarded the nine of diamonds, and then I had a sure thing with my chain of hearts. One-play-two-contra-three-schneider-four-times-clubs-is-forty-eight-or-twelve-pfennigs. It wasn't until the next hand, when I attempted a more than risky grand without two that things began to get exciting. Kobyella, who had had both jacks but only bid up to thirty-three, took my jack of diamonds with the jack of clubs. Then, as though revived by the trick he had taken, he followed up with the ace of diamonds and I had to follow suit. Jan threw in the ten, Kobyella took the trick and played the king, I should have taken but didn't, instead I discarded the eight of clubs, Jan threw in what he could, he even led once with the ten of spades, I bettered it and I'm damned if Kobyella didn't top the pile with the jack of spades, I'd forgotten that fellow or rather thought Jan had it, but no, Kobyella had it. Naturally he led another spade, I had to discard, Jan played something or other, the rest of the tricks were mine but it was too late: grand-without-two-play-three-makes-sixty-hundred-and-twenty-for-the-loser-makes-thirty-pfennigs. Jan loaned me two gulden in change, and I paid up, but despite the hand he had won, Kobyella had collapsed again, he didn't take his winnings and even the first antitank shell bursting on the stairs didn't mean a thing to the poor janitor, though it was his staircase that he had cleaned and polished relentlessly for years.

Fear regained possession of Jan when the door to our mailroom rattled and the flames of our tallow candles didn't know what had come over them or in which direction to lie down. Then it grew relatively still in the stairwell and the next antitank shell burst far off against the façade. But even so, Jan Bronski shuffled with an insane frenzy and misdealt twice, but I let it pass. As long as there was shooting to be heard, Jan was too overwrought to hear anything I could say, he neglected to follow suit, even forgot to discard the skat, and sometimes sat motionless, his sensory ear attuned to the outer world while we waited impatiently for him to get on with the game. Yet, while Jan's play became more and more distraught, Kobyella kept his mind pretty well on the game though from time to time he needed a poke in the ribs to keep him from sagging. His playing wasn't nearly as bad as the state he seemed to be in. He only collapsed after he had won a hand or had spoiled a grand for Jan or me. He didn't care one bit whether he had won or lost. It was only the game itself that could hold his attention. As we counted up the score, he would sag on the borrowed braces, giving no sign of life except for the terrifying spasms of his Adam's apple.

This card game was a great strain on Oskar too. Not that the sounds connected with the siege and defense of the post office bothered him particularly. For me the nerve-racking part of it was that for the first time I had suddenly dropped all disguises – though not, I resolved, for long. Up until then I had been my true unvarnished self only for Master Bebra and his somnambulistic Lady Roswitha. And now I had laid myself bare not only to my uncle and presumptive father but also to an invalid janitor (neither of whom, to be sure, looked much like a future witness) as the fifteen-year-old inscribed in my birth certificate, who, despite his diminutive stature, played a rather foolhardy but not unskillful hand of skat. My will was up to it, but the exertion was too much for my gnomelike proportions. After barely an hour of skat-playing, my limbs and head were aching abominably.

Oskar felt inclined to give up; it would not have been hard for him to slip away between two of the shell hits which were shaking the building in quick succession, if a feeling of responsibility, such as he had never before experienced, had not bidden him hold on and counter his presumptive father's terror by the one effective means: skat-playing.

And so we played and refused to let Kobyella die. He just couldn't get around to it, for I took good care that the cards should be in movement at all times. When, after an explosion on the stairs, the candles toppled over and the flames vanished, it was I who had the presence of mind to do the obvious, to take a match from Jan's pocket, and Jan's gold-tipped cigarettes too while I was at it; it was I who restored light to the world, lit a comforting Regatta for Jan, and pierced the night with flame upon flame before Kobyella could take advantage of the darkness to make his getaway.

Oskar stuck two candles on his new drum and set down the cigarettes within reach. He wanted none for himself, but from time to time he would pass Jan a cigarette and put one between Kobyella's distorted lips. That helped; the tobacco appeased and consoled, though it could not prevent Jan Bronski from losing game after game. Jan perspired and, as he had always done when giving his whole heart to the game, tickled his upper lip with the tip of his tongue. He grew so excited that in his enthusiasm he began to call me Alfred or Matzerath and to take Kobyella for my poor mama. When out in the corridor someone screamed: 'They've got Konrad!' he looked at me reproachfully and said: 'For goodness' sake, Alfred, turn off the radio. A man can't hear himself think in here.'

Jan became really irritated when the door was torn open and the lifeless Konrad was dragged in.

'Close that door. You're making a draft!' he protested. There was indeed a draft. The candles flickered alarmingly and came to their senses only when, after dumping Konrad in a corner, the men had closed the door behind them. A strange threesome we made. Striking us from below, the candlelight gave us the look of all-powerful wizards. Kobyella bid his hearts without two; twenty-seven, thirty, he said, or rather gurgled. His eyes had a way of rolling out of sight and there was something in his right shoulder that wanted to come out, that quivered and jumped like mad. It finally stopped, but Kobyella sagged face foremost, setting the mail basket which he was tied to rolling with the dead braceless man on top of it. With one blow into which he put all his strength Jan brought Kobyella and the laundry basket to a standstill, whereupon Kobyella, once more prevented from sneaking out on us, finally piped 'Hearts.' To which Jan hissed 'Contra' and Kobyella 'Double contra.' At this moment it came to Oskar that the defense of the Polish Post Office had been successful, that the assailants, having scarcely begun the war, had already lost it, even if they succeeded in occupying Alaska and Tibet, the Easter Islands and Jerusalem.

The only bad part of it was that Jan was unable to play out his beautiful, sure-thing grand hand with four and a declaration of schneider schwarz.

He led clubs; now he was calling me Agnes while Kobyella had become his rival Matzerath. With an air of false innocence he played the jack of diamonds – I was much happier to be my poor mama for him than to be Matzerath – then the jack of hearts – it didn't appeal to me one bit to be mistaken for Matzerath. Jan waited impatiently for Matzerath, who in reality was a crippled janitor named Kobyella, to play; that took time, but then Jan slammed down the ace of hearts and was absolutely unwilling and unable to understand, the truth is he had never fully understood, he had never been anything but a blue-eyed boy, smelling of cologne and incapable of understanding certain things, and so he simply could not understand why Kobyella suddenly dropped all his cards, tugged at the laundry basket with the letters in it and the dead man on top of the letters, until first the dead man, then a layer of letters, and finally the whole excellently plaited basket toppled over, sending us a wave of letters as though we were the addressees, as though the thing for us to do now was to put aside our playing cards and take to reading our correspondence or collecting stamps. But Jan didn't feel like reading and he didn't feel like collecting, he had collected too much as a child, he wanted to play, he wanted to play out his grand hand to the end, he wanted to win, Jan did, to triumph. He lifted Kobyella up, set the basket back on its wheels, but let the dead man lie and also neglected to put the letters back in the basket. Anyone could see that the basket was too light, yet Jan showed the utmost astonishment when Kobyella, dangling from the light, unstable basket, just wouldn't sit still but sagged lower and lower. Finally Jan shouted at him: 'Alfred, I beg of you, don't be a spoilsport. Just this one little game and then we'll go home. Alfred, will you listen to me!'

Oskar arose wearily, fought down the increasing pains in his limbs and head, laid his wiry little drummer's hands on Jan Bronski's shoulders, and forced himself to speak, gently but with authority: 'Leave him be, Papa. He can't play any more. He's dead. We can play sixty-six if you like.'

Jan, whom I had just addressed as my father, released the janitor's mortal envelope, gave me an overflowing blue stare, and wept nononono . . . I patted him, but still he said no. I kissed him meaningly, but still he could think of nothing but his interrupted grand.

'I would have won it, Agnes. It was a sure thing.' So he lamented to me in my poor mama's stead, and I – his son – threw myself into the role, yes, he was right, I said, I swore that he would have won, that to all intents and purposes he actually had won, that he simply must believe what his Agnes was telling him. But Jan wouldn't believe; he believed neither me nor my mama. For a time his weeping was loud and articulate; then his plaint subsided into an unmodulated blubbering, and he began to dig skat cards from beneath the cooling Mount Kobyella; some he scraped from between his legs, and the avalanche of mail yielded a few. Jan would not rest before he had recovered all thirty-two. One by one, he cleaned them up, wiping away the sticky blood. When he had done, he shuffled and prepared to deal. Only then did his well-shaped forehead – it would have been unjust to call it low, though it was rather too smooth, rather too impenetrable – admit the thought that there was no third skat hand left in this world.

It grew very still in the storeroom for undeliverable mail. Outside, as well, a protracted minute of silence was dedicated to the memory of the world's last skat hand. To Oskar it seemed, though, that the door was slowly opening. Looking over his shoulder, expecting heaven knows what supernatural apparition, he saw Victor Weluhn's strangely blind empty face. 'I've lost my glasses, Jan. Are you still there? We'd better run for it. The French aren't coming or, if they are, they'll be too late. Come with me, Jan. Lead me, I've lost my glasses.'

Maybe Victor thought he had got into the wrong room. For when he received no answer and no guiding arm was held out to him, he withdrew his unspectacled face and closed the door. I could still hear Victor's first few steps as, groping his way through the fog, he embarked on his flight.

Heaven knows what comical incident may have transpired in Jan's little head to make him start laughing, first softly and plaintively but then loudly and boisterously, making his fresh, pink little tongue quiver like a bell clapper. He tossed the cards into the air, caught them, and finally, when a Sunday quietness descended on the room with its silent men and silent letters, began, with wary measured movements and bated breath, to build an ever so fragile house of cards. The seven of spades and the queen of clubs provided the foundation. Over them spanned the king of diamonds. The nine of hearts and the ace of spades, spanned by the eight of clubs, became a second foundation adjacent to the first. He then proceeded to join the two with tens and jacks set upright on their edges, using queens and aces as crossbeams, so that one part of the edifice supported another. Then he decided to set a third story upon the second, and did so with the spellbinding hands that my mother must have known in connection with other rituals. And when he leaned the queen of hearts against the king with the red heart, the edifice did not collapse; no, airily it stood, breathing softly, delicately, in that room where the dead breathed no more and the living held their breath. That house of cards made it possible for us to sit back with folded hands, and even the skeptical Oskar, who was quite familiar with the rules of statics governing the construction of card houses, was enabled to forget the acrid smoke and stench that crept, in wisps and coils, through the cracks in the door, making it seem as though the little room with the card house in it were right next door and wall to wall with hell.

They had brought in flame throwers; fearing to make a frontal assault, they had decided to smoke out the last defenders. The operation had been so successful that Dr. Michon resolved to surrender the post office. Removing his helmet, he had picked up a bed sheet and waved it; and when that didn't satisfy him, he had pulled out his silk handkerchief with his other hand and waved that too.

It was some thirty scorched, half-blinded men, arms upraised and hands folded behind their necks, who left the building through the left-hand side door and lined up against the wall of the courtyard where they waited for the slowly advancing Home Guards. Later the story went round that in the brief interval while the Home Guards were coming up, three or four had got away: through the post office garage and the adjoining police garage they had made their way to an evacuated and hence unoccupied house on the Rähm, where they had found clothes, complete with Party insignia. Having washed and dressed, they had vanished singly into thin air. One of them, still according to the story, had gone to an optician's in the Altstädtischer Graben, had himself fitted out with a pair of glasses, his own having been lost in the battle of the post office. Freshly bespectacled, Victor Weluhn – for it was he – allegedly went so far as to have a beer on the Holzmarkt, and then another, for the flame throwers had made him thirsty. Then with his new glasses, which dispersed the environing mists up to a certain point, but not nearly as well as his old ones had done, had started on the flight that continues – such is the doggedness of his pursuers! – to this day.

The others, however – as I have said, there were some thirty of them who couldn't make up their minds to run for it – were standing against the wall across from the side entrance when Jan leaned the queen of hearts against the king of hearts and, thoroughly blissful, took his hands away.

What more shall I say? They found us. They flung the door open, shouting 'Come out!' stirred up a wind, and the card house collapsed. They had no feeling for this kind of architecture. Their medium was concrete. They built for eternity. They paid no attention whatever to Postal Secretary Bronski's look of indignation, of bitter injury. They didn't see that before coming out Jan reached into the pile of cards and picked up something, or that I, Oskar, wiped the candle ends from my newly acquired drum, took the drum but spurned the candle ends, for light was no problem with all those flashlights shining in our eyes. They didn't even notice that their flashlights blinded us and made it hard for us to find the door. From behind flashlights and rifles, they shouted: 'Come out of there,' and they were still shouting 'Come out' after Jan and I had reached the corridor. These 'come outs' were directed at Kobyella, at Konrad from Warsaw, at Bobek and little Wischnewski, who in his lifetime had kept the telegraph window. The invaders were alarmed at these men's unwillingness to obey. I gave a loud laugh every time the Home Guards shouted 'Come out' and after a while they saw they were making fools of themselves, stopped shouting, and said, 'Oh!' Then they led us to the thirty in the courtyard with arms upraised and hands folded behind their necks, who were thirsty and having their pictures taken for the newsreels.

The camera had been mounted on top of an automobile. As we were led out through the side door, the photographers swung it around at us and shot the short strip that was later shown in all the movie houses.

I was separated from the thirty defenders by the wall. At this point Oskar remembered his gnomelike stature, he remembered that a three-year-old is not responsible for his comings and goings.

Again he felt those disagreeable pains in his head and limbs; he sank to the ground with his drum, began to thrash and flail, and ended up throwing a fit that was half real and half put on, but even during the fit he hung on to his drum. They picked him up and handed him into an official car belonging to the SS Home Guard. As the car drove off, taking him to the City Hospital, Oskar could see Jan, poor Jan, smiling stupidly and blissfully into the air. In his upraised hands he held a few skat cards and with one hand – holding the queen of hearts, I think – he waved to Oskar, his departing son.

He Lies in Saspe

I have just reread the last paragraph. I am not too well satisfied, but Oskar's pen ought to be, for writing tersely and succinctly, it has managed, as terse, succinct accounts so often do, to exaggerate and mislead, if not to lie.

Wishing to stick to the truth, I shall try to circumvent Oskar's pen and make a few corrections: in the first place, Jan's last hand, which he was unhappily prevented from playing out and winning, was not a grand hand, but a diamond hand without two; in the second place, Oskar, as he left the storeroom, picked up not only his new drum but also the old broken one, which had fallen out of the laundry basket with the dead braceless man and the letters. Furthermore, there is a little omission that needs filling in: No sooner had Jan and I left the storeroom for undeliverable mail at the behest of the Home Guards with their 'Come outs,' their flashlights, and their rifles, than Oskar, concerned for his comfort and safety, made up to two Home Guards who struck him as good-natured, uncle-like souls, put on an imitation of pathetic sniveling, and pointed to Jan, his father, with accusing gestures which transformed the poor man into a villain who had dragged off an innocent child to the Polish Post Office to use him, with typically Polish inhumanity, as a buffer for enemy bullets.

Oskar counted on certain benefits for both his drums, and his expectations were not disappointed: the Home Guards kicked Jan in the small of the back and battered him with their rifle stocks, but left me both drums, and one middle-aged Home Guard with the careworn creases of a paterfamilias alongside of his nose and mouth stroked my cheeks, while another, tow-headed fellow, who kept laughing and in laughing screwed up his eyes so you couldn't see them, picked me up in his arms, which was distasteful and embarrassing to Oskar.

Even today, if fills me with shame to think, as I sometimes do, of this disgusting behavior of mine, but I always comfort myself with the thought that Jan didn't notice, for he was still preoccupied with his cards and remained so to the end, that nothing, neither the funniest nor the most fiendish inspiration of the Home Guards, could ever again lure his attention away from those cards. Already Jan had gone off to the eternal realm of card houses and castles in Spain, where men believe in happiness, whereas the Home Guards and I – for at this moment Oskar counted himself among the Home Guards – stood amid brick walls, in stone corridors, beneath ceilings with plaster cornices, all so intricately interlocked with walls and partitions that the worst was to be feared for the day when, in response to one set of circumstances or another, all this patchwork we call architecture would lose its cohesion.

Of course this belated perception cannot justify me, especially when it is remembered that I have never been able to look at a building under construction without fancying this same building in process of being torn down and that I have always regarded card houses as the only dwellings worthy of humankind. And there is still another incriminating factor. That afternoon I felt absolutely certain that Jan Bronski was no mere uncle or presumptive father, but my real father. Which put him ahead of Matzerath then and for all time: for Matzerath was either my father or nothing at all.

September 1, 1939 – I assume that you too, on that ill-starred afternoon, recognized Bronski, the blissful builder of card houses, as my father – that date marks the inception of my second great burden of guilt.

Even when I feel most sorry for myself, I cannot deny it: It was my drum, no, it was I myself, Oskar the drummer, who dispatched first my poor mama, then Jan Bronski, my uncle and father, to their graves.

But on days when an importunate feeling of guilt, which nothing can dispel, sits on the very pillows of my hospital bed, I tend, like everyone else, to make allowances for my ignorance – the ignorance which came into style in those years and which even today quite a few of our citizens wear like a jaunty and oh, so becoming little hat.

Oskar, the sly ignoramus, an innocent victim of Polish barbarism, was taken to the City Hospital with brain fever. Matzerath was notified. He had reported my disappearance the night before, although his ownership of me had never been proved.

As for the thirty men with upraised arms and hands folded behind their necks, they – and Jan – after having their pictures taken for the newsreels, were taken first to the evacuated Victoria School, then to Schiesstange Prison. Finally, early in October, they were entrusted to the porous sand behind the wall of the run-down, abandoned old cemetery in Saspe.

How did Oskar come to know all this? I heard it from Leo Schugger. For of course there was never any official announcement to tell us against what wall the thirty-one men were shot and what sand was shoveled over them.

Hedwig Bronski first received a notice to vacate the flat in Ringstrasse, which was taken over by the family of a high-ranking officer in the Luftwaffe. While she was packing with Stephan's help and preparing to move to Ramkau – where she owned a house and a few acres of forest and farmland – she received the communication which made her officially a widow. She gazed at it out of eyes which mirrored but did not penetrate the sorrows of the world, and it was only very slowly, with the help of her son Stephan, that she managed to distil the sense of it.

Here is the communication:

COURT-MARTIAL, EBERHARDT ST. L. GROUP 41/39
ZOPPOT, 6 OCT. 1939

MRS. HEDWIG BRONSKI,
You are hereby informed that Bronski, Jan, has been sentenced to death for irregular military activity and executed.

ZELEWSKI
(*Inspector of Courts-Martial*)

So you see, not a word about Saspe. Out of solicitude for the men's relatives, who would have been crushed by the expense of caring for so large and flower-consuming a mass grave, the authorities assumed full responsibility for maintenance and perhaps even for transplantation. They had the sandy soil leveled and the cartridge cases removed, except for one – one is always overlooked – because cartridge cases are out of place in any respectable cemetery, even an abandoned one.

But this one cartridge case, which is always left behind, the one that concerns us here, was found by Leo Schugger, from whom no burial, however discreet, could be kept secret. He, who knew me from my poor mama's funeral and from that of my scar-covered friend Herbert Truczinski, who assuredly knew where they had buried Sigismund Markus – though I never asked him about it – was delighted, almost beside himself with joy, when late in November, just after I was discharged from the hospital, he found an opportunity to hand me the telltale cartridge case.

But before I guide you in the wake of Leo Schugger to Saspe Cemetery with that slightly oxidized cartridge case, which perhaps had harbored the lead kernel destined for Jan, I must ask you to compare two hospital beds, the one I occupied in the children's section of the Danzig City Hospital, and the one I am lying in now. Both are metal, both are painted with white enamel, yet there is a difference. The bed in the children's section was shorter but higher, if you apply a yardstick to the bars. Although my preference goes to the shorter but higher cage of 1939, I have found peace of mind in my present makeshift bed, intended for grownups, and learned not to be too demanding. Months ago I put in a petition for a higher bed, though I am perfectly satisfied with the metal and the white enamel. But let the management grant my petition or reject it; I await the result with equanimity.

Today I am almost defenseless against my visitors; then, on visiting days in the children's section, a tall fence separated me from Visitor Matzerath, from Visitors Greff (Mr. and Mrs.) and Scheffler (Mr. and Mrs.). And toward the end of my stay at the hospital, the bars of my fence divided the mountain-of-four-skirts named after my grandmother Anna Koljaiczek, into worried, heavily breathing compartments. She came, sighed, raised her great multifarious hands, disclosing her cracked pink palms, then let hands and palms sink in despair. So violent was her despair that they slapped against her thighs, and I can hear that slapping to this day, though I can give only a rough imitation of it on my drum.

On the very first visit she brought along her brother Vincent Bronski, who clutched the bars of my bed and spoke or sang softly but incisively and at great length about the Virgin Mary, Queen of Poland. Oskar was glad when there was a nurse nearby. For those two were my accusers, they turned their unclouded Bronski eyes on me and, quite oblivious of the time I was having with this brain fever I had acquired while playing skat in the Polish Post Office, expected me to comfort them with a kind word, to reassure them about Jan's last hours, spent between terror and card houses. They wanted a confession from me that would put Jan in the clear; as though I had it in my power to clear him, as though my testimony carried any weight.

Supposing I had sent an affidavit to the court-martial of the Eberhardt Group. What would I have said? I, Oskar Matzerath, avow and declare that on the evening of August 31 I waited outside Jan Bronski's home for him to come home and lured him, on the ground that my drum needed repairing, back to the Polish Post Office, which Jan Bronski had left because he did not wish to defend it.

Oskar made no such confession; he did nothing to exculpate his presumptive father. Every time he decided to speak, to tell the old people what had happened, he was seized with such convulsions that at the demand of the head nurse his visiting hours were curtailed and the visits of his grandmother Anna and his presumptive grandfather Vincent were forbidden.

The two old people, who had walked in from Bissau and brought me apples, left the children's ward with the wary, helpless gait of country folk in town. And with each receding step of my grandmother's four skirts and her brother's black Sunday suit, redolent of cow dung, my burden of guilt, my enormous burden of guilt increased.

So much happened at once. While Matzerath, the Greffs, the Schefflers crowded round my bed with fruit and cakes, while my grandmother and Uncle Vincent walked in from Bissau by way of Goldkrug and Brenntau because the railroad line from Karthaus to Langfuhr had not yet been cleared, while nurses, clad in anesthetic white, babbled hospital talk and substituted for angels in the children's ward, Poland was not yet lost, almost lost, and finally, at the end of those famous eighteen days, Poland was lost, although it was soon to turn out that Poland was not yet lost; just as today, despite the efforts of the Silesian and East Prussian patriotic societies, Poland is not yet lost.

O insane cavalry! Picking blueberries on horseback. Bearing lances with red and white pennants. Squadrons of melancholy, squadrons of tradition. Picture-book charges. Racing across the fields before Lodz and Kutno. At Modlin substituting for the fortress. Oh, so brilliantly galloping! Always waiting for the sunset. Both foreground and background must be right before the cavalry can attack, for battles were made to be picturesque and death to be painted, poised in mid-gallop, then falling, nibbling blueberries, the dog roses crackle and break, providing the itch without which the cavalry will not jump. There are the Uhlans, they've got the itch again, amid haystacks – another picture for you – wheeling their horses, they gather round a man, his name in Spain is Don Quixote, but here he is Pan Kichot, a pure-blooded Pole, a noble, mournful figure, who has taught his Uhlans to kiss ladies' hands on horseback, ah, with what aplomb they will kiss the hand of death, as though death were a lady; but first they gather, with the sunset behind them – for color and romance are their reserves – and ahead of them the German tanks, stallions from the studs of the Krupps von Bohlen und Halbach, no nobler steeds in all the world. But Pan Kichot, the eccentric knight in love with death, the talented, too talented knight, half-Spanish half-Polish, lowers his lance with the red-and-white pennant and calls on his men to kiss the lady's hand. The storks clatter white and red on the rooftops, and the sunset spits out pits like cherries, as he cries to his cavalry: 'Ye noble Poles on horseback, these are no steel tanks, they are mere windmills or sheep, I summon you to kiss the lady's hand.'

So rode the squadrons out against the grey steel foe, adding another dash of red to the sunset glow.

Oskar hopes to be forgiven for the poetic effects. He might have done better to give figures, to enumerate the casualties of the Polish cavalry, to commemorate the so-called Polish Campaign with dry but eloquent statistics. Or another solution might be to let the poem stand but append a footnote.

Up to September 20, I could hear, as I lay in my hospital bed, the roaring of the cannon firing from the heights of the Jeschkental and Oliva forests. Then the last nest of resistance on Hela Peninsula surrendered. The Free Hanseatic City of Danzig celebrated the Anschluss of its brick Gothic to the Greater German Reich and gazed jubilantly into the blue eyes (which had one thing in common with Jan Bronski's blue eyes, namely their success with women) of Adolf Hitler, the Führer and Chancellor, as he stood in his black Mercedes distributing rectangular salutes.

In mid-October Oskar was discharged from the City Hospital. It was hard for me to take leave of the nurses. When one of them – her name was Berni or maybe Erni, I think – when Sister Erni or Berni gave me my two drums, the battered one that had made me guilty and the whole one that I had conquered during the battle of the Polish Post Office, it came to me that I hadn't thought of my drums for weeks, that there was something else in the world for me beside drums, to wit, nurses.

Matzerath held me by the hand as, still rather shaky on my three-year-old pins, I left the City Hospital with my instruments and my new self-knowledge, for the flat in Labesweg, there to face the tedious weekdays and still more tedious Sundays of the first war year.

One Tuesday late in November, I was allowed to go out for the first time after weeks of convalescence. As he was gloomily drumming through the streets, paying little attention to the cold rain, whom should Oskar run into on the corner of Max-Halbe-Platz and Brösener-Weg but Leo Schugger, the former seminarist.

We stood for some time exchanging embarrassed smiles, and it was not until Leo plucked a pair of kid gloves from the pockets of his morning coat and pulled the yellowish-white, skinlike coverings over his fingers and palms, that I realized whom I had met and what this encounter would bring me. Oskar was afraid.

For a while we examined the windows of Kaiser's grocery store, looked after a few streetcars of lines Number 5 and 9, which crossed on Max-Halbe-Platz, skirted the uniform houses on Brösener-Weg, revolved several times round an advertising pillar, studied a poster telling when and how to exchange Danzig guldens for reichsmarks, scratched a poster advertising Persil soap powder, and found a bit of red under the blue and white but let well enough alone. We were just starting back for Max-Halbe-Platz when suddenly Leo Schugger pushed Oskar with both hands into a doorway, reached under his coat-tails with the gloved fingers of his left hand, poked about in his pants pocket, sifted the contents, found something, studied it for a moment with his fingers, then, satisfied with what he had found, removed his closed fist from his pocket, and let his coat-tail fall back into place. Slowly he thrust forward the gloved fist, forward and still forward, pushing Oskar against the wall of the doorway; longer and longer grew his arm, but the wall did not recede. That arm, I was beginning to think, was going to jump out of its socket, pierce my chest, pass through it, and make off between my shoulder blades and the wall of this musty doorway. I was beginning to fear that Oskar would never see what Leo had in his fist, that the most he would ever learn in this doorway was the text of the house regulations, which were not very different from those in his own house in Labesweg. And then the five-fingered skin opened.

Pressing against one of the anchor buttons on my sailor coat, Leo's glove opened so fast that I could hear his finger joints crack. And there, on the stiff, shiny leather that protected the inside of his hand, lay the cartridge case.

When Leo closed his fist again, I was prepared to follow him. That little scrap of metal had spoken to me directly. We walked side by side down Brösener-Weg; this time no shopwindow, no advertising pillar detained us. We crossed Magdeburger-Strasse, left behind us the last two tall, boxlike buildings on Brösener-Weg, topped at night by warning lights for planes that were taking off or about to land, skirted the fence of the airfield for a time, but then moved over to the asphalt road, where the going was less wet, and followed the rails of the Number 5 streetcar line in the direction of Brösen.

We said not a word, but Leo still held the cartridge case in his glove. The weather was miserably cold and wet, but when I wavered and thought of going back, he opened his fist, made the little piece of metal hop up and down on his palm, and so lured me on, a hundred paces, then another hundred paces, and even resorted to music when, shortly before the city reservation in

Saspe, I seriously decided to turn back. He turned on his heel, held the cartridge case with the open end up, pressed the hole like the mouthpiece of a flute against his protruding, slavering lower lip, and projected a new note, now shrill, now muffled as though by the fog, into the mounting whish of the rain. Oskar shivered. It wasn't just the music that made him shiver; the wretched weather, which seemed made to order for the occasion, had more than a little to do with it. So intense was my misery that I hardly bothered to hide my shivering.

What lured me to Brösen? Leo, the pied piper, of course, piping on his cartridge case. But there was more to it than that. From the roadstead and from Neufahrwasser, from behind the November fog, the sirens of the steamships and the hungry howling of a torpedo boat entering or leaving the harbor carried over to us past Schottland, Schellmühl, and Reichskolonie. In short, it was child's play for Leo, supported by foghorns, sirens, and a whistling cartridge case, to draw a frozen Oskar after him.

Not far from the wire fence which turns off in the direction of Pelonken and divides the airfield from the new drill ground, Leo Schugger stopped and stood for a time, his head cocked on one side, his saliva flowing over the cartridge case, observing my trembling little body. He sucked in the cartridge case, held it with his lower lip, then, following a sudden inspiration, flailed wildly with his arms, removed his long-tailed morning coat, and threw the heavy cloth, smelling of moist earth, over my head and shoulders.

We started off again. I don't know whether Oskar was any less cold. Sometimes Leo leapt five steps ahead and then stopped; as he stood there in his rumpled but terrifying white shirt, he seemed to have stepped directly out of a medieval dungeon, perhaps the Stockturm, to illustrate a disquisition on What the Lunatics Will Wear. Whenever Leo turned his eyes on Oskar staggering along in the long coat, he burst out laughing and flapped his wings like a raven. I must indeed have looked like a grotesque bird, a raven or crow, especially with those coat-tails dragging over the asphalt highway like a train or a huge mop and leaving a broad majestic track, which filled Oskar with pride whenever he looked back, and foreshadowed, if it did not symbolize, the tragic fate, not yet fully implemented, that slumbered within him.

236

Even before leaving Max-Halbe-Platz, I had suspected that Leo had no intention of taking me to Brösen or Neufahrwasser. From the very start it was perfectly clear that our destination could only be the cemetery in Saspe, near which a modern rifle range had been laid out for the Security Police.

From September to April the cars serving the seaside resorts ran only every thirty-five minutes. As we were leaving the suburb of Langfuhr, a car without trailer approached from the direction of Brösen and passed us by. A moment later the car that had been waiting on the Magdeburger-Strasse siding came up behind us and passed by. It was not until we had almost reached the cemetery, near which there was a second siding, that another car moved up clanking and tinkling behind us, and soon its companion piece, which we had long seen waiting in the mist up ahead, its yellow light shining wet in the fog, started up and passed us by.

The flat morose face of the motorman was still sharp in Oskar's mind when Leo Schugger led him off the asphalt road, through loose sand not very different from that of the dunes by the beach. The cemetery was square with a wall running round it. We went in on the south side, through a little gate that was covered with ornamental rust and only supposed to be locked. Most of the tombstones were of black Swedish granite or diorite, rough hewn on the back and sides and polished in front. Some leaned perilously, others had already toppled. Unfortunately Leo left me no time to look at them more closely. The place was poor in trees; five or six gnarled and moth-eaten scrub pines, that was all. Mama in her lifetime had admired this tumble-down graveyard; as she often said, it was her favorite among last resting places. And now she lay in Brenntau. There the soil was richer, elms and maples grew.

By way of an open gate that had lost its grating, Leo led me out of the cemetery through the northern wall, before I could attune my thoughts to its romantic decay. Close behind the wall the soil was flat and sandy. Amid the steaming fog, broom, scrub pine, and dog rose stretched out toward the coast. When I looked back toward the cemetery, it struck me at once that a piece of the northern wall had been freshly whitewashed.

Close to this stretch of wall, which gave the impression of

being new, as painfully white as Leo's rumpled shirt, Leo became very active. He took great long strides which he appeared to count; at all events, he counted aloud and, as Oskar believes to this day, in Latin. Whatever this litany was, he chanted it as he had no doubt learned to do at the seminary. Leo marked a spot some ten yards from the wall and also set down a piece of wood not far from the whitewashed portion, where, it seemed pretty obvious, the wall had been mended. All this he did with his left hand, for in his right hand he held the cartridge case. Finally, after interminable searching and measuring, he bent down near the piece of wood and there deposited the hollow metallic cylinder, slightly tapered at the front end, which had lodged a lead kernel until someone with a curved forefinger had exerted just enough pressure to evict the lead projectile and start it on its death-dealing change of habitat.

We stood and stood. The spittle flowed from Leo Schugger's mouth and hung down in threads. Wringing his gloves, he chanted for a time in Latin, but stopped after a while as there was no one present who knew the responses. From time to time he turned about and cast a peevish, impatient look over the wall toward the highway, especially when the streetcars, empty for the most part, stopped at the switch and clanged their bells as they passed one another by and moved off in opposite directions. Leo must have been waiting for mourners. But neither on foot nor by car did anyone arrive to whom he could extend a glove in condolence.

Once some planes roared over us, preparing to land. We did not look up, we submitted to the noise without bothering to ascertain that three planes of the Ju-52 type, with blinking lights on their wing tips, were preparing to land.

Shortly after the motors had left us – the stillness was as painful as the wall facing us was white – Leo Schugger reached into his shirt and pulled something out. A moment later he was standing beside me. Tearing his crow costume from Oskar's shoulders, he darted off coastward, into the broom, dog rose, and scrub pine, and in departing dropped something with a calculated gesture suggesting that it was meant to be found.

Only when Leo had vanished for good – for a time he could be seen moving about in the foreground like a spook, until at last he was swallowed up by low-lying pools of milky mist – only when I was all alone with the rain, did I reach out for the object that lay in the sand: it was a skat card, the seven of spades.

A few days after this meeting at Saspe Cemetery, Oskar met his grandmother Anna Koljaiczek at the weekly market in Langfuhr. Now that there was no more borderline at Bissau, she was able once again to bring her eggs, butter, cabbages, and winter apples to market. The people bought plentifully, they had begun to lay in stocks, for food rationing was in the offing. Just as Oskar caught sight of his grandmother sitting behind her wares, he felt the skat card on his bare skin, beneath his coat, sweater, and undershirt. At first, while riding back from Saspe to Max-Halbe Platz, after a streetcar conductor had invited me to come along free of charge, I had meant to tear up that seven of spades. But Oskar did not tear it up. He gave it to his grandmother. She seemed to take fright behind her cabbages when she saw him. Maybe it passed through her mind that Oskar's presence could bode no good. But then she motioned the three-year-old urchin, half-hiding behind some baskets of fish, to come over. Oskar took his time; first he examined a live codfish nearly a yard long, lying in a bed of moist seaweed, then watched some crabs crawling about in a basket; finally, himself adopting the gait of a crab, he approached his grandmother's stand with the back of his sailor coat and, turning to show her his gold anchor buttons, jostled one of the sawhorses under her display and started the apples rolling.

Schwerdtfeger came over with his hot bricks wrapped in newspaper, shoved them under my grandmother's skirts, removed the cold bricks with his rake as he had done ever since I could remember, made a mark on the slate that hung from his neck, and proceeded to the next stand while my grandmother handed me a shining apple.

What could Oskar give her if she gave him an apple? He gave her first the skat card and then the cartridge case, for he hadn't abandoned that in Saspe either. For quite some time Anna Koljaiczek stared uncomprehending at these two so disparate objects. Then Oskar's mouth approached her aged cartilaginous ear beneath her kerchief and, throwing caution to the winds, I whispered, thinking of Jan's pink, small, but fleshy ear with the long, well-shaped lobes. 'He's lying in Saspe,' Oskar whispered and ran off, upsetting a basket of cabbages.

Maria

While history, blaring special communiqués at the top of its lungs, sped like a well-greased amphibious vehicle over the roads and waterways of Europe and through the air as well, conquering everything in its path, my own affairs, which were restricted to the belaboring of lacquered toy drums, were in a bad way. While the history-makers were throwing expensive metal out the window with both hands, I, once more, was running out of drums. Yes, yes, Oskar had managed to save a new instrument with scarcely a scratch on it from the Polish Post Office, so lending some significance to the defense of said post office, but what could Naczalnik Junior's drum mean to me, Oskar, who in my least troubled days had taken barely eight weeks to transform a drum into scrap metal?

Distressed over the loss of my nurses, I began to drum furiously soon after my discharge from the City Hospital. That rainy afternoon in Saspe Cemetery did nothing to diminish my drumming; on the contrary, Oskar redoubled his efforts to destroy the last witness to his shameful conduct with the Home Guards, namely, that drum.

But the drum withstood my assaults; as often as I struck it, it struck back accusingly. The strange part of it is that during this pounding, whose sole purpose was to eradicate a very definite segment of my past, Victor Weluhn, the carrier of funds, kept turning up in my mind, although, nearsighted as he was, his testimony against me couldn't have amounted to much. But hadn't he managed to escape despite his nearsightedness? Could it be that the nearsighted see more than others, that Weluhn, whom I usually speak of as poor Victor, had read my gestures like the movements of a black silhouette, that he had seen through my betrayal and that now, on his flight, he would carry Oskar's secret, Oskar's shame, all over the world with him?

It was not until the middle of December that the accusations of the serrated red and white conscience round my neck began to carry less conviction: the lacquer cracked and peeled; the tin grew thin and fragile. Condemned to look on at this death agony, I was eager, as one always is in such cases, to shorten the sufferings of the moribund, to hasten the end. During the last weeks of Advent, Oskar worked so hard that Matzerath and the neighbors held their heads, for he was determined to settle his accounts by Christmas Eve; I felt confident that for Christmas I should receive a new and guiltless drum.

I made it. On the twenty-fourth of December I was able to rid my body and soul of a rusty, dissipated, shapeless something suggestive of a wrecked motor car; by discarding it, I hoped, I should be putting the defense of the Polish Post Office behind me forever.

Never has any human being – if you are willing to accept me as one – known a more disappointing Christmas than Oskar, who found everything imaginable under the Christmas tree, save only a drum.

There was a set of blocks that I never opened. A rocking swan, viewed by the grownups as the most sensational of presents, was supposed to turn me into Lohengrin. Just to annoy me, no doubt, they had had the nerve to put three or four picture books on the gift table. The only presents that struck me as in some sense serviceable were a pair of gloves, a pair of boots, and a red sweater knitted by Gretchen Scheffler. In consternation Oskar looked from the building blocks to the swan, and stared at a picture in one of the picture books, showing an assortment of teddy bears which were not only too cute for words but, to make matters worse, held all manner of musical instruments in their paws. One of these cute hypocritical beasts even had a drum; he looked as if he knew how to drum, as if he were just about to strike up a drum solo; while as for me, I had a swan but no drum, probably more than a thousand building blocks but not one single drum; I had mittens for bitter-cold winter nights, but between my gloved fists no round, smooth-lacquered, metallic, and ice-cold object that I might carry out into the winter nights, to warm their icy heart.

Oskar thought to himself: Matzerath has hidden the drum. Or

Gretchen Scheffler, who has come with her baker to polish off our Christmas goose, is sitting on it. They are determined to enjoy my enjoyment of the swan, the building blocks, the picture books, before disgorging the real treasure. I gave in; I leafed like mad through the picture books, swung myself upon the swan's back and, fighting back my mounting repugnance, rocked for at least half an hour. Despite the overheated apartment I let them try on the sweater; aided by Gretchen Scheffler, I slipped into the shoes. Meanwhile the Greffs had arrived, the goose had been planned for six, and after the goose, stuffed with dried fruit and masterfully prepared by Matzerath, had been consumed, during the dessert, consisting of stewed plums and pears, desperately holding a picture book which Greff had added to my four other picture books; after soup, goose, red cabbage, boiled potatoes, plums, and pears, under the hot breath of a tile stove which had hot breath to spare, we all sang, Oskar too, a Christmas carol and an extra verse, Rejoice, and Ochristmastree, ochristmastree, greenarethybellstingalingtingelingyearafteryear, and I was good and sick of the whole business; outside the bells had already started in, and I wanted my drum; the alcoholic brass band, to which Meyn the musician had formerly belonged, blew so the icicles outside the window ... but I wanted my drum, and they wouldn't give it to me, they wouldn't cough it up. Oskar: 'Yes!' The others: 'No!' Whereupon I screamed, it was a long time since I had screamed, after a long rest period I filed my voice once again into a sharp, glass-cutting instrument; I killed no vases, no beer glasses nor light bulbs, I opened up no showcase nor deprived any spectacles of their power of vision – no, my vocal rancor was directed against all the balls, bells, light refracting silvery soap bubbles that graced the Ochristmastree: with a tinkle tinkle and a klingaling, the tree decorations were shattered into dust. Quite superfluously several dustpans full of fir needles detached themselves at the same time. But the candles went on burning, silent and holy, and with it all Oskar got no drum.

Matzerath had no perception. I don't know whether he was trying to wean me away from my instrument or whether it simply didn't occur to him to keep me supplied, amply and punctually, with drums. I was threatened with disaster. And it was only the coincidence that just then the mounting disorder in our shop could no longer be overlooked which brought help, before it was too late, both to me and the shop.

Since Oskar was neither big enough nor in any way inclined to stand behind a counter selling crackers, margarine, and synthetic honey, Matzerath, whom for the sake of simplicity I shall once more call my father, took on Maria Truczinski, my poor friend Herbert's youngest sister, to work in the store.

She wasn't just called Maria; she was one. It was not only that she managed, in only a few weeks, to restore the reputation of our shop; quite apart from her firm though friendly business management, to which Matzerath willingly submitted, she showed a definite understanding for my situation.

Even before Maria took her place behind the counter, she had several times offered me an old washbasin as a substitute for the lump of scrap metal with which I had taken to stamping accusingly up and down the more than hundred steps of our stairway. But Oskar wanted no substitute. Steadfastly he refused to drum on the bottom of a washbasin. But no sooner had Maria gained a firm foothold in the shop than she succeeded, Matzerath to the contrary notwithstanding, in fulfilling my desires. It must be admitted that Oskar could not be moved to enter a toystore with her. The inside of one of those emporiums bursting with multicolored wares would surely have inspired painful comparisons with Sigismund Markus' devastated shop. The soul of kindness, Maria would let me wait outside while she attended to the purchases alone; every four or five weeks, according to my needs, she would bring me a new drum. And during the last years of the war, when even toy drums had grown rare and come to be rationed, she resorted to barter, offering the storekeepers sugar or a sixteenth of a pound of real coffee and receiving my drum under the counter in return. All this she did without sighing, shaking her head, or glancing heavenward, but seriously and attentively and as matter-of-factly as though dressing me in freshly washed, properly mended pants, stockings, and school smocks. Though, in the years that followed, the relations between Maria and me were in constant flux and have not been fully stabilized to this day, the way in which she hands me a drum has remained unchanged, though the prices are a good deal higher than in 1940.

Today Maria subscribes to a fashion magazine. She is becoming more chic from one visiting day to the next. But what of those days?

Was Maria beautiful? She had a round, freshly washed face and the look in her somewhat too prominent grey eyes with their short but abundant lashes and their dark, dense brows that joined over the nose, was cool but not cold. High cheekbones – when it was very cold, the skin over them grew taut and bluish and cracked painfully – gave the planes of which her face was constructed a reassuring balance which was scarcely disturbed by her diminutive but not unbeautiful or comical nose, which though small was very well shaped. Her forehead was small and round, marked very early by thoughtful vertical creases toward the middle. Rising from the temples, her brown, slightly curly hair, which still has the sheen of wet tree trunks, arched tightly over her little round head, which, like Mother Truczinski's, showed little sign of an occiput. When Maria put on her white smock and took her place behind the counter in our store, she still wore braids behind her florid, healthy ears, the lobes of which unfortunately did not hang free but grew directly into the flesh of her lower jaws – there were no ugly creases, but still the effect was degenerate enough to admit of inferences about Maria's character. Later on, Matzerath talked her into a permanent and her ears were hidden. Today, beneath tousled, fashionably short-cropped hair, Maria exhibits only the lobes of her ears; but she hides the flaw in her beauty beneath large clips that are not in very good taste.

Similar in its way to her small head with its full cheeks, prominent cheekbones, and large eyes on either side of her small, almost insignificant nose, Maria's body, which was distinctly on the small side, disclosed shoulders that were rather broad, full breasts swelling upward from her armpits, and an ample pelvis and rear end, which in turn were supported by legs so slender, though quite robust, that you could see between them beneath her pubic hair.

It is possible that Maria was a trifle knock-kneed in those days. Moreover, it seemed to me that in contrast to her figure, which was that of a grown woman, her little red hands were childlike and her fingers reminded me rather of sausages. To this day there is something childlike about those paws of hers. Her feet, however, shod at the time in lumpy hiking shoes and a little later in my poor mama's chic, but outmoded high heels, which were scarcely becoming to her, gradually lost their childish redness and drollness in spite of the ill-fitting hand-me-downs they were forced into and gradually adapted themselves to modern shoe fashions of West German and even Italian origin.

Maria did not talk much but liked to sing as she was washing the dishes or filling blue pound and half-pound bags with sugar. When the shop closed and Matzerath busied himself with his accounts, or on Sundays, when she sat down to rest, Maria would play the harmonica that her brother Fritz had given her when he was drafted and sent to Gross-Boschpol.

Maria played just about everything on her harmonica. Scout songs she had learned at meetings of the League of German Girls, operatta tunes, and song hits that she had heard on the radio or learned from her brother Fritz, who came to Danzig for a few days at Easter 1940 on official business. But Maria never took out her 'Hohner' during business hours. Even when there were no customers about, she refrained from music and wrote price tags and inventories in a round childlike hand.

Though it was plain for all to see that it was she who ran the store and had won back a part of the clientele that had deserted to our competitors after my poor mama's death, her attitude toward Matzerath was always respectful to the point of servility; but that didn't embarrass Matzerath, who had never lacked faith in his own worth.

'After all,' he argued when Greff the greengrocer and Gretchen Scheffler tried to nettle him, 'it was me that hired the girl and taught her the business.' So simple were the thought processes of this man who, it must be admitted, became more subtle, more sensitive, and in a word more interesting only when engaged in his favorite occupation, cookery. For Oskar must give the devil his due: his Kassler Rippchen with sauerkraut, his pork kidneys in mustard sauce, his Wiener Schnitzel, and, above all, his carp with cream and horse radish, were splendid to look upon and delectable to smell and taste. There was little he could teach Maria in the shop, because the girl had a native business sense whereas Matzerath himself knew little about selling over the counter though he had a certain gift for dealing with the wholesalers, but he did teach Maria to boil, roast, and stew; for though she had spent two years working for a family of civil servants in Schidlitz, she could barely bring water to a boil when she first came to us.

Soon Matzerath's program was very much what it had been in my poor mama's lifetime: he reigned in the kitchen, outdoing himself from Sunday roast to Sunday roast, and spent hours of his time contentedly washing the dishes. In addition, as a sideline so to speak, he attended to the buying and ordering, the accounts with the wholesale houses and the Board of Trade – occupations which became more and more complicated as the war went on – carried on, and not without shrewdness, the necessary correspondence with the fiscal authorities, decorated the showcase with considerable imagination and good taste, and conscientiously performed his so-called Party duties. All in all – while Maria stood imperturbably behind the counter – he was kept very busy.

You may ask: what am I getting at with these preparatory remarks, why have I gone into so much detail about a young girl's cheekbones, eyebrows, ear lobes, hands, and feet? I agree with you perfectly, I too am opposed to this kind of description. Oskar knows perfectly well that he has succeeded at best in distorting Maria's image in your mind, perhaps for good. For this reason I will add one sentence that should make everything clear: If we disregard all the anonymous nurses, Maria was Oskar's first love.

I became aware of this state of affairs one day when, as seldom happened, I listened to my drumming. I could not help noticing the insistent new note of passion which Oskar, despite all his precautions, was communicating to his drum. Maria took this drumming in good part. But I was none too pleased when she set her harmonica to her lips, assumed an unprepossessing frown, and felt called upon to accompany me. Often, though, while darning stockings or filling sugar bags, her quiet eyes would gaze earnestly and attentively at me and my drumsticks and, before resuming her work, she would run her hand slowly and sleepily over my short-cropped hair.

Oskar, who ordinarily could not bear the slightest contact, however affectionately meant, accepted Maria's hand and became so enslaved to this caress that he would often, quite consciously, spend hours drumming the rhythms that brought it on, until at last Maria's hand obeyed and brought him well-being.

After a while Maria began to put me to bed at night. She

undressed me, washed me, helped me into my pajamas, advised me to empty my bladder one last time before going to sleep, prayed with me, although she was a Protestant, an Our Father, three Hail Mary's and from time to time a JesusfortheeIlivejesusfortheeIdie, and finally tucked me in with a friendly, drowsymaking face.

Pleasant as were the last minutes before putting out the light – gradually I exchanged Our Father and JesusfortheeIlive for the tenderly allusive StaroftheseaIgreetthee and MaryIlovethee – these daily preparations for bed embarrassed me. They almost shattered my self-control, reducing Oskar – who had always prided himself on his mastery over his features – to the telltale blushes of starry-eyed maidens and tormented young men. Oskar must own that every time Maria undressed me, put me in the zinc tub, scrubbed the dust of a drummer's day off me with washcloth, brush, and soap, every time it was brought home to me that I, almost sixteen, was standing or sitting mother-naked in the presence of a girl somewhat older than myself, I blushed long and loud.

But Maria did not seem to notice my change of color. Could she have thought that washcloth and brush brought such a flush to my cheeks? Or was Maria modest and tactful enough to see through my daily evenglow and yet to overlook it?

I am still subject to this sudden flush, impossible to hide, that may last as much as five minutes or longer. Like my grandfather, Koljaiczek the firebug, who turned flaming red whenever the word 'match' was dropped in his hearing, the blood rushes to my head whenever anyone, even a total stranger, speaks in my presence of small children being tubbed and scrubbed before they go to bed at night. Oskar stands there like an Indian; those around me call me eccentric if not vicious; for what can it mean to them that little children should be soaped, scrubbed, and visited with a washcloth in their most secret places?

Maria, on the other hand, was a child of nature: she did the most daring things in my presence without embarrassment. Before scrubbing the living room or bedroom floor, she would hoist her skirt to mid-thigh and take off her stockings, a gift from Matzerath, for fear of soiling them. One Saturday after the shop had closed – Matzerath had business at the local Party headquarters

– Maria shed her skirt and blouse, stood beside me in a pitiful but clean petticoat, and began to remove some spots from her skirt and artificial silk blouse with gasoline.

What could it have been that gave Maria, whenever she removed her outer garments and as soon as the smell of gasoline had worn off, a pleasantly and naively bewitching smell of vanilla? Did she rub herself with some such extract? Was there a cheap perfume with this sort of smell? Or was this scent as specific to her as, for example, ammonia to Mrs. Kater or rancid butter to my grandmother's skirts? Oskar, who liked to get to the bottom of things, investigated the vanilla: Maria did not anoint herself. Maria just smelled that way. Yes, I am still convinced that she was not even aware of the scent that clung to her; for on Sunday, when, after roast veal with mashed potatoes and cauliflower in brown butter, a vanilla pudding trembled on the table because I was tapping my foot on the table leg, Maria, who was wild about other varieties of pudding, ate but little and with evident distaste, while Oskar to this day is in love with this simplest and perhaps most commonplace of all puddings.

In July, 1940, shortly after the special communiqués announcing the rapid success of the French campaign, the Baltic bathing season opened. While Maria's brother Fritz, now a corporal, was sending the first picture postcards from Paris, Matzerath and Maria decided that Oskar must go to the beach, that the sea air would surely be good for his health. It was decided that Maria should take me at midday – the shop was closed from one to three – to the beach at Brösen, and if she stayed out until four, Matzerath said, it didn't matter; he liked to stand behind the counter from time to time and show himself to the customers.

A blue bathing suit with an anchor sewn on it was purchased for Oskar. Maria already had a green one with red trimmings that her sister Guste had given her as a confirmation present. Into a beach bag from Mama's days were stuffed a white woolen bathrobe of the same vintage and, quite superfluously, a pail and shovel and a set of sand molds. Maria carried the bag, while I carried my drum.

Oskar was apprehensive of the streetcar ride past the cemetery at Saspe. Was it not to be feared that the sight of this silent, yet so eloquent spot would put a crimp in his enthusiasm about bathing, which was no more than moderate to begin with? What, Oskar asked himself, will the ghost of Jan Bronski do when his assassin, dressed for summer, goes jingling past his grave in a streetcar?

The Number 9 car stopped. The conductor announced Saspe. I looked fixedly past Maria in the direction of Brösen, whence the other car crept toward us, growing gradually larger. Mustn't let my eyes wander. What, after all, was there to look at? Scrub pines, rusty ironwork, a maze of tumble-down tombstones with inscriptions that only the thistles and wild oats could read. Under such circumstances, it was better to look out the open window and up into the sky: there they hummed, the fat Ju-52's, as only trimotored planes or enormous flies can hum in a cloudless July sky.

We moved up with a great clanging of bells and the other car cut off our view. The moment we passed the trailer, my head turned of its own accord and I was treated to the whole tumble-down cemetery and also a bit of the north wall; the white patch lay in the shadow, but it was still painfully white . . .

Then the cemetery was gone, we approached Brösen, and once again I looked at Maria. She had on a light summer dress with a flower pattern. On her round neck with its faintly radiant skin, over her well-upholstered collarbone, she wore a necklace of red wooden cherries, all the same size and simulating bursting ripeness. Was it my imagination or did I really smell it? Maria seemed to be taking her vanilla scent along with her to the Baltic. Oskar leaned slightly forward, took a long whiff of it, and in an instant vanquished the moldering Jan Bronski. The defense of the Polish Post Office had receded into history even before the flesh had fallen from the defenders' bones. Oskar, the survivor, had very different smells in his nostrils than that of his presumptive father, once so elegant a figure, now dust.

In Brösen Maria bought a pound of cherries, took me by the hand – well she knew that only she was permitted to do so – and led me through the pine woods to the bathing establishment. Though I was nearly sixteen – the attendant had no eye for such things – I was allowed into the ladies' section. Water: 65, said the blackboard, air: 80; wind: east; forecast: fair. Beside the blackboard hung a poster, dealing with artificial respiration. The victims all had on striped bathing suits, the rescuers wore mustaches, straw hats floated upon treacherous, turbulent waters.

The barefooted girl attendant went ahead. Around her waist, like a penitent, she wore a cord from which hung the enormous key that opened the cabins. Plank walks. Railings. Alongside the cabins a hard runner of coconut fiber. We had cabin Number 53. The wood of the cabin was warm, dry, and of a natural bluish-white hue that I should call blind. Beside the window hung a mirror that had ceased to take itself seriously.

First Oskar had to undress. This I did with my face to the wall and it was only reluctantly that I let Maria help me. Then Maria turned me round in her sturdy, matter-of-fact way, held out my new bathing suit, and forced me ruthlessly into the tight-fitting wool. No sooner had I buttoned the shoulder straps than she lifted me up on the wooden bench against the back wall of the cabin, put my drum and sticks on my lap, and began, with quick energetic movements, to undress.

First I drummed a little and counted the knotholes in the floor-boards. Then I stopped counting and drumming. It was quite beyond me why Maria, with oddly pursed lips, should whistle while removing her shoes, two high notes, two low notes, and while stripping off her socks. Whistling like the driver of a brewery truck, she took off the flowery dress, whistling she hung up her petticoat over her dress, dropped her brassiere, and still without finding a tune, whistled frantically while pulling her panties, which were really gym shorts, down to her knees, letting them slip to the floor, climbing out of the rolled-up pants legs, and kicking the shorts into the corner with one foot.

Maria frightened Oskar with her hairy triangle. Of course he knew from his poor mama that women are not bald down there, but for him Maria was not a woman in the sense in which his mama had shown herself to be a woman in her dealings with Matzerath or Jan Bronski.

And I recognized her at once. Rage, shame, indignation, disappointment, and a nascent half-comical, half-painful stiffening of my watering can under my bathing suit made me forget drum and drumsticks for the sake of the new stick I had developed.

Oskar jumped up and flung himself on Maria. She caught him with her hair. He buried his face in it. It grew between his lips.

Maria laughed and tried to pull him away. I drew more and more of her into me, looking for the source of the vanilla smell. Maria was still laughing. She even left me to her vanilla, it seemed to amuse her, for she didn't stop laughing. Only when my feet slipped and I hurt her – for I didn't let go the hair or perhaps it was the hair that didn't let me go – only when the vanilla brought tears to my eyes, only when I began to taste mushrooms or some acrid spice, in any case, something that was not vanilla, only when this earthy smell that Maria concealed behind the vanilla brought me back to the smell of the earth where Jan Bronski lay moldering and contaminated me for all time with the taste of perishability – only then did I let go.

Oskar slipped on the blind-colored boards of the bathhouse cabin and was still crying when Maria, who was laughing once more, picked him up, caressed him, and pressed him to the necklace of wooden cherries which was all she had on.

Shaking her head, she picked her hairs from between my lips and said in a tone of surprise: 'What a little rascal you are! You start up and you don't know what's what and then you cry.'

Fizz Powder

D does that mean anything to you? Formerly, you could buy it at any time of year in little flat packages. In our shop my mama sold woodruff fizz powder in a nauseatingly green little bag. Another sack that had the color of not-quite-ripe oranges claimed to have an orange flavor. There was also a raspberry flavor, and another variety which, if you poured fresh water over it, hissed, bubbled, and acted excited, and if you drank it before it quieted down, tasted very remotely like lemon, and had a lemon color in the glass, only more so: an artificial yellow masquerading as poison.

What else was on the package except for the flavor? Natural Product, it said. Patented. Protect Against Moisture, and, under a dotted line, Tear Here.

Where else could you buy this fizz powder? Not only in my

mama's shop was it for sale, but in all grocery stores, except for Kaiser's and the cooperatives. In the stores and at all refreshment stands a package cost three pfennigs.

Maria and I got ours free of charge. Only when we couldn't wait to get home were we obliged to stop at a grocery store or refreshment stand and pay three pfennigs or even six, because we could never get enough of it and often asked for two packages.

Who started up with the fizz powder? The old, old quarrel between lovers. I say Maria started it. Maria never claimed that Oskar started it. She left the question open and the most she would say, if pressed, was: 'The fizz powder started it.'

Of course everyone will agree with Maria. Only Oskar could not accept this verdict. Never would I have admitted that Oskar was seduced by a little package of fizz powder at three pfennigs. I was sixteen, I wanted to blame myself or Maria if need be, but certainly not a powder demanding to be protected against moisture.

It began a few days after my birthday. According to the calendar, the bathing season was drawing to an end. But the weather would hear nothing of September. After a rainy August, the summer showed its mettle; its belated accomplishment could be read on the bulletin board beside the artificial-respiration poster: air: 84; water: 68; wind: southwest; forecast: generally fair.

While Fritz Truczinski, a corporal in the air corps, sent postcards from Paris, Copenhagen, Oslo, and Brussels – the fellow was always traveling on official buisiness – Maria and I acquired quite a tan. In July we had occupied a place on the family beach. But here Maria had been exposed to the inept horseplay of some boys from the Conradinum and to interminable declarations of love emanating from a student at the Petri School; in mid-August we moved to the beach reserved for ladies, where we found a quiet spot near the water. Buxom ladies panted and puffed as they submerged their varicose veins up to their knees, and naked, misbehaved urchins waged war on fate; that is, they piled up sand into crude castles that kept toppling down.

The ladies' beach: when women are by themselves and think themselves unobserved, a young man – and Oskar was well aware of being a young man beneath the surface – will do well to close his eyes rather than become a witness, however involuntary, to uninhibited womanhood.

We lay in the sand, Maria in her green bathing suit bordered with red, I in my blue one. The sand slept, the sea slept, the shells had been crushed and did not listen. Amber, which allegedly keeps you awake, was elsewhere; the wind, which according to the bulletin board came from the southwest, fell gradually asleep; the whole wide sky, which had surely been overexerting itself, did nothing but yawn; Maria and I were also somewhat tired. We had already bathed and we had eaten after, not before, bathing. Our cherries, reduced to moist pits, lay in the sand beside bleached cherry pits from the previous year.

At the sight of so much transience, Oskar took to picking up handfuls of sand mingled with fresh young cherry pits and others that were one or a thousand years old, and sifting it over his drum; so he impersonated an hourglass and at the same time tried to think himself into the role of death by playing with bones. Under Maria's warm, sleepy flesh I imagined parts of her surely wide-awake skeleton; I relished the view between radius and ulna, played counting games up and down her spine, reached in through her iliac fossae and played with her sternum.

Despite all the fun I was having playing the part of death with my hourglass and my skeleton, Maria moved. Blindly, trusting wholly to her fingers, she reached into the beach bag and looked for something, while I dropped what was left of my sand and cherry pits on the drum, which was almost half-buried. When she failed to find what she was looking for, probably her harmonica, Maria turned the bag inside out: a moment later, something lay on the beach towel; but it was not a harmonica; it was a package of woodruff fizz powder.

Maria affected surprise. Or maybe she really was surprised. As for me, my surprise was real: over and over I asked myself, as I still ask myself: how did this package of fizz powder, this miserable cheap stuff, bought only by the children of dock workers and the unemployed, because they had no money for real pop, how did this unsalable article get into our beach bag?

While Oskar pondered, Maria grew thirsty. And breaking off my meditations, I too, quite against my will, had to confess to an irresistible thirst. We had no cup, and besides it was at least thirty-five paces to the drinking water if Maria went and nearly fifty if I did. To borrow a cup from the attendant and use the tap by the bathhouse, it was necessary to pass over burning sand between mountains of flesh shining with Nivea oil, some lying on their backs, others on their bellies.

We both dreaded the errand and left the package lying on the towel. Finally I picked it up, before Maria showed any sign of picking it up. But Oskar only put it back on the towel in order that Maria might reach out for it. Maria did not reach out. So I reached out and gave it to Maria. Maria gave it back to Oskar. I thanked her and made her a present of it. But she wanted no presents from Oskar. I had to put it back on the towel. There it lay a long while without stirring.

Oskar wishes to make it clear that it was Maria who after an oppressive pause picked up the package again. But that was not all: she tore off a strip of paper exactly on the dotted line where it said to Tear Here. Then she held out the opened package – to me. This time Oskar declined with thanks. Maria managed to be vexed. She resolutely laid the open package down on the towel. What was there for me to do but to pick the package up before sand should get into it, and offer it to Maria.

Oskar wishes to make it clear that it was Maria who made one finger disappear into the opening of the package, who coaxed the finger out again, and held it up vertically for inspection: something bluish-white, fizz powder, was discernible on the fingertip. She offered me the finger. I took it of course. Although it made my nose prickle, my face succeeded in registering pleasure. It was Maria who held out a hollow hand. Oskar could hardly have helped pouring some fizz powder into the pink bowl. What she would do with the little pile of powder, she did not know. This mound in the cup of her hand was something too new, too strange. At this point I leaned forward, summoning up all my spit, and directed it at the powder; I repeated the operation and leaned back only when I was out of saliva.

In Maria's hand a hissing and bubbling set in. The woodruff erupted like a volcano, seethed like the greenish fury of some exotic nation. Something was going on that Maria had never seen and probably never felt, for her hand quivered, trembled, and tried to fly away, for woodruff was biting her, woodruff penetrated her skin, woodruff excited her, gave her a feeling, a feeling, a feeling . . .

The green grew greener, but Maria grew red, raised her hand to her mouth, and licked her palm with a long tongue. This she did several times, so frantically that Oskar was very close to supposing that her tongue, far from appeasing the woodruff feeling that so stirred her, raised it to the limit, perhaps beyond the limit, that is appointed to all feeling.

Then the feeling died down. Maria giggled, looked around to make sure there had been no witnesses, and when she saw that the sea cows breathing in bathing suits were motionless, indifferent, and Nivea-brown, she lay down on the towel; against the white background, her blushes died slowly away.

Perhaps the seaside air of that noonday hour might still have sent Oskar off to sleep, if Maria, after only a few minutes, had not sat up again and reached out once more for the package, which was still half-full. I do not know whether she struggled with herself before pouring the rest of the powder into her palm, which was no longer a stranger to the effect of woodruff. For about as long as a man takes to clean his glasses, she held the package on the left and the bowl on the right, motionless and antagonistic. Not that she directed her gaze toward the package or the hollow hand, or looked back and forth between half-full and empty; no, Maria looked between package and hand with a stern scowl. But her sternness was soon to prove weaker than the half-full package. The package approached the hollow hand, the hand came to meet the package, the gaze lost its sternness sprinkled with melancholy, became curious, and then frankly avid. With painstakingly feigned indifference, she piled up the rest of the woodruff fizz powder in her well-upholstered palm, which was dry in spite of the heat, dropped package and indifference, propped up the filled hand on the now empty one, rested her grey eyes on the powder for a time, then looked at me, gave me a grey look, her grey eyes were demanding something of me. It was my saliva she wanted, why didn't she take some of her own, Oskar had hardly any left, she certainly had much more, saliva doesn't replenish itself so quickly, she should kindly take her own, it was just as good, if not better, in any case she surely had more than I, because I couldn't make it so quickly and also because she was bigger than Oskar.

Maria wanted my saliva. From the start it was perfectly plain that only my spit could be considered. She did not avert those demanding eyes from me, and I blamed this cruel obstinacy of hers on those ear lobes which, instead of hanging free, grew straight into her lower jaws. Oskar swallowed; he thought of things which ordinarily made his mouth water, but – it was the fault of the sea air, the salt air, the salty sea air no doubt – my salivary glands were on strike. Goaded by Maria's eyes, I had to get up and start on my way. My labor was to take more than fifty steps through the burning sand, looking neither to left nor right, to climb the still more burning steps to the bathhouse, to turn on the tap, to twist my head and hold my mouth under it, to drink, to rinse, to swallow in order that Oskar might be replenished.

When I had completed the journey, so endless and bordered by such terrible sights, from the bathhouse to our white towel, I found Maria lying on her belly, her head nestling in her arms. Her braids lay lazy on her round back.

I poked her, for Oskar now had saliva. Maria didn't budge. I poked her again. Nothing doing. Cautiously I opened her left hand. She did not resist: the hand was empty, as though it had never seen any woodruff. I straightened the fingers of her right hand: pink was her palm, with moist lines, hot and empty.

Had Maria resorted to her own saliva? Had she been unable to wait? Or had she blown away the fizz powder, stifling that feeling before feeling it; had she rubbed her hand clean on the towel until Maria's familiar little paw reappeared, with its slightly superstitious mound of the moon, its fat Mercury, and its solidly padded girdle of Venus?

Shortly after that we went home, and Oskar will never know whether Maria made the fizz powder fizz for the second time that same day or whether it was not until a few days later that the mixture of fizz powder with my spittle became, through repetition, a vice for herself and for me.

Chance, or if you will a chance pliant to our wishes, brought it about that on the evening of the bathing day just described – we were eating blueberry soup followed by potato pancakes – Matzerath informed Maria and me, ever so circumspectly, that he had joined a little skat club made up of members of the local Party group, that he would meet his new skat partners, who were all unit leaders, two evenings a week at Springer's restaurant, that Sellke, the new local group leader, would attend from time to time, and that that in itself obliged him to be present, which unfortunately meant leaving us alone. The best arrangement, he thought, would be for Oskar to sleep at Mother Truczinski's on skat nights.

Mother Truczinski was agreed, all the more so as this solution appealed to her far more than the proposal which Matzerath, without consulting Maria, had made her the day before, to wit, that instead of my spending the night at Mother Truczinski's, Maria should sleep on our sofa two nights a week.

Up until then Maria had slept in the broad bed where my friend Herbert had formerly laid his scarred back. This extraordinarily heavy piece of furniture stood in the small rear room. Mother Truczinski had her bed in the living room. Guste Truczinski, who still waited on table at the snack bar in the Hotel Eden, lived at the hotel; she occasionally came home on her day off, but rarely spent the night, and when she did, it was on the couch. When Fritz Truczinski, laden with presents, came home on furlough from distant lands, he slept in Herbert's bed, Maria took Mother Truczinski's bed, while the old woman camped on the couch.

This order of things was disturbed by my demands. Originally I was expected to sleep on the couch. This plan I rejected out of hand. Then Mother Truczinski offered to cede me her bed and take the couch for herself. Here Maria objected, her mother needed her sleep, her mother must not be made uncomfortable. Very simply and directly Maria expressed her willingness to share Herbert's former bed with me. 'I'll be all right in the same bed with Oskar,' she said. 'He's only an eighth of a portion.'

And so, twice weekly, beginning a few days later, Maria carried my bedclothes from our ground-floor apartment to the Truczinski dwelling on the second floor and prepared a night lodging for me and my drum on the left side of her bed. On Matzerath's first skat night nothing at all happened. Herbert's bed seemed frightfully big to me. I lay down first, Maria came in later. She had washed herself in the kitchen and entered the bedroom in an old-fashioned, absurdly long and absurdly starched nightgown. Oskar had expected her to be naked and hairy and was disappointed at first, but soon he was perfectly happy, because the heirloom nightgown made pleasant bridges, reminding him of trained nurses and their white draperies.

Standing at the washstand, Maria undid her braids and whistled. Maria always whistled while dressing or undressing, doing or undoing her braids. Even while combing her hair, she never wearied of squeezing out those two notes between her pursed lips, without ever arriving at a tune.

The moment Maria put her comb aside, the whistling stopped. She turned, shook her hair once again, put the washstand in order with a few quick strokes. Order made her frolicsome: she threw a kiss at her photographed, retouched, and mustachioed father in the ebony frame, then with exaggerated gusto jumped into bed and bounced a few times. At the last bounce she pulled up the eiderdown and vanished beneath the mountain as far as her chin. I was lying under my own quilt and she didn't touch me at all; she stretched out a well-rounded arm from under the eiderdown, groped about overhead for the light cord, found it, and switched out the light. Only when it was dark did she say, in much too loud a voice: 'Good night!'

Maria was soon breathing evenly. I do not think she was pretending; it is quite likely that she did drop right off to sleep, for the quantities of work she did each day certainly called for corresponding quantities of sleep.

For quite some time, absorbing and sleep-dispelling images passed before Oskar's eyes. For all the dense darkness between the far walls and the blacked-out windows, blonde nurses bent over to examine Herbert's scarred back, from Leo Schugger's white rumpled shirt arose – what else would you expect? – a sea gull, which flew until it dashed itself to pieces against a cemetery wall, which instantly took on a freshly whitewashed look. And so on. Only when the steadily mounting, drowsy-making smell of vanilla made the film flicker before his eyes did Oskar begin to breathe as peacefully as Maria had been doing for heaven knows how long.

Three days later I was treated to the same demure tableau of maidenly going-to-bed. She entered in her nightgown, whistled while undoing her braids, whistled while combing her hair, put the comb down, stopped whistling, put the washstand in order, threw the photo a kiss, made her wild leap, took hold of the eiderdown, and caught sight – I was contemplating her back – caught sight of a little package – I was admiring her lovely long hair – discovered something green on the quilt – I closed my eyes, resolved to wait until she had grown used to the sight of the fizz powder. The bedsprings screamed beneath the weight of a Maria flopping down backward, I heard the sound of a switch, and when I opened my eyes because of the sound, Oskar was able to confirm what he already knew; Maria had put out the light and was breathing irregularly in the darkness; she had been unable to accustom herself to the sight of the fizz powder. However, it seemed not unlikely that the darkness by her ordained had only given the fizz powder an intensified existence, bringing woodruff to bloom and mingling soda bubbles with the night.

I am almost inclined to think that the darkness was on Oskar's side. For after a few minutes – if one can speak of minutes in a pitch-dark room – I became aware of stirrings at the head end of the bed; Maria was fishing for the light cord, the cord bit, and an instant later I was once more admiring the lovely long hair falling over Maria's sitting nightgown. How steady and yellow shone the light bulb behind the pleated lampshade cover! The eiderdown still bulged untouched on the foot end of the bed. The package on top of the mountain hadn't dared to budge in the darkness. Maria's ancestral nightgown rustled, a sleeve rose up with the little hand belonging to it, and Oskar gathered saliva in his mouth.

In the course of the weeks that followed, the two of us emptied over a dozen little packages of fizz powder, mostly with woodruff flavoring, then, when the woodruff ran out, lemon or raspberry, according to the very same ritual, making it fizz with my saliva, and so provoking a sensation which Maria came to value more and more. I developed a certain skill in the gathering of saliva, devised tricks that sent the water running quickly and abundantly to my mouth, and was soon able, with the contents of one package, to give Maria the desired sensation three times in quick succession.

Maria was pleased with Oskar; sometimes, after her orgy of fizz powder, she pressed him close and kissed him two or three times, somewhere in the face. Then she would giggle for a moment in the darkness and quickly fall asleep.

It became harder and harder for me to get to sleep. I was sixteen years old; I had an active mind and a sleep-discouraging need to associate my love for Maria with other, still more amazing possibilities than those which lay dormant in the fizz powder and, awakened by my saliva, invariably provoked the same sensation.

Oskar's meditations were not limited to the time after lights out. All day long I pondered behind my drum, leafed through my tattered excerpts from Rasputin, remembered earlier educational orgies between Gretchen Scheffler and my poor mama, consulted Goethe, whose *Elective Affinities* I possessed in excerpts similar to those from Rasputin; from the faith healer I took his elemental drive, tempered it with the great poet's world-encompassing feeling for nature; sometimes I gave Maria the look of the Tsarina or the features of the Grand Duchess Anastasia, selected ladies from among Rasputin's following of eccentric nobles; but soon, repelled by this excess of animal passion, I found Maria in the celestial transparency of an Ottilie or the chaste, controlled passion of a Charlotte. Oskar saw himself by turns as Rasputin in person, as his murderer, often as a captain, more rarely as Charlotte's vacillating husband, and once – I have to own – as a genius with the well-known features of Goethe, hovering over a sleeping Maria.

Strange to say, I expected more inspiration from literature than from real, naked life. Jan Bronski, whom I had often enough seen kneading my mother's flesh, was able to teach me next to nothing. Although I knew that this tangle, consisting by turns of Mama and Jan or Matzerath and Mama, this knot which sighed, exerted itself, moaned with fatigue, and at last fell stickily apart, meant love, Oskar was still unwilling to believe that love was love; love itself made him cast about for some other love, and yet time and time again he came back to tangled love, which he hated until the day when in love he practiced it; then he was obliged to defend it in his own eyes as the only possible love.

Maria took the fizz powder lying on her back. As soon as it bubbled up, her legs began to quiver and thrash and her nightgown, sometimes after the very first sensation, slipped up as far as her thighs. At the second fizz, the nightgown usually managed to climb past her belly and to bunch below her breasts. One night after I had been filling her left hand for weeks, I quite spontaneously – for there was no chance to consult Goethe or Rasputin first – spilled the rest of a package of raspberry powder into the hollow of her navel, and spat on it before she could protest. Once the crater began to seethe, Maria lost track of all the arguments needed to bolster up a protest: for the seething, foaming navel had many advantages over the palm of the hand. It was the same fizz powder, my spit remained my spit, and indeed the sensation was no different, but more intense, much more intense. The sensation rose to such a pitch that Maria could hardly bear it. She leaned forward, as though to quench with her tongue the bubbling raspberries in her navel as she had quenched the woodruff in the hollow of her hand, but her tongue was not long enough; her bellybutton was farther away than Africa or Tierra del Fuego. I, however, was close to Maria's bellybutton; looking for raspberries, I sank my tongue into it and found more and more of them; I wandered far afield, came to places where there was no forester to demand a permit to pick berries; I felt under obligation to cull every last berry, there was nothing but raspberries in my eyes, my mind, my heart, my ears, all I could smell in the world was raspberries, and so intent was I upon raspberries that Oskar said to himself only in passing: Maria is pleased with your assiduity. That's why she has turned off the light. That's why she surrenders so trustingly to sleep and allows you to go on picking; for Maria was rich in raspberries.

And when I found no more, I found, as though by chance, mushrooms in other spots. And because they lay hidden deep down beneath the moss, my tongue gave up and I grew an eleventh finger, for my ten fingers proved inadequate for the purpose. And so Oskar acquired a third drumstick – he was old enough for that. And instead of drumming on tin, I drummed on moss. I no longer knew if it was I who drummed or if it was Maria or if it was my moss or her moss. Do the moss and the eleventh finger belong to someone else and only the mushrooms to me? Did the little gentleman down there have a mind and a will of his own? Who was doing all this: Oskar, he, or I?

And Maria, who was sleeping upstairs and wide awake downstairs, who smelled upstairs of innocent vanilla and under the moss of pungent mushrooms, who wanted fizz powder, but not this little gentleman whom I didn't want either, who had declared his independence, who did just what he was minded to, who did things I hadn't taught him, who stood up when I lay down, who had other dreams than I, who could neither read nor write and nevertheless signed for me, who goes his own way to this very day, who broke with me on the very day I first took notice of him, who is my enemy with whom I am constrained, time and time again, to ally myself, who betrays me and leaves me in the lurch, whom I should like to auction off, whom I am ashamed of, who is sick of me, whom I wash, who befouls me, who sees nothing and flairs everything, who is so much a stranger to me that I should like to call him Sir, who has a very different memory from Oskar: for today when Maria comes into my room and Bruno discreetly slips off into the corridor, he no longer recognizes Maria, he can't, he won't, he sprawls most phlegmatically while Oskar's leaping heart makes my mouth stammer: 'Listen to me, Maria, tender suggestions. I might buy a compass and trace a circle around us; with the same compass, I might measure the angle of inclination of your neck while you are reading, sewing, or as now, tinkering with the buttons of my portable radio. Let the radio be, tender suggestions: I might have my eyes vaccinated and find tears again. At the nearest butcher shop Oskar would put his heart through the meat grinder if you would do the same with your soul. We might buy a stuffed animal to have something quiet between us. If I had the worms and you the patience, we might go fishing and be happier. Or the fizz powder of those days? Do you remember? You call me woodruff, I fizz up, you want still more, I give you the rest – Maria, fizz powder, tender suggestions.

'Why do you keep playing with those radio knobs, all you care about nowadays is the radio, as though you were taken with a mad passion for special communiqués.'

Special Communiqués

I t is hard to experiment on the white disk of my drum. I ought to have known that. My drum always wants the same wood. It wants to be questioned with drumsticks and to beat out striking answers or, with an easy, conversational roll, leave questions and answers open. So you see, my drum is neither a frying pan which, artificially heated, cooks raw meat to a crisp, nor a dance floor for couples who do not know whether they belong together. Consequently, even in the loneliest hours, Oskar has never strewn fizz powder on his drum, mixed his saliva with it, and put on a show that he has not seen for years and that I miss exceedingly. It is true that Oskar couldn't help trying an experiment with said powder, but he proceeded more directly and left the drum out of it; and in so doing, I exposed myself, for without my drum I am always exposed and helpless.

It was hard to procure the fizz powder. I sent Bruno to every grocery store in Grafenberg, I sent him to Gerresheim by streetcar. I asked him to try in town, but even at refreshment stands of the sort you find at the end of streetcar lines, Bruno could find no fizz powder. Young salesgirls had never heard of it, older shopkeepers remembered loquaciously; thoughtfully – as Bruno reported – they rubbed their foreheads and said: 'What is it you want? Fizz powder? That was a long time ago. Under Wilhelm they sold it, and under Adolf just in the beginning. Those were the good old days. But if you'd like a bottle of soda or a Coke?'

My keeper drank several bottles of soda pop or Coke at my expense without obtaining what I wanted, and nevertheless Oskar got his fizz powder in the end: yesterday Bruno brought me a little white package without a label; the laboratory technician of our mental hospital, a certain Miss Klein, had sympathetically agreed to open her drawers, phials, and reference works, to take a few grams of this and a few grams of that, and finally, after several attempts, had mixed up a fizz powder which, as Bruno reported, could fizz, prickle, turn green, and taste very discreetly of woodruff.

And today was visiting day. Maria came. But first came Klepp. We laughed together for three-quarters of an hour about something worth forgetting. I was considerate of Klepp and spared his Leninist feelings, avoided bringing up current events, and said nothing of the special announcement of Stalin's death, which had come to me over my little portable radio – given to me by Maria a few weeks ago. But Klepp seemed to know, for a crepe was sewn incompetently to the sleeve of his brown checked overcoat. Then Klepp arose and Vittlar came in. The two friends seem to have quarreled again, for Vittlar greeted Klepp with a laugh and made horns at him. 'Stalin's death surprised me as I was shaving this morning,' he said sententiously and helped Klepp into his coat. His broad face coated with unctuous piety, Klepp lifted up the black cloth on his sleeve: 'That's why I am in mourning,' he sighed and, giving an imitation of Armstrong's trumpet, intoned the first funereal measures of New Orleans Function: trrah trah-daha traah dada dadada – then he slipped through the door.

But Vittlar stayed; he didn't want to sit down, but hopped about in front of the mirror and for a few minutes we exchanged understanding smiles that had no reference to Stalin.

I don't know whether I meant to confide in Vittlar or to drive him away. I motioned him to come close, to incline an ear, and whispered in his great-lobed spoon: 'Fizz powder! Does that mean anything to you, Gottfried?' A horrified leap bore Vittlar away from my cage-bed; he thrust out his forefinger and in tones of theatrical passion that came easy to him, declaimed: 'Wilt thou seduce me with fizz powder, O Satan? Dost thou not know I am an angel?'

And like an angel, Vittlar, not without a last look at the mirror over the washbasin, fluttered away. The young folks outside the mental hospital are really an odd and affected lot.

And then Maria arrived. She has a new tailor-made spring suit and a stylish mouse-grey hat with a discreet, sophisticated strawcolored trimming. Even in my room she does not remove this *objet d'art*. She gave me a cursory greeting, held out her cheek to be kissed, and at once turned on the portable radio which was, to be sure, a present from her to me, but seems to have been intended for her own use, for it is the function of that execrable plastic box to replace a part of our conversation on visiting days. 'Did you hear the news this morning? Isn't it exciting? Or didn't you?' 'Yes, Maria,' I replied patiently. 'They haven't kept Stalin's death secret from me, but please turn off the radio.'

Maria obeyed without a word, sat down, still in her hat, and we spoke as usual about little Kurt.

'Just imagine, Oskar, the little rascal don't want to wear long stockings no more, when it's only March and more cold weather coming, they said so on the radio.' I ignored the weather report but sided with Kurt about the long stockings. 'The boy is twelve, Maria, he's ashamed to go to school in wool stockings, his friends make fun of him.'

'Well, as far as I'm concerned, his health comes first; he wears the stockings until Easter.'

This date was stated so unequivocally that I tried another tack. 'Then you should buy him ski pants, because those long woolen stockings are really ugly. Just think back to when you were his age. In our court in Labesweg. Shorty always had to wear stockings until Easter, you remember what they did to him? Nuchi Eyke, who was killed in Crete, Axel Mischke, who got his in Holland just before the war was over, and Harry Schlager, what did they do to Shorty? They smeared those long woolen stockings of his with tar so they stuck to his skin, and Shorty had to be taken to the hospital.'

'That wasn't the fault of the stockings, Susi Kater was to blame,' cried Maria furiously. Although Susi had joined the Blitz Girls at the very beginning of the war and was rumored to have married in Bavaria later on, Maria bore Susi, who was several years her senior, a lasting grudge such as women and only women can carry with them from childhood to a ripe old age. Even so, my allusion to Shorty's tar-daubed stockings produced a certain effect. Maria promised to buy Kurt ski pants. We were able to go on to something else. There was good news about Kurt. The school principal had spoken well of him at the parents' and teachers' meeting. 'Just imagine. He's second in his class. And he helps me in the shop, I can't tell you what a help he is to me.'

I nodded approval and listened as she described the latest purchases for the delicatessen store. I encouraged Maria to open a branch in Oberkassel. The times were favorable, I said, the wave of prosperity would continue – I had just picked that up on the radio. And then I decided it was time to ring for Bruno. He came in and handed me the little white package containing the fizz powder.

Oskar had worked out his plan. Without explanation I asked Maria for her left hand. She started to give me her right hand, but then corrected herself. Shaking her head and laughing, she offered me the back of her left hand, probably expecting me to kiss it. She showed no surprise until I turned the hand around and poured the powder from the package into a pile between mound of the Moon and mound of Venus. But even then she did not protest. She took fright only when Oskar bent down over her hand and spat copiously on the mound of fizz powder.

'Hey, what is this?' she cried with indignation, moved her hand as far from her as possible, and stared in horror at the frothing green foam. Maria blushed from her forehead down. I was beginning to hope, when three quick steps carried her to the washbasin. She let water, disgusting water, first cold, then hot, flow over the fizz powder. Then she washed her hands with my soap.

'Oskar, you're really impossible. What do you expect Mr. Münsterberg to think of us?' She turned to Bruno, who during my experiment had taken up a position at the foot end of the bed, as though pleading with him to overlook my insane behavior. To spare Maria any further embarrassment, I sent the keeper out of the room, and as soon as he had closed the door behind him, called her back to my bedside: 'Don't you remember? Please remember. Fizz powder! Three pfennigs a package. Think back! Woodruff, raspberry, how beautifully it foamed and bubbled, and the sensation, Maria, the way it made you feel.'

Maria did not remember. She was taken with an insane fear of me, she hid her left hand, tried frantically to find another topic of conversation, told me once again about Kurt's good work in school, about Stalin's death, the new icebox at Matzerath's delicatessen, the projected new branch in Oberkassel. I, however, remained faithful to the fizz powder, fizz powder, I said, she stood up, fizz powder, I begged, she said a hasty good-by, plucked at her hat, undecided whether to go or stay, and turned on the radio, which began to squeak. But I shouted above it: 'Fizz powder, Maria, remember!'

Then she stood in the doorway, wept, shook her head, and left me alone with the squeaking, whistling radio, closing the door as cautiously as though she were leaving me on my death-bed.

And so Maria can't remember the fizz powder. Yet for me, as long as I may breathe and drum, that fizz powder will never cease to fizz and foam; for it was my spittle which in the late summer of 1940 aroused woodruff and raspberry, which awakened feelings, which sent my flesh out questing, which made me a collector of morels, chanterelles, and other edible mushrooms unknown to me, which made me a father, yes indeed, young as I was, a father, from spittle to father, kindler of feelings, gathering and begetting, a father; for by early November, there was no room for doubt, Maria was pregnant, Maria was in her second month and I, Oskar, was the father.

Of that I am convinced to this day, for the business with Matzerath happened much later; two weeks, no, ten days after I had impregnated the sleeping Maria in the bed of her brother Herbert, rich in scars, in plain sight of the postcards sent by her younger brother, the corporal, and then in the dark, between walls and blackout paper, I found Maria, not sleeping this time but actively gasping for air on our sofa; under Matzerath she lay, and on top of her lay Matzerath.

Oskar, who had been meditating in the attic, came in from the hallway with his drum and entered the living room. The two of them didn't notice me. Their heads were turned toward the tile stove. They hadn't even undressed properly. Matzerath's under-drawers were hanging down to his knees. His trousers were piled up on the carpet. Maria's dress and petticoat had rolled up over her brassiere to her armpits. Her panties were dangling round one foot which hung from the sofa on a repulsively twisted leg. Her other leg lay bent back, as though unconcerned, over the head rest. Between her legs Matzerath. With his right hand he turned her head aside, the other hand guided him on his way. Through Matzerath's parted fingers Maria stared at the carpet and seemed to follow the pattern under the table. He had sunk his teeth into a cushion with a velvet cover and only let the velvet go when they talked together. For from time to time they talked, though without interrupting their labours. Only when the clock struck three quarters did the two of them pause till the last stroke, and then, resuming his efforts, he said: 'It's a quarter of.' Then he wanted to know if she liked it the way he was doing it. She said yes several times and asked him to be careful. He promised. She commanded, no, entreated him to be particularly careful. Then he inquired if it was time. And she said yes, very soon. Then she must have had a cramp in her foot that was hanging down off the sofa, for she kicked it up in the air, but her panties still hung from it. Then he bit into the velvet cushion again and she screamed: go away, and he wanted to go away, but he couldn't, because Oskar was on top of them before he could go away, because I had plunked down my drum on the small of his back and was pounding it with the sticks, because I couldn't stand listening any more to their go away go away, because my drum was louder than their go away, because I wouldn't allow him to go away as Jan Bronski had always gone away from my mother; for Mama had always said go away to Jan and go away to Matzerath, go away, go away. And then they fell apart. But I couldn't bear to see it. After all, I hadn't gone away. That's why I am the father and not this Matzerath who to the last supposed himself to be my father. But my father was Jan Bronski. Jan Bronski got there ahead of Matzerath and didn't go away; he stayed right where he was and deposited everything he had; from Jan Bronski I inherited this quality of getting there ahead of Matzerath and staying put; what emerged was my son, not his son. He never had any son at all. He was no real father. Even if he had married my poor mama ten times over, even if he did marry Maria because she was pregnant. That, he thought, is certainly what the people in the neighborhood think. Of course they thought Matzerath had knocked up Maria and that's why he's marrying her though she's only seventeen and he's going on forty-five. But she's a mighty good worker for her age and as for little Oskar, he can be very glad to have such a stepmother, for Maria doesn't treat the poor child like a stepmother but like a real mother, even if little Oskar isn't quite right in the head and actually belongs in the nuthouse in Silberhammer or Tapiau.

On Gretchen Scheffler's advice, Matzerath decided to marry my sweetheart. If we think of this presumptive father of mine as my father, it follows inevitably that my father married my future wife, called my son Kurt his son Kurt, and expected me to acknowledge his grandson as my half-brother, to accept the presence of my darling vanilla-scented Maria as a stepmother and to tolerate her presence in his bed, which stank of fish roe. But if, more in conformance to the truth, I say: this Matzerath is not even your presumptive father, he is a total stranger to you, deserving neither to be liked nor disliked, who is a good cook, who with his good cooking has thus far been a father of sorts to you, because your poor mother handed him down to you, who now in the eyes of all has purloined the best of women away from you, who compels you to witness his marriage and five months later a baptism, to play the role of guest at two family functions where you should properly have been the host, for *you* should have taken Maria to the City Hall, *you* should have picked the child's godfather and godmother. When I considered the miscasting of this tragedy, I had to despair of the theater, for Oskar, the real lead, had been cast in the role of an extra, that might just as well have been dropped.

Before I give my son the name of Kurt, before I name him as he should never have been named – for I would have named the boy after his great-grandfather Vincent Bronski – before I resign myself to Kurt, Oskar feels obliged to tell you how in the course of Maria's pregnancy he defended himself against the expected event.

On the evening of the very same day on which I surprised the two of them on the sofa, the day when I sat drumming on Matzerath's sweat-bathed back and frustrated the precautions demanded by Maria, I made a desperate attempt to win back my sweetheart.

Matzerath succeeded in shaking me off when it was already too late. As a result, he struck me. Maria took Oskar under her protection and reviled Matzerath for not taking care. Matzerath defended himself like an old man. It was Maria's fault, he protested, she should have been satisfied with once, but she never had enough. Maria wept and said with her things didn't go so quick, in and out before you can say Pilsener beer, he'd better get somebody else, yes, she admitted she was inexperienced but her sister Guste that was at the Eden knew what was what and she said it don't go so quick, Maria had better watch out, some men just wanted to shoot their snot, the sooner the better, and it looked like Matzerath was one of that kind, but he could count her out from now on, her bell had to ring too, like last time. But just the same he should have been careful, he owed her that much consideration. Then she cried some more and stayed sitting on the sofa. And Matzerath in his underdrawers shouted that he couldn't abide her wailing any more; then he was sorry he had lost his temper and blundered again, that is, he tried to pat her bare ass under her dress, and that really threw Maria into a tizzy.

Oskar had never seen her that way. Red spots came out all over her face and her grey eyes got darker and darker. She called Matzerath a mollycoddle, whereupon he picked up his trousers, stepped in, and buttoned up. She screamed for all she was worth: he could clear out for all she cared, he could join his unit leaders, a bunch of quick-squirts the whole lot of them. Matzerath picked up his jacket and gripped the doorknob, there'd be changes, he assured her, he had women up to here; if she was so hot, why didn't she get her hooks on one of the foreign laborers, the Frenchie that brought the beer would surely do it better. To him, Matzerath, love meant something more than piggishness, he was going to shoot some skat, in a skat game at least you knew what to expect.

And then I was alone with Maria in the living room. She had stopped crying and was thoughtfully pulling on her panties, whistling, but very sparingly. For a long while she smoothed out her dress that had lain on the sofa. Then she turned on the radio and tried to listen to the announcement of the water level of the Vistula and Nogat. When, after announcing the level of the lower Mottlau, the speaker promised a waltz and his promise was directly kept, she suddenly removed her panties again, went into the kitchen, plunked down a basin, and turned the water on; I heard the puffing of the gas and guessed that Maria had decided to take a sitz bath.

In order to dispel this rather unpleasant image, Oskar concentrated on the strains of the waltz. If I remember aright, I even drummed a few measures of Strauss and enjoyed it. Then the waltz was broken off for a special communiqué. Oskar bet on news from the Atlantic and was not mistaken. Several U-boats had succeeded in sinking seven or eight ships of so and so many thousand tons off the west coast of Ireland. Another group of subs had sent almost as much tonnage to the bottom. A U-boat under Lieutenant Schepke – or it may have been Lieutenant Kretschmar, in any case it was one or the other of them unless it was a third equally famous submarine captain – had especially distinguished itself, sinking not only the most tonnage but also a British destroyer of the XY class.

While I on my drum picked up the ensuing 'Sailing against England' and almost turned it into a waltz, Maria came into the living room with a Turkish towel under her arm. In an undertone she said: 'Did you hear that, Oskar, another special communiqué. If they keep on like that . . .'

Without letting Oskar know what would happen if they kept on like that, Maria sat down in the chair on which Matzerath customarily hung his jacket. She twisted the wet towel into a sausage and whistled 'Sailing against England' along with the radio; she whistled loudly and in tune. She repeated the final chorus once more after it had stopped on the radio, and switched off the radio as soon as the strains of immortal waltz resumed. She left the sausaged towel on the table, sat down, and rested her sweet little hands on her thighs.

A deep silence fell in our living room, only the grandfather clock spoke louder and louder and Maria seemed to be wondering whether it might not be better to turn on the radio again. But then she made another decision. She pressed her face to the sausaged towel on the table, let her arms hang down between her knees to carpetward, and began, steadily and silently, to weep.

Oskar wondered if Maria was ashamed because of the embarrassing situation I had found her in. I decided to cheer her up; I crept out of the living room and in the dark shop, beside the waxed paper and packages of pudding, found a little package which in the corridor, where there was some light, proved to be a package of fizz powder with woodruff flavoring. Oskar was pleased with his blind choice, for at the time it seemed to me that Maria preferred woodruff to all other flavors.

When I entered the living room, Maria's right cheek still lay on the bunched-up towel. Her arms still dangled helplessly between her thighs. Oskar approached her from the left and was disappointed when he saw that her eyes were closed and dry. I waited patiently until her eyelids stickily opened, and held out the package, but she didn't notice the woodruff, she seemed to look through the package and Oskar too.

Her tears must have blinded her, I thought, for I wanted to forgive her; after a moment's deliberation, I decided on a more direct approach. Oskar crawled under the table, and huddled at Maria's feet – the toes were turned slightly inward – took one of her dangling hands, twisted it till I could see the palm, tore open the package with my teeth, strewed half the contents into the inert bowl, and contributed my saliva. Just as the powder began to foam, I received a sharp kick in the chest that sent Oskar sprawling under the table.

In spite of the pain I was on my feet in an instant and out from under the table. Maria stood up too, and we stood face to face, breathing hard. Maria picked up the towel, wiped her hand clean, and flung the towel at my feet; she called me a loathsome pig, a vicious midget, a crazy gnome, that ought to be chucked in the nuthouse. She grabbed hold of me, slapped the back of my head, and reviled my poor mama for having brought a brat like me into the world. When I prepared to scream, having declared war on all the glass in the living room and in the whole world, she stuffed the towel in my mouth; I bit into it and it was tougher than tough boiled beef.

Only when Oskar made himself turn red and blue did she let me go. I might easily have screamed all the glasses and window-panes in the room to pieces and repeated my childhood assault on the dial of the grandfather clock. I did not scream, I opened the gates of my heart to a hatred so deep-seated that to this day, whenever Maria comes into the room, I feel it between my teeth like that towel.

Capricious as Maria could be, she forgot her anger. She gave a good-natured laugh and with a single flip turned the radio back on again. Whistling the radio waltz, she came toward me, meaning to make up, to stroke my hair. The fact is that I liked her to stroke my hair.

Oskar let her come very close. Then with both fists he landed an uppercut in the exact same spot where she had admitted Matzerath. She caught my fists before I could strike again, whereupon I sank my teeth into the same accursed spot and, still clinging fast, fell with Maria to the sofa. I heard the radio promising another special communiqué, but Oskar had no desire to listen; consequently he cannot tell you who sank what or how much, for a violent fit of tears loosened my jaws and I lay motionless on Maria, who was crying with pain, while Oskar cried from hate and love, which turned to a leaden helplessness but could not die.

How Oskar Took His Helplessness to Mrs. Greff

I didn't like Greff. Greff didn't like me. Even later on, when Greff made me the drumming machine, I didn't like him. Lasting antipathies require a fortitude that Oskar hasn't really got, but I still don't care much for Greff, even now that Greff has gone out of existence.

Greff was a greengrocer. But don't be deceived. He believed neither in potatoes nor in cabbage, yet he knew a great deal about vegetable-raising and liked to think of himself as a gardener, a friend of nature, and a vegetarian. But precisely because Greff ate no meat, he was not an authentic greengrocer. It was impossible for him to talk about vegetables as vegetables. 'Will you kindly look at this extraordinary potato,' I often heard him say to a customer. 'This swelling, bursting vegetable flesh, always devising new forms and yet so chaste. I love a potato because it speaks to me.' Obviously, no real greengrocer will embarrass his customers with such talk. Even in the best potato years, my grandmother Anna Koljaiczek, who had grown old in potato fields, would never say anything more than: 'Hm, the spuds are a little bigger than last year.' Yet Anna Koljaiczek and her brother Vincent Bronski were far more dependent on the potato harvest than Greff, for in his line of business a good plum year could make up for a bad potato year.

Everything about Greff was overdone. Did he absolutely have to wear a green apron in the shop? The presumption of the man! The knowing smile he would put on to explain that this spinach-green rag of his was 'God's green gardener's apron.' Worst of all, he just couldn't give up boy-scouting. He had been forced to disband his group in '38 – his boys had been put into brown shirts or dashing black winter uniforms – but the former scouts, in civilian clothes or in their new uniforms, came regularly to see their former scout leader, to sing morning songs, evening songs, hiking songs, soldier's songs, harvest songs, hymns to the Virgin, and folk songs native and foreign. Since Greff had joined the National Socialist Motorists' Corps before it was too late and from 1941 on termed himself not only greengrocer but air raid warden as well; since, moreover, he had the support of two former scouts who had meanwhile made places for themselves, one as a squad leader, the other as a platoon leader, in the Hitler Youth, the song feasts in Greff's potato cellar were tolerated if not exactly authorized by the district bureau of the Party. Greff was even asked by Löbsack, the district chief of training, to organize song festivals during the training courses at Jenkau Castle. Early in 1940 Greff and a certain schoolteacher were commissioned to compile a young people's songbook for the district of Danzig-West Prussia, under the title: 'Sing with Us.' The book was quite a success. The greengrocer received a letter from Berlin, signed by the Reich Youth Leader, and was invited to attend a meeting of song leaders in Berlin.

Greff certainly had ability. He knew all the verses of all the songs; he could pitch tents, kindle and quench campfires without provoking forest fires, and find his way in the woods with a compass, he knew the first names of all the visible stars and could reel off no end of stories of both the funny and exciting variety; he knew the legends of the Vistula country and gave lectures on 'Danzig and the Hanseatic League.' He could list all the grand masters of the Teutonic Knights with the corresponding dates, and even that did not satisfy him; he could talk for hours about the Germanic mission in the territories of the Order, and it was only very rarely that locutions smacking too strongly of boy scout turned up in his lectures.

Greff liked young people. He liked boys more than girls. Actually he didn't like girls at all, just boys. Often he liked boys more than the singing of songs could express. Possibly it was Mrs. Greff, a sloven with greasy brassieres and holes in her underwear, who made him seek a purer measure of love among wiry, cleancut boys. But perhaps, on the other hand, the tree on whose branches Mrs. Greff's dirty underwear blossomed at every season of the year had another root. Perhaps, that is, Mrs. Greff became a sloven because the greengrocer and air raid warden lacked sufficient appreciation of her carefree and rather stupid *embonpoint*.

Greff liked everything that was hard, taut, muscular. When he said 'nature', he meant asceticism. When he said 'asceticism', he meant a particular kind of physical culture. Greff was an expert on the subject of his body. He took elaborate care of it, exposing it to heat and, with special inventiveness, to cold. While Oskar sang glass, far and near, to pieces, occasionally thawing the frost flowers on the windowpanes, melting icicles and sending them to the ground with a crash, the greengrocer was a man who attacked ice at close quarters, with hand tools.

Greff made holes in the ice. In December, January, February, he made holes in the ice with an ax. Long before dawn, he would haul his bicycle up from the cellar and wrap his ice ax in an onion sack. Then he would ride via Saspe to Brösen, whence he would take the snow-covered beach promenade in the direction of Glettkau. Between Brösen and Glettkau he would alight. As the day slowly dawned, he would push his bicycle over the icy beach, and then two or three hundred yards out into the frozen Baltic. The scene was immersed in coastal fog. No one could have seen from the beach how Greff laid down the bicycle, unwrapped the ax from the onion sack, and stood for a while in devout silence, listening to the foghorns of the icebound freighters in the roadstead. Then he would throw off his smock, do a bit of gymnastics, and finally begin, with steady, powerful strokes, to dig a circular hole in the Baltic Sea.

Greff needed a good three-quarters of an hour for his hole. Don't ask me, please, how I know. Oskar knew just about everything in those days, including the length of time it took Greff to dig his hole in the ice. Drops of salt sweat formed on his high bumpy forehead and flew off into the snow. He handled his ax well; its strokes left a deep circular track. When the circle had come full circle, his gloveless hands lifted a disk, perhaps six or seven inches thick, out of the great sheet of ice that extended, it seems safe to say, as far as Hela if not Sweden. The water in the hole was old and grey, shot through with ice-grits. It steamed a bit, though it was not a hot spring. The hole attracted fish. That is, holes in the ice are said to attract fish. Greff might have caught lampreys or a twenty-pound cod. But he did not fish. He began to undress. He took off his clothes and he was soon stark naked, for Greff's nakedness was always stark.

Oskar is not trying to send winter shudders running down your spine. In view of the climate, he prefers to make a long story short: twice a week, during the winter months, Greff the greengrocer bathed in the Baltic. On Wednesday he bathed alone at the crack of dawn. He started off at six, arrived at half-past, and dug until a quarter past seven. Then he tore off his clothes with quick, excessive movements, rubbed himself with snow, jumped into the hole, and, once in it, began to shout. Or sometimes I heard him sing: 'Wild geese are flying through the night' or 'Oh, how we love the storm . . .' He sang, shouted, and bathed for two minutes, or three at most. Then with a single leap he was standing, terrifyingly distinct, on the ice: a steaming mass of lobstery flesh, racing round the hole, glowing, and still shouting. In the end, he was dressed once more and departing with his bicycle. Shortly before eight, he was back in Labesweg and his shop opened punctually.

Greff's other weekly bath was taken on Sunday, in the company of several boys, youths, striplings, or young men. This is something Oskar never saw or claimed to have seen. But the word got round. Meyn the musician knew stories about the greengrocer and trumpeted them all over the neighborhood. One of his trumpeter's tales was that every Sunday in the grimmest winter months Greff bathed in the company of several boys. Yet even Meyn never claimed that Greff made the boys jump naked into the hole in the ice like himself. He seems to have been perfectly satisfied if, lithe and sinewy, they tumbled and gamboled about on the ice, half naked or mostly naked, and rubbed each other with snow. So appealing to Greff were striplings in the snow that he often romped with them before or after his bath, helped them with their reciprocal rubdowns, or allowed the entire horde to rub him down. Meyn the musician claimed that despite the perpetual fog he once saw from the Glettkau beach promenade how an appallingly naked, singing, shouting Greff lifted up two of his naked disciples and, naked laden with naked, a roaring, frenzied troika raced headlong over the solidly frozen surface of the Baltic.

It is easy to guess that Greff was not a fisherman's son, although there were plenty of fishermen named Greff in Brösen and Neufahrwasser. Greff the greengrocer hailed from Tiegenhof, but he had met Lina Greff, née Bartsch, at Praust. There he had helped an enterprising young vicar to run an apprentices' club, and Lina, on the same vicar's account, went to the parish house every Saturday. To judge by a snapshot, which she must have given me, for it is still in my album, Lina, at the age of twenty, was robust, plump, light-headed, and dumb. Her father raised fruit and vegetables on a considerable market garden at Sankt Albrecht. As she later related on every possible occasion, she was quite inexperienced when at the age of twenty-three she married Greff on the vicar's advice. With her father's money they opened the vegetable store in Langfuhr. Since her father provided them with a large part of their vegetables and nearly all their fruit at low prices, the business virtually ran itself and Greff could do little damage.

Without Greff's childish tendency to invent mechanical contrivances, he could easily have made a gold mine of this store, so well situated, so far removed from all competition, in a suburb swarming with children. But when the inspector from the Bureau of Weights and Measures presented himself for the third or fourth time, checked the scales, confiscated the weights, and decreed an assortment of fines, some of Greff's regular customers left him and took to buying at the market. There was nothing wrong with the quality of Greff's vegetables, they said, and his prices were not too high, but the inspectors had been there again, and something fishy must be going on.

Yet I am certain Greff had no intention of cheating anyone. This is what had happened: After Greff had made certain changes in his big potato scales, they weighed to his disadvantage. Consequently, just before the war broke out, he equipped these selfsame scales with a set of chimes which struck up a tune after every weighing operation; what tune depended on the weight registered. A customer who brought twenty pounds of potatoes was regaled, as a kind of premium, with 'On the Sunny Shores of the Saale'; fifty pounds of potatoes got you 'Be True and Upright to the

Grave', and a hundredweight of winter potatoes made the chimes intone the naively bewitching strains of 'Ännchen von Tharau.'

Though I could easily see that these musical fancies might not be to the liking of the Bureau of Weights and Measures, Oskar was all in favor of the greengrocer's little hobbies. Even Lina Greff was indulgent about her husband's eccentricities, because, well, because the essence and content of the Greff marriage was forbearance with each other's foibles. In this light the Greff marriage may be termed a good marriage. Greff did not beat his wife, was never unfaithful to her with other women, and was neither a drinker nor a debauchee; he was a good-humored man who dressed carefully and was well liked for his sociable, helpful ways, not only by lads and striplings but also by those of his customers who went on taking music with their potatoes.

And so Greff looked on calmly and indulgently as his Lina from year to year became an increasingly foul-smelling sloven. I remember seeing him smile when sympathetic friends called a sloven a sloven. Blowing into and rubbing his own hands, which were nicely kept in spite of the potatoes, he would sometimes, in my hearing, say to Matzerath, who had been chiding him over his wife: 'Of course you're perfectly right, Alfred. Our good Lina does rather let herself go. But haven't we all got our faults?' If Matzerath persisted, Greff would close the discussion in a firm though friendly tone: 'You may be right on certain points, but Lina has a good heart. I know my Lina.'

Maybe he did. But she knew next to nothing of him. Like the neighbors and customers, she never saw anything more in Greff's relations with his frequent youthful visitors than the enthusiasm of young men for a devoted, though nonprofessional, friend and educator of the young.

As for me, Greff could neither educate me nor fire me with enthusiasm. Actually Oskar was not his type. If I had made up my mind to grow, I might have become his type, for my lean and lank son Kurt is the exact embodiment of Greff's type, though he takes mostly after Maria, bears little resemblance to me, and none whatever to Matzerath.

Greff was one witness to the marriage of Maria Truczinski and Alfred Matzerath; the other was Fritz Truczinski, home on furlough. Since Maria, like the bridegroom, was a Protestant, they only had a civil marriage. That was in the middle of December. Matzerath said 'I do' in his Party uniform. Maria was in her third month.

The stouter my sweetheart became, the more Oskar's hate mounted. I had no objection to her being pregnant. But that the fruit by me engendered should one day bear the name of Matzerath deprived me of all pleasure in my anticipated son and heir. Maria was in her fifth month when I made my first attempt at abortion, much too late of course. It was in Carnival. Maria was fastening some paper streamers and clown's masks with potato noses to the brass bar over the counter, where the sausage and bacon were hung. Ordinarily the ladder had solid support in the shelves; now it was propped up precariously on the counter. Maria high above with her hands full of streamers, Oskar far below, at the foot of the ladder. Using my drumsticks as levers, helping with my shoulder and firm resolve, I raised the foot of the ladder, then pushed it to one side: amid streamers and masks, Maria let out a faint cry of terror. The ladder tottered, Oskar jumped to one side, and beside him fell Maria, drawing colored paper, sausages, and masks in her wake.

It looked worse than it was. She had only turned her ankle, she had to lie down and be careful, but there was no serious injury. Her shape grew worse and worse and she didn't even tell Matzerath who had been responsible for her turned ankle.

It was not until May of the following year when, some three weeks before the child was scheduled to be born, I made my second try, that she spoke to Matzerath, her husband, though even then she didn't tell him the whole truth. At table, right in front of me, she said: 'Oskar has been awful rough these days. Sometimes he hits me in the belly. Maybe we could leave him with my mother until the baby gets born. She has plenty of room.'

Matzerath heard and believed. In reality, a fit of murderous frenzy had brought on a very different sort of encounter between Maria and me.

She had lain down on the sofa after lunch. Matzerath had finished washing the dishes and was in the shop decorating the window. It was quiet in the living room. Maybe the buzzing of a fly, the clock as usual, on the radio a newscast about the exploits of the paratroopers on Crete had been turned low. I perked up an ear only when they put on Max Schmeling, the boxer. As far as I could make out, he had hurt his world's champion's ankle, landing on the stony soil of Crete, and now he had to lie down and take care of himself; just like Maria, who had had to lie down after her fall from the ladder. Schmeling spoke with quiet modesty, then some less illustrious paratroopers spoke, and Oskar stopped listening: it was quiet, maybe the buzzing of a fly, the clock as usual, the radio turned very low.

I sat by the window on my little bench and observed Maria's belly on the sofa. She breathed heavily and kept her eyes closed. From time to time I tapped my drum morosely. She didn't stir, but still she made me breathe in the same room with her belly. The clock was still there, and the fly between windowpane and curtain, and the radio with the stony island of Crete in the background. But quickly all this was submerged; all I could see was that belly; I knew neither in what room that bulging belly was situated, nor to whom it belonged, I hardly remembered who had made it so big. All I knew was that I couldn't bear it: it's got to be suppressed, it's a mistake, it's cutting off your view, you've got to stand up and do something about it. So I stood up. You've got to investigate, to see what can be done. So I approached the belly and took something with me. That's a malignant swelling, needs to be deflated. I lifted the object I had taken with me and looked for a spot between Maria's hands that lay breathing with her belly. Now is the time, Oskar, or Maria will open her eyes.

Already I felt that I was being watched, but I just stood gazing at Maria's slightly trembling left hand, though I saw her right hand moving, saw she was planning something with her right hand, and was not greatly surprised when Maria, with her right hand, twisted the scissors out of Oskar's fist. I may have stood there for another few seconds with hand upraised but empty, listening to the clock, the fly, the voice of the radio announcer announcing the end of the Crete program, then I turned about and before the next program – light music from two to three – could begin, left our living room, which in view of that space-filling abdomen had become too small for me.

Two days later Maria bought me a new drum and took me to Mother Truczinski's third-floor flat, smelling of ersatz coffee and fried potatoes. At first I slept on the couch; for fear of lingering vanilla Oskar refused to sleep in Herbert's old bed. A week later old man Heilandt carried my wooden crib up the stairs. I allowed them to set it up beside the bed which had harbored me, Maria, and our fizz powder.

Oskar grew calmer or more resigned at Mother Truczinski's. I was spared the sight of the belly, for Maria feared to climb the stairs. I avoided our apartment, the store, the street, even the court, where rabbits were being raised again as food became harder to come by.

Oskar spent most of his time looking at the postcards that Sergeant Fritz Truczinski had sent or brought with him from Paris. I had my ideas about the city of Paris and when Mother Truczinski brought me a postcard of the Eiffel Tower, I took up the theme and began to drum Paris, to drum a musette though I had never heard one.

On June 12, two weeks too soon according to my calculations, in the sign of Gemini and not as I had reckoned in that of Cancer, my son Kurt was born. The father in a Jupiter year, the son in a Venus year. The father dominated by Mercury in Virgo, which makes for skepticism and ingenuity; the son likewise governed by Mercury but in the sign of Gemini, hence endowed with a cold, ambitious intelligence. What in me was attenuated by the Venus of Libra in the house of the ascendant was aggravated in my son by Aries in the same house; I was to have trouble with his Mars.

With mousy excitement, Mother Truczinski imparted the news: 'Just think, Oskar, the stork has brought you a little brother. Just when I was beginning to think if only it isn't a girl that makes so much worry later on.' I scarcely interrupted my drumming of the Eiffel Tower and the Arc de Triomphe, which had arrived in the meantime. Even in the guise of Grandma Truczinski, Mother Truczinski seemed to expect no congratulations from me. Though it was Sunday, she decided to put on a little color, rubbed her cheeks with the good old chicory wrapping, and thus freshly painted, went downstairs to give Matzerath, the alleged father, a hand.

As I have said, it was June. A deceptive month. Victories on all fronts – if you choose to lend so high-sounding a term to victories in the Balkans – but still greater triumphs were imminent on the

Eastern Front. An enormous army was moving forward. The railroads were being kept very busy. Fritz Truczinski, who until then had been having so delightful a time of it in Paris, was also compelled to embark on an eastward journey which would prove to be a very long one and could not be mistaken for a trip home on furlough. Oskar, however, sat quietly looking at the shiny postcards, dwelling in the mild Paris springtime, and lightly drumming 'Trois jeunes tambours'; having no connection with the Army of Occupation, he had no reason to fear that any partisans would attempt to toss him off the Seine bridges. No, it was clad as a civilian that I climbed the Eiffel Tower with my drum and enjoyed the view just as one is expected to, feeling so good and despite the tempting heights so free from bittersweet thoughts of suicide, that it was only on descending, when I stood three feet high at the foot of the Eiffel Tower, that I remembered the birth of my son.

Voilà, I thought, a son. When he is three years old, he will get a tin drum. We'll see who's the father around here, that Mr. Matzerath or I, Oskar Bronski.

In the heat of August – I believe that the successful conclusion of another battle of encirclement, that of Smolensk, had just been announced – my son Kurt was baptized. But how did my grandmother Anna Koljaiczek and her brother Vincent Bronski come to be invited? Of course if you accept – as I do – the version according to which Jan Bronski was my father and the silent, increasingly eccentric Vincent Bronski my paternal grandfather, there was reason enough for the invitation. After all my grandparents were my son Kurt's great-grandparents.

But it goes without saying that no such reasoning ever occurred to Matzerath, who had sent the invitation. Even in his moments of darkest self-doubt, even after losing a game of skat by six lengths, he regarded himself as twice a progenitor, father, and provider. It was other considerations that gave Oskar the opportunity to see his grandparents. The old folks had been turned into Germans. They were Poles no longer and spoke Kashubian only in their dreams. German Nationals, Group 3, they were called. Moreover, Hedwig Bronski, Jan's widow, had married a Baltic German who was local peasant leader in Ramkau. Petitions were already under way, which, when approved, would entitle

Marga and Stephan Bronski to take the name of their stepfather Ehlers. Seventeen-year-old Stephan had volunteered, he was now in the Infantry Training Camp at Gross-Boschpol and had good prospects of visiting the war theaters of Europe, while Oskar, who would soon be of military age, was reduced to waiting behind his drum until there should be an opening for a three-year-old drummer in the Army or Navy, or even in the Air Corps.

It was Local Peasant Leader Ehlers who took the first steps. Two weeks before the baptism he drove up to Labesweg with Hedwig beside him on the seat of a carriage and pair. He had bowlegs and stomach trouble and was not to be mentioned in the same breath with Jan Bronski. A good head shorter than Jan, he sat beside cow-eyed Hedwig at our living room table. The looks of the man came as a surprise, even to Matzerath. The conversation refused to get started. They spoke of the weather, observed that all sorts of things were happening in the East, that our troops were getting ahead fine – much faster than in '15, as Matzerath, who had been there in '15, remembered. All took great pains not to speak of Jan Bronski, until I spoiled their game by making a droll infantile pout and crying out loudly and more than once for Oskar's Uncle Jan. Matzerath gave himself a jolt and said something affectionate followed by something thoughtful about his former friend and rival. Ehlers joined in effusively, although he had never laid eyes on his predecessor. Hedwig even produced a few authentic tears that rolled slowly down her cheeks and finally said the words that closed the topic of Jan: 'He was a good man. He wouldn't hurt a fly. Who'd have thought he'd come to such an end, a scarecat like him that was scared of his shadow.'

These words having been spoken, Matzerath bade Maria, who was standing behind him, to bring in a few bottles of beer and asked Ehlers if he played skat. No, Ehlers was sorry to say he didn't, but Matzerath magnanimously forgave the peasant leader this little shortcoming. He even gave him a tap on the shoulder and assured him, after the beer glasses had been filled, that it didn't matter if he wasn't a skat player, they could still be good friends.

Thus Hedwig Bronski in the guise of Hedwig Ehlers found her way back to our flat and brought with her, to attend the baptism of my son Kurt, not only her local peasant leader but also her former father-in-law Vincent Bronski and his sister Anna. Matzerath gave the old folks a loud, friendly welcome out in the street, beneath the neighbors' windows, and in the living room, when my grandmother reached under her four skirts and brought forth her baptismal gift, a fine fat goose, he said: 'You didn't have to do that, Grandma. I'd be glad to have you even if you didn't bring a thing.' But this was going too far for my grandmother, who wanted her goose to be appreciated. Smacking the noble bird with the palm of her hand, she protested: 'Don't make so much fuss, Alfred. She's no Kashubian goose, she's a German National bird and tastes just like before the war.'

With this all problems of nationality were solved and everything went smoothly until it came time for the baby to be baptized and Oskar refused to set foot in the Protestant church. They took my drum out of the taxi and tried to lure me with it, assuring me not once but several times that drums were allowed in Protestant churches. I persevered, however, in the blackest Catholicism; I would rather at that moment have poured a detailed and compre-hensive confession into the apostolic ear of Father Wiehnke than listen to a Protestant baptismal sermon. Matzerath gave in, prob-ably dreading my voice and attendant damage claims. While my son was being baptized, I remained in the taxi, staring at the back of the driver's head, scrutinizing Oskar's features in the rear view mirror, thinking of my own baptism, already far in the past, and of Father Wiehnke's valiant effort to drive Satan out of the infant Oskar.

Afterwards we ate. Two tables had been put together. First came mock turtle soup. The countryfolk lapped. Greff crooked his little finger. Gretchen Scheffler bit into the soup. Guste smiled broadly over her spoon. Ehlers spoke with the spoon in his mouth. Vincent's hands shook as he looked for something that wouldn't come into the spoon. Only the old women, Grandma Anna and Mother Truczinski, were committed heart and soul to their spoons. As for Oskar, he dropped his and slipped away while the others were still spooning and sought out his son's cradle in the bedroom, for he wanted to think about his son, while the others, behind their spoons, shriveled more and more into unthinking, spooned-out emptiness, even though the soup was being spooned, not out of, but into them.

Over the basket on wheels a sky-blue canopy of tulle. The edge of the basket was too high and all I could see at first was a puckered little reddish-bluish head. By laying my drum on the floor and standing on it, I was able to observe my sleeping son, who twitched nervously as he slept. O paternal pride, ever on the lookout for grand words! Gazing upon my infant son, I could think of nothing but the short sentence: When he is three years old, he shall have a drum. My son refused to grant me the slightest insight into his intellectual situation, and I could only hope that he might, like me, belong to the race of clairaudient infants. Quite at a loss, I repeated my promise of a drum for his third birthday, descended from my pedestal, and once more tried my chance with the grownups in the living room.

They were just finishing the mock turtle soup. Maria brought in canned green peas with melted butter. Matzerath, who was responsible for the pork roast, dressed the platter in person; he took his coat off and, standing in his shirtsleeves, cut slice after slice, his features so full of unabashed tenderness over the tender, succulent meat that I had to avert my eyes.

Greff was served separately: he was given canned asparagus, hard-boiled eggs, and black radish with cream, because vegetarians eat no meat. Like the others, he took a dab of mashed potatoes: however, he moistened them not with meat gravy but with brown butter which the attentive Maria brought in from the kitchen in a sizzling frying pan. While the others drank beer, he drank apple juice. The encirclement of Kiev was discussed, the prisoners taken counted on fingers. Ehlers, a native of the Baltic, showed a special aptitude for counting Russian prisoners; at every hundred thousand, a finger shot up; when his two outstretched hands had completed a million, he went right on counting by decapitating one finger after another. When the subject of prisoners, whose mounting numbers made them increasingly useless and uninteresting, was exhausted, Scheffler spoke of the U-boats at Gotenhafen and Matzerath whispered in my grandmother Anna's ear that they were launching two subs a week at Schichau. Thereupon Greff explained to all present why submarines had to be launched sideways instead of stern first. He was determined to make it all very clear and visual; for every operation he had a gesture which those of the guests who were fascinated by U-boats imitated attentively and awkwardly. Trying to impersonate a diving submarine, Vincent Bronski's left hand upset his beer glass. My grandmother started to scold him. But Maria smoothed her down, saying it didn't matter, the table cloth was due for the laundry anyway, you couldn't celebrate without making spots. Mother Truczinski came in with a cloth and mopped up the pool of beer; in her left hand she carried our large crystal bowl, full of chocolate pudding with crushed almonds.

Ah me, if that chocolate pudding had only had some other sauce or no sauce at all! But it had to be vanilla sauce, rich and yellow and viscous: vanilla sauce! Perhaps there is nothing so joyous and nothing so sad in this world as vanilla sauce. Softly the vanilla scent spread round about, enveloping me more and more in Maria, to the point that I couldn't bear to look at her, root and source of all vanilla, who sat beside Matzerath, holding his hand in hers.

Oskar slipped off his baby chair, clung to the skirts of Lina Greff, lay at her feet as above board she wielded her spoon. For the first time I breathed in the effluvium peculiar to Lina Greff, which instantly outshouted, engulfed, and killed all vanilla.

Acrid as it was to my nostrils, I clung to the new perfume until all recollections connected with vanilla seemed to be dulled. Slowly, without the slightest sound or spasm, I was seized with a redeeming nausea. While the mock turtle soup, the roast pork in chunks, the canned green peas almost intact, and the few spoonfuls I had taken of chocolate pudding with vanilla sauce escaped me, I became fully aware of my helplessness, I wallowed in my helplessness. Oskar's helplessness spread itself out at the feet of Lina Greff – and I decided that from then on and daily I should carry my helplessness to Lina Greff.

165 Lbs.

Vyazma and Bryansk; then the mud set in. In the middle of October, 1941, Oskar too began to wallow intensively in mud. I hope I shall be forgiven for drawing a parallel between the muddy triumphs of Army Group Center and my own triumphs in the impassable and equally muddy terrain of Mrs. Lina Greff. Just as tanks and trucks bogged down on the approaches to Moscow, so I too bogged down; just as the wheels went on spinning, churning up the mud of Russia, so I too kept on trying – I feel justified in saying that I churned the Greffian mud into a foaming lather – but neither on the approaches to Moscow nor in the Greff bedroom was any ground gained.

I am not quite ready to drop my military metaphor: just as future strategists would draw a lesson from these unsuccessful operations in the mud, so I too would draw my conclusions from the natural phenomenon named Lina Greff. Our efforts on the home front during the Second World War should not be under-estimated. Oskar was only seventeen, and despite his tender years Lina Greff, that endless and insidious infiltration course, made a man of him. But enough of military comparisons. Let us measure Oskar's progress in artistic terms: If Maria, with her naively bewitching clouds of vanilla, taught me to appreciate the small, the delicate: if she taught me the lyricism of fizz powder and mushroom-picking, then Mrs. Greff's acrid vapors, compounded of multiple effluvia, may be said to have given me the broad epic breath which enables me today to mention military victories and bedroom triumphs in the same breath. Music! From Maria's child-like, sentimental, and yet so sweet harmonica I was transported, without transition, to the concert hall, and I was the conductor; for Lina Greff offered me an orchestra, so graduated in depth and breadth that you will hardly find its equal in Bayreuth or Salzburg. There I mastered brasses and wood winds, the per-cussion, the strings, bowed and pizzicato; I mastered harmony and counterpoint, classical and diatonic, the entry of the scherzo and the tempo of the andante; my beat could be hard and precise or soft and fluid; Oskar got the maximum out of his instrument, namely Mrs. Greff, and yet, as befits a true artist, he remained dis- if not un-satisfied.

The Greff vegetable shop was only a few steps across and down the street from our store. A convenient location, much handier for me than the quarters of Alexander Scheffler, the master baker, in Kleinhammer-Weg. Maybe the convenient situation was the main reason why I made rather more progress in female anatomy than in the study of my masters Goethe and Rasputin. But perhaps this discrepancy in my education, which remains flagrant to this day, can be explained and in part justified by the difference between my two teachers. While Lina Greff made no attempt to instruct me but passively and in all simplicity spread out all her riches for me to observe and experiment with, Gretchen Scheffler took her pedagogic vocation far too seriously. She wanted to see results, to hear me read aloud, to see my drummer's finger engaged in penmanship, to establish a friendship between me and fair Grammatica and benefit by it her own self. When Oskar refused to show any visible sign of progress, Gretchen Scheffler lost patience; shortly after the death of my poor mama – by then, it must be admitted, she had been teaching me for seven years – she reverted to her knitting. From then on her interest in me was expressed only by occasional gifts of hand-knitted sweaters, stockings, and mittens – her marriage was still childless – bestowed for the most part on the principal holidays. We no longer read or spoke of Goethe or Rasputin, and it was only thanks to the excerpts from the works of both masters which I still kept hidden in various places, mostly in the attic of our apartment house, that this branch of Oskar's studies was not wholly forgotten; I educated myself and formed my own opinions.

Moored to her bed, the ailing Lina Greff could neither escape nor leave me, for her ailment, though chronic, was not serious enough to snatch Lina, my teacher Lina, away from me prematurely. But since on this planet nothing lasts forever, it was Oskar who left his bedridden teacher the moment it seemed to him that his studies were complete.

You will say: how limited the world to which this young man was reduced for his education! A grocery store, a bakery, and a vegetable shop circumscribed the field in which he was obliged to piece together his equipment for adult life. Yes, I must admit that Oskar gathered his first, all-important impressions in very musty *petit-bourgeois* surroundings. However, I had a third teacher. It was he who would open up the world to Oskar and make him what he is today, a person whom, for want of a better epithet, I can only term cosmopolitan.

I am referring, as the most attentive among you will have noted, to my teacher and master Bebra, direct descendant of Prince

Eugene, scion from the tree of Louis XIV, the midget and musical clown Bebra. When I say Bebra, I also, it goes without saying, have in mind the woman at his side, Roswitha Raguna, the great somnambulist and timeless beauty, to whom my thoughts were often drawn in those dark years after Matzerath took my Maria away from me. How old, I wondered, can the signora be? Is she a fresh young girl of nineteen or twenty? Or is she the delicate, the graceful old lady of ninety-nine, who in a hundred years will still indestructibly embody the diminutive format of eternal youth.

If I remember correctly, I met these two, so kindred to me in body and spirit, shortly after the death of my poor mama. We drank mocha together in the Café of the Four Seasons, then our ways parted. There were slight, but not negligible political differences; Bebra was close to the Reich Propaganda Ministry, frequented, as I easily inferred from the hints he dropped, the privy chambers of Messrs. Goebbels and Goering – corrupt behavior which he tried, in all sorts of ways, to explain and justify to me. He would talk about the influence wielded by court jesters in the Middle Ages, and show me reproductions of Spanish paintings respresenting some Philip or Carlos with his retinue; in the midst of these stiff, pompous gatherings, one could distinguish fools about the size of Bebra or even Oskar, in ruffs, goatees, and baggy pantaloons. I liked the pictures – for without exaggeration I can call myself an ardent admirer of Diego Velasquez – but for that very reason I refused to be convinced, and after a while he would drop his comparisons between the position of the jester at the court of Philip IV of Spain and his own position in the entourage of the Rhenish upstart Joseph Goebbels. He would go on to speak of the hard times, of the weak who must temporarily incline, of the resistance that thrives in concealment, in short, the words 'inward emigration' cropped up, and for Oskar that was the parting of the ways.

Not that I bore the master a grudge. In the years that followed, I searched vaudeville and circus posters for Bebra's name. Twice I found it, side by side with that of Signora Raguna, yet I did nothing that might have led to a meeting with my friends.

I left it to chance, but chance declined to help, for if Bebra's ways and mine had crossed in the autumn of '42 rather than in the following year, Oskar would never have become the pupil of

Lina Greff, but would have become the disciple of Bebra the master. As it was, I crossed Labesweg every day, sometimes early in the morning, entered the vegetable shop, for propriety's sake spent half an hour in the vicinity of the greengrocer, who was becoming more and more crotchety and devoting more and more of his time to his inventions. I looked on as he constructed his weird, tinkling, howling, screaming contraptions, and poked him when customers entered the shop; for Greff had ceased to take much notice of the world around him. What had happened? What was it that made the once so open-hearted, so convivial gardener and friend of the young so silent? What was it that transformed him into a lonely, eccentric, rather unkempt old man?

The young people had stopped coming to see him. The new generation didn't know him. His following from the boy scout days had been dispersed by the war. Letters came from various fronts, then there were only postcards, and one day Greff indirectly received the news that his favorite, Horst Donath, first scout, then squad leader, then lieutenant in the Army, had fallen by the Donets.

From that day Greff began to age, neglected his appearance, and devoted himself exclusively to his inventions, until there were more ringing and howling machines to be seen in his shop than potatoes or cabbage. Of course the general food shortage had something to do with it; deliveries to the shop were few and far between, and Greff was not, like Matzerath, a good buyer with good connections in the wholesale market.

The shop was pitiful to look upon, and one could only be grateful to Greff's silly noise machines for taking up space in their absurd but decorative way. I liked the creations that sprang from Greff's increasingly fuzzy brain. When today I look at the knotted string spooks of Bruno my keeper, I am reminded of Greff's exhibits. And just as Bruno relishes my smiling yet serious interest in his artistic amusements, so Greff, in his distraught way, was glad when I took pleasure in one of his music machines. He who for years had paid no attention to me was visibly disappointed when after half an hour I left his vegetable and work shop to call on his wife, Lina Greff.

What shall I tell you about my visits to the bedridden woman, which generally took from two to two and a half hours? When Oskar entered, she beckoned from the bed: 'Ah, it's you, Oskar. Well, come on over, come in under the covers if you feel like it, it's cold and Greff hasn't made much of a fire.' So I slipped in with her under the featherbed, left my drum and the two sticks I had just been using outside, and permitted only a third drumstick, a used and rather scrawny one, to accompany me on my visit to Lina.

It should not be supposed that I undressed before getting into bed with Lina. In wool, velvet, and leather, I climbed in. And despite the heat generated by my labors, I climbed out of the rumpled feathers some hours later in the same clothing, scarcely disarranged.

Then, fresh from Lina's bed, her effluvia still clinging to me, I would pay another call on Greff. When this had happened several times, he inaugurated a ritual that I was only too glad to observe. Before I arose from the palace of matrimony, he would come into the room with a basin full of warm water and set it down on a stool. Having disposed soap and towel beside it, he would leave the room without a word or so much as a glance in the direction of the bed.

Quickly Oskar would tear himself out of the warm nest, toddle over to the washbasin, and give himself and his bedtime drumstick a good wash; I could readily understand that even at second hand the smell of his wife was more than Greff could stomach.

Freshly washed, however, I was welcome to the inventor. He would demonstrate his machines and their various sounds, and I find it rather surprising to this day that despite this late intimacy no friendship ever developed between Oskar and Greff, that Greff remained a stranger to me, arousing my interest no doubt, but never my sympathy.

It was in September, 1942 – my eighteenth birthday had just gone by without pomp or ceremony, on the radio the Sixth Army, was taking Stalingrad – that Greff built the drumming machine. A wooden framework, inside it a pair of scales, evenly balanced with potatoes; when a potato was removed from one pan the scales were thrown off balance and released a lever which set off the drumming mechanism installed on top of the frame. There followed a rolling as of kettledrums, a booming and clanking, basins struck together, a gong rang out, and the end of it all was a tinkling, transitory, tragically cacophonous finale.

The machine appealed to me. Over and over again I would ask Greff to demonstrate it. For Oskar imagined that the greengrocer had invented and built it for him. Soon my mistake was made clear to me. Greff may have taken an idea or two from me, but the machine was intended for himself; for its finale was his finale.

It was a clear October morning such as only the northwest wind delivers free of charge. I had left Mother Truczinski's flat early and Matzerath was just raising the sliding shutter in front of his shop as I stepped out into the street. I stood beside him as the green slats clanked upward; a whiff of pent-up grocery store smell came out at me, then Matzerath kissed me good morning. Before Maria showed herself, I crossed Labesweg, casting a long westward shadow on the cobblestones, for to the right of me, the East, the sun rose up over Max-Halbe-Platz by its own power, resorting to the same trick as Baron Münchhausen when he lifted himself out of the swamp by his own pigtail.

Anyone who knew Greff the greengrocer as well as I would have been just as surprised to find the door and showcase of his shop still curtained and closed at that hour. The last few years, it is true, had transformed Greff into more and more of a crank. However, the shop had always opened on time. Maybe he is sick, thought Oskar, but dismissed this notion at once. For how could Greff, who only last winter, though perhaps not as regularly as in former years, had chopped holes in the Baltic Sea to bathe in – how, despite certain signs that he was growing older, could this nature lover suddenly fall sick from one day to the next? The privilege of staying in bed was reserved for his wife, who managed for two; moreover, I knew that Greff despised soft mattresses, preferring to sleep on camp beds and wooden planks. There existed no ailment that could have fastened the greengrocer to his bed.

I took up my position outside the closed shop, looked back toward our store, and ascertained that Matzerath was inside; only then did I roll off a few measures on my drum, hoping to attract Mrs. Greff's sensitive ear. Barely a murmur was needed, already the second window to the right beside the shop door opened. La Greff in her nightgown, her hair full of curlers, shielding her bosom with a pillow, appeared over the window box and its ice plants. 'Why, Oskar, come in, come in. What are you waiting for when it's so chilly out?'

I explained by tapping the iron curtain over the shop window with one drumstick.

'Albrecht,' she cried. 'Albrecht, where are you? What's the matter?'

Still calling her husband, she removed herself from the window. Doors slammed, I heard her rattling round the shop, then she began to scream again. She screamed in the cellar, but I couldn't see why she was screaming, for the cellar transom, through which potatoes were poured on delivery days, but more and more seldom in the war years, was also closed. Pressing an eye to the tarred planks covering the transom, I saw that the light was burning in the cellar. I could also distinguish the top part of the cellar steps, on which lay something white, probably Mrs. Greff's pillow.

She must have dropped the pillow on the stairs, for she was no longer in the cellar but screaming again in the shop and a moment later in the bedroom. She picked up the phone, screamed, and dialed; she screamed into the telephone; but Oskar couldn't tell what it was about, all he could catch was accident and the address, Labesweg 24, which she screamed several times. She hung up, and a moment later, screaming in her nightgown, pillowless but still in curlers, she filled the window frame, pouring the vast bipartite bulk with which I was so familiar into the window box, over the ice plants, and thrusting both her hands into the fleshy, pale-red leaves. She screamed upward, so that the street became narrow and it seemed to Oskar that glass must begin to fly. But not a windowpane broke. Windows were torn open, neighbors appeared, women called out questions, men came running, Laubschad the watchmaker, pulling on his jacket, old man Heilandt, Mr. Reissberg, Libischewski the tailor, Mr. Esch, emerged from the nearest house doors; even Probst, not the barber but the coal dealer, appeared with his son. Matzerath came sailing up in his white smock, while Maria, holding Kurt in her arms, stood in the doorway of our store.

I had no difficulty in submerging myself in the swarm of excited grownups and in evading Matzerath, who was looking for me. He and Laubschad the watchmaker were the first to spring into action. They tried to enter the house through the window. But Mrs Greff wouldn't let anybody climb up, much less enter. Scratching, flailing, and biting, she still managed to find time to scream louder than ever and in part intelligibly. The ambulance men should be first to go in; she had telephoned long ago, there was no need for anyone to telephone again, she knew what had to be done in such cases. They should attend to their own shops, things were already bad enough without their meddling. Curiosity, nothing but curiosity, you could see who your friends were when trouble came. In the middle of her lament, she must have caught sight of me outside her window, for she called me and, after shaking off the men, held out her bare arms to me, and someone – Oskar still thinks it was Laubschad the watchmaker – lifted me up, tried, despite Matzerath's opposition, to hand me in. Close by the window box, Matzerath nearly caught me, but then Lina Greff reached out, pressed me to her warm nightgown, and stopped screaming. After that she just gave out a falsetto whimpering and between whimpers gasped for air.

A moment before, Mrs. Greff's screams had lashed the neighbors into a shamelessly gesticulating frenzy; now her high, thin whimpering reduced those pressing round the window box to a silent, scraping, embarrassed mob which seemed almost afraid to look her lamentations in the face and projected all its hope, all its curiosity and sympathy into the moment when the ambulance should arrive.

Oskar too was repelled by Mrs. Greff's whimpering. I tried to slip down a little lower, where I wouldn't be quite so close to the source of her lamentations; I managed to relinquish my hold on her neck and to seat myself partly on the window box. But soon Oskar felt he was being watched; Maria, with the child in her arms, was standing in the doorway of the shop. Again I decided to move, for I was keenly aware of the awkwardness of my situation. But I was thinking only of Maria; I didn't care a hoot for the neighbors. I shoved off from the Greffian coast, which was quaking too much for my taste and reminded me of bed.

Lina Greff was unaware of my flight, or else she lacked the strength to restrain the little body which had so long provided her with compensation. Or perhaps she suspected that Oskar was slipping away from her forever, that with her screams a sound had been born which, on the one hand, would become a wall, a sound barrier between the drummer and the bedridden woman, and on the other hand would shatter the wall that had arisen between Maria and myself.

I stood in the Greff bedroom. My drum hung down askew and insecure. Oskar knew the room well, he could have recited the sap-green wallpaper by heart in any direction. The washbasin with the grey soapsuds from the previous day was still in its place. Everything had its place and yet the furniture in that room, worn with sitting, lying, and bumping, looked fresh to me, or at least refreshed, as though all these objects that stood stiffly on four legs along the walls had needed the screams, followed by the falsetto whimpering of Lina Greff, to give them a new terrifyingly cold radiance.

The door to the shop stood open. Against his will Oskar let himself be drawn into that room, redolent of dry earth and onions. Seeping in through cracks in the shutters, the daylight designed stripes of luminous dust particles in the air. Most of Greff's noise and music machines were hidden in the half-darkness, the light fell only on a few details, a little bell, a wooden prop, the lower part of the drumming machine, the evenly balanced potatoes.

The trap door which, exactly as in our shop, led down to the cellar, stood open. Nothing supported the plank cover which Mrs. Greff must have opened in her screaming haste: nor had she inserted the hook in its eye affixed to the counter. With a slight push Oskar might have tipped it back and closed the cellar.

Motionless, I stood behind those planks, breathing in their smell of dust and mold and staring at the brightly lit rectangle enclosing a part of the staircase and a piece of concrete cellar floor. Into this rectangle, from the upper right, protruded part of a platform with steps leading up to it, obviously a recent acquisition of Greff's, for I had never seen it on previous visits to the cellar. But Oskar would not have peered so long and intently into the cellar for the sake of a platform; what held his attention was those two woolen stockings and those two black laced shoes which, strangely foreshortened, occupied the upper righthand corner of the picture. Though I could not see the soles, I knew them at once for Greff's hiking shoes. It can't be Greff, I thought, who is standing there in the cellar all ready for a hike for the shoes are not standing but hanging in midair, just over the platform, though it seems possible that the tips of the shoes, pointing sharply downward, are in contact with the boards, not much, but still in contact. For a second I fancied a Greff standing on tiptoes, a comical and strenuous exercise, yet quite conceivable in this athlete and nature lover.

To check this hypothesis, meaning, if it were confirmed, to have a good laugh at the greengrocer's expense, I climbed cautiously down the steep stairs, drumming, if I remember correctly, something or other of a nature to create and dispel fear: 'Where's the Witch, black as pitch?'

Only when Oskar stood firmly on the concrete floor did he pursue his investigation – by detours, via bundles of empty onion bags, via piles of empty fruit crates – until, grazing a scaffolding he had never seen before, his eyes approached the spot where Greff's hiking shoes must have been hanging or standing on tiptoes.

Of course I knew Greff was hanging. The shoes hung, consequently the coarsely knitted dark green stockings must also be hanging. Bare adult knees over the edges of the stockings, hairy thighs to the edges of the trousers; at this point a cutting, prickling sensation rose slowly from my private parts, slowly following my rump to my back, which grew suddenly numb, climbed my spinal coard, settled down in the back of my neck, struck me hot and cold, raced down again between my legs, made my scrotum, tiny to begin with, shrivel to nothingness, leapt upward again, over my back, my neck, and shrank – to this day Oskar feels that same gagging, that same knife thrust, when anyone speaks of hanging in his presence, even of hanging out washing. It wasn't just Greff's hiking shoes, his woolen stockings, knees, and knee breeches that were hanging; the whole of Greff hung by the neck, and the strained expression of his face, above the cord, was not entirely free from theatrical affectation.

Surprisingly soon, the cutting, prickling sensation died down. I grew accustomed to the sight of Greff; for basically the posture of a man hanging is just as normal and natural as that of a man walking on his hands or standing on his head, or of a human who puts himself in the truly unfortunate position of mounting a four-legged horse with a view to riding.

Then there was the setting. Only now did Oskar appreciate the trouble Greff had gone to. The frame, the setting in which Greff hung, was studied to the point of extravagance. The greengrocer had aimed at a form of death appropriate to himself, a well-balanced death. He who in his lifetime had had difficulties and unpleasant correspondence with the Bureau of Weights and Measures, whose weights had several times been confiscated, who had had to pay fines for inaccuracy in the weighing of fruit and vegetables, had weighed himself to the last ounce with potatoes.

The faintly shiny rope, soaped I should think, ran, guided by pulleys, over two beams which, for the last day of his life, Greff had fashioned into a scaffolding whose sole purpose it was to serve as his last scaffolding. Obviously the greengrocer had spared no expense, he had used the very best wood. What with the wartime shortage of building materials, those planks and beams must have been hard to come by. Greff must have bartered fruit for wood. The scaffolding was not lacking in superfluous but decorative struts and braces. The platform and the steps leading up to it – Oskar had seen a corner of it from the shop – gave the whole edifice a quality verging on the sublime.

As in the drumming machine, which the inventor may have taken as his model, Greff and his counterweight hung inside a frame. Forming a sharp contrast to the four whitewashed cross-beams, a graceful little green ladder stood between him and the potatoes that counterbalanced him. With an ingenious knot such as scouts know how to tie, he had fastened the potato baskets to the main rope. Since the interior of the scaffolding was illumined by four light bulbs which, though painted white, gave off an intense glow, Oskar was able, without desecrating the platform with his presence, to read the inscription on a cardboard tag fastened with wire to the scout knot over the potato basket: 165 lbs. (less 3 oz.).

Greff hung in the uniform of a boy scout leader. On his last day he had resumed the uniform of the pre-war years. But it was now too tight for him. He had been unable to close the two uppermost trouser buttons and the belt, a jarring note in his otherwise trim costume. In accordance with scout ritual Greff had crossed two fingers of his left hand. Before hanging himself, he had tied his scout hat to his right wrist. He had had to forgo the neckerchief. He had also been unable to button the collar of his shirt, and a bush of curly black hair burst through the opening.

On the steps of the platform lay a few asters, accompanied inappropriately by parsley stalks. Apparently he had run out of flowers to strew on the steps, for he had used most of the asters and a few roses to wreathe the four little pictures that hung on the four main beams of the scaffolding. Left front behind glass, hung Baden-Powell, founder of the Boy Scouts. Left rear, unframed, St. George. Right rear, without glass, the head of Michelangelo's David. On the right front post, provided with frame and glass, hung the photo of an expressively handsome boy, aged perhaps sixteen: an early picture of his favorite, Horst Donath, later Lieutenant Donath, who had fallen by the Donets.

Perhaps I should say a word about the four scraps of paper on the platform steps between the asters and the parsley. They were disposed in such a way that they could easily be pieced together Oskar pieced them together and deciphered a summons to appear in court on a morals charge.

The ambulance siren aroused me from my meditations about the greengrocer's death. A moment later they came hobbling down the cellar stairs, mounted the steps to the platform, and took the dangling Greff in hand. No sooner had they lifted him than the potato baskets making a counterweight fell with a crash, releasing a mechanism similar to that of the drumming machine, housed on top of the scaffolding but discreetly sheathed in plywood. While down below potatoes rolled over the platform or fell directly to the concrete floor, up above clappers pounded upon tin, wood, bronze, and glass, an orchestra of drums was unleashed: Albrecht Greff's grand finale.

Oskar finds it very difficult to reproduce on his drum an echo of that avalanche of potatoes – a windfall, incidentally, to some of the ambulance orderlies – and of the organized din of Greff's drumming machine. And yet, perhaps because my drum accounted in good part for the form Greff imprinted upon his death, I occasionally manage to drum a pretty faithful tone-poem of Greff's death. When friends, or Bruno my keeper, ask me what my piece is called, I tell them the title is '165 Lbs.'

Bebra's Theater at the Front

In mid-June, 1942, my son Kurt was one year old. Oskar, the father, attached little importance to this birthday; two years more, he thought to himself. In October, '42, Greff, the greengrocer, hanged himself on a gallows so ingeniously conceived that I, Oskar, have ever since looked upon suicide as one of the noble forms of death. In January, '43, there was a good deal of talk about the city of Stalingrad. But since Matzerath uttered the name of this city very much in the same tone as previously Pearl Harbor, Tobruk, and Dunkirk, I paid no more attention to the happenings there than I had to those in the other cities whose names had been made familiar to me by special communiqués; for Wehrmacht communiqués and newscasts had become Oskar's school of geography. How else would I have learned the situation of the Kuban, Mius, and Don rivers, who could have taught me more about the Aleutian Islands, Atu, Kiska, and Adak than than radio commentaries on the events in the Far East? So it came about that in January, 1943, I learned that the city of Stalingrad is situated on the Volga; but I was far less interested in the fate of the Sixth Army than in Maria, who had a slight case of grippe at the time.

As Maria's grippe drew to a close, the geography lesson went on: to this day, Oskar can locate Rzev and Demyansk instantly and with his eyes shut on any map of Soviet Russia. No sooner was Maria well again than my son Kurt came down with the whooping cough. While I struggled to retain the difficult names of a few hotly disputed Tunisian oases, Kurt's whooping cough, simultaneously with the Afrika Korps, came to an end.

Oh, merry month of May: Maria, Matzerath, and Gretchen Scheffler made preparations for little Kurt's second birthday. Oskar, too, took considerable interest in the impending celebration; for from June 12, 1943 it would be only a brief year. If I had been present, I might have whispered into my son's ear on his second birthday: 'Just wait, soon you too will be drumming.'

But it so happened that on June 12, 1943, Oskar was no longer in Danzig-Langfuhr but in Metz, an ancient city founded by the Romans. My absence was indeed so protracted that Oskar had considerable difficulty in getting back to his native place by June 12, 1944, before the big air raids and in time for Kurt's third birthday.

What business took me abroad? I won't beat around the bush. Outside the Pestalozzi School, which had been turned into an Air Force barracks, I met my master Bebra. But Bebra by himself could not have persuaded me to go out into the world. On Bebra's arm hung Raguna, Signora Roswitha, the great somnambulist.

Oskar was coming from Kleinhammer-Weg. He had paid Gretchen Scheffler a call and had leafed through the *Struggle for Rome*. Even then, even in the days of Belisarius, he had discovered, history had its ups and downs, even then victories and defeats at river crossings and cities were celebrated or deplored with a fine geographical sweep.

I crossed the Fröbelwiese, which in the course of the last few years had been turned into a storehouse for the Organization Todt; I was thinking about Taginae – where in the year 552 Narses defeated Totila – but it was not the victory that attracted my thoughts to Narses, the great Armenian; no, what interested me was the general's build; Narses was a misshapen hunchback, Narses was undersized, a dwarf, a gnome, a midget. Narses, I reflected, was a child's head taller than Oskar. By then I was standing outside the Pestalozzi School. Eager to make comparisons, I looked at the insignia of some Air Force officers who had shot up too quickly. Surely, I said to myself, Narses hadn't worn any insignia, he had no need to. And there, in the main entrance to the school, stood the great general in person; on his arm hung a lady – why shouldn't Narses have had a lady on his arm? As they stepped toward me, they were dwarfed by the Air Force giants, and yet they were the hub and center, round them hung an aura of history and legend, they were old as the hills in the midst of these half-baked heroes of the air – what was this whole barracks full of Totilas and Tejas, full of mast-high Ostrogoths, beside a single Armenian dwarf named Narses? With measured tread Narses approached Oskar; he beckoned and so did the lady on his arm. Respectfully the Air Force moved out of our way as

Bebra and Signora Roswitha Raguna greeted me. I moved my lips close to Bebra's ear and whispered: 'Beloved master, I took you for Narses the great general; I hold him in far higher esteem than the athlete Belisarius.'

Modestly Bebra waved my compliment away. But Raguna was pleased by my comparison. How prettily her lips moved when she spoke: 'Why, Bebra, is our young *amico* so mistaken? Does not the blood of Prince Eugene flow in your veins? *E Lodovico quattordicesimo?* Is he not your ancestor?'

Bebra took my arm and led me aside, for the Air Force kept admiring us and annoying us with their stares. After a lieutenant and a moment later two sergeants had saluted Bebra – the master bore the stripes of a captain and on his sleeve an armband with the legend 'Propaganda Company' – after the fliers had asked Raguna for autographs and obtained them, Bebra motioned the driver of his official car and we got in. As we drove off, there was more applause from the Air Force.

We drove down Pestalozzi-Strasse, Madgeburger-Strasse, Heeresanger. Bebra sat beside the driver. It was in Magdeburger-Strasse that Raguna started in, taking my drum as a springboard: 'Still faithful to your drum, dear friend?' she whispered with her Mediterranean voice that I had not heard in so long. 'And in general how faithful have you been?' Oskar gave no answer, spared her the narrative of his complicated sex life, but smilingly permitted the great somnambulist to caress first his drum, then his hands, which were clutching the drum rather convulsively, to caress his hands in a more and more meridional way.

As we turned into the Heeresanger and followed the rails of the Number 5 car line, I even responded, that is, I stroked her left hand with mine, while her right hand bestowed tenderness on my right hand. We had passed Max-Halbe-Platz, it was too late for Oskar to get out, when, looking into the rear view mirror, I saw Bebra's shrewd, light-brown, age-old eyes observing our caresses. But Raguna held on to my hands, which, out of consideration for my friend and master, I should have liked to withdraw. Bebra smiled in the rear view mirror, then looked away and struck up a conversation with the driver, while Roswitha for her part, warmly caressing and pressing my hands, embarked in Mediterranean tones upon a discourse addressed simply and directly to my heart, fluid, lyrical words which, after taking a brief practical turn, became sweeter than ever, paralyzing all my scruples and thoughts of flight. We were at Reichskolonie, heading for the Women's Clinic, when Raguna owned to Oskar that she had never stopped thinking of him all these years, that she still had the glass from the Four Seasons Café, upon which I had sung an inscription, that Bebra was an excellent friend and working companion, but marriage was out of the question; Bebra had to live alone, said Raguna, in answer to a question from me; she allowed him complete freedom, and he too, although extremely jealous by nature, had come to understand in the course of the years that Raguna could not be tied, and anyway Bebra, as director of the Theater at the Front, had little time for conjugal duties, but as for the troupe, it was tops, in peacetime it could perfectly well have played at the Wintergarten or the Scala, would I, Oskar, with all my divine talent that was just going to waste, be interested in a trial year, I was certainly old enough, a trial year, she could promise me I would like it, but presumably I, Oskar, had other obligations, *vero?* So much the better, they were leaving today, they had just given their last performance in the military district of Danzig-West Prussia, now they were going to France, there was no danger of being sent to the Eastern Front for the present, they had that behind them, thank goodness, I, Oskar, could be very glad that the East was passé, that I would be going to Paris, yes, they were certainly going to Paris, had I, Oskar, ever been in Paris. Well, then, *amico*, if Raguna cannot seduce your hard drummer's heart, let Paris seduce you, *andiamo!*

As the great somnambulist spoke these last words, the car stopped. Green grew the trees on Hindenburg-Allee, at regular Prussian intervals. We got out, Bebra told the driver to wait. I wasn't in the mood for the Four Seasons, my head was spinning and in need of fresh air. We strolled about the Steffens-Park, Bebra to my right, Roswitha to my left. Bebra explained the nature and purpose of the Propaganda Company. Roswitha related anecdotes from the daily life of the Propaganda Company. Bebra spoke of war artists, war correspondents, and his theater. From Roswitha's Mediterranean lips poured the names of distant cities I had heard of on the radio. Bebra said Copenhagen, Roswitha murmured Palermo. Bebra sang Belgrade; Athens, lamented

Roswitha in the tones of a tragedienne. But both of them raved about Paris; even if I never saw those other cities, they assured me, Paris would compensate for my loss. And finally Bebra, speaking as director and captain of a front-line theater, made me what sounded like an official offer: 'Join us, young man, drum, sing beer glasses and light bulbs to pieces. The German Army of Occupation in fair France, in Paris the city of eternal youth, will reward you with gratitude and applause.'

Purely for the sake of form, Oskar asked for time to think it over. For a good half an hour I walked about in the springtime shrubbery, apart from Raguna, apart from Bebra my friend and master; I gave myself an air of tormented reflection, I rubbed my forehead, I hearkened, as I had never done before, to the little birds in the trees; a little robin would tell me what to do. Suddenly some winged creature was heard to outchirp all the rest, and I said: 'Mother Nature in her wisdom and benevolence advises me, revered master, to accept your offer. You may look upon me from this moment on as a member of your troupe.'

Then we went to the Four Seasons after all, drank an anemic mocha, and discussed the details of my getaway, but we didn't call it a getaway, we spoke of it rather as a departure.

Outside the café we recapitulated the details of our plan. Then I took my leave of Raguna and Captain Bebra of the Propaganda Company, who insisted on putting his official car at my disposal. While the two of them sauntered up Hindenburg-Allee in the direction of town, the captain's driver, a middle-aged corporal, drove me back to Langfuhr. He let me off at Max-Halbe-Platz, an Oskar driving into Labesweg in an official Wehrmacht car would have attracted far too much attention.

I hadn't too much time ahead of me. A farewell visit to Matzerath and Maria. For a while I stood by the playpen of my son Kurt; if I remember right, I even managed a few paternal thoughts and tried to caress the blond little rascal. Little Kurt rebuffed my caresses, but not so Maria. With some surprise she accepted my fondlings, the first in years, and returned them affectionately. I found it strangely hard to take leave of Matzerath. He was standing in the kitchen cooking kidneys in mustard sauce; utterly at one with his cooking spoon, he may even have been happy. I feared to disturb him. But when he reached behind him and groped blindly for something on the kitchen table, Oscar guessed his intention, picked up the little board with the chopped parsley on it, and handed it to him; to this day, I am convinced that long after I had left the kitchen Matzerath must have stood there surprised and bewildered with his parsley board; for never before had Oskar handed Matzerath anything.

I ate supper with Mother Trunczinski; I let her wash me and put me to bed, waited until she had retired and was snoring, each snore followed by a soft whistle. Then I located my slippers, picked up my clothes, and tiptoed through the room where the grey-haired mouse was snoring, whistling, and growing older; in the hallway I had a little trouble with the key, but finally coaxed the bolt out of its groove. Still in my nightgown, I carried my bundle of clothes up the stairs to the attic. Stumbling over the air defense sand pile and the air defense bucket, I came to my hiding place behind piles of roofing tiles and bundles of newspapers, stored there in defiance of air defense regulations. There I unearthed a brand-new drum that I had set aside unbeknownst to Maria. And I also found Oskar's one-volume library: Rasputin and Goethe. Should I take my favourite authors with me?

While slipping into his clothes, adjusting the drum round his neck, stowing his drumsticks under his braces, Oskar carried on negotiations with his two gods Dionysus and Apollo. The god of unreflecting drunkenness advised me to take no reading matter at all, or if I absolutely insisted on reading matter, then a little stack of Rasputin would do; Apollo, on the other hand, in his shrewd, sensible way, tried to talk me out of this trip to France altogether, but when he saw that Oskar's mind was made up, insisted on the proper baggage; very well, I would have to take the highly respectable yawn that Goethe had yawned so long ago, but for spite, and also because I knew that *The Elective Affinities* could never solve all my sexual problems, I also took Rasputin and his naked women, naked but for their black stockings. If Apollo strove for harmony and Dionysus for drunkenness and chaos, Oskar was a little demigod whose business it was to harmonize chaos and intoxicate reason. In addition to his mortality, he had one advantage over all the full divinities whose characters and careers had been established in the remote past: Oskar could read what he pleased, whereas the gods censored themselves.

How accustomed one becomes to an apartment house and the kitchen smells of nineteen tenants. I took my leave of every step, every story, every apartment door with its name plate: O Meyn the musician, whom they had sent home as unfit for service, who played the trumpet again, drank gin again, and waited for them to come for him again – and later on they actually did come for him, but this time they didn't let him take his trumpet. O Axel Mischke, for what did you exchange your whip? Mr. and Mrs. Woiwuth, who were always eating kohlrabi. Because Mr. Heinert had stomach trouble, he was working at Schichau instead of serving in the infantry. And next door lived Heinert's parents, who were still called Heimowski. O Mother Truczinski; gently slumbered the mouse behind her apartment door. My ear to the wood, I heard her whistling. Shorty, whose name was really Retzel, had made lieutenant, even though as a child he had always been compelled to wear long woolen stockings. Schlager's son was dead, Eyke's son was dead, Kollin's son was dead. But Laubschad the watchmaker was still alive, waking dead clocks to life. And old man Heilandt was still alive, hammering crooked nails straight. And Mrs. Schwerwinski was sick, and Mr. Schwerwinski was in good health but nevertheless died first. And what of the ground floor? Who lived there? There dwelt Alfred and Maria Matzerath and a little rascal almost two years old, named Kurt. And who was it that left the large, heavily breathing apartment house? It was Oskar, little Kurt's father. What did he take out with him into the darkened street? He took his drum and a big educational book. Why did he stop still amid all the blacked-out houses, amid all those houses that put there trust in the air-defense regulations, why did he stop outside one of these blacked-out houses? Because there dwelt the widow Greff, to whom he owed not his education but certain delicate skills. Why did he take off his cap outside the black house? Because he was thinking of Greff the greengrocer, who had curly hair and an aquiline nose, who weighed and hanged himself both at the same time, who hanging still had curly hair and an aquiline nose, though his brown eyes, which ordinarily lay thoughtfully in their grottoes, were now strained and protuberant. Why did Oskar put his sailor cap with the flowing ribbons back on again and plod off? Because

305

he had an appointment at the Langfuhr freight station. Did he get there on time? He did.

At the last minute, that is, I reached the railway embankment, not far from the Brünshofer-Weg underpass. No, I did not stop at the nearby office of Dr. Hollatz. In my thoughts I took leave of Sister Inge and sent greetings to the baker couple in Kleinhammer-Weg, but all this I did while walking, and only the Church of the Sacred Heart forced me to pause a moment – a pause that almost made me late. The portal was closed. But only too vividly my mind's eye saw that pink boy Jesus perched on the Virgin Mary's left thigh. My poor mama, there she was again. She knelt in the confessional, pouring her grocery wife's sins into Father Wiehnke's ear very much as she had poured sugar into blue pound and half-pound bags. And Oscar knelt at the left-side altar, trying to teach the boy Jesus how to drum, but the little monster wouldn't drum, wouldn't give me a miracle. Oskar had sworn at the time, and today outside the closed church door he swore again; I'll teach him to drum yet. Sooner or later.

Having a long journey ahead of me, I settled for later and turned a drummer's back on the church door, confident that Jesus would not escape me. Not far from the underpass, I scrambled up the railway embankment, losing a little Goethe and Rasputin in the process, but most of my educational baggage was still with me when I reached the tracks. Then I stumbled on a few yards, over ties and crushed stone, and nearly knocked Bebra over in the darkness.

'If it isn't our virtuoso drummer!' cried the captain and musical clown. Bidding one another to be careful, we groped our way over tracks and intersections, lost our bearings amid a maze of stationary freight cars, and finally found the furlough train, in which a compartment had been assigned to Bebra's troupe.

Oskar had many a streetcar ride behind him, but now he was going to ride in a train. When Bebra pushed me into the compartment, Raguna looked up with a smile from something she was sewing and kissed me on the cheek. Still smiling, but without interrupting her needlework, she introduced the other two members of the troupe: the acrobats Felix and Kitty. Kitty, honey-blonde with a rather grey complexion, was not unattractive and seemed to be about the signora's size. She had a slight Saxon accent that added to her charm. Felix, the acrobat, was no doubt the tallest member of the troupe. He must have measured almost four feet. The poor fellow suffered from his disproportionate stature. The arrival of my trim three feet made him more self-conscious than ever. His profile was rather like that of a highly bred race horse, which led Raguna to call him 'Cavallo' or 'Felix Cavallo'. Like Captain Bebra, the acrobat wore a field-grey Army uniform, though with the insignia of a corporal. The ladies, too, wore field-grey tailored into traveling uniforms which were not very becoming. Raguna's sewing also proved to be field-grey, my future uniform. Felix and Bebra had purchased the cloth, Ros-witha and Kitty took turns sewing, snipping away more and more of the material until trousers, jacket, and cap were the right size for me. As to shoes, it would have been useless to search the clothing depots of the Wehrmacht for Oskar's size. I had to content myself with my civilian laced shoes, and I never did get any Army boots.

My papers were forged. Felix the acrobat proved very clever at this delicate work. Sheer courtesy deterred me from protesting when the great somnambulist adopted me as her brother, her elder brother, I might add: Oskarnello Raguna, born on October 21, 1912 in Naples. I have used all sorts of names in my time. Oskarnello Raguna was certainly not the least mellifluous.

The train pulled out. By way of Stolp, Stettin, Berlin, Hanover, and Cologne, it carried us to Metz. Of Berlin I saw next to nothing. We had a five-hour stopover. Naturally there was an air raid. We had to take refuge in the Thomaskeller. The soldiers from the train were packed like sardines in the vaulted rooms. There was quite a to-do as an MP tried to fit us in. A few of the boys who had just come from the Eastern Front knew Bebra and his troupe from earlier performances; they clapped and whistled and Raguna blew kisses. We were asked to perform; in a few minutes something resembling a stage was improvised at one end of the former beer hall. Bebra could hardly say no, especially when an Air Force major requested him amiably and with exaggerated deference to give the men a treat.

For the first time, Oskar was to appear in a real theatrical performance. Though not wholly unprepared – in the course of the train trip Bebra had several times rehearsed my number with me – I was stricken with stage fright and Raguna found occasion to soothe me by stroking my hands.

With loathsome alacrity the boys handed in our professional luggage and a moment later Felix and Kitty started their act. They were both made of rubber. They tied themselves into knot, twined in and out and around it, exchanged arms and legs. The spectacle gave the pushing, wide-eyed soldiers fierce pains in their joints and sore muscles that would plague them for days. While Felix and Kitty were still tying and untying themselves, Bebra embarked on his musical clown number. On beer bottles ranging from full to empty, he played the most popular hits of the war years; he played 'Erika' and 'Mamatchi, Give Me a Horse'; he made the 'Stars of the Homeland' twinkle and resound from the bottlenecks, and when that didn't quite take, fell back on his old standby: 'Jimmy the Tiger' raged and roared among the bottles. That appealed to the soldiers and even to Oskar's jaded ear; and when after a few ridiculous but successful tricks of magic Bebra announced Roswitha Raguna the great somnambulist and Oskarnello Raguna the glass-slaying drummer, the audience was nicely warmed up: the success of Roswitha and Oskarnello was assured. I introduced our performance with a light roll on my drum, led up to the climaxes with crescendo rolls, and after each phase invited applause with a loud and accurately timed boom. Raguna would invite a soldier, even an officer or two, to step forward; she would bid a leathery old corporal or a bashfully cocky young ensign sit down beside her. And then she would look into his heart – yes, Raguna saw into the hearts of men. She would reveal not only the data, always correct, out of her subject's paybook, but details of his intimate life as well. Her indiscretions were always full of delicacy and wit. In conclusion she rewarded one of her victims with a bottle of beer and asked him to hold it up high so the audience could see it. Then she gave me, Oskarnello, the signal: my drum rolled crescendo and I lifted up my voice, a voice designed for far more exacting tasks. It was child's play to shatter that beer bottle, not without a resounding explosion: the bewildered, beer-bespattered face of a case-hardened corporal or of a milk-faced ensign – I don't remember which – wrote finis to our act – and then came applause, long and thunderous, mingled with the sounds of a major air raid on the capital.

Our offering was hardly in the international class, but it entertained the men, it made them forget the front and the furlough
that was ended, and it made them laugh and laugh; for when the
aerial torpedoes landed overhead, shaking and burying the cellar
and everything in it, dousing the light and the emergency light,
when everything about us was tossed topsy-turvy, laughter still
rang through the dark, stifling coffin, accompanied by cries of
'Bebra! We want Bebra!' And good old indestructible Bebra spoke
up, played the clown in the darkness, wrung volleys of laughter
from the buried mob. And when voices demanded Raguna and
Oskarnello, he blared out: 'Signora Raguna is very tired, my dear
tin soldiers. And Oskarnello must also take a little nap for the
sake of the Greater German Reich and final victory.'

She, Roswitha, lay with me and was frightened. Oskar, on the
other hand, was not frightened, and yet he lay with Raguna. Her
fear and my courage brought our hands together. I felt her fear
and she felt my courage. At length I became rather fearful, and
she grew courageous. And after I had banished her fear and given
her courage, my manly courage raised its head a second time.
While my courage was eighteen glorious years old, she, in I
know not what year of her life, recumbent for I know not the
howmanieth time, fell a prey once more to the fear that aroused
my courage. For like her face, her body, sparingly measured but
quite complete, showed no trace of time. Timelessly courageous
and timelessly fearful, Roswitha offered herself to me. And never
will anyone learn whether that midget, who during a major air
raid on the capital lost her fear beneath my courage in the buried
Thomaskeller until the air-raid wardens dug us out, was nineteen
or ninety-nine years old; what makes it all the easier for Oskar
to be discreet is that he himself has no idea whether this first
embrace truly suited to his physical dimensions was conferred
upon him by a courageous old woman or by a young girl made
submissive by fear.

Inspection of Concrete, or Barbaric, Mystical, Bored

For three weeks we played every night in the venerable case-
mates of Metz, long a city of garrisons and once a Roman
outpost. We did the same program for two weeks in Nancy. A
few words of French had begun to sprout from Oskar's lips. In
Reims we had an opportunity to admire damage created by the
previous World War. Sickened by humanity, the stone menagerie
of the world-famous cathedral spewed water and more water on
the cobblestones round about, which is a way of saying that it
rained all day in Reims even at night. But Paris gave us a mild
and resplendent September. I spent my nineteenth birthday strolling on the *quais* with Roswitha on my arm. Although Paris was
well known to me from Sergeant Fritz Truczinski's postcards, I
wasn't a bit disappointed. The first time Roswitha and I – she
measured three feet three, three inches more than myself – stood
arm in arm at the foot of the Eiffel Tower, looking up, we
became aware – this too for the first time – of our grandeur and
uniqueness. We exchanged kisses wherever we went, but that's
nothing new in Paris.

How wonderful it is to rub shoulders with art and history! Still
with Roswitha on my arm, I visited the Dôme des Invalides,
thinking of the great Emperor and feeling very close to him,
because, though great, he was not tall. Recalling how, at the tomb
of Frederick the Great, himself no giant, Napoleon had said: 'If
he were still alive, we should not be standing here,' I whispered
tenderly into my Roswitha's ear: 'If the Corsican were still alive,
we should not be standing here, we should not be kissing each
other under the bridges, on the *quais, sur le trottoir de Paris.*'

In collaboration with other groups, we put on colossal programs
at the Salle Pleyel and the Théâtre Sarah Bernhardt. Oskar
quickly grew accustomed to the theatrical style of the big city,
perfected his repertory, adapted himself to the jaded tastes of the

Paris occupation troops: No longer did I waste my vocal prowess on common German beer bottles; here, in the city of light, I shattered graceful, invaluable vases and fruit bowls, immaterial figments of blown glass, taken from French castles. My number was conceived along historical lines. I started in with glassware from the reign of Louis XIV, and continued, like history itself, with the reign of Louis XV. With revolutionary fervor I attacked the crockery of the unfortunate Louis XVI and his headless and heedless Marie Antoinette. Finally, after a sprinkling of Louis-Philippe, I carried my battle to the vitreous fantasies of the Third Republic.

Of course the historical significance of my act was beyond the reach of the field-grey mass in the orchestra and galleries; they applauded my shards as common shards; but now and then there was a staff officer or a newspaperman from the Reich who relished my historical acumen along with the damage. A scholarly character in uniform complimented me on my art when we were introduced to him after a gala performance for the Kommandantur. Oskar was particularly grateful to the correspondent for a leading German newspaper who described himself as an expert on France and discreetly called my attention to a few trifling mistakes, not to say stylistic inconsistencies, in my program.

We spent the whole winter in Paris. They billeted us in first-class hotels, and I shall not deny that all winter long Roswitha joined me in investigating the superior qualities of French beds. Was Oskar happy in Paris? Had he forgotten his dear ones at home, Maria, Matzerath, Gretchen and Alexander Scheffler; had Oskar forgotten his son Kurt and his grandmother Anna Koljaiczek?

Though I had not forgotten them, I missed none of them. I wrote no Army postcards, gave no sign of life, but on the contrary gave the folks at home every opportunity to live a whole year without me; for from the moment of my departure I had been resolved to return, whence it followed that I would have been rather interested to know how they were getting along in my absence. On the street or during performances, I sometimes searched the soldiers' faces for familiar features. Perhaps, Oskar speculated, Fritz Truczinski or Axel Mischke has been transferred here from the Eastern Front, and once or twice he thought he had recognized Maria's handsome brother amid a horde of infantrymen; but it wasn't he; field-grey can be misleading.

Only the Eiffel Tower made me homesick. Don't go supposing that I rode to the top and that remote vistas made me dream of home. Oskar had mounted the Eiffel Tower so often on postcards and in his thoughts that an actual ascension could only have brought him disappointment. As I stood or sat at the foot of the Eiffel Tower, but without Roswitha, alone beneath those towering girders flung upward by the pioneers of steel construction, the great vault, which seems so solidly closed despite spaces on all sides, became for me the sheltering vault of my grandmother Anna: sitting beneath the Eiffel Tower, I was sitting beneath her four skirts, the Champ de Mars was a Kashubian potato field, the Paris October rain slanted endlessly down between Bissau and Ramkau, and on such days all Paris, even the Metro, smelled of slightly rancid butter. I grew silent and thoughtful. Roswitha respected my sorrow and was very kind and considerate on these occasions; she was a sensitive soul.

In April, 1944 – from all fronts came communiqués announcing that our lines had been successfully shortened – we were obliged to pack up and leave Paris for a tour of the Atlantic Wall. Our first stop was Le Havre. It seemed to me that Bebra was becoming taciturn and distraught. Though he never lost his grip during performances and still had the laughs on his side, his age-old Narses face turned to stone once the last curtain had fallen. At first I thought he was jealous, or, worse, that he had capitulated in the face of my youthful vigor. In whispers Roswitha dispelled my error; she didn't know exactly what was going on, but she had noticed that certain officers were meeting with Bebra behind closed doors after the show. It looked as though the master were emerging from his inward emigration, as though, inspired by the blood of his ancestor Prince Eugene, he were planning some direct action. His plans had carried him so far away from us, had involved him in preoccupations so vast and far-reaching, that Oskar's intimacy with his former Roswitha could arouse no more than a weary wrinkled smile. One day in Trouville – we were lodged at the Casino – he found us intertwined on the carpet of the dressing room he shared with us. Our impulse was to leap apart, but with a gesture he gave us to understand that there was no need to. Looking into his make-up glass, he said: 'Enjoy yourselves, children, hug and kiss, tomorrow we inspect concrete, and the day after tomorrow it's concrete you'll have between your lips. Gather ye rosebuds while ye may.'

That was in June, '44. By that time we had done the Atlantic Wall from the Bay of Biscay to Holland, but we spent most of our time inland and saw little of the legendary pillboxes. It wasn't until Trouville that we played directly on the coast. Here we were offered an opportunity to visit the Atlantic Wall. Bebra accepted. After our last show in Trouville, we were driven to the village of Bavent near Caen, three miles behind the shore dunes. We were lodged with peasants. Pasture, hedgerows, apple trees. That is where the apple brandy called calvados is distilled. We had a drink of it and went to bed. Brisk air came in through the window, a frog pond croaked until morning. Some frogs are good drummers. I heard them in my sleep and said to myself: Oskar, you've got to go home, soon your son Kurt will be three years old, you've got to give him his drum, you've promised. Thus admonished, Oskar, the tormented father, awoke each hour, groped about in the darkness, made sure his Roswitha was there, breathed in her smell: Raguna smelled ever so slightly of cinnamon, crushed cloves, and nutmeg; even in summer she had that scent of Christmas, of cake spice.

In the morning an armored personnel carrier drove up to the farm. We stood in the doorway, chatting into the sea wind, all of us shivering a little. It was early and very chilly. We got in: Bebra, Raguna, Felix and Kitty, Oskar, and a Lieutenant Herzog who was taking us to his battery west of Cabourg.

To say Normandy is green is to disregard the spotted brown and white cows which were chewing their cuds on misty meadows, wet with dew, to the right and left of the straight highway, greeted our armored vehicle with such indifference that the armor plate would have turned red with shame had it not previously been daubed with camouflage paint. Poplars, hedgerows, creepers, the first hulking beach hotels, empty, their shutters clattering in the wind. We turned into the beach promenade, got out, and plodded along behind the lieutenant, who showed Captain Bebra a condescending yet properly military respect, across the dunes, against a wind full of sand and surf roar.

This wasn't the mild, bottle-green Baltic, sobbing like a tender-hearted maiden as it waited for me to come in. It was the Atlantic carrying out its immemorial maneuver, pressing forward at high tide, receding at low tide.

And then we had our concrete. We could admire it and even pat it to our heart's content; it didn't budge. 'Attention!' cried someone inside the concrete and leapt, tall as a mast, from the pillbox, which was shaped like a flattened-out turtle, lay amid sand dunes, was called 'Dora Seven', and looked out upon the shifting tides through gun embrasures, observation slits, and machine-gun barrels. The man's name was Corporal Lankes. He reported to Lieutenant Herzog and at the same time to our Captain Bebra.

LANKES: (*saluting*): Dora seven, one corporal and four men. Nothing special to report.

HERZOG: Thank you. At ease, Corporal Lankes. Did you hear that, Captain? Nothing special to report. That's how it's been for years.

BEBRA: There's still the tide. Ebbing and flowing. Nature's contribution.

HERZOG: That's just what keeps our men busy. That's why we go on building pillboxes one after another. They're already in each other's field of fire. Pretty soon we'll have to demolish a few of them to make room for more concrete.

BEBRA (*knocks on the concrete; the members of his troupe do likewise*): And you have faith in concrete?

HERZOG: Faith is hardly the right word. We haven't much faith in anything any more. What do you say, Lankes?

LANKES: Right, sir. No more faith.

BEBRA: But they keep on mixing and pouring.

HERZOG: Between you and me, Captain, we're getting valuable experience. I'd never built a thing until I came here. I was in school when the war started. Now I've learned a thing or two about cement and I hope to make use of it after the war. The whole of Germany is going to have to be rebuilt. Take a good look at this concrete. (BEBRA *and his troupe poke their noses into the concrete.*) What do you see? Shells. We've got all we we need right at the doorstep. Just have to take the stuff and mix. Stones, shells, sand, cement . . . What else can I tell you, Captain, you are an artist, you know how it is. Lankes, tell the captain what we put in our cement.

LANKES: Yes, sir. I'll tell the captain. Puppies, sir. Every one of our pillboxes has a puppy in it. Walled up in the foundation.

BEBRA'S TROUPE: A puppy?

LANKES: Pretty soon there won't be a single puppy left in the whole sector from Caen to Le Havre.

BEBRA'S TROUPE: No more puppies.

LANKES: That's what eager beavers we are.

BEBRA'S TROUPE: What eager beavers!

LANKES: Pretty soon we'll have to use kittens.

BEBRA'S TROUPE: Meow!

LANKES: But cats aren't as good as dogs. That's why we hope there'll be a little action here soon.

BEBRA'S TROUPE: The big show! (*They applaud.*)

LANKES: We've rehearsed enough. And if we run out of puppies . . .

BEBRA'S TROUPE: Oh!

LANKES: . . . we'll have to stop building. Cats are bad luck.

BEBRA'S TROUPE: Meow! Meow!

LANKES: Would you like me to tell you short and sweet why we put in puppies . . .

BEBRA'S TROUPE: Puppies!

LANKES: Personally I think it's the bunk . . .

BEBRA'S TROUPE: For shame!

LANKES: But my buddies, here, are mostly from the country. And in the country when they build a house or a barn or a village church, it's the custom to put something living in the foundations . . . and . . .

HERZOG: That's enough, Lankes. At ease. As you've heard, sir, we're given to superstition here on the Atlantic Wall. Like you theater people who mustn't whistle before an opening night or spit over your shoulders before the curtain goes up . . .

BEBRA'S TROUPE: Toi-toi-toi! (*Spit over each other's shoulders.*)

HERZOG: But joking aside, we've got to let the men have their fun. Recently they've started decorating the entrances to the pillboxes with improvisations in concrete or sea-shell mosaics, and it's tolerated by order from way up. The men like to be kept busy. Those concrete pretzels get on our C.O.'s nerves, but what I tell him is: better pretzels in the concrete, sir, than pretzels in the head. We Germans are no good at sitting idle. That's a fact.

BEBRA: And we, too, do our bit to distract the men who are waiting on the Atlantic Wall . . .

BEBRA'S TROUPE: Bebra's front-line theater sings for you, plays for you, boosts your morale for the final victory.

HERZOG: Yes, you've got the right point of view. But the theater alone isn't enough. Most of the time we have only ourselves to depend on, and we do our best. Am I right, Lankes?

LANKES: Right, sir. We do our best.

HERZOG: There you have it. And if you'll excuse me now, sir, I've got to take a run over to Dora Four and Dora Five. Take your time, have a good look at our concrete. It's worth it. Lankes will show you everything . . .

LANKES: Everything, sir.

(Lankes and Bebra exchange salutes. Herzog goes out right, Raguna, Oskar, Felix, and Kitty, who have thus far been standing behind Bebra, jump out. Oskar is holding his drum, Raguna is carrying a basket of provisions. Felix and Kitty climb up on the concrete roof of the pillbox and begin doing acrobatic exercises. Oskar and Raguna play with pails and shovels, make it plain that they are in love, yodel, and tease Felix and Kitty.)

BEBRA: *(wearily, after examining the pillbox from all sides)*: Tell me, Corporal, what is your civilian occupation?

LANKES: Painter, sir, but that was a long time ago.

BEBRA: House painter?

LANKES: Houses too, but mostly pictures.

BEBRA: Hear, hear! You mean you emulated the great Rembrandt, or maybe Velasquez?

LANKES: Sort of in between.

BEBRA: Why, good God man! Why are you mixing, pouring, guarding concrete? You ought to be in the Propaganda Company. Why, a war artist is just what we need!

LANKES: It's not my line, sir. My stuff slants too much for present tastes. But if you've got a cigarette . . .

316

(BEBRA *hands him a cigarette.*)

BEBRA: Slants? I suppose you mean it's modern?

LANKES: What do you mean by modern? Well, anyway, before they started up with their concrete, slanting was modern for a while.

BEBRA: Oh.

LANKES: Yep.

BEBRA: I guess you lay it on thick. With a trowel maybe?

LANKES: Yeah, I do that too. I stick my thumb in, automatic like, I put in nails and buttons, and before '33 I had a period when I put barbed wire on cinnabar. Got good reviews. A private collector in Switzerland has them now. Makes soap.

BEBRA: Oh, this war! This awful war! And today you're pouring concrete. Hiring out your genius for fortification work. Well, I've got to admit, Leonardo and Michelangelo did the same thing in their day. Designed military machines and fortifications when they didn't have a madonna on order.

LANKES: See! There's always something cockeyed. Every real artist has got to express himself. If you'd like to take a look at the ornaments over the entrance, sir, I did them.

BEBRA: (*after a thorough examination of them*): Amazing! What wealth of form. What expressive power!

LANKES: Structural formations I call them.

BEBRA: And your creation, your picture, or should I call it a relief, has it a title?

LANKES: I just told you: Formations, or Oblique Formations if you like that better. It's a new style. Never been done before.

BEBRA: Even so, you ought to give it a title. Just to avoid misunderstandings. It's your work, after all.

LANKES: What for? What good are titles? Except to put in the catalog when you have a show.

BEBRA: You're putting on airs, Lankes. Think of me as an art lover, not as an officer. Cigarette? (LANKES *takes it.*) Well then, what's on your mind?

LANKES: Oh, all right, if you put it that way. This is how I figure it. When this war is over – one way or another, it will be over some day – well, then, when the war is over, the pillboxes will still be here. These things were made to last. And then my time will come. The centuries ... (*He puts the last cigarette in bis pocket.*) Maybe you've got another cigarette, sir? Thank you, sir . . . the centuries start coming and going, one after another like nothing at all. But the pillboxes stay put just like the Pyramids stayed put. And one fine day one of those archaeologist fellows comes along. And he says to himself: what an artistic void there was between the First and the Seventh World Wars! Dull drab concrete; here and there, over a pill-box entrance, you find some clumsy amateurish squiggles in the old-home style. And that's all. Then he discovers Dora Five, Six, Seven; he sees my Structural Oblique Formations, and he says to himself, Say, take a look at that, Very, very interesting, magic, menacing, and yet shot through with spirituality. In these works a genius, perhaps the only genius of the twentieth century, has expressed himself clearly, resolutely, and for all time. I wonder, says our archaeologist to himself, I wonder if it's got a name? A signature to tell us who the master was? Well, sir, if you look closely, sir, and hold your head on a slant, you'll see, between those Oblique Formations . . .

BEBRA: My glasses. Help me, Lankes.

LANKES: All right, here's what it says: Herbert Lankes, anno nineteen hundred and forty-four. Title: BARBARIC, MYSTICAL, BORED.

BEBRA: You have given our century its name.

LANKES: See!

BEBRA: Perhaps when they restore your work in five hundred or a thousand years, they will find a few puppy bones in the concrete.

LANKES: That will only give additional force to my title.

BEBRA (*excited*): What are the times and what are we, my friend, if our works . . . but take a look at Felix and Kitty, my acrobats. They are performing on the concrete.

> (*For some time a piece of paper has been passing back and forth between Roswitha and Oskar and Felix and Kitty, each pair writing on it by turns.*)

KITTY (*with a slight Saxon accent*): Mr Bebra, see what we can do on the concrete. (*She walks on her hands.*)

FELIX: Nobody ever did a back flip on concrete before. Not even a front flip. (*He does both.*)

KITTY: We oughta have a stage like this.

FELIX: It's a bit too windy for me.

KITTY: But it's not hot and stinky like the movie houses. (*She ties herself into a knot.*)

FELIX: And we've just composed a poem up here.

KITTY: What do you mean *we*? Oskarnello and Roswitha made it up.

FELIX: But we helped out when they were stuck for a rhyme.

KITTY: Just one word is missing, then it'll be done.

FELIX: Oskar wants to know what those spikes in the sand are called.

KITTY: 'Cause he needs them for the poem.

FELIX: They're too important to leave out.

KITTY: Won't you tell us, Mr Corporal? What are they called?

FELIX: Maybe he's not allowed to. On account of enemy ears.

KITTY: We promise not to tell anybody.

FELIX: It's for art.

KITTY: Oskarnello has gone to so much trouble.

FELIX: And how beautifully he writes. In Sütterlin script.

KITTY: I wonder where he learned it.

FELIX: Oh, Oskar's educated. He knows everything, except what those spikes are called.

LANKES: I'll tell you if the captain has no objection.

BEBRA: But maybe it's top secret.

FELIX: But Oskar needs to know.

KITTY: Or the poem will be ruined.

ROSWITHA: And we're all so curious.

BEBRA: You might as well tell us. It's an order.

LANKES: Well, we put them in as a defense against tanks and landing craft. They look like asparagus, don't they? Well, that's why we call them Rommel asparagus.

FELIX: Rommel . . .

KITTY: . . . asparagus? Does it fit Oskarnello?

OSKAR: It fits! (*He writes the word on the paper, hands the poem to Kitty on top of the pillbox. She knots herself still more and recites the following lines like a schoolchild.*)

KITTY: On the Atlantic Wall

Rommel has sent us steel asparagus

And here we sit, bristling and camouflaged,
Dreaming of the land of carpet slippers,
Of Sunday's roasts and Friday's kippers,
Where everything is soft and snug:
The trend is toward the bourgeois-smug.
We live in concrete and barbed wire,

We bury mines in the latrines.
But then we dream of garden bowers
Of frigidaires and happy hours
Bestowed by an electric plug:
The trend is toward the bourgeois-smug.
Though some of us are sure to die
And many a mother's heart must break,

Though death still wears a parachute
And Martian harness on his suit,
The thought of comfort's like a drug:
The trend is toward the bourgeois-smug.

(*All applaud, including Lankes.*)

LANKES: It's low tide.

ROSWITHA: That's time for breakfast. (*She brandishes her big basket, which is decorated with bows and artificial flowers.*)

KITTY: Oh, yes, a picnic in the open.

FELIX: Nature has whetted our appetites.

ROSWITHA: Oh, sacred act of belly-filling that will unite the nations as long as men eat breakfast!

BEBRA: Let us feast on the concrete. Let us have human rituals built on solid foundations! (*All except for Lankes climb up on the pillbox. Roswitha spreads out a bright flowery tablecloth. From the bottomless basket she produces little cushions with tassels and fringes. A pink and bright green parasol is opened, a tiny gramophone with loudspeaker is set up. Little plates, little spoons, little knives, egg cups, and napkins are distributed.*)

FELIX: I'd like some of the pâté de foie gras.

KITTY: Have you still got any of that caviar we rescued from Stalingrad?

OSKAR: You oughtn't to spread the Danish butter so thick, Roswitha.

BEBRA: I'm glad to see you looking out for her figure. That's the right spirit, son.

ROSWITHA: But I like it and it's good for me. Oh! When I think of the cake and whipped cream the Air Force served us in Copenhagen.

BEBRA: The Dutch chocolate in the thermos bottle is still nice and warm.

KITTY: I'm just crazy about these canned American cookies.

ROSWITHA: But they're only good if you spread some of the South African ginger preserve on top.

OSKAR: A little moderation, Roswitha, I beseech you.

ROSWITHA: What about you? Look at the big thick slices of that nasty English corned beef you've been helping yourself to.

BEBRA: What about you, my dear corporal? May I offer you a paper-thin slice of raisin bread with plum jam?

LANKES: If I weren't on duty, sir.

ROSWITHA: He needs an official order.

KITTY: Yes, do give him an order.

BEBRA: Very well. Corporal Lankes, you are hereby ordered to accept a slice of raisin bread with French plum jam, a softboiled Danish egg, a spot of Soviet caviar, and a little cup of genuine Dutch chocolate.

LANKES: Yes, sir. (*He joins the others on top of the pillbox.*)

BEBRA: Haven't we another cushion for the corporal?

OSKAR: He can have mine. I'll sit on my drum.

ROSWITHA: Mustn't catch cold, precious. Concrete is treacherous, and you're not used to it.

KITTY: He can have my cushion too. I'll just knot myself up a little, it helps my digestion anyway.

FELIX: But do eat over the tablecloth or you'll get honey on the concrete. We wouldn't want to damage the defenses! (*All giggle.*)

BEBRA: Ah, the sea air! How fine it makes us feel.

ROSWITHA: Feel!

BEBRA: The breast expands.

ROSWITHA: Expands!

BEBRA: The heart casts off its crust.

ROSWITHA: Crust!

BEBRA: The soul is reborn.

ROSWITHA: Reborn!

BEBRA: The eyes soar aloft.

ROSWITHA: Aloft!

BEBRA: Over the sea, the endless sea ... I say, Corporal, I see something black down there on the beach. Whatever it is, there's five of them.

KITTY: So do I. With five umbrellas.

FELIX: Six.

KITTY: Five! One, two, three, four, five!

LANKES: It's the nuns from Lisieux. They've been evacuated and shipped over here with their kindergarten.

KITTY: I don't see any children. Just five umbrellas.

LANKES: They leave the children at Bavent. Sometimes they come. down here at low tide to pick up the crabs and shellfish that get stuck in the Rommel asparagus.

KITTY: Poor things!

ROSWITHA: Shouldn't we offer them some corned beef and cookies?

OSKAR: I suggest raisin bread with plum jam. It's Friday; nuns aren't allowed to eat corned beef on Friday.

KITTY: They're running now. They seem to be gliding on their umbrellas.

LANKES: They always do that when they've finished picking. Then they begin to play. Especially Agneta, the novice, she's just a kid that doesn't know which way is up. May be you could spare another cigarette? Thank you, sir. And the one back there, the fat one that isn't running is Scholastica, the mother superior. She doesn't like them to play on the beach, she thinks it might be against the rule of their order.

(*Nuns with umbrellas are seen running in the background. Roswitha puts on the gramophone*: 'Sleigh Bells in St. Petersburg.' *The nuns dance and shout*.)

AGNETA: Yoohoo, Sister Scholastica!

SCHOLASTICA: Agneta, Sister Agneta!

AGNETA: Yoohoo, Sister Scholastica!

SCHOLASTICA: Come back now, child! Sister Agneta!

AGNETA: I can't. It carries me away.

SCHOLASTICA: Then you must pray, sister, for a conversion.

AGNETA: A sorrowful one?

SCHOLASTICA: A merciful one.

AGGNETA: A joyful one?

SCHOLASTICA: Just pray, Sister Agneta!

AGNETA: I'm praying to beat the band. But I'm still being carried away.

SCHOLASTICA (*her voice dying away in the distance*): Agneta, Sister Agneta.

AGNETA: Yoohoo, Sister Scholastica!

(*The nuns disappear, but from time to time their umbrellas appear in the background. The phonograph record runs down. Beside the pillbox entrance the telephone rings. Lankes jumps down and picks up the receiver, the others go on eating.*)

ROSWITHA: Telephones, telephones, wherever you go. Between the sea and the sky, telephones.

LANKES: Dora Seven speaking. Corporal Lankes.

HERZOG: (*comes in slowly from the right, holding a telephone and dragging the wire after him. He stops repeatedly and talks into the phone*): Are you asleep, Lankes? There's something moving in front of Dora Seven. I'm sure of it.

LANKES: It's the nuns, sir.

HERZOG: What are nuns doing down there? And suppose they're not nuns.

LANKES: But they are nuns. I can see them plain as day.

HERZOG: Never hear of camouflage? Never hear of the fifth column? The English have been at it for centuries. They come in with their Bibles and before you know what they're up to, boom!

LANKES: They're picking up crabs, sir . . .

HERZOG: I want that beach cleared immediately. Is that clear?

LANKES: Yes, sir, but they're just picking up crabs.

HERZOG: Lankes, I want you to get your ass behind your MG!

LANKES: But suppose they're just looking for crabs, 'cause it's low tide and the children in their kindergarten . . .

HERZOG: That's an official order, Lankes.

LANKES: Yes, sir. (*Lankes disappears into the pillbox. Herzog goes out right with the telephone.*)

OSKAR: Roswitha, stop your ears, there's going to be shooting like in the newsreels.

KITTY: Oh, how awful! I'm going to knot myself still tighter.

323

BEBRA: I myself am almost inclined to think that we shall soon hear some noise.

FELIX: Let's put on another record. That will help some. (*He puts on the gramophone: The Platters singing 'The Great Pretender'. The rat-tat-tat of the machine gun punctuates the slow mournful music. Roswitha holds her ears. Felix stands on his head. In the background five nuns with umbrellas are seen flying heavenward. The record sticks in its groove and repeats. Felix returns to his feet. Kitty unties herself. Roswitha begins to clear the table and repack her basket. Oskar and Bebra help her. They leave the roof of the pillbox. Lankes appears in the entrance.*)

LANKES: Captain, sir, if you could spare another cigarette . . .

BEBRA: (*his frightened troupe huddle behind him*): You smoke too much, Corporal.

BEBRA'S TROUPE: He smokes too much.

LANKES: That's on account of the concrete, sir.

BEBRA: And suppose some day there's no more concrete?

BEBRA'S TROUPE: No more concrete.

LANKES: Concrete is immortal, sir. Just us and our cigarettes . . .

BEBRA: I know, I know, we vanish like a puff of smoke.

BEBRA'S TROUPE: (*slowly going out*): Smoke!

BEBRA: But in a thousand years they will still be coming to see the concrete.

BEBRA'S TROUPE: In a thousand years!

BEBRA: They'll find puppy bones.

BEBRA'S TROUPE: Puppy bones.

BEBRA: And your Oblique Formations in the concrete.

BEBRA'S TROUPE: BARBARIC, MYSTICAL, BORED!

(*Lankes is left alone, smoking*)

Though Oskar hardly opened his mouth in the course of that breakfast on the concrete, the mere fact that such words should be spoken on the eve of the invasion has impelled me to record them. Moreover, we haven't seen the last of Corporal Lankes, the master of 'concrete' art; we shall meet him again when the time comes to speak of the postwar period and the present apotheosis of bourgeois comfort.

On the beach promenade, our armored personnel carrier was still waiting for us. With long strides Lieutenant Herzog returned to his protégés and breathlessly apologized to Bebra for the little incident, adding, however, that the beach was off limits for civilians and 'Off limits is off limits.' He helped the ladies into the vehicle, gave the driver some instructions, and back we rode to Bavent. We had to hurry, there was no time for lunch, for at two o'clock we had a show at the charming little Norman château nestling among the poplars at the edge of the village.

We had barely half an hour in which to test the lighting; then Oskar raised the curtain with a drum flourish. We were playing to an audience of enlisted men. We laid it on thick and the laughter was hearty and frequent. I sang at a glass chamber pot containing a pair of hot dogs with mustard. Bebra, in white grease paint, wept clown's tears over the broken pot, salvaged the sausages from the shards, and devoured them to the joy of the field-grey mass. Felix and Kitty had taken to appearing in leather shorts and Tyrolian hats, which lent their act a special cachet. Roswitha wore a close-fitting silvery gown and long pale-green gloves; her tiny feet were encased in gold-embroidered sandals. Her half-closed bluish eyelids and drowsy Mediterranean voice produced their usual effect of eerie magic. Oskar – or have I mentioned it before? – required no special costume. I wore my good old sailor hat with s.m.s. *Seydlitz* on the band, my navy-blue shirt, and my jacket with the golden anchor buttons. As the camera eye descended, it registered the bottoms of my knee-pants, rolled stockings, and a very dilapidated pair of boots. From my neck hung my red and white lacquered drum, serene in the knowledge that there were five more like it in my luggage.

That night we repeated the same show for officers and for the Blitz Girls from the Cabourg message center. Roswitha was a trifle nervous. She made no mistakes, but in the middle of her number she put on a pair of sunglasses with blue rims and abruptly changed her tone. Here revelations became more direct; for instance, she informed an anemic-looking Blitz Girl, whose embarrassment made her snippish, that she was having an affair with her commanding officer. This, it seemed to me, was in poor taste, but there were plenty of laughs, for there was an officer sitting beside the Blitz Girl, and there was good reason to suppose . . .

After the show the regimental staff officers, who were billeted in the château, gave a party. Bebra, Kitty, and Felix stayed on, but Raguna and Oskar slipped quietly away and went to bed. It had been a trying day. We dropped off quickly and slept until 5 A.M. when the invasion woke us up.

What shall I tell you about the invasion? Canadians landed in our sector, not far from the mouth of the Orne. Bavent had to be evacuated. Our luggage was already stowed in the truck. We were pulling out with the regimental staff. A motorized field kitchen had stopped in the court of the château. Roswitha asked me to get her a cup of coffee. Rather nervous and afraid of missing the truck, I refused. I was even a little rude to her. Thereupon she herself ran over to the field kitchen in her high-heeled shoes, and reached the steaming hot-coffee exactly at the same time as a shell from a naval gun.

O Roswitha, I know not how old you were, I know only that you measured three foot three, that the Mediterranean spoke from your lips, that you smelled of cinnamon and nutmeg, and that you could see into the hearts of men; but you couldn't see into your own heart, or else you would have stayed with me instead of running after that coffee, which was much too hot.

In Lisieux Bebra managed to wangle marching orders for Berlin. We waited for him outside the Kommandantur, and it was only when he joined us that he mentioned Roswitha's death for the first time: 'We dwarfs and fools have no business dancing on concrete made for giants. If only we had stayed under the rostrums where no one suspected our presence!'

In Berlin I parted from Bebra. 'What,' he said with a smile as thin as a spiderweb, 'will you do in all those air-raid shelters without your Roswitha?' Then he kissed me on the forehead. He made me a present of the five remaining drums and sent Kitty and Felix to Danzig with official travel orders to keep me company. So it was that armed with six drums and my 'book', I returned on June 11, 1944, the day before my son's third birthday, to my native city, which was still intact and medieval and which still resounded with bells of every size ringing out the hour from belfries high and low.

The Imitation of Christ

Ah, yes, homecoming! At four minutes after twenty hundred, the furlough train pulled into Danzig station. Felix and Kitty accompanied me as far as Max-Halbe-Platz. Kitty burst into tears as they were saying goodbye. Then – it was almost twenty-one hundred – they went on to Propaganda Troop headquarters in Hochstriess, while Oskar toted his luggage down Labesweg.

Homecoming indeed! Nowadays every young man who forges a little check, joins the Foreign Legion, and spins a few yarns when he gets home a few years later, tends to be regarded as a modern Ulysses. Maybe on his way home our young man gets into the wrong train which takes him to Oberhausen instead of Frankfurt, and has some sort of experience on the way – why not? – and the moment he reaches home, he begins to bandy mythological names about: Circe, Penelope, Telemachus.

Oskar was no Ulysses, if only because on his return home he found everything unchanged. Far from being beset by lecherous suitors, his beloved Maria, who, had he been Ulysses, would have had to play the role of Penelope, still had her Matzerath, in whose favor she had decided long before Oskar's departure. And I do hope the more classical-minded among my readers will not, because of her somnambulism, mistake my poor Roswitha for Circe, the enchantress who turned men into beasts. Lastly, my son Kurt didn't raise a finger for his returning father; accordingly, he was no Telemachus, even if he did fail to recognize me.

If comparison there must be – and I can see that homecomers must put up with a comparison or two – I prefer to be looked upon as the Prodigal Son; for Matzerath opened the door and welcomed me like a true, not a presumptive, father. In fact, he managed to be so happy over Oskar's return, to the point of shedding real, speechless tears, that from that day on I ceased to call myself exclusively Oskar Bronski and called myself Oskar Matzerath as well.

Maria's reception of me was less emotional but not unfriendly.

She was sitting at the table, pasting up food stamps for the Board of Trade, having previously piled up a few birthday presents for little Kurt. Practical as she was, she thought first of my physical well-being, undressed me, bathed me as in times gone by, over-looked my blushes, and set me down in my pajamas at the table, Matzerath having meanwhile served up a dish of fried eggs and browned potatoes. I drank milk with my food, and as I ate and drank, the questions began: 'Where have you been? We looked all over like mad; we even had to go to the police and swear we hadn't done you in. Well, here you are and thank the Lord for that. But plenty of trouble you made us and there's going to be more, because now we've got to report you back again. I only hope they won't put you in an institution. That's what you deserve. Running away without a word.'

Maria was right. There was plenty of bother. A man came from the Ministry of Public Health and spoke to Matzerath in private, but Matzerath shouted so loud you could hear him all over the house; 'It's out of the question. I promised my wife on her death-bed. *I'm* his father, not the Board of Health.'

So I was not sent to an institution. But every two weeks an official letter came, asking Matzerath for a little signature; Matz-erath refused to sign, but his forehead was creased with care.

Oskar has been getting ahead of himself; now he must smooth the creases out of Matzerath's brow, for on the night of my arrival he beamed; he was much less worried than Maria, also asked fewer questions, and was happy just to have me home. All in all, he behaved like a true father. 'Won't Kurt be glad to have a little brother again!' he said as they were putting me to bed in the flat of the rather bewildered Mother Truczinski. 'And just imagine, tomorrow is Kurt's third birthday.'

On his birthday table my son Kurt found a cake with three candles, a crimson sweater knitted by Gretchen Scheffler, to which he paid no attention at all, and various other articles. There was a ghastly yellow ball, which he sat on, rode about on, and finally punctured with a potato knife. From the wound in the rubber he sucked the sickly sweet fluid that gathers inside all air-filled balls, and when he had enough of that began to dismantle and wreck the sailboat. The whistling top and the whip that went with it lay untouched, but frighteningly close at hand.

Oskar, who had long been thinking of this birthday, who had hastened eastward amid one of history's wildest frenzies, determined not to miss the third birthday of his son and heir – Oskar stood aside viewing the little fellow's destructive efforts, admiring his resolution, comparing his own dimensions with those of his son. I had to face the facts. While you were gone, I said to myself in some alarm, Kurt has grown by more than a head. He is already a good inch taller than the three feet you've kept yourself down to ever since your third birthday nearly seventeen years ago; it is time to make a drummer of him and call a halt to that immoderate growth.

I had stored away my drums along with my one-volume library behind the roof tiles in the attic. I picked out a gleaming, brand new instrument, resolved – since the grownups weren't doing anything about it – to offer my son the same opportunity as my poor mother, faithful to her promise, had offered me on *my* third birthday.

In my own infancy Matzerath had chosen me as his successor in the shop. Now that I had failed him, there was every reason to suppose that he had transferred his designs to Kurt. This, I said to myself, must be prevented at all costs. But I should not like you to see in Oskar a sworn enemy of the retail trade. If my son had been offered the ownership of a factory, or even of a kingdom complete with colonies, I should have felt exactly the same. Oskar had wanted no hand-me-downs for himself and he wanted none for his son. What Oskar wanted – and here was the flaw in my logic – was to make Kurt a permanently three-year-old drummer, as though it were not just as nauseating for a young hopeful to take over a tin drum as to step into a ready-made grocery store.

This is Oskar's present opinion. But at the time he was consumed by one desire: to see a drummer son beside a drummer father, two diminutive drummers looking on at the doings of the grown-up world; to establish a dynasty of drummers, capable of perpetuating itself and of handing down my work, drummed on tin encased in red and white lacquer, from generation to generation.

What a life lay ahead of us! How we might have drummed. Side by side, but also in different rooms, side by side, but also he in Labesweg and I in Luisenstrasse, he in the cellar, I in the attic, Kurt in the kitchen, Oskar in the toilet, father and son, hither and yon but occasionally together; and when we had the chance, the two of us might have slipped under the skirts of Anna Koljaiczek, my grandmother and his great-grandmother, to live and drum and breathe in the smell of slightly rancid butter. Squatting by her portal, I should have said to Kurt: 'Look inside, my son. That's where we come from. And if you're a good little boy, we shall be allowed to go back for an hour or more and visit those who are waiting.'

And bending low, little Kurt would have peeped in. And ever so politely he would have asked me, his father, for explanations.

And Oskar would have whispered: 'The lovely lady sitting there in the middle, playing with her lovely hands, the lovely lady whose sweet oval face brings the tears to my eyes, and yours no doubt as well, is my poor mama, your good grandmother, who died of eating eel soup, or maybe because her heart was too tender.'

'Tell me more, Papa, tell me more,' little Kurt would have clamored. 'Who is the man with the mustache?'

With an air of mystery, I should have lowered my voice: 'That's Joseph Koljaiczek, your great-grandfather. Take a good look at those flashing incendiary eyes, at his divine Polish wildness and the practical Kashubian shrewdness of his brow. Observe, if you please, the webs between his toes. In the year 1913, when the *Columbus* ran down the ways, he was hiding under a timber raft. After that he had to swim a long way; he swam and swam till he came to America and became a millionaire. But sometimes he takes to the water, swims back, and dives in here, where the fugitive firebug first found shelter and contributed his part toward my mama.'

'But what about the handsome gentleman who has been hiding behind the lady who is my grandmother, who is sitting down now beside her and stroking her hands with his hands? His eyes are just as blue as yours, Papa.'

Then I, unnatural son and traitor that I was, should have summoned up all my courage to answer my dear child: 'Those are the dreamy blue eyes of the Bronskis that are looking at you, my boy. Your eyes, it is true, are grey. They come to you from your mother. And yet, just like this Jan who is kissing my poor mama's hands, or his father Vincent, for that matter, you too are a Bronski, a dreamer through and through, yet with a practical Kashubian side. One day we will go back there, one day we shall follow the source whence flows that smell of slightly rancid butter. It's something to look forward to.'

In those days it seemed to me that true family life was possible only in the interior of my grandmother Koljaiczek, in the grandmotherly butter tub, as I liked to call it. Today many things have changed. With a snap of my fingers I can equal if not surpass God the Father, the only begotten Son, and most important of all, the Holy Ghost. The imitation of Christ has become an occupation with me, that I practice with the same distaste as all my other occupations. And yet, though nothing is farther away from me today than the entrance to my grandmother, it is among my forebears that I picture the most beautiful family scenes.

These fantasies come to me mostly on rainy days: my grandmother sends out invitations and we all meet inside her. Jan Bronski comes with flowers, carnations mostly, in the bullet holes perforating his Polish Post Office defender's breast. Timidly Maria, who at my behest has also received an invitation, approaches my mama; currying favor, she shows her the account books impeccably set up by my mama and impeccably carried on by Maria, and Mama, with her most Kashubian laugh, draws my darling to her, kisses her on the cheek, and says with a twinkle: 'Why child, there's nothing to be ashamed of. Haven't the both of us married a Matzerath and nursed a Bronski?'

I must sternly forbid myself any further reflections along these lines, speculations for example about a son begotten by Jan, deposited by my mama inside Grandma Koljaiczek, and finally born in the butter tub. Such notions would inevitably lead too far. Might it not occur to my half brother Stephan Bronski, who is after all one of us, to cast first a glance, and thereafter heaven knows what else, at my Maria? My imagination prefers to limit itself to an innocent family gathering. Renouncing a third and fourth drummer, I content myself with Oskar and Little Kurt. For the benefit of those present, I drum something or other about that Eiffel Tower which replaced my grandmother for me in a strange land, quite satisfied if the guests and Anna Koljaiczek, our hostess, enjoy our drumming and clap each other on the knees in obedience to the rhythm.

Delightful as it may be to see the world and its relationships unfolding inside my own grandmother, to be profound in a limited area, Oskar must now – since like Matzerath he is only a presumptive father – turn back to the events of June 12, 1944, to Kurt's third birthday.

I repeat: the child had been given a sweater, a ball, a sailboat, a whistling top, and the whip that went with it, and was going to get a drum, lacquered red and white. When he had finished dismantling his sailboat, Oskar approached, the new gift drum hidden behind his back, the battered old one dangling beneath his belly. We stood face to face, only a short step apart: Oskar, the Lilliputian; Kurt, he too a Lilliputian but an inch taller. He had a furious, vicious look on his face, for he was still busy demolishing the sailing vessel. Just as I drew forth the drum and held it up, he cracked the last remaining mast of the *Pamir*, for that was the windjammer's name.

Kurt dropped the wreck, took the drum, and turned it over; he seemed to have calmed down a bit, but his expression was still tense. It was time to hand him the drumsticks. Unfortunately, he misinterpreted my twin movements, felt threatened, and instantly knocked the sticks out of my fingers with the edge of the drum. As I bent down to pick up the sticks, he reached behind himself. I tried again to hand him the sticks, whereupon he hauled off with his birthday present and struck me. It wasn't the top that he whipped but Oskar, not the whistling top, that was meant to be whipped, but his father. Determined to teach his father to spin and to whistle, he whipped me, thinking: just wait, little brother. Thus did Cain whip Abel until Abel began to spin, staggering at first, then faster and with greater precision, until he began to sing at first in a low, disagreeable grumble, then higher and more steadily, till at last he was singing the song of the whistling top. And higher and higher Cain made me sing with his whip; I sang like a tenor singing his morning prayers, like angels forged of silver, like the Vienna Sängerknaben, like a chorus of eunuchs – I sang as Abel may have sung before he collapsed, as I too collapsed under the whip of my son Kurt.

When he saw me lying there, moaning like a run-down top,

he lashed at the air as though his arm had not yet exhausted its fury. At length he examined the drum carefully while at the same time keeping a suspicious eye on me. First he chipped off the lacquer against the edge of a chair; then he threw my gift to the floor and armed himself with the massive hull of the erstwhile sailing vessel and began to beat the drum. But the sounds he produced were not drumbeats. Not even the most rudimentary rhythm was discernible. With a look of frantic concentration he hammered ruthlessly at an instrument that had never expected such a drummer, that was made for a light roll, a playful flourish, and not for the blows of a nautical battering ram. The drum buckled, tried to escape by breaking away from its casing, tried to conceal its identity by shedding its red and white lacquer. In the end it was dull-grey tin that sued for mercy. But toward the father's birthday present the son was unrelenting. And when the father tried again to make peace, to cross the carpet to his son in spite of his many aches and pains, the son resorted once more to his whip. The weary top said uncle and ceased to spin, moan, or whistle, and the drum gave up all hope of a sensitive drummer who would wield the sticks with authority but without brutality.

When Maria came in, the drum was ready for the scrap heap. She took me in her arms, kissed my swollen eyes and lacerated ear, licked my blood and the welts on my hands.

Oh, if only Maria had not kissed the maltreated, backward, deplorably abnormal child! If she had recognized the beaten father and in every wound the lover. What a consolation, what a loyal though secret husband I might have been to her during the dark months to come!

The first blow – though it cannot have meant too much to Maria – was the death or the Arctic front of my half brother, Stephan Bronski, or Ehlers, if you will, for by then he had taken his stepfather's name. He had just been promoted to lieutenant, but now his career was cut short forever. Unlike his father, Jan who, when shot in Saspe Cemetery for defending the Polish Post Office, had borne a skat card under his shirt, the lieutenant was buried with the Iron Cross Second Class, the Infantry Badge, and the so-called Cold Storage Medal.

At the end of June, Mother Truczinski suffered a slight stroke when the mailman brought her bad news. Sergeant Truczinski had fallen for three things at once: Führer, Folk, and Fatherland. This had happened in the Center Sector, and Fritz' belongings – his wallet containing snapshots taken in Heidelberg, Brest, Paris, Bad Kreuznach, and Saloniki, of pretty girls, most of them smiling, the Iron Cross First and Second Class, various medals for various wounds, the bronze close-combat clasp, his two antitank patches, and a few letters – had been sent directly from Headquarters Center Sector to Labesweg, Langfuhr, by a certain Captain Kanauer.

Matzerath helped as much as he could and soon Mother Truczinski felt better, though she never fully recovered. All day she sat in her chair by the window, periodically asking me or Matzerath, who would come up two or three times a day with something to eat or drink, where this 'Center Sector' was, whether it was far away, and whether you could go there by train over Sunday.

With all his good intentions Matzerath could tell her nothing. Oskar, however, had learned geography from the special newscasts and Wehrmacht communiqués. I spent many a long afternoon trying with my drum to tell Mother Truczinski, who sat motionless in her chair except for her wagging head, all I could about Center Sector and its increasingly precipitate movements.

Maria had been very fond of her handsome brother. His death made her religious. All through July, she tried the religion she had been raised in; every Sunday she went to hear Pastor Hecht preach at Christ Church; once or twice Matzerath went with her, although she preferred to go alone.

Protestant services failed to satisfy Maria. One weekday – a Thursday or maybe a Friday – Maria entrusted the shop to Matzerath's care, took me, the Catholic, by the hand, and left the house. Starting off in the direction of the Neue Markt, we turned into Elsenstrasse, then took Marienstrasse, past Wohlgemuth's butcher shop, as far as Kleinhammer-Park – we're headed for Langfuhr Station, Oskar was beginning to think, we're going to take a little trip, maybe to Bissau in Kashubia. But then we turned left, waited superstitiously near the underpass for a freight train to go by, and went on through the oozing, dripping tunnel. On the far side, instead of going straight ahead toward the Film-Palast, we turned left along the embankment. Either, I figured, she is dragging me to see Dr. Hollatz in Brunshofer-Weg or else she's going to Sacred Heart to be converted.

The church door faced the railway tracks. Between the embankment and the open door we stopped still. An afternoon in late August, full of humming and buzzing. Behind us some Ukrainian women in white kerchiefs were picking and shoveling on the ballast. We stood there, peering into the cool, shady belly of the church. Far in the distance, ingeniously alluring, a violently inflamed eye: the eternal light. Behind us on the embankment the Ukrainian women stopped their picking and shoveling. A horn blew, a train was coming, there it was, still there, not yet past, gone, the horn tooted, and the women set to work again. Maria was undecided, perhaps uncertain which foot to put forward, and put all the responsibility on me, who by birth and baptism was closer to the only-saving Church; for the first time in years, for the first time since those two weeks full of fizz powder and love, she resigned herself to Oskar's guidance.

We left the embankment and its sounds, August and its buzzing, outside. Rather mournfully, letting my fingertips under my smock play sleepily over my drum, while outwardly a look of indifference settled on my features, I recalled the Masses, pontifical offices, Vespers services and Saturday confessions I had experienced at the side of my mother, who shortly before her death was rendered pious by the intensity of her relations with Jan Bronski, who Saturday after Saturday cast off her burden by confessing, who fortified herself with sacraments on Sunday in order, thus unburdened and fortified, to meet Jan in Tischlergasse the following Thursday. Who was the priest in those days? His name, then as now, for he was still priest of Sacred Heart, was Father Wiehnke, his sermons were pleasantly soft-spoken and unintelligible, his singing of the Credo was so thin and plaintive that even I should have been invaded by something resembling faith in those days if not for that left side-altar with the Virgin, the boy Jesus, and the boy John the Baptist.

And yet it was that altar which impelled me to pull Maria from the sunshine into the doorway and then across the flags into the nave.

Oskar took his time, sat quietly beside Maria in the oak pew, feeling more and more at his ease. Years had passed, and yet it seemed to me that the same people were still leafing through their missals, working out their strategy while waiting for Father Wiehnke's ear. We were sitting slightly to one side of the center aisle. I wanted to let Maria do the choosing, but to make the choice easier for her. On the one hand, the confessional was not so close as to upset her, thus her conversion could be leisurely, unofficial as it were; on the other hand, she was in a position to see how people behaved while preparing to confess and, while looking on, make up her mind. She had not far to go to consult Father Wiehnke in the confessional, to discuss with him the details of her conversion to the only saving faith. I felt sorry for her; she seemed so little, so awkward as she knelt amid dust, incense, plaster, tortuous angels, refracted light, convulsed saints, as she knelt beneath and amid the sweetness and sorrow, the sorrowful sweetness of Catholicism and for the first time crossed herself the wrong way around. Oskar gave Maria a poke and showed her the right way. She was eager to learn. He showed her where behind her forehead, where deep in her heart, exactly where in the joints of her shoulders Father, Son, and Holy Ghost have their dwelling places, and how you must fold your hands if your amen is to be successful. Maria obeyed, her hands came to rest in amen, and she began to pray.

At first Oskar, too, tried to pray for some of the dead, but while praying to the Lord for his Roswitha, while trying to negotiate peace for her and admission to heavenly joys, he so lost himself in earthly details that in the end peace and heavenly joys settled down in a Paris hotel. Accordingly, I took refuge in the Preface, because here there is nothing much to pin you down; for all eternity I said, *sursum corda*, *dignum et justum* – it is just and right. Then I let well enough alone and took to watching Maria from the side.

Catholic prayer was becoming to her. She was pretty as a picture in her devotions. Prayer lengthens the lashes, lifts the eyebrows, inflames the cheeks, makes the forehead grave, lends suppleness to the neck, and makes the nostrils quiver. Maria's features, flowering in sorrow, almost beguiled me into a display of affection. But one must not disturb those who are praying, one must neither seduce them nor let oneself be seduced by them, even if it is pleasant for those who pray and conducive to prayer, to know that someone considers them worth watching.

Oskar slipped off the smooth bench and fled from Maria. My hands, under my smock, were still quietly folded over my drum, as we, my drum and I, made our way over the flags, past the stations of the Cross in the left aisle of the nave; we did not stop with St. Anthony – pray for us! – for we had lost neither a purse nor a house key, nor with St. Adalbert of Prague who was slain by the heathen Prussians. We did not halt until, hopping from flag to flag as over a checkerboard, we reached the carpeted steps to the left side-altar.

You will not doubt my word when I tell you that nothing had changed in the Neo-Gothic brick Church of the Sacred Heart or, *a fortiori*, on the left side-altar. The boy Jesus still sat pink and naked on the Virgin's pink thigh – I shall not call her the Virgin Mary for fear of confusion with my Mary, my Maria, then busy with her conversion. Young John the Baptist, scantily clad in the same old shaggy, chocolate-colored pelt, was still pressing against the Virgin's right knee. She herself was still pointing her left forefinger at Jesus, but looking at John.

Yet even after years of absence, Oskar was less interested in the Virgin's maternal pride than in the constitutions of the two boys. Jesus was about the size of my son Kurt on his third birthday, in other words, he was about an inch taller than Oskar. John, who according to the documents was older than the Nazarene, was my size. But both of them had the same precocious expression as I, the eternal three-year-old. Nothing had changed. They had had that same sly look on their faces years before, in the days when I had frequented the Church of the Sacred Heart with my poor mama.

Climbing the carpeted steps, though without saying the Introit, I examined every fold in the drapery; slowly, carefully, I explored the painted plaster exterior of those two little nudists with my drumstick, which had more feeling than all my fingers together; omitting nothing, I covered the thighs, the bellies, the arms, taking in every crease and dimple. Jesus was the spit and image of Oskar, my healthy flesh, my strong, rather plump knees, my short but muscular drummer's arms. And the little rascal's posture was that of a drummer too. He sat on the Virgin's thigh, arms

337

and fists upraised as though he were planning to beat a drum, as though Jesus, not Oskar, were the drummer, as though he were just waiting for my drum, as though this time he seriously intended to imprint some charming rhythm on the drum for the benefit of the Virgin, John and myself. I did what I had done years before: I removed the drum from my belly and put Jesus to the test. Cautiously, careful not to harm the painted plaster, I set Oskar's red and white drum on his pink thighs. This time, however, I was driven by sheer malice, I had lost my idiotic faith in miracles, all I wanted was to show him up. For though he sat there with upraised fists, though he had my dimensions and rugged build, though he was a plaster copy of the three-year-old that I – by dint of what effort, what privations! – had remained, he could not drum, he could only give himself an air of knowing how to drum. If I had one, I could do it, he seemed to be thinking; ha-ha, I said, now you've got one, what are you going to do? Shaking with laughter, I pressed both sticks into his little sausage fingers, ten of them – sweet little plaster Jesus, go on and drum! Oskar steps back, descends three steps; he leaves the carpet for the flags, go on and drum, little boy Jesus. Oskar takes a long step backward for detachment. Oskar begins to laugh himself sick, because all Jesus can do is sit there, unable to drum, though maybe he'd like to. Boredom is beginning to gnaw at me as a mouse gnaws at a side of bacon when – I'm damned if he doesn't begin to drum.

While round us nothing stirred, he started in with his right stick, then a tap or two with the left, then both together. Blessed if he isn't crossing his sticks, say, that roll wasn't bad. He was very much in earnest and there was plenty of variety in his playing. He did some very complicated things but his simple rhythms were just as successful. There was nothing phony about his playing, he steered clear of gimmicks and just played the drum. His style wasn't even religious, and there was no military vulgarity about it. He was a musician through and through, but no snob. He knew all the hits. He played 'Everything Passes,' which everyone was singing at the time, and, of course, 'Lili Marlene.' Slowly, a little jerkily perhaps, he turned his curly head with the blue Bronski eyes toward me, smiled, rather arrogantly it seemed to me, and proceeded to weave Oskar's favorites into a pot-pourri:

it began with 'Smash a Little Windowpane' and there was a bare suggestion of 'The Schedule'; just like me, the little scoundrel played off Rasputin against Goethe; he climbed up the Stockturm with me, crawled under the rostrum with me, caught eels on the breakwater, walked with me behind the coffin, tapered at the foot end, of my poor mama, and, what flabbergasted me most of all, took refuge again and again beneath the four skirts of my grandmother Anna Koljaiczek.

Oskar stepped closer. Something drew him forward. He wanted to be on the carpet, he didn't want to stand on the flags any more. One stair sent him up the next. I climbed up, though I would rather have had him climb down. 'Jesus,' I said, summoning up what little voice was left me, 'that wasn't our bargain. Give me back my drum this minute. You've got your cross, that should do you.' He stopped playing, but gently, without abruptness, crossed the sticks over the drum with exaggerated care, and without a word of discussion returned what Oskar had unthinkingly lent him.

I was on the point of racing down the steps without thanks, of running away from Catholicism as fast as my legs would carry me, when a pleasant though imperious voice touched my shoulder: 'Dost thou love me, Oskar?' Without turning, I replied: 'Not that I know of.' Whereupon he, without raising his voice: 'Dost thou love me, Oskar?' This time my tone was more biting: 'Sorry, old man, I'm afraid not.' For the third time he came at me with that irritating voice of his: 'Oskar, dost thou love me?' I turned around and looked him full in the face: 'You bastard, I hate you, you and all your hocus-pocus.'

Strange to say, my hostility, far from getting him down, was his occasion to triumph. Raising his forefinger like a lady school-teacher, he gave me an assignment: 'Thou art Oskar, the rock, and on this rock I will build my Church. Follow thou me!'

You can imagine my indignation. I had gooseflesh with rage. I broke off one of his plaster toes, but he didn't budge. 'Say that again,' Oskar hissed, 'and I'll scratch the paint off you.'

After that, not a single word came forth; what came, as always, was the old man who is forever shuffling about all the churches in the world. He cast a glance at the left side-altar but failed to see me, and shuffled on. He had already reached St. Adalbert of

Prague when I stumbled down the steps, passed from the carpet to the flags, and, without looking back, crossed the checkerboard pattern to Maria, who just then crossed herself correctly in accordance with my instructions.

I took her by the hand and led her to the holy water font; just before the door, I bade her cross herself again in the direction of the high altar, but I did not join in, and when she wanted to genuflect, I pulled her out into the sunlight.

It was late in the afternoon. The Ukrainian women were gone from the railroad tracks. In their place, a freight train was being shunted about, not far from Langfuhr Station. Clusters of gnats hung in mid-air. From overhead came the sound of bells, mingling with the railroad noises. The gnats still hung in clusters. Maria's face was wet with tears. Oskar would have liked to scream. What was I going to do about Jesus? I felt like loading my voice. What had I to do with his Cross? But I was perfectly well aware that my voice was powerless against the windows of his church. Let him go on building his temple on people called Peter. 'Watch out, Oskar, leave those church windows alone,' Satan whispered within me. 'One of these days that fellow's going to ruin your voice.' I cast one solitary glance upward, took the measure of one of those Neo-Gothic windows, and wrenched myself away. I did not sing, I did not follow Him, I just trotted along by Maria's side to the underpass in Bahnhofstrasse. Through the oozing, dripping tunnel, up the hill to Kleinhammer-Park, right turn into Marienstrasse, past Wohlgemuth's butcher shop, left turn into Elsenstrasse, across the Striessbach to the Neue Markt, where they were building a water tank for the air-raid defense. Labesweg was endless, but then we were home. Leaving Maria, Oskar climbed over a hundred steps to the attic. Bed sheets had been hung up to dry; behind the bed sheets a mound of air-defense sand; behind sand and buckets, behind bundles of newspaper and piles of roofing tiles, were secreted my book and my supply of drums. But there was also a shoe box containing several burned-out, but still pear-shaped light bulbs. Oskar selected one and sang it to pieces; he took another, turned it to pulverized glass, cut a third neatly in two. Upon a fourth his voice inscribed JESUS in Sütterlin script, then pulverized both bulb and inscription. He wanted to do it again, but there were no more bulbs. Exhausted,

I sank down on the air-defense sand: Oskar still had his voice. Maybe Jesus had a disciple. As for me, my first disciples were to be the Dusters.

The Dusters

Oskar was not cut out to be a follower of Christ; for one thing, he has no aptitude for enlisting disciples. Nevertheless Christ's 'follow thou me' found its way indirectly, circuitously, to my heart and I became his follower though I did not believe in him. But, as they say, he who doubts, believes, and it is the unbeliever who believes longest. Jesus had treated me to little private miracle in the Church of the Sacred Heart and I was unable to stifle that miracle under my doubts; quite on the contrary, I did all I could to make Jesus put on a repeat performance.

After that Oskar returned to Sacred Heart a number of times without Maria. It was not very difficult to slip away from Mother Truczinski, who was glued to her chair. What had Jesus to offer me? Why did I spend half the night in the left-hand aisle of the nave and let the sacristan lock me in? Why did Oskar stand at the left side-altar until his limbs congealed and his ears were frozen stiff? For with all my crushing humility and no less crushing blasphemies, I never got to hear either my drum or Jesus' voice again.

Miserere. Never in all my life have I heard my teeth chatter as they did in those midnight hours in Sacred Heart. What jester could ever have found a better rattle than Oskar? I sounded like a machine-gun nest, I had a bevy of typists between my upper and lower jaws. My teeth chattered in all directions, calling forth echoes and applause. Pillars shivered, arches had gooseflesh, and when my teeth weren't chattering, I coughed. My cough hopped over the checkerboard pattern of the flags, down the transept, up the nave, hoisted itself into the choir. Multiplied by sixty, it organized a Bach society that did not sing but specialized in coughing, and just as I was beginning to think that Oskar's cough had crawled away into the organ pipes and wouldn't be heard again until the Sunday chorale, a cough rang out in the sacristy, and another from the pulpit, until at length the cough died down, coughed out its soul behind the high altar, not far from the Athlete on the Cross. It is accomplished, said my cough; but nothing was accomplished. The boy Jesus sat there stiff and proud, holding my drumsticks and my drum, but drum he would not, he refused to confirm my mission. For Oskar wanted to have it in writing.

A sorry habit has remained with me from that period. Whenever I visit a church or even a famous cathedral I begin to cough. Even if I am in the best of health. The moment I set foot inside, I embark on a sustained cough which takes on a Gothic, Romanesque, perhaps even a Baroque character according to the style of the church. I feel certain that years hence I shall still be able to give you a drum rendition of Oskar's cough in the Cathedral of Ulm, or of Speyer for that matter. At that time, however, in the days when I was suffering the effects of the most glacial Catholicism in mid-August, there was no opportunity to visit churches in distant lands, unless you happened to be a soldier participating in the planned withdrawals of the Reichswehr, noting perhaps in your diary: 'Evacuated Orvieto today; wonderful church, must come back with Monica after the war and look at it properly.'

It was easy for me to become a churchgoer, for there was nothing to keep me at home. There was Maria. But Maria had Matzerath. There was my son Kurt. But he was getting more and more insufferable, throwing sand in my eyes and clawing me so ferociously that his fingernails broke off in my parental flesh. Moreover, my son showed me a pair of fists with knuckles so white that the mere sight of them sent the blood gushing from my nose.

Strange to say, Matzerath defended me, awkwardly perhaps but not without tenderness. In his surprise, Oskar would allow this man, who had never meant a thing to him, to pick him up on his lap, hug him, gaze at him, and once even to kiss him. With tears in his eyes Matzerath had said, more to himself than to Maria: 'It's impossible. I can't send my own son away. The doctors can say what they like. They don't stop to think. I bet they have no children of their own.'

Maria, who was sitting at the table, pasting food stamps in ledgers as she did every evening, looked up: 'Take it easy, Alfred. You talk as if I didn't care. But when they say it's the modern way to do, I don't know what to think.'

Matzerath pointed at the piano, which had produced no music since the death of my poor mama: 'Agnes would never have done that, she'd never have allowed it.'

Maria cast a glance at the piano, shrugged her shoulders, and let them drop back into place only when she opened her mouth to speak. 'Of course not, she was his mother, she kept hoping he'd get better. But you see how it is: nothing has happened he's always being pushed around, he don't know how to live and he don't know how to die.'

Was it the likeness of Beethoven, who still hung over the piano, glumly mustering the glum Hitler, who gave Matzerath the strength? 'No,' he shouted. 'Never!' and banged his fist on the table and its damp sticky papers. He asked Maria to hand him the letter from the institution, he read it and read it again, then tore it up and scattered the scraps among the bread stamps, fat stamps, food stamps, travel stamps, heavy-labor stamps, extra-heavy-labor stamps, and the stamps for pregnant women and nursing mothers. Though, thanks to Matzerath, Oskar never fell into the hands of those doctors, he beheld a vision, and to this day, whenever he lays eyes on Maria, he beholds a vision of a beautiful clinic situated in the mountain air, of a light, airy, friendly, and modern operating room; outside its padded door, Maria, shy but smiling, hands me over confidently, to a group of first-class physicians, who are smiling too and ever so confidence-inspiring and holding first-class, confidence-inspiring and immediately effective syringes behind their white, sterile aprons.

The whole world had forsaken me and it was only the shadow of my poor mama, falling across Matzerath's fingers and paralyzing them whenever he thought of signing the authorization form drawn up by the Ministry of Public Health, that kept me alive.

Oskar would not like to seem ungrateful. I still had my drum. I still had my voice, which is of no use to you now that you have heard all about my triumphs with glass and is probably beginning to bore the lovers of novelty among you – but to me Oskar's voice, even more than his drum, was proof of my existence and as such forever new; for as long as I sang glass to pieces, I existed.

In that period, Oskar sang a good deal. He sang with an energy born of desperation. Every time I left the Church of the Sacred Heart at a late hour, I sang something to pieces. I did not go looking for targets of particular interest. On my way home, I would select an attic window that hadn't been properly blacked out or a street lamp painted regulation blue. Each time I went to church, I chose a different way home. One evening Oskar would take Anton-Möller-Weg and Marienstrasse. Another, he would pass by the Conradinum and shatter the glass in the main entrance. One day toward the end of August, I reached the church too late and found the door locked. Wishing to walk off my fury, I picked a particularly circuitous way home. I started off on Bahnhofstrasse, where I demolished every third street lamp, passed the Film-Palast and turned right into Adolf-Hitler-Strasse. I ignored the windows of the infantry barracks, but vented my rage on an almost empty streetcar coming toward me from Oliva, stripping one side of it of all its lugubrious blackout glass.

Brakes screeched, the car stopped, the people got out, cursed a while, and got back in again. A triumph, if you will, but Oskar gave it little thought. He started off in search of a dessert for his rage, a tasty morsel in that period so poor in tasty morsels, and did not stop until, approaching Langfuhr, he saw the Baltic Chocolate Factory spread out in the moonlight between Berendt's carpentry shop and the spacious hangars of the airfield.

By this time, however, my rage had lost some of its intensity. Instead of introducing myself to the factory at once, I took my time and counted the moonlit windows. That done, I was just about ready to introduce myself, but first wanted to find out what the youngsters who had been following me from Hochstriess, and perhaps all the way from Bahnhofstrasse, were up to. Six or seven of them were standing by the shelter at the nearby streetcar stop, and I could make out five more behind the trees on the avenue.

I had already decided to postpone my visit to the chocolate factory, to give them a wide berth and make for home by way of the overpass and the Aktien Brewery, when Oskar heard an exchange of whistle signals. One group was signaling from the overpass. There was no room for doubt: this troop movement was for my benefit.

I had seen my pursuers, but the hunt had not yet begun. In such situations one tends to enumerate the remaining possibilities of escape with great relish and thoroughness: Oskar might have cried out for Mama and Papa. I might have summoned heaven knows whom, a policeman maybe, on my drum. My stature would assuredly have won me grown-up support, but even Oskar had his principles and occasionally stuck to them. And so I resolved to do without the help of any policemen or other adults who might be within earshot. Spurred by curiosity and flattered at so much attention, I decided to let things take their course and did the stupidest thing imaginable: I went looking for a hole in the tarred fence surrounding the chocolate factory. I found none. Slowly and nonchalantly, the young bandits converged: from the car-stop shelter, from under the trees on the avenue, and at length from the overpass. Oskar moved along the fence, still looking for that hole. They gave me just the time I needed to find the place where the plank was missing. But when I squeezed through, tearing my pants in the process, there were four of these characters in windbreakers on the other side, waiting for me with their hands in the pockets of their ski pants.

Recognizing that nothing could be done about my situation, I ran my hands over my pants, looking for the tear. It was in the seat. I measured it with outspread fingers, found it annoyingly large but put on a show of indifference, and before looking up to face the music, waited until all the boys from the car stop, the avenue, and the overpass had climbed over the fence, for they were too big to squeeze through the gap.

This was in the last days of August. From time to time the moon hid behind a cloud. I counted about twenty of these young fellows. The youngest were fourteen, the oldest sixteen, almost seventeen. The summer of '44 was hot and dry. Four of the larger boys had on Air Force Auxiliary uniforms. It was a good cherry year, I remember. They stood round Oskar in small groups, talked in an undertone, using a jargon that I made no effort to understand. They gave each other weird names, only a few of which I bothered to take note of. A little fifteen-year-old with rather misty doe's eyes was addressed, I recall, as Ripper and occasionally as Bouncer. The one beside him was Putty. The smallest, though surely not the youngest, with a protruding upper lip and a lisp, was called Firestealer. One of the Air Force Auxiliaries was addressed as Mister and another, very aptly, as Soup Chicken. There were also historical names such as Lionheart and Bluebeard – Bluebeard had the look of a milksop – and old friends of mine like Totila and Teja. Two of them even had the impudence to call themselves Belisarius and Narses. The leader was a sixteen-year-old named Störtebeker after the celebrated pirate. He had on a genuine velours hat with the crown battered in to look like a duck pond, and a raincoat that was too long for him.

No one paid any attention to Oskar; they were trying to wear him down with suspense. Half-amused and half-annoyed at myself for bothering with these adolescent Romantics, I sat wearily down on my drum, studied the moon, which was just about full, and tried to dispatch a part of my thoughts to the Church of the Sacred Heart.

Just today He might have drummed and said a word or two. And here I was, sitting in the yard of the Baltic Chocolate Factory, wasting my time with cops and robbers. Maybe He was waiting for me, maybe after a brief introduction on the drum, He was planning to open His mouth again, to elaborate on the ways of imitating Christ. Disappointed at my failure to show up, He was probably, at this very moment, lifting His eyebrows in that arrogant way of His. What would Jesus think of these young scamps? What could Oskar, his likeness, his disciple and vicar, be expected to do with this horde? Could he have addressed the words of Jesus: 'Suffer little children to come unto me!' to a gang of young hoodlums calling themselves Putty, Bluebeard, Firestealer, and Störtebeker?

Störtebeker approached, accompanied by Firestealer, his right hand. Störtebeker: 'Stand up!'

Oskar's eyes were still on the moon, his thoughts by the left side-altar of the Church of the Sacred Heart. He did not stand up, and Firestealer, at a signal from Störtebeker, kicked the drum out from under me.

Rising for want of anything to sit on, I put the drum under my smock to protect it against further damage.

Nice-looking boy, this Störtebeker, Oskar thought. The eyes

are a bit too deep-set and close together, but there's life and imagination in the cut of his mouth.

'Where are you from?'

So they were going to question me. Displeased at this overture, I turned back to the moon, thinking to myself – the moon doesn't seem to care what one thinks – that it looked like a drum, and smiled at my harmless megalomania.

'He's got a grin on his face, Störtebeker.'

Firestealer looked me over and suggested an activity that he called 'dusting'. Others in the background, pimple-faced Lionheart, Mister, Bouncer, and Putty were also in favor of dusting.

Still on the moon, I mentally spelled out the word 'dusting'. A nice word, but it was sure to stand for something unpleasant.

Störtebeker asserted his authority: 'I'm the one that says who's going to be dusted around here and when.' Then he addressed me: 'We've been seeing quite a lot of you in Bahnhofstrasse. How come? Where you been?'

Two questions at once. Oskar would have to give at least one answer if he was to remain master of the situation. I turned away from the moon, faced him with my blue persuasive eyes, and said calmly: 'Church.'

From behind Störtebeker's raincoat came commentaries on my answer. Firestealer figured out that by church I meant Sacred Heart.

'What's your name?'

An inevitable question, a question that arises wherever man meets man and that plays a vital role in human conversation. It provides the substance of whole plays, even operas – *Lohengrin*, for instance.

I waited for the moon to pass between two clouds, let the sheen in my eyes work on Störtebeker for the time it takes to eat three spoonfuls of soup. Then I spoke, intent on the effect, named myself – what would I have got but a laugh if I had owned to the name of Oskar? 'My name is Jesus,' I said. A long silence ensued. Finally Firestealer cleared his throat: 'We'll have to dust him after all, chief.'

This time Firestealer met with no opposition; with a snap of his fingers, Störtebeker gave his permission, and Firestealer seized me, dug his knuckles into my arm just above the elbow, and gouged, producing a hot, painful sensation, until Störtebeker snapped his fingers again as a sign to stop – so that was dusting!

'Well now, what *is* your name?' The chief in the velours hat gave himself an air of boredom, did a little shadow boxing, which made the long sleeves of his raincoat slide up to his elbows, and held up his wristwatch in the moonlight. 'You've got one minute to think it over,' he whispered. 'Then I give the boys the green light.'

Oskar had a whole minute in which to study the moon with impunity, to look for a solution among the craters, to reconsider his idea of stepping into Christ's shoes. This green light talk was not to my liking, and I certainly was not going to let any half-baked hoodlums put me on a schedule. I waited about thirty-five seconds; then Oskar said: 'I am Jesus.'

What happened next was pretty good, but I can't say I planned it. Immediately after my second announcement that I was Jesus, before Störtebeker could snap his fingers or Firestealer could dust, the air-raid sirens let loose.

' . . . Jesus,' said Oskar and took a breath. Thereupon my identity was confirmed, successively, by the sirens at the nearby airfield, the siren on the main building of the Hochstriess Infantry Barracks, the siren on the roof of Horst-Wessel High School, the siren on Sternfeld's Department Store, and far in the distance, from the direction of the Hindenburg-Allee, the siren of the Engineering School. It was some time before all the sirens in the suburb, like a choir of iron-lunged, overenthusiastic archangels, took up my glad tidings, made the night rise and fall, made dreams flare up and crash, crept into the ears of the sleeping population, and transformed the cold, disinterested moon into a merciless light that there was no way to black out.

Oskar knew that the alarm was on his side; not so Störtebeker, the sirens made him nervous. For some of his henchmen the alarm was a call to duty. The four Air Force Auxiliaries had to climb the fence, rush back to their batteries between the car barn and the airfield, and help man the 88's. Three others, including Belisarius, were wardens at the Conradinum. Störtebeker managed to keep his hold on the rest, some fifteen of them. Since nothing more was doing in the sky, he went on questioning me:

'Very well, if my ears do not deceive me, you are Jesus. O.K. One more question: that trick of yours with the street lights and window-panes, how do you do it? You'd better come clean. We know all about it.'

Of course they didn't know a thing. They had witnessed one or two of my vocal triumphs and that was that. Oskar told himself that he must not be too severe in his appraisal of these junior hoodlums, or juvenile delinquents as we should call them today. Their way of doing things was amateurish, too eager, too direct, but boys will be boys; I was determined to be patient with them. So these were the notorious Dusters that everybody had been talking about for the last few weeks, the gang that the police and several Hitler Youth patrols had been trying to track down. As it later turned out, they were schoolboys, students at the Conradinum, the Petri and Horst-Wessel High Schools. There was a second group of Dusters in Neufahrwasser, led by high school students but made up chiefly of apprentices at the Schichau shipyards and the railroad car factory. The two groups worked separately, joining forces only for night expeditions to the Steffens-Park and Hindenburg-Allee, where they would waylay leaders of the League of German Girls on their way home after training sessions. Friction between the groups was avoided; their territories were marked out with precision, and Störtebeker looked upon the leader of the Neufahrwasser group more as a friend than a rival. The Dusters were against everything. They raided the offices of the Hitler Youth, attacked soldiers found necking in the parks to strip them of their medals and insignia of rank, and with the help of their members among the Air Force Auxiliaries stole arms, ammunition, and gasoline from the AA batteries. But their main project, which they had been maturing ever since their inception, was an all-out attack on the Rationing Office.

At the time Oskar knew nothing about the Dusters, their organization or plans, but he was feeling low and forsaken, and he thought these young men might give him a sense of security, a sense of belonging somewhere. Despite the difference in our ages – I would soon be twenty – I already considered myself secretly as one of them. Why, I said to myself, shouldn't you give them a sample of your art? The young are always eager to learn. You yourself were fifteen or sixteen once. Set them an example, show them your accomplishments. They will look up to you. Maybe they will choose you as their leader. Now at last you will be able to exert influence, to bring your intelligence and experience to bear; this is your chance to heed your vocation, to gather disciples and walk in the footsteps of Christ.

Perhaps Störtebeker suspected that there was thought behind my thoughtfulness. He gave me time to think, and I was grateful to him for that. A moonlit night toward the end of August. Slightly cloudy. Air-raid alarm. Two or three searchlights on the coast. Maybe a reconnaissance plane. Paris was just being evacuated. Facing me the front, rich in windows, of the Baltic Chocolate Factory. After a long retreat, Army Group Center had dug in on the Vistula. Baltic was no longer working for the retail market, its whole output went to the Air Force. Oskar was having to get used to the idea of General Patton's soldiers strolling beneath the Eiffel Tower in American uniforms. In response to this painful thought – ah, the happy hours with Roswitha! – Oskar lifted a drumstick. Störtebeker noticed my gesture, his eye followed my drumstick to the chocolate factory. While in broad daylight the Japanese were being cleaned out of some Pacific island, on our side of the globe the moon was shining on the windows of a chocolate factory. And to all those who had ears to hear, Oskar said: 'The voice of Jesus will now demolish some glass.'

Before I had disposed of the first three panes, I heard the buzzing of a fly far above me. While two more panes were surrendering their share of moonlight, I thought: that fly must be dying or it wouldn't buzz so loud. Thereupon I blackened the rest of the windows on the top floor. Awfully pale, those searchlight beams, I said to myself before expelling the reflected lights – probably from the battery near Camp Narvik – from several first- and second-floor windows. The coastal batteries fired, then I finished off the second floor. A moment later the batteries at Altschottland, Pelonken, and Schellmühl let loose. Three ground-floor windows, then the pursuit planes took off and flew low over the factory. Before I had finished off the ground floor, the AA suspended fire to let the pursuit planes take care of a four-motored bomber that was receiving the attentions of three searchlights at once over Oliva.

At first Oskar feared the spectacular efforts of the antiaircraft batteries might distract my new friends' attention. My work done, I was overjoyed to see them all gaping at my alterations in the chocolate factory. Even when applause and cries of 'Bravo' rose up from nearby Hohenfriedberger-Weg as from a theater, because the bomber had been hit and could be seen falling in flames over Jeschkenthal Forest, only a few members of the gang, among then Putty, looked away from the unglassed factory. Neither Störtebeker nor Firestealer, and it was they who mattered, showed any interest in the bomber.

Once more the heavens were bare, except for the moon and the small-fry stars. The pursuit planes landed. Far in the distance fire engines could be heard. Störtebeker turned, showing me the contemptuous curve of his mouth, and put up his fists, disengaging his wristwatch from the long sleeve of his raincoat. Taking off the watch, he handed it to me without a word. Then he sighed and tried to say something, but had to wait for the all-clear signal to die down. At last, amid the applause of his henchmen, he got the words out: 'O.K., Jesus. If you feel like it, you're in. We're the Dusters if that means anything to you.'

Oskar weighed the wristwatch in his hand, a cute little thing with a luminous dial and hands indicating twenty-three minutes after midnight, and handed it to Firestealer. Firestealer cast a questioning look at his boss. Störtebeker nodded his consent. Shifting his drum to a comfortable position for the homeward march, Oskar said: 'Jesus will lead you. Follow Him.'

The Christmas Play

There was a good deal of talk in those days about secret weapons and final victory. We, the Dusters, discussed neither one, but we had the secret weapon.

Oskar's first move after taking over the leadership of the thirty to forty members of the gang was to have Störtebeker introduce me to the leader of the Neufahrwasser outfit. Moorkähne, a sixteen-year-old with a limp, was the son of an official at the Neufahrwasser pilot office; his physical defect – his right leg was almost an inch shorter than his left – had prevented him from being drafted or taken on as an Air Force Auxiliary. Though a bit ostentatious about his limp, Moorkähne was shy and soft-spoken. There was always an artful smile on his lips, and he was regarded as the best student in the graduating class at the Conradinum. He had every prospect, if the Russian Army should raise no objection, of passing his final examination brilliantly; he was planning to study philosophy.

Like Störtebeker, whose unstinting respect I had won, Moork-ähne recognized me as Jesus, first in command of the Dusters. Oskar insisted at once on being shown the storehouse and treas-ury, for both groups kept their loot in the same place, the spacious cellar of a quiet, fashionable villa on Jeschkenthaler-Weg in Lang-fuhr. This house, covered with ivy and creepers and separated from the street by a gently sloping meadow, was the abode of Putty's parents, whose name was Von Puttkamer. Mr. von Puttka-mer, a nobleman of Pomeranian, Polish, and Prussian descent and a wearer of the Knight's Cross, was off commanding a division in fair France; Mrs. Elisabeth von Puttkamer had been spending the last few months in the Bavarian highlands for reasons of health. Wolfgang von Puttkamer, whom the Dusters called Putty, had been left in charge of the house; as for the elderly, half-deaf maid who ministered to the young gentleman's needs, she never went below the ground floor, and we never saw her, for we entered the cellar through the laundry room.

In the storeroom were piled canned goods, tobacco, and several bolts of parachute silk. From one of the shelves hung two dozen Army watches, which Putty had orders from Störtebeker to keep running and properly set. Another of his duties was to keep the two tommy guns, the rifle, and the pistols clean. I was shown a bazooka, some machine-gun ammunition, and twenty-five hand grenades. All this and an impressive supply of gasoline in jerrycans was intended for the assault on the Rationing Office. Oskar-Jesus' first order was: 'Bury the arms and gasoline in the garden. Hand over all bolts and firing pins to Jesus. Our weapons are of a different kind.'

When the boys produced a cigar box full of stolen decorations and insignia, I smiled and said they could keep them. But I should have taken away the paratroopers' knives. Later on they made use of the blades which fitted so neatly into their handles, as though just begging to be used.

Then they brought me the treasury. Oskar ordered a counting and checked it over. The Dusters' liquid assets amounted to two thousand four hundred and twenty Reichsmarks. This was at the beginning of September, 1944. When, in mid-January, 1945, Koniev and Zhukov broke through on the Vistula, Putty confessed and we were obliged to hand over our treasury to the authorities. Thirty-six thousand Reichsmarks were counted into piles and bundles on the bench of the District Court.

In keeping with my nature, Oskar remained in the background during operations. In the daytime I would go out alone or with Störtebeker, to find worth-while targets for the Dusters' night expeditions. I let Störtebeker or Moorkähne do the actual organizing. After nightfall I never stirred from Mother Truczinski's apartment. That brings us to the secret weapon. I would stand at my bedroom window and send out my voice, farther than ever before, to demolish windows at the other end of town. I unglassed several Party headquarters, a printshop that turned out ration cards, and once, acceding reluctantly to the request of my comrades-in-arms, shattered the kitchen windows of an apartment belonging to a high school principal who had incurred their displeasure.

That was in November. While V-1 and V-2 rockets were winging their way to England, my voice winged its way over Langfuhr and along the file of trees on Hindenburg-Allee, hopped over the Central Station and the Old City, and sought out the museum in Fleischergasse; my men had orders to look for Niobe, the wooden figurehead.

They did not find her. In the adjoining room Mother Truczinski sat motionless but for the wagging of her head. In a way we had something in common; for while Oskar engaged in long-distance song, she was occupied with long-distance thoughts. She searched God's heaven for her son Herbert and the front lines of Center Sector for her son Fritz. She also had to look far away for eldest daughter Guste, who early in 1944 had married and gone off to distant Düsseldorf, for it was there that Headwaiter Köster had his home; though he personally was spending most of his time in Courland. A scant two weeks' furlough was all the time Guste had to keep him for herself and get to know him.

353

Those were peaceful evenings. Oskar sat at Mother Truczinski's feet, improvised a bit on his drum, took a baked apple from the recess in the tile stove, and with this wrinkled fruit meant for old women and little children vanished into the dark bedroom. He would raise the blackout paper and open the window just a crack, letting in a little of the frosty night. Then he would take aim and dispatch his long-distance song. He did not sing at the stars, the Milky Way was not on his route. His song was directed at Winterfeld-Platz, not at the Radio Building but at the boxlike structure across the way, which housed the district headquarters of the Hitler Youth.

In clear weather my work took hardly a minute. Meanwhile my baked apple had cooled a little by the open window. Munching, I returned to Mother Truczinski and my drum, and soon went to bed with every assurance that while Oskar slept the Dusters, in Jesus' name, were looting Party treasuries, stealing food cards, rubber stamps, printed forms, or a membership list of the Hitler Youth Patrol.

Indulgently I allowed Störtebeker and Moorkähne to engage in all sorts of monkey business with forged documents. The gang's main enemy was the Patrol Service. It was all right with me if they chose to kidnap their adversaries, dust them, and – as Fire-stealer, who had charge of this activity, called it – polish their balls.

Since I remained aloof from these expeditions, which were a mere prologue that can give you no idea of my real plans, I cannot say for sure whether it was the Dusters who in September, 1944, tied up two high officers of the Patrol Service, including the dreaded Helmut Neitberg, and drowned them in the Mottlau, above the Cows' Bridge.

However, I, Oskar-Jesus, who gave the Dusters their orders, feel the need to deny certain stories that gained currency later on: that the Dusters had connections with the Edelweiss Pirates of Cologne or that Polish partisans from Tuchlerheide had exerted an influence on us or even directed our movement. All this is pure legend.

At our trial we were also accused of having ties with the July 20th conspirators, because Putty's father, August von Puttkamer, had been close to Field Marshal Rommel and had committed suicide. Since the beginning of the war, Putty had seen his father no more than five or six times, and then scarcely long enough to get used to his changing insignia of rank. It was not until our trial that he first heard about this officer's foolishness, which, to tell the truth, was a matter of utter indifference to us. When he did hear about it, he cried so shamefully, so shamelessly that Firestealer, who was sitting beside him, had to dust him right in front of the judges.

Only once in the course of our activity did any grownups approach us. Some shipyard workers – with Communist affiliations, as I could tell at a glance – tried to gain influence over us through our apprentices at the Schichau dockyards and turn as into a Red underground movement. The apprentices were not unwilling. But the schoolboys among us rejected all political trends. Mister, an Air Force Auxiliary who was the cynic and theoretician of the gang, stated his views at one of our meetings: 'We have nothing to do with parties,' he declared. 'Our fight is against our parents and all other grownups, regardless of what they may be for or against.'

He put it rather too strongly, no doubt, but all the schoolboys agreed; the outcome was a factional split. The shipyard apprentices started a club of their own – I was sorry to lose them, they were good workers. Despite the objections of Störtebeker and Moorkähne, they continued to call themselves Dusters. At the trial – their outfit was caught at the same time as ours – the burning of the training sub in the shipyard basin was pinned on them. Over a hundred U-boat captains and ensigns had met a terrible death in the fire which broke out below decks; the U-boat crews were blocked in their quarters, and when the ensigns, lads of eighteen, tried to escape through portholes, their hips wouldn't pass and the fire caught them from behind. They had hung there screaming and the only way of putting them out of their misery had been to bring a cutter alongside and shoot them.

We had nothing to do with that fire. It may have been the Schichau apprentices and it may have been the Westerland Society. The Dusters were not firebugs though I, their spiritual guide, may have inherited an incendiary gene or two from my grandfather Koljaiczek.

I remember well the mechanic, recently transferred to Schichau from the Deutsche Werke at Kiel, who came to see us in our cellar shortly before the split. Erich and Horst Pietzger, the sons of a longshoreman in Fuchswall, had brought him. He inspected our storehouse with a professional air, deplored the absence of any weapons in working order, but uttered a few grudging words of approval. When he asked to speak to the chief, Störtebeker promptly, and Moorkähne with some hesitation, referred him to me. Thereupon he flew into a gale of laughter so long and so insolent that Oskar came very close to handing him over to the dusters for a dusting.

'What kind of a sawed-off runt do you call that?' he said to Moorkähne, pointing his thumb at me over his shoulder.

Moorkähne smiled in visible embarrassment. Before he could think of anything to say, Störtebeker replied with ominous calm: 'He is our Jesus.'

That was too much for the mechanic, whose name was Walter; he took it on himself to insult us right there in our own headquarters. 'Say, are you revolutionaries or a bunch of choirboys getting ready for a Christmas play?'

The blade of a paratrooper's knife popped out of Störtebeker's sleeve; he opened the cellar door, gave Firestealer a sign, and said, more to the gang than to the mechanic: 'We're choirboys and we're getting ready for a Christmas play.'

But nothing drastic happened to the mechanic. He was blindfolded and led away. A few days later this same Walter organized the dockyard apprentices into a club of their own, and I am quite sure it was they who set the training sub on fire.

From my point of view Störtebeker had given the right answer. We were not interested in politics. Once we had so intimidated the Hitler Youth Patrols that they scarcely left their quarters except occasionally to check the papers of flighty young ladies at the railroad stations, we shifted our field of operations to the churches and began, as the Communist mechanic had put it, to occupy ourselves with Christmas plays.

Our first concern was to find replacements for the invaluable Schichau apprentices. At the end of October, Störtebeker swore in the brothers Felix and Paul Rennwand, both choirboys at Sacred Heart. Störtebeker had approached them through their sister Lucy, a girl of sixteen who, over my protest, was allowed to attend the swearing-in ceremony. Setting their left hands on my drum, which the boys, incurable Romantics that they were, liked to think of as some sort of symbol, the Rennwand brothers repeated the oath of allegiance, a text so absurd and full of hocuspocus that I can no longer remember it.

Oskar watched Lucy during the ceremony. In one hand she held a sandwich that seemed to quiver slightly, she shrugged her shoulders and gnawed at her lower lip. Her triangular fox face was expressionless, and she kept her eyes riveted on Störtebeker's back. Suddenly I had misgivings about the Dusters' future.

We began to redecorate our basement. In close collaboration with the choirboys, I oversaw the acquisition of the required furnishings. From St. Catherine's we took a sixteenth-century half-length Joseph who turned out to be authentic, a few candelabra, some chalices, patens, and cruets, and a Corpus Christi banner. A night visit to the Church of the Trinity brought us a wooden, trumpet-blowing angel of no artistic interest, and a colored tapestry, copied from an older original, showing a lady who seemed ever so prim, prissy, and deceitful, and a mythical animal known as a unicorn, who was obviously very much under her influence. The lady's smile, as Störtebeker observed, had the same playful cruelty as that which predominated in Lucy's fox face, and I hoped my lieutenant would not prove as submissive as the unicorn. We hung the tapestry on the rear wall of our cellar, formerly decorated with death's heads, black hands, and other such absurdities, and soon the unicorn motif seemed to dominate all our deliberations. Meanwhile Lucy had made herself at home in our midst, coming and going as she pleased and sniggering behind my back. Why then, I asked myself, did we have to bring in this second, woven Lucy, who is turning your lieutenants into unicorns, who alive or woven is really out to get you, Oskar, for you alone of the Dusters are truly fabulous and unique, you are the human unicorn.

But then Advent was upon us, and I was mighty glad of it. We began to collect Nativity figures from all the churches in the neighborhood, and soon the tapestry was so well hidden behind them that the fable — or so I thought — was bound to lose its influence. In mid-December Rundstedt opened his offensive in the Ardennes and we completed preparations for our major coup.

Several Sundays running I attended ten o'clock Mass with Maria, who, to Matzerath's chagrin, had become thoroughly immersed in Catholicism. The Dusters, too, at my behest, had become regular churchgoers. This was our way of casing the joint. Finally, on the night of September 18, we broke into the Church of the Sacred Heart. 'Broke' is a manner of speaking. Thanks to our choirboys, there was no need to break anything, not even for Oskar to sing at any glass.

It was snowing, but the snow melted as it fell. We stowed the three handcarts behind the sacristy. The younger Rennwand had the key to the main door. Oskar went in first, led the boys one by one to the holy-water font, where at his bidding they genuflected toward the high altar. Then I had them throw a Labor Service blanket over the statue of Jesus bearing his Sacred Heart, lest his blue gaze interfere with our work. Bouncer and Mister carried the tools to the scene of action, the left side-altar. The manger with its Nativity figures and evergreen boughs had to be cleared out of the way. We already had all the shepherds and angels, all the sheep, asses, and cows we needed. Our cellar was full of extras; all that was lacking were the central figures. Belisarius removed the flowers from the altar. Totila and Teja rolled up the carpet. Firestealer unpacked the tools. Oskar, on his knees behind a pew, supervised the operations.

The first to be sawed off was little John the Baptist in his chocolate-colored pelt. Luckily, we had a metal saw, for inside the plaster there were metal rods as thick as your finger connecting the boy Baptist with the cloud. Firestealer did the sawing. He went about it like an intellectual, that is to say, clumsily. Once again the Schichau apprentices were sorely missed. Störtebeker relieved Firestealer. He was somewhat handier and after half an hour's rasping and squeaking we were able to topple the boy Baptist over and wrap him in a woolen blanket. Then for a moment we breathed in the midnight ecclesiastical silence.

It took a little longer to saw off the child Jesus, whose whole rear end rested on the Virgin's thigh. Bouncer, the elder Rennwand, and Lionheart were at work for fully forty minutes. But where, I wondered, was Moorkähne? His idea had been that our movements would attract less attention if he and his men came directly from Neufahrwasser and met us in the church.

Störtebeker seemed nervous and irritable. Several times he asked the Rennwand brothers about Moorkähne. When at length, as we all expected, Lucy's name came up, Störtebeker stopped asking questions, wrenched the metal saw out of Lionheart's unpracticed hands, and working feverishly gave the boy Jesus the *coup de grâce*.

As they laid Jesus down, his halo broke off. Störtebeker apologized to me. Controlling myself with some difficulty – for I too was succumbing to the general irritability – I told them to pick up the pieces, which were gathered into two caps. Firestealer thought the halo could be glued together again. Jesus was bedded in cushions and wrapped in blankets.

Our plan was to saw off the Virgin at the waist, making a second cut between the cloud and the soles of her feet. We would leave the cloud where it was and take only the figures, Jesus, the two halves of the Virgin, and the boy Baptist if there was still room in one of the carts. The figures, as we were glad to discover, weighed less than we had expected. The whole group was hollow cast. The walls were no more than an inch thick, and the only heavy part was the iron skeleton.

The boys were exhausted, especially Firestealer and Lionheart. Operations had to be suspended while they rested, for the others, including the Rennwand brothers, could not saw. The gang sat shivering in the pews. Störtebeker stood crumpling his velours hat, which he had removed on entering the church. The atmosphere was not to my liking. Something had to be done. The boys were suffering the effects of the religious architecture, full of night and emptiness. Some were worried about Moorkähne's absence. The Rennwand brothers seemed to be afraid of Störtebeker; they stood to one side, whispering until Störtebeker ordered them to be still.

Slowly, I seem to remember, slowly and with a sigh, I rose from my prayer cushion and went straight up to the Virgin, who was still in her place. Her eyes, which had been turned toward John, were now resting on the altar steps, white with plaster dust. Her right forefinger, hitherto aimed at Jesus, pointed into the void, or rather, the dark left aisle of the nave. I took one step after another, then looked behind me, trying to catch Störtebeker's attention. His deep-set eyes were far away until Firestealer gave him a poke. Then he looked at me, but with a lack of assurance such as I had never seen in him. At first he failed to understand, then he understood, or partly so, and stepped slowly, much too slowly forward. However, he took the altar steps at one bound and then lifted me up on the white, jagged, incompetent saw cut on the Virgin's thigh, which roughly reproduced the imprint of the boy Jesus' behind.

Störtebeker turned back at once and with one step he was back on the flags. He almost fell back into his reverie, but then he gave himself a jolt, and his eyes narrowed. No more than our henchmen in the pews could he conceal his emotion at the sight of me sitting so naturally in Jesus' place, all ready to be worshipped.

He soon saw what I was after and even gave me more than I had bargained for. He ordered Narses and Bluebeard to shine their Army flashlights upon me and the Virgin. When the glare blinded me, he told them to use the red beam. Then he summoned the Rennwand brothers and held a whispered conference with them. They were reluctant to do his bidding; Firestealer stepped over to the group and exhibited his knuckles, all ready for dusting; the brothers gave in and vanished into the sacristy with Firestealer and Mister. Oskar waited calmly, moved his drum into position, and was not even surprised when Mister, who was a tall, gangling fellow, came back attired as a priest, accompanied by the two Rennwand brothers in the red and white raiment of choirboys. Firestealer, wearing some of the vicar's clothing, brought in everything needed for Mass, stowed his equipment on the cloud, and withdrew. The elder Rennwand bore the vestments, Mister gave a fair imitation of Father Wiehnke. At first he performed with a schoolboy's cynicism, but then, letting himself be carried away by the words and gestures, offered us all, and myself in particular, not a silly parody, but a Mass which even at our trial was consistently referred to as a Mass, though a black one to be sure.

The three of them began with the gradual prayers; the boys in the pews and on the flags genuflected, crossed themselves, and Mister, who knew the words up to a point, embarked on the Mass with the expert support of the two choir boys. I began to drum, cautiously in the Introit, but more forcefully in the Kyrie. *Gloria in excelsis Deo* – I praised the Lord on my drum, summoned the congregation to prayer, substituted a drum solo of some length for the Epistle. My Halleluia was particularly successful. In the Credo, I saw that the boys believed in me; for the Offertory, I drummed rather more softly as Mister presented the bread and mixed wine with water. Sharing a whiff of incense with the chalice, I looked on to see how Mister would handle the Lavabo. *Orate, fratres,* I drummed in the red glow of the flash-lights, and led up to the Transubstantiation: This is My body. *Oremus,* sang Mister, in response to orders from above – the boys in the pews offered me two different versions of the Lord's Prayer, but Mister managed to reconcile Protestants and Catholics in one Communion. Even before the meal was over, my drum introduced the Confiteor. The Virgin pointed her finger at Oskar, the drummer. I had indeed taken the place of Christ. The Mass was going like clockwork. Mister's voice rose and fell. How splendidly he pronounced the benediction: pardon, absolution, and remission. '*Ite, missa est* – Go, you are dismissed.' By the time these words were spoken, every one of us, I believe, had experienced a spiritual liberation. When the secular arm fell, it was upon a band of Dusters confirmed in the faith in Oskar's and Jesus's name.

I had heard the motors during the Mass and Störtebeker too had turned his head. We alone showed no surprise when voices were heard and heavy heels converged on us from the front and side doors and from the sacristy.

Störtebeker wanted to lift me down from the Virgin's thigh. I motioned him away. He understood, nodded, and made the boys keep kneeling. There they remained, waiting for the police. They trembled, a few lost their balance, some dropped on two knees, but they waited in silence until the law, converging in three groups, had surrounded the left side-altar.

The police had flashlights too, but favored a white beam. Störtebeker arose, crossed himself, stepped forward into the light, and handed his velours hat to Firestealer, who was still kneeling. Moving quickly around a bloated shadow without a flashlight – Father Wiehnke – Störtebeker seized a thin figure that thrashed about and tried to defend itself – Lucy Rennwand. He slapped and punched the pinched triangular face under the beret until a blow from one of the policemen sent him rolling among the pews.

Still perched on my Virgin, I heard one of the cops exclaiming: 'Good God, Jeschke, that's the boss's kid.'

To Oskar it was a source of modest satisfaction to learn that my excellent lieutenant had been the son of the chief of police. I offered no resistance, but stepped automatically into the role of a sniveling three-year-old who had been led astray by gangsters. All I wanted was to be comforted and protected. Father Wiehnke picked me up in his arms.

Everyone was quiet except for the policemen. The boys were led away. Father Wiehnke felt faint and had to sit down, but first he deposited me on the floor not far from our equipment. Behind hammers and crowbars, I found the basket full of sandwiches that Bouncer had made before we started on our expedition.

I took the basket, went over to Lucy, who was shivering in her light coat, and offered her the sandwiches. She picked us both up, Oskar and basket. A moment later she had a sandwich between her teeth. I studied her flaming, battered, swollen face: restless eyes in black slits, a chewing triangle, a doll, a wicked witch devouring sausage and, even as she ate, growing skinnier, hungrier, more triangular, more doll-like. The sight set its stamp on me. Who will efface that triangle from my mind? How long will it live within me, chewing sausage, chewing men, and smiling as only triangles, or lady unicorn-tamers on tapestries, can smile.

As he was led away between two inspectors, Störtebeker turned his blood-smeared face toward Lucy and Oskar. I looked past him. I recognized him no longer. When all my erstwhile followers had left, I too was led away, still in the arms of the sandwich-eating Lucy.

Who stayed behind? Father Wiehnke with our flashlights, still shining red, and the vestments hurriedly shed by Father Mister and his assistants. Chalice and ciborium lay on the steps to the altar. The sawed-off John and the sawed-off Jesus were still there with the Virgin, who was to have formed a counterweight to the lady with the unicorn in our cellar headquarters.

Oskar, however, was carried away to a trial that I still call the second trial of Jesus, a trial that ended with the acquittal of Oskar, hence also of Jesus.

The Ant Trail

Imagine, if you please, a swimming pool lined with azure-blue tiles. Quite a few sunburned, athletic young people in the water, and more sunburned young men and women sitting or reclining on the tiles round the edges. Perhaps a bit of soft music from the loudspeaker. Healthy boredom and a mild, noncommittal sexuality. The tiles are smooth, but no one slips. Only a few signs prohibiting anything; no need of them, the bathers come only for an hour or two and have other places to do what is forbidden. Now and then someone dives from the ten-foot springboard but fails to attract the attention of those in the water, or to lure the eyes of those reclining on the tiles away from their illustrated weeklies. Suddenly a breeze! No, not a breeze, but a young man who slowly, resolutely, reaching from rung to rung, climbs the ladder to the thirty-foot diving tower. Magazines droop, eyes rise, recumbent bodies grow longer, a young woman shades her forehead, someone forgets what he was thinking about, a word remains unspoken, a flirtation, just begun, comes to a sudden end in the middle of the sentence – for there he stands virile and well built, jumps up and down on the platform, leans on gently curved tubular railing, casts a bored look downward, moves away from the railing with a graceful swing of the haunches, ventures out on the springboard that sways at every step, focuses his eyes on an azure-blue, alarmingly small swimming pool, full of intermingling bathing caps: yellow, green, white, red, yellow, green, white, red, yellow, green. . . . That's where his friends must be sitting, Doris and Erika Schüler, and Jutta Daniels with her boy friend, who isn't right for her. They wave, Jutta waves too. Rather worried about his balance, he waves back. They shout. What can they want? He should go ahead, they shout, dive, cries Jutta. But he had climbed up with no such intention, he had just wanted to see how things looked from up here, and then climb down, slowly, rung by rung. And now they are shouting so everybody can hear: Dive! Go ahead and dive! Go ahead.

This, you will admit, though a diving tower may be a step nearer heaven, is a desperate plight to be in. In January, 1945, the Dusters and I, though it was not the bathing season, found ourselves in a similar situation. We had ventured high up, we were all crowded together on the diving tower, and below, forming a solemn horseshoe round a waterless pool, sat the judges, witnesses, and court clerks.

Störtebeker stepped out on the supple, railingless springboard. 'Dive!' cried the judges.

But Störtebeker didn't feel like it.

Then from the witnesses' bench there arose a slender figure with a grey pleated skirt and a little Bavarian-style jacket. A pale but not indistinct face which, I still maintain, formed a triangle, rose up like a target indicator: Lucy Rennwand did not shout. She only whispered: 'Jump, Störtebeker, jump!'

Then Störtebeker jumped. Lucy sat down again on the witnesses' bench and pulled down the sleeves of her Bavarian jacket over her fists.

Moorkähne limped onto the springboard. The judges ordered him to dive. But Moorkähne didn't feel like it; smiling in embarrassment at his fingernails, he waited for Lucy to pull up her sleeves, let her fists fall out of the wool, and display the black-framed triangle with the slits for eyes. Then he plunged furiously at the triangle, but missed it.

Even on the way up, Firestealer and Putty hadn't been exactly lovely-dovey; on the springboard they came to blows. Putty was dusted, and even when he plunged, Firestealer wouldn't let him go.

Bouncer, who had long silky eyelashes, closed his deep, sad doe's eyes before taking the leap.

The Air Force Auxiliaries had to take off their uniforms before plunging.

Nor were the Rennwand brothers permitted to take their heavenward plunge attired as choirboys; that would have been quite unacceptable to their sister Lucy, sitting on the witnesses' bench in her jacket of threadbare wartime wool and encouraging young men to dive.

In defiance of history, Belisarius and Narses dove first, then Totila and Teja. Bluebeard plunged, Lionheart plunged, then the rank and file: The Nose, Bushman, Tanker, Piper, Mustard Pot, Yatagan, and Cooper.

The last to jump was Stuchel, a high school student so cross-eyed it made you dizzy to look at him; he had only half belonged to the gang and that by accident. Only Jesus was left on the platform. Addressing him as Oskar Matzerath, the judges asked him to dive, but Jesus did not comply. Lucy, the stern and unbending, Lucy with the scrawny Mozart pigtail hanging between her shoulders, rose from the witnesses' bench, spread her sweater arms, and whispered without visibly moving her compressed lips: 'Jump, sweet Jesus, jump.' At this moment I understood the fatal lure of a thirty-foot springboard; little grey kittens began to wriggle in my knee joints, hedgehogs mated under the soles of my feet, swallows took wing in my armpits, and at my feet I saw not only Europe but the whole world. Americans and Japanese were doing a torch dance on the island of Luzon, dancing so hard that slant-eyes and round-eyes alike lost the buttons off their uniforms. But at the very same moment a tailor in Stockholm was sewing buttons on a handsome suit of evening clothes. Mountbatten was feeding Burmese elephants shells of every caliber. A widow in Lima was teaching her parrot to say 'Caramba'. In the middle of the Pacific two enormous aircraft carriers, done up to look like Gothic cathedrals, stood face to face, sent up their planes, and simultaneously sank one another. The planes had no place to land, they hovered helplessly and quite allegorically like angels in mid-air, using up their fuel with a terrible din. This was all one to the streetcar conductor in Haparanda, who had just gone off duty. He was breaking eggs into a frying pan, two for himself and two for his fiancée, whom he was expecting any minute, having planned the whole evening in advance. Obviously the armies of Koniev and Zhukov could be expected to resume their forward drive; while rain fell in Ireland, they broke through on the Vistula, took Warsaw too late and Königsberg too soon, and even so were powerless to prevent a woman in Panama, who had five children and only one husband, from burning the milk she was warming up on her gas range. Inevitably the thread of events wound itself into loops and knots which became known as the fabric of History. I also saw that activities such as thumb-twiddling, frowning, looking up and down, handshaking, making babies, counterfeiting, turning out the light, brushing teeth, shooting people, and changing diapers were being practiced all over the world, though not always with the same skill. My head swimming at the thought of so much purposive movement, I turned back to the trial which was continuing in my honor at the foot of the diving tower. 'Jump, sweet Jesus, jump,' whispered Lucy Rennwand, the witness and virgin temptress. She was sitting on Satan's lap, and that brought out her virginity. He handed her a sandwich. She bit into it with pleasure, but lost none of her chastity. 'Jump, sweet Jesus,' she chewed, offering me her triangle, still intact.

I did not jump, and you will never catch me jumping or diving from a diving tower. This was not to be Oskar's last trial. Many attempts have been made, one very recently, to persuade me to jump. At the ring-finger trial – which I prefer to call the third trial of Jesus – there were again plenty of spectators at the edge of the waterless swimming pool. They sat on witnesses' benches, determined to enjoy and survive my trial.

But I made an about-face, stifled the fledgling swallows in my armpits, squashed the hedgehogs mating under the soles of my feet, starved the grey kittens out from under my kneecaps. Scorning the exaltation of plunging, I went stiffly to the railing, swung myself onto the ladder, descended, let every rung in the ladder reinforce my conviction that diving towers can not only be climbed but also relinquished without diving.

Down below, Maria and Matzerath were waiting for me. Father Wiehnke gave me his blessing though I hadn't asked for it. Gretchen Scheffler had brought me a little winter coat and some cake. Kurt had grown and refused to recognize me either as a father or as a half brother. My grandmother Koljaiczek held her brother Vincent by the arm. He knew the world and talked incoherent nonsense.

As we were leaving the courthouse, an official in civilian clothes approached Matzerath, handed him a paper, and said: 'You really ought to think it over, Mr. Matzerath. You've got to get the child off the streets. You see how helpless and gullible he is, always ready to be taken in by disreputable elements.'

Maria wept and gave me my drum, which Father Wiehnke had taken care of during the trial. We went to the streetcar stop by the Central Station. Matzerath carried me the last bit of the way. I looked back over his shoulder, searching the crowd for a triangular face, wondering whether she too had had to climb the tower, whether she had jumped after Störtebeker and Moorkähne, or whether like me she had availed herself of the alternative possibility, of climbing down the ladder.

To this day I have not been able to dispel the habit of looking about in streets and public places for a skinny teenage girl, neither pretty nor ugly, but always biting men. Even in my bed in the mental hospital I am frightened when Bruno announces an unexpected visitor. My nightmare is that Lucy Rennwand will turn up in the shape of a wicked witch and for the last time bid me to plunge.

For ten days Matzerath pondered whether to sign the letter and send it to the Ministry of Public Health. When on the eleventh day he signed and mailed it, the city was already under artillery fire, and it was doubtful that his letter would cover much ground. Armored spearheads of Marshal Rokossovski's army reached Elbing. The German Second Army, commanded by Weiss, took up positions on the heights surrounding Danzig. Like everyone else, we began to live in the cellar.

As we all know, our cellar was under the shop. You could reach it by way of the cellar door in the hallway across from the toilet; you went down eighteen steps, past Heilandt's cellar and Kater's cellar, but before Schlager's. Old man Heilandt was still in the house. But Mrs. Kater, Laubschad the watchmaker, the Eykes, and the Schlagers had slipped away with a few bundles. Later the story went round that they, and with them Alexander and Gretchen Scheffler, had managed at the last minute to board a Strength through Joy ship which had either reached Stettin or Lubeck or struck a mine; in any case over half of the flats and cellars were empty.

Our cellar had the advantage of a second entrance which, as we also all of us know, consisted of a trap door behind the counter of our shop. Consequently, no one could see what Matzerath put into the cellar or removed from it. Otherwise Matzerath's accumulation of provisions during the war years would never have been tolerated. The warm, dry room was full of dried peas and beans, noodles, sugar, artificial honey, wheat flour, and margarine.

Boxes of Swedish bread rested on cases of Crisco. Matzerath was clever with his hands. He himself had put up shelves, which were well stocked with canned fruit and vegetables. Thanks to a few uprights which Matzerath, at Greff's instigation, had wedged between floor and ceiling toward the middle of the war, the storeroom was as safe as a regulation air-raid shelter. On several occasions Matzerath had thought of removing the uprights, for there had been no heavy air raids. But when Greff the air-raid warden was no longer there to remonstrate with him, Maria insisted that he leave the props in place. She demanded safety for little Kurt, and occasionally even for me.

During the first air raids at the end of January, old man Heilandt and Matzerath joined forces to remove Mother Truczinski and her chair to our cellar. Then, perhaps at her request, possibly to avoid the effort of carrying her, they left her in her flat, sitting beside the window. After the big raid on the inner city, Maria and Matzerath found the old woman with her jaw hanging down, squinting as though a sticky little gnat had got caught in her eye.

The door to the bedroom was lifted off its hinges. Old man Heilandt brought his tools and a few boards, mostly disassembled crates. Smoking Derby cigarettes that Matzerath had given him, he took measurements. Oskar helped him with his work. The others vanished into the cellar, for the artillery shelling had started in again.

Old man Heilandt was in a hurry, he had in mind a simple rectangular box. But Oskar insisted on the traditional coffin shape. I held the boards in place, making him saw to my specifications, and the outcome was a coffin tapered at the foot end, such as every human corpse has a right to demand.

It was a fine-looking coffin in the end. Lina Greff washed Mother Truczinski, took a fresh nightgown from the cupboard, cut her fingernails, arranged her bun and propped it up on three knitting needles. In short, she managed to make Mother Truczinski look, even in death, like a grey mouse who had been given to potato pancakes and Postum in her lifetime.

The mouse had stiffened in her chair during the bombing and her knees refused to unbend. Before he could put on the coffin lid, old man Heilandt was obliged, when Maria left the room for a few moments, to break her legs.

Unfortunately there was no black paint, only yellow. Mother Truczinski was carried out of the flat and down the stairs in boards unpainted, but properly tapered at the foot end. Oskar followed with his drum, reading the inscription on the coffin lid: Vitello Margarine – Vitello Margarine – Vitello Margarine: evenly spaced and thrice repeated, these words bore witness to Mother Truczinski's taste in household fat. For indeed she had preferred that good Vitello Margarine, made exclusively from vegetable oils, to the best butter, because margarine stays fresh, is wholesome and nutritious, and makes for good humor.

Old man Heilandt loaded the coffin on the handcart belonging to Greff's vegetable shop, and pulled it through Luisenstrasse, Marienstrasse, down Anton-Möller-Weg, where two houses were burning, toward the Women's Clinic. Little Kurt had remained with the widow Greff in our cellar. Maria and Matzerath pushed, Oskar sat in the cart beside the coffin, he would have liked to climb on top, but was not allowed to. The streets were clogged with refugees from East Prussia and the Delta. It was just about impossible to get through the underpass by the Sports Palace. Matzerath suggested digging a hole in the park of the Conradinum. The idea did not appeal to Maria or to old man Heilandt, who was the same age as Mother Truczinski. I too was opposed to the school park. Still, there was no hope of reaching the city cemetery, for from the Sports Palace on, Hindenburg-Allee was closed to all but military vehicles. And so, unable to bury the mouse beside her son Herbert, we chose a place for her in Steffens-Park, not far from the Maiwiese.

The ground was frozen. While Matzerath and old man Heilandt took turns with the pickax and Maria tried to dig up some ivy beside the stone benches, Oskar slipped away to Hindenburg-Allee. What traffic! Tanks retreating from the heights and the Delta, some being towed. From the trees – lindens if I remember rightly – dangled soldiers and Volkssturm men. To their jackets were affixed cardboard signs identifying them quite legibly as traitors. I looked into the convulsed faces of several of these hanging men and drew comparisons – with other hanged men as such and in general and with Greff the greengrocer in particular. There were also whole clusters of youngsters strung up in uniforms that were too big for them, and several times I thought I

369

recognized Störtebeker – but youngsters at the end of a rope all look alike. Nevertheless, I said to myself: so now they've hanged Störtebeker, I wonder if they've strung up Lucy Rennwand.

That thought gave Oskar wings. He searched the trees to left and right for a skinny, dangling girl, and even crossed the street in between the tanks, but there too he found only soldiers, old men in Volkssturm uniforms, and youngsters who looked like Störtebeker. Disappointed, I trotted along as far as the half-demolished Four Seasons Café, and turned back only reluctantly. As I stood by Mother Truczinski's grave, helping Maria to strew ivy and leaves over the fresh earth, the vision, clear in every detail, of a dangling Lucy was still with me.

We didn't return the cart to the vegetable shop. Matzerath and old man Heilandt took it apart and piled up the pieces by the counter. 'Maybe we'll be needing the cart again,' said Matzerath. 'Here it's fairly safe.' Then he gave the old man three packs of Derby cigarettes.

Old man Heilandt said nothing but helped himself to several packages of noodles and two bags of sugar from the near-empty shelves. Then he shuffled off in his felt slippers, which he had worn for the funeral, leaving Matzerath to remove what little remained of his stock from the shelves and carry it down to the cellar.

After that we seldom emerged from our hole. The Russians were said to be in Zigankenberg, Pietzgendorf, and on the out-skirts of Schidlitz. There was no doubt that they occupied the heights, for they were firing straight down into the city. Inner City and Outer City, Old City, New City and Old New City, Lower City and Spice City – what had taken seven hundred years to build burned down in three days. Yet this was not the first fire to descend on the city of Danzig. For centuries Pomerellians, Brandenburgers, Teutonic Knights, Poles, Swedes, and a second time Swedes, Frenchmen, Prussians, and Russians, even Saxons, had made history by deciding every few years that the city of Danzig was worth burning. And now it was Russians, Poles, Germans, and Englishmen all at once who were burning the city's Gothic bricks for the hundredth time. Hook Street, Long Street, and Broad Street, Big Weaver Street and Little Weaver Street were in flames; Tobias Street, Hound Street, Old City Ditch,

Outer City Ditch, the ramparts and Long Bridge, all were in flames. Built of wood, Crane Gate made a particularly fine blaze. In Breechesmaker Street, the fire had itself measured for several pairs of extra-loud breeches. The Church of St. Mary was burning inside and outside, festive light effects could be seen through its ogival windows. What bells had not been evacuated from St. Catherine, St. John, St. Brigit, Saints Barbara, Elisabeth, Peter, and Paul, from Trinity and Corpus Christi, melted in their belfries and dripped away without pomp or ceremony. In the Big Mill red wheat was milled. Butcher Street smelled of burnt Sunday roast. The Municipal Theater was giving a première, a one-act play entitled The Firebug's Dream. The town fathers decided to raise the firemen's wages retroactively after the fire. Holy Ghost Street was burning in the name of the Holy Ghost. Joyously, the Franciscan Monastery blazed in the name of St. Francis, who had loved fire and sung hymns to it. Our Lady Street burned for Father and Son at once. Needless to say the Lumber Market, Coal Market, and Haymarket burned to the ground. In Baker Street the ovens burned and the bread and rolls with them. In Milk Pitcher Street the milk boiled over. Only the West Prussian Fire Insurance Building, for purely symbolic reasons, refused to burn down.

Oskar has never been very much interested in fires. I would have stayed in the cellar when Matzerath ran up the stairs for a view of Danzig in flames, if I had not improvidently stored my few, highly inflammable belongings in the attic. I was determined to save the last of the drums Bebra had given me and my volume of Goethe-Rasputin. Between the pages of the book, I had been saving a fan, light as gossamer and delicately painted, that my Roswitha had wielded, so gracefully, so graciously, in her lifetime. Maria remained in the cellar. But little Kurt wanted to go up on the roof with me and Matzerath, to see the fire. Though irritated by my son's uncontrollable enthusiasm, Oskar told himself that Kurt must have inherited his interest in fire from his great-grandfather, my grandfather, Koljaiczek the firebug. Maria kept Kurt downstairs, I was allowed to go up with Matzerath. I took my belongings, cast a glance through the window of the loft, and was amazed to see what a burst of vitality our venerable old city had been able to summon up.

When shells began to land nearby, we went downstairs. Later on, Matzerath wanted to go up again, but Maria wouldn't let him. He gave in and burst into tears while giving a detailed description of the fire to the widow Greff, who had remained below. Once more he returned to the flat and turned on the radio, but nothing came out. You couldn't even hear the crackling flames of the burning radio station, let alone a special newscast.

Matzerath stood there in the middle of the cellar, tugging at his braces, as bewildered as a child who can't make up his mind whether to go on believing in Santa Claus, and for the first time expressed doubts about the final victory. On the widow Greff's advice, he removed his Party pin from his lapel, but couldn't figure out what to do with it: for the cellar had a concrete floor, Lina Greff was unwilling to take it, Maria said he should bury it in the winter potatoes, but the potatoes didn't seem safe, and he was afraid to go upstairs, because they were bound to come soon, they were on their way, they had already reached Brenntau and Oliva when he had looked from the attic, and he was sorry now that he hadn't left it up there in the air-defense sand, for it would be a fine kettle of fish if they found him with the thing in his hand. He dropped it on the concrete, meaning to stamp on it, to grind it to powder, but Kurt and I leapt at it both together. I had it first and I kept my hold on it when Kurt began to punch as he always did when he wanted something, but I wouldn't give my son the Party badge for fear of endangering him, because you didn't joke with the Russians. Oskar remembered that from his readings in Rasputin, and I wondered, while Kurt pummeled me and Maria tried to separate us, whether it would be White Russians or Great Russians, Cossacks or Georgians, Kalmucks or Crimean Tartars, Ruthenians or Ukrainians, or maybe even Kirghizes who would find the Party badge on Kurt if Oskar were to give way under his son's blows.

When Maria with the widow Greff's help parted us, I was clutching the pin victoriously in my fist. Matzerath was glad to be rid of it. Maria was busy with Kurt, who was bawling. The open pin pricked my hand. I had never liked the thing much and I still didn't. But just as I was trying to pin it to the back of Matzerath's jacket – what business of mine, after all, was that

Party of his? – they were in the shop over our heads and, to judge by the screaming women, in the neighboring cellars as well.

When they lifted the trap door, the pin was still sticking into me. There was nothing to do but sit down by Maria's trembling knees and watch the ants which had laid out a military highway running from the winter potatoes, across the concrete floor, to a sack of sugar. Perfectly normal Russians, slight racial mixture, I said to myself, as six or seven of them appeared on the stairs with big eyes and tommy guns. Amid all the screaming it was reassuring to note that the ants were in no way affected by the arrival of the Russian Army. They still had the same interests – potatoes and sugar – despite the men with the tommy guns who put other conquests first. It struck me as perfectly normal that the grownups should put up their hands. I knew about that from the newsreels, and I had witnessed the same gesture of submission after the fall of the Polish Post Office. But why Kurt should ape the grownups was more than I could see. He should have taken an example from me, his father – or if not from his father, then from the ants. Instantly three of the rectangular uniforms turned their attentions to Lina Greff, and that put some life into the hitherto static ensemble. La Greff, who after her long widowhood and the lean years preceding it, had scarcely expected such sudden popularity, let out a few screams of surprise but soon reaccustomed herself to an occupation she had almost forgotten.

I had read in Rasputin that the Russians are great lovers of children. This, as I was soon to learn, is perfectly true. Maria trembled needlessly. She failed to understand why the four Ivans who were not busy with la Greff left Kurt sitting on her lap instead of taking turns at it themselves; she was amazed to see them fondle him and say dadada, and pat him on the cheeks with an occasional pat for herself.

Someone picked up me and my drum from the floor; I could no longer observe the ants and judge the life of my times by their purposeful industry. My drum hung on my belly, and with his thick fingers the big Russian with the dilated pores tapped out a few measures one might have danced to; not bad for a grown-up, I thought. Oskar would have liked to show off his own talents, but that was impossible because Matzerath's party pin was still sticking into his hand.

A peaceful atmosphere, one would almost have called it cozy, settled on our cellar. More and more calmly la Greff lay spread out beneath one after another of the three Ivans. When one of them decided to call it a day, my gifted drummer handed Oskar on to a sweating young fellow with slanting eyes, a Kalmuck no doubt. Holding me with his left hand, he buttoned his fly with his right, while his predecessor, the drummer, did the exact opposite. For Matzerath, however, nothing had changed. He was still standing by the shelf full of Leipzig stew with his hands up, clearly displaying their lines; but nobody wanted to read his palms. The women meanwhile showed a remarkable aptitude for adjustment: Maria learned her first words of Russian, her knees stopped shaking, she even laughed, and would have played her harmonica had it been within reach.

Oskar, who was less adaptable, looked about for something to take the place of his ants and discovered a colony of flat greyish-brown insects that were strolling about on the edge of my Kalmuck's collar. I wanted to catch one of them and examine it, for I had read a good deal about lice, not so much in Goethe but all the more in Rasputin. However, it is difficult to chase lice with one hand, so I decided to get rid of the Party pin. Oskar feels that he ought to explain his behavior at this point. Well, this is the best he can do: This pin was sticking me and preventing me from catching lice. The Kalmuck's chest was already covered with medals and insignia. So I held out my loosely closed hand to Matzerath, who was standing beside me.

You may say that I shouldn't have done it. But perhaps I am entitled to reply that Matzerath shouldn't have grasped at my hand.

Anyway, he grasped, I was rid of the thing. Little by little, fear took possession of Matzerath as he felt the emblem of his Party between his fingers. Now that my hands were free, I didn't want to see what Matzerath did with the pin. Too distraught to pursue the lice, Oskar tried to concentrate on the ants, but couldn't help taking in a swift movement of Matzerath's hand. Unable to remember what I thought at the time, I can only say in retrospect that it would have been wiser of him to keep the little colored lozenge in his hand.

But he wanted desperately to get rid of it, and despite the rich imagination he had shown as a cook and window dresser, he could think of no other hiding place than his mouth.

How important a trifling gesture can be! That little move from hand to mouth was enough to startle the two Ivans who had been sitting peacefully to left and right of Maria and make them jump up from the air-defense cot. They thrust their tommy guns at Matzerath's belly, and it was plain for all to see that Matzerath was trying to swallow something.

If only he had first, with an adroit finger maneuver, closed the pin. As it was, he gagged, his face went purple, his eyes stood out of his head, he coughed, cried, laughed, and all this turn made it impossible for him to keep his hands up. But on that point the Ivans were firm. They shouted at him, they wanted to see the palms of his hands. Matzerath, however, was pre-occupied with his windpipe. He couldn't even cough properly. He began to dance and thrash about with his arms and swept a can of Leipzig stew off the shelf. My Kalmuck, who until then had been quietly looking on, deposited me carefully on the floor, reached behind him, brought something or other into a horizontal position, and shot from the hip. He had emptied a whole magazine before Matzerath finished suffocating.

What strange things one does at the moments when fate puts on its act! While my presumptive father was swallowing the Party and dying, I, involuntarily and unaware of what I was doing, squashed between my fingers a louse I had just caught on the Kalmuck. Matzerath had fallen across the ant highway. The Ivans left the cellar by way of the stairs leading to the shop, taking with them a few packages of artificial honey. My Kalmuck went last, but he took no honey, for he had to change the magazine of his tommy gun. The widow Greff lay disheveled and undone between the margarine crates. Maria clutched little Kurt to her as though to crush him. A phrase from Goethe passed through my mind. The ants found themselves facing a new situation but, undismayed by the detour, soon built a new highway round the doubled-up Matzerath; for the sugar that trickled out of the burst sack had lost none of its sweetness while Marshal Rokossovski was occupying the city of Danzig.

Should I or Shouldn't I?

First came the Rugii, then the Goths and Gepidae, then the Kashubes from whom Oskar is descended in a straight line. A little later the Poles sent in Adalbert of Prague, who came with the Cross and was slain with an ax by the Kashubes or Borussians. This happened in a fishing village called Gyddanyzc. Gyddanyzc became Danczik, which was turned into Dantzig, later written without the t, and today the city is called Gdansk.

But before this orthographic development and after the arrival of the Kashubes, the dukes of Pomerelia came to Gyddanyzc. They bore such names as Subislaus, Sambor, Mestwin, and Swantopolk. The village became a small town. Then came the wild Borussians, intent on pillage and destruction. Then came the distant Brandenburgers, equally given to pillage and destruction. Boleslaw of Poland did his bit in the same spirit and no sooner was the damage repaired than the Teutonic Knights stepped in to carry on the time-honored tradition.

The centuries passed. The city was destroyed and rebuilt in turn by the dukes of Pomerelia, the grand masters of the Teutonic Order, the kings and antikings of Poland, the counts of Brandenburg, and the bishops of Wloclawek. The directors of the building and wrecking enterprises were named Otto and Waldemar, Bogussa, Heinrich von Plotzke – and Dietrich von Altenberg, who built the fortress of the Teutonic Knights on the spot which became the Hevelius-Platz, where in the twentieth century the Polish Post Office was defended.

The Hussites came, made a little fire here and there, and left. The Teutonic Knights were thrown out of the city and the fortress was torn down because the townspeople were sick of having a fortress in their city. The Poles took over and no one was any the worse for it. The king who brought this to pass was Kazimierz, who became known as the Great, son of Wladyslaw the First. Then came Louis of Hungary and after Louis his daughter Jadwiga. She married Jagiello of Lithuania, founder of the Jagellon dynasty. After Wladyslaw II came Wladyslaw III, then another Kazimierz, who lacked the proper enthusiasm and nevertheless, for thirteen long years, squandered the good money of the Danzig merchants making war on the Teutonic Knights. The attentions of John Albert, on the other hand, were more taken up by the Turks. Alexander was followed by Zygmunt Stary, or Sigismund the Elder. After the chapter about Sigismund Augustus comes the one about Stefan Batory, for whom the Poles like to name their ocean liners. He besieged the city and shot cannon balls into it for Lord knows how long (as we may read in our books), but never succeeded in taking it. Then came the Swedes and continued in the same vein. They got so fond of besieging the city that they repeated the performance several times. In the same period, the Gulf of Danzig also became exceedingly popular with the Dutch, Danes, and English, and a number of these foreign sea captains came to be heroes of the sea just by cruising around the Danzig roadstead.

The Peace of Cliva. How sweet and peaceful it sounds! There the great powers noticed for the first time that the land of the Poles lends itself admirably to partition. Swedes, Swedes, and more Swedes – Swedish earthworks, Swedish punch, Swedish gallows. Then came the Russians and Saxons, because Stanislaw Leszczynski, the poor King of Poland, was hidden in the city. On account of this one king, eighteen hundred houses were destroyed, and when poor Leszczynski fled to France because that's where his son-in-law Louis was living, the people of Danzig had to cough up a round million.

Then Poland was divided in three. The Prussians came uninvited and painted the Polish eagle over with their own bird on all the city gates. Johannes Falk, the educator, had just time to write his famous Christmas carol 'O Du fröhliche . . .' when the French turned up. Napoleon's general was called Rapp and after a miserable siege the people of Danzig had to rap out twenty million francs to him. The horrors of the French occupation should not necessarily be held in doubt. But it lasted only seven years. Then came the Russians and the Prussians and set the Speicherinsel on fire with their artillery. That was the end of the Free State that Napoleon had dreamed up. Again the Prussians found occasion to paint their bird on all the city gates. Having

377

done so with Prussian thoroughness, they proceeded to establish a garrison consisting of the 4th Regiment of Grenadiers, the 1st Artillery Brigade, the 1st Battalion of Engineers, and the 1st Regiment of Leib-Hussars. The 30th Infantry Regiment, the 18th Infantry Regiment, the 3rd Regiment of Foot Guards, the 44th Infantry Regiment, and the 33rd Regiment of Fusiliers were all at one time or another garrisoned in the city, though none of them for very long. But the famous 128th Infantry Regiment did not leave until 1920. For the sake of completeness it may be worth mentioning that in the course of the Prussian period the First Artillery Brigade was expanded to include the 1st Battalion of Fortress Artillery, the 2nd Infantry Battalion, the 1st East-Prussian Artillery Regiment, and later the 2nd Pomeranian Foot Artillery Regiment, which was subsequently replaced by the 16th West Prussian Foot Artillery Regiment. The 1st Regiment of Leib Hussars was succeeded by the 2nd Regiment of Leib Hussars. The 8th Regiment of Uhlans, on the other hand, spent only a brief time within the city's walls, while the 17th West-Prussian Quartermaster Battalion was stationed outside the walls, in the suburb of Langfuhr.

In the days of Burckhardt, Rauschning, and Greiser, German authority was represented in the Free State only by the green-uniformed security police. This changed in '39 under Forster. The brick barracks filled rapidly with happy lads in uniform, who juggled with every known weapon. We might go on to list all the units that were quartered in Danzig and environs from '39 to '45 or shipped out from Danzig to fight on the Arctic front. This Oskar will spare you and merely say: then, as we have already seen, came Marshal Rokossovski. At the sight of the still intact city, he remembered his great international precursors and set the whole place on fire with his artillery in order that those who came after him might work off their excess energies in rebuilding.

This time, strange to say, no Prussians, Swedes, Saxons, or Frenchmen came after the Russians; this time it was the Poles who arrived.

The Poles came with bag and baggage from Vilna, Bialystok, and Lwow, all looking for living quarters. To us came a gentleman by the name of Fajngold; he was all alone in the world, but he behaved as though surrounded by a large family that couldn't manage for one minute without his instructions. Mr. Fajngold took over the grocery store at once and proceeded to show his wife Luba, who remained invisible and unresponsive, the scales, the kerosene tank, the brass rod to hang sausages on, the empty cash drawer, and with the utmost enthusiasm, the provisions in the cellar. He engaged Maria as salesgirl and introduced her very verbosely to his imaginary Luba, whereupon Maria showed Mr. Fajngold our Matzerath, who had been lying in the cellar for three days under a square of canvas. We had been unable to bury him because the streets were swarming with Russians avid for bicycles, sewing machines, and women.

When Mr. Fajngold saw the corpse, which we had turned over on his back, he clapped his hands over his head in the same expressive gesture as Oskar had seen Sigismund Markus, his toy dealer, make years before. He called not only Luba his wife, but his whole family into the cellar, and there is no doubt that he saw them all coming, for he called them by name: Luba, Lev, Jakub, Berek, Leon, Mendel, and Sonya. He explained to them all who it was who was lying there dead and went on to tell us that all those he had just summoned as well as his sister-in-law and her other brother-in-law who had five children had lain in the same way, before being taken to the crematoria of Treblinka, and the whole lot of them had been lying there – except for him because he had had to strew lime on them.

Then he helped us to carry Matzerath upstairs to the shop. His family was about him again, and he asked his wife Luba to help Maria wash the corpse. She didn't stir a finger, but Mr. Fajngold didn't notice, for by now he was moving supplies from the cellar up to the shop. This time Lina Greff, who had washed Mother Truczinski, wasn't there to help us; she had a houseful of Russians and we could hear her singing.

Old man Heilandt had found work as a shoemaker. He was busy resoling the boots the Russians had worn out during their rapid advance and was unwilling at first to make us a coffin. But after Mr. Fajngold had drawn him into a business deal – Derby cigarettes from our shop for an electric motor from his shed – he set his boots aside and took up other tools and the last of his boards.

At that time – until we were evicted and Mr. Fajngold turned the cellar over to us – we were living in Mother Truczinski's flat, which had been stripped bare by neighbors and Polish immigrants. Old man Heilandt removed the door between the kitchen and living room from its hinges, for the door between the living room and bedroom had been used for Mother Truczinski's coffin. Down below, in the court, he was smoking Derby cigarettes and throwing the box together. We remained upstairs. I took the one chair that was left in the flat and pushed open the broken window. It grieved me to see that the old fellow was taking no pains at all with his work and turning out a plain rectangular box without the tapering characteristic of self-respecting coffins.

Oskar didn't see Matzerath again, for when the box was lifted onto the widow Greff's handcart, the Vitello Margarine slats had already been nailed down, although in his lifetime Matzerath, far from eating margarine, had despised it even for cooking.

Maria asked Mr. Fajngold to come with us; she was afraid of the Russian soldiers in the streets. Fajngold, who was squatting on the counter, spooning artificial honey out of a cardboard cup, expressed misgivings at first; he was afraid Luba might object, but then apparently his wife gave him permission to go, for he slipped off the counter, giving me the honey. I passed it on to Kurt, who made short shrift of it, while Maria helped Mr. Fajngold into a long black coat with grey rabbit fur. Before he closed the shop, bidding his wife to open for no one, he put on a top hat, considerably too small for him, which Matzerath had worn at various weddings and funerals.

Old man Heilandt refused to pull the cart as far as the City Cemetery. He hadn't the time, he said, he still had boots to mend. At Max-Halbe-Platz, the ruins of which were still smoldering, he turned left into Brösener-Weg and I guessed he was heading for Saspe. The Russians sat outside the houses in the thin February sun, sorting out wristwatches and pocket watches, polishing silver spoons with sand, experimenting to see how brassieres worked out as ear muffs, and doing stunt bicycle-riding over an obstacle course fashioned of oil paintings, grandfather clocks, bathtubs, radios, and clothes trees. Enthusiastically applauded for their skill, they did figure eights, twists, and spirals, all the while dodging the baby carriages, chandeliers, and such like that were being thrown out of the windows. As we passed, they broke off their sport for a few seconds. A few soldiers with negligees over their uniforms helped us to push and tried to make passes at Maria, but were called to order by Mr. Fajngold, who spoke Russian and had an official pass. A soldier in a lady's hat gave us a birdcage containing a live lovebird on a perch. Kurt, who was hopping along beside the cart, tried to pull out its feathers. Afraid to decline the gift, Maria lifted the cage out of Kurt's reach and handed it up to me on the cart. Oskar, who was in no mood for lovebirds, put the cage down on Matzerath's enlarged margarine crate. I was sitting in the rear end of the cart, dangling my legs and looking into the folds of Mr. Fajngold's face, which bore a look of thoughtful gloom, suggesting a mind at work on a complicated problem that refused to come out.

I beat my drum a little, something sprightly, in an effort to dispel Mr. Fajngold's somber thoughts. But his expression remained unchanged, his eyes were somewhere else, maybe in far-away Galicia; one thing they did not see was my drum. Oskar gave up, and after that there was no sound but Maria's weeping and the rumbling of the wheels.

What a mild winter, I thought when we had left the last houses of Langfuhr behind us; I also took some notice of the lovebird, which was puffing out its feathers in consideration of the afternoon sun hovering over the airfield.

The airfield was guarded, the road to Brösen closed. An officer spoke with Mr. Fajngold, who during the interview held his top hat between his fingers, letting his thin, reddish-blond hair blow in the wind. After tapping for a moment on Matzerath's crate as though to determine its contents and tickling the lovebird with his forefinger, the officer let us pass, but assigned two young fellows, who couldn't have been more than sixteen, with caps that were too little and tommy guns that were too big, to escort us, perhaps for our protection or perhaps to keep an eye on us.

Old man Heilandt pulled, without ever once turning around. He had a trick of lighting his cigarette with one hand, without slowing down. Planes darted about overhead. The engines were so clearly audible because of the season, late February or early March. Only in the vicinity of the sun were there a few clouds which gradually took on color. The bombers were heading for

Hela or returning from Hela Peninsula, where what was left of the Second Army was still holding out.

The weather and the droning of the planes made me sad. There is nothing so tedious, nothing that makes for such a feeling of surfeit and disgust, as a cloudless March sky full of airplane motors crescendo and decrescendo. To make matters worse, the two Russian puppies kept trying, quite unsuccessfully, to march in step.

Perhaps some of the boards of the hastily assembled coffin had been jolted loose, first on the cobblestones, then on battered asphalt; we were heading into the wind and, as we have seen, I was sitting in back; in any case, it smelled of dead Matzerath, and Oskar was glad when we reached Saspe Cemetery.

We couldn't take the cart as far as the iron gate, for the road was blocked shortly before the cemetery by the charred wreckage of a T-34. Other tanks, obliged to detour around it on their way to Neufahrwasser, had left their tracks in the sand to the left of the highway and flattened a part of the cemetery wall. Mr. Fajng-old asked old man Heilandt to take the rear. They carried the coffin, which sagged slightly in the middle, along the tracks of the tank treads, traversed with some difficulty the stone pile into which the cemetery wall had been transformed, and finally, with their last strength, took a few steps among the tumble-down tombstones. Old man Heilandt tugged avidly at his cigarette and blew out smoke over the coffin. I carried the cage with the lovebird. Maria dragged two shovels behind her. Little Kurt carried or rather brandished a pickax, attacking the grey granite tombstones at the risk of his life, until Maria took it away from him and helped the men to dig.

How fortunate that the soil here is sandy and not frozen, I said to myself, while looking for Jan Bronski's place behind the northern wall. It must be here, I thought, or maybe there. I couldn't be sure, for the changing seasons had turned the telltale fresh whitewash a crumbling grey like all the walls in Saspe.

I came back through the hind gate, looked up at the stunted pines: So now they're burying Matzerath, I thought, for fear of thinking something irrelevant. And I found at least partial meaning in the circumstance that the two skat brothers, Bronski and

Matzerath, should lie here in the same sandy ground, even if my poor mama was not here to keep them company.

Funerals always make you think of other funerals.

The sandy soil put up a fight, it probably wanted more experienced gravediggers. Maria paused, leaned panting on her pick, and began to cry again when she saw Kurt throwing stones at the lovebird in its cage. Kurt missed, his stones overshot the mark; Maria wept loudly and in all sincerity, because she had lost Matzerath, because she had seen something in Matzerath which in my opinion wasn't there, but which, as far as she was concerned, was to remain henceforth real and lovable. Mr. Fajngold said a few comforting words, which gave him a chance to rest, for the digging was too much for him. Old man Heilandt wielded his shovel with the regularity of a seeker after gold, tossed the earth behind him, and blew out puffs of smoke, also at measured intervals. The two Russian puppies sat on the cemetery wall a few steps away from us, chatting into the wind. Overhead, airplanes and a sun growing steadily riper.

They may have dug about three feet. Oskar stood idle and perplexed amid the old granite, amid the stunted pines, between Matzerath's widow and a Kurt throwing stones at a lovebird.

Should I or shouldn't I? You are going on twenty-one, Oskar. Should you or shouldn't you? You are an orphan. Actually you should, it's high time. When your poor mama died, you were left half an orphan. That was when you should have made up your mind. Then they laid Jan, your presumptive father, under the crust of the earth. That made you a presumptive full orphan. You stood here on this sand named Saspe, holding a slightly oxidized cartridge case. It was raining and a Ju-52 was getting ready to land. Wasn't this 'Should I or shouldn't I?' audible even then, if not in the sound of the rain, then in the roaring of the landing transport plane? You said to yourself: it's the rain, it's the sound of airplanes engines; uninspired interpretations of this sort can be read into any text you please. You wanted everything to be perfectly plain and not just presumptive.

Should I or shouldn't I? Now they are digging a hole for Matzerath, your second presumptive father. As far as you know, you have no more presumptive fathers. Why, then, do you keep juggling with two bottle-green bottles: should I or shouldn't I?

Who else is there to question? These stunted pines, themselves so questionable?

I found a slender cast-iron cross with crumbling ornaments and encrusted letters adding up to Mathilde Kunkel – or Runkel. In the sand – should I or shouldn't I? – between thistles and wild oats – should I? – I found – or shouldn't I? – three or four rusty metal wreaths the size of dinner plates – should I? – which once upon a time – or shouldn't I? – were no doubt supposed to look like oak leaves or laurel – or should I after all? – weighed them in my hand, took aim – should I? – the top end of the ironwork cross – or shouldn't I? – had a diameter of – should I? – maybe an inch and a half – or shouldn't I? – I ordered myself to stand six feet away – should I? – tossed – or shouldn't I? – and missed – should I try again? – the cross was too much on a slant – should I? – Mathilde Kunkel or was it Runkel – should I Runkel, should I Kunkel? – that was the sixth throw and I had allowed myself seven, six times I shouldn't and now seven – *should*, the wreath was on the cross – *should* – wreathed Mathilde – *should* – laurel for Miss Kunkel – should I? I asked young Mrs. Runkel – yes, said Mathilde; she had died young, at twenty-seven, and born in '68. As for me, I was going on twenty-one when I made it on the seventh throw, when my problem – should I or shouldn't I? – was simplified, transformed into a demonstrated, wreathed, aimed, and triumphant 'I should'.

As Oskar, with his new 'I should' on his tongue and in his heart, made his way back to the gravediggers, the lovebird let out a squeak and shed several yellow-blue feathers, for one of Kurt's stones had struck home. I wondered what question may have impelled my son to keep throwing stones at a lovebird until at last a hit gave him his answer.

They had moved the crate to the edge of the pit, which was about four feet deep. Old man Heilandt was in a hurry, but had to wait while Maria completed her Catholic prayers, while Mr. Fajngold stood there with his silk hat over his chest and his eyes in Galicia. Kurt, too, came closer. After his bull's-eye he had probably arrived at a decision; he approached the grave for reasons of his own but just as resolutely as Oskar.

The uncertainty was killing me. After all, it was my son who had decided for or against something. Had he decided at last to recognize and love me as his only true father? Had he, now that it was too late, decided to take up the drum? Or was his decision: death to my presumptive father Oskar, who killed my presumptive father Matzerath with a Party pin for no other reason than because he was sick of fathers? Perhaps he, too, could express only by homicide the childlike affection that would seem to be desirable between fathers and sons.

While old man Heilandt flung rather than lowered the crate containing Matzerath, the Party pin in Matzerath's windpipe and the magazineful of Russian tommy-gun ammunition in Matzerath's belly, into the grave, Oskar owned to himself that he had killed Matzerath deliberately, because in all likelihood Matzerath was not just his presumptive father, but his real father; and also because he was sick of dragging a father around with him all his life.

And so it was not true that the pin had been open when I picked up the badge from the concrete floor. The pin had been opened within my closed hand. It was a jagged, pointed lozenge that I had passed on to Matzerath, intending that they find the insignia on him, that he put the Party in his mouth and choke on it – on the Party, on me, his son; for this situation couldn't go on forever.

Old man Heilandt began to shovel. Little Kurt helped him clumsily but with alacrity. I had never loved Matzerath. Occasionally I liked him. He took care of me, but more as a cook than as a father. He was a good cook. If today I sometimes miss Matzerath, it is his Königsberg dumplings, his pork kidneys in vinegar sauce, his carp with horseradish and cream, his green eel soup, his Kassler Rippchen with sauerkraut, and all his unforgettable Sunday roasts, which I can still feel on my tongue and between my teeth. They forgot to put a cooking spoon in the coffin of this man who transformed feelings into soups. They also forgot to put a deck of skat cards in his coffin. He was a better cook than skat player. Still, he played better than Jan Bronski and almost as well as my poor mama. Such was his endowment, such was his tragedy. I have never been able to forgive him for taking Maria away from me, although he treated her well, never beat her, and usually gave in when she picked a fight. He hadn't turned me over to the Ministry of Public Health, and had signed the letter only after the mails had stopped running. When I came into the world under the light bulbs, he chose the shop as my career. To avoid standing behind a counter, Oskar had spent more than seventeen years standing behind a hundred or so toy drums, lacquered red and white. Now Matzerath lay flat and could stand no more. Smoking Matzerath's Derby cigarettes, old man Heilandt shoveled him in. Oskar should have taken over the shop. Meanwhile Mr. Fajngold had taken over the shop with his large, invisible family. But I inherited the rest: Maria, Kurt, and the responsibility for them both.

Maria was still crying authentically and praying Catholically. Mr. Fajngold was sojourning in Galicia or solving some knotty reckoning. Kurt was weakening but still shoveling. The Russian puppies sat chatting on the cemetery wall. With morose regularity old man Heilandt shoveled the sand of Saspe over the margarine-crate coffin. Oskar could still read three letters of the word Vitello. At this point he unslung the drum from his neck, no longer saying 'Should I or shouldn't I?' but instead: 'It must be,' and threw the drum where the sand was deep enough to muffle the sound. I tossed in the sticks too. They stuck in the sand. That was my drum from the Duster days, the last of those Bebra had given me. What would the Master have thought of my decision? Jesus had beaten that drum, as had a Russian with large, open pores and built like a bank safe. There wasn't much life left in it. But when a shovelful of sand struck its surface, it sounded. At the second shovelful, it still had something to say. At the third it was silent, only showing a little white lacquer until that too was covered over. The sand piled up on my drum, the sand mounted and grew – and I too began to grow; the first symptom being a violent nosebleed

Kurt was the first to notice the blood. 'He's bleeding, he's bleeding,' he shouted, calling Mr. Fajngold back from Galicia, calling Maria from her prayers, and even making the two young Russians, who had been sitting on the wall the whole while, chatting in the direction of Brösen, look up in momentary fright.

Old man Heilandt left his shovel in the sand, took the pickax, and rested my neck against the blue-black iron. The cool metal produced the desired effect. The bleeding began to subside. Old man Heilandt returned to his shoveling. There was still a little sand left beside the grave when the bleeding stopped entirely, but the growth continued, as I could tell by the rumbling and cracking and grinding inside me.

When old man Heilandt had finished shoveling, he took a dilapidated wooden cross with no inscription on it from a nearby tomb and thrust it into the fresh mound, approximately between Matzerath's head and my buried drum. 'That does it!' said the old man and picked up Oskar, who was unable to walk, in his arms. Carrying me, he led the others, including the Russian puppies with the tommy guns, out of the cemetery, across the crushed wall, along the tank tracks to the handcart on the highway. I looked back over my shoulder toward the cemetery. Maria was carrying the cage with the lovebird, Mr. Fajngold was carrying the tools, Kurt was carrying nothing, the two Russians with the caps that were too small were carrying the tommy guns that were too big for them, and the scrub pines were bent beneath so much carrying.

From the sand to the asphalt highway, still blocked by the burned-out tank. On the tank sat Leo Schugger. High overhead planes coming from Hela, headed for Hela. Leo Schugger was careful not to blacken his gloves on the charred T-34. Surrounded by puffy little clouds, the sun descended on Tower Mountain near Zoppot. Leo Schugger slid off the tank and stood very straight.

The sight of Leo Schugger handed old man Heilandt a laugh. 'D'you ever see the like of it? The world comes to an end, but they can't get Leo Schugger down.' In high good humor, he gave the black tailcoat a slap on the back and explained to Mr. Fajngold: 'This is our Leo Schugger. He wants to give us sympathy and shake hands with us.'

He spoke the truth. Leo Schugger made his gloves flutter and, slavering as usual, expressed his sympathies to all present. 'Did you see the Lord?' he asked. 'Did you see the Lord?' No one had seen Him. Maria, I don't know why, gave Leo the cage with the lovebird.

When it was the turn of Oskar, whom old man Heilandt had stowed on the handcart, Leo Schugger's face seemed to decompose itself, the winds inflated his garments, and a dance seized hold of his legs. 'The Lord, the Lord!' he cried, shaking the lovebird in its cage. 'See the Lord! He's growing, he's growing!'

Then he was tossed into the air with the cage, and he ran, flew, danced, staggered, and fled with the screeching bird, himself a bird. Taking flight at last, he fluttered across the fields in the direction of the sewage land and was heard shouting through the voices of the tommy guns: 'He's growing, he's growing!' He was still screaming when the two young Russians reloaded. 'He's growing!' And even when the tommy guns rang out again, even after Oskar had fallen down a stepless staircase into an expanding, all-engulfing faint, I could hear the bird, the voice, the raven, I could hear Leo proclaiming to all the world: 'He's growing, he's growing, he's growing . . .'

Disinfectant

Last night I was beset by hasty dreams. They were like friends on visiting days. One dream after another; one by one they came and went after telling me what dreams find worth telling; preposterous stories full of repetitions, monologues which could not be ignored, because they were declaimed in a voice that demanded attention and with the gestures of incompetent actors. When I tried to tell Bruno the stories at breakfast, I couldn't get rid of them, because I had forgotten everything; Oskar has no talent for dreaming.

While Bruno cleared away the breakfast, I asked him as though in passing: 'My dear Bruno, how tall am I exactly?'

Bruno set the little dish of jam on my coffee cup and said in tones of concern: 'Why, Mr. Matzerath, you haven't touched your jam.'

How well I know those words of reproach. I hear them every day after breakfast. Every morning Bruno brings me this dab of strawberry jam just to make me build a newspaper roof over it. I can't even bear to look at jam, much less eat it. Accordingly I dismissed Bruno's reproach with quiet firmness: 'You know how I feel about jam, Bruno. Just tell me how tall I am.'

Bruno's eyes took on the expression of an extinct octopod. He always casts this prehistoric gaze up at the ceiling whenever he has to think, and if he has anything to say, it is also the ceiling he addresses. This morning, then, he said to the ceiling: 'But it's strawberry jam.' Only when after a considerable pause – for by my silence I sustained my question about Oskar's size – Bruno's gaze came down from the ceiling and twined itself round the bars of my bed, was I privileged to hear that I measured four feet one.

'Wouldn't you kindly measure me again, Bruno, just to be sure?'

Without batting an eyelash, Bruno drew a folding rule from his back pants pocket, threw back my covers with a gesture that was almost brutal, pulled down my nightgown, which had bunched up, unfolded the ferociously yellow ruler which had broken off at five feet eleven, placed it alongside me, shifted its position, checked. His hands worked efficiently, but his eyes were still dwelling in the age of dinosaurs. At length the ruler came to rest and he declared, as though reading off his findings: 'Still four feet one.'

Why did he have to make so much noise folding up his ruler and removing my breakfast tray? Were my measurements not to his liking?

After leaving the room with the breakfast tray, with the eggyellow ruler beside the revoltingly natural-colored strawberry jam, Bruno cast a last glance back through the peephole in the door – a glance that made me feel as old as the hills. Then at length he left me alone with my four feet and my one inch.

So Oskar is really so tall! Almost too big for a dwarf, a gnome, a midget? What was the altitude of la Raguna's, my Roswitha's, summit? At what height did Master Bebra, who was descended from Prince Eugene, succeed in keeping himself? Today I could look down even on Kitty and Felix. Whereas all those I have just mentioned once looked down with friendly envy upon Oskar, who, until the twenty-first year of his life, had measured a spare three feet.

It was only when that stone hit me at Matzerath's funeral in Saspe Cemetery that I began to grow.

Stone, Oskar has said. I had better fill in my record of the events at the cemetery.

After I had found out, thanks to my little game of quoits, that for me there could be no more 'Should I or shouldn't I?' but only an 'I should, I must, I will!' I unslung my drum, cast it complete with drumsticks into Matzerath's grave, and made up my mind to grow. At once I felt a buzzing, louder and louder, in my ears. Just then I was struck in the back of the head by a stone about the size of a walnut, which my son Kurt had thrown with all his four-year-old might. Though the blow came as no surprise to me – I had suspected that my son was cooking up something against me – I nevertheless made a dash for my drum in Matzerath's grave. Old man Heilandt pulled me out of the hole with his dry, old man's grip, but left drum and drumsticks where they were. Then when my nose began to bleed, he laid me down with my neck against the iron of the pickax. The nosebleed, as we know, soon subsided, but I continued to grow, though so slowly that only Leo Schugger noticed, whereupon he proclaimed my growth to the world with loud cries and birdlike fluttering.

So much for my addendum, which is actually superfluous; for I had started to grow even before I was hit by the stone and flung myself into Matzerath's grave. But from the very first Maria and Mr. Fajngold saw but one reason for my growth, or sickness as they called it, namely, the stone that had hit me in the head, my leap into the grave. Even before we had left the cemetery, Maria gave Kurt a sound spanking. I was sorry for Kurt. For after all he may have thrown that stone at me to help me, to accelerate my growth. Perhaps he wanted at last to have a real grown-up father, or maybe just a substitute for Matzerath; for to tell the truth, he has never acknowledged or honored the father in me.

In the course of my growth, which went on for nearly a year, there were plenty of doctors of both sexes who confirmed the theory that the stone and my headlong leap into the grave were responsible, who said and wrote in my case history: Oskar Matzerath is a deformed Oskar because a stone hit him in the back of the head, etc. etc.

Here it seems relevant to recall my third birthday. What had the grownups said about the beginning of my biography proper? This is what they had said: At the age of three, Oskar Matzerath fell from the cellar stairs to the concrete floor. This fall put an end to his growth, etc. etc.

In these explanations we find man's understandable desire to find physical justification for all alleged miracles. Oskar must admit that he too examines all alleged miracles with the utmost care before discarding them as irresponsible hokum.

On our return from Saspe Cemetery, we found new tenants in Mother Truczinski's flat. They were nice enough people and offered to take us in until we had found something else, but Mr. Fajngold refused to countenance such overcrowding and said we could have the bedroom of the ground-floor flat, he could manage for the present with the living room. To this arrangement Maria objected, feeling that it would not be right in her recently widowed state to live at such close quarters with a gentleman alone. At the time Fajngold was unaware of being a gentleman alone, but Luba's energetic presence made it easier in a way for him to appreciate Maria's arguments. For Luba's sake as well, they would make a different arrangement, he would turn the cellar over to us. He even helped us to rearrange the storeroom, but he would not let me move into the cellar, for I was sick, a poor sick child, and so a bed was set up for me in the living room, beside my poor mama's piano.

It was hard to find a doctor. Most of the doctors had left with the troops, because in January the medical insurance fund had been evacuated westward and patients had become exceedingly rare. After a long search, Mr. Fajngold managed to scare up a lady doctor from Elbing, who was amputating at the Helene Lange School, where wounded from the Wehrmacht and the Red Army lay side by side. She promised to look in, and four days later she actually did. She sat down by my sickbed, smoked three or four cigarettes in a row while examining me, and on the last cigarette fell asleep.

Mr. Fajngold was afraid to wake her up. Maria gave her a timid poke. But the lady doctor didn't wake up until her cigarette burned down and singed her finger. She stood up and stamped out the butt on the carpet. She spoke tersely in a tone of nervous irritation: 'You'll have to excuse me. Haven't closed an eye in three weeks. I was in Käsemark with a trainload of children from East Prussia. Couldn't get the kids on the ferry. Only took troops. Four thousand kids. All blown to pieces.' There was the same terseness in the way she stroked my cheek. Thrusting a fresh cigarette into her face, she rolled up her left sleeve and took an ampoule out of her briefcase. While giving herself a shot in the arm, she said to Maria: 'I can't tell you what's the matter with the boy. Ought to be in a hospital, but not here. You've got to get away. To the West. The joints of his wrists, knees, and shoulders are swollen. It's bound to attack his brain in the end. Make him cold compresses. I'm leaving you a few pills in case the pain prevents him from sleeping.'

I liked this terse lady doctor, who didn't know what was wrong with me and admitted as much. In the few weeks that followed, Maria and Mr. Fajngold made me several hundred cold compresses which soothed me, but didn't prevent my knee, wrist, and shoulder joints, and my head as well, from swelling and aching. What horrified Maria and Mr. Fajngold the most was my swelling head. She gave me the pills, but they were soon gone. He began to plot fever curves, took to experimenting with pencil and ruler, constructed bold fantastic shapes round my temperature, which he took five times a day with a thermometer obtained on the black market in exchange for synthetic honey. My fever chart looked like a mountain range with terrifying chasms – I thought of the Alps, the snowy peaks of the Andes. In reality, there was nothing so fantastic about my temperature: in the morning I usually had a hundred and five-tenths; by evening it had risen to something over a hundred and two and the most I ever had during my period of growth was a hundred and two point seven. I saw and heard all sorts of things in my fever; I was riding a merry-go-round, I wanted to get off but I couldn't. I was one of many little children sitting in fire engines and hollowed-out swans, on dogs, cats, pigs, and stags, riding round and round. I wanted to get off but I wasn't allowed to. All the little children were crying, like me they wanted to get out of the fire engines and hollowed-out swans, down from the backs of the cats, dogs, pigs, and stags, they didn't want to ride on the merry-go-round any more, but they weren't allowed to get off. The Heavenly Father was standing beside the merry-go-round and every time it stopped, he paid for another turn. And we prayed: 'Oh, our Father who art in heaven, we know you have lots of loose change, we know you like to treat us to rides on the merry-go-round, we know you like to prove to us that this world is round. Please put your pocket-book away, say stop, finished, *fertig, basta, stoi*, closing time – we poor little children are dizzy, they've brought us, four thousand of us, to

Käsemark on the Vistula, but we can't get across, because your merry-go-round, your merry-go-round . . .'

But God our Father, the merry-go-round owner, smiled in his most benevolent manner and another coin came sailing out of his purse to make the merry-go-round keep on turning, carrying four thousand children with Oskar in their midst, in fire engines and hollowed-out swans, on cats, dogs, pigs, and stags, round and round in a ring, and every time my stag – I'm still quite sure it was a stag – carried us past our Father in heaven, the merry-go-round owner, he had a different face: He was Rasputin, laughing and biting the coin for the next ride with his faith healer's teeth; and then he was Goethe, the poet prince, holding a beautifully embroidered purse, and the coins he took out of it were all stamped with his father-in-heaven profile; and then again Rasputin, tipsy, and again Herr von Goethe, sober. A bit of madness with Rasputin and a bit of rationality with Goethe. The extremists with Rasputin, the forces of order with Goethe. The tumultuous masses round Rasputin, calendar mottoes with Goethe . . . until at length the merry-go-round slowed down – not because my fever subsided, but because a soothing presence bent down over my fever, because Mr. Fajngold bent over me and stopped the merry-go-round. He stopped the fire engines, the swan, and the stag, devaluated Rasputin's coins, sent Goethe back to the Mothers, sent four thousand dizzy little children floating off to Käsemerk, across the Vistula, to the kingdom of heaven – and picked Oskar up from his sickbed, and lifted him up on a cloud of Lysol, that is to say, he disinfected me.

It started on account of the lice and then became a habit. He first discovered the lice on little Kurt, then on me, Maria, and himself. The lice had probably been left behind by the Kalmuck who had taken Matzerath from Maria. How Mr. Fajngold yelled when he discovered them. He summoned his wife and children; the whole lot of them, he suspected, were infested with vermin. Then, having bartered rolled oats and synthetic honey for different kinds of disinfectant, he took to disinfecting himself, his whole family, Maria, and myself every single day. He rubbed us, sprayed us, and powdered us. And while he sprayed, powdered, and rubbed, my fever blazed, his tongue wagged, and I learned about the whole carloads of carbolic acid, lime, and Lysol that he had sprayed, strewn, and sprinkled when he was disinfector in Treblinka Concentration Camp. Every day at 2 p.m., in his official capacity as Disinfector Mariusz Fajngold, he had sprinkled Lysol on the camp streets, over the barracks, the shower rooms, the cremating furnaces, the bundles of clothing, over those who were waiting to shower, over those who lay recumbent after their showers, over all that came out of the ovens and all who were about to go in. He listed the names, for he knew them all. He told me about Bilauer, who one hot day in August had advised the disinfector to sprinkle the camp streets with kerosene instead of Lysol. Mr. Fajngold had taken his advice. And Bilauer had the match. Old Zev Kurland of the ZOB had administered the oath to the lot of them. And Engineer Galewski had broken into the weapons room. Bilauer had shot Hauptsturmführer Kutner. Sztulbach and Warynski got Zisenis by the throat; the others tackled the guards from Trawniki Camp. Some were electrocuted cutting the high-tension fence. SS Sergeant Schöpke, who had always made little jokes while taking his protégés to the showers, stood by the camp gate shooting. But it didn't help him, they were all on top of him at once: Adek Kave, Motel Levit, and Henoch Lerer; Hersz Rotblat and Letek Zegel were there too, and Tosias Baran with his Deborah. And Lolek Begelmann shouted: 'What about Fajngold? Got to get him out of here before the planes come.' Mr. Fajngold was waiting for Luba, his wife. But even then she had stopped coming when he called her. So they seized him left and right, Jakub Gelernter on the left side, Mordechaj Szwarcbard on the right. And in front of him ran little Dr. Atlas, who, in the camp at Treblinka and later in the woods round Vilna, had recommended a thorough sprinkling with Lysol and maintained that Lysol is more important than life. This Mr. Fajngold could corroborate, for he had sprinkled the dead, not one corpse but many, why bother with figures; he had sprinkled dead men and dead women with Lysol and that was that. And he knew names, so many that it became tedious, that to me who was also swimming in Lysol the question of the life and death of a hundred thousand names became less important than the question of whether life and, if not life, then death, had been disinfected adequately and on time with Mr. Fajngold's disinfectants.

Gradually my fever left me and it was April. Then the fever went up again, the merry-go-round spun, and Mr. Fajngold sprinkled Lysol on the living and the dead. Then the fever was down again and April was at an end. Early in May, my neck grew shorter and my chest grew broader and higher, so that I could rub Oskar's collarbone with my chin without lowering my head. Again there was fever and Lysol. And I heard Maria whispering words that floated in Lysol: 'If only he don't grow crooked! If only he don't get a hump! If only he don't get water on the brain!'

Mr. Fajngold comforted Maria, telling her about people he had known who in spite of humps and dropsy had made a success of life. There was a certain Roman Frydrych, for instance, who had gone to the Argentine with his hump and started a sewing-machine business which got to be big-time and very well known.

The story of Frydrych the successful hunchback failed to comfort Maria but filled the narrator, Mr. Fajngold, with such enthusiasm that he resolved to give our grocery store a new face. In the middle of May, shortly after the war ended, new merchandise made its appearance. He began to sell sewing machines and spare parts for sewing machines, but to facilitate the transition, he still carried groceries for a while. What blissful times. Hardly anything was paid for in cash. Everything was done by barter. Synthetic honey, oat flakes, sugar, flour, margarine, and the last little bags of Dr. Oetker's Baking Powder were transformed into bicycles; the bicycles and bicycle spare parts into electric motors, and these into tools; the tools became furs, and as though by magic Mr. Fajngold turned the furs into sewing machines. Little Kurt made himself useful at this game of swap and swap again; he brought in customers, negotiated deals, and caught on much more quickly than Maria to the new line. It was almost as in Matzerath's days. Maria stood behind the counter, waiting on those of the old customers who were still in town, and trying hard, with her painful Polish, to find out what the new customers wanted. Kurt was a born linguist. Kurt was all over the place. Mr. Fajngold could rely on him. Though not quite five, he became an expert on sewing machines. Amid the hundred-odd middling to miserable models displayed on the black market in Bahnhofstrasse he detected the first-class Singers and Pfaffs at a glance, and Mr. Fajngold valued his knowledge.

At the end of May my grandmother Anna Koljaiczek came to see us and flung herself panting on the sofa. She had walked all the way from Bissau by way of Brenntau. Mr. Fajngold was full of praise for little Kurt and had plenty of good things to say about Maria as well. He told my grandmother the story of my illness at great length, coming back over and over again to the utility of his disinfectant. For Oskar, too, he had words of praise: I had been so quiet and well behaved and during the whole of my illness hadn't cried once.

My grandmother wanted kerosene because there was no light in Bissau. Mr. Fajngold told her about his experience with kerosene in the camp at Treblinka and about his multifarious duties as camp disinfector. He told Maria to fill two quart bottles with kerosene, added a package of synthetic honey and a whole assortment of disinfectants, and listened, nodding absently, as my grandmother listed all the many things that had burned down in Bissau and Bissau Quarry during the fighting. She also described the damage in Viereck, which had been renamed Firoga as in times gone by. And Bissau had again been given its pre-war name of Bysew. As for Ehlers, who had been local peasant leader in Ramkau and very competent, who had married her brother's son's wife, Hedwig, widow of Jan who had lost his life at the post office, the farm laborers had hanged him outside his office. They had came very close to hanging Hedwig for marrying Ehlers when she was the widow of a Polish hero, and also because Stephan had been a lieutenant and Marga had belonged to the League of German Girls.

'Well,' said my grandmother, 'they couldn't hurt Stephan no more, because he was killed up there in the Arctic. They wanted to take Marga away and put her in a camp. But then Vincent opened his mouth and spoke like he never spoke in all his life. And now Hedwig and Marga are both with us, helping in the fields. But Vincent was knocked out from talking so much and I think maybe he won't last long. As for old Grandma, I've had my share of trouble too; pains all over, in the heart and in the head where some numbskull hit me 'cause he thought it was the right thing to do.'

Such were the lamentations of Anna Koljaiczek; holding her head and stroking mine as it grew, she thought things over and came up with the following wisdom: 'Yes, Oskar, that's how it is with the Kashubes. They always get hit on the head. You'll be going away where things are better, only Grandma will be left. The Kashubes are no good at moving. Their business is to stay where they are and hold out their heads for everybody else to hit, because we're not real Poles and we're not real Germans, and if you're a Kashube, you're not good enough for the Germans or the Polacks. They want everything full measure.'

My grandmother gave a loud laugh, hid the bottle of kerosene, the synthetic honey, and the disinfectant under her four skirts, which despite the most violent military, political, and historical upheavals had never lost their potato color.

She was about to go, but Mr. Fajngold asked her to wait a few moments, he wanted her to meet his wife Luba and the rest of his family. When Luba failed to appear, my grandmother said: 'Never mind. I'm always calling people, too: Agnes, I say, Agnes, my daughter, come and help your old mother wring out the wash. And she don't come no more than your Luba. And Vincent, my brother, in the black of night he stands outside the door though he's a sick man and shouldn't and wakes up the neighbors hollering for his son Jan that was in the post office and got killed.'

She was already in the doorway, putting on her kerchief, when I called from my bed: 'Babka, Babka,' which means Grandma, Grandma. She turned around and lifted her skirt a little as though to let me in and take me with her. But then she probably remembered that the haven and refuge was already occupied by kerosene bottles, honey, and disinfectant, and went off without me, without Oskar.

At the beginning of June the first convoys left for the West. Maria said nothing, but I could see that she was taking leave of the furniture, the shop, the house, the tombs on both sides of Hindenburg-Allee, and the mound in Saspe Cemetery.

Sometimes in the evening, before going down in the cellar with Kurt, she would sit beside my bed, at my poor mama's piano, playing the harmonica with her left hand and trying to accompany her little tune on the piano with one finger of her right hand.

The music made Mr. Fajngold unhappy; he asked Maria to stop, and then, when she had taken the harmonica out of her mouth and was going to close the piano, he would ask her to play a little more.

Then he proposed to her. Oskar had seen it coming. Mr. Fajngold called his Luba less and less often, and one summer evening full of humming and buzzing, when he was sure she was gone, he proposed to Maria. He promised to take care of her and both children, Oskar, the sick one, too. He offered her the flat and a partnership in the business.

Maria was twenty-two. The beauty of her younger days, which seemed to have been pieced together by chance, had taken on firmer, perhaps harder contours. The last few months before and after the end of the war had uncurled the permanents Matzerath had paid for. She no longer wore pigtails as in my day; now her hair hung long over her shoulders, giving her the look of a rather solemn, perhaps somewhat soured young girl – and this young girl said no, rejected Mr. Fajngold's proposal. Maria stood on the carpet that had once been ours with Kurt to one side of her and pointed her thumb at the tile stove. Mr. Fajngold and Oskar heard her say: 'It can't be done. Here the whole place is washed up and finished. We're going to the Rhineland where my sister Guste is. She's married to a headwaiter. His name is Köster and he'll take us in temporarily, all three of us.'

Next day she filled out the application and three days later we had our papers. After that Mr. Fajngold was silent. He closed the shop. While Maria was packing, he sat in the dark shop on the counter, beside the scale; he hadn't even the heart to spoon out honey. But when Maria came to say goodbye, he slid off the counter, got out the bicycle and trailer, and said he would take us to the station.

Oskar and the baggage – we were allowed fifty pounds each – were loaded on the two-wheeled rubber-tired trailer. Mr. Fajngold pushed the bicycle. Maria held Kurt by the hand and took a last look back as we turned left into Elsenstrasse. I couldn't look back at Labesweg because it hurt me to twist my neck. Oskar's head remained motionless on his shoulders, and it was only with my eyes, which had preserved their mobility, that I took leave of Marienstrasse, Striessbach, Kleinhammer-Park, the underpass, which still oozed as disgustingly as ever, Bahnhofstrasse, my undestroyed Church of the Sacred Heart, and the Langfuhr station – Langfuhr was now called Wrzeszcz, but who can pronounce that?

We had to wait. When a train finally rolled in, it was a freight. There were hordes of people and far too many children. The baggage was inspected and weighed. Soldiers threw a bale of straw into each car. There was no music, but at least it wasn't raining. The weather was partly cloudy with an easterly wind.

We found a place in the fourth car from the end. Mr. Fajngold stood below us on the tracks, his thin, reddish hair blowing in the wind. When the locomotive revealed its arrival with a jolt, he stepped closer, handed Maria three packages of margarine and two of synthetic honey, and when orders in Polish, screaming and wailing, announced that the train was pulling out, he added a package of disinfectant to our provisions – Lysol is more important than life. Then we began to move, leaving Mr. Fajngold behind. He stood there with his reddish hair blowing in the wind, becoming smaller and smaller, as is fitting and proper when trains leave, until nothing was left of him but a waving arm, and soon he had ceased to exist altogether.

Growth in a Freight Car

Those aches and pains are still with me. They have thrown me back on my pillows. I have taken to grinding my teeth to keep from hearing the grinding in my bones and joints. I look at my ten fingers and have to admit that they are swollen. A last attempt to beat my drum has proved to me that Oskar's fingers are not only somewhat swollen but temporarily no good for drumming; they just can't hold the drumsticks.

My fountain pen also refuses my guidance. I shall have to ask Bruno for cold compresses. Then, when my hands, feet, and knees are all wrapped and cool, when Bruno has put a cool cloth on my forehead too, I shall give him paper and pencil; for I don't like lending him my fountain pen. Will Bruno be willing and able to listen properly? Will his record do justice to that journey in a freight car, begun on June 12, 1945? Bruno is sitting at the table under the picture of the anemones. Now he turns his head, showing me the side of it that calls itself face, while with the eyes of a mythical animal he looks past me, one eye to the left, the other to the right of me. He lays the pencil slantwise over his thin, puckered lips. That is his way of impersonating someone who is waiting. But even admitting that he is really waiting for me to speak, waiting for the signal to begin taking down my story, his thoughts are busy with his knotted fantasies. He will knot strings together, whereas Oskar's task will be to disentangle my knotted history with the help of many words. Now Bruno writes:

I, Bruno Münsterberg, of Altena in Sauerland, unmarried and childless, am a male nurse in the private pavilion of the local mental hospital. Mr. Matzerath, who has been here for over a year, is my patient. I have other patients, of whom I cannot speak here. Mr. Matzerath is my most harmless patient. He never gets so wild that I have to call in other nurses. Today, in order to rest his overstrained fingers, he has asked me to write for him and to stop making my knotted figures. However, I have put a supply of string in my pocket and as he tells his story, I shall start on the lower limbs of a figure which, in accordance with Mr. Matzerath's story, I shall call 'Refugee from the East.' This will not be the first figure I have derived from my patient's stories. So far, I have done his grandmother, whom I call 'Potato in Four Skirts,' and his grandfather, the raftsman, whose string image I have called, rather pretentiously perhaps, 'Columbus'; my strings have turned his poor mama into 'The Beautiful Fish Eater,' and his two fathers, Matzerath and Jan Bronski, have become 'The Two Skat Players.' I have also rendered the scarry back of his friend Herbert Truczinski; this piece is entitled 'Rough Going.' In addition, I have drawn inspiration from such sites and edifices as the Polish Post Office, the Stockturm, the Stadt-Theater, Arsenal Passage, the Maritime Museum, the cellar of Greff's vegetable store, Pestalozzi School, the Brösen bathing establishment, the Church of the Sacred Heart, the Four Seasons Café, the Baltic Chocolate Factory, the pillboxes of the Atlantic Wall, the Eiffel Tower, the Stettin Station in Berlin, Reims Cathedral, and neither last nor least the apartment house where Mr. Matzerath first saw the light of this world. The fences and tombstones of the cemeteries of

Saspe and Brenntau suggested ornaments; with knot upon knot, I have made the Vistula and the Seine flow and set the waves of the Baltic and Atlantic dashing against coasts of pure disembodied string. I have shaped pieces of string into Kashubian potato fields and Norman pastures, and peopled the resulting landscape, which I call Europe for short, with such figures as post office defenders, grocers, people on rostrums, people at the foot of the rostrums, schoolboys with cornucopias, expiring museum attendants, juvenile delinquents preparing for Christmas, Polish cavalrymen at sunset, ants that make history, Theater at the Front, standing men, disinfecting recumbent figures in Treblinka Camp. I have just begun 'Refugee from the East,' which will probably develop into a group of refugees from the East.

On June 12, 1945, at approximately 11 A.M., Mr. Matzerath pulled out of Danzig, which at the time was already called Gdansk. He was accompanied by the widow Maria Matzerath, whom my patient refers to as his former mistress, and by Kurt Matzerath, my patient's alleged son. In addition, he tells me, there were thirty-two other persons in the freight car, including four Franciscan nuns, dressed as such, and a young girl with a kerchief on her head, whom Mr. Oskar Matzerath claims to have recognized as one Lucy Rennwand. In response to repeated questions, my patient admits that this young lady's real name was Regina Raeck, but he continues to speak of a nameless triangular fox face and call it by name, namely Lucy. All this to the contrary notwithstanding, the young lady's real name, as I here beg leave to state, was Miss Regina Raeck. She was traveling with her parents, her grandparents, and a sick uncle who for his part was accompanied by, in addition to his family, an acute cancer of the stomach. The sick uncle was a big talker and lost no time in identifying himself as a former Social Democrat.

As far as my patient can remember, the trip was uneventful as far as Gdynia, which for four and a half years had borne the name of Gotenhafen. Two women from Oliva, several children, and an elderly gentleman from Langfuhr cried until the train had passed Zoppot, while the nuns resorted to prayer.

In Gdynia the convoy stopped for five hours. Two women with six children were shown into the car. The Social Democrat, as my patient tells me, protested on the ground that he was sick and was entitled, as a prewar Social Democrat, to special treatment. But when he refused to sit down and hold his tongue, the Polish officer in charge of the convoy slapped him in the face and gave him to understand in very fluent German that he, the Polish officer, didn't know what 'Social Democrat' meant. During the war he had paid forced visits to various parts of Germany, and never had the word Social Democrat been dropped in his hearing. The Social Democrat with the stomach cancer never did get a chance to explain the aims, nature, and history of the Social Democratic Party of Germany to the Polish officer, for the Polish officer left the car, closed the doors, and bolted them from outside.

I have forgotten to write that everyone was sitting or lying on straw. When the train started to move late that afternoon, some of the women screamed: 'We're going back to Danzig.' But they were mistaken. It was just some sort of switching maneuver, and soon they were on their way westward, headed for Stolp. The trip to Stolp, my informant tells me, took four days; the train was constantly stopped in the open fields by former partisans and young Polish gangsters. The youngsters opened the sliding doors, letting in a little fresh air, and each time removed part of the travelers' baggage along with the carbon dioxide. Whenever the young bandits occupied Mr. Matzerath's car, the four nuns rose to their feet and held up their crucifixes. The four crucifixes made a profound impression on the young fellows, who never failed to cross themselves before tossing the travelers' suitcases and knapsacks out on the roadbed.

When the Social Democrat held out a paper in which the Polish authorities in Danzig or Gdansk attested that he had been a dues-paying member of the Social Democratic Party from '31 to '37, the boys did not cross themselves, but knocked the paper out of his fingers and took his two suitcases and his wife's knapsack; the fine winter coat with the large checks, on which the Social Democrat had been lying, was also carried out into the fresh Pomeranian air.

Even so, Mr. Matzerath says the boys had seemed well disciplined and in general made a favorable impression on him. This he attributes to the influence of their leader, who despite his tender years, just sixteen of them, had cut quite a figure and reminded Mr. Matzerath, to his pleasure and sorrow, of Störtebeker, commander of the Dusters.

When this young man who so resembled Störtebeker was pulling the knapsack out of Mrs. Maria Matzerath's hands, Mr. Matzerath reached in at the last moment and removed the family photograph album, which was fortunately lying on top. The young bandit was on the point of getting angry. But when my patient opened the album and showed him a picture of his grandmother Koljaiczek, the boy dropped Maria's knapsack, thinking no doubt of his own grandmother. Raising two fingers to his pointed Polish cap in salute, he said 'Do widzenia, good-by,' in the general direction of the Matzerath family, and taking someone else's suitcase instead of the Matzerath knapsack, left the car with his men.

Apart from a small amount of underwear, this knapsack, which remained in the family's possession thanks to the family photograph album, contained the books, bankbooks, and tax vouchers of the Matzerath grocery enterprise, and a ruby necklace, once the property of Mr. Matzerath's mother, which my patient had hidden in a package of disinfectant; the educational tome, consisting half of excerpts from Rasputin and half of selections from Goethe, also accompanied Mr. Matzerath on his journey westward.

My patient tells me that in the course of the trip he often perused the photo album and occasionally consulted the educational tome and that despite the violent pains in his joints he derived a good many happy though pensive hours from both volumes.

He has also asked me expressly to say that all the shaking and jolting, the switches and intersections, the constant vibration of the front axle on which he was lying, promoted his growth. He ceased to broaden and began to grow lengthwise. His joints, which were swollen but not inflamed, were given an opportunity to relax. Even his ears, nose, and sex organ, I am told, grew perceptibly, aided by the pounding of the rails. As long as the train was in motion, Mr. Matzerath seems to have felt no pain. Only when the train stopped for partisans or juvenile delinquents did he, so he tells me, suffer the shooting, pulling pains which he soothed as best he could with the photograph album.

He tells me that apart from the Polish Störtebeker several other youthful bandits and a middle-aged partisan took an interest in the family photos. The hardened warrior went so far as to sit down, light a cigarette, and leaf thoughtfully through the album, omitting not a single rectangle. He began with the likeness of grandfather Koljaiczek, followed the richly imaged rise of the family, and continued on to the snapshots of Mrs. Maria Matzerath with her one-, two-, three-, four-year-old son Kurt. My patient even saw him smile at some of the family idylls. The partisan took umbrage only at the unmistakable Party insignia on the lapels of the late Mr. Matzerath senior and of Mr. Ehlers, formerly a local peasant leader in Ramkau, who had married the widow of Jan Bronski, the post office defender. My patient tells me that he scratched out the offending insignia with his penknife before the eyes, and to the satisfaction, of his critic.

Mr. Matzerath has just seen fit to inform me that this partisan, unlike so many of them, was an authentic partisan. For – to quote the rest of my patient's lecture – there is no such thing as a parttime partisan. Real partisans are partisans always and as long as they live. They put fallen governments back in power and overthrow governments that have just been put in power with the help of partisans. Mr. Matzerath contended – and his thesis struck me as perfectly plausible – that among all those who go in for politics your incorrigible partisan, who undermines what he has just set up, is closest to the artist because he consistently rejects what he has just created.

My own situation is rather similar. No sooner have I applied the coat of plaster that gives my knot sculptures body than as likely as not I smash them with my fist. In this connection I am reminded of the commission my patient gave me some months ago. He wished me, with plain, ordinary string, to combine Rasputin, the Russian faith healer, and Goethe, the German poet prince, into a single figure which, moreover, should present a striking resemblance to himself. He even knows how many miles of string I have tied into knots, trying to create a valid synthesis of the two extremes. But like the partisan whom Mr. Matzerath so admires, I remain restless and dissatisfied; what I knot with my right hand, I undo with my left, what my left hand creates, my right fist shatters.

But Mr. Matzerath himself is unable to keep his story running in a straight line. Take those four nuns in the freight car. First he refers to them as Franciscans and the next time he calls them Vincentians. But what throws his story out of kilter more than anything else is this young lady with her two names and her one supposedly foxlike face. To be really conscientious, I should have to write two or more separate versions of his journey from East to West. But that kind of thing is not in my line. I prefer to concentrate on the Social Democrat, who managed with one name and, my patient assures me, one story, which he repeated incessantly until shortly before Stolp, to the effect that up to 1937 he had been a kind of partisan, risking his health and sacrificing his free time pasting posters, for he had been one of the few Social Democrats to put up posters even when it was raining.

He told the same story when shortly before Stolp the convoy was stopped for the nth time by a large gang of youthful bandits. Since there was hardly any baggage left, the visitors devoted their attentions to the travelers' clothing. But they took a very reasonable attitude, all they wanted was gentlemen's outer garments. To the Social Democrat, however, their procedure seemed the very opposite of reasonable; he was of the opinion, which he also stated, that a clever tailor could make several excellent suits from the yards and yards of material in which the nuns were draped. The Social Democrat, as he piously proclaimed, was an atheist. The young bandits made no pious proclamations, but their attachment to the only-saving Church could not be held in doubt. Despite the wood fiber that had gone into the material, the atheist's single-breasted suit interested them far more than the nuns' ample woolens. The atheist declined to remove his jacket, vest, and trousers; instead, he told them about his brief but brilliant career as a Social Democratic poster paster, and when he refused either to stop talking or to take off his suit, he received a kick in the stomach with a boot formerly the property of the German Army.

The Social Democrat vomited. His vomiting fit was long and violent and at the end he threw up blood. He vomited without regard for his clothing, and our young delinquents lost all interest in the suit though it could easily have been salvaged with a good dry cleaning. Turning their backs on men's clothing, they removed a light-blue imitation silk blouse from Mrs. Maria Matzerath and a Bavarian-style knitted jacket from the young lady whose name was not Lucy Rennwand but Regina Raeck. Then they closed the car doors, but not entirely, and the train started up, while the Social Democrat began to die.

A mile or two before Stolp the train was switched onto a siding where it remained all night – a clear, starry night but rather cool, my informant tells me, for the month of June.

The Social Democrat, who had set too much store by his single-breasted suit, died that night. He died without dignity, loudly blaspheming God and summoning the working class to struggle. His last words, as in the movies, were 'Long live freedom!' Then he expired in a fit of vomiting that filled the whole car with horror.

Afterwards, my patient says, there was no screaming or wailing. A long silence fell, broken only by the chattering teeth of Mrs. Maria Matzerath, who was cold without her blouse and had put all the clothing she had left on her son Kurt and Mr. Matzerath. Toward morning two nuns with stout hearts and strong stomachs took advantage of the open door and swept out quantities of wet straw, the feces of children and grownups, and the Social Democrat's vomit.

In Stolp the train was inspected by Polish officers. Hot soup and a beverage resembling coffee substitute were distributed. The corpse in Mr. Matzerath's car was confiscated because of the danger of contagion, laid on a plank, and carried away by some medical corps men. At the request of the nuns, a superior officer gave the members of the family time for a short prayer. They were also permitted to remove the dead man's shoes, socks, and suit. During the undressing scene – later the body was covered with cement bags – my patient watched the former Social Democrat's niece. Once again, though the young lady's name was Raeck, he was reminded, to his concurrent loathing and fascination, of Lucy Rennwand, whose image in knotted string I have entitled 'The Sandwich Eater'. The girl in the freight car, it is true, did not reach for a sandwich at the sight of her despoiled uncle, but she did participate in the pillage, appropriating the vest of her uncle's suit, putting it on in place of the knitted jacket that had been taken from her, and studying her not unbecoming new costume in a pocket mirror. And then Mr. Matzerath tells me – he is still seized with panic when he thinks of it – she captured him in this same mirror and coolly, coldly, observed him out of eyes that were slits in a triangle.'

The trip from Stolp to Stettin took two days. There were still plenty of involuntary stops and more visits from juvenile delinquents with tommy guns and paratrooper's knives. But though frequent, the visits became shorter and shorter, because there was very little left to take.

My patient claims that he grew three and a half to four inches between Danzig-Gdansk and Stettin. The stretching was mostly the legs, there was little change in the chest or head. However, though my patient lay on his back throughout the trip, he could not prevent the emergence of a hump, rather high up and slightly displaced to leftward. Mr. Matzerath also admits that the pain increased after Stettin – meanwhile German railroad men had taken over – and that leafing through the family photograph album didn't help much. Though the screams that escaped him were loud and protracted, they caused no damage in the glass of any of the stations (Matzerath: 'my voice had lost its power to demolish glass') but they brought the four nuns scurrying over to his tick of pain, where they began to pray interminably.

A good half of his fellow travelers, including Miss Regina and the other members of the deceased Social Democrat's family, left the convoy at Schwerin. Mr. Matzerath was sorry. He had grown so accustomed to looking at the young girl. The sight of her had indeed become so necessary to him that when she had gone, he was seized with convulsions accompanied by high fever. According to Mrs. Maria Matzerath, he cried out desperately for a certain Lucy, called himself a mythical animal, a unicorn, and seems to have been afraid of falling, but at the same time eager to plunge, from a thirty-foot diving tower.

In Lüneburg Mr. Oskar Matzerath was taken to a hospital. There in his fever he made the acquaintance of several nurses but was soon transferred to the University Clinic in Hanover, where they managed to bring his fever down. For a time Mr. Matzerath saw little of Maria Matzerath and her son Kurt; it was only after she had found work as a cleaning woman in the clinic that she was able to visit him every day. Mrs. Matzerath was not lodged at the clinic; she and her little boy ended up in a refugee camp on the outskirts of the·city and she spent at least three hours traveling back and forth, always in overcrowded trains, usually on the running board. Soon she was thoroughly exhausted, and the doctors, despite grave misgivings, granted permission to move the patient to Düsseldorf, where Mrs. Matzerath had a sister. This sister, whose name was Guste, was married to a headwaiter whom she had met during the war. The headwaiter was receiving free board and lodging in Russia at the time, and that enabled her to give Mrs. Matzerath one of her two and a half rooms. Mr. Matzerath was admitted to the Düsseldorf City Hospital.

The apartment was conveniently located. There were several streetcar lines going directly to the City Hospital.

There Mr. Matzerath lay from August, 1945, to May, 1946. For the last hour or more he has been telling me about several nurses at once. Their names are Sister Monica, Sister Helmtrud, Sister Walburga, Sister Ilse, and Sister Gertrude. He remembers all sorts of the most tedious chitchat and seems to be obsessed by nurses' uniforms and the details of their daily life. Not a word about the hospital food, which, if my memory does not mislead me, was unspeakable in those days, or about the freezing-cold rooms. All he can talk about is nurses, he goes on and on about this most boring of all social groups. It seems that Sister Ilse had told the head nurse, in the strictest confidence, whereupon the head nurse had had the gall to inspect the quarters of the nurses in training shortly after lunch hour; something or other had been stolen and some nurse from Dortmund – Gertrude I think he said – was accused unjustly. Then there were the young doctors who were always chasing after the nurses and they wanted just one thing – the nurses' cigarette stamps. On top of all this he sees fit to tell me about a laboratory assistant – not a nurse, for once – who was accused of giving herself an abortion, perhaps abetted by one of the interns. It is beyond me why my patient wastes his time and brains on such trivialities.

Mr. Matzerath has just asked me to describe him. It will be a pleasure. Now I shall be able to omit several dozen of his sententious and interminable stories about nurses.

My patient is four feet one inch tall. He carries his head, which would be too large even for a person of normal proportions, between his shoulders on an almost nonexistent neck. His eyes are blue, brilliant, alive with intelligence; occasionally they take on a dreamy, ecstatic, wide-eyed look. He has dense, slightly wavy, dark-brown hair. He likes to exhibit his arms, which are powerful in comparison with the rest of the body, and his hands, which, as he himself says, are beautiful. Especially when Mr. Matzerath plays the drum – which the management allows for three or at most four hours a day – his fingers move as though of their own accord and seem to belong to another, better proportioned body. Mr. Matzerath has made a fortune on phonograph records and they are still bringing in money. Interesting people come to see him on visiting days. Even before his trial, before he was brought here to us, his name was familiar to me, for Mr. Oskar Matzerath is a well-known performer. I personally believe him to be innocent and am not sure whether he will stay here with us or be let out and resume his successful career. Now he wants me to measure him, though I did so only two days ago.

Without bothering to read over what Bruno my keeper has written, I, Oskar, take up my pen again.

Bruno has just measured me with his folding rule. He has left the rule lying alongside me, and hurried out of the room, loudly proclaiming the result. He even dropped the knot creation he was secretly working on while I was telling him my story. I presume that he has gone to get Dr. (Miss) Hornstetter.

But before she comes in and confirms Bruno's measurements, Oskar will tell you what it is all about: In the three days during which I told my keeper the story of my growth, I grew a whole inch.

And so, as of today, Oskar measures four feet two. He will now relate how he fared after the war when in relatively good health, despite my deformity, writing with difficulty, but fluent at talking and reading, I was discharged from the Düsseldorf City Hospital in the hope that I might embark – as people discharged from hospitals are always expected to do – on a new and adult life.

BOOK THREE

Firestones and Tombstones

Fat, sleepy, good-natured. There had been no need for Guste Truczinski to change in becoming Guste Köster, especially as her association with Köster had been so very limited: they had been engaged for two weeks when he was shipped out to the Arctic Front; when he came home on furlough, they had married and spent a few nights together, most of them in air-raid shelters. Though there was no news of Köster's whereabouts after the army in Courland surrendered, Guste, when asked about her husband, would reply with assurance, at the same time gesturing toward the kitchen: 'Oh, he's a prisoner in Russia. There's going to be some changes around here when he gets back.'

The changes she had in mind involved Maria and more particularly little Kurt. Discharged from the hospital, I said goodbye to the nurses, promising to come and see them as soon as I had the chance. Then I took the streetcar to Bilk, where the two sisters and my son Kurt were living. The apartment house stopped at the fourth floor; the rest, including the roof, had been destroyed by fire. Entering the third-floor flat, I found Maria and my son busily engaged in black market operations. Kurt, who was six years old, counted on his fingers. Even in the black market Maria remained loyal to her Matzerath. She dealt in synthetic honey. She spooned the stuff from unlabeled pails and weighed out quarter-pounds on the kitchen scales. I had barely time to get my bearings in the cramped flat before she put me to work doing up packages.

Kurt was sitting behind his counter – a soap box. He looked in the direction of his homecoming father, but his chilly grey eyes seemed to be concerned with something of interest that could be seen through me. Before him on his counter lay a sheet of paper on which he was adding up imaginary columns of figures. After just six weeks of schooling in overcrowded, poorly heated classrooms, he had the look of a very busy self-made man.

Guste Köster was drinking coffee, real coffee, as Oskar noticed when she presented me with a cupful. While I busied myself with the honey, she observed my hump with curiosity and a look suggesting commiseration with her sister Maria. It was all she could do to sit still and not caress my hump, for like all women she was convinced that it's good luck to touch, pat, or stroke a hump. To Guste good luck meant the return of Köster, who would change everything. She restrained herself, patted her coffee cup instead, and heaved a sigh, followed by the litany that I was to hear several times a day for several months: 'When Köster gets home there's going to be changes around here before you can say Jakob Schmidt. You can bet your bottom taler on that.'

Guste frowned on black market activities but was not averse to drinking the real coffee obtained for synthetic honey. When customers came, she left the living room and padded away into the kitchen, where she raised an ostentatious clatter in protest.

There was no shortage of customers. At nine o'clock, right after breakfast, the bell began to ring: short, long, short. At 10 P.M. Guste disconnected the bell, often amid protests from Kurt, whose schooling made distressing inroads on his business day.

'Synthetic honey?' said the visitor.

Maria nodded gently and asked: 'A quarter or a half a pound?' But there were other customers who didn't want honey. They would say: 'Flints?' Whereupon Kurt, who had school alternately in the morning and afternoon, would emerge from his columns of figures, grope about under his sweater for a little cloth bag, and project his challenging childlike voice into the living room air: 'Would you like three or four? My advice is to take five. They'll be up to twenty-four before you know it. Last week they were eighteen, and this morning I had to ask twenty. If you'd come two hours ago, right after school, I could have let you have them for twenty-one.'

In a territory six blocks long and four blocks wide, Kurt was the only dealer in flints. He had a 'source'; he never told anybody who or what it was, though he never stopped talking about it. Even before going to sleep at night, he would say, instead of his prayers: 'I've got a source.'

As his father, I claimed that I was entitled to know my son's source. He didn't even trouble to inject a note of mystery into his voice when he said 'I've got a source.' If his tone conveyed anything at all, it was pride and self-assurance. 'Where did you get those flints?' I roared at him. 'You will tell me this minute.'

Maria's standing remark in that period, whenever I tried to get at the source, was: 'Leave the kid alone. In the first place, it's none of your business; in the second place, if anybody's going to ask questions, it's me; in the third place, don't take on like you was his father. A few months ago, you couldn't even say boo.'

When I went on too long about Kurt's source, Maria would smack her hand down on the honey pail and, indignant to the elbow, launch into a diatribe against me and also Guste, who sometimes supported Oskar in his effort to penetrate the source: 'A fine lot you are. Trying to ruin the kid's business. Biting the hand that feeds you. When I think of the ten calories Oskar gets for sick relief that he gobbles up in two days, it makes me good and sick, in fact, it makes me laugh.'

Oskar can't deny it: I had a monstrous appetite in those days: it was thanks to Kurt and his source, which brought in more than the honey, that Oskar was able to regain his strength after the meager hospital fare.

Oskar was reduced to shamefaced silence; taking the ample pocket money with which little Kurt deigned to provide him, he would leave the flat in Bilk and stay away as much as he could, to avoid having his nose rubbed in his shame.

Today there are plenty of well-heeled critics of the economic miracle who proclaim nostalgically – and the less they remember about the situation in those days the more nostalgic they become – 'Ah, those were the days, before the currency reform! Then people were still alive! Their empty stomachs didn't prevent them from waiting in line for theater tickets. And the wonderful parties we used to improvise with two pretzels and a bottle of potato schnaps, so much more fun than the fancy doings today, with all their caviar and champagne.'

This is what you might call the romanticism of lost opportunities. I could lament with the best of them if I chose, for in the days when Kurt's 'source' was gushing, I developed a sudden interest in adult education and imbibed a certain amount of culture almost free of charge. I took courses at night school, became a steady visitor at the British Center, also known as 'Die Brücke', discussed collective guilt with Catholics and Protestants alike, and shared the guilt feelings of all those who said to themselves: 'Let's do our stint now; when things begin to look up we'll have it over with and our consciences will be all right.'

Be that as it may, it is to night school that I owe what education I possess; I am the first to own that it doesn't amount to much, though there is something rather grandiose about the gaps in it. I began to read avidly, no longer satisfied, now that I had grown, with an oversimplified world evenly divided between Goethe and Rasputin or with the information that could be culled from the 1904–1916 issues of Köhler's *Naval Calendar*. I was always reading, though I don't remember what. I read in the toilet. I read while waiting in line for theater tickets, surrounded by young girls with Mozart pigtails, also reading. I read while Kurt sold his flints and while I myself was packaging synthetic honey. And when the current was shut off, I read by the light of tallow candles also obtained from Kurt's 'source'.

I am ashamed to say that what I read in those days did not become a part of me, but went in one eye and out the other. I have retained a few turns of phrase, an aphorism or two, and that is about all. And the theater? A few names of actors: Hoppe, Peter Esser, Flickenschildt and her special way of pronouncing the letter r. I recall some drama students in experimental theaters, who tried to improve on Flickenschildt's r's; I remember Gründgens as Tasso, he wore the regulation black, but had discarded the laurel wreath called for in Goethe's text, alleging that the greenery burned his hair. And Gründgens again, still in black as Hamlet. And la Flickenschildt claiming that Hamlet is fat. Yorick's skull made quite an impression on me because of the impressive remarks it drew from Gründgens. *Draussen vor der Tür* played in unheated theaters to spellbound audiences; to me Beckmann as the man with the broken glasses was Köster, Guste's husband, who would change everything on his return home and stop up my son Kurt's source forever.

Now all that is behind me; today I know that a postwar binge is only a binge and therefore followed by a hangover, and one symptom of this hangover is that the deeds and misdeeds which only yesterday were fresh and alive and real, are reduced to history and explained as such. Today I am able once more to appreciate the instruction Gretchen Scheffler meted out to me amid her travel souvenirs and her knitting: not too much Rasputin, Goethe in moderation, Keyser's *History of the City of Danzig*, the armament of a battleship that has long been lying on the bottom of the sea, the speed (in knots) of all the Japanese torpedo boats that took part in the battle of Tsushima, not to mention Belisarius and Narses, Totila and Teja, as represented in Felix Dahn's *A Struggle for Rome*.

In the spring of '47 I abandoned night school, the British Center, and Pastor Niemöller, and took my leave, from the second balcony, of Gustaf Gründgens, who still figured on the program as Hamlet.

Two years had not passed since at Matzerath's grave I had resolved to grow, and already I had lost interest in grown-up life. I dreamed of my lost three-year-old dimensions. I wanted to be three feet tall again, smaller than my friend Bebra, smaller than the dear departed Roswitha. Oskar missed his drum. I took long walks which often ended up at the City Hospital. In any event I was expected to call once a month on Professor Irdell, who regarded Oskar as an interesting case. At regular intervals Oskar visited the nurses he had known during his illness, and even when they had no time for him, their hurrying white uniforms, betokening recovery or death, gave him a feeling bordering on happiness.

The nurses liked me, they played childish, but not malicious, games with my hump, gave me good things to eat, and told me interminable, pleasantly soporific stories about the complexities of hospital life. I listened, gave advice, and was able even to arbitrate some of their little disputes, for I enjoyed the sympathy of the head nurse. On these days Oskar was the only man among twenty or more young or not so young girls camouflaged beneath nurse's uniforms – and in some strange way he was an object of desire.

As Bruno has already said, Oskar has lovely, expressive hands, fine wavy hair, and those winning, ever so blue, Bronski eyes. Possibly the attractiveness of my hands, eyes, and hair was accentuated by my hump and the shocking proximity of my chin to my narrow, vaulted chest. It was not infrequent, in any case, that as I was sitting in the nurses' room, they would take hold of my hands, play with my fingers, fondle my hair, and say to one another in leaving: 'When you look into his eyes, you forget all the rest.'

Thus I was superior to my hump and I might well have attempted a conquest in the hospital if I had still had my drum, if I had been able to count on my reliable drummer's potency of former years. As it was, I felt unsure of myself and my physical reactions and I would leave the hospital after these affectionate hors d'oeuvres, fearing to reach out for the main course. I would take the air, go for a walk in the garden or around the wire fence which, with its close-meshed regularity, gave me a peace of mind that I expressed by whistling. I would watch the street-cars headed for Wersten and Benrath or stroll along the park promenade beside the bicycle path, smiling in pleasant boredom at the efforts of nature, which was playing spring and, following the program to a T, making buds burst open almost audibly.

Across the way, our Sunday painter who art in heaven, was each day adding a little more green fresh from the tube to the trees of Wersten Cemetery. Cemeteries have always had a lure for me. They are well kept, free from ambiguity, logical, virile, and alive. In cemeteries you can summon up courage and arrive at decisions, in cemeteries life takes on distinct contours – I am not referring to the borders of the graves – and if you will, a meaning.

Along the northern wall of the cemetery ran a street called Bittweg, occupied by no less than six manufacturers of tombstones. There were two large establishments: C. Schnoog and Julius Wöbel. The rest were small artisans: R. Haydenreich, J. Bois, Kühn & Müller, and P. Korneff. Sheds and workshops with large signs hanging from the roofs, some freshly painted, others barely legible, indicating the name of the firm and the nature of its wares: Tombstones – Mortuary Monuments and Borders – Natural and Artificial Stone – Mortuary Art. Korneff's sign, in such disrepair that I had to spell it out, said: P. Korneff, Stone-cutter and Mortuary Sculptor.

Between the workshop and the wire fence enclosing the yard stood neat rows of monuments on simple and double pedestals; they were of different sizes, calculated to adorn anything from a solitary one-man grave to a family vault with room for four. Just behind the fence, reflecting its diamond-shaped pattern in sunny weather, an assortment of tombstones: shell-lime cushions for modest pocketbooks, polished diorite slabs with unpolished palms, standard thirty-inch children's tombstones of slightly cloudy Silesian marble, surrounded by fluting and adorned toward the top with sunken reliefs, most of which represented broken roses. Next came a row of plain, red sandstone slabs taken from the facades of bombed-out banks and department stores. At the center the prize piece was displayed: a monument of bluish-white Tyrolian marble with three pedestals, two side-pieces, and a large richly carved slab featuring what is known in the trade as a corpus. This corpus was beardless; his distinguishing features were: head and knees turned leftward, a crown of thorns, three nails, open hands, and stylized bleeding from the wound in his flank, five drops, I seem to recall.

This was far from being the only mortuary monument in Bittweg showing a corpus turned leftward – sometimes there were as many as ten of them getting ready for the spring season. But Korneff's Jesus Christ had made a particular impression on me, because, well, because he showed a marked resemblance to my Athlete on the Cross, flexing his muscles and expanding his chest over the main altar of the Church of the Sacred Heart. I spent hours by that fence, scraping a stick along the close wire meshes, thinking of everything and nothing and toying perhaps with a wish or two. For a long while Korneff remained in hiding. A stovepipe full of knees and elbows emerged from one of the windows of the shop and jutted over the flat roof. You couldn't get very good coal in those days. Yellow smoke arose in fitful puffs and fell back on the roofing paper. More smoke seeped from the windows, slid down the drainpipe, and lost itself amid tombstones in various stages of completion. Outside the sliding door of the workshop stood a three-wheeled truck under several tarpaulins, as though camouflaged against attack from low-flying planes. Sounds from the shop – wood striking iron, iron chipping stone – bore witness to the stonecutter at work.

In May the canvas was gone from over the three-wheeler, the sliding door stood open. I could see inside the workshop grey on grey, stones on the cutting bench, a polishing machine that looked like a gallows, shelves full of plaster models, and at last Korneff. He walked with a stoop and permanently bent knees, his head thrust rigidly forward. The back of his neck was criss-crossed with grimy, once pink adhesive tape. He stepped out of the shop with a rake and, assuming no doubt that spring had come, began to clean up the grounds. He raked carefully between the tombstones, leaving tracks in the gravel, occasionally stopping to remove dead leaves from one of the monuments. As he was raking between the shell-lime cushions and diorite slabs near the fence, I was suddenly surprised by his voice: 'What's the matter, boy; don't they want you at home no more?'

'I'm very fond of your tombstones,' I said. 'Mustn't say that out loud,' he replied. 'Bad luck. Talk like that and they'll be putting one on top of you.'

Only then did he move his stiff neck, catching me, or rather my hump, in a sidelong glance: 'Say, what they done to you? Don't it get in your way for sleeping?'

I let him have his laugh. Then I explained that a hump was not necessarily a drawback, that it didn't get me down, that, believe it or not, some women and even young girls had a special weakness for humps and were only too glad to adapt themselves to the special proportions and possibilities of a hunchback.

Leaning his chin on his rake handle, Korneff pondered: 'Maybe so. I've heard tell of it.'

He went on to tell me about his days in the basalt quarries when he had had a woman with a wooden leg that could be unbuckled. This, to his way of thinking, was something like my hump, even if my gas meter, as he insisted on calling it, was not removable. The stonecutter's memory was long, broad, and thorough. I waited patiently for him to finish, for his woman to buckle her leg on again. Then I asked if I could visit his shop.

Korneff opened the gate in the fence and pointed his rake in invitation at the open sliding door. Gravel crunched beneath my feet and a moment later I was engulfed in the smell of sulphur, lime, and dampness.

Heavy, pear-shaped wooden mallets with fibrous hollows showing frequent repetition of the same expert blow, rested on roughly hewn slabs of stone. Stippling irons for the embossing mallet, stippling tools with round heads, freshly reforged and still blue from tempering; long, springy etching-chisels and bull chisels for marble, polishing paste drying on four-cornered sawing trestles, and, on wooden rollers, ready to move, an up-ended, polished travertine slab, fatty, yellow, cheesy, porous for a double grave.

'That's a bush hammer, that's a spoon chisel, that's a groove cutter, and that,' Korneff lifted a board a hand's breadth wide and three feet long and examined the edge closely, 'that's a straight edge; I use it to whack the apprentices with if they don't keep moving.'

My question was not one of pure politeness: 'You employ apprentices then?'

Korneff told me his troubles: 'I could keep five boys busy. But you can't get none. All the young pantywaists wants to learn nowadays is how to turn a crooked penny on the black market.' Like me, the stonecutter was opposed to the dark machinations that prevented so many a young hopeful from learning a useful trade. While Korneff was showing me carborundum stones ranging from coarse to fine and their effect on a Solnhof slab, I was playing with a little idea. Pumice stones, chocolate-brown sandstone for rough polishing, tripoli for high polish, and there was my little idea popping up again, but it had taken on a higher, shinier polish. Korneff showed me models of lettering, spoke of raised and sunken inscriptions, and told me about gilding; that it wasn't nearly so expensive as generally supposed, that you could gild a horse and rider with one genuine old taler. This made me think of the equestrian monument of Kaiser Wilhelm on the Heumarkt in Danzig, which the Polish authorities would maybe decide to gild, but neither horse nor rider could make me give up my little idea, which seemed to become shinier and shinier. I continued to toy with it, and went so far as to formulate it while Korneff was explaining the workings of a three-legged stippling machine for sculpture and tapping his knuckles on some plaster models of Christ crucified: 'So you're thinking of taking on an apprentice?' This was my first formulation. My little idea gained ground. What I actually said was: 'I gather you're looking for an apprentice, or am I mistaken?' Korneff rubbed the adhesive tape covering the boils on his neck. 'I mean, would you consider taking me on as an apprentice, other things being equal?' I had put it awkwardly and corrected myself at once: 'Don't underestimate my strength, my dear Mr Korneff. It's just my legs that are underdeveloped. There's plenty of strength in my arms.' Delighted with my resolution and determined to go the whole hog, I bared my left arm and asked Korneff to feel my muscle, which was small but tough. When he made no move to feel it, I picked up an embossing chisel that was lying on some shell lime and made the metal bob up and down on my biceps. I continued my demonstration until Korneff turned on the polishing machine; a carborundum disk raced screeching over the travertine pedestal of a slab for a double grave. After a while Korneff, his eyes glued to the machine, shouted above the noise: 'Sleep on it, boy. It's hard work. Come back and see me when you've thought it over. I'll take you on if you still feel like it.'

Following Korneff's instructions, I slept a whole week on my little idea; I weighed and compared: on the one hand Kurt's firestones, on the other, Korneff's tombstones. Maria was always finding fault: 'You're a drain on our budget, Oskar. Why don't you start something? Tea or cocoa maybe, or powdered milk.' I started nothing; instead, I basked in the approval of Guste, who held up the absent Köster as the example to follow and praised me for my negative attitude toward the black market. What really troubled me was my son Kurt, who sat there writing columns of imaginary figures and overlooking me just as I had managed for years to overlook Matzerath.

We were having our lunch. Guste had disconnected the bell so our customers wouldn't find us eating scrambled eggs with bacon. Maria said: 'You see, Oskar, we have nice things to eat. Why? Because we don't sit with our hands folded.' Kurt heaved a sigh. Flints had dropped to eighteen. Guste ate heartily and in silence. I too. I savored the eggs, but even while savoring, I felt miserable, perhaps because powdered eggs are not really so very appetizing, and suddenly, while biting into some gristle, experienced a yearning for happiness so intense that it made my cheeks tingle. Against all my better judgment, despite my ingrained skepticism, I wanted happiness. I wanted to be boundlessly happy. While the others were still eating, content with scrambled egg-powder, I left the table and went to the cupboard, as though it contained happiness. Rummaging through my compartment, I found, not happiness, but behind the photograph album, two packages of Mr. Fajngold's disinfectant. From one package I took – no, not happiness, but the thoroughly disinfected ruby necklace which had belonged to my mother, which Jan Bronski years ago, on a winter's night that smelled of more snow to come, had removed from a shopwindow with a circular hole cut out a short while before by Oskar, who in those days was still happy and able to cut glass with his voice. And with that necklace I left the flat. The necklace, I felt, would be my start, my jumping-off place. I took the car to the Central Station, thinking if all goes well ... and throughout the lengthy negotiations, the same thoughts were with me. But the one-armed man and the Saxon, whom the other called the Assessor, were aware only of my article's material value, they failed to suspect what pathways of happiness they laid out before me when in return for my poor mama's necklace they gave me a real leather briefcase and twelve cartons of 'Ami' cigarettes, Lucky Strikes.

That afternoon I was back in Bilk. I unloaded twelve cartons of Lucky Strikes, a fortune. I savored their amazement, thrust the mountain of blond tobacco at them, and said: this is for you. From now on I want you to leave me alone. It's not too much to ask for all these cigarettes. Aside from that I want a lunchbox with lunch in it, beginning tomorrow. I hope you will be happy with your honey and flints, I said without anger or resentment; as for me, I shall practice another art, my happiness will be written, or to put it more professionally, incised on tombstones.

Korneff took me on as his helper for a hundred reichsmarks a month. Not much money, but I worked hard for it just the same. It was clear by the end of the first week that I was not strong enough for the heavy work. I had been given the job of embossing a slab of Belgian granite, fresh from the quarry, for a family vault. In an hour's time I could scarcely hold the chisel and my mallet hand was numb. I also had to leave the blunt chiseling for Korneff, but thanks to my skill, I was able to take over the fine chiseling and scalloping, to square off the slabs, draw the lines for the four blows, and finish the dolomite borders. Sitting on an improvised stool, in my right hand the chisel and in my left, despite the objections of Korneff, who wished to make me right-handed, a pear-shaped wooden mallet or an iron bush hammer; metal rang on stone, the sixty-four teeth of the bush hammer bit simultaneously into the stone to soften it. Here was happiness; not my drum, to be sure, just an ersatz, but there is also such a thing as ersatz happiness, perhaps happiness exists only as an ersatz, perhaps all happiness is an ersatz for happiness. Here I was, then, in a storehouse of ersatz happiness: Marble happiness, sandstone happiness. Hard happiness: Carrara. Cloudy, brittle happiness: alabaster. The happiness of chrome steel cutting into diorite. Dolomite: green happiness; gentle happiness: tufa. Colored happiness from the river Lahn. Porous happiness: basalt. Cold happiness from the Eifel. Like a volcano the happiness erupted and fell in a layer of dust, of grit between my teeth. I proved most talented at cutting inscriptions. I soon outdid Korneff and he entrusted me with all the ornamental work, the acanthus leaves, the broken roses for those who died in their tender years, such Christian symbols as XP or INRI, the flutes and beads, the eggs and anchors, chamfers and double chamfers. Oskar provided tombstones at all prices with all manner of ornaments. And when I had spent eight hours clouding a polished diorite slab with my breath and incising an inscription such as: Here rests in God my beloved husband – new line – Our beloved father, brother, and uncle – new line – Joseph Esser – new line – b. April 3, 1885, d. June 22, 1946 – new line – Death is the Gateway to Life – I was conscious, as I reread the text, of an ersatz happiness, that is, I was pleasantly happy. In gratitude to Joseph Esser, who had passed away at the age of sixty-one, and to the little green clouds of diorite raised by my chisel, I took special care with the O's in Esser's epitaph; Oskar was particularly fond of the letter O, and there was always a fine regularity and endlessness about my O's, though they tended to be rather too large.

At the end of May I went to work as a stonecutter's helper; at the beginning of October Korneff developed two new boils, and it was time to set up the travertine slab for Hermann Webknecht and Else Webknecht, née Freytag, in the South Cemetery. Until then Korneff, doubting my strength, had refused to take me with him to the cemetery. When he had a tombstone to haul and set up, he usually borrowed one of Julius Wöbel's helpers, who was almost stone-deaf but otherwise a satisfactory worker. In return Korneff would give Wöbel – who employed eight men – a hand in emergencies. Time and time again I had offered my services for work at the cemetery; cemeteries had retained their attraction for me, though at the time there were no decisions to be made. Fortunately, the beginning of October was the rush season at Wöbel's, he would need all his men until the frosts set in; Korneff had to fall back on me.

We put the travertine slab on hardwood rollers and rolled it up the ramp onto the back of the three-wheel truck. We set the pedestal beside it, cushioned the edges in empty paper sacks, loaded on tools, cement, sand, gravel, and the rollers and crates for unloading; I shut the tail gate, Korneff got in and started the motor. Then he stuck his head and boil-infested neck out of the cab and shouted: 'Come along, boy. Get your lunchbox and pile in.'

We drove slowly round the City Hospital. Outside the main gate white clouds of nurses, including one I knew, Sister Gertrude. I waved, she waved back. Lucky seeing her like that, I thought, I ought to ask her out one of these days, even if she has disappeared now that we've turned off toward the Rhine, invite her to do something with me, heading for Kappeshamm; the movies maybe, or to the theater to see Gründgens; ha, there it is, that yellow brick building, but it doesn't necessarily have to be the theater, smoke rising from the crematory over autumnal trees, a change of surroundings might do you good, Sister Gertrude. Another cemetery, other makers of tombstones: Beutz & Kranich, Pottgiesser, natural stones, Bohm, mortuary art, Gockeln, mortuary gardening and landscaping; questions at the entrance, it's not so easy to get into a cemetery: travertine for grave Number 79, Section Eight, Webknecht Hermann. Guard raises two fingers to his cap, leave lunchpails at the crematory to be warmed up, and in front of the ossuary stood Leo Schugger.

'The fellow with the white gloves,' I ask Korneff, 'isn't that Leo Schugger?'

Korneff, feeling his boils: 'No, no, never heard of any Leo Schugger. That's Willem Slobber; he lives here.'

How could I have contented myself with this information? I myself, after all, had been in Danzig and now I was in Düsseldorf, but I was still called Oskar: 'In Danzig there was a fellow who hung around the centuries and looked exactly like this fellow. His name was Leo Schugger; before he was in the cemeteries he was called just plain Leo and he was a student at the seminary.'

Korneff, left hand on his boils, right hand turning the wheel as we curved round the crematory: 'I don't doubt it. I know a whole raft of them that look the same, that started out at the seminary, and now they're living in cemeteries under different names. This one here is Willem Slobber.'

We drove past Willem Slobber. He waved a white glove at us, and I felt at home at the South Cemetery.

October, cemetery paths, the world losing its hair and teeth, which is just another way of saying that yellow leaves kept falling from the trees. Silence, sparrows, people out for a stroll, our three-wheeler chugging along on its way to Section Eight, which is still far off. Here and there old women with watering cans and grandchildren, sun on black Swedish granite, obelisks, truncated columns – symbolic or real war damage – a tarnished green angel behind a yew tree or something that looked like a yew tree. A woman shading her eyes with a marble hand, dazzled by her own marble. Christ in stone sandals blessing the elm trees, and in Section Four another Christ, blessing a birch. Delicious daydreams on the path between Section Four and Section Five: the ocean for instance. And this ocean casts, among other things, a corpse up on the beach. From the direction of the Zoppot beach promenade, violin music and the bashful beginnings of a fireworks display for the benefit of the war blind. Oskar, aged three, bends down over the flotsam, hoping it will prove to be Maria, or perhaps Sister Gertrude, whom I should ask out some time. But it is fair Lucy, pale Lucy, as I can see by the light of the fireworks, now hurrying toward their climax. Even if I couldn't see her face, I'd recognize her by the knitted Bavarian jacket she always has on when she is planning evil. When I take it off her, the wool is wet. Wet too is the jacket she has on under the jacket. Another little Bavarian jacket. And at the very end, as the fireworks die down and only the violins are left, I find, under wool on wool on wool, her heart wrapped in an athletic jersey marked League of German Girls, her heart, Lucy's heart, a little cold tombstone, on which is written: Here lies Oskar – Here lies Oskar – Here lies Oskar . . .

'Wake up, boy,' Korneff interrupted my daydreams, washed ashore by the sea, illumined by the fireworks. We turned left and Section Eight, a new section without trees and with but few tombstones, lay flat and hungry before us. The graves were all alike, too fresh to be decorated, but the last five burials were easily recognizable: moldering mounds of brown wreaths with faded, rain-soaked ribbons.

We quickly found Number 79 at the beginning of the fourth row, adjoining Section Seven, which already had a more settled look with its sprinkling of young, quick-growing trees and its considerable number of tombstones, mostly of Silesian marble, arranged with a certain regularity. We approached 79 from the rear, unloaded the tools, cement, gravel, and the travertine slab with its slightly oily sheen. The three-wheeler gave a jump as we rolled the slab down on the crates waiting to receive it. Korneff removed the temporary cross, bearing the names of H. Webknecht and E. Webknecht, from the head end of the grave; I handed him the drill and he began to dig the two holes – depth five feet three inches, stipulated the cemetery regulations – for the concrete posts, while I brought water from Section Seven and mixed concrete. I had finished just as he, having dug five feet, said he had finished. I began to fill the holes with concrete while Korneff sat catching his breath on the travertine slab, reaching behind him and feeling his boils. 'Coming to a head,' he said. 'I can always feel it when they're ready to bust.' My mind just about vacant, I rammed in the concrete. Coming from Section Seven, a Protestant funeral crawled through Section Eight to Section Nine. As they were passing three rows away from us, Korneff slid off the travertine slab and, in compliance with the cemetery regulations, we took our caps off for the procession from the pastor to the next of kin. Immediately after the coffin came, all alone, a lopsided little woman in black. Those who followed her were all much bigger and solidly built.

'Gawd a'mighty,' Korneff groaned. 'I got a feeling they're going to pop before we can get that slab up.'

Meanwhile the funeral party had reached Section Nine, where it arranged itself and poured forth the pastor's voice, rising and falling. The concrete had contracted, and we could have put the pedestal on its foundations. But Korneff lay prone on the travertine slab. He slipped his cap under his forehead and pulled down the collar of his jacket and shirt, baring his neck, while the biography of the dear departed drifted over to us from Section Nine. I had to climb up on the slab and sit on Korneff's back. I took in the situation at a glance; there were two of them almost on top of each other. A straggler with an enormous wreath hurried toward Section Nine and the sermon that was drawing slowly to an end. I tore off the plaster at one tug, wiped away the ichthyol salve with a beech leaf, and examined the two indurations. They were almost the same size, tar-brown shading into yellow. 'Let us pray,' said the breeze from Section Nine. Taking this as a sign, I turned my head to one side and simultaneously pressed and pulled the beech leaves under my thumbs. 'Our Father . . .' Korneff croaked: 'Don't squeeze, pull.' I pulled. ' . . . be Thy name.' Korneff managed to join in the prayer: ' . . . Thy Kingdom come.' Pulling didn't help, so I squeezed again. 'Will be done, on as it is in.' A miracle that there was no explosion. And once again: 'give us this day.' And again Korneff caught up the thread: 'trespasses and not into temptation . . .' There was more of it than I had expected. 'Kingdom and the power and the glory.' I squeezed out the last colorful remnant. ' . . . and ever, amen.' While I give a last squeeze, Korneff: 'Amen,' and, a last pull: 'Amen.' As the folks over in Section Nine started on their condolences, Korneff said another amen. Still flat on the travertine slab, he heaved a sigh of relief: 'Amen,' to which he added: 'Got some concrete left for under the pedestal?' Yes, I had. And he: 'Amen.'

I spread the last shovelfuls as a binder between the two posts. Then Korneff slid down off the polished inscription and Oskar showed him the autumnal beech leaves and the similarly colored contents of his boils. We put our caps back on, took hold of the stone, and, as the funeral in Section Nine dispersed, put up the slab that would mark the grave of Hermann Webknecht and Else Webknecht, née Freytag.

426

Fortuna North

In those days only people who left something valuable behind them on the surface of the earth could afford tombstones. It didn't have to be a diamond or a string of pearls. For five sacks of potatoes, you could get a plain but good-sized stone of Grenzheim shell lime. A Belgian granite monument on three pedestals for a tomb for two brought us material for two three-piece suits. The tailor's widow, who gave us the goods, still had an apprentice working for her; she agreed to make the suits in return for a dolomite border.

One evening after work Korneff and I took the Number 10 car out to Stockum, where we dropped in on the Widow Lennert and had our measurements taken. Absurd as it may sound, Oskar was wearing an armored infantry uniform with alterations by Maria. The buttons on the jacket had been moved, but even so, what with my peculiar build, it was impossible to button them.

The suit which Anton the apprentice proceeded to make me was dark blue with a pin stripe and light grey lining; it was single-breasted, adequately but not misleadingly padded at the shoulders; it did not conceal my hump, but made the most of it, though without exaggeration; cuffs on the trousers but not ostentatiously wide. My model, in matters of dress, was still Master Bebra, hence no loops for a belt but buttons for braces; waistcoat shiny in back, subdued in front, lined with old rose. The whole thing took five fittings.

While Anton was still working on Korneff's double-breasted and my single-breasted suit, a trafficker in shoes came to see us about a tombstone for his wife, who had been killed in an air raid in '43. First he tried to palm off ration coupons on us, but we demanded merchandise. For Silesian marble with fancy border plus installation Korneff obtained for himself one pair of dark-brown oxfords and one of carpet slippers and for me a pair of high, old-fashioned but wonderfully supple black shoes size five, which supported my weak ankles and, despite their archaic cut, had a pleasingly elegant look.

Laying a bundle of reichsmarks on the honey scales, I asked Maria to buy me two white shirts, one with pin stripes, and two ties, one light grey, the other dark brown. 'The rest,' I said, 'is for Kurt and for you, my dear Maria, who never think of yourself but only of others.'

While my giving spree lasted, I gave Guste an umbrella with a real bone handle and a deck of almost new skat cards, for she liked to lay out cards, but it painted her to borrow a deck from the neighbors every time she was curious to know when Köster would come home.

Maria carried out my commission without delay. With the money that was left – and there was quite a lot – she bought herself a raincoat and Kurt a school satchel of imitation leather, which was horrible to look upon but served its purpose for the time. To my shirts and ties she added three pairs of grey socks that I had forgotten to order.

When Korneff and Oskar called for our suits, we were embarrassed at our reflections in the glass, but quite impressed by one another. Korneff hardly dared to turn his ravaged neck. His arms hung forward from drooping shoulders, and he tried to straighten his bent knees. My new clothes give me a demonic, intellectual look, especially when I folded my arms over my chest, so adding to my upper horizontal dimension, and, supporting my weight on my feeble right leg, held out my left at a nonchalant angle. Smiling at Korneff and his astonishment, I approached the mirror, stood close enough to kiss my reverse image, but was satisfied to cloud myself over with my breath and said as though in passing: 'Ho, there, Oskar. You still need a tie pin.'

When, one Sunday afternoon a week later, I visited my nurses in the City Hospital and not without vanity displayed my spruce, brand-new self, I was already in possession of a silver tie pin with a pearl in it.

The dear girls were speechless when they saw me sitting in the nurses' room. That was late in the summer of '47. I crossed my arms over my chest in the traditional way and played with my leather gloves. For more than a year now I had been a stonecutter's helper, a master at fluting and grooving. I crossed my legs, careful not to disturb the crease in my trousers. Our good Guste took care of my suit as though it had been made to order for Köster, whose homecoming was going to change everything. Sister Helmtrud wanted to feel the material and of course I let her. In the spring of '47 we celebrated Kurt's seventh birthday with home-mixed egg liqueur and homemade sand cake – take two pounds of butter. Take this, take that – and I gave him a mouse-grey loden coat. Meanwhile Sister Gertrude had joined the other nurses and I passed around some candy which, in addition to twenty pounds of brown sugar, we had been given for a diorite slab. Little Kurt, it seemed to me, was much too fond of school. His teacher, who was young and attractive and in no way resembled la Spollenhauer, spoke well of him; she said he was bright, though a trifle solemn. How gay nurses can be when you bring them candy. When left alone for a moment with Sister Gertrude, I inquired about her free Sundays.

'Well, today for instance, I'm off at five. But,' said Sister Gertrude with resignation, 'there's nothing doing in town.'

I said it was worth trying. Her reaction was: 'What's the use?' Her idea was to have her sleep out. I made my invitation more definite, and when she still couldn't make up her mind, concluded mysteriously with the words: 'A little gumption, Sister Gertrude. We're only young once. I know someone who's got plenty of cake stamps.' I illustrated this last remark with a light, stylized tap on my breast pocket and offered her another piece of candy. Strange to say, I was rather terrified when this strapping Westphalian lass, who was not my type at all, said as though to the medicine chest: 'All right, if you feel like it. Let's say six o'clock, but not here, how about Cornelius-Platz?'

As though I would ever have expected Sister Gertrude to meet me or anyone else in or near the hospital entrance! At six o'clock I was waiting for her under the Cornelius-Platz clock, which was still feeling the effects of the war and did not tell time. She was punctual, as I could tell by the not very expensive pocket watch I had bought some weeks before. I hardly recognized her; if I had seen her a little sooner, on her descent for instance from the streetcar some fifty paces away, before she could notice me, I should have slipped quietly away; for Sister Gertrude did not come as Sister Gertrude in white with a Red Cross pin, she came in miserably cut civilian dress as Miss Gertrude Wilms from Hamm or Dortmund or one of those towns between Dortmund and Hamm.

She didn't notice my dismay, but told me she had nearly been late because, just to be mean, the head nurse had given her something to do just before five.

'Well, Miss Gertrude, may I offer a few suggestions? Let's first relax a while in a pastry shop and after that whatever you say: we could go to the movies, it's too late to get theater tickets, or how about a little dance?'

'Oh, yes, let's go dancing,' she cried with enthusiasm. It was too late when she realized, but then with ill-concealed distress, that despite my finery I was hardly cut out to be her dancing partner.

With a certain malice – why hadn't she come in the nurse's uniform I was so fond of? – I confirmed the arrangements; she, for lack of imagination, soon forgot her fright, and joined me in consuming – I one piece, she three – some cake that must have had cement in it. After I had paid with money and cake stamps, we boarded the Gerresheim car, for if Korneff were to be believed, there was a dance hall below Grafenberg.

We did the last bit of the way slowly on foot, for the car stopped before the uphill stretch. A September evening by the book. Gertrude's wooden sandals, obtainable without coupons, clattered like the mill on the floss. The sound made me feel gay. The people coming downhill turned around to look at us. Miss Gertrude was embarrassed. I was used to it and took no notice. After all it was my cake stamps that had fed her three slices of cement cake at Kürten's Pastry Shop.

The dance hall was called Wedig's and subtitled The Lions' Den. There was tittering before we left the ticket window, and heads turned as we entered. Sister Gertrude was ill at ease in her civilian clothing and would have fallen over a folding chair if a waiter and I hadn't held her up. The waiter showed us a table near the dance floor, and I ordered two iced drinks, adding in an undertone audible only to the waiter: 'But toss in a couple of shots, if you please.'

The Lions' Den consisted chiefly of a large room that must once have been a riding academy. The rafters and bomb-scarred ceiling had been decorated with streamers and garlands from last year's carnival. Muted colored lights swung in circles, casting reflections on the resolutely slicked hair of the young black marketeers, some of them fashionably dressed, and the taffeta blouses of the girls, who all seemed to know each other.

When the drinks were served, I bought ten American cigarettes from the waiter, offered Sister Gertrude one and gave another to the waiter, who stored it behind his ear. After giving my companion a light, I produced Oskar's amber cigarette holder and smoked half a Camel. The tables around us quieted down. Sister Gertrude dared to look up. When I crushed out my enormous Camel butt in the ash tray and left it there, Sister Gertrude picked it up with a practiced hand and tucked it away in the side pocket of her oilskin handbag.

'For my fiancé in Dortmund,' she said. 'He smokes like mad.'

I was glad I wasn't her fiancé and glad too that the music had started up.

The five-piece band played 'Don't Fence Me In.' Males in crêpe soles dashed across the dance floor without colliding and appropriated young ladies who as they arose gave their bags to girl friends for safekeeping.

A few of the couples danced with a smoothness born of long practice. Quantities of gum were being ruminated; now and then a group of young black marketeers would stop dancing for a few measures to confer in Rhenish leavened with American slang while their partners, held vaguely by the arm, bobbed and joggled impatiently. Small objects exchanged hands: a true black marketeer never takes time off.

We sat the first dance out and the next foxtrot as well. Oskar took an occasional look at the men's feet. When the band struck up 'Rosamund,' he asked a bewildered Sister Gertrude to dance.

Remembering Jan Bronski's choreographic arts, I, who was almost two heads shorter than Sister Gertrude, decided to try a *schieber*; I was well aware of the grotesque note we struck and determined to accentuate it. With resignation she let herself be led. I held her firmly by the rear end, thirty percent wool content; cheek to blouse, I pushed her, every pound of her, backward and followed in her footsteps. Sweeping away obstacles with our unbending side arms, we crossed the dance floor from corner to corner. It went better than I had dared to hope. I risked a variation or two. My cheek still clinging to her blouse, my hand still supported by her hips, I danced around her without relinquishing the classical posture of the *schieber*, whose purpose it is to suggest that she is about to fall backward and that he is about to fall on top of her, though because they are such good dancers, they never actually fall.

Soon we had an audience. I heard cries such as: 'Didn't I tell you it was Jimmy? Hey, take a look at Jimmy. Hello, Jimmy. Come on, Jimmy. Let's go, Jimmy.'

Unfortunately, I couldn't see Sister Gertrude's face and could only hope that she was taking the applause in her stride as a well-meant homage. A nurse, after all, should be used to embarrassing flattery.

When we sat down, those around us were still clapping. The five-piece band did a flourish and another and another; the percussion man outdid himself. There were cries of 'Jimmy!' And 'Say, did you see those two?' At this point Sister Gertrude arose, mumbled something about going to the ladies' room, took her handbag containing the cigarette butt for her fiancé in Dortmund, and blushing scarlet, shoved her way, colliding with everything in her path, between chairs and tables, toward the ladies' room, which happened to be near the exit.

She never came back. Before leaving, she had drained her drink at one long gulp, a gesture that apparently means goodbye; Sister Gertrude had walked out on me.

And Oskar? An American cigarette in his amber holder, he ordered a straight schnaps from the waiter who was discreetly removing Sister Gertrude's empty glass. He was determined to smile at all costs. His smile may have been a bit sorrowful, but it was still a smile; folding his arms and crossing his legs, he waggled one delicate black shoe, size five, and savored the superiority of the forsaken.

The young habitués of the Lions' Den were very nice; it was a swing number, and they winked at me from the dance floor as they swung by. 'Hello,' cried the boys and 'Take it easy' the girls. With a wave of my cigarette holder I thanked the repositories of true humanity and smirked indulgently as the percussion man gave a sumptuous roll and did a solo number on the drums, cymbals, and triangle, which reminded me of my good old rostrum days. The next dance, he then announced, would be ladies' invitation.

A hot number, 'Jimmy the Tiger,' meant for me no doubt, though no one at the Lions' Den could have known about my career as a disrupter of mass meetings. A fidgety little thing with a henna mop came over to me and, pausing a moment in her gum chewing, whispered in my ear with a voice husky from smoking: 'Jimmy the Tiger.' I was the partner of her choice. Conjuring up jungle menaces, we danced Jimmy; the Tiger walked – for about ten minutes – on velvet paws. Again a flourish, applause and another flourish, because my hump was well dressed and I was nimble on my legs and cut a pretty good figure as Jimmy the Tiger. I asked my admirer to my table, and Helma – that was her name – asked if her girl friend Hannelore could come too. Hannelore was silent, sedentary, and hard-drinking. Helma, on the other hand, was addicted to American cigarettes, and I had to ask the waiter for some more.

A fine evening. I danced 'Hey Bob A Re Bop,' 'In the Mood,' 'Shoeshine Boy,' chatted between dances, and entertained the two young ladies, who were not very exacting and told me that they worked in the telephone exchange on Graf-Adolf-Platz and that lots of girls from the exchange came to Wedig's every Saturday and Sunday night. They themselves came regularly when they weren't on duty, and I too promised to come often, because Helma and Hannelore were so nice, and because telephone operators seemed so easy to get along with when there was no telephone – a little joke that they were good enough to laugh at.

It was a long while before I went back to the City Hospital. When I resumed my occasional visits, Sister Gertrude had been transferred to gynecology. I never saw her again except to wave to from a distance. I became a welcome habitué at the Lions' Den. The girls exploited me but not immoderately. Through them I made the acquaintance of several members of the British Army of Occupation and picked up a few dozen words of English, I made friends with a couple of the musicians, but controlled myself, that is, I kept away from the drums and contented myself with the modest happiness of cutting inscriptions at Korneff's.

During the hard winter of 1947 to 1948, I kept up my contact with the telephone girls. At no great expense, I obtained a certain amount of warmth from the silent, sedentary Hannelore, though we never went beyond the noncommittal manual stage.

In the winter the stonecutter took care of his equipment. The tools had to be reforged, a few leftover blocks were trimmed and made ready for their inscriptions. Korneff and I replenished our stores, which had been thinned out during the autumn season, and made a few artificial stones from shell-lime waste. I also tried my hand at some simple sculpture with the stippling machine, did reliefs representing angels' heads, heads of Christ with crowns of thorns, and doves of the Holy Ghost. When snow fell, I shoveled it away, and when there was none, thawed out the water pipe leading to the polishing machine.

At the end of February, '48, soon after Ash Wednesday – I had lost weight during carnival and may have been looking rather ethereal, for some of the girls at the Lions' Den took to calling me Doctor – the first peasants from the left bank of the Rhine came over to look at our offerings. Korneff was absent on his annual rheumatism cure, tending a blast furnace in Duisburg. When he came back two weeks later, parched and boilless, I had already sold three stones, one of them for a tomb for three, on favorable terms. Korneff sold two slabs of Kirchheim shell lime; and early in March we began to set them up. One slab of Silesian marble went to Grevenbroich; the two Kirchheim stones are in a village cemetery near Neuss; the red sandstone with my angels' heads can still be admired in the cemetery at Stomml. At the end of March we loaded the diorite slab with the thorn-crowned Christ and drove slowly, because the three-wheeler was over-loaded, in the direction of Kappes-Hamm, meaning to cross the Rhine at Neuss. From Neuss via Grevenbroich to Rommerskir-chen, then left on the road to Bergheim Erft. Leaving Rheydt and Niederaussem behind us, we reached Oberaussem without breaking an axle. The cemetery was situated on a hill sloping gently toward the village.

Ah, the view! At our feet the Erftland soft coal country. The eight chimneys of the Fortuna Works, steaming heavenward. The new Fortuna North power plant, hissing as though about to explode. The mountains of slag surmounted by telpher lines. Every three minutes a train empty or full of coke, no larger than a toy, moving to or from the power plant; a larger toy, a toy for giants, was the high-tension line that swept across one corner of the cemetery on its way, three abreast, buzzing with high tension, to Cologne. Other lines hurried horizonward in other directions, to Belgium and Holland: hub of the world. We set up the diorite slab for the Flies family – electricity is generated by ... The gravedigger with his helper, who substituted for Leo Schugger on this occasion, passed by with their implements. We were standing in a field of tension. Three rows away, they started to dig up a grave preparatory to moving its occupant – war reparations flowing over high-tension wires – the wind carried the smells typical of a premature exhumation – not so bad, it was only March. Amid the coke piles the green fields of spring. The bows of the gravedigger's glasses were mended with string, he was arguing in an undertone with his Leo Schugger, until for exactly one minute the Fortuna siren gave a gasp, leaving us breathless, not to mention the woman whose remains were being moved, only the high tension lines got on with their work. The siren tipped, fell overboard, and drowned – while from the slate-grey slate roofs of the village rose coils of smoke betokening the lunch hour, followed by the church bells: pray and work, industry and religion, boon companions. Change of shifts at Fortuna. We unwrapped our smoked pork sandwiches, but exhumation suffers no delay and the high-tension current continued without interruption on its way to the victor powers, to light the lamps of Holland, while here the juice was constantly being shut off – but the dead woman saw the light.

While Korneff dug the five-foot holes for the foundation, she was brought up into the fresh air. She hadn't been lying very long down in the darkness, only since the fall, and already she had made progress, keeping pace with the improvements that were everywhere under way. Those who were dismantling industrial plants in the Ruhr and Rhineland had progressed like anything; during the winter that I had frittered away at the Lions' Den, this woman had made serious progress and now, as we were laying on concrete and putting the pedestal in place, it was piece by piece that she had to be persuaded to let herself be dug up. But that's what the zinc casket was for, to prevent anything, even the most negligible part of her, from getting lost. Just as when free coal was distributed at Fortuna, children ran behind the over-loaded trucks and picked up the chunks that fell out, because Cardinal Frings had proclaimed from the pulpit: Verily I say unto you, it is not a sin to filch coal. But for this woman there was no longer any need to keep up a fire. I don't think she was cold in the proverbially chilly March air, she had quite a good deal of skin left; to be sure it had sprung leaks and runners; but these were compensated for by vestiges of cloth and hair, the latter still permanently waved, hence the term. The coffin fittings were also worth moving and there were even bits of wood that wanted to go along to the other cemetery, where there would be no peasants or miners from Fortuna, for this next last resting place was in the city where there was always something doing, nineteen movie houses operating all at once. For as the grave-digger told us, she wasn't from around here, she had been evacuated: 'She was from Cologne, and now they're taking her to Mülheim on the other side of the Rhine.' He would have said more if the siren hadn't gone off again for another minute. Taking advantage of the siren, I approached the grave; tacking against the siren, I wanted to witness this exhumation, and I took something with me which turned out, when I reached the zinc casket, to be my spade, which I put into action, not in order to help but because I happened to have it with me. On the blade I picked up something that had fallen on the ground. This spade had formerly been the property of the Reich Labor Service. And what I picked up on the Reich Labor Service spade was or had been the middle finger and, as I am still convinced, the ring finger of the evacuated woman; they had not fallen off but had been chopped off by the gravedigger, an unfeeling sort. But it seemed to me that they had been beautiful and adroit. Similarly the woman's head, which had already been placed in the casket, had preserved a certain regularity through the winter of '47 to '48, which was a severe one as you surely remember, and it was reasonably possible to speak of beauty, though on the decline. Moreover, this woman's head and fingers were closer to me, more human, than the beauty of Fortuna North. It seems safe to say that I enjoyed the industrial landscape as I had enjoyed Gustaf Gründgens at the theater – a surface beauty which I have always distrusted, though assuredly there was art in it, whereas the effect produced by this evacuee was only too natural. Granted that the high-tension lines, like Goethe, gave me a cosmic feeling, but the woman's fingers touched my heart. They still touched my heart when I began to think of her as a man, because it was more compatible with my thing about making decisions and with the fancy that transformed me into Yorick and the woman – half of her still in the earth, half in the zinc casket – into Hamlet. And I, Yorick, Act V, the fool, 'I knew him, Horatio,' Scene I, I who on all the stages of this world – 'Alas, poor Yorick!' – lend Hamlet my skull so that some Gründgens or Sir Laurence Olivier in the role of Hamlet may ponder over it: 'Where be your gibes now? your gambols?' I held Gründgens' Hamlet fingers on the blade of the Labor Service shovel, stood on the solid ground of the Rhenish soft coal fields, amid the graves of miners, peasants, and their families, and looked down on the slate roofs of the village of Oberaussem. The village cemetery became for me the center of the world, while Fortuna North stood there as the redoubtable demigod, my antagonist. The fields were the fields of Denmark; the Erft was my Belt, whatever rot lay round about was rotten in the state of Denmark – and I was Yorick. Charged with high tension, crackling, the high-tension angels, in lines of three, sang as they made their way to the horizon, to Cologne with its fabulous Gothic monster, heavenly hosts over the beet fields. But the earth yielded up coal and the corpse, not of Yorick but of Hamlet. As to the others, who had no parts in the play, they lay buried for good – 'The rest is silence' – weighed down with tombstones just as we were weighing down the Flies family with this ponderous diorite slab. But for me, Oskar Matzerath Bronski Yorick, a new era was dawning, and scarcely aware of it, I took another quick look at Hamlet's worn-out fingers on the blade of my shovel – 'He is fat and scant of breath' – I looked on as Gründgens, Act III, Scene I, labored his dilemma about being or not being, rejected this absurd formulation, and put the question more concretely: 'My son and my son's lighter flints, my presumptive earthly and heavenly father, my grandmother's four skirts, the beauty, immortalized in photographs, of my poor mama, the maze of scars on Herbert Truczinski's back, the blood-absorbing mail baskets at the Polish Post Office, America – but what is America compared to Streetcar Number 9 that went to Brösen? I considered Maria's scent of vanilla, still perceptible now and then, and my hallucination of Lucy Rennwand's triangular face; I asked Mr. Fajngold, that disinfector unto death, to search for the Party pin that had disappeared in Matzerath's windpipe. And at last, turning to Korneff, or more to the pylons of the power line, I said – my decision was made, but before coming out with it, I felt the need of a theatrical question that would cast doubt on Hamlet but legitimize me, Yorick, as a citizen – turning, then, to Korneff, who had called me because it was time to join our slab to the pedestal, I, stirred by the desire to become an honest citizen, said, slightly imitating Gründgens, although he could scarcely have played Yorick, said across the shovel blade: 'To marry or not to marry, that is the question.'

After this crisis at the cemetery facing Fortuna North, I gave up dancing at Wedig's Lions' Den, broke off all connections with the girls at the telephone exchange, whose foremost quality had been their ability to provide connections.

In May I took Maria to the movies. After the show we went to a restaurant and ate relatively well. We had a heart to heart talk. Maria was dreadfully worried because Kurt's source was drying up, because the honey business was falling off, because I, weakling, so she put it, that I was, had been supporting the whole family for several months. I comforted Maria, told her that Oskar was glad to be doing what he could, that Oskar liked nothing better than to bear a heavy responsibility, complimented her on her looks, and finally came out with a proposal.

She asked for time to think it over. For weeks the only answer to my Yorick's question was silence and evasion; in the end it was answered by the currency reform.

Maria gave me innumerable reasons. She caressed my sleeve, called me 'dear Oskar,' said I was too good for this world, begged me to understand and always be her friend, wished me the best of everything for my future as a stonecutter and otherwise, but when asked more explicitly and urgently, declined to marry me.

And so Yorick did not become a good citizen, but a Hamlet, a fool.

Madonna 49

The currency reform came too soon, it made a fool of me, compelling me in turn to reform Oskar's currency. I was obliged to capitalize, or at least to make a living from, my hump.

Yet I might have been a good citizen. The period following the currency reform, which — it has now become perfectly clear — contained all the seeds of the middle-class paradise we are living in today, might have brought out the bourgeois Oskar. As a husband and family man I should have participated in the reconstruction of Germany, I should now be the owner of a medium-sized stonecutting business, giving thirty workers their livelihood and providing office buildings and insurance palaces with the shell-lime and travertine façades that have become so popular: I should be a businessman, a family man, a respected member of society. But Maria turned me down.

It was then that Oskar remembered his hump and fell a victim to art. Before Korneff, whose existence as a maker of tombstones was also threatened by the currency reform, could dismiss me, I walked out. I took to standing on streetcorners when I wasn't twiddling my thumbs in Guste Köster's kitchen-living room; I gradually wore out my tailor-made suit and began to neglect my appearance. There were no fights with Maria, but for fear of fights I would leave the flat in Bilk in the early forenoon. First I went to see the swans in Graf-Adolf-Platz, then I shifted to the swans in the Hofgarten. Small, thoughtful, but not embittered, I would sit on a park bench across the street from the Municipal Employment Agency and the Academy of Art, which are neighbors in Düsseldorf.

It is amazing how long a man can sit on a park bench; he sits till he turns to wood and feels the need of communicating with other wooden figures: old men who come only in good weather, old women gradually reverting to garrulous girlhood, children shouting as they play tag, lovers who will have to part soon, but not yet, not yet. The swans are black, the weather hot, cold, or medium according to the season. Much paper is dropped; the scraps flutter about or lie on the walks until a man in a cap, paid by the city, spears them on a pointed stick.

Oskar was careful in sitting to blouse the knees of his trousers evenly. Of course I noticed the two emaciated young men and the girl in glasses before the girl – she had on a leather overcoat with an ex-Wehrmacht belt – addressed me. The idea seemed to have originated with her companions, who despite their sinister underworldly look were afraid to approach me, the hunchback, for they sensed my hidden greatness. It was the girl who summoned up the courage. She stood before me on firm, widely spaced columns until I asked her to sit down. There was a mist blowing up from the Rhine and her glasses were clouded over; she talked and talked, until I asked her to wipe her glasses and state her business intelligibly. Then she beckoned to her sinister companions. I had no need to question them; they introduced themselves at once as painters in search of a model. I was just what they were looking for, they said with an enthusiasm that was almost frightening. When I rubbed my thumb against my index and middle finger, they told me the Academy paid one mark eighty an hour, or two marks for posing in the nude, but that, said the stout girl, didn't seem very likely.

Why did Oskar say yes? Was it the lure of art? Or of lucre? No need to choose. It was both. I arose, leaving the park bench and the joys and sorrows of park bench existence behind me forever, and followed my new friends – the stout girl marching with determination, the two young men, stooped as though carrying their genius on their backs – past the Employment Agency to the partially demolished Academy of Art.

Professor Kuchen – black beard, coal-black eyes, black soft hat, black fingernails – agreed that I would be an excellent model.

For a time he walked around me, darting coal-black looks, breathing black dust from his nostrils. Throttling an invisible enemy with his black fingers, he declared: 'Art is accusation, expression, passion. Art is a fight to the finish between black charcoal and white paper.'

Professor Kuchen led me to a studio, lifted me up with his own hands on a revolving platform, and spun it about, not in order to make me dizzy, but to display Oskar's proportions from all sides.

Sixteen easels gathered round. The coal-breathing professor gave his disciples a short briefing: What he wanted was expression, always expression, pitch-black, desperate expression. I, Oskar, he maintained, was the shattered image of man, an accusation, a challenge, timeless yet expressing the madness of our century. In conclusion he thundered over the easels: 'I don't want you to sketch this cripple, this freak of nature, I want you to slaughter him, crucify him, to nail him to your paper with charcoal!'

This was the signal to begin. Sixteen sticks of charcoal rasped behind sixteen easels; charcoal came to grips with my expression, that is, my hump, blackened it, and put it on paper. Professor Kuchen's students took so black a view of my expression that inevitably they exaggerated the dimensions of my hump; it refused to fit on the paper though they took larger and larger sheets.

Professor Kuchen gave the sixteen charcoal-crushers a piece of good advice: not to begin with the outlines of my hump – which was allegedly so pregnant with expression that no format could contain it – but first to black in my head on the upper fifth of the paper, as far to the left as possible.

My beautiful hair is a glossy chestnut-brown. They made me a scraggly-haired gypsy. Not a one of them ever noticed that Oskar has blue eyes. During an intermission – for every model is entitled to fifteen minutes' rest after posing for three-quarters of an hour – I took a look at the sixteen sketches. On all sides my cadaverous features thundered condemnation, but nowhere did I see the blue radiance of my eyes; where there should have been a clear, winning sparkle, I saw narrow, sinister orbs of crumbling coal-black charcoal.

However, the essence of art is freedom. I took an indulgent view. These sons and daughters of the Muses, I said to myself, have recognized the Rasputin in you; but will they ever discover the Goethe who lies dormant in your soul, will they ever call him to life and put him on paper, not with expressive charcoal but with a sensitive and restrained pencil point? Neither the sixteen students, gifted as they may have been, nor Professor Kuchen with his supposedly unique charcoal stroke, succeeded in turning out an acceptable portrait of Oskar. Still, I made good money and was treated with respect for six hours a day. Facing the clogged washbasin, a screen, or the sky-blue, slightly cloudy studio windows, I posed for six hours a day, displaying an expression valued at one mark and eighty pfennigs an hour.

In a few weeks' time the students produced a number of pleasant little sketches. The 'expression' became more moderate, the dimensions of my hump more plausible; sometimes they even managed to get the whole of me into the picture from top to toe, from the jacket buttons over my chest to the hindmost promontory of my hump. Occasionally there was room for a background. Despite the currency reform, these young people had not forgotten the war; behind me they erected ruins with accusing black holes where the windows had been. Or they would represent me as a forlorn, undernourished refugee, amid blasted tree trunks; or their charcoal would imprison me, weave ferociously barbed barbed-wire fences behind me, and build menacing watchtowers above me; they dressed me as a convict and made me hold an empty tin bowl, dungeon windows lent me graphic charm. And all in the name of artistic expression.

But since it was a black-haired gypsy-Oskar who was made to look upon all this misery out of coal-black eyes, and not my true blue-eyed self, I stood (or sat) still and kept my peace though I well knew that barbed wire is no fit subject for drawing. Nevertheless I was glad when the sculptors, who, as everyone knows, have to manage without timely backgrounds, asked me to pose for them in the nude.

This time it was not a student but the master in person who spoke to me. Professor Maruhn was a friend of my charcoal-crusher. One day when I was standing motionless in Kuchen's private studio, a dismal repair full of framed charcoal sketches, letting the black beard with the inimitable black stroke put me on paper, Professor Maruhn dropped in. A short, stocky man in his fifties, whose neat white smock might have suggested a surgeon if a dusty beret hadn't identified him as an artist.

Maruhn, as I could see at a glance, was a lover of classical form. He thoroughly disapproved of my build and began to poke fun at Kuchen: couldn't he be satisfied with the gypsy models who had earned him the nickname of Gypsy Cake? Must he try his hand at freaks? The gypsy period had sold well, there was that to be said for it; did the charcoal-crusher entertain hopes that a midget period would sell still better?

Smarting under his friend's mockery, Professor Kuchen translated it into furious strokes of charcoal: of all his pictures of Oskar this was the blackest. It was all black except for a touch of murky dawn on the cheekbones, nose, forehead, and hands – Kuchen always made my hands enormous, swollen with gout, screaming with expression, and put them in the middle ground of his charcoal orgies. In this drawing, however, which was later admired at exhibitions, my eyes are blue, that is, the usual somber glow has given way to a distinctly light tone. Oskar attributes this anomaly to the influence of Maruhn, who was not a fanatic of coal-black expression but a classicist, alert to the Goethean clarity of my eyes. It can only have been Oskar's eyes that persuaded this lover of classical harmony to select me as a fit model for sculpture, his sculpture.

Maruhn's studio was light, dusty, and bare. It contained not a single piece of finished work. But everywhere there were skeletons for projected sculptures, so perfectly thought out that wire, iron, and bare lead tubing, even without modeling clay, gave promise of future harmony.

I posed in the nude for five hours a day, and he paid me two marks an hour. A chalk mark on the platform showed where my right foot was to take root. An imaginary vertical rising from the instep had to pass directly between my collarbones. The left leg was 'free moving'. Illusory freedom. I was expected to bend the knee slightly and hold this leg slightly to one side, with an air of negligence, but I was not allowed to move it. It too was rooted in a chalk mark on the platform.

I spent several weeks posing for Maruhn. In all that time he was able to find no set pose for my arms comparable to that of the legs. He made me try everything: left arm drooping, right arm curved over my head; both arms folded over my chest or crossed under my hump; hands on hips; the possibilities were legion and the sculptor tried just about everything, first on me, then on the iron skeleton with the flexible lead joints.

When finally, after a month of strenuous effort, he decided to do me in clay, either with hands folded behind my head or as an armless torso, he was so exhausted from building and rebuilding his skeleton that he could do no more. He would pick up a handful of clay, sometimes he would even move forward to apply it, but then he would drop the dull, unformed clod back in the box. Then he would sit and stare at me and my skeleton, trembling as with fever: the skeleton was too perfect.

He sighed with resignation, said he had a headache, and without resentment toward Oskar gave up. He picked up the hump-backed skeleton, with fixed leg and free-moving leg, with tubular arms and upraised wire fingers joined behind iron neck, and put it in the corner with all his other prematurely finished skeleton. Gently, without mockery, aware of their own futility, the wooden bars, known also as butterflies, which were to have borne the weight of the clay, quivered in the spacious cage that was my hump.

After that we drank tea and chatted for an hour or so, which was counted as posing time. He spoke of former times when, vigorous and uninhibited as a young Michelangelo, he had spread whole wagonloads of clay on skeletons and completed innumerable sculptures, most of which had been destroyed during the war. I told him about Oskar's activity as a stonecutter and engraver of inscriptions. We talked shop a while and then he took me to pose for his students.

If long hair is an indication of sex, six of Professor Maruhn's ten pupils can be designated as girls. Four were homely and talented. Two were pretty, lively, and scatterbrained: real girls. It has never embarrassed me to pose in the nude. On the contrary, Oskar savored the astonishment of the two pretty, scatterbrained sculptresses when they viewed me on the platform for the first time and observed, not without a certain dismay, that Oskar, despite his hump, despite his small size, carried with him a sex organ which could, in a pinch, have borne comparison with just about anyone else's.

The students' trouble was rather different from the master's. The framework was complete in two days; with the frenzy of genius, they would fling clay on the hastily and inexpertly fastened lead tubes, but apparently they hadn't put enough wooden butterflies into my hump. For no sooner was the moist modeling clay in place, representing an Oskar who looked for all the world like a rugged mountain landscape, than this mountain-Oskar, or rather ten of them, would begin to sag. My head fell between my feet, the clay parted from the tubing, my hump drooped nearly to my knees, and I came to appreciate Maruhn, the master, whose skeletons were so perfect that there was no need to hide them beneath vile flesh.

The homely but gifted sculptresses wept when the clay Oskar parted from the skeleton Oskar. The pretty but scatterbrained sculptresses laughed as the perishable flesh fell symbolically from my bones. After several weeks, however, the class managed to turn out a few passable sculptures, first in clay, then in plaster and imitation marble. They were shown at the End of Term Exhibition and I had occasion to draw new comparisons between the homely but gifted sculptresses and the pretty but scatterbrained young ladies. While the homely but not untalented young ladies reproduced my head, limbs, and hump with the utmost care but, seized with a strange diffidence, either ignored my sex organ or stylized it ad absurdum, the pretty young ladies with the big blue eyes, with the shapely but awkward fingers, gave little heed to the articulations and proportions of my body, but reproduced my imposing genitals with the utmost precision. But while I am on this subject, I mustn't forget the four male sculptors: they abstracted me; making use of flat, grooved boards, they slapped me into a cube. As for the object that the homely young ladies neglected and the pretty ones rendered with carnal verism, they, with their masculine intellects, saw it as two cubes of like size, surmounted by an elongated rectangular block: Priapus in terms of solid geometry.

Was it because of my blue eyes or because of the sun-bowl heaters with which the sculptors surrounded the nude Oskar: in any case, some young painters who had come to see the pretty young sculptresses discovered a picturesque charm either in the blue of my eyes or in my glowing, irradiated, lobster-red skin and carried me away to the upper floors where the painting classes were held.

At first the painters were too much under the influence of my blue eyes and saw the whole of me as blue. Oskar's fresh complexion, his brown wavy hair, his fresh, pink mouth – all were submerged in macabre blues; here and there, serving only to intensify the putrefaction, a moribund green, a nauseous yellow crept in between the patches of blue flesh.

Oskar did not take on other colors until carnival week, when,

445

in the course of festivities held in the basement of the Academy, he discovered Ulla and brought her to the painters to be their Muse.

Was it on Shrove Monday? Yes, it was on Shrove Monday that I decided to join in the festivities, to put on a costume and to add a costumed Oskar to the motley throng.

When Maria saw me at the mirror, she said: 'You'd better stay home, Oskar. They'll just step on you.' Nevertheless, she helped me with my costume, cutting out patches which her sister Guste, with garrulous needle, joined into a jester costume. My first idea had been one of Velasquez' dwarfs. I should also have liked to appear as Narses or as Prince Eugene. When at length I stood before the big mirror, whose image was slightly distorted by a diagonal crack left over from the war, when the whole motley costume, baggy, slashed, and hung with bells came to light, making my son Kurt laugh so hard that he couldn't stop coughing, I said to myself softly and none too happily: Now, Oskar, you are Yorick, the fool. But where is the king for you to play the fool to?

In the streetcar that took me to Ratinger Tor, near the Academy, I soon noted that Oskar-Yorick did not bring laughter to the populace – all these cowboys and Spanish dancers trying to forget their tawdry daily occupations. No, I frightened them. They edged away from me, so much so that though the car was jammed, I easily found a seat. Outside the Academy, policemen were wielding genuine billies which had no connection with carnival make-believe.

The art students' ball was jam-packed and still there were crowds trying to get in. The resulting forays with the police were more colorful than bloody.

When Oskar made his bells tinkle, the throng parted like the Red Sea, and a policeman, his eye sharpened by his occupation, perceived my true stature. He looked down, saluted, and swinging his billy escorted me to the cellar festivities. When I arrived, the pot was on the fire but hadn't quite come to a boil.

No one should suppose that an artists' ball is an affair at which artists have themselves a ball. Most of the actual artists, looking rather worried and serious through their carnival paint, were standing behind amusingly decorated but very unstable counters, trying to make a little extra money selling beer, schnaps, champagne, and sausages. The merrymakers, for the most part, were workaday citizens who thought it would be fun, just this once, to carouse and fling money about like artists.

After spending an hour or so on staircases, in nooks and corners, under tables, frightening couples who seemed to be investigating the charms of discomfort, I made friends with two Chinese girls from Lesbos, or should I say Lesbians from China? They were very much wrapped up in one another. Though they left no finger unturned in their mutual dealings, they did not trespass on my more critical zones and offered me a spectacle that was entertaining at times. We drank warm champagne together and at length, with my permission, they made use of my hump, which was sharp and horny at the extremity, for experiments which were crowned with success, once more confirming my thesis that a hump is good luck to women.

In the long run, however, these occupations made me more and more morose. Thoughts plagued me, I began to worry about the political situation; I painted the blockade of Berlin on the table top with champagne and sketched out a picture of the air lift. Contemplating these Chinese girls who couldn't get together, I despaired of the reunification of Germany and did something that is very unlike me. Oskar, in the role of Yorick, began to look for the meaning of life.

When my girl friends could think of nothing more to show me, they began to cry, leaving telltale traces in their oriental make-up. Slashed and baggy and powdered, I stood up, ringing my bells. Two-thirds of me wanted to go home, but the remaining third still hoped for some little carnivalesque experience. It was then that I caught sight of Corporal Lankes, that is, he spoke to me.

Do you remember? We met on the Atlantic Wall during the summer of '44. He had guarded concrete and smoked my master Bebra's cigarettes.

A dense crowd sat necking on the stairs. I tried to squeeze through. I had just lighted up when someone poked me and a corporal from the last war spoke: 'Hi, buddy, can you spare a butt?'

Quite aside from these familiar words, he was costumed in field

447

grey. Small wonder that I recognized him at once. Even so, I should have made no move to revive our acquaintance if the young lady sitting on the corporal and concrete painter's field-grey lap had not been the Muse in person.

Let me speak with the painter first and describe the Muse afterwards. I not only gave him a cigarette, but even lighted it for him, and said as the first cloud of smoke arose: 'Corporal Lankes, do you remember? Bebra's Theater at the Front? Barbaric, mystical, bored?'

A tremor ran through the painter as I addressed him in these terms; he managed to keep a hold on his cigarette, but the Muse fell from his knees. She was hardly more than a child, long-legged and very drunk. I caught her in mid-air and returned her to him. As the two of us, Lankes and Oskar, exchanged reminiscences with a disparaging remark or two for Lieutenant Herzog, whom Lankes called a nut, and a thought for Bebra my master as well as the nuns who had been picking up crabs that day amid the Rommel asparagus, I gazed in amazement at the Muse. She had come as an angel and had on a hat molded from the variety of cardboard that is used for shipping eggs. Despite her drooping wings and far-advanced drunkenness, she still exerted the some what artsy-craftsy charm of a dweller in heaven.

'This here is Ulla,' Lankes informed me. 'She studied to be a dressmaker, but now she wants to be an artist, but I say to hell with it, with dressmaking she can bring in some dough.'

Oskar, who made a good living on art, offered forthwith to introduce Ulla to the painters at the Academy, who would be sure to take her on as a model and Muse. Lankes was so delighted with my proposal that he helped himself to three cigarettes at once, but in return asked me to come see his studio if I didn't mind paying the taxi fare.

Off we rode, leaving the carnival behind us. I paid the fare, and Lankes, on his alcohol stove, made us some coffee that revived the Muse. Once she had relieved the weight on her stomach with the help of my right forefinger, she seemed almost sober.

Only then did I see the look of wonderment in her light-blue eyes and hear her voice, which was a little birdlike, a little tinny perhaps, but touching in its way and not without charm. Lankes submitted my proposal that she should pose at the Academy, putting it more as an order than as a suggestion. At first she refused; she wished to be neither a Muse nor a model for other painters, but to belong to Lankes alone.

Thereupon he, as talented painters sometimes do, gave her a resounding slap in the face; then he asked her again and chuckled with satisfaction when, weeping just as angels would weep, she professed her willingness to become the well-paid model and maybe even the Muse of the painters at the Academy.

It must be borne in mind that Ulla measures roughly five feet ten; she is exceedingly slender, lithe, and fragile, reminding one of Botticelli, Cranach, or both. We posed together in the nude. Lobster meat has just about the color of her long smooth flesh, which is covered by a light childlike down. The hair on her head is perhaps a trifle thin, but long and straw-blonde. Her pubic hair is reddish and curly, restricted to a small triangle. Ulla shaves under her arms regularly once a week.

As one might have expected, the run-of-the-mill students couldn't do much with us, they made her arms too long, my head too big, and were unable to squeeze us into any known format. It was only when Ziege and Raskolnikov discovered us that pictures worthy of Oskar and the Muse came into being. She asleep, I startling her awake: faun and nymph.

I sitting; she, with small, always slightly shivering breasts, leaning over me, stroking my hair: Beauty and the beast.

She lying, I between her legs, playing with the mask of a horned horse: The lady with the unicorn.

All this in the style of Ziege or Raskolnikov; color or delicate grey tones laid on with a fine brush (Raskolnikov) or with the impetuous palette knife of genius (Ziege). Some of these paintings carried an intimation of the mystery surrounding Ulla and Oskar; they were the work of Raskolnikov, who, with our help, found his way to surrealism: Oskar's face became a honey-yellow dial like that of our grandfather clock; in my hump bloomed mechanical roses which Ulla picked; Ulla, smiling on one end and long-legged on the other, was cut open in the middle and inside sat Oskar between her spleen and liver, turning over the pages of a picture book. Sometimes they put us in costume, turning Ulla into a Columbine and me into a mournful mime covered with white grease paint. It was Raskolnikov – so nicknamed because

449

he never stopped talking of crime and punishment, guilt and atonement – who turned out the masterpiece: I sitting on Ulla's milk-white, naked thigh, a crippled child – she was the Madonna, while I sat still for Jesus.

This painting, entitled 'Madonna 49', was shown at a number of exhibitions; it also proved effective as a poster, which came to the eyes of my ever so respectable Maria and brought on a domestic quarrel. However, it was purchased for a considerable sum by a Rhenish industrialist and today it is hanging in the boardroom of a big business firm, influencing the board of directors.

I was amused by the ingenious monstrosities perpetrated on the basis of my hump and proportions. Ulla and I were in great demand, and received two marks fifty each for posing together. Ulla was delighted with her new career. Now that she was bringing in a regular income, the horny-handed Lankes treated her better and beat her only when his own abstractions demanded an angry mood. He could make no use of her as a model, but for him too she was a kind of Muse, for it was only by boxing her ears that his hand could achieve its true creative power.

I too was fired to acts of violence by Ulla's plaintive fragility, which was actually the indestructibility of an angel; however, I kept myself under control, and whenever the desire to whip her became too strong, I took her out to a pastry shop. Or else, with a certain dandyism inspired by my association with artists, I would exhibit her as a rare plant, highlighted by the contrast with my own proportions, on the busy Königs-Allee, where we would be much gaped at. Or as a last resort I would buy her lavender stockings and pink gloves.

It was a different story with Raskolnikov, who, without ever touching her, kept up the most intimate relations with her. He would have her pose sitting down, her legs far apart. On such occasions he did not paint. He would settle himself on a stool a few steps away, stare at her private parts, and talk, in a hoarse, impassioned whisper, of guilt and atonement. The Muse's private parts became moist and distended, and after a while Raskolnikov, by dint of looking and listening to himself, would experience exultation and release. Thereupon, he would jump up from his stool and belabor the 'Madonna 49' on his easel with grandiose brushstrokes.

Sometimes Raskolnikov stared at me as well, but for other reasons. It seemed to him that I lacked something. He spoke of a vacuum between my fingers and kept putting one object after another – what with his surrealist imagination he was never at a loss for an object – into my hands. He armed Oskar with a pistol, made Oskar-Jesus take aim at the Madonna. Or I would hold out an hourglass to her or a mirror which, being convex, would distort her horribly. He made me hold scissors, fishbones, telephone receivers, death's heads, little airplanes, armored cars, steamships, but none of these filled the vacuum. Oskar dreaded the day when the painter would turn up with the object which alone of all objects was made to be held by me. When at length he brought the drum, I cried out: 'No!'

Raskolnikov: 'Take the drum, Oskar. I have seen through you.'

I, trembling: 'Never again. All that is ended.'

He, darkly: 'Nothing is ended, everything returns, guilt, atonement, more guilt.'

I, with my last strength: 'Oskar has atoned, spare him the drum. I'll hold anything you say, anything but a drum.'

I wept when the Muse Ulla bent over me. Blinded with tears, I could not prevent her from kissing me, I could not prevent the Muse from giving me that terrible kiss. All of you who have ever been kissed by the Muse will surely understand that Oskar, once branded by that kiss, was condemned to take back the drum he had rejected years before, the drum he had buried in the sand of Saspe Cemetery.

But I did not drum. I merely posed – but that was plenty – and was painted as Jesus the drummer boy, sitting on the nude left thigh of the Madonna 49.

It was thus that Maria saw me on a poster advertising an art show. Unbeknownst to me, she attended the exhibition and looked at the picture; she must have stood there long and cloud-gathering, for when she spoke of it, she struck me with my son Kurt's school ruler. She, who for some months had been holding down a well-paid job in a luxury delicatessen store, first as a salesgirl, then, thanks to her obvious ability, as cashier, was now an established citizen of West Germany and no longer a black marketing refugee from the East. Thus it was with a certain conviction that she was able to call me a pig, a pimp, a degenerate. She went so far as to shout that she wanted no more of the filthy money I made with my filthy occupations, nor of me either for that matter.

Though Maria soon took back this last remark and only two weeks later was again accepting a considerable share of my modeling fees in return for my board and lodging, I nevertheless decided to stop living with her, her sister Guste, and my son Kurt. My first idea was to go far away, to Hamburg or perhaps to the seashore, but Maria, who had no objection to my moving, persuaded me, with her sister Guste's support, to look for a room not too far away from herself and Kurt, in any case in Düsseldorf.

The Hedgehog

It was only as a subtenant that Oskar learned the art of drumming back the past. It wasn't just the room; the Hedgehog, the coffin warehouse in the court, and Mr. Münzer helped – not to mention Sister Dorothea.

Do you know *Parsifal?* I don't know it very well either. All that has stuck with me is the story about the three drops of blood in the snow. There is truth in that story, because it fits me like a glove. It is probably the story of everyone who has an idea.

I was still a servant of the arts; I let myself be painted in blue, green, and earth tones; I let myself be sketched in charcoal and put in front of backgrounds; in collaboration with the Muse Ulla, I inspired a whole winter semester at the Academy and the following summer semester as well, but already the snow had fallen which was to receive those three drops of blood, the sight of which transfixed me as it had transfixed Parsifal the fool, about whom Oskar the fool knows so little that it costs him no effort at all to identify himself with this same Parsifal.

My image is clumsy but clear enough, I think: the snow is the uniform of a nurse; the red cross, which most nurses, including Sister Dorothea, wear in the middle of the brooch that holds their collar together, was for me the three drops of blood. There I sat and couldn't take my eyes off it.

But before I could sit in the erstwhile bathroom of the Zeidler apartment, I had to go room-hunting. The winter semester was drawing to a close; some of the students, those who were not planning to return after Easter vacation, would be giving up their rooms. My associate, the Muse Ulla, was helpful; she took me to the students' housing office, where they gave me several addresses and a recommendation from the Academy.

Before looking up the addresses, I went to see Korneff the stonecutter at his shop in Bittweg. It was a long time since I had seen him. I was drawn by my fondness for him, but I was also in search of work during the vacation period; I had a few hours of private posing with or without Ulla, but that could hardly be expected to keep me for the next six weeks, and moreover if I was to take a room, I would have to raise the rent.

I found Korneff unchanged – one boil that had not yet come to a head and two that were nearly healed – over a block of Belgian granite that he had roughed out and was now engaged in polishing. We spoke a while; I began to play suggestively with the lettering chisels and looked round for stones that were already cut and polished, waiting for an inscription. Two stones, one of shell lime, the other of Silesian marble, looked as if Korneff had sold them and they were waiting for an expert cutter of inscriptions. I congratulated Korneff on his success in weathering the hard times after the currency reform. Yet even at the time we had drawn comfort from the thought that a currency reform, however vigorous, vital, and optimistic, cannot deter people from dying and ordering tombstones.

Our prediction had been confirmed. Once more people were dying and buying. In addition, moreover, the currency reform had brought new business: butchers were having their fronts and sometimes even the insides of their shops faced with fancy marble; certain banks and department stores were obliged, in order to recapture their old prestige, to have their damaged sandstone and tufa façades repaired and redecorated.

I complimented Korneff on his industry and asked him if he was able to handle all the work. At first he replied evasively, then he admitted that he had sometimes wished he had four hands, and finally he made me a proposition: I could cut inscriptions for him on a half-time basis; he would pay forty-five pfennigs a letter for hollow lettering in limestone, fifty-five in granite and diorite, while for raised lettering he was prepared to pay sixty and seventy-five.

I started right in on a piece of shell lime. Quickly recovering my knack, I cut out: Aloys Küfer, September 3, 1887 – June 10, 1946. I had the thirty-four letters and figures done in just three hours and received fifteen marks and thirty pfennigs on leaving.

This was more than a third of the monthly rent I had decided I could afford. I was determined to pay no more than forty, for Oskar still felt in duty bound to help with the unkeep of the household in Bilk.

The people in the Housing Office had been kind enough to give me four addresses. My first choice was: Zeidler, Jülicher-Strasse 7, because it was near the Academy.

Early in May, a warm, misty day typical of spring in the lower Rhineland, I started out, provided with sufficient cash. Maria had ironed my suit, I looked presentable. Crumbling stucco façade, in front of it a dusty chestnut tree. As Jülicher-Strasse was half in ruins, it would be unrealistic to speak of the house next door or across the street. To the left, a mound of rubble overgrown with grass and dandelions, here and there disclosing part of a rusty T-girder, suggested the previous existence of a four-story building. To the right a partly damaged house had been repaired as far as the third floor. But the builders had apparently run out of funds; the façade of polished, black Swedish granite was cracked in many places and in urgent need of repair. The inscription 'Schornemann, Undertaker' lacked several letters, I don't remember which. Fortunately, the two palm branches incised in the mirror-smooth granite were still intact and helped to give the shop a certain air of piety and respectability.

This enterprise had been in existence for seventy-five years. Its coffin warehouse was in the court, across from my window, and I often found it worth looking at. In good weather I watched as the workmen rolled a coffin or two out of the shed and set them up on sawhorses, to refresh their polish. All of these last dwelling places, as I noted with pleasure, were tapered at the foot end in the old familiar way.

It was Zeidler in person who opened at my ring. Short, squat, breathless, and hedgehoggy, he stood in the doorway; he had on thick glasses and the lower half of his face was hidden beneath a dense shaving lather. He held his shaving brush against his cheek, appeared to be an alcoholic, and sounded like a Westphalian.

'If you don't like the room, don't shilly-shally. I'm shaving and after that I've got to wash my feet.'

Clearly Zeidler didn't stand on ceremony. I took a look at the room. Of course I didn't like it; it was a decommissioned bathroom, half in turquoise tile, half in wallpaper with a convulsive sort of pattern. However, I kept my feelings to myself. Disregarding Zeidler's drying lather and unwashed feet, I asked if the bathtub could be taken out, especially as it had no drainpipe in the first place.

Smiling, Zeidler shook his grey hedgehog's head, and tried in vain to whip up a lather. That was his reply. Thereupon I expressed my willingness to take the room with bathtub for forty marks a month.

We returned to the dimly lighted, tubular corridor, disclosing several partly glassed doors, painted in various colors, and I asked who else lived in the flat.

'Wife and roomers.'

I tapped on a frosted-glass door, hardly a step from the entrance to the flat.

'A nurse,' said Zeidler. 'But it's no skin off *your* nose. You'll never see her. She only comes here to sleep and sometimes she doesn't.'

I am not going to tell you that Oskar trembled at the word 'nurse'. He nodded his head, not daring to ask about the other roomers, but noted the situation of his room with bathtub; it was on the right-tapped side, at the end of the hall.

Zeidler tapped me on the lapel: 'You can cook in your room if you've got an alcohol stove. You can use the kitchen off and on too, for all I care, if the stove isn't too high for you.'

That was his first allusion to Oskar's stature. He gave my recommendation from the Academy a cursory glance; it was signed by Professor Reuser, the director, and seemed to impress him favorably. I agreed to all his do's and don'ts, impressed it on my mind that the kitchen was next to my room on the left, and promised to have my laundry done outside; he was afraid the steam would be bad for the bathroom wallpaper. It was a promise I could make with a clear conscience; Maria had agreed to do my washing.

At this point I should have left, announcing that I was going to get my baggage and fill out the police registration forms. But Oskar did nothing of the sort. He couldn't bear to leave that apartment. For no reason at all, he asked his future landlord to show him the toilet. With his thumb mine host pointed to a plywood door reminiscent of the war and postwar years. When something in Oskar's movements suggested a desire to use it – the toilet, that is – Zeidler, his face itching with crumbling shaving soap, turned on the light.

Once within, I was vexed, for Oskar didn't have to go. However, I waited stubbornly for Oskar to make a little water. In view of my insufficient bladder pressure and also because the wooden seat was too close, I had to be very careful not to wet the seat or the tile floor. Even so, I had to daub a few drops off the worn-down seat with my handkerchief and efface a few unfortunate traces on the tiles with the soles of my shoes.

Zeidler had not taken advantage of my absence to wash the hardened soap from his face. He had preferred to wait in the hallway, perhaps because he had sensed the joker in me. 'Aren't you the funny guy! Using the toilet before you've even signed your lease.'

He approached me with a cold crusty shaving brush, surely planning some silly joke. But he did nothing, just opened the door for me. While Oskar slipped not backward into the stairway, keeping an eye on the Hedgehog as I passed him, observed that the toilet door was situated between the kitchen door and the frosted-glass door behind which a trained nurse sometimes, not always, spent her nights.

When late that afternoon Oskar, with his baggage including the new drum given him by Raskolnikov, the painter of madonnas, returned brandishing the registration form, a freshly shaved Hedgehog, who had meanwhile no doubt washed his feet, led me into the living room.

The living room smelled of cold cigar smoke. Of cigars that had been lighted several times. There was also a smell of carpets, valuable carpets perhaps, which lay in several layers all over the room. It also smelled of old calendars. But I didn't see any calendars, so it must have been the carpets. Strange to say, the comfortable, leather-upholstered chairs had in themselves no smell. This came as a disappointment to me, for Oskar, who had never sat in a leather chair, had so vivid a notion of what leather upholstery must smell like that he suspected this leather of being artificial.

In one of these smooth, unsmelling, and, as I later ascertained, genuine leather chairs, sat Mrs. Zeidler. She had on a grey tailored suit, which fitted her only very approximately. Her skirt had slipped up over her knees, revealing three fingers' breadths of slip. Since she made no move to arrange her clothing and, it seemed to Oskar, had been crying, I did not dare to greet her or to introduce myself in words. My bow was a silent one; in its last stages, it turned back to Zeidler, who had introduced his wife with a motion of his thumb and a slight cough.

The room was large and square. The shadow of the chestnut tree in front of the house made it seem larger and smaller. I left my suitcase and drum near the door and, holding my registration form, approached Zeidler, who was standing near the windows. Oskar did not hear his own steps, for he walked on four carpets – I counted them later – four superimposed carpets of decreasing size which, with their fringed or unfringed edges of different colors, added up to a strange color pattern. The bottom most carpet was reddish-brown and began near the walls; the next, approximately green, was largely hidden by furniture, the heavy sideboard, the china closet filled entirely with liqueur glasses, dozens of them, and the spacious marriage bed. The third carpet was of a blue design and ran from corner to corner. The fourth, a solid claret-color, supported the extensible dining table covered with protective oilcloth, and four leather-upholstered chairs with evenly spaced brass rivets.

Since there were more rugs, hardly intended for that purpose, hanging on the walls, and still others rolled up in the corners, Oskar assumed that the Hedgehog had traded in carpets before the currency reform and been stuck with them afterwards.

The only picture was a glass-covered likeness of Bismarck, hanging on the outer wall between two seemingly oriental rugs. The Hedgehog sat in a leather chair beneath the Iron Chancellor,

457

to whom he showed a certain family resemblance. He took the form from my hand, studied both sides of the official document alertly, critically, and impatiently. His wife asked him in a whisper if anything was wrong. Her question threw him into a fit of rage which made him look still more like the Chancellor. The chair spewed him out. Standing on four carpets, he held the form out to one side and filled himself and his waistcoat with air. With one bound he was on the first and second carpets, looking down on his wife, who had meanwhile taken up her needlework, and pouring forth words on the order of: Whoaskedyoul'dliketoknow? Nobody'sgoingtodoanytalkingaroundherebutmeme! Shutthatmouthofyoursandkeepitshut!

Since Mrs. Zeidler kept her peace and attended unflustered to her sewing, the problem for the Hedgehog, as he treated the carpets, was to let his fury rise and fall with an air of plausibility. A single step took him to the china closet, which he opened with such violence as to call forth a general tinkling. Carefully, each outstretched finger a precision mechanism, he picked up eight liqueur glasses, removed them undamaged from the case, tiptoed – like a host planning to divert himself and seven guests with an exercise in dexterity – toward the green tiled stove, and then, suddenly throwing all caution to the winds, hurled his fragile freight at the cold, cast-iron stove door.

The most amazing part of it was that during this performance, which required a certain accuracy of aim, the Hedgehog kept a bespectacled eye on his wife, who had risen and was trying to thread a needle by the right-hand window. Scarcely a second after his annihilation of the glasses, she carried this delicate operation, which required a steady hand, to a successful conclusion. Then she went back to her chair and sat down, and again her skirt slipped up disclosing three fingers' breadths of pink slip. With a malevolent though submissive look, the Hedgehog had followed his wife's movement to the window, her threading of the needle, her return to the chair. No sooner had she resumed her seat than he reached behind the stove, took up dustpan and brush, swept up the fragments, and poured them into a newspaper, which was already half full of shattered liqueur glasses. There would not have been room for a third outburst.

If the reader should suppose that Oskar recognized his old

glass-shattering self in the glass-shattering Hedgehog, I can only say that the reader is not entirely mistaken; I too once tended to transform my rage into shattered glass – but never in those days did anyone see me resort to dustpan and brush!

Having removed the traces of his wrath, Zeidler sat down again. Once more Oskar handed him the registration form that the Hedgehog had been obliged to drop in order to have both hands free for the liqueur glasses.

Zeidler signed the form and gave me to understand that he expected order to reign in his flat, where would we be if everyone did as he pleased, he was in a position to know, he had been a salesman for fifteen years, sold hair clippers, was I familiar with this article?

Oskar made certain movements from which Zeidler could infer that I was adequately informed on the subject of hair clippers. Zeidler's well-clipped brush suggested confidence in his merchandise, hence effectiveness as a salesman. After he had explained his work schedule – a week on the road, two days at home – he lost interest in Oskar. More hedgehoggy than ever, he sat rocking himself in the squeaky light-brown leather, his eyeglasses sparkled, and with or without reason he muttered: jajajajaja. It was time for me to go.

First Oskar took leave of Mrs. Zeidler. Her hand was cold, boneless, but dry. The Hedgehog from his chair waved me toward the door where Oskar's baggage stood. I already had my hands full when his voice came to me: 'What you got there, tied to your suitcase?'

'That's my drum.'

'You expect to play it here?'

'Not necessarily. There was a time when I played quite a lot.'

'Go ahead as far as I care. I'm never home anyway.'

'It is very unlikely that I shall ever drum again.'

'And what made you stay so little?'

'An unfortunate accident hampered my growth.'

'Well, I only hope you don't give us any trouble, fits and that kind of thing.'

'The state of my health has improved steadily in the last few years. See how nimble I am.' Thereupon Oskar, for the benefit of the Zeidlers, did a few flips and semi-acrobatic exercises he had learned in his theatrical period. Mrs. Zeidler tittered while Mr. Zeidler assumed the look of a Hedgehog on the point of slapping his thighs. Then I was in the hallway. Past the nurse's frosted-glass door, the toilet door, and the kitchen door, I carried my belongings, including drum, to my room.

This was in the beginning of May. From that day on I was tempted, possessed, overwhelmed by the mystery of the trained nurse. My feeling for nurses is a kind of sickness. Perhaps it is incurable, for even today, with all that far behind me, I contradict Bruno my keeper when he says that only men can be proper nurses, that a patient's desire to be cared for by lady nurses is just one more symptom of his disease. Whereas, still according to Bruno, your male nurse takes conscientious care of his patient and sometimes cures him, his female counterpart, woman that she is, beguiles the patient, sometimes into recovery, sometimes into a death pleasantly seasoned with eroticism.

So speaks Bruno my keeper. Perhaps he is right, but I should be very reluctant to admit it. One who has been brought back to life every two or three years by lady nurses cannot help being grateful; he is not going to allow any grumpy old male nurse, however likable, to sully my image of my beloved lady nurses, especially as his one and only motive is professional jealousy.

It began with my fall down the cellar steps on the occasion of my third birthday. I think she was called Sister Lotte and came from Praust. Dr. Hollatz' Sister Inge was with me for several years. After the defense of the Polish Post Office, I fell into the hands of several nurses at once. I remember only one of them by name: Sister Erni or Berni. Nameless nurses in Lüneburg, then at the University Clinic in Hanover. Then the nurses at the City Hospital in Düsseldorf, first and foremost Sister Gertrude. And then, without my having to go to any hospital, She came. In the best of health, Oskar succumbed to a nurse who was a roomer in the Zeidler flat. From that day on my world was full of nurses.

When I went to work in the early morning, to cut inscriptions at Korneff's, my streetcar stop was named: Marien-Hospital. Outside the brick gateway and in the flower-choked grounds, nurses came and went, on their way to and from work. I often found myself riding in the same trailer car, on the same platform with several of these exhausted, or at least weary-looking nurses. At first I breathed in their scent with repugnance, soon I sought it out, stationed myself as near as possible to their uniforms.

Then Bittweg. In good weather I worked outside amid the display of tombstones and saw them passing arm in arm, two by two, four by four, on their hour off, compelling Oskar to look up from his granite, to neglect his work, for every upward look cost me twenty pfennigs.

Movie posters: the Germans have always been addicted to films about nurses. Maria Schell lured me to the movies. She wore a nurse's uniform, laughed and wept; her days were full of self-sacrifice; smiling and still wearing her nurse's cap, she played somber music. Later on, in a fit of despair, she came very close to tearing her nightgown. But after her attempted suicide she sacrificed her love – Borsche as the doctor – remained true to her profession, and retained her cap and Red Cross pin. While Oskar's conscious mind laughed and wore an endless chain of obscenities into the film, Oskar's eyes wept tears, I wandered about half-blind in a desert of white-clad anonymous lady Samaritans, searching for Sister Dorothea, who – and that was all I knew about her – rented the room behind the frosted-glass door in the Zeidler flat.

Sometimes I heard her steps as she came home from night duty. I also heard her toward nine o'clock at night, after the day shift. Oskar did not always remain seated in his chair when he heard her in the hall. Quite often he played with his doorknob. Who could have resisted? Who does not look up at the passage of something which is passing perhaps for him? Who can sit still in his chair when every nearby sound seems to serve the sole purpose of making him jump up?

Still worse is the silence. We have seen the power of silence in connection with the female figurehead, wooden, silent, and passive. There lay the first museum attendant in his blood. And everyone said Niobe had killed him. The director looked for a new attendant, for the museum had to be kept open. When the second attendant was dead, everyone screamed that Niobe had killed him. The museum director had difficulty in finding a third attendant – or was it already the eleventh he was looking for? One day, in any case, this attendant it had been so hard to find was dead. And everyone screamed: Niobe, Niobe of the green paint and amber eyes; wooden Niobe, naked, unbreathing, unsweating, untrembling, suffering neither heat nor cold; Niobe, wormless because, what with her historical value, she had been sprayed against worms. A witch was burned on her account, the woodcarver's hand was cut off, ships sank, but she floated, she survived. Niobe was wooden but fireproof, Niobe killed and remained valuable. Schoolboys, students, an elderly priest, and a bevy of museum attendants all fell prey to her silence. My friend Herbert Truczinski jumped her and died; but Niobe, still dry, only increased in silence.

When the nurse left her room, the hallway, and the Hedgehog's apartment early in the morning, at about six o'clock, it became very still, though when present she had never made any noise. Unable to stand the silence, Oskar had to coax a squeak or two from his bed, move a chair, or roll an apple in the direction of the bathtub.

Toward eight o'clock a rustling. That was the postman dropping letters and postcards through the slit in the outer door. Not only Oskar, but Mrs. Zeidler as well had been waiting for that sound. She was a secretary at the offices of the Mannesmann Company and didn't go to work until nine o'clock. She let me go first; it was Oskar who first looked into the rustling. I moved quietly though I knew she could hear me just the same, and left my room door open in order not to have to switch on the light. I picked up all the mail at once. Regularly once a week there was a letter from Maria, giving a complete account of herself, the child, and her sister Guste. Having secreted it in my pajama pocket, I would look quickly through the rest of the mail. Everything addressed to the Zeidlers or to a certain Mr. Münzer who lived at the end of the hallway, I would replace on the floor. As for Sister Dorothea's mail, I would turn it over, smell it, feel it, and examine the return address.

Sister Dorothea received more mail than I, but not very much. Her full name was Dorothea Köngetter; but I called her only Sister Dorothea and occasionally forgot her last name — what, indeed, does a trained nurse need a last name for? She received letters from her mother in Hildesheim. There were also postcards from all over West Germany, most of them with pictures of ivy-covered hospitals, written by nurses she had known at training school, obviously in reply to Sister Dorothea's halting efforts to keep up with her old friends.

Nearly all these communications, as Oskar soon found out, were quite rapid and unrevealing. Nevertheless, they threw some light on Sister Dorothea's past; she had worked at the Vinzent-Hospital in Cologne, at a private clinic in Aachen, and in Hildesheim, where her mother was still living. It could be inferred either that she was from Lower Saxony or that like Oskar she was a refugee from the East and had settled there after the war. I also found out that Sister Dorothea was working nearby, at the Marien-Hospital, that she had a close friend by the name of Beata, for the postcards were full of references to, and regards for, this Sister Beata.

The existence of a girl friend gave me wild ideas. I composed letters to Beata, in one I asked her to intercede for me, in the next I said nothing about Dorothea, my idea being to approach Beata first and switch to Dorothea later on. I drafted five or six letters and even addressed one or two; several times I started for the mailbox, but none was ever sent.

Yet perhaps, in my madness, I would actually have mailed one of these pleas to Sister Beata had I not – one Monday it was, the day Maria started up with Mr. Stenzel, her boss, an occurrence that left me surprisingly cold – found on the floor, below the letter slot, the missive which transformed my passion from love to jealous love.

The name and address printed on the envelope told me that the letter had been written by a Dr. Erich Werner at the Marien-Hospital. On Tuesday a second letter came. Thursday brought a third. What shall I say of my state of mind on that Thursday? Oskar tottered back to his room, fell on one of the kitchen chairs which helped to turn my bathroom into a place of residence, and drew Maria's weekly letter from his pajama pocket – in spite of her love affair Maria continued to write punctually, neatly, and exhaustively. Oskar even tore open the envelope and gazed at the letter with sightless eyes; he heard Mrs. Zeidler in the hall, calling Mr. Münzer, who did not answer. But Münzer must have been in, for Mrs. Zeidler opened his room door, handed in the mail, and kept on talking to him.

Mrs. Zeidler was still talking but I could no longer hear her. I surrendered myself to the madness of the wallpaper, the vertical, horizontal, diagonal madness, the curved madness, reproduced a thousandfold; I saw myself as Matzerath, eating the alarmingly nutritious bread of cuckolds; and no shame or scruple deterred me from representing my Jan Bronski as a seducer in Satanic make-up, clad by turns in the traditional overcoat with velvet collar, in Dr. Hollatz' white smock, and in the equally white smock of Dr. Werner, in every case seducing, corrupting, desecrating, insulting, scourging, and torturing, in short, doing everything a seducer has to do if he is to be plausible.

Today I can smile when I recall the idea which then turned Oskar as yellow and mad as the wallpaper: I decided to study medicine. I would graduate in no time. I would become a doctor, at the Marien-Hospital, of course. I would expose Dr. Werner, demonstrate his incompetence, nay more, prove that his criminal negligence had been responsible for the death of a patient in the course of a larynx operation. It would turn out that this Mr. Werner had never attended medical school. He had picked up a smattering of medicine while working as an orderly in a field hospital during the war. Off to jail with the charlatan. And Oskar, despite his youth, becomes head physician. A new Professor Sauerbruch, with Sister Dorothea at his side, followed by a white-clad retinue, strides down resounding corridors, visits his patients, decides at the last minute to operate. How fortunate that this film was never made!

In the Clothes Cupboard

It should not be supposed that Oskar's whole life was taken up with nurses. After all, I had my professional occupations. I had to give up cutting inscriptions, the summer semester at the Academy had begun. Once again Ulla and I received good money for sitting still while art students, employing methods old or new, subjected us to their vision or blindness. There were many who destroyed our objective existence, rejected and negated us, covering paper and canvas with lines, rectangles, spirals, producing wallpaper designs which had everything in them but Oskar and Ulla, or mystery and tension if you will, and giving these absurdities high-sounding titles such as: 'Plaited Upward,' 'Hymn above Time', 'Red in New Spaces'.

This manner was particularly favored by the younger students who had not yet learned to draw. We fared better at the hands of my old friends from the studios of Kuchen and Maruhn, not to mention the prize students Ziege and Raskolnikov.

In her earthly existence the Muse Ulla revealed a marked taste for applied art. Lankes had left her but in her enthusiasm for the new wallpaper designs she soon forgot him and convinced herself that the decorative abstractions of a middle-aged painter named Meitel were sweet, amusing, cute, fantastic, terrific, and even chic. Meitel had a special fondness for forms suggesting sugary-syrupy Easter eggs, but that is hardly worth mentioning; since then she has found many other occasions to become engaged and at the present moment – as she informed me when she came to see me the day before yesterday, with candy for me and Bruno – is on the point of entering upon a serious and lasting relationship, as she has always put it.

At the beginning of the semester, Ulla wanted to pose only for the 'new trends' – a flea that Meiter, her Easter egg painter, had put in her ear; his engagement present to her had been a vocabulary which she tried out in conversations with me. She spoke of relationships, constellations, accents, perspectives, granular structures, processes of fusion, phenomena of erosion. She, whose daily fare consisted exclusively of bananas and tomato juice, spoke of proto-cells, color atoms which in their dynamic flat trajectories found their natural positions in their fields of forces, but did not stop there; no, they went on and on . . . This was the tone of her conversation with me during our rest periods or when we went out for an occasional cup of coffee in Ratinger-Strasse. Even when her engagement to the dynamic painter of Easter eggs had ceased to be, even when after a brief episode with a Lesbian she took up with one of Kuchen's students and returned to the objective world, she retained this vocabulary which so strained her little face that two sharp, rather fanatical creases formed on either side of her mouth.

Here I must admit that it was not entirely Raskolnikov's idea to dress the Muse Ulla as a nurse and paint her with Oskar. After the 'Madonna 49' he put us into 'The Abduction of Europa' – I was the bull. And immediately after the rather controversial 'Abduction' came 'Fool Heals Nurse'.

It was a little word of mine that fired Raskolnikov's imagination. Somber, red-haired, and crafty, he cleaned his brushes and brooded; staring fixedly at Ulla, he began to speak of guilt and atonement. At this I advised him to picture me as guilt, Ulla as atonement; my guilt, I said, was patent; as for Atonement, why not dress her as a nurse?

If this excellent picture later bore another, misleadingly different title, it was Raskolnikov's doing. I myself should have called it 'Temptation', because my right, painted hand was gripping and turning a doorknob, opening the door to a room where The Nurse is standing. Or it might have been called 'The Doorknob', for if I were asked to think up a new name for temptation, I should recommend the word 'doorknob', because what are these protuberances put on doors for if not to tempt us, because the doorknob on the frosted-glass door of Sister Dorothea's room was to me temptation itself whenever I knew that Hedgehog Zeidler was on the road, Sister Dorothea at the hospital, and Mrs. Zeidler in the office at Mannesmann's.

Oskar would emerge from his room with the drainless bathtub, cross the hallway, approach the nurse's room, and grip the doorknob.

Until about the middle of June – and I made the experiment almost every day – the door had resisted my temptation. I was beginning to think that Sister Dorothea's work had just made her too orderly in her ways, that I might as well give up hope of her ever neglecting to lock it. And that is why, when one day the door opened under my pressure, my dull-witted, mechanical reaction was close it again.

For several minutes Oskar stood there in a very tight skin, a prey to so many thoughts of the most divergent origins that his heart had difficulty in imposing any sort of arrangement upon them.

It was only after I had transferred my thoughts to another context – Maria and her lover, I thought; Maria has a lover, lover gives her a coffee pot, lover and Maria go to the Apollo on

Saturday night, Maria addresses lover as Mr. So-and-So during working hours, he is her boss, owner of the store where she works – only after I had thus considered Maria and her lover from various angles, that I managed to create a little order in my poor brain . . . and opened the frosted-glass door.

I had already figured out that the room must be windowless, for never had the upper, dimly transparent part of the door revealed the slightest trace of daylight. Reaching to the right, exactly as in my own room, I found the switch. The forty-watt bulb was quite sufficient for this cubbyhole which hardly deserved to be called a room. I was rather distressed to find myself face to face with my bust in the mirror. Though his reverse image had nothing to tell him, Oskar did not move away; he was too fascinated by the objects on the dressing table in front of the mirror.

There were blue-black spots in the white enamel of the washbasin. The table top in which the washbasin was sunk almost to the rim also had blemishes. The left corner was missing and the missing piece lay on the table top under the mirror, showing the mirror its veins. Traces of peeling glue on the broken edge bore witness to a bungled attempt to repair the damage. My stonecutter's fingers itched. I thought of Korneff's homemade marble cement, which transformed even the most dilapidated marble into enduring slabs fit to adorn the façades of large butcher stores.

Once these familiar thoughts had diverted me from my cruelly distorted image in the mirror, I was able to give the smell that had struck me the moment I came in a name.

It was vinegar. Later, and again only a few weeks ago, I justified that acrid smell by the assumption that Sister Dorothea must have washed her hair the day before and had put vinegar in the rinse water. However, there was no vinegar bottle on the dressing table. Nor did I detect vinegar in any of the containers otherwise labeled; moreover, I have often said to myself, would Sister Dorothea be likely to heat water in the Zeidler kitcher, for which she would have required Zeidler's permission, and go through the bother of washing her hair in her room, when the hospital is full of the best showers and bathrooms? Yet possibly the head nurse or the hospital management had forbidden the nurses to use certain sanitary installations in the hospital; perhaps Sister Dorothea actually was obliged to wash her hair in this enamel bowl, in front of this deceitful mirror.

Though there was no vinegar bottle on the table, there were plenty of other bottles and jars on the clammy marble. A package of cotton and a half-empty package of sanitary napkins discouraged Oskar from investigating the contents of the little jars. But I am still of the opinion that they contained nothing but routine cosmetics or harmless medicinal ointments.

Sister Dorothea had left her comb in her brush. It cost me a struggle to pull it out and take a good look at it. How fortunate that I did so, for in that instant Oskar made his important discovery; the nurse's hair was blonde, perhaps ashblonde, but one cannot be too suspicious of conclusions drawn from the dead hair that comes out in a comb. Suffice it to say that Sister Dorothea had blonde hair.

In addition, the alarmingly abundant contents of the comb told me that Sister Dorothea suffered from falling hair, an ailment that must have distressed her. It's the fault of her nurse's caps, I said to myself; but I did not condemn them, for how can a hospital be run properly without nurses' caps?

Distasteful as the vinegar smell was to Oskar, the only sentiment aroused in me by the thought that Sister Dorothea was losing her hair was love, seasoned with solicitude and compassion. It is characteristic of the state I was in that I thought of several hair lotions I had heard recommended and resolved to supply Sister Dorothea with one or more of them at the first opportunity. Dreaming of our first meeting, which would take place beneath a warm summer sky, amid fields of waving grain, I plucked the homeless hairs from the comb and arranged them in a bundle, which I secured by tying a knot in it. I blew off some of the dust and dandruff and carefully secreted my treasure in a compartment of my wallet from which I had quickly removed its previous contents.

Having stowed my wallet in my jacket, I picked up the comb, which I had laid down on the table top for want of hands. I held it up to the naked light bulb, making it transparent, examined the two rows of prongs, coarse and fine, and noted that two of the finer prongs were missing. I could not resist the temptation to run the nail of my left forefinger over the tips of the coarse prongs, and while thus playing Oskar was gladdened by the glitter of a few hairs which, to avert suspicion, I had intentionally neglected to remove.

At length I dropped the comb back into the brush and left the dressing table, which, it seemed to me, was giving me an unbalanced picture. On my way to Sister Dorothea's bed I bumped into a chair on which hung a brassiere – much washed, I noted, and faded at the edges.

Oskar had nothing but his fists with which to fill the two concavities. They were inadequate. Too hard, too nervous, they were alien and unhappy in these bowls which in my ignorance of their contents I should gladly have lapped up with a teaspoon day after day; I might have experienced a little nausea now and then, for too much of any fare will unsettle the stomach, but after nausea sweetness, such sweetness as to make nausea desirable, the seal of true love.

I thought of Dr. Werner and took my fists out of the brassiere. But then Dr. Werner vanished and I was able to approach Sister Dorothea's bed. So this was her bed! How often Oskar had tried to visualize it, and now it was the same hideous wooden structure, painted brown, that served as a setting for my own repose and occasional insomnia. What I should have wished for her was a white-enameled metal bed with brass knobs, a light, immaterial frame, and not this cumbersome and loveless object. Immobile, with heavy head, devoid of passion, incapable even of jealousy, I stood for a time gazing at this altar of sleep – the comforter, it seemed to me, must be granite. Then I turned away from the loathsome sight. Never could Oskar have visualized Sister Dorothea and her slumbers in this repulsive tomb.

I started back toward the dressing table, planning perhaps to open the presumed ointment jars. On my way, the clothes cupboard commanded me to note its dimensions, to qualify its paint as black-brown, to follow the contours of its molding, and at last to open it; for where is the cupboard that does not demand to be opened?

There was no lock, the doors were held together by a bent nail; I turned it to a vertical position and at once, with no help from me, the doors swung apart with a sigh, offering me so wide a vista that I had to step backward to take it all in. Oskar didn't want to lose himself in details as he had at the dressing table; nor did he wish, as in the case of the bed, to let prejudice pass judgment; no, he was determined to give himself to that cupboard, which opened out its arms to him, with the freshness of the first day of Creation.

Nevertheless Oskar, the incorrigible esthete, could not refrain entirely from criticism: some barbarian had hurriedly sawed off the legs, tearing splinters out of the wood, and set the disfigured cupboard down flat on the floor.

The inside was in the best of order. On the right there were three deep shelves piled with undergarments and blouses; white, pink, and a light blue which Oskar felt certain would not discolor. Two red and green oilcloth bags hung inside the right-hand door, one containing stockings with runs, the other stockings Sister Dorothea had mended. These stockings, it seemed to me, were equal in quality to those that Maria's employer and boy friend had given her, but of closer weave and more durable. To the left hung starched, gleaming white nurse's uniforms. In the hat compartment on top, in beauty and simplicity, sat the fragile nurse's caps, fearing the touch of any unpracticed hand. I cast only a brief glance at the civilian clothes to the left of the under-garments. The cheap, haphazard assortment confirmed my secret hope: Sister Dorothea was not deeply interested in this depart-ment of her clothing. And the same impression was conveyed by the three or four pot-shaped hats with imitation flowers, which, tossed negligently in a heap beside the caps, suggested nothing so much as an unsuccessful cake. The hat compartment also contained ten or a dozen books with colored backs, leaning on a shoe box filled with wool left over from knitting.

Oskar had to step closer and tilt his head in order to read the titles. It was with an indulgent smile that my head resumed a vertical position: so our good Sister Dorothea read crime novels. But I have said enough about the civilian section of the cupboard. Lured closer by the books, I did not retreat; quite on the contrary, I stuck my head in the cupboard and ceased to resist my mounting desire to belong to it, to become a part of the clothes cupboard where Sister Dorothea kept a not inappreciable part of her visible presence.

I didn't even have to move the sensible low-heeled shoes that stood on the cupboard floor, meticulously polished and waiting to go out. As though to invite me in, the contents of the cupboard were so arranged that Oskar was able, without crushing a single garment, to take shelter in the middle of it. Full of anticipation, I crawled in and squatted on my heels.

At first, however, my mind was not at rest. Oskar felt himself observed by the furniture and the light bulb. Wishing to make my sojourn in the cupboard more intimate, I tried to pull the doors shut. It was none too easy, the catch was worn out, the doors refused to close properly. Light still entered, but not enough to disturb me. The smell became more concentrated. An old-fashioned, clean smell, no longer of vinegar, but of some mild moth deterrent; a good smell.

What did Oskar do as he sat in the cupboard? He leaned his forehead against Sister Dorothea's nearest uniform, which opened the door to every aspect of life. My left hand, perhaps in search of something for me to lean on, reached backward, past the civilian clothes, went astray, lost its hold, shot out, gripped something smooth and flexible, and finally – still holding the smoothness – found a horizontal strut, intended to support the rear wall of the cupboard, but willing to do the same for me. My hand was free, I brought it forward and showed myself what I had found behind me.

I saw a black leather belt, but instantly I saw more than the belt because it was so grey in the cupboard that a patent-leather belt could easily be something else. It might just as well have been something different, something just as smooth and long, something I had seen as an incorrigible three-year-old drummer on the harbor breakwater at Neufahrwasser: my poor mama in her light-blue spring coat with the raspberry-colored facings, Matzerath in his brown overcoat, Jan Bronski with his velvet collar, Oskar in his sailor hat with the gold-embroidered inscription 's.m.s. *Seydlitz*'; ulster and velvet collar jumped on ahead of me and Mama, who because of her high heels could not jump from stone to stone as far as the beacon, at the foot of which sat the longshoreman with the clothesline and the potato sack full of salt and movement. At the sight of the sack and clothesline, we asked the man under the beacon why he was fishing with a clothesline, but this fellow from Neufahrwasser or Brösen just laughed and spat out viscous brown juice, which bobbed up and down in the water beside the breakwater and didn't stir from the spot until a seagull carried it away; for a seagull will pick up anything under the sun, it's not one of your picky-and-choosy doves, nor is it by any stretch of the imagination a nurse – wouldn't it be just too simple if you could lump everything white under one head and toss it into a cupboard? And the same goes for black, for in those days I was not yet afraid of the wicked black Witch, I sat fearless in the cupboard and then again not in the cupboard, but equally fearless on the breakwater in Neufahrwasser, in the one case holding a patent-leather belt, in the other something else, which was also black and slippery but not a belt. Because I was in the cupboard, I cast about for a comparison, for cupboards force comparisons, called the wicked black Witch by name, but at that time she meant little to me, I was farther gone on the subject of white, scarcely able to distinguish between a gull and Sister Dorothea. Nevertheless, I expelled doves, pigeons, and all such rot from my thoughts, all the more readily as it wasn't Pentecost but Good Friday when we rode out to Brösen and continued on to the breakwater – besides, there were no pigeons over the breakwater where this fellow from Neufahrwasser was sitting with his clothesline, sitting and spitting. And when the longshoreman from Brösen pulled the line in until the line stopped and showed why it had been so hard to pull it out of the brackish waters of the Mottlau, when my poor mama laid her hand on Jan Bronski's shoulder and velvet collar, because her face was as green as green cheese, because she wanted to go away but had to look on as this longshoreman flung the horse's head down on the stones, as the smaller, sea-green eels fell out of the mane and he pulled the larger, darker-ones out of the cadaver. Someone ripped open a featherbed which is just a way of saying that the gulls swooped down and set to, because gulls, when there are three or more of them, can easily finish off a small eel, though they have a bit of trouble with the bigger fellows. The longshoreman wrenched open the horse's mouth, forced a piece of wood between the teeth, which made the horse laugh, and reached in with his hairy arm, groped and reached some more, like me in the cupboard, and extracted, as I in the cupboard had extracted the patent-leather belt, two eels at once.

He swung them through the air and dashed them against the stones, until my poor mama's face disgorged her whole breakfast, consisting of café au lait, egg white and egg yolk, a bit of jam, and a few lumps of white bread. So copious was that breakfast that in an instant the gulls had assumed an oblique position, come a story lower, and fallen to – I won't even mention the screams, and that gulls have wicked eyes is generally known. They wouldn't be driven off, not in any case by Jan Bronski, for he was scared stiff of gulls and held both hands before his frantic blue eyes. They wouldn't even pay any attention to my drum, but gobbled, while I with fury, but also with enthusiasm, created many a new rhythm on my drum. But to my poor mama it was all one, she was too busy; she gagged and gagged, but nothing more would come up, she hadn't eaten so very much, for my mama was trying to lose weight and did gymnastics twice a week at the Women's Association, but it didn't help because she kept eating in secret and always found some little loophole in her resolutions. As for the man from Neufahrwasser, when all present thought it was over, there could be no more, he, in defiance of all theory, pulled one last eel out of the horse's ear. It was all full of white porridge, it had been exploring the horse's brains. But the longshoreman swung it about until the porridge fell off, until the eel showed its varnish and glittered like a patent-leather belt. What I am trying to get at is that Sister Dorothea wore just such a belt when she went out in civvies, without her Red Cross pin.

We started homeward although Matzerath wanted to stay on because a Finnish ship of some eighteen hundred tons was putting into port and making waves. The longshoreman left the horse's head on the breakwater. A moment later the horse turned white and screamed. But he didn't scream like a horse, he screamed more like a cloud that is white and voracious and descends on a horse's head. Which was all to the good, because now the horse was hidden from sight, though one could imagine what was at the bottom of that white frenzy. The Finn diverted us too; he was as rusty as the fence in Saspe Cemetery and was carrying timber. But my poor mama turned to look neither at the Finn nor the gulls. She was done in. Though formerly she had not only played 'Fly, little seagull, fly away to Heligoland' on our piano, but sung it as well, she never sang that song again or anything else for that matter; at first she wouldn't eat any more fish, but suddenly she began to eat so much fish, such big fish and fat fish, that one day she couldn't, wouldn't eat any more, that she was sick of it, sick of eels and sick of life, especially of men, perhaps also of Oskar, in any case she, who had never been able to forgo anything, became frugal and abstemious and had herself buried in Brenntau. I have inherited this combination of self-indulgence and frugality. I want everything but there's nothing I cannot do without – except for smoked eels; whatever the price, I can't live without them. And another such exception was Sister Dorothea, whom I had never seen, whose patent-leather belt I was not really wild about – and yet I could not tear myself away from it, it was endless, it multiplied, and with my free hand I unbuttoned my trousers in order to reclarify my image of Sister Dorothea, which had been blurred by the Finnish merchantman and those innumerable varnished eels.

Finally Oskar, with the help of the gulls, managed to shake off his obsession with the breakwater and rediscover Sister Dorothea's world amid her empty, yet winsome uniforms. But when at last I could see her before me and distinguish certain of her features, suddenly, with a screech and a whine, the cupboard doors swung open; the bright light upset me, and it cost me an effort not to soil the smock that hung closest to me.

Only in order to create a transition, to relax the tension of my stay in the cupboard, which had been more strenuous than I had expected, I did something I had not done for years; I drummed a few measures, nothing very brilliant, on the dry rear wall of the cupboard. Then I emerged, checked once more for neatness; I had created no disorder, even the patent-leather belt had preserved its sheen, no, there were a few dull spots that had to be breathed on and rubbed before the belt became once again an object capable of suggesting eels that were caught many years before on the harbor breakwater at Neufahrwasser.

I, Oskar, cut off the current from the forty-watt bulb that had watched me throughout my visit and left Sister Dorothea's room.

Klepp

There I was in the hallway with a bundle of pale blonde hair in my pocket book. For a second I tried to feel the hair through the leather, through the lining of my jacket, through my waistcoat, shirt, and undershirt; but I was too weary, too satisfied in a strangely morose way to look upon my treasure as anything more than leavings found on a comb.

Only then did Oskar own to himself that he had been looking for treasures of a very different kind. What I had really wanted was to demonstrate the presence of Dr. Werner somewhere in Sister Dorothea's room, if only by finding a letter or one of those envelopes I knew so well. I found nothing. Not so much as an envelope, let alone a sheet of paper with writing on it. Oskar owns that he removed the crime novels, one by one, from the hat compartment and opened them, looking for dedications and bookmarks. I was also looking for a picture, for Oskar knew most of the doctors of the Marien-Hospital by sight though not by name – but there was no photograph of Dr. Werner.

Sister Dorothea's room seemed unknown to Dr. Werner, and if he had ever seen it, he had not succeeded in leaving any traces. Oskar had every reason to be pleased. Didn't I have a considerable advantage over the doctor? Wasn't the absence of any trace of him proof positive that the relations between doctor and nurse were confined to the hospital, hence purely professional, and that if there was anything personal about them, it was unilateral?

Nevertheless, Oskar's jealousy clamored for a motive. Though the slightest sign of Dr. Werner would have come as a blow to me, it would at the same time have given me a satisfaction incommensurable with my brief little adventure in the cupboard.

I don't remember how I made my way back to my room, I do recall hearing a mock cough, calculated to attract attention, behind Mr. Münzer's door at the end of the hall. What was this Mr. Münzer to me? Didn't I have my hands full with Sister Dorothea? Was it any time to burden myself with this Münzer –

475

who knows what the name might conceal? And so Oskar failed to hear the inviting cough, or rather, I failed to understand what was wanted of me, and realized only after I was back in my room that this Mr. Münzer, this total stranger who meant nothing to me, had coughed in order to lure Oskar to his room.

I admit it: for a long while I was sorry I had not reacted to that cough, for my room seemed so cramped and at the same time so enormous that a conversation, even of the most force and tedious kind, with the coughing Mr. Münzer would have done me good. But I could not summon up the courage to establish a delayed contact – I might, for instance, have gone out into the corridor and given an answering cough – with the gentleman behind the door at the end of the hallway. I surrendered passively to the unyielding angularity of my kitchen chair, grew restless as I always do when sitting in chairs, took up a medical reference book from the bed, dropped the expensive tome I had spent my good money on in a disorderly heap, and picked up Raskolnikov's present, the drum, from the table. I held it, but neither could I take the sticks to it nor was Oskar able to burst into tears that would have fallen on the round white lacquer and brought me a rhythmical relief.

Here I could embark on an essay about lost innocence, a comparison between two Oskars, the permanently three-year-old drummer and the voiceless, tearless, drumless hunchback. But that would be an oversimplification and would not do justice to the facts: even in his drumming days, Oskar lost his innocence more than once and recovered it or waited for it to grow in again; for innocence is comparable to a luxuriant weed – just think of all the innocent grandmothers who were once loathsome, spiteful infants – no, it was not any absurd reflections about innocence and lost innocence that made Oskar jump up from the kitchen chair: no, it was my love for Sister Dorothea that commanded me to replace the drum undrummed, to leave room, hallway, and flat, and hasten to the Academy although my appointment with Professor Kuchen was not until late in the afternoon.

When Oskar left the room with faltering tread, stepped out into the corridor, opened the apartment door as ostentatiously as possible, I listened for a moment in the direction of Mr. Münzer's door. He did not cough. Shamed, revolted, satiated and hungry, sick of living and avid for life, I was on the verge of tears as I left, first the flat, then the house in Jülicher-Strasse.

A few days later I carried out a long-cherished plan, which I had spent so much time rejecting that I had prepared it in every detail. That day I had the whole morning free. Not until three were Oskar and Ulla expected to pose for the ingenious Raskolnikov, I as Ulysses who in homecoming presents Penelope with a hump – something he had grown during his absence no doubt. In vain I tried to talk the artist out of this idea. For some time he had been successfully exploiting the Greek gods and demigods and Ulla felt quite at home in mythology. In the end I gave in and allowed myself to be painted as Vulcan, as Pluto with Proserpina, and finally, that afternoon, as a humpbacked Ulysses. But because I am more concerned with the events of the morning, Oskar will not tell you how the Muse Ulla looked as Penelope, but say instead: all was quiet in the Zeidler flat. The Hedgehog was on the road with his hair clippers, Sister Dorothea was on the day shift and had left the house at six o'clock, and Mrs. Zeidler was still in bed when, shortly after eight, the mail came.

At once I looked it over, found nothing for myself – Maria had written only two days before – but discovered at the very first glance an envelope mailed in town and addressed unmistakably in Dr. Werner's handwriting.

First I put the letter in with the others, addressed to Mr. Münzer and Mrs. Zeidler, went to my room and waited until Mrs. Zeidler had emerged, brought Münzer his letter, gone to the kitchen, then back to the bedroom, and in just ten minutes left the flat, for her work at Mannesmann's began at nine o'clock.

For safety's sake Oskar waited, dressed very slowly, cleaned his fingernails with a show (for his own benefit) of perfect calm, and only then resolved to act. I went to the kitchen, set an aluminum pot half-full of water on the largest of the three gas burners, and turned the flame on full, but reduced it as soon as the water came to a boil. Then, carefully supervising my thoughts, holding them as close as possible to the action in hand, I crossed over to Sister Dorothea's room, took the letter, which Mrs. Zeidler had thrust half under the frosted-glass door, returned to the kitchen, and held the back of the envelope cautiously over the steam until I was able to open it without damage. It goes without saying that

Oskar had turned off the gas before venturing to hold Dr. Werner's letter over the pot.

I did not read the doctor's communication in the kitchen, but lying on my bed. At first I was disappointed, for neither the salutation, 'Dear Miss Dorothea,' nor the closing formula, 'Sincerely yours, Erich Werner,' threw any light on the relations between doctor and nurse.

Nor in reading the letter did I find one frankly tender word. Werner expressed his regret at not having spoken to Sister Dorothea the previous day, although he had seen her from the doorway of the Men's Private Pavilion. For reasons unknown to Dr. Werner, Sister Dorothea had turned away when she saw him in conference with Sister Beata – Dorothea's friend, as we all remember. Dr. Werner merely requested an explanation. His conversation with Sister Beata, he begged leave to state, had been of a purely professional nature. Sister Beata was rather impetuous, but as she, Sister Dorothea, knew, he had always done his best to keep her at a distance. This was no easy matter, as she, Dorothea, knowing Beata, must surely realize. There were times when Sister Beata made no attempt to conceal her feelings, which he, Dr. Werner, had never reciprocated. The last sentence of the letter ran: 'Please believe me that you are free to drop in on me at any time.' Despite the formality and coldness bordering on arrogance of these lines, I had no great difficulty in seeing through Dr. E. Werner's epistolary style and recognizing the note for what it was, a passionate love letter.

Mechanically I put the letter back in its envelope. Forgetting the most elementary measures of hygiene, I moistened the flap, which Werner may well have licked, with Oskar's tongue. Then I burst out laughing. Still laughing, I began to slap my forehead and occiput by turns. It was only after this had been going on for some time that I managed to divert my right hand from Oskar's forehead to the doorknob of my room, opened the door, stepped out into the hallway, and slipped the letter half under Sister Dorothea's door.

I was still crouching with one, maybe two fingers on the letter, when I heard Mr. Münzer's voice from the other end of the hall. He spoke slowly and emphatically as though dictating; I could make out every word: 'Would you, kind sir, please bring me some water?'

I stood up. It ran through my mind that the man must be sick, but I realized at once that the man behind the door was not sick and that Oskar had hit on this idea only to have an excuse for bringing him water. Never would I have set foot in a total stranger's room in response to any ordinary unmotivated call!

At first I was going to bring him the still tepid water that had helped me to open Dr. Werner's letter. But then I poured the used water into the sink, let fresh water gush into the pot, and carried pot and water to the door behind which dwelt the voice that had cried out for me and water, perhaps only for water.

Oskar knocked, entered, and was hit by the smell that is so very characteristic of Klepp. To call this effluvium acrid would be to overlook its density and sweetness. The air surrounding Klepp had, for example, nothing in common with the vinegary scent of Sister Dorothea's room. To say sweet and sour would also be misleading. This Münzer, or Klepp as I call him today, this corpulent, indolent, yet not inactive, superstitious, readily perspiring, unwashed, but not derelict flutist and jazz clarinettist, had, though something or other was always preventing him from dying, and still has, the smell of a corpse that never stops smoking cigarettes, sucking peppermints, and eating garlic. So smelled he even then, and so smells he and breathes he today when, injecting transience and love of life into the atmosphere along with, and I might say enveloped in, his aroma, he descends upon me on visiting days, compelling Bruno to fling open every available door and window the moment Klepp, after elaborate farewells and promises to come again, has left the room.

Today Oskar is bedridden. Then, in the Zeidler flat, I found Klepp in the leftovers of a bed, cheerfully rotting. Within reaching distance of him, I observed an old-fashioned, extremely baroque-looking alcohol lamp, a dozen or more packages of spaghetti, several cans of olive oil, a few tubes of tomato paste, some damp, lumpy salt wrapped in newspaper, and a case of beer which turned out to be lukewarm. Into the empty beer bottles he urinated lying down, then, as he told me confidentially an hour or so later, he recapped the greenish receptacles, which held about as much as he did and for the most part were full to the brim.

These, to avoid any misunderstanding born of sudden thirst, he set aside, careful to segregate them from the beer bottles still properly deserving of the name. Although he had running water in his room – with a little spirit of enterprise he might have urinated in the washbasin – he was too lazy, or rather too busy with himself, to get up, to leave the bed he had taken such pains adjusting to his person, and put fresh water in his spaghetti pot.

Since Klepp, Mr. Münzer I mean, was always careful to cook his spaghetti in the same water and guarded this several times drained-off, increasingly viscous liquid like the apple of his eye, he was often able, aided by his supply of beer bottles, to lie flat on his back for upward of four days at a time. The situation became critical only when his spaghetti water had boiled down to an oversalted, glutinous sludge. On such occasions Klepp might, of course, have let himself starve to death; but in those days he lacked the ideological foundations for that kind of thing, and moreover, his asceticism seemed by its very nature to fall into four- or five-day periods. Otherwise, he might easily have made himself still more independent of the outside world with the help of Mrs. Zeidler, who brought him his mail, or of a larger spaghetti pot.

On the day when Oskar violated the secrecy of the mails, Klepp had been lying independently in bed for five days. The remains of his spaghetti water might have been fine for posting bills. This was his situation when he heard my irresolute step, a step preoccupied with Sister Dorothea and her correspondence, in the corridor. Having observed that Oskar did not react to his mock cough, he threw his voice into the breach on the day when I opened Dr. Werner's coolly passionate love letter, and said: 'Would you, kind sir, please bring me some water?'

And I took the pot, poured out the tepid water, turned on the faucet, let the water gush until the little pot was half-full, added a little, and brought him the fresh water. I was the kind sir he had guessed me to be; I introduced myself as Matzerath, stone-cutter and maker of inscriptions.

He, equally courteous, raised the upper part of his body a degree or two, identified himself as Egon Münzer, jazz musician, but asked me to call him Klepp, as his father before him had borne the name of Münzer. I understood this request only too well; it was sheer humility that impelled me to keep the name of Matzerath and it was only on rare occasions that I could make up my mind to call myself Oskar Bronski; I preferred to call myself Koljaiczek or just plain Oskar. Consequently I had no difficulty whatever in calling this corpulent and recumbent young man – I gave him thirty but he proved to be younger – just plain Klepp. He, unable to get his tongue around Koljaiczek, called me Oskar.

We struck up a conversation, taking pains at first to give it an easy flow and sticking to the most frivolous topics. Did he, I asked, believe in predestination? He did. Did he believe that all men were doomed to die? Yes, he felt certain that all men would ultimately have to die, but he was much less sure that all men had to be born; he was convinced that he himself had been born by mistake, and again Oskar felt a strong sense of kinship with him. We both believed in heaven, but when Klepp said 'heaven,' he gave a nasty little laugh and scratched himself under the bed covers: it was clear that Mr. Klepp, here and now, was hatching out indecent projects that he was planning to carry out in heaven. When the subject of politics came up, he waxed almost passionate; he reeled off the names of some three hundred noble German families to which he wished to hand over the whole of Germany on the spot, all except the Duchy of Hanover, which Klepp magnanimously ceded to the British Empire. When I asked him who was to rule over the erstwhile Free City of Danzig, he said he was sorry, he had never heard of the place, but even so, could offer me one of the counts of Berg, descended, he could assure me, in an almost direct line from Jan Wellem himself. Finally – we had been trying to define the concept of truth and making definite progress – I found out by an adroitly interpolated question or two that Mr. Klepp had been rooming at Zeidler's for the last three years. We expressed our regrets at not having met sooner. I said it was the fault of the Hedgehog, who had not told me nearly enough about his bedridden roomer, just as it had never occurred to him to say anything about Sister Dorothea, except that a nurse was living behind the frosted-glass door.

Oskar didn't wish to start right in burdening Mr. Münzer with his troubles. And so I did not ask for any information about the nurse. Instead, I asked him about himself. 'Apropos of nurses,' I said, 'are you unwell?'

Again Klepp raised his body by one degree, but when it became clear to him that he would never arrive at a right angle, he sank back again and confided his true reason for lying in bed: he was trying to find out whether his health was good, middling, or poor. He hoped in a few weeks to gain the assurance that it was middling.

Then it happened. This was just what I had feared, but hoped that a long and widely ramified conversation might avoid. 'Ah, my dear sir, won't you please join me in a plate of spaghetti!' There was no help for it. We ate spaghetti prepared in the fresh water I had brought. I should have liked to give his pasty cooking pot a thorough scouring in the kitchen sink, but I was afraid to say a word. Klepp rolled over on one side and silently, with the assured movements of a somnambulist, attended to his cookery. When the spaghetti was done, he drained off the water into a large empty can, then, without noticeably altering the position of his body, reached under the bed and produced a plate incrusted with grease and tomato paste. After what seemed like a moment's hesitation, he reached again under the bed, fished out a wad of newspaper, wiped the plate with it, and tossed the paper back under the bed. He breathed on the smudged plate as though to blow away a last grain of dust, and finally, with a gesture of noblesse oblige, handed me the most loathsome dish I have ever seen and invited Oskar to help himself.

After you, I said. But nothing doing, he was the perfect host. After providing me with a fork and spoon so greasy they stuck to my fingers, he piled an immense portion of spaghetti on my plate; upon it, with another of his noble gestures, he squeezed a long worm of tomato paste, to which, by deft movements of the tube, he succeeded in lending an ornamental line; finally he poured on a plentiful portion of oil from the can. He himself ate out of the pot. He served himself oil and tomato paste, sprinkled pepper on both helpings, mixed up his share, and motioned me to do like-wise. 'Ah, dear sir,' he said when all was in readiness, 'forgive me for having no grated parmesan. Nevertheless, I wish you the best of appetites.'

To this day Oskar is at a loss to say how he summoned up the courage to ply his fork and spoon. Strange to say, I enjoyed that spaghetti. In fact, Klepp's spaghetti became for me a culinary ideal, by which from that day on I have measured every menu that is set before me.

In the course of our repast, I managed to take a good look round the bedridden gentleman's room – but without attracting his attention. The main attraction was an open chimney hole, just under the ceiling, through which a black breath invaded the room. There were two windows, and it was windy out. Apparently it was the gusts of wind that sent clouds of soot puffing intermittently from the chimney hole into the room, where the soot settled evenly on the furniture. Since the furniture consisted solely of the bed in the middle of the room and several rolled carpets covered with wrapping paper, it was safe to say that nothing in the room was more blackened than the once-white bed sheet, the pillow slip under Klepp's head, and a towel with which Klepp always covered his face when a gust of wind wafted a soot cloud into the room.

Both windows, like those of the Zeidler living room, looked out on Jülicher-Strasse, or, more precisely, on the green leaves of the chestnut tree that stood in front of the house. The only picture in the room was a color photo of Elizabeth of England, probably cut out of an illustrated weekly. Under the picture bagpipes hung on a hook, the plaid pattern still recognizable beneath the pervading blackness. While I contemplated the colored photo, thinking less of Elizabeth and her Philip than of Sister Dorothea, torn, poor thing, perhaps desperately, between Oskar and Dr. Werner, Klepp informed me that he was a loyal and enthusiastic supporter of the British Royal Family and had consequently taken bagpipe lessons from the pipers of a Scottish regiment in the British Army of Occupation; Elizabeth, it so happened, was colonel of said regiment, which was all the more reason for him to take these particular pipers for his bagpipe teachers; Klepp had seen her in newsreels, wearing a kilt as she reviewed the regiment.

Here, strange to say, the Catholic in me began to stir. I said I doubted whether Elizabeth knew a thing about bagpipe music, tossed in a word or two about the cruel and unjust execution of the Catholic Mary Stuart, and, in short, gave Klepp to understand that in my opinion Elizabeth was tone-deaf.

I had been expecting an outburst of rage on the royalist's part. But he smiled like one graced with superior knowledge and asked me for an explanation: had I any grounds for setting myself up as an authority on music?

For a long while Oskar gazed at Klepp. Unwittingly, he had touched off a spark within me, and from my head that spark leapt to my hump. It was as though all my old, battered, exhausted drums had decided to celebrate a Last Judgment of their own. The thousand drums I had thrown on the scrap heap and the one drum that lay buried in Saspe Cemetery were resurrected, arose again, sound of limb; their resonance filled my whole being. I leapt up from the bed, asked Klepp to excuse me for just one moment, and rushed out of the room. Passing Sister Dorothea's frosted-glass door – half the letter still protruded – I ran to my own room, where I was met by the drum which Raskolnikov had given me while he was painting his 'Madonna 49.' I seized the drum and the two drumsticks, I turned or was turned, left the room, rushed past the forbidden room, and entered Klepp's spaghetti kitchen as a traveler returns from long wanderings. I sat on the edge of the bed and, without waiting to be asked, put my red and white lacquered cylinder into position. Feeling a little awkward at first, I toyed for a moment with the sticks, made little movements in the air. Then, looking past the astonished Klepp, I let one stick fall on the drum as though at random, and ah, the drum responded to Oskar, and Oskar brought the second stick into play. I began to drum, relating everything in order: in the beginning was the beginning. The moth between the light bulbs drummed in the hour of my birth; I drummed the cellar stairs with their sixteen steps and my fall from those same stairs during the celebration of my legendary third birthday; I drummed the schedule at the Pestalozzi School, I climbed the Stockturm with my drum, sat with it beneath political rostrums, drummed eels and gulls, and carpet-beating on Good Friday. Drumming, I sat on the coffin, tapered at the foot end, of my poor mama; I drummed the saga of Herbert Truczinski's scarry back. As I was drumming out the defense of the Polish Post Office, I noted a movement far away, at the head end of the bed I was sitting on: with half an eye, I saw Klepp sitting up, taking a preposterous wooden flute from under his pillow, setting it to his lips, and

bringing forth sounds that were so sweet and unnatural, so perfectly attuned to my drumming that I was able to lead Klepp to
the cemetery in Saspe and, after Leo Schugger had finished his
dance, Klepp helped me to make the fizz powder of my first love
foam up for him; I even led Klepp into the jungles of Mrs. Lina
Greff; I made Greff's drumming machine with its 165-pound
counterweight play its grand finale and run down; I welcomed
Klepp to Bebra's Theater at the Front, made Jesus speak, and
drummed Störtebeker and his fellow Dusters off the diving tower
– and down below sat Lucy. I let ants and Russians take possession
of my drum, but I did not guide Klepp back to the cemetery in
Saspe, where I threw my drum into the grave after Matzerath,
but struck up my main, never-ending theme: Kashubian potato
fields in the October rain, there sits my grand-mother in her four
skirts; and Oskar's heart nearly turned to stone when I heard the
October rain trickling from Klepp's flute, when, beneath the rain
and the four skirts, Klepp's flute discovered Joseph Koljaiczek the
firebug and celebrated, nay represented, the begetting of my poor
mama.

We played for several hours. After a number of variations on
my grandfather's flight over the timber rafts, we concluded our
concert, happy though exhausted, with a hymn, a song of hope,
suggesting that perhaps the vanished arsonist had been miraculously saved.

Before the last tone had quite left his flute, Klepp jumped up
from his warm, deep-furrowed bed. Cadaverous smells followed
him, but he tore the windows open, stuffed newspaper in the
chimney hole, tore the picture of Elizabeth of England to tatters,
announced that the royalist era was ended, ran water into the
washbasin and washed himself: yes, Klepp washed, there was
nothing he feared to wash away. This was no mere washing, it
was a purification. And when the purified one turned away from
the water and stood before me in his dripping, naked corpulence,
his ungainly member hanging down at a slant, and, bursting with
vigor, lifted me, lifted me high in the air – for Oskar was and still
is a lightweight – when laughter burst out of him and dashed
against the ceiling, I understood that Oskar's drum had not been
alone in rising from the dead, for Klepp too was as one resur-

rected. And so we congratulated one another and kissed each other on the cheeks.

That same day – we went out toward evening, drank beer and ate blood sausage with onions – Klepp suggested that we start a jazz band together. I asked for time to think it over, but Oskar had already made up his mind to give up his modeling and stonecutting activities and become percussion man in a jazz band.

On the Fiber Rug

There can be no doubt that on the day just recorded Oskar supplied Klepp with grounds for getting out of bed. He leapt overjoyed from his musty bedclothes; he allowed water to touch him, he was a new man, the kind that says 'Terrific' and 'The world is my oyster.' And yet today, now that it is Oskar who is privileged to lie in bed, here is what I think: Klepp is trying to get even with me, he is trying to throw me out of my bed in this mental hospital, because I made him forsake his bed in the spaghetti kitchen.

Once a week I have to put up with his visits, listen to his tirades about jazz and his musico-Communist manifestoes, for no sooner had I deprived him of his bed and his Elizabeth-of-the-bagpipes than he, who as long as he lay in bed was a royalist, devoted heart and soul to the English royal family, became a dues-paying member of the Communist Party, and Communism has been his illegal hobby ever since: drinking beer, devouring blood sausage, he holds forth to the harmless little men who stand at bars, studying the labels on bottles, about the benefits of collective endeavour, of a jazz band working full time, or a Soviet kolkhoz.

In these times of ours, there isn't very much an awakened dreamer can do. Once alienated from his sheltering bed, Klepp had the possibility of becoming a comrade, and illegally at that, which added to the charm. Jazz was the second religion available to him. Thirdly Klepp, born a Protestant, could have been converted to Catholicism.

You've got to hand it to Klepp: he left the roads to all religions open. Caution, his heavy, glistening flesh, and a sense of humor that lives on applause, enabled him to devise a sly system, combining the teachings of Marx with the myth of jazz. If one day a left-wing priest of the worker-priest type should cross his path, especially if this priest should happen to have a collection of Dixieland records, you will see a Marxist jazz fan starting to take the sacraments on Sunday and mingling his above-mentioned body odor with the scent of a Neo-Gothic Cathedral.

Between me and such a fate stands my bed, from which Klepp tries to lure me with throbbing, life-loving promises. He sends petition after petition to the court and works hand in glove with my lawyer in demanding a new trial: he wants Oskar to be acquitted, set free – he wants them to turn me out of my hospital – and why? Just because he envies me my bed.

Even so, I have no regret that while rooming at Zeidler's I transformed a recumbent friend into a standing, stamping, and occasionally even running friend. Apart from the strenuously thoughtful hours that I devoted to Sister Dorothea, I now had a carefree private life. 'Hey, Klepp,' I would cry, slapping him on the shoulder, 'what about that jazz band?' And he would fondle my hump, which he loved almost as much as his belly. 'Oskar and me,' he announced to the world, 'we're going to start a jazz-band. All we need is a good guitarist who can handle the banjo maybe if he has to.'

. He was right. Drum and flute would not have been enough. A second melodic instrument was needed. A plucked bass wouldn't have been bad, and visually there was certainly something to be said for it, but even then bass players were hard to come by. So we searched frantically for a guitarist. We went to the movies a good deal, had our pictures taken twice a week as you may remember, and over beer, blood sausage, and onions, did all sorts of silly tricks with our passport photos. It was then that Klepp met his redheaded Ilse, thoughtlessly gave her a picture of himself, and just for that had to marry her. But we didn't find a guitarist.

In the course of my life as a model, I had gained some knowledge of the Old City of Düsseldorf, with its bull's-eye window-panes, its mustard and cheese, its beer fumes and Lower Rhenish coziness, but it was only with Klepp that I became really familiar with it. We looked for a guitarist all around St. Lambert's Church in all the bars, and most particularly in Ratinger-Strasse, at the Unicorn, because Bobby, who led the dance band, would sometimes let us join in with our flute and toy drum and was enthusiastic about my drumming, though he himself, despite the finger that was missing from his right hand, was no slouch as a percussion man.

We found no guitarist at the Unicorn, but I got a certain amount of practice. What with my wartime theatrical experience, I would have gotten back into the swing of it very quickly if not for Sister Dorothea, who occasionally made me miss my cue.

Half my thoughts were still with her. That would have been all right if the rest had remained entirely on my drum. But as it worked out, my thoughts would start with my drum and end up with Sister Dorothea's Red Cross pin. Klepp was brilliant at bridging over my lapses with his flute; but it worried him to see Oskar so half-immersed in his thoughts. 'Are you hungry? I'll order some sausage.'

Behind all the sorrows of this world Klepp saw a ravenous hunger; all human suffering, he believed, could be cured by a portion of blood sausage. What quantities of fresh blood sausage with rings of onion, washed down with beer, Oskar consumed in order to make his friend Klepp think his sorrow's name was hunger and not Sister Dorothea.

Usually we left the Zeidler flat early in the morning and took our breakfast in the Old City. I no longer went to the Academy except when we needed money for the movies. The Muse Ulla, who had meanwhile become engaged for the third or fourth time to Lankes, was unavailable, because Lankes was getting his first big industrial commissions. But Oskar didn't like to pose without Ulla, for when I posed alone, they would always distort me horribly and paint me in the blackest colors. And so I gave myself up entirely to my friend Klepp. I could still go to see Maria and little Kurt, but their apartment offered me no peace. Mr. Stenzel, her boss and married lover, was always there.

One day in the early fall of '49, Klepp and I left our rooms and converged in the hallway, not far from the frosted-glass door. We were about to leave the flat with our instruments when Zeidler opened the door of his living room by a crack and called out to us.

He was pushing a bulky roll of narrow carpeting and wanted

us to help him lay it – a coconut-fiber runner it proved to be – in the hallway. The runner measured twenty-eight feet, but the hallway came to just twenty-five feet and seven inches; Klepp and I had to cut off the rest. This we did sitting down, for the cutting of coconut fiber proved to be hard work. When we were through, the runner was almost an inch too short, though the width was just right. Next Zeidler, who said he had trouble bending down, asked us to do the tacking. Oskar hit on the idea of stretching the runner as we tacked, and we managed to make up the gap, or very close to it. We used tacks with large, flat heads; small heads wouldn't have held in the coarse weave. Neither Oskar nor Klepp brought the hammer down on his thumb; we did bend a few tacks, though. But it wasn't our fault, it was the quality of the tacks, which were from Zeidler's stock, that is to say, manufactured before the currency reform. When the runner was half in place, we laid down our hammers crosswise and gave the Hedgehog, who was supervising our work, a look which while not insolently demanding must surely have been wistful. He disappeared into his bed-living room and came back with three of his famous liqueur glasses and a bottle of schnaps. We drank to the durability of the carpet; the first glass drained, we remarked – and again our tone was more wistful than demanding – that coconut fiber makes a man thirsty. I feel sure those liqueur glasses must have been glad of the opportunity to hold schnaps several times in a row before being reduced to smithereens by one of the Hedgehog's temper tantrums. When Klepp accidentally dropped an empty glass on the carpet, it did not break or even make a sound. We all sang the praises of the carpet. When Mrs. Zeidler, who was watching our work from the bed-living room, joined us in praising the fiber carpet because it protected falling liqueur glasses from harm, the Hedgehog flew into a rage. He stamped on the part of the runner that had not yet been tacked down, seized the three empty glasses, and vanished into the bed-living room. The china closet rattled – he was taking more glasses, three were not enough – and a moment later Oskar heard the familiar music: to his mind's eye appeared the Zeidler tile stove, eight shattered liqueur glasses beneath its cast-iron door, Zeidler bending down for the dustpan and brush, Zeidler sweeping up all the breakage that the Hedgehog had created. Mrs. Zeidler remained in the doorway while the glasses went tinkle-tinkle and crash-bang behind her. She took a considerable interest in our work; during the Hedgehog's tantrum we had picked up our hammers again. He never came back, but he had left the schnaps bottle. At first Mrs. Zeidler's presence embarrassed us, as alternately we set the bottle to our lips. She gave us a friendly nod. That put us at our ease, but it never occurred to us to pass the bottle and offer her a nip. However, we made a neat job of it, and our tacks were evenly spaced. As Oskar was wielding his hammer outside Sister Dorothea's room, the panes of frosted glass rattled at every stroke. This stirred him to the quick and for an anguished moment he let the hammer drop. But once he had passed the frosted-glass door, he and his hammer felt better.

All things come to an end, and so did that fiber runner. The broad-headed tacks ran from end to end, up to their necks in the floorboards, holding just their heads above the surging, swirling coconut fibers. Well pleased with ourselves, we strode up and down the hallway, enjoying the length of the carpet, complimented ourselves on our work, and intimated just in passing that it was not so easy to lay a carpet before breakfast, on an empty stomach. At last we achieved our end: Mrs. Zeidler ventured out on the brand-new, virgin runner and found her way over it to the kitchen, where she poured out coffee and fried some eggs. We ate in my room; Mrs. Zeidler toddled off, it was time for her to go to the office at Mannesmann's. We left the door open, chewed, savored our fatigue, and contemplated our work, the fiber runner running fibrously toward us.

Why so many words about a cheap carpet which might at most have had a certain barter value before the currency reform? The question is justified. Oskar anticipates it and replies: it was on this fiber runner that Oskar, in the ensuing night, met Sister Dorothea for the first time.

It must have been close to midnight when I came home full of beer and blood sausage. I had left Klepp in the Old City, still looking for the guitarist. I found the keyhole of the Zeidler flat, found the fiber runner in the hallway, found my way past the dark frosted glass to my room, and, having taken my clothes off, found my bed. I did not find my pajamas, they were at Maria's in the wash; instead I found the extra piece of fiber runner we had cut off, laid it down beside my bed, got into bed, but found no sleep.

There is no reason to tell you everything that Oskar thought or revolved unthinking in his head because he could not sleep. Today I believe I have discovered the reason for my insomnia. Before climbing into bed, I had stood barefoot on my new bedside rug, the remnant from the runner. The coconut fibers pierced my bare skin and crept into my bloodstream: long after I had lain down, I was still standing on coconut fibers, and that is why I was unable to sleep; for nothing is more stimulating, more sleep-dispelling, more thought-provoking than standing barefoot on a coconut-fiber mat.

Long after midnight Oskar was still standing on the mat and lying in bed both at once; toward three in the morning he heard a door and another door. That, I thought, must be Klepp coming home without a guitarist but full of blood sausage; yet I knew it was not Klepp who opened first one door and then another. In addition, I thought, as long as you are lying in bed for nothing, with coconut fibers cutting into the soles of your feet, you might as well get out of bed and really, not just in your imagination, stand on the fiber mat beside your bed. Oskar did just this. There were consequences. The moment I set foot on the mat, it reminded me, via the soles of my feet, of its origin and source, the twenty-five-foot-six-inch runner in the hallway. Was it because I felt sorry for the cut-off remnant? Was it because I had heard the doors in the hallway and presumed, without believing, that it was Klepp? In any event, Oskar, who in going to bed had failed to find his pajamas, bent down, picked up one corner of the mat in each hand, moved his legs aside until he was no longer standing on the mat but on the floor, pulled up the thirty-inch mat between his legs and in front of his body, which, as we recall, measured four feet one. His nakedness was decently covered, but from knees to collarbone he was exposed to the influence of the coconut fiber. And that influence was further enhanced when behind his fibrous shield he left his dark room for the dark corridor and set his feet on the runner.

Is it any wonder if I took hurried little steps in order to escape the fibrous influence beneath my feet, if, in my search for salvation and safety, I made for the one place where there was no coconut fiber on the floor – the toilet?

This recess was as dark as the hallway or Oskar's room but was occupied nonetheless, as a muffled feminine scream made clear to me. My fiber pelt collided with the knees of a seated human. When I made no move to leave the toilet – for behind me threatened the coconut fibers – the seated human tried to expel me. 'Who are you? what do you want? go away!' said a voice that could not possibly belong to Mrs. Zeidler. There was a certain plaintiveness in that 'Who are you?'

'Well, well, Sister Dorothea, just guess.' I ventured a little banter which, I hoped, would distract her from the slightly embarrassing circumstances of our meeting. But she wasn't in the mood for guessing; she stood up, reached out for me in the darkness and tried to push me out onto the runner, but she reached too high, into the void over my head. She tried lower down, but this time it wasn't I but my fibrous apron, my coconut pelt that she caught hold of. Again she let out a scream – oh, why do women always have to scream? Sister Dorothea seemed to have mistaken me for somebody, for she began to tremble and whispered: 'Oh, heavens, it's the Devil!' I couldn't repress a slight giggle, but it wasn't meant maliciously. She, however, took it as the Devil's sniggering. That word Devil was not to my liking and when she again, but now in a very cowed tone, asked: 'Who are you?' Oskar replied: 'I am Satan, come to call on Sister Dorothea!' And she: 'Oh, heavens, what for?'

Slowly I felt my way into my role, and Satan was my prompter. 'Because Satan is in love with Sister Dorothea!' 'No, no, no, I won't have it,' she cried. She tried again to escape, but once again encountered the Satanic fibers of my coconut pelt – her nightgown must have been very thin. Her ten fingers also encountered the jungle of seduction, and suddenly she felt faint. She fell forward; I caught her in my pelt, managed to hold her up long enough to arrive at a decision in keeping with my Satanic role. Gently giving way, I let her down on her knees, taking care that they should not touch the cold tiles of the toilet but come to rest on the fiber rug in the hallway. Then I let her slip down backward on the carpet, her head pointing westward in the direction of Klepp's room. The whole dorsal length of her – she must have measured at least five feet four – was in contact with the runner; I covered her over with the same fibrous stuff, but I had only thirty inches available. First I put the top end under her chin, but then the lower edge came down too far over her thighs. I had to move the mat up a couple of inches; now it covered her mouth, but her nose was still free, she could still breathe. She did more than breathe; she heaved and panted as Oskar lay down on his erstwhile mat, setting all its thousand fibers in vibration, for instead of seeking direct contact with Sister Dorothea, he relied on the effects of the coconut fiber. Again he tried to strike up a conversation, but Sister Dorothea was still in a half-faint. She could only gasp 'Heavens, heavens!' and ask Oskar over and over who he was and where he was from. There was shuddering and trembling between fiber runner and fiber mat when I said I was Satan, pronounced the name with a Satanic hiss, gave hell as my address, and described it with a picturesque touch or two. I thrashed about vigorously on my bedside mat to keep it in motion, for my ears told me plainly that the fibers gave Sister Dorothea a sensation similar to that which fizz powder had given my beloved Maria years before, the only difference being that the fizz powder had allowed me to hold up my end successfully, nay triumphantly, while here on the fiber mat, I suffered a humiliating failure. I just couldn't throw anchor. My little friend who in the fizz powder days and frequently thereafter had stood erect, full of purpose and ambition, now drooped his head; here on the coconut fiber he remained puny, listless, and unresponsive. Nothing could move him, neither my intellectual arguments nor the heart-rending appeals of Sister Dorothea, who whimpered and moaned: 'Come, Satan, come!' I tried to comfort her with promises: 'Satan is coming,' I said in a Satanic tone, 'Satan will be ready in a minute.' At the same time I held a dialogue with the Satan who has dwelt within me since my baptism. I scolded: Don't be a kill-joy, Satan. I pleaded: For goodness' sake, Satan, don't disgrace me this way. And cajoled: It's not a bit like you, old boy. Think back, think of Maria, or better still of the widow Greff, or of how you and I used to frolic with my darling Roswitha in gay Paree? Satan's reply was morose and repetitious: I'm not in the mood, Oskar. When Satan's not in the mood, virtue triumphs. Hasn't even Satan a right not to be in the mood once in a while?

With these and similar saws, Satan refused me his support. I kept the fiber mat in motion, scraping poor Sister Dorothea raw, but I was gradually weakening. 'Come, Satan,' she sighed, 'oh, please come.' And at length I responded with a desperate, absurd, utterly unmotivated assault beneath the mat: I aimed an unloaded pistol at the bull's-eye. She tried to help her Satan, her arms came out from under the mat, she flung them around me, found my hump, my warm, human, and not at all fibrous skin. But this wasn't the Satan she wanted. There were no more murmurs of 'Come, Satan, come.' Instead, she cleared her throat and repeated her original question but in a different register: 'For heaven's sake who are you, what do you want?' I could only pull in my horns and admit that according to my papers my name was Oskar Matzerath, that I was her neighbor, and that I loved her, Sister Dorothea, with all my heart.

If any malicious soul imagines that Sister Dorothea cursed me and pushed me down on the fiber runner, Oskar must assure him, sadly yet with a certain satisfaction, that Sister Dorothea removed her hands very slowly, thoughtfully as it were, from my hump, with a movement resembling an infinitely sad caress. She began to cry, to sob, but without violence. I hardly noticed it when she wriggled out from under me and the mat, when she slipped away from me and I slipped to the floor. The carpet absorbed the sound of her steps. I heard a door opening and closing, a key turning; then the six squares of the frosted-glass door took on light and reality from within.

Oskar lay there and covered himself with the mat, which still had a little Satanic warmth in it. My eyes were fixed on the illumined squares. From time to time a shadow darted across the frosted glass. Now she is going to the clothes cupboard, I said to myself, and now to the washstand. Oskar attempted a last diabolical venture. Taking my mat with me I crawled over the runner to the door, scratched on the wood, raised myself a little, sent a searching, pleading hand over the two lower panes. Sister Dorothea did not open; she kept moving busily between cupboard and washstand. I knew the truth and admitted as much: Sister Dorothea was packing, preparing to take flight, to take flight from me.

Even the feeble hope that in leaving the room she would show me her electrically illumined face was to be disappointed. First the light went out behind the frosted glass, then I heard the key, the door opened, shoes on the fiber runner – I reached out for her, struck a suitcase, a stockinged leg. She kicked me in the chest with one of those sensible hiking shoes I had seen in the clothes cupboard, and when Oskar pleaded a last time: 'Sister Dorothea,' the apartment door slammed: a woman had left me.

You and all those who understand my grief will say now: Go to bed, Oskar. What business have you in the hallway after this humiliating episode? It is four in the morning. You are lying naked on a fiber rug, with no cover but a small and scraggly mat. You've scraped the skin off your hands and knees. Your heart bleeds, your member aches, your shame cries out to high heaven. You have waked Mr. Zeidler. He has waked his wife. In another minute they'll get up, open the door of their bed-living room, and see you. Go to bed, Oskar, it will soon strike five.

This was exactly the advice I gave myself as I lay on the fiber runner. But I just shivered and lay still. I tried to call back Sister Dorothea's body. I could feel nothing but coconut fibers, they were everywhere, even between my teeth. Then a band of light fell on Oskar: the door of the Zeidler bed-living room opened a crack. Zeidler's hedgehog-head, above it a head full of metal curlers, Mrs. Zeidler. They stared, he coughed, she giggled, he called me, I gave no reply, she went on giggling, he told her to be still, she asked what was wrong with me, he said this won't do, she said it was a respectable house, he threatened to put me out, but I was silent, for the measure was not yet full. The Zeidlers opened the door, he switched on the light in the hall. They came toward me, making malignant little eyes; he had a good rage up, and it wasn't on any liqueur glasses that he was going to vent it this time. He stood over me, and Oskar awaited the Hedgehog's fury. But Zeidler never did get that tantrum off his chest. A hubbub was heard in the stair well, an uncertain key groped for, and at last found, the keyhole, and Klepp came in, bringing with him someone who was just as drunk as he: Scholle, the long-sought guitarist.

The two of them pacified Zeidler and wife, bent down over Oskar, asked no questions, picked me up, and carried me, me and my Satanic mat, to my room.

Klepp rubbed me warm. The guitarist picked up my clothes. Together they dressed me and dried my tears. Sobs. Daybreak outside the window. Sparrows. Klepp hung my drum round my neck and showed his little wooden flute. Sobs. The guitarist picked up his guitar. Sparrows. Friends surrounded me, took me between them, led the sobbing but unresisting Oskar out of the flat, out of the house in Jülicher-Strasse, toward the sparrows, led him away from the influence of coconut fiber, led me through dawning streets, through the Hofgarten to the planetarium and the banks of the river Rhine, whose grey waters rolled down to Holland, carrying barges with flowing clotheslines.

From six to nine that misty September morning, Klepp the flutist, Scholle the guitarist, and Oskar the percussion man sat on the right bank of the river Rhine. We made music, played ourselves into the groove, drank out of one bottle, peered across at the poplars on the opposite bank, and regaled the steamers that were bucking the current after taking on coal in Duisburg, with hot jazz and sad Mississippi music. Meanwhile we wondered about a name for the jazz band we had just founded.

When a bit of sun colored the morning mist and a craving for breakfast crept into our music, Oskar, who had put his drum between himself and the preceding night, arose, took some money from his coat pocket, by which he meant and they understood breakfast, and announced to his friends the name of the newborn band: We agreed to call ourselves 'The Rhine River Three' and went to breakfast.

In the Onion Cellar

We loved the Rhine meadows, and it so happened that Ferdinand Schmuh, the restaurant and night-spot owner, also loved the right bank of the Rhine between Düsseldorf and Kaiserswerth. We did most of our practicing above Stockum. Meanwhile Schmuh, carrying a small-caliber rifle, searched the riverside hedges and bushes for sparrows. That was his hobby, his recreation. When business got on his nerves, Schmuh bade his wife take the wheel of the Mercedes; they would drive along the river and park above Stockum. Slightly flat-footed, his rifle pointing at the ground, he set off across the meadows, followed by his wife, who would rather have stayed in the car. At the end of their cross-country jaunt, he deposited her on a comfortable stone by the riverbank and vanished amid the hedges. While we played our ragtime, he went pop pop in the bushes. While we made music, Schmuh shot sparrows.

When Scholle, who like Klepp knew every bar owner in town, heard shooting in the shrubbery, he announced:

'Schmuh is shooting sparrows.'

Since Schmuh is no longer living, I may as well put in my obituary right here: Schmuh was a good marksman and perhaps a good man as well; for when Schmuh went sparrow-shooting, he kept ammunition in the left-hand pocket of his coat, but his right-hand pocket was full of bird food, which he distributed among the sparrows with a generous sweeping movement, not before, but after he had done his shooting, and he never shot more than twelve birds in an afternoon.

One cool November morning in 1949, when Schmuh was still among the living and we for our part had been rehearsing for some weeks on the banks of the Rhine, he addressed us in a voice too loud and angry to be taken quite seriously: 'How do you expect me to shoot birds when you scare them away with your music?'

'Oh,' Klepp apologized, holding out his flute as though presenting arms. 'You must be the gentleman with the superb sense of rhythm, whose shooting keeps such perfect time with our melodies. My respects, Mr. Schmuh!'

Schmuh was pleased that Klepp knew him by name, but inquired how so. Klepp, with a show of indignation: Why, everybody knows Schmuh. In the street I can always hear somebody saying: There's Schmuh, there goes Schmuh, did you see Schmuh just now, where is Schmuh today, Schmuh is out shooting sparrows.

Thus transformed into a public figure, Schmuh offered us cigarettes, asked us our names, and requested a piece from our repertory. We obliged with a tiger rag, whereupon he called his wife, who had been sitting in her fur coat on a stone, musing over the waters of the Rhine. Fur-coated, she joined us and again we played; this time it was 'High Society', and when we had finished, she said in her fur coat: 'Why, Ferdy, that's just what you need for the Cellar.' He seemed to be of the same opinion; indeed, he was under the impression that he personally had gone scouting for us and found us. Nevertheless, Schmuh, pondering, maybe calculating, sent several flat stones skipping over the waters of the Rhine before he made his offer: would we play at the Onion Cellar from nine to two, for ten marks an evening apiece, well, let's say twelve? Klepp said seventeen in order that Schmuh might say fifteen; Schmuh said fourteen fifty, and we called it a deal.

Seen from the street, the Onion Cellar looked like many of the newer night clubs which are distinguished from the older bars and cabarets by, among other things, their higher prices. The higher prices were justified by the outlandish decoration of these night spots, many of which termed themselves 'Artists' clubs' and also by their names. There was 'The Ravioli Room' (discreet and refined), 'The Taboo' (mysterious and existentialist), 'The Paprika' (spicy and high-spirited). And of course there was 'The Onion Cellar'.

The words 'Onion Cellar' and a poignantly naive likeness of an onion had been painted with deliberate awkwardness on an enamel sign which hung in the old German manner from elaborate wrought-iron gallows in front of the house. The one and only window was glassed with bottle-green bull's-eye panes. The iron door, painted with red lead, had no doubt seen service outside an air-raid shelter in the war years. Outside it stood the doorman in a rustic sheepskin. Not everyone was allowed in the Onion Cellar. Especially on Fridays, when wages turn to beer, it was the doorman's business to turn away certain Old City characters, for whom the Onion Cellar was too expensive in the first place. Behind the red-lead door, those who were allowed in found five concrete steps. You went down, found yourself on a landing some three feet square, to which a poster for a Picasso show lent an original, artistic turn. Four more steps took you to the check-room. 'Please pay later,' said a little cardboard sign, and indeed, the young man at the counter, usually an art student with a beard, refused to take money in advance, because the Onion Cellar was not only expensive but also and nevertheless high class.

The owner in person welcomed every single guest with elaborate gestures and mobile, expressive eyebrows, as though initiating him into a secret rite. As we know, the owner's name was Ferdinand Schmuh; he was a man who shot sparrows now and then, and had a keen eye for the society which had sprung up in Düsseldorf (and elsewhere, though not quite so quickly) since the currency reform.

The Onion Cellar – and here we see the note of authenticity essential to a successful night club – was a real cellar; in fact, it was quite damp and chilly under foot. Tubular in shape, it measured roughly thirteen by sixty, and was heated by two authentic cast-iron stoves. Yet in one respect the Cellar wasn't a cellar after all. The ceiling had been taken off, so that the club actually included the former ground-floor apartment. The one and only window was not a real cellar window, but the former window of the ground-floor apartment. However, since one might have looked out of the window if not for its opaque bull's-eye panes; since there was a gallery that one reached by a highly original and highly precipitous staircase, the Onion Cellar can reasonably be termed 'authentic', even if it was not a real cellar – and besides, why should it have been?

Oskar has forgotten to tell you that the staircase leading to the gallery was not a real staircase but more like a companionway, because on either side of its dangerously steep steps there were two extremely original clotheslines to hold on to; the staircase swayed a bit, making you think of an ocean voyage and adding to the price.

The Onion Cellar was lighted by acetylene lamps such as miners carry, which broadcast a smell of carbide – again adding to the price – and transported the customer unto the gallery of a mine, a potash mine for instance, three thousand feet below the surface of the earth: cutters bare to the waist hack away at the rock, opening up a vein; the scraper hauls out the salt, the windlass roars as it fills the cars; far behind, where the gallery turns off to Friedrichshall Two, a swaying light; that's the head foreman and here he comes with a cheery hello, swinging a carbide lamp that looks exactly like the carbide lamps that hung from the unadorned, slapdashly whitewashed walls of the Onion Cellar, casting their light and smell, adding to the prices, and creating an original atmosphere.

The customers were uncomfortably seated on common crates covered with onion sacks, yet the plank tables, scrubbed and spotless, recalled the guests from the mine to a peaceful peasant inn such as we sometimes see in the movies.

That was all! But what about the bar? No bar. Waiter, the menu please! Neither waiter nor menu. In fact, there was no one else but ourselves, the Rhine River Three. Klepp, Scholle, and Oskar sat beneath the staircase that was really a companionway. We arrived at nine, unpacked our instruments, and began to play at about ten. But for the present it is only a quarter past nine and I won't be able to speak about us until later. Right now let us keep an eye on Schmuh, who occasionally shot sparrows with a small-caliber rifle.

As soon as the Onion Cellar had filled up – half-full was regarded as full – Schmuh, the host, donned his shawl. This shawl had been specially made for him. It was cobalt-blue silk, printed with a golden-yellow pattern. I mention all this because the donning of the shawl was significant. The pattern printed on the shawl was made up of golden-yellow onions. The Onion Cellar was not really 'open' until Schmuh had put on his shawl.

The customers – businessmen, doctors, lawyers, artists, journalists, theater and movie people, well-known figures from the sporting world, officials in the provincial and municipal government, in short, a cross section of the world which nowadays calls itself intellectual – came with wives, mistresses, secretaries, interior decorators, and occasional male mistresses, to sit on crates covered with burlap. Until Schmuh put on his golden-yellow onions, the conversation was subdued, forced, dispirited. These people wanted to talk, to unburden themselves, but they couldn't seem to get started; despite all their efforts, they left the essential unsaid, talked around it. Yet how eager they were to spill their guts, to talk from their hearts, their bowels, their entrails, to forget about their brains just this once, to lay bare the raw, unvarnished truth, the man within. Here and there a stifled remark about a botched career, a broken marriage. One gathers that the gentleman over there with the massive head, the intelligent face and soft, almost delicate hands, is having trouble with his son, who is displeased about his father's past. Those two ladies in mink, who still look quite attractive in the light of the carbide lamp, claim to have lost their faith, but they don't say in what. So far we know nothing about the past of the gentleman with the massive head, nor have we the slightest idea what sort of trouble his son is making for him on account of this unknown past; if you'll forgive Oskar a crude metaphor, it was like laying eggs; you push and push . . .

The pushing in the Onion Cellar brought meager results until Schmuh appeared in his special shawl. Having been welcomed with a joyful 'Ah!' for which he thanked his kind guests, he vanished for a few minutes behind a curtain at the end of the Onion Cellar, where the toilets and storeroom were situated.

But why did a still more joyous 'Ah', an 'Ah' of relief and release, welcome the host on his reappearance? The proprietor of a successful nightclub disappears behind a curtain, takes something from the storeroom, flings a choice selection of insults in an undertone at the washroom attendant who is sitting there reading an illustrated weekly, reappears in front of the curtain, and is welcomed like the Saviour, like the legendary uncle from Australia!

Schmuh came back with a little basket on his arm and moved among the guests. The basket was covered with a blue-and-yellow checkered napkin. On the cloth lay a considerable number of little wooden boards, shaped like pigs or fish. These he handed out to his guests with little bows and compliments which showed, beyond the shadow of a doubt, that he had grown up in Budapest and Vienna; Schmuh's smile was like the smile on a copy of a copy of the supposedly authentic Mona Lisa.

The guests, however, looked very serious as they took their little boards. Some exchanged boards with their neighbors, for some preferred the silhouette of a pig, while others preferred the more mysterious fish. They sniffed at the pieces of wood and moved them about. Schmuh, after serving the customers in the gallery, waited until all the little boards had come to rest.

Then – and every heart was waiting – he removed the napkin, very much in the manner of a magician: beneath it lay still another napkin, upon which, almost unrecognizable at first glance, lay the paring knives.

These too he proceeded to hand out. But this time he made his rounds more quickly, whipping up the tension that permitted him to raise his prices; he paid no more compliments, and left no time for any exchanges of knives; a calculated haste entered into his movements. 'On your mark, get set,' he shouted. At 'Go' he tore the napkin off the basket, reached into the basket, and handed out, dispensed, distributed among the multitude ... onions – onions such as were represented, golden-yellow and slightly styli- zed, on his shawl, plain ordinary onions, not tulip bulbs, but onions such as women buy in the market, such as the vegetable woman sells, such as the peasant, the peasant's wife, or the hired girl plants and harvests, onions such as may be seen, more or less faithfully portrayed in the still lifes of the lesser Dutch masters. Such onions, then, Schmuh dispensed among his guests until each had an onion and no sound could be heard but the purring of the stoves and the whistling of the carbide lamps. For the grand distribution of onions was followed by silence. Into which Ferdi- nand Schmuh cried: 'Ladies and gentlemen, help yourselves.' And he tossed one end of his shawl over his left shoulder like a skier just before the start. This was the signal.

The guests peeled the onions. Onions are said to have seven skins. The ladies and gentlemen peeled the onions with the paring knives. They removed the first, third, blond, golden-yellow, rust- brown, or better still, onion-colored skin, they peeled until the onion became glassy, green, whitish, damp, and water-sticky, until it smelled, smelled like an onion. Then they cut it as one cuts onions, deftly or clumsily, on the little chopping boards shaped like pigs or fish; they cut in one direction and another until the juice spurted or turned to vapor – the older gentlemen were not very handy with paring knives and had to be careful not to cut their fingers; some cut themselves even so, but didn't notice it – the ladies were more skillful, not all of them, but those at least who were housewives at home, who knew how one cuts up onions for hash-brown potatoes, or for liver with apples and onion rings; but in Schmuh's onion cellar there was neither, there was nothing whatever to eat, and anyone who wanted to eat had to go else- where, to the 'Fischl', for instance, for at the Onion Cellar onions were only cut. Why all these onions? For one thing, because of the name. The Onion Cellar had its specialty: onions. And moreover, the onion, the cut onion, when you look at it closely . . . but enough of that, Schmuh's guests had stopped looking, they could see nothing more, because their eyes were running over and not because their hearts were so full; for it is not true that when the heart is full the eyes necessarily overflow, some people can never manage it, especially in our century, which in spite of all the suffering and sorrow will surely be known to posterity as the tearless century. It was this drought, this tearlessness that brought those who could afford it to Schmuh's Onion Cellar, where the host handed them a little chopping board – pig or fish – a paring knife for eighty pfennigs, and for twelve marks an ordinary field-, garden-, and kitchen-variety onion, and induced them to cut their onions smaller and smaller until the juice – what did the onion juice do? It did what the world and the sorrows of the world could not do: it brought forth a round, human tear. It made them cry. At last they were able to cry again. To cry properly, without restraint, to cry like mad. The tears flowed and washed everything away. The rain came. The dew. Oskar has a vision of floodgates opening. Of dams bursting in the spring floods. What is the name of that river that overflows every spring and the government does nothing to stop it?

After this cataclysm at twelve marks eighty, human beings who have had a good cry open their mouths to speak. Still hesitant, startled by the nakedness of their own words, the weepers poured out their hearts to their neighbors on the uncomfortable, burlap-covered crates, submitted to questioning, let themselves be turned inside-out like overcoats. But Oskar, who with Klepp and Scholle sat tearless behind the staircase or companionway, will be discreet; from among all the disclosures, self-accusations, confessions that fell on his ears, he will relate only the story of Miss Pioch, who lost her Mr. Vollmer many times over, so acquiring a strong heart and a tearless eye, which necessitated frequent visits to Schmuh's Onion Cellar.

We met, said Miss Pioch when she had finished crying, in the streetcar. I had just come from the store – she owns and operates an excellent bookstore. The car was full and Willy – that's Mr Vollmer – stepped on my right foot. He stepped so hard that I couldn't stand on it any more, and we loved each other at first sight. I couldn't walk either, so he offered me his arm, escorted, or rather carried, me home, and from that day on he took loving care of the toenail which had turned black and blue under his heel. He loved me, not just my toe, until the toenail came loose from its toe – the right big toe – and there was nothing to prevent a new toenail from growing in. The day the dead toenail fell, his love began to cool. Both of us were miserable about it. It was then that Willy – he still cared for me in a way and, besides, we had so much in common – had his terrible idea. Let me, he pleaded, trample your left big toe until the nail turns a light, then a darker purple. I consented and he trampled. Again he loved me with his whole being, and his love endured until my big toenail, the left one it was, fell away like a withered leaf; and then it was autumn again for our love. Willy wanted to start in again on my right big toe, the nail had meanwhile grown in again. But I wouldn't let him. If your love for me is really so overpowering, I said, it ought to outlast a toenail. He couldn't seem to understand. He left me. Months later, we met at a concert. The seat beside me happened to be unoccupied and after the intermission he sat down in it. They were doing the *Ninth Symphony*. When the chorus started up, I removed the shoe from my right foot and held the foot out in front of him. He stepped on it with might and main, but I didn't do anything to interfere with the concert. Seven weeks later Willy left me again. We had two more brief reprieves; twice more I held out my toe, first the left one, then the right one. Today both my toes are maimed. The nails won't grow in again. From time to time Willy comes to see me; shaken, full of pity for me and for himself, he sits at my feet on the rug and stares, unloving and unweeping, at the two nailless victims of our love. Sometimes I say: Come along Willy, let's go to Schmuh's Onion Cellar and have a good cry. But so far he has refused to come. What the poor soul must suffer without the consolation of tears!

Later – this Oskar relates only to satisfy the curious among you – Mr. Vollmer (he sold radios, I might mention in passing) did come to our Cellar. They cried together and it seems, as Klepp told me yesterday in visiting hour, that they have just been married.

It was from Tuesday to Saturday – the Onion Cellar was closed on Sunday – that the onion brought the more basic tragedies of human existence welling to the surface. But the most violent weeping was done on Mondays, when our cellar was patronized by the younger set. On Monday Schmuh served onions to students at half-price. The most frequent guests were medical and pre-medical students – of both sexes. Quite a few art students as well, particularly among those who were planning to teach drawing later on, spent a portion of their stipends on onions. But where, I have wondered ever since, did the boys and girls in their last year of high school get the money for onions?

Young people have a different way of crying. They have entirely different problems from their elders, but this doesn't mean that examinations are their only source of anguish. Oh, what conflicts between father and son, mother and daughter, were aired in the Onion Cellar! A good many of the young people felt that they were not understood, but most of them were used to it; nothing to cry about. Oskar was glad to see that love, and not just sexual frustration, could still wring tears from the young folks. Gerhard and Gudrun for instance.

At first they sat downstairs; it was only later that they wept side by side in the gallery. She, large and muscular, a handball player and student of chemistry. She wore her hair over her neck in a big bun. Most of the time she looked straight ahead of her out of grey, motherly eyes, a clean forthright gaze that reminded me of the Women's Association posters during the war.

In spite of her fine forehead, smooth, milky-white, and radiant with health, her face was her misfortune. Her cheeks and her round, firm chin down to her Adam's apple bore the distressing traces of a vigorous growth of beard that the poor thing kept trying in vain to shave off. Her sensitive skin reacted violently to the razor blade. Gudrun wept for her red, cracked, pimply complexion, she wept for the beard that kept growing back in. They had not met in the streetcar like Miss Pioch and Mr. Vollmer, but in the train. He was sitting opposite her, they were both on their way back from their between-semesters vacation. He loved her instantly in spite of the beard. She, because of her beard, was afraid to love him, but was full of admiration for what to him was his misfortune, his chin, which was as smooth and beardless as a baby's bottom, and made him bashful in the presence of girls. Nevertheless, Gerhard spoke to Gudrun, and by the time they left the train at the Düsseldorf station, they were friends at least. After that they saw each other every day. They spoke of this and that, and shared a good part of their thoughts, but never alluded to the beard that was missing or the beard that was all too present. Gerhard was considerate of Gudrun; knowing that her skin was sensitive, he never kissed her. Their love remained chaste, though neither of them set much store by chastity, for she was interested in chemistry while he was studying medicine. When a friend suggested the Onion Cellar, they smiled contemptuously with the skepticism characteristic of chemists and medical men. But finally they went, for purposes of documentation, as they assured each other. Never has Oskar seen young people cry so. They came time and time again; they went without food to save up the six marks forty it cost them, and wept about the beard that was absent and the beard that devastated the soft, maidenly skin. Sometimes they tried to stay away from the Onion Cellar. One Monday they didn't come, but the following Monday they were back again. Rubbing the chopped onion between their fingers, they admitted that they had tried to save the six marks forty; they had tried doing it by themselves in her room with a cheap onion, but it wasn't the same. You needed an audience. It was so much easier to cry in company. It gave you a real sense of brotherhood in sorrow when to the right and left of you and in the gallery overhead your fellow students were all crying their hearts out.

This was another case in which the Onion Cellar bestowed not only tears but also, little by little, a cure. Apparently the tears washed away their inhibitions and brought them, as the saying goes, closer together. He kissed her tortured cheeks, she fondled his smooth chin, and one day they stopped coming to the Onion Cellar; they didn't need it any more. Oskar met them months later in Königs-Allee. He didn't recognize them at first. He, the glabrous Gerhard, sported a waving, reddish-blond beard; she, the prickly Gudrun, had barely a slight dark fuzz on her upper lip, very becoming to her. Her chin and cheeks were smooth, radiant, free from vegetation. Still studying but happily married, a student couple. Oskar can hear them in fifty years talking to their grandchildren. She, Gudrun: 'That was long ago, before Grandpa had his beard.' And he, Gerhard: 'That was in the days when your Grandma was having trouble with her beard and we went to the Onion Cellar every Monday.'

But to what purpose, you may ask, are three musicians still sitting under the companionway or staircase? What use had the onion shop, what with all this weeping, wailing, and gnashing of teeth, for a regular, and regularly paid, band?

Once the customers had finished crying and unburdening themselves, we took up our instruments and provided a musical transition to normal, everyday conversation. We made it easy for the guests to leave the Onion Cellar and make room for more guests. Klepp, Scholle, and Oskar were not personally lovers of onions. Besides, there was a clause in our contract forbidding us to 'use' onions in the same way as the guests. We had no need of them anyway. Scholle, the guitarist, had no ground for sorrow, he always seemed happy and contented, even when two strings on his banjo snapped at once in the middle of a rag. As to Klepp, the very concepts of crying and laughing are to this day unclear to him. Tears make him laugh; I have never seen anyone laugh as hard as Klepp did at the funeral of the aunt who used to wash his shirts and socks before he got married. But what of Oskar? Oskar had plenty of ground for tears. Mightn't he have used a few tears to wash away Sister Dorothea and that long, futile night spent on a still longer coconut-fiber runner? And my Maria? There is no doubt that she gave me cause enough for grief. Didn't Stenzel, her boss, come and go as he pleased in the flat in Bilk? Hadn't Kurt, my son, taken to calling the grocery-store-owner first 'Uncle Stenzel' and then 'Papa Stenzel'? And what of those who lay in the faraway sand of Saspe Cemetery or in the clay at Brenntau: my poor mama, the foolish and lovable Jan Bronski, and Matzerath, the cook who knew how to transform feelings into soups? All of them needed to be wept for. But Oskar was one of the fortunate who could still weep without onions. My drum helped me. Just a few very special measures were all it took to make Oskar melt into tears that were no better or worse than the expensive tears of the Onion Cellar.

As for Schmuh, the proprietor, he never touched his onions either. In his case the sparrows he shot out of hedges and bushes in his free time filled the bill. Sometimes, after shooting, Schmuh would line up his twelve dead sparrows on a newspaper, shed tears over the little bundles of feathers before they even had time to grow cold, and, still weeping, strew bird food over the Rhine meadows and the pebbles by the water. In the Cellar he had still another outlet for his sorrow. He had gotten into the habit of giving the washroom attendant a ferocious tongue-lashing once a week, making more and more use of archaic expressions like 'slut', 'miserable strumpet', 'blasted old harridan'. 'Out of my sight!' we could hear him bellow, 'Despicable monster! You're fired!' He would dismiss his victim without notice and hire a new one. But soon he ran into difficulty, there were no washroom attendants left. There was nothing for it but to hire back those he had previously fired. They were only too glad to accept; most of Schmuh's insults didn't mean much to them anyway, and they made good money. The guests at the Onion Cellar – an effect of so much weeping no doubt – made exorbitant use of the facilities, and moreover Homo lacrimans tends to be more generous than his dry-eyed counterpart. Especially the gentlemen, who, after begging leave in voices choked with tears to step out for a minute, could be counted on to reach deep into their purses. Another source of income for the washroom attendant was the sale of the famous onion-print handkerchiefs inscribed with the legend: 'In the Onion Cellar'. They sold like hotcakes, for when they were no longer needed to wipe the eyes with they made attractive souvenirs and could be worn on the head. They could also be made into pennants which the habitués of the Onion Cellar would hang in the rear windows of their cars, so bearing the fame of Schmuh's Onion Cellar, in vacation time, to Paris, the Côte d'Azur, Rome, Ravenna, Rimini, and even remote Spain.

We musicians and our music had still another function. Occasionally some of the guests would partake of two onions in quick succession; the result was an outbreak that might easily have degenerated into an orgy. Schmuh insisted on a certain restraint; when gentlemen began taking off their ties and ladies undoing their blouses, he would order us to step in with our music and counteract the stirrings of lewdness. However, Schmuh himself was largely responsible for these ticklish situations, what with his insidious habit of serving up a second onion to particularly vulnerable customers.

The most spectacular outburst I can recall was to influence

Oskar's whole career, though I shall not go so far as to speak of a crucial turning point. Schmuh's wife, the vivacious Billy, did not come to the Cellar very often, and when she did, it was in the company of friends to whom Schmuh was far from partial. One night she turned up with Woode, the music critic, and Wackerlei, the architect and pipe-smoker. Both of them were regular customers, but their sorrows were of the most boring variety. Woode wept for religious reasons – he was always being converted or reconverted to something or other; as for Wackerlei, the pipe-smoker, he was still bewailing a professorship he had turned down in the twenties for the sake of a little Danish fly-by-night who had gone and married a South American and had six children by him, which was still a source of grief to Wackerlei and made his pipe go out year after year. It was the somewhat malicious Woode who persuaded Madame Schmuh to cut into an onion. She cut, the tears flowed, and she began to spill. She laid Schmuh bare, told stories about him that Oskar will tactfully pass over in silence; it took several of the more powerful customers to prevent Schmuh from flinging himself on his spouse; don't forget that there were paring knives on every table. In any case, Schmuh was forcibly restrained until the indiscreet Billy could slip away with her friends Woode and Wackerlei.

Schmuh was very upset. I could see that by the way his hands flew about arranging and rearranging his onion shawl. Several times he vanished behind the curtain and reviled the washroom attendant. Finally he came back with a full basket and informed his guests in a tone of hysterical glee that he, Schmuh, was in a generous mood and was going to hand out a free round of onions. Which he proceeded to do.

Every human situation, however painful, strikes Klepp as a terrific joke, but on this occasion he was tense and held his flute at the ready. For we knew how dangerous it was to offer these high-strung people a double portion of tears, of the tears that wash away barriers.

Schmuh saw that we were holding our instruments in readiness and forbade us to play. At the tables the paring knives were at work. The beautiful outer skins, colored like rosewood, were thrust heedlessly aside. The knives bit into vitreous onion flesh with pale-green stripes. Oddly enough, the weeping did not begin with the ladies. Gentlemen in their prime – the owner of a large flour mill, a hotel-owner with his slightly rouged young friend, a nobleman high in the councils of an important business firm, a whole tableful of men's clothing manufacturers who were in town for a board meeting, the bald actor who was known in the Cellar as the Gnasher, because he gnashed his teeth when he wept – all were in tears before the ladies joined in. But neither the ladies nor the gentlemen wept the tears of deliverance and release that the first onion had called forth; this was a frantic, convulsive crying jag. The Gnasher gnashed his teeth blood-curdlingly; had he been on the stage, the whole audience would have joined in; the mill-owner hanged his carefully groomed grey head on the table top; the hotel-owner mingled his convulsions with those of his delicate young friend. Schmuh, who stood by the stairs, let his shawl droop and peered with malicious satisfaction at the near-unleashed company. Suddenly, a lady of ripe years tore off her blouse before the eyes of her son-in-law. The hotel-owner's young friend, whose slightly exotic look had already been remarked on, bared his swarthy torso, and leaping from table top to table top performed a dance which exists perhaps somewhere in the Orient. The orgy was under way. But despite the violence with which it began, it was a dull, uninspired affair, hardly worth describing in detail.

Schmuh was disappointed; even Oskar lifted his eyebrows in disgust. One or two cute strip tease acts; men appeared in ladies' underwear, Amazons donned ties and braces; a couple or two disappeared under the table; the Gnasher chewed up a brassiere and apparently swallowed some of it.

The hubbub was frightful, wows and yippees with next to nothing behind them. At length Schmuh, disgusted and maybe fearing the police, left his post by the stairs, bent down over us, gave first Klepp, then me a poke, and hissed: 'Music! Play something, for God's sake. Make them stop.'

But it turned out that Klepp, who was easy to please, was enjoying himself. Shaking with laughter, he couldn't do a thing with his flute. Shaking with laughter, he couldn't do a thing with his flute. Scholle, who looked on Klepp as his master, imitated everything Klepp did, including his laughter. Only Oskar was left

– but Schmuh could rely on me. I pulled my drum from under the bench, nonchalantly lit a cigarette, and began to drum.

Without any notion of what I was going to do, I made myself understood. I forgot all about the usual café concert routine. Nor did Oskar play jazz. For one thing I didn't like to be taken for a percussion maniac. All right, I was a good drummer, but not a hepcat. Sure, I like jazz, but I like Viennese waltzes too. I could play both, but I didn't have to. When Schmuh asked me to step in with my drum, I didn't play anything I had ever learned, I played with my heart. It was a three-year-old Oskar who picked up those drumsticks. I drummed my way back, I drummed up the world as a three-year-old sees it. And the first thing I did to these postwar humans incapable of a real orgy was to put a harness on them: I led them to Posadowski-Weg, to Auntie Kauer's kindergarten. Soon I had their jaws hanging down; they took each other by the hands, turned their toes in, and waited for me, their Pied Piper. I left my post under the staircase and took the lead. 'Bake, bake, bake a cake': that was my first sample. When I had registered my success – childlike merriment on every hand – I decided to scare them out of their wits. 'Where's the Witch, black as pitch?' I drummed. And I drummed up the wicked black Witch who gave me an occasional fright in my childhood days and in recent years has terrified me more and more; I made her rage through the Onion Cellar in all her gigantic, coal-black frightfulness, so obtaining the results for which Schmuh required onions; the ladies and gentlemen wept great round, childlike tears, the ladies and gentlemen were scared pink and green; their teeth chattered, they begged me to have mercy. And so, to comfort them, and in part to help them back into their outer and undergarments, their silks and satins, I drummed: 'Green, green, green is my raiment' and 'Red, red, red is my raiment', not to mention 'Blue, blue, blue . . .' and 'Yellow, yellow, yellow'. By the time I had gone through all the more familiar colors, my charges were all properly dressed. Thereupon I formed them into a procession, led them through the Onion Cellar as though it were Jeschkentaler-Weg. I led them up the Erbsberg, round the hideous Gutenberg Monument, and on the Johannis-Wiese grew daisies which they, the ladies and gentlemen, were free to pick in innocent merriment. Then, at last, wishing to give all those present, including Schmuh the head man, something by which to remember their day in kindergarten, I gave them all permission to do number one. We were approaching Devil's Gulch, a sinister place it was, gathering beechnuts, when I said on my drum: now, children, you may go. And they availed themselves of the opportunity. All the ladies and gentlemen, Schmuh the host, even the far-off wash-room attendant, all the little children wet themselves, psss, psss they went, they all crouched down and listened to the sound they were making and they all wet their pants. It was only when the music had died down – Oskar had left the infant sound effects to themselves except for a soft distant roll – that I ushered in unre-strained merriment with one loud, emphatic boom. All about me the company roared, tittered, babbled childish nonsense:

> Smash a little windowpane
> Put sugar in your beer,
> Mrs. Biddle plays the fiddle,
> Dear, dear, dear.

I led them to the cloakroom, where a bewildered student gave Schmuh's kindergarteners their wraps; then, with the familiar ditty 'Hard-working washerwomen scrubbing out the clothes,' I drummed them up the concrete steps, past the doorman in the rustic sheepskin. I dismissed the kindergarten beneath the night sky of spring, 1950, a trifle cool perhaps, but studded with fairytale stars, as though made to order for the occasion. Forgetful of home, they continued for quite some time to make childish mis-chief in the Old City, until at length the police helped them to remember their age, social position, and telephone number.

As for me, I giggled and caressed my drum as I went back to the Onion Cellar, where Schmuh was still clapping his hands, still standing bowlegged and wet beside the staircase, seemingly as happy in Auntie Kauer's kindergarten as on the Rhine meadows when a grown-up Schmuh went shooting sparrows.

On the Atlantic Wall or Concrete Eternal

I had only been trying to help him. But Schmuh, owner and guiding spirit of the Onion Cellar, could not forgive me for my drum solo which had transformed his well-paying guests into babbling, riotously merry children who wet their pants and cried because they had wet their pants, all without benefit of onions.

Oskar tries to understand him. Could he help fearing my competition when his guests began to push aside the traditional onions and cry out for Oskar, for Oskar's drum, for me who on my drum could conjure up the childhood of every one of them, however old and feeble?

Up until then, Schmuh had contented himself with dismissing his washroom attendants without notice. Now it was the whole Rhine River Three that he fired. In our place he took on an ambulatory fiddler who, if you closed an eye or two, might have been taken for a gypsy.

But when, as a result of our dismissal, several of the guests, the most faithful at that, threatened to leave the Onion Cellar for good, Schmuh had to accept a compromise. Three times a week the fiddler fiddled. Three times a week we performed, having demanded and obtained a raise: twenty DM a night. There were good tips too; Oskar started a savings account and rejoiced as the interest accrued.

Only too soon my savings account was to become a friend in need and indeed, for then came Death and carried away our Ferdinand Schmuh, our job, and our earnings.

I have already said that Schmuh shot sparrows. Sometimes he took us along in his Mercedes and let us look on. Despite occasional quarrels about my drum, which involved Klepp and Scholle, because they took my part, relations between Schmuh and his musicians remained friendly until, as I have intimated, death came between us.

We piled in. As usual, Schmuh's wife was at the wheel. Klepp beside her. Between Oskar and Scholle sat Schmuh, holding his rifle over his knees and caressing it from time to time. We stopped just before Kaiserswerth. On both banks of the Rhine lines of trees: the stage was set. Schmuh's wife stayed in the car and unfolded a newspaper. Klepp had bought some raisins which he munched with noteworthy regularity. Scholle, who had been a student of something or other before taking up the guitar in earnest, managed to conjure up from his memory a number of poems about the river Rhine, which had indeed put its poetic foot forward and, apart from the usual barges, was giving us quite a display of swaying autumnal foliage in the direction of Duisburg, though according to the calendar it was still summer. If Schmuh's rifle had not spoken up from time to time, that afternoon below Kaiserswerth might well have been termed peaceful or even serene.

By the time Klepp had finished his raisins and wiped his fingers on the grass, Schmuh too had finished. Beside the eleven cold balls of feathers on the newspaper, he laid a twelfth – still quivering, as he remarked. The marksman was already packing up his 'bag' – for some unfathomable reason Schmuh always took his victims home with him – when a sparrow settled on a tree root that the river had washed ashore not far from us. The sparrow was so cocky about it, so grey, such a model specimen of a sparrow, that Schmuh couldn't resist; he who never shot more than twelve sparrows in an afternoon shot a thirteenth – he shouldn't have.

After he had laid the thirteenth beside the twelve, we went back to the black Mercedes and found Madame Schmuh asleep. Scholle and Klepp got into the back seat. I was about to join them but didn't; I felt like a little walk, I said, I'd take the streetcar, no need to bother about me. And so they drove off without Oskar, who had been very wise not to ride with them.

I followed slowly. I didn't have far to go. There was a detour round a stretch of road that was under repair. The detour passed by a gravel pit. And in this gravel pit, some twenty feet below the surface of the road, lay the black Mercedes with its wheels in the air.

Some workmen from the gravel pit had removed the three injured persons and Schmuh's body from the car. The ambulance was on its way. I climbed down into the pit – my shoes were soon full of gravel – and busied myself a little with the injured; in spite of the pain they were in, they asked me questions, but I didn't tell them Schmuh was dead. Stiff and startled, he stared up at the sky, which was mostly cloudy. The newspaper containing his afternoon's bag had been flung out of the car. I counted twelve sparrows but couldn't find the thirteenth; I was still looking for it when they eased the ambulance down into the gravel pit.

Schmuh's wife, Klepp, and Scholle had nothing very serious the matter with them: bruises, a few broken ribs. When I went to see Klepp in the hospital and asked him what had caused the accident, he told me an amazing story: As they were driving past the gravel pit, slowly because of the poor condition of the road, hundreds maybe thousands of sparrows had swarmed out of the hedges, bushes, and fruit trees, casting a great shadow over the Mercedes, crashing against the windshield, and frightening Mrs. Schmuh. By sheer sparrow power, they had brought about the accident and Schmuh's death.

You are free to think what you please of Klepp's story; Oskar is skeptical, especially when he considers that when Schmuh was buried in the South Cemetery, he, Oskar, was able to count no more sparrows than years before when he had come here to set up tombstones. Be that as it may, as I, in a borrowed top hat, was following the coffin with the mourners, I caught a glimpse of Korneff in Section Nine, setting up a diorite slab for a two-place grave, with an assistant unknown to me. As the coffin with Schmuh in it was carried past the stonecutter on its way to the newly laid-out Section Ten, Korneff doffed his cap in accordance with cemetery regulations; perhaps because of the top hat, he failed to recognize me, but he rubbed his neck in token of ripening or over-ripe boils.

Funerals! I have been obliged to take you to so many cemeteries. Somewhere, I went so far as to say that funerals remind one of other funerals. Very well, I will refrain from speaking at length of Schmuh's funeral or of Oskar's retrospective musings at the time. Suffice it to say that Schmuh had a normal, decent burial and that nothing unusual happened. All I really have to tell you is that when they had finished burying Schmuh – the widow was in the hospital, or perhaps a little more decorum would have been maintained – I was approached by a gentleman who introduced himself as Dr. Dösch.

Dr. Dösch ran a concert bureau but the concert bureau did not belong to him. He had been a frequent guest, he told me, at the Onion Cellar. I had never noticed him, but he had been there when I transformed Schmuh's customers into a band of babbling, happy children. Dösch himself, in fact, as he told me in confidence, had returned to childhood bliss under the influence of my drum, and he was dead set on making a big thing out of me and my 'terrific stunt', as he called it. He had been authorized to offer me a contract, a terrific contract; why wouldn't I sign it on the spot? Outside the crematorium, where Leo Schugger, who in Düsseldorf bore the name of Willem Slobber, was waiting in his white gloves for the mourners, Dr. Dösch pulled out a paper which, in return for enormous sums of money, committed the undersigned, hereinafter referred to as 'Oskar, the drummer', to give solo performances in large theaters, to appear all by myself on the stage before audiences numbering two to three thousand. Dösch was inconsolable when I said I could not sign right away. As my reason, I gave Schmuh's death; Schmuh, I said, had been very close to me, I just couldn't go to work for someone else before he was cold in his grave, I'd have to think the matter over, maybe I'd take a little trip somewhere; I'd look up Dr. Dösch the moment I got back and then perhaps I would sign this paper that he called a contract.

However, though I signed no contract at the cemetery, Oskar's financial situation impelled him to accept an advance which Dr. Dösch handed me discreetly, hidden away in an envelope with his visiting card, outside the cemetery where he had parked his car.

And I did take the trip, I even found a traveling companion. Actually I should have liked Klepp to go with me. But Klepp was in the hospital, Klepp couldn't even laugh, for he had four broken ribs. I should have liked to take Maria. But the summer holidays were still on, little Kurt would have to come with us. And besides, she was still tied up with Stenzel, her boss, who had got Kurt to call him Papa Stenzel.

In the end I set out with Lankes. You remember him no doubt as Corporal Lankes and as the Muse Ulla's sometime fiancé. When, with my advance and my savings book in my pocket, I repaired to Lankes' studio in Sittarder-Strasse, I was hoping to find Ulla, my former partner; I thought I would ask the Muse to come along on my trip.

Ulla was there. Right in the doorway she told me: We're engaged. Been engaged for two weeks. It hadn't worked with Hänschen Krages, she had been obliged to break it off. Did I know Hänschen Krages?

No, said Oskar, to his infinite regret he hadn't known Ulla's former fiancé. Then Oskar made his generous offer but before Ulla could accept, Lankes, emerging from the studio, elected himself Oskar's travel companion and boxed the long-legged Muse on the ear because she didn't want to stay home and had burst into tears in her disappointment.

Why didn't Oskar defend himself? Why, if he wanted the Muse as his traveling companion, didn't he take the Muse's part? Much as I was attracted by the prospect of a journey with Ulla by my side, Ulla so slender, Ulla so fuzzy and blond, I feared too close an intimacy with a Muse. Better keep the Muses at a distance, I said to myself, or the kiss of the Muses will get to be a domestic habit. It will be wiser to travel with Lankes, who gives his Muse a good licking when she tries to kiss him.

There was little discussion about our destination. Normandy, of course, where else? We would visit the fortifications between Caen and Cabourg. For that is where we had met during the war. The only difficulty was getting visas. But Oskar isn't one to waste words on visas.

Lankes is a stingy man. The lavishness with which he flings paint – cheap stuff to be sure, and scrounged as often as not – on poorly prepared canvas is equalled only by his tight-fistedness with money, coins as well as paper. A constant smoker, he has never been known to buy a cigarette. Moreover his stinginess is systematic: whenever someone gives him a cigarette, he takes a ten-pfennig piece out of his left pants pocket, raises his cap in a brief gesture of recognition, and drops the coin into his right pants pocket where it takes its place among other coins – how many depends on the time of day. As I have said, he is always smoking, and one day when he was in a good humor, he confided in me: 'Every day I make about two marks, just by smoking.'

Last year Lankes bought a bombed-out lot in Wersten. He paid for it with the cigarettes of his friends and acquaintances.

This was the Lankes with whom Oskar went to Normandy. We took the train – an express. Lankes would rather have hitch-hiked. But since he was my guest and I was paying, he had to give in. We rode past poplars, behind which there were meadows bounded by hedgerows. Brown and white cows gave the country-side the look of an advertisement for milk chocolate, though of course for advertising purposes one would have had to block out the war damage. The villages, including the village of Bavent where I had lost my Roswitha, were still in pretty bad shape.

From Cabourg we walked along the beach toward the mouth of the Orne. It wasn't raining. As we approached Le Home, Lankes said: 'We're home again, my boy. Give me a butt.' Before he had finished transferring his coin from pocket to pocket, he stretched out his wolf's head toward one of the numerous unharmed pillboxes in the dunes. With one long arm he toted his knapsack, his traveling easel, and his dozen frames; with the other, he pulled me toward the concrete. Oskar's luggage con-sisted of a suitcase and his drum.

On the third day of our stay on the Atlantic Coast – we had meanwhile cleared the drifted sand out of Dora Seven, removed the distasteful traces of lovers who had found a haven there, and furnished the place with a crate and our sleeping bags – Lankes came up from the beach with a good-sized codfish. Some fisher-men had given it to him in return for a picture he had done of their boat.

In view of the fact that we still called the pillbox Dora Seven, it is hardly surprising that Oskar's thoughts, as he cleaned the fish, turned to Sister Dorothea. The liver and milt spurted over both my hands. While scaling, I faced the sun, which gave Lankes a chance to dash off a water color. We sat behind the pillbox, sheltered from the wind. The August sun beat down on the concrete dome. I larded the fish with garlic. The cavity once occupied by the milt, liver, and entrails, I stuffed with onions, cheese, and thyme; but I didn't throw away the milt and liver; I lodged both delicacies between the fish's jaws, which I wedged open with a lemon. Lankes reconnoitred. He disappeared into Dora Four, Dora Three, and so on down the line. Soon he returned with boards and some large cartons. The cartons he kept to paint on; the wood was for the fire.

There was no difficulty in keeping up the fire; the beach was covered with pieces of dry, feather-light driftwood, casting a variety of shadows. Over the hot coals I laid part of an iron balcony grating which Lankes had torn off a deserted beach villa. I rubbed the fish with olive oil and set it down on the hot grate, which I had also smeared with oil. I squeezed lemon juice over the crackling codfish and let it broil slowly – one should never be in a hurry about cooking fish.

We had made a table by laying a big piece of tarboard over some empty buckets. We had our own forks and tin plates. To divert Lankes – he was circling round the fish like a hungry sea gull – I went to the pillbox and brought out my drum. Bedding it in the sand, I drummed into the wind, variations on the sounds of the surf and the rising tide: Bebra's Theater at the Front had come to inspect the concrete. From Kashubia to Normandy. Felix and Kitty, the two acrobats, tied themselves into knots on top of the pillbox and, just as Oskar was drumming against the wind, recited against the wind a poem the refrain of which, in the very midst of the war, announced the coming of an era of cozy comfort: ' . . . The thought of comfort's like a drug: The trend is toward the bourgeois-smug,' declaimed Kitty with her Saxon accent; and Bebra, my wise Bebra, captain of the Propaganda Company, nodded; and Roswitha, my Raguna from the Mediterranean, took up the picnic basket and set the table on the concrete, on top of Dora Seven; and Corporal Lankes, too, ate our white bread, drank our chocolate, and smoked Captain Bebra's cigarettes . . .

'Man!' Lankes called me back from the past. 'Man, Oskar! If I could only paint like you drum; give me a butt.'

I stopped drumming, gave my traveling companion a cigarette, examined the fish, and saw that it was good: the eyes were white, serene, and liquid. Slowly I squeezed a last lemon, omitting not the slightest patch of the skin, which had cracked in places but was otherwise a beautiful brown.

'I'm hungry,' said Lankes. He showed his long yellow fangs and, apelike, beat his breast with both fists through his checkered shirt.

'Head or tail?' I asked, setting the fish down on a sheet of waxed paper, which we had spread over the tarboard in lieu of a tablecloth.

'What's your advice?' Lankes pinched out his cigarette and put away the butt.

'As a friend, I'd say: Take the tail. As a cook, I can only recommend the head. On the other hand, if my mama, who was a big fish-eater, were here now, she'd say: Mr. Lankes, take the tail, then you know what you've got. On the third hand, the doctor used to advise my father . . .'

'I'm not interested in doctors,' said Lankes distrustfully.

'Dr. Hollatz advised my father always to eat the head of the codfish.'

'Then I'll take the tail. I see you're trying to sell me a bill of goods.' Lankes was still suspicious.

'So much the better for Oskar. The head is what I prefer.'

'Well, if you're so crazy about it, I'll take the head.'

'You're having a tough time, aren't you, Lankes,' I said. 'All right, the head is yours, I'll take the tail.' This, I hoped, would be the end of our dialogue.

'Heh, heh!' said Lankes. 'I guess I put one over on you.'

Oskar admitted that Lankes had put one over on him. Well I knew that his portion wouldn't taste right unless it were seasoned with the assurance that he had put one over on me. A shrewd article, a lucky bastard, I called him – then we fell to.

He took the head piece, I squeezed what was left of the lemon juice over the white, crumbling flesh of the tail piece, whence, as I picked it up, two or three butter-soft wedges of garlic detached themselves.

Sucking at his bones, Lankes peered over at me and the tail piece: 'Give me a taste of your tail.' I nodded, he took his taste, and was undecided until Oskar took a taste of his head piece and assured him once again that he, Lankes, had as usual got the better deal.

We drank red Bordeaux with the fish. I felt sorry about that, I should have preferred to see white wine in our coffee cups. Lankes swept my regrets aside; when he was a corporal in Dora Seven, he remembered, they had never drunk anything but red wine. They had still been drinking red wine when the invasion started: 'Boy, oh boy, were we liquored up! Kowalski, Scherbach, and little Leuthold didn't even notice anything was wrong. And now they're all in the same cemetery, the other side of Cabourg. Over by Arromanches, it was Tommies, here in our sector, Canadians, millions of them. Before we could get our braces up, there they were, saying, "How are you?" '

A little later, waving his fork and spitting out bones: 'Say, who do you think I ran into in Cabourg today? Herzog, Lieutenant Herzog, the nut, you met him on your tour of inspection. You remember him, don't you?'

Of course Oskar remembered Lieutenant Herzog. Lankes went on to tell me over the fish that Herzog returned to Cabourg year in, year out, with maps and surveying instruments, because the thought of these fortifications gave him no sleep. He was planning to drop in at Dora Seven and do a bit of measuring.

We were still on the fish – little by little the contours of the backbone were emerging – when Lieutenant Herzog turned up. Khaki knee breeches, plump calves, tennis shoes; a growth of grey-brown hair emerged from the open neck of his linen shirt. Naturally we kept our seats. Lankes introduced me as Oskar, his peacetime friend and wartime buddy, and addressed Herzog as Reserve Lieutenant Herzog.

The reserve lieutenant began at once to inspect Dora Seven. He began with the outside, and Lankes raised no objection. Herzog filled out charts and examined the land and sea through his binoculars. Then for a moment he caressed the gun embrasures of Dora Six as tenderly as though fondling his wife. When he wished to inspect the inside of Dora Seven, our villa, our summer house, Lankes wouldn't hear of it: 'Herzog, man, what's the matter with you? Poking around in concrete. Maybe it was news ten years ago. Now it's passé.'

'Passé' is a pet word with Lankes. Everything under the sun is either news or passé. But the reserve lieutenant held that nothing was passé, that the accounts were still unclear, that some of the figures would have to be rectified, that men would always be called upon to give an account of themselves before the judgment seat of history, and that was why he wanted to inspect the inside of Dora Seven: 'I hope, Lankes, that I have made myself clear.'

Herzog's shadow fell across our table and fish. He meant to pass around us to the pillbox entrance, over which concrete ornaments still bore witness to the creative hand of Corporal Lankes.

But Herzog never got past our table. Rising swiftly, Lankes' fist, still gripping its fork but making no use of it, sent Reserve Lieutenant Herzog sprawling backward on the sand. Shaking his head, deploring the interruption of our meal, Lankes stood up, seized a fistful of the lieutenant's shirt, dragged him to the edge of the dune – the track in the sand was remarkably straight, I recall – and tossed him off. He had vanished from my sight but not, unfortunately, from my hearing. He gathered together his surveying instruments, which Lankes had thrown after him, and went away grumbling and conjuring up all the historical ghosts that Lankes had dismissed as passé.

'He's not so very wrong,' said Lankes, 'even if he is a nut. If we hadn't been so soused when the shooting started, who knows what would have happened to those Canadians.'

I could only nod assent, for just the day before, at low tide, I had found the telltale button of a Canadian uniform in among the empty crab shells. As pleased as though he had found a rare Etruscan coin, Oskar had secreted the button in his wallet.

Brief as it was, Lieutenant Herzog's visit had conjured up memories: 'Do you remember, Lankes, when our theatrical group was inspecting your concrete and we had breakfast on top of the pillbox? There was a little breeze just like today. And suddenly there were six or seven nuns, looking for crabs in the Rommel asparagus, and you, Lankes, you had orders to clear the beach; which you did with a murderous machine gun.'

Sucking bones, Lankes remembered; he even remembered their names: Sister Scholastica, Sister Agneta... he described the novice as a rosy little face with lots of black around it. His portrait of her was so vivid that it partly, but only partly, concealed the image, which never left me, of my trained nurse, my secular Sister Dorothea. A few minutes later – I wasn't surprised enough to put it down as a miracle – a young nun came drifting across the dunes from the direction of Cabourg. Pink little face, with lots of black around it, there was no mistaking her.

She was shielding herself from the sun with a black umbrella such as elderly gentlemen carry. Over her eyes arched a poison-green celluloid shade, suggesting dynamic movie directors in Hollywood. Off in the dunes someone was calling her. There seemed to be more nuns about. 'Sister Agneta!' the voice cried, 'Sister Agneta, where are you?'

And Sister Agneta, the young thing who could be seen over the backbone of our codfish: 'Here I am, Sister Scholastica. There's no wind here.'

Lankes grinned and nodded his wolf's head complacently, as though he himself had conjured up this Catholic parade, as though nothing in the world could startle him.

The young nun caught sight of us and stopped still, to one side of the pillbox. 'Oh!' gasped her rosy face between slightly protruding but otherwise flawless teeth.

Lankes turned head and neck without stirring his body: 'Hiya, Sister, taking a little walk?'

How quickly the answer came: 'We always go to the seashore once a year. But for me it's the first time. I never saw the ocean before. It's so big.'

There was no denying that. To this day I look upon her description of the ocean as the only accurate one.

Lankes played the host, poked about in my portion of fish and offered her some: 'Won't you try a little fish, Sister? It's still warm.'

I was amazed at the ease with which he spoke French, and Oskar also tried his hand at the foreign language: 'Nothing to worry about. It's Friday anyway.'

But even this tactful allusion to the rules of her order could not move the young girl, so cleverly dissimulated in the nun's clothes, to partake of our repast.

'Do you always live here?' her curiosity impelled her to ask. Our pillbox struck her as pretty and a wee bit comical. But then, unfortunately, the mother superior and five other nuns, all with black umbrellas and green visors, entered the picture over the crest of the dune. Agneta whished away. As far as I could understand the flurry of words clipped by the east wind, she was given a good lecture and made to take her place in the group.

Lankes dreamed. He held his fork in his mouth upside down and gazed at the group floating over the dunes. 'That ain't no nuns, it's sailboats.'

'Sailboats are white,' I objected.

'It's black sailboats.' It wasn't easy to argue with Lankes. 'The one out there on the left is the flagship. Agneta's a fast corvette. Good sailing weather. Column formation, jib to stern-post, mainmast, mizzenmast, and foremast, all sails set, off to the horizon and England. Think of it: tomorrow morning the Tommies wake up, look out the window, and what do they see: twenty-five thousand nuns, all decked with flags. And here comes the first broadside . . .'

'A new war of religion,' I helped him. The flagship, I suggested, should be called the Mary Stuart or the De Valera or, better still, the Don Juan. A new, more mobile Armada avenges Trafalgar. 'Death to all Puritans!' was the battle cry and this time the English had no Nelson on hand. Let the invasion begin, England has ceased to be an island.

The conversation was getting too political for Lankes.

'The nuns are steaming away,' he announced.

'Sailing,' I corrected.

Whether steaming or sailing, they were floating off in the direction of Cabourg, holding umbrellas between themselves and the sun. Only one lagged behind a little, bent down between steps, picked up something, and dropped something. The rest of the fleet made its way slowly, tacking into the wind, toward the gutted beach hotel in the background.

'Looks like her steering gear is damaged or maybe she can't get her anchor up,' said Lankes, running his nautical image into the ground. 'Hey, that must be Agneta, the fast corvette.'

Frigate or corvette, it was indeed Sister Agneta, the novice, who came toward us, picking up shells and throwing some of them away.

'What are you picking up there, Sister?' Lankes could see perfectly well what she was picking up.

'Shells,' she pronounced the word very clearly and bent down.

'You allowed to do that? Ain't they earthly goods?'

I came out for Sister Agneta: 'You're wrong, Lankes. There's nothing earthly about sea shells.'

'Whether they come from the earth or the sea, in any case they are goods and nuns shouldn't have any. Poverty, poverty, and more poverty, that's what nuns should have. Am I right, Sister?'

Sister Agneta smiled through her protruding teeth: 'I only take a few. They are for the kindergarten. The children love to play with them. They have never been to the seashore.'

Agneta stood outside the entrance to the pillbox and cast a furtive, nun's glance inside.

'How do you like our little home?' I asked, trying to make friends. Lankes was more direct: 'Come in and take a look at our villa. Won't cost you a penny.'

Her pointed high shoes fidgeted under her long skirt, stirring sand that the wind picked up and strewed over our fish. Losing some of her self-assurance, she examined us and the table between us out of eyes that were distinctly light brown. 'It surely wouldn't be right.'

'Come along, Sister,' Lankes swept aside all her objections and stood up. 'There's a fine view. You can see the whole beach through the gun slits.'

Still she hesitated; her shoes, it occurred to me, must be full of sand. Lankes waved in the direction of the entrance. His concrete ornament cast sharp ornamental shadows. 'It's tidy inside.'

Perhaps it was Lankes' gesture of invitation that decided the nun to go in. 'But just a minute!' And she whished into the pillbox ahead of Lankes. He wiped his hands on his trousers – a typical painter's gesture – and flung a threat at me before disappearing: 'Careful you don't take none of my fish.'

But Oskar had his fill of fish. I moved away from the table, surrendered myself to the sandy wind and the exaggerated bellowing of Strong Man Sea. I pulled my drum close with one foot and tried, by drumming, to find a way out of this concrete landscape, this fortified world, this vegetable called Rommel asparagus.

First, with small success, I tried love; once upon a time I too had loved a sister. Not a nun, to be sure, but Sister Dorothea, a nurse. She lived in the Zeidler flat, behind a frosted-glass door. She was very beautiful, but I never saw her. It was too dark in the Zeidler hallway. A fiber runner came between us.

After following this theme to its abortive end on the fiber rug, I tried to convert my early love for Maria into rhythm and set it down on the concrete like quick-growing creepers. But there was Sister Dorothea again, interfering with my love of Maria. A smell of carbolic acid blew in from the sea, gulls in nurse's uniforms waved at me, the sun insisted on glittering like a Red Cross pin.

Oskar was glad when his drumming was interrupted. Sister

Scholastica, the mother superior, was coming back with her five nuns. They looked tired and their umbrellas slanted forlornly: 'Have you seen a little nun, our little novice? The child is so young. The child had never seen the ocean before. She must have got lost. Sister Agneta, where are you?'

There was nothing I could do but send the little squadron, now with the wind in their stern, off toward the mouth of the Orne, Arromanches, and Port Winston, where the English had wrested an artificial harbor from the sea. There would hardly have been room for all of them in the pillbox. For a moment, I have to admit, I was tempted to surprise Lankes with their visit, but then friendship, disgust, malice, all in one, bade me hold out my thumb in the direction of the Orne estuary. The nuns obeyed my thumb and gradually turned into six receding, black, wind-blown spots on the crest of the dune; their plaintive 'Sister Agneta, Sister Agneta' came to me more and more diluted with wind, until at last it was swallowed up in the sand.

Lankes was first to come out. Again the typical painter's gesture: he wiped his hands on his trousers, demanded a cigarette, put it into his shirt pocket, and fell upon the cold fish. 'It whets the appetite,' he said with a leer, pillaging the tail end which was my share. Then he sprawled himself out in the sun.

'She must be unhappy now,' I said accusingly, savoring the word 'unhappy.'

'How so? Got nothing to be unhappy about.'

It was inconceivable to Lankes that his version of human relations might make anyone unhappy.

'What's she doing now?' I asked, though I really meant to ask him something else.

'Sewing,' said Lankes with his fork. 'Ripped her habit a bit, now she's mending it.'

The seamstress came out of the pillbox. At once she opened the umbrella and started to babble gaily, yet, it seemed to me, with a certain strain: 'The view is really divine. The whole beach and the ocean too.'

She stopped by the wreckage of our fish.

'May I?'

Both of us nodded at once.

'The sea air whets the appetite,' I encouraged her. Nodding, she dug into our fish with chapped, reddened hands revealing her hard work in the convent, and filled her mouth. She ate gravely, with pensive concentration, as though mulling over, with the fish, something she had had before the fish.

I looked under her coif. She had left her green reporter's eyeshade in the pillbox. Little beads of sweat, all of equal size, lined up on her smooth forehead, which, in its white starched frame, had a madonna-like quality. Lankes asked for another cigarette though he hadn't smoked the previous one. I tossed him the pack. While he stowed three in his shirt pocket and stuck a fourth between his lips, Sister Agneta turned, threw the umbrella away, ran – only then did I see that she was barefoot – up the dune, and vanished in the direction of the surf.

'Let her run,' said Lankes in an oracular tone. 'She'll be back or maybe she won't.'

For an instant I managed to sit still and watch Lankes smoking. Then I climbed on top of the pillbox and looked out at the beach. The tide had risen and very little beach was left.

'Well?' Lankes asked.

'She's undressing.' That was all he could get out of me. 'Probably means to go swimming. Wants to cool off.'

That struck me as dangerous at high tide, especially so soon after eating. Already she was in up to the knees; her back was bent forward and she sank deeper and deeper. The water could not have been exactly warm, but that didn't seem to bother her: she swam, she swam well, practicing several different strokes, and dove through the waves.

'Let her swim, and come down off that pillbox.' I looked behind me and saw Lankes sprawling in the sand and puffing away. The smooth backbone of the codfish glistened white in the sun, dominating the table.

As I jumped off the concrete, Lankes opened his painter's eyes and said: 'Christ, what a picture! Nuns at High Tide.'

'You monster,' I shouted. 'Supposing she drowns?' Lankes closed his eyes: 'Then we'll call it: Nuns Drowning.'

'And if she comes back and flings herself at your feet?'

Wide-eyed, the painted declaimed: 'Then she and the picture will be called: Fallen Nun.'

With him it was always either-or, head or tail, drowned on

fallen. He took my cigarettes, threw the lieutenant off the dune, ate my fish, showed the inside of a pillbox to a little girl who was supposed to be the bride of Christ, and while she was still swimming out to sea, drew pictures in the air with his big lumpy foot. He even listed the titles and plotted the formats: Nuns at High Tide, eight by five, Nuns Drowning, Fallen Nuns, Twenty-five Thousand Nuns. Nuns at Trafalgar. Nuns Defeat Lord Nelson. Nuns Bucking the Wind. Nuns Before the Breeze. Nuns Tacking. Black, lots of black; dingy white and cold blue: The Invasion, or Barbaric, Mystical, Bored. And on our return to the Rhineland Lankes actually painted all these pictures, in formats ranging from wide and low to high and narrow. He did whole series of nuns, found a dealer who was wild about nuns, exhibited forty-three of these nunsuch canvases and sold seventeen to collectors, industrialists, museums, and an American; some of the critics even saw fit to compare him, Lankes, to Picasso. It was Lankes success that persuaded me, Oskar, to dig up the visiting card of Dr. Dösch, the concert manager, for Lankes' art was not alone in clamoring for bread. The time had come to transmute the prewar and wartime experience of Oskar, the three-year-old drummer, into the pure, resounding gold of the postwar period.

The Ring Finger

'So that's it,' said Zeidler. 'So you've decided not to work any more.' It riled him that Klepp and Oskar should spend the whole day sitting either in Klepp's or Oskar's room, doing just about nothing. I had paid the October rent on both rooms out of what was left of Dr. Dösch's advance, but the prospects, financial and otherwise, for November, were bleak.

And yet we had plenty of offers. Any number of dance halls or night clubs would have taken us on. But Oskar was sick of playing jazz. That put a strain on my relations with Klepp. Klepp said my new drum style had no connection with jazz. He was right and I didn't deny it. He said I was disloyal to the jazz ideal. Early in November Klepp found a new percussion man, and a good one at that, namely Bobby from the Unicorn, and was able to accept an engagement in the Old City. After that we were friends again, even though Klepp was already beginning to think, or perhaps it would be safer to say talk, along Communist lines.

In the end Dr. Dösch was my only resort. I couldn't have gone back to live with Maria even if I had wanted to; Stenzel was getting a divorce, meaning to convert my Maria into a Maria Stenzel. From time to time I knocked out an inscription for Korneff or dropped in at the Academy to be blackened or abstracted. Quite frequently I went calling, with nothing definite in mind, on Ulla, who had been obliged to break her engagement to Lankes shortly after our trip to the Atlantic Wall, because Lankes wasn't doing anything but nuns and didn't even want to beat Ulla any more.

Dr. Dösch's visiting card lay silently clamoring on my table beside the bathtub. One day, having decided that I wanted none of Dr. Dösch, I tore it up and threw it away. To my horror I discovered that the address and telephone number were graven on my memory. I could read them off like a poem. I not only could but did. This went on for three days; the telephone number kept me awake at night. On the fourth day, I went to the nearest telephone booth. Dösch spoke as though he had been expecting my call from one minute to the next and asked me to drop in at the office that same afternoon; he wanted to introduce me to the boss, in fact the boss was expecting me.

The West Concert Bureau had its offices on the eighth floor of a new office building. Expensive carpeting, quantities of chrome, indirect lighting, soundproofing, crisp, long-legged secretaries, wafting their boss's cigar smoke past me; two seconds more and I would have fled.

Dr. Dösch received me with open arms though he did not actually hug me – a narrow escape, it seemed to Oskar. Beside him a green sweater girl was typing; her machine stopped as I entered, but speeded up almost instantly to make up for lost time. Dösch announced me to the boss. Oskar sat down on the front left sixth of an armchair upholstered in English vermilion. A folding door opened, the typewriter held its breath, a hidden force raised me to my feet, the doors closed behind me, a carpet, flowing through the large, luminous room, led me forward until an enormous oak table top supported by steel tubing said to me: now Oskar is standing in front of the boss's desk, I wonder how much he weighs. I raised my blue eyes, looked for the boss behind the infinitely empty oak surface, and found, in a wheelchair that could be cranked up and tipped like a dentist's chair, my friend and master Bebra, paralyzed, living only with his eyes and fingertips.

He still had his voice though. And Bebra's voice spoke: 'So we meet again, Mr. Matzerath. Did I not tell you years ago, when you still chose to face the world as a three-year old, that our kind can never lose one another? However, I see to my regret that you have altered your proportions, immoderately so, and not all to your advantage. Did you not measure exactly three feet in those days?'

I nodded, on the verge of tears. The wall behind the master's wheelchair – it was operated by an electric motor which gave off a low, steady hum – had just one picture on it: a life-size bust of Roswitha, the great Raguna, in a baroque frame. Bebra didn't have to follow my eyes to know what I was looking at. His lips, when he spoke, were almost motionless: 'Ah, yes, our good Roswitha! How, I wonder, would she have liked the new Oskar? Not too well, I think. It was another Oskar that she cared for, a three-year-old with cheeks like a cherub, but oh, so loving! She worshipped him, as she never wearied of telling me. But one day he was disinclined to bring her a cup of coffee; she herself went for it and lost her life. And if I am not mistaken, that is not the only murder committed by our cherubic little Oskar. Is it not true that he drummed his poor mama into her grave?'

I nodded. I looked up at Roswitha, I was able to cry, thank the Lord. Bebra recoiled for the next blow; 'And what of Jan Bronski, the postal secretary, whom three-year-old Oskar liked to call his presumptive father? Oskar handed him over to the centurions who shot him. And now perhaps, Mr. Oskar Matzerath, you who have had the audacity to change your shape, now perhaps you can tell me what became of your second presumptive father, Matzerath the grocer?'

Again I confessed. I admitted that I had murdered Matzerath, because I wanted to be rid of him, and told my judge how I had made him choke to death. I no longer hid behind a Russian tommy gun, but said: 'It was I, Master Bebra. I did it; this crime, too, I committed, I am not innocent of this death. Have mercy!'

Bebra laughed, though I don't know what with. His wheelchair trembled, winds ruffled his gnome's hair over the hundred thousand wrinkles that constituted his face.

Again I begged for mercy, charging my voice with a sweetness which I knew to be effective and covering my face with my hands, which I knew to be touchingly beautiful: 'Mercy, dear Master Bebra! Have mercy!'

Bebra, who had set himself up as my judge and played the role to perfection, pressed a button on the little ivory-white switchboard that he held between his hands and knees.

The carpet behind me brought in the green sweater girl, carrying a folder. She spread out the contents of the folder on the oak table top, which was roughly on a level with my collarbone, too high for me to see exactly what she was spreading out. Then she handed me a fountain pen: I was to purchase Bebra's mercy with my signature.

Still, I ventured to ask a few questions. I couldn't just sign with my eyes closed.

'The document before you,' said Bebra, 'is a contract for your professional services. Your full name is required. We have to know whom we are dealing with. First name and last name: Oskar Matzerath.'

The moment I had signed, the hum of the electric motor increased in force. I looked up from the fountain pen just in time to see a wheelchair race across the room and vanish through a side door.

The reader may be tempted to believe that the contract in duplicate to which I affixed my signature provided for the sale of my soul or committed me to some monstrous crime. Nothing of the sort. With the help of Dr. Dösch I studied the contract in the foyer and found no difficulty in understanding that all Oskar had to do was to appear in public all by himself with his drum, to drum as I had drummed as a three-year-old and once again, more recently, in Schmuh's Onion Cellar. The West Concert Bureau undertook to organize tours for me and to provide suitable advance publicity.

I received a second generous advance, on which I lived while the publicity campaign was in progress. From time to time I dropped in at the office and submitted to interviewers and photographers. Dr. Dösch and the sweater girl were always most obliging, but I never saw Master Bebra again.

Even before the first tour I could well have afforded better lodgings. However, I stayed on at Zeidler's for Klepp's sake. Klepp resented my dealings with an agency; I did what I could to placate him but I did not give in, and there were no more expeditions to the Old City to drink beer or eat fresh blood sausage with onions. Instead, to prepare myself for the life of a traveling man, I treated myself to excellent dinners at the railroad station.

Oskar hasn't space enough to describe his success at length. The publicity posters, building me up as a miracle man, a faith-healer, and little short of a Messiah, proved scandalously effective. I made my debut in the cities of the Ruhr Valley in halls with a seating capacity of fifteen hundred to two thousand. The spotlight discovered me in a dinner jacket, all alone against a black velvet curtain. I played the drum, but my following did not consist of youthful jazz addicts. No, those who flocked to hear me were the middle-aged, the elderly, and the doddering. My message was addressed most particularly to the aged, and they responded. They did not sit silent as I awakened my three-year-old drum to life; they gave vent to their pleasure, though not in the language of their years, but burbling and babbling like three-year-olds. 'Rashu, Rashu!' they piped when Oskar drummed up an episode from the miraculous life of the miraculous Rasputin. But most of my listeners were not really up to Rasputin. My biggest triumphs were with numbers evoking not any particular happenings, but stages of infancy and childhood. I gave these numbers such titles as: 'Baby's First Teeth', 'That Beastly Whooping Cough', 'Itchy Stockings', 'Dream of Fire and You'll Wet Your Bed'.

That appealed to the old folks. They went for it hook, line, and sinker. They cut their first teeth and their gums ached. Two thousand old folks hacked and whooped when I infected them with whooping cough. How they scratched when I put woolen stockings on them! Many an old lady, many an aged gentleman wet his or her underwear, not to mention the upholstery he or she was sitting on, when I made the children dream of a fire. I don't recall whether it was in Wuppertal or in Bochum; no, it was in Recklinghausen: I was playing to a house of aged miners, the performance was sponsored by the union. These old-timers, I said to myself, have been handling black coal all their lives; surely they'll be able to put up with a little black fright. Whereupon Oskar drummed 'The Wicked Black Witch' and lo and behold, fifteen hundred crusty old miners, who had lived through cave-ins, explosions, flooded pits, strikes, and unemployment, let out the most bloodcurdling screams I have ever heard. Their screams – and this is why I mention the incident – demolished several windows in spite of the heavy drapes covering them. Indirectly, I had recovered my glass-killing voice. However, I made little use of it; I didn't want to ruin my business.

Yes, business was good. When the tour was over and I reckoned up with Dr. Dösch, it turned out that my tin drum was a gold mine.

I hadn't even asked after Bebra the master and had given up hope of seeing him again. But as Dr. Dösch soon informed me, Bebra was waiting for me.

My second meeting with the master was quite different from the first. This time Oskar was not made to stand in front of the oak table top. Instead, I sat in an electric wheelchair, made to order for Oskar. Dr. Dösch had made tape recordings of my press notices, and Bebra and I sat listening as he ran them off. Bebra seemed pleased. To me the effusions of the newspapers were rather embarrassing. They were building me up into a cult, Oskar and his drum had become healers of the body and soul. And what we cured best of all was loss of memory. The word 'Oskarism' made its first appearance, but not, I am sorry to say, its last.

Afterward, the sweater girl brought me tea and put two pills on the master's tongue. We chatted. He had ceased to be my accuser. It was like years before at the Four Seasons Café, except that the Signora, our Roswitha, was missing. When I couldn't help noticing that Master Bebra had fallen asleep over some longwinded story about my past, I spent ten or fifteen minutes playing with my wheelchair, making the motor hum, racing across the floor, circling to left and right. I had difficulty in tearing myself away from this remarkable piece of furniture, which offered all the possibilities of a harmless vice.

My second tour was at Advent. I conceived my program accordingly and was highly praised in the religious press. For I succeeded in turning hardened old sinners into little children, singing Christmas carols in touching watery voices. 'Jesus, for thee I live, Jesus, for thee I die,' sang two thousand five hundred aged souls, whom no one would have suspected of such childlike innocence or religious zeal.

My third tour coincided with carnival, and again I rearranged my program. No so-called children's carnival could have been merrier or more carefree than those evenings that turned palsied grandmas into Carmens and Indian maidens, while Grampa went bang-bang and led his robbers into battle.

After carnival I signed a contract with a record company. The recording was done in soundproof studios. The sterile atmosphere cramped my style at first, but then I had the walls plastered with enormous photographs of old people such as one sees in homes for the aged and on park benches. By fixing my attention on them, I was able to drum with the same conviction as in concert halls full of human warmth.

The records sold like hotcakes. Oskar was rich. Did that make me give up my miserable sometime bathroom in the Zeidler flat? No. Why not? Because of my friend Klepp and also because of the empty room behind the frosted-glass door, where Sister Dorothea had once lived and breathed. What did Oskar do with all his money? He made Maria, his Maria, a proposition.

This is what I said to Maria: If you give Stenzel his walking papers, if you not only forget about marrying him but throw him out altogether, I'll buy you a modern, up-and-coming delicatessen store. Because after all, my dear Maria, you were born for business and not for any no-good Mr. Stenzel.

I was not mistaken in Maria. She gave up Stenzel and with my financial assistance built up a first-class delicatessen store in Friedrichstrasse. The business prospered and three years later, last week that is – as Maria informed me only yesterday, bursting with joy and not without gratitude – she opened a branch store in Ober-Kassel.

Was it on my return from my seventh or from my eighth tour? In any case it was July and very hot. From the Central Station, where I was besieged by aged autograph hunters, I took a cab straight to the concert bureau and was besieged on alighting by some more aged autograph hunters, who should have been look-ing after their grandchildren. I sent in my name; the folding doors were open, the carpet still led to the big desk, but behind the desk there was no Bebra and no wheelchair was waiting for me. There was only a smiling Dr. Dösch.

Bebra was dead. He had died several weeks ago. He had not wished them to inform me of his illness. Nothing, not even his death, he had said, must interfere with Oskar's tour. The will was soon read; I inherited a small fortune and the picture of Roswitha that hung over his desk. At the same time I incurred a severe financial loss, for I was in no state to perform. I called off two whole tours – in Southern Germany and Switzerland – on in-sufficient notice and was sued for breach of contract.

And alas, my loss was more than financial. Bebra's death was a severe blow to me and I did not recover overnight. I locked up my drum and refused to stir from my room. To make matters worse, this was the moment my friend Klepp chose to get married, to take a redheaded cigarette girl as his life companion, and all because he had once given her a photograph of himself. Shortly before the wedding, to which I was not invited, he gave up his room and moved to Stockum. Oskar was left as Zeidler's only roomer.

My relations with the Hedgehog had changed. Now that the papers carried my name in banner headlines, he treated me with respect; in return for a bit of change, he even gave me the key to Sister Dorothea's room. Later I rented the room to prevent anyone else from doing so.

My sorrow had its itinerary. I opened the doors of both rooms, dragged myself from my bathtub down the fiber runner to Doro-thea's room, gazed into the empty clothes cupboard, faced the ridicule of the washstand mirror, despaired at the sight of the gross, coverless bed, retreated to the hallway, and fled to my room. But there too it was intolerable.

Speculating no doubt on the needs of lonely people, an enter-prising East Prussian who had lost his Masurian estates had opened, not far from Jülicher-Strasse, an establishment specializ-ing in the rental of dogs.

There I rented Lux, a rottweiler – glossy black, powerful, a trifle too fat. As the only alternative to racing back and forth between my bathtub and Sister Dorothea's empty clothes cup board, I began to take walks with Lux.

Lux often led me to the Rhine, where he barked at the ships. He often led me to Rath, to Grafenberg Forest, where he barked at lovers. At the end of July, 1951, he led me to Gerresheim, a suburb which, with the help of a few factories including a large glassworks, is rapidly losing its rural character. Beyond Gerresheim the path winds between kitchen gardens separated by fences from the outlying pastures and grainfields.

Have I said that it was hot on the day when Lux led me to Gerresheim and past Gerresheim between the grain – rye, it was, I think – and the gardens? When the last houses of the suburb were behind us, I let Lux off the leash. Still he tagged along at my heels; he was a faithful dog, an unusually faithful dog when you consider that in his line of business he had to be faithful to several masters.

The fact is he was too well behaved for my liking, I should rather have seen him run about, and indeed I kicked him to give him the idea. But when he did run off, it was plain that his conscience troubled him; on his return, he would hang his glossy black head and look up at me with those proverbially faithful eyes.

'Run along now, Lux,' I demanded. 'Get going.'

Lux obeyed several times but so briefly that I was delighted when at length he disappeared into the rye field and stayed and stayed. Lux must be after a rabbit, I thought. Or maybe he just feels the need to be alone, to be a dog, just as Oskar would like for a little while to be a human without a dog.

I paid no attention to my surroundings. Neither the gardens nor Gerresheim nor the low-lying city in the mist behind it attracted my eye. I sat down on a rusty iron drum, on which cable had at one time been wound, and hardly had Oskar taken his mety seat when he began to drum on the cable drum with his knuckles. It was very hot. My suit was too heavy for this kind of weather. Lux was gone and did not come back. Of course no cast-iron cable drum could take the place of my little tin drum, but even so: gradually I slipped back into the past. When I bogged down, when the images of the last few years, full of hospitals and nurses, insisted on recurring, I picked up two dry sticks, and said to myself: Just wait a minute, Oskar. Let's see now who you are and where you're from. And there they glowed, the two sixty-watt bulbs of the hour of my birth. Between them the moth drummed, while the storm moved furniture in the distance. I heard Matzerath speak, and a moment later my mama. He promised me the store, she promised me a toy; at the age of three I would be given a drum, and so Oskar tried to make the three years pass as quickly as possible; I ate, drank, evacuated, put on weight, let them weigh me, swaddle, bathe, brush, powder, vaccinate, and admire me; I let them call me by name, smiled when expected to, laughed when necessary, went to sleep at the proper time, woke up punctually, and in my sleep made the face that grownups call an angel face. I had diarrhea a few times and several colds, caught whooping cough, hung on to it, and relinquished it only when I had mastered its difficult rhythm, when I had it in my wrists forever, for, as we know, 'Whooping Cough' is one of the pieces in my repertory, and when Oskar played 'Whooping Cough' to an audience of two thousand, two thousand old men and women hacked and whooped.

Lux whimpered at my feet, rubbed against my knees. Oh, this rented dog that my loneliness had made me rent! There he stood four-legged and tail-wagging, definitely a dog, with that doggy look and something or other in his slavering jaws: a stick, a stone, or whatever may seem desirable to a dog.

Slowly my childhood – the childhood that means so much to me – slipped away. The pain in my gums, foreshadowing my first teeth, died down; tired, I leaned back: an adult hunchback, carefully though rather too warmly dressed, with a wristwatch, identification papers, a bundle of banknotes in his billfold. I put a cigarette between my lips, set a match to it, and trusted the tobacco to expel that obsessive taste of childhood from my oral cavity.

And Lux? Lux rubbed against me. I pushed him away, blew cigarette smoke at him. He didn't like that but he held his ground and kept on rubbing. He licked me with his eyes. I searched the nearby telegraph wires for swallows, a remedy it seemed to me against importunate dogs. There were no swallows and Lux refused to be driven away. He nuzzled in between my trouser legs, finding his way to a certain spot with as much assurance as if his East Prussian employer had trained him for that kind of thing.

The heel of my shoe struck him twice. He retreated a few feet and stood there, four-legged and quivering, but continued to offer me his muzzle with its stick or stone as insistently as if what he was holding had been not a stick or stone but my wallet which I could feel in my jacket or my watch that was ticking audibly on my wrist.

What then was he holding? What was so important, so eminently worth showing me?

I reached out between his warm jaws, I had the thing in my hand, I knew what I was holding but pretended to be puzzled, as though looking for a word to name this object that Lux had brought me from the rye field.

There are parts of the human body which can be examined more easily and accurately when detached, when alienated from the center. It was a finger. A woman's finger. A ring finger. A woman's ring finger. A woman's finger with an attractive ring on it. Between the metacarpus and the first finger joint, some three-quarters of an inch below the ring, the finger had allowed itself to be chopped off. The section was neat, clearly revealing the tendon of the extensor muscle.

It was a beautiful finger, a mobile finger. The stone on the ring was held in place by six gold claws. I identified it at once – correctly, it later turned out – as an aquamarine. The ring itself was worn so thin at one place that I set it down as an heirloom. Despite the line of dirt, or rather of earth under the nail, as though the finger had been obliged to scratch or dig earth, the nail seemed to have been carefully manicured. Once I had removed it from the dog's warm muzzle, the finger felt cold and its peculiarly yellowish pallor also suggested coldness.

For several months Oskar had been wearing a silk handkerchief in his breast pocket. He laid the ring finger down on this square of silk and observed that the inside of the finger up to the third joint was marked with lines indicating that this had been a hard-working finger with a relentless sense of duty.

After folding up the finger in the handkerchief, I rose from the cable drum, stroked Lux's neck, and started for home, carrying handkerchief and finger in my right hand. Planning to do this and that with my find, I came to the fence of a nearby garden. It was then that Vittlar, who had been lying in the crook of an apple tree, observing me and the dog, addressed me.

The Last Streetcar Or Adoration of a Preserving Jar

That voice for one thing, that arrogant, affected whine! Besides, he was lying in the crook of an apple tree. 'That's a smart dog you've got there,' he whined.

I, rather bewildered: 'What are you doing up there?' He stretched languidly: 'They are only cooking apples. I assure you, you have nothing to fear.'

He was beginning to get on my nerves: 'Who cares what kind of apples you've got? And what do you expect me to fear?'

'Oh. well!' His whine was almost a hiss. 'You might mistake me for the Snake. There were cooking apples even in those days.'

I, angrily: 'Allegorical rubbish!'

He, slyly: 'I suppose you think only eating apples are worth sinning for?'

I was about to go. I hadn't the slightest desire to discuss the fruit situation in Paradise. Then he tried a more direct approach. Jumping nimbly down from the tree, he stood long and willowy by the fence: 'What did your dog find in the rye?'

I can't imagine why I said: 'A stone.'

'And you put the stone in your pocket?' Blessed if he wasn't beginning to cross-examine me.

'I like to carry stones in my pocket.'

'It looked more like a stick to me.'

'That may well be. But I still say it's a stone.'

'Aha! So it is a stick?'

'For all I care: stick or stone, cooking apples or eating apples . . .'

'A flexible little stick?'

'The dog wants to go home. I'll have to be leaving.'

'A flesh-colored stick?'

'Why don't you attend to your apples? Come along, Lux.'

'A flesh-colored, flexible little stick with a ring on it?'

'What do you want of me? I'm just a man taking a walk with this dog I borrowed to take a walk with.'

'Splendid. See here, I should like to borrow something too. Won't you let me, just for a second, try on that handsome ring that sparkled on the stick and turned it into a ring finger? My name is Vittlar. Gottfried von Vittlar. I am the last of our line.'

So it was that I made Vittlar's acquaintance. Before the day was out, we were friends, and I still call him my friend. Only a few days ago, when he came to see me, I said: 'I am so glad, my dear Gottfried, that it was you who turned me in to the police and not some common stranger.'

If angels exist, they must look like Vittlar: long, willowy, vivacious, collapsible, more likely to throw their arms around the most barren of lampposts than a soft, eager young girl.

You don't see Vittlar at first. According to his surroundings, he can make himself look like a thread, a scarecrow, a clothestree, or the limb of a tree. That indeed is why I failed to notice him when I sat on the cable drum and he lay in the apple tree. The dog didn't even bark, for dogs can neither see, smell, nor bark at an angel.

'Will you be kind enough, my dear Gottfried,' I asked him the day before yesterday, 'to send me a copy of the statement you made to the police just about two years ago?' It was this statement that led to my trial and formed the basis of Vittlar's subsequent testimony.

Here is the copy, I shall let him speak as he testified against me in court:

On the day in question, I, Gottfried Vittlar, was lying in the crook of an apple tree that grows at the edge of my mother's garden and bears each year enough apples to fill our seven preserving jars with applesauce. I was lying on my side, my left hip embedded in the bottom of the crook, which is somewhat mossy. My feet were pointing in the direction of the Gerresheim glassworks. What was I looking at? I was looking straight ahead, waiting for something to happen within my field of vision.

The accused, who is today my friend, entered my field of vision. A dog came with him, circling round him, behaving like a dog. His name, as the accused later told me, was Lux, he was a rottweiler, and could be rented at a 'dog rental shop' not far from St. Roch's Church.

The accused sat down on the empty cable drum which has been lying ever since the war outside the aforesaid kitchen garden belonging to my mother, Alice von Vittlar. As the court knows, the accused is a small man. Moreover, if we are to be strictly truthful, he is deformed. This fact caught my attention. What struck me even more was his behavior. The small, well-dressed gentleman proceeded to drum on the rusty cable drum, first with his fingers, then with two dry sticks. If you bear in mind that the accused is a drummer by trade and that, as has been established beyond any shadow of a doubt, he practices his trade at all times and places; if you consider, furthermore, that there is something about a cable drum which, as the name suggests, incites people to drum on it, it seems in no wise unreasonable to aver that one sultry summer day the accused Oskar Matzerath sat on a cable drum situated outside the kitchen garden of Mrs. Alice von Vittlar, producing rhythmically arranged sound with the help of two willow sticks of unequal length.

I further testify that the dog Lux vanished for some time into a field of rye; yes, the rye was about ready to mow. If asked exactly how long he was gone, I should be unable to reply, because the moment I lie down in the crook of our apple tree, I lose all sense of time. If I say notwithstanding that the dog disappeared for a considerable time, it means that I missed him, because I liked his black coat any floppy ears.

The accused, however – I feel justified in saying – did not miss the dog.

When the dog Lux came back out of the ripe rye, he was carrying something between his teeth. I thought of a stick, a stone, or perhaps, though even then it did not seem very likely, a tin can or even a tin spoon. Only when the accused removed the corpus delicti from the dog's muzzle did I definitely recognize it for what it was. But between the moment when the dog rubbed his muzzle, still holding the object, against the trouser leg of the accused – the left trouser leg, I should say – to the moment when the accused took possession of it, several minutes passed – exactly how many I should not venture to say.

The dog tried very hard to attract the attention of his temporary master; the accused, however, continued to drum in his monotonous, obsessive, disconcerting, I might say childish way. Only when the dog resorted to indecency, forcing his moist muzzle between the legs of the accused, did he drop the willow sticks and give the dog a kick with his right – yes, of that I am perfectly sure – foot. The dog described a half-circle, came back, trembling like a dog, and once again presented his muzzle and the object it held. Without rising, the accused – with his left hand – reached between the dog's teeth. Relieved of his find, the dog Lux backed away a few feet. The accused remained seated, held the object in his hand, closed his hand, opened it, closed it, and the next time he opened his hand, I could see something sparkle. When the accused had grown accustomed to the sight of the object, he held it up with his thumb and forefinger, approximately at eye level.

Only then did I identify the object as a finger, and a moment later, because of the sparkle, more specifically as a ring finger. Unsuspecting, I had given a name to one of the most interesting criminal cases of the postwar period. And indeed, I, Gottfried Vittlar, have frequently been referred to as the star witness in the Ring Finger Case.

Since the accused remained motionless, I followed suit. In fact, his immobility communicated itself to me. And when the accused wrapped the finger and ring carefully in the handkerchief he had previously worn in his breast pocket, I felt a stirring of sympathy for the man on the cable drum: how neat and methodical he is; now there's a man I'd like to know.

So it was that I called out to him as he was about to leave in the direction of Gerresheim with his rented dog. His first reaction, however, was irritable, almost arrogant. To this day, I cannot understand why, just because I was lying in a tree, he should have taken me for a symbolic snake and even suspected my mother's cooking apples of being the Paradise variety.

It may well be a favorite habit with the Tempter to lie in the crooks of trees. In my case, it was just boredom, a state of mind I come by without effort, that impelled me to assume a recumbent position several times a week in the aforesaid tree. Perhaps boredom is in itself the absolute evil. And now let me ask: What motive drove the accused to Gerresheim in the outskirts of Düsseldorf that sultry day? Loneliness, as he later confessed to me. But are not loneliness and boredom twin sisters? I bring up these points only in order to explain the accused, not in order to confound him. For what made me take a liking to him, speak to him, and finally make friends with him was precisely his particular variety of evil, that drumming of his, which resolved evil into its rhythmical components. Even my denunciation of him, the act which has brought us here, him as the accused, myself as a witness, was a game we invented, a means of diverting and entertaining our boredom and our loneliness.

After some hesitation the accused, in response to my request, slipped the ring off the ring finger – it came off without difficulty – and onto my little finger. It was a good fit and I was extremely pleased. It hardly seems necessary to tell you that I came down out of the tree before trying on the ring. Standing on either side of the fence, we introduced ourselves and chatted a while, touching on various political topics, and then he gave me the ring. He kept the finger, which he handled with great care. We agreed that it was a woman's finger. While I held the ring and let the light play on it, the accused, with his left hand, beat a lively little dance rhythm on the fence. The wooden fence surrounding my mother's garden is in a very dilapidated state: it rattled, clattered, and vibrated in response to the accused's drumming. I do not know how long we stood there, conversing with our eyes. We were engaged in this innocent pastime when we heard airplane engines at a moderate altitude; the plane was probably getting ready to land in Lohhausen. Although both of us were curious to know whether it was going to land on two or four engines, we did not interrupt our exchange of glances nor look up at the plane; later on, when we had occasion to play the game again, we gave it a name: Leo Schugger's asceticism; Leo Schugger, it appears, is the name of a friend with whom the accused had played this game years before, usually in cemeteries.

After the plane had found its landing field – whether on two or four engines I am at a loss to say – I gave back the ring. The accused put it on the ring finger, which he folded up again in the handkerchief, and asked me to go with him some of the way.

543

That was on July 7, 1951. We walked as far as the streetcar terminus in Gerresheim, but the vehicle we mounted was a cab. Since then the accused has found frequent occasion to treat me with the utmost generosity. We rode into town and had the taxi wait outside the dog rental shop near St. Roch's Church. Having got rid of the dog Lux, we rode across town, through Bilk and Oberbilk to Wersten Cemetery, where Mr. Matzerath had more than twelve marks fare to pay. Then we went to Korneff's stone-cutting establishment.

The place was disgustingly filthy and I was glad when the stonecutter had completed my friend's commission – it took about an hour. While my friend lovingly lectured to me about the tools and the various kinds of stone, Mr. Korneff, without a word of comment on the finger, made a plaster cast of it – without the ring. I watched him with only half an eye. First the finger had to be treated; that is, he smeared it with fat and ran a string round the edge. Then he applied the plaster, but before it was quite hard split the mold in two with the string. I am by trade a decorator and the making of plaster molds is nothing new to me; nevertheless, the moment Mr. Korneff had picked up that finger, it took on – or so I thought – an unesthetic quality which it lost only after the cast was finished and the accused had recovered the finger and wiped the grease off it. My friend paid the stonecut-ter, though at first Mr. Korneff was reluctant to take money, for he regarded Mr. Matzerath as a colleague, and further pointed out that Oskar, as he called Mr. Matzerath, had squeezed out his boils free of charge. When the cast had hardened, the stonecutter opened the mold, gave Mr. Matzerath the cast, and promised to make him a few more in the next few days. Then he saw us out to Bittweg through his display of tombstones.

A second taxi ride took us to the Central Station. There the accused treated me to a copious dinner in the excellent station restaurant. From his familiar tone with the waiters I inferred that he must be a regular customer. We ate boiled beef with fresh horseradish, Rhine salmon, and cheese, the whole topped off with a bottle of champagne. When the conversation drifted back to the finger, I advised him to consider it as someone else's property, to send it in to the Lost and Found, especially as he had a cast of it. To this the accused replied very firmly that he regarded

544

himself as the rightful owner, because he had been promised just such a finger on the occasion of his birth – in code to be sure, the word actually employed being 'drumstick'; further, certain finger-length scars on the back of his friend Herbert Truczinski had forecast this ring finger; finally, the cartridge case he had found in Saspe Cemetery had also had the dimensions and implications of a future ring finger.

Though at first I smiled at my new-found friend's arguments, I had to admit that a man of discernment could not fail to see through the sequence: drumstick, scar, cartridge case, ring finger.

A third taxi took me home after dinner. We made an appointment to meet again, and when I visited my friend three days later, he had a surprise for me.

First he showed me his rooms. Originally, he had rented only one, a wretched little place formerly used as a bathroom, but later on, when his drum recitals had brought him wealth and fame, he had undertaken to pay a second rent for a windowless recess which he referred to as Sister Dorothea's room, and ultimately he had rented a third room, formerly occupied by a Mr. Münzer, a musician and associate of the accused. All this cost him a pretty penny, for Mr. Zeidler, the landlord, was well aware of Mr. Matzerath's prosperity and determined to profit by it.

It was in Sister Dorothea's room that the accused had prepared his surprise. On the marble top of a washstand – or perhaps I should call this article of furniture a dressing table because of the mirror behind it – stood a preserving jar about the size of those which my mother, Alice von Vittlar, uses for putting up the applesauce she makes from our cooking apples. This preserving jar, however, contained not applesauce but the ring finger, swimming in alcohol. Proudly the accused showed me several thick scientific books which he had consulted while preserving the finger. I leafed absently through them, pausing only at the illustrations, but admitted that the accused had done an excellent job and that the finger's appearance was unchanged. Speaking as a decorator, I also told him that the glass with its contents looked interestingly decorative at the foot of the mirror.

When the accused saw that I had made friends with the preserving jar, he informed me that he sometimes worshipped it and prayed to it. My curiosity was aroused and I asked him for a sample of his prayers. He asked me a favor in return: providing me with paper and pencil, he asked me to write his prayer down. I could ask questions as he went along; while praying, he would answer to the best of his knowledge.

Here I give in testimony the words of the accused, my questions, his answers: Adoration of a preserving jar: I adore. Who, I? Oskar or I? I, piously; Oskar, with distraction. Devotion, perpetual, never mind about repetitions. I, discerning because without recollections; Oskar, discerning because full of recollections. I, cold, hot, lukewarm. Guilty under examination. Innocent without examination. Guilty because of, succumbed because of, remitted my guilt, unloaded the guilt on, fought through to, kept free of, laughed at and about, wept for, over, without, blasphemed in speech, blasphemed in silence, I speak not, I am not silent, I pray. I adore. What? A glass jar. What kind of a jar? A preserving jar. What is preserved in it? A finger. What sort of finger? A ring finger. Whose finger? Blond. Who's blond? Medium height. Five feet four? Five feet five. Distinguishing marks? A mole. Where? Inside of arm. Left, right? Right. Ring finger where? Left. Engaged? Yes, but not married. Religion? Protestant. Virgin? Virgin. Born? Don't know. Where? Near Hanover. When? December. Sagittarius or Capricorn? Sagittarius. Character? Timid. Good-natured? Conscientious, talkative. Sensible? Economical, matter-of-fact, but cheerful. Shy? Fond of goodies, straightforward, and bigoted. Pale, dreams of traveling, menstruation irregular, lazy, likes to suffer and talk about it, lacks imagination, passive, waits to see what will happen, good listener, nods in agreement, folds her arms, lowers eyelids when speaking, opens eyes wide when spoken to, light-grey with brown close to pupil, ring a present from boss, married man, didn't want to take it at first, took it, terrible experience, fibers, Satan, lots of white, took trip, moved, came back, couldn't stop, jealous, too, but for no reason. Sickness but not, death but not, yes, no, don't know, I can't go on. Picking cornflowers when murderer arrived, no, murderer was with her all along . . . Amen? Amen.

I, Gottfried Vittlar, append this prayer only because, confused as it may seem, the indications contained in it concerning the owner of the ring finger coincide very largely with the testimony regarding the murdered woman, Sister Dorothea Köngetter.

However, I am not trying to cast doubt on the accused's allegation that he did not murder Dorothea Köngetter and never saw her face to face.

It seems to me, in any case, that the extreme devotion with which the accused prayed and drummed – he was kneeling and had wedged his drum between his knees – to that preserving jar argues in his favor.

I had further occasion, in the year or more that followed, to see the accused pray and drum, for he was soon to offer me a generous salary – which I accepted – to accompany him on his tours, which he had interrupted for a considerable period but resumed shortly after finding the ring finger. We visited the whole of Western Germany and had offers to play in the East Zone and even abroad. But Mr. Matzerath preferred to remain within the boundaries of the Federal Republic; as he himself put it, he didn't want to get into the usual international rat race. He never drummed or prayed to the jar before performing. But after his appearance and a long-drawn-out dinner we would repair to his hotel room: then he drummed and prayed, while I asked questions and wrote; afterwards we would compare his prayer with those of the previous days and weeks. The prayers vary in length. Sometimes the words clashed violently, on other days the rhythm was fluid, almost meditative. Yet the prayers I collected, which I herewith submit to the court, contain no more information than my first transcript, which I incorporated in my deposition.

In the course of the year, I became superficially acquainted, between tours, with a few of Mr. Matzerath's friends and relatives. I met his stepmother, Mrs. Maria Matzerath, whom the accused adores, though with a certain restraint. And the same afternoon I made the acquaintance of Kurt Matzerath, the accused's half brother, a well-behaved boy of eleven. Mrs. Augusta Köster, the sister of Mrs. Maria Matzerath, also made a favorable impression on me. As the accused confessed to me, his relations with his family became more than strained during the first postwar years. It was only when Mr. Matzerath helped his stepmother to set up a large delicatessen store, which also carries tropical fruit, and helped financially whenever business difficulties arose, that relations between stepmother and stepson became really friendly.

Mr. Matzerath also introduced me to a number of former colleagues, for the most part jazz musicians. Mr. Münzer, whom the accused calls familiarly Klepp, struck me as a cheerful and amiable sort, but so far I have not had the energy or desire to develop these contacts.

Though, thanks to the generosity of the accused, I had no need to practice my trade during this period, love of my profession led me, between tours, to decorate a showcase or two. The accused took a friendly interest in my work. Often, late at night, he would stand out in the street, looking on as I practiced my modest arts. Occasionally, when the work was done, we would do the town a bit, though we avoided the Old City because the accused, as he himself explained, couldn't stand the sight of any more bull's-eye panes or signs in old-fashioned Gothic lettering. One of these excursions – and I am coming to the end of my deposition – took us through Unterrath to the car barn. It was past midnight.

We stood there at peace with the world and each other, watching the last cars pull in according to schedule. It's quite a sight. The dark city round about. In the distance, because it was Friday, the roaring of a drunken workman. Otherwise silence, because the last cars, even when they ring their bells and squeak on the curves, make no noise. Most of the cars ran straight into the barn. But a few stood outside, facing every which way, empty, but festively lighted. Who had the idea? Both of us, but it was I who said: 'Well, my dear friend, what do you say?' Mr. Matzerath nodded, we got in without haste, I took the motorman's place and immediately felt quite at home. I started off gently, but gradually gathered speed. I turned out to be a good motorman. Matzerath – by now the brightly lit barn was behind us – acknowledged my prowess with these words: 'You must have been baptized a Catholic, Gottfried, to be able to run a streetcar so well.'

Indeed, this unaccustomed occupation gave me great pleasure. At the car barn no one seemed to have noticed our departure, for we were not followed, and they could easily have stopped us by turning off the current. I took the direction of Flingern; after Flingern I thought of turning left at Haniel and going on toward Rath and Ratingen, but Mr. Matzerath asked me to head for Grafenberg and Gerresheim. Though I had misgivings about the hill below the Lions' Den Dance Hall, I acceded to the request of the accused. I made the hill, the dance hall was behind me, but then I had to jam on the brakes because three men were standing on the tracks.

Shortly after Haniel, Mr. Matzerath had gone inside the car to smoke a cigarette. So it was I, the motorman, who had to cry 'All aboard!' Two of the men were wearing green hats with black bands; the third, whom they held between them, was hatless. I observed that in getting on this third man missed the running board several times, either because of clumsiness or poor eyesight. His companions or guards helped him, or perhaps it would be more accurate to say that they dragged him brutally, onto my motorman's platform and then into the car.

I had started off again when suddenly from behind me, from inside the car, I heard a pitiful whimpering and a sound as of someone being slapped. But then I was reassured to hear the firm voice of Mr. Matzerath giving the new arrivals a piece of his mind, telling them to stop hitting an injured, half-blind man who had lost his glasses.

'You mind your own business,' I heard one of the green hats roar. 'This time he's going to get what's coming to him. It's been going on long enough.'

While I drove on slowly in the direction of Gerresheim, my friend Matzerath asked what the poor fellow had done. Then the conversation took a strange turn: We were carried back to the days, in fact to the very first day, of the war: September 1, 1939; it seemed that this man, who was so nearsighted as to be almost blind, had participated as an irregular in the defense of some Polish post office. Strange to say, Mr. Matzerath, who could not have been more than fifteen at the time, knew all about it; he even recognized the poor devil as one Victor Weluhn, a nearsighted carrier of money orders, who had lost his glasses in the battle, escaped while the battle was still on, and given his pursuers the slip. But the chase had continued, they had pursued him till the end of the war, and even then they had not given up. They produced a paper issued in 1939, an execution order. At last they had him, cried the one green hat; the other agreed: 'And damn glad to get it over with. I've given up all my free time, even my vacations. An order, if you please, is an order, and this one has been hanging fire since '39. You think I've nothing else to do. I've got my work.' He was a salesman, it appeared, and his associate had his troubles too, he had lost a good business in the East Zone and been obliged to start up from scratch. 'But enough's enough; tonight we carry out that order, and that's an end to the past. Damn lucky we were to catch the last car!'

Thus quite unintentionally I became a motorman on a streetcar carrying two executioners and their intended victim to Gerresheim. The Gerresheim marketplace was deserted and looked rather lopsided; here I turned right, meaning to unload my passengers at the terminus near the glassworks and start home with Mr. Matzerath. Three stations before the terminus, Mr. Matzerath came out on the platform and deposited his briefcase, in which as I knew the preserving jar stood upright, approximately in the place where professional motormen put their lunchboxes.

'We've got to save him. It's Victor, poor Victor!' Mr. Matzerath was very upset.

'He still hasn't found glasses to fit him. He's terribly near-sighted, they'll shoot him and he'll be looking in the wrong direction.' The executioners looked unarmed to me. But Mr. Matzerath had noticed the ungainly lumps in their coats.

'He carried money orders at the Polish Post Office. Now he has the same job at the Federal Post Office. But they hound him after working hours; they still have an order to shoot him.'

Though I could not entirely follow Mr. Matzerath's explanations, I promised to attend the shooting with him and help him if possible to prevent it.

Behind the glassworks, just before the first gardens – if the moon had been out I could have seen my mother's garden with its apple tree – I put on the brakes and shouted into the car: 'Last stop! All out!' And out they came with their green hats and black hatbands. Again poor Victor had trouble with the running board. Then Mr. Matzerath got out, but first he pulled out his drum from under his coat and asked me to take care of his briefcase with the jar in it.

We followed the executioners and their victim. The lights of the car were still on, and looking back we could see it far in the distance.

We passed along garden fences. I was beginning to feel very tired. When the three of them stopped still ahead of us, I saw that my mother's garden had been chosen as the execution site. Both of us protested. Paying no attention, they knocked down the board fence, not a very difficult task for it was about to collapse of its own accord, and tied poor Victor to the apple tree just below my crook. When we continued to protest, they turned their flashlight on the crumpled execution order. It was signed by an inspector of courts-martial by the name of Zelewski and dated, if I remember right, Zoppot, October 5, 1939. Even the rubber stamps seemed to be right. The situation looked hopeless. Nevertheless, we talked about the United Nations, collective guilt, Adenauer, and so on; but one of the green hats swept aside all our objections, which were without juridical foundation, he assured us, because the peace treaty had never been signed, or even drawn up. 'I vote for Adenauer just the same as you do,' he went on. 'But this execution order is still valid; we've consulted the highest authorities. We are simply doing our duty and the best thing you can do is to run along.'

We did nothing of the sort. When the green hats produced the machine pistols from under their coats, Mr. Matzerath put his drum in place. At that moment the moon – it was almost full, just the slightest bit battered – burst through the clouds. And Mr. Matzerath began to drum . . . desperately.

A strange rhythm, yet it seemed familiar. Over and over again the letter O took form: lost, not yet lost, Poland is not yet lost! But that was the voice of poor Victor, he knew the words to Mr. Matzerath's drumming: While we live, Poland cannot die. The green hats, too, seemed to know that rhythm, I could see them take fright behind their hardware in the moonlight. And well they might. For the march that Mr. Matzerath and poor Victor struck up in my mother's garden awakened the Polish cavalry to life. Maybe the moon helped, or maybe it was the drum, the moon, and poor, nearsighted Victor's cracking voice all together that sent those multitudes of horsemen springing from the ground: stallions whinnied, hoofs thundered, nostrils fumed, spurs jangled, hurrah, hurrah! . . . No, not at all: no thundering, no jangling, whinnying, or shouts of hurrah; silently they glided over the harvested fields outside of Gerresheim, but beyond any doubt they were a squadron of Polish Uhlans, for red and white like Mr. Matzerath's lacquered drum, the pennants clung to the lances;

no, clung is not right, they floated, they glided, and indeed the whole squadron floated beneath the moon, coming perhaps from the moon, floated off, wheeled to the left, toward our garden, floated, seemingly not of flesh and blood, floated like toys fresh out of the box, phantoms, comparable perhaps to the spooklike figures that Mr. Matzerath's keeper makes out of knotted string: Polish cavalry of knotted string, soundless yet thundering, flesh-less, bloodless, and yet Polish, down upon us they thundered, and we threw ourselves upon the ground while the moon and Poland's horsemen passed over us and over my mother's garden and all the other carefully tended gardens. But they did not harm the gardens. They merely took along poor Victor and the two executioners and were lost in the open fields under the moon – lost, not yet lost, they galloped off to the east, toward Poland beyond the moon.

Panting, we waited for the night to quiet down, for the heavens to close again and remove the light that alone could have per-suaded those riders long dead, long dust, to mount a last charge. I was first to stand up. Though I did not underestimate the influence of the moon, I congratulated Mr. Matzerath on his brilliant performance; a triumph I called it. He waved me aside with a weary, dejected gesture: 'Triumph, my dear Gottfried? I have had too many triumphs, too much success in my life. What I would like is to be unsuccessful for once. But that is very difficult and calls for a great deal of work.'

This speech was not to my liking, because I am the hard-working, conscientious type and have never met with the least success, let alone a triumph. It seemed to me that Mr. Matzerath showed a lack of gratitude, and I told him as much. 'You are being very arrogant, Oskar,' I ventured – by then we were calling each other by our first names. 'All the papers are full of you. You've made a name for yourself. I'm not thinking of money. But do you suppose that it is easy for me, whom no newspaper has ever so much as mentioned, to live side by side with a darling of fame like you. Oh, how I long to do something big, unique, spectacular like what you have just done, to do it all by myself and get into the newspapers, to appear in print: This was the achievement of Gottfried von Vittlar.'

I was offended at Mr. Matzerath's laughter. He lay on his back, rolling his hump in the loose earth, pulling out clumps of grass with both hands, tossing them up in the air, and laughing like an inhuman god who can do anything he pleases: 'Nothing could be simpler, my friend. Here, take this briefcase. Luckily, the Polish cavalry hasn't crushed it. I make you a present of it; it contains a jar with a ring finger in it. Take it; run to Gerresheim, the streetcar is still there with all the lights on. Get in, drive to the Fürstenwall, take my present to Police Headquarters. Report me, and tomorrow you'll see your name in all the papers.'

At first I rejected his offer; I argued that he wouldn't be able to live without his jar and his finger. But he reassured me; he said he was sick of the whole finger business, besides he had several plaster casts, he had even had a gold cast made. So would I please make up my mind, pick up the briefcase, get in that car, and go to the police.

So off I went. I could long hear Mr. Matzerath laughing behind me. He stayed there, lying on his back, he wanted to savor the charms of the night while I rode off ting-a-ling into town. I didn't go to the police until the following morning, but my report, thanks to Mr. Matzerath's kindness, brought me quite a lot of attention in the papers.

Meanwhile I, the kindly Mr. Matzerath, lay laughing in the night-black grass outside Gerresheim, rolled with laughter within sight of several deadly serious stars, laughed so hard that I worked my hump into the warm earth, and thought: Sleep, Oskar, sleep a little while before the police come and wake you up. Never again will you lie so free beneath the moon.

And when I awoke, I noticed, before noticing that it was broad daylight, that something, someone was licking my face: the quality of the sensation was warm, rough but not very, and moist.

Could that be the police so soon, awakened by Vittlar and now licking you awake? Nevertheless, I was in no hurry to open my eyes, but let myself be licked a while: warmly, moistly, not too roughly, it was quite pleasant. I chose not to care who was licking me: it's either the police, Oskar conjectured, or a cow. Only then did I open my blue eyes.

Spotted black and white, she breathed on me and licked me until I opened my eyes. It was broad daylight, clear to cloudy, and I said to myself: Oskar, don't waste your time on this cow even if there is something divine in her way of looking at you. Don't let that rasping-soothing tongue of hers tranquilize you by shutting off your memory. It is day, the flies are buzzing, you must run for your life. Vittlar is turning you in; consequently, you must flee. You can't have a bona fide denunciation without a bona fide flight. Leave the cow to her mooing and make your getaway. They will catch you either way, but why let that worry you?

And so, licked, washed, and combed by a cow, I fled. After the very first steps of my flight, I burst into a gale of fresh, early morning laughter. Leaving my drum with the cow, who lay still and mooed, I embarked, laughing, upon my flight.

Thirty

Ah, yes, my flight, my getaway. There's still that to tell you about. I fled in order to enhance the value of Vittlar's denunciation. A getaway, I said to myself, requires first of all a destination. Whither, O Oskar, will you flee? Political obstacles, the so-called Iron Curtain, forbade me to flee eastward. It was not possible to head for my grandmother Anna Koljaiczek's four skirts, which to this day billow protectively in the Kashubian potato fields, although I told myself that if flight there must be, my grandmother's skirts were the only worthwhile destination.

Just in passing: today is my thirtieth birthday. At the age of thirty, one is obliged to discuss serious matters like flight as a man and not as a boy. As she brought in the cake with the thirty candles, Maria said: 'You're thirty now, Oskar. It's time you were getting some sense into your head.'

Klepp, my friend Klepp, gave me as usual some jazz records and used five matches to light the thirty candles on my cake: 'Life begins at thirty!' said Klepp; he is twenty-nine.

Vittlar, however, my friend Gottfried, who is dearest to my heart, gave me sweets, bent down over the bars of my bed, and whined: 'When Jesus was thirty years of age, he set forth and gathered disciples round him.'

Vittlar has always liked to mess things up for me. Just because I am thirty, he wants me to leave my bed and gather disciples. Then my lawyer came, brandishing a paper and trumpeting congratulations. Hanging his nylon hat on my bedpost, he proclaimed to me and all my birthday guests: 'What a happy coincidence! Today my client is celebrating his thirtieth birthday; and just today I've received news that the Ring Finger Case is being reopened. A new clue has been found. Sister Beata, her friend, you remember . . .'

Just what I have been dreading for years, ever since my getaway: that they would find the real murderer, reopen the case, acquit me, discharge me from this mental hospital, take away my lovely bed, put me out in the cold street, in the wind and rain, and oblige a thirty-year-old Oskar to gather disciples round himself and his drum.

So apparently it was Sister Beata who murdered my Sister Dorothea out of festering green jealousy.

Perhaps you remember? There was this Dr. Werner who – the situation is only too common in life as it is in the movies – stood between the two nurses. A nasty business: Beata was in love with Dr. Werner. Dr. Werner was in love with Dorothea. And Dorothea wasn't in love with anyone, unless it was secretly, deep down, with little Oskar. Werner fell sick. Dorothea took care of him, because he was put into her section. Sister Beata couldn't bear it. She inveigled Dorothea into taking a walk with her and killed or, if you prefer, did away with her in a rye field near Gerresheim. Now Beata was free to take care of Dr. Werner. But it seems that she took care of him in a special way, so much so that he did not get well; just the opposite. Perhaps the love-crazed nurse said to herself: As long as he is sick, he belongs to me. Did she give him too much medicine? Did she give him the wrong medicine? In any case, Dr. Werner died; but when she testified in court, Sister Beata said nothing about wrong or too much, and not one word about her stroll in the rye fields with Sister Dorothea. And Oskar, who similarly confessed to nothing, but was the owner of an incriminating finger in a preserving jar, was convicted of the crime in the rye field. But esteeming that Oskar was not fully responsible for his actions, they sent me to the mental hospital for observation. Be that as it may, before they convicted him and sent him to the mental hospital, Oskar fled, for I wished, by my disappearance, to heighten the value of my friend Gottfried's denunciation.

At the time of my flight, I was twenty-eight. A few hours ago thirty candles were still dripping phlegmatically over my birthday cake. On the day of my flight it was September, just as it is today. I was born in the sign of Virgo. At the moment, though, it's my getaway I'm talking about, not my birth beneath the light bulbs.

As I have said, the eastward escape route, the road to my grandmother, was closed. Accordingly, like everyone else nowadays, I saw myself obliged to flee westward. If, Oskar, I said to myself, the inscrutable ways of politics prevent you from going to your grandmother, why not run to your grandfather, who is living in Buffalo, U.S.A.? Take America as your destination; we'll see how far you get.

This thought of Grandfather Koljaiczek in America came to me while my eyes were still closed and the cow was licking me in the meadow near Gerresheim. It must have been about seven o'clock and I said to myself: the stores open at eight. Laughing, I ran off, leaving my drum with the cow, saying to myself: Gottfried was tired, I doubt if he goes to the police before eight or maybe half-past. Take advantage of your little head start. It took me ten minutes, in the sleepy suburb of Gerresheim, to get a cab by telephone. The cab carried me to the Central Station. On the way I counted my money; several times I had to start counting all over again, because I couldn't help laughing, sending out gales of fresh early-morning laughter. Then I leafed through my passport and found that, thanks to the efforts of the West Concert Bureau, I possessed visas for France as well as the U.S.; Dr. Dösch had always hoped that one day Oskar the Drummer would consent to tour those countries.

Voilà, I said to myself, let us flee to Paris, it looks good and sounds good, it could happen in the movies, with Gabin smoking his pipe and tracking me down, inexorably but with kindness and understanding. But who will play *me*? Chaplin? Picasso? Laughing, stimulated by my thoughts of flight, I was still slapping the thighs of my slightly rumpled trousers when the driver asked me for seven DM. I paid up and had breakfast in the station restaurant. I laid out the timetable beside my soft-boiled egg and found a suitable train. After breakfast I had time to provide myself with foreign exchange and buy a small suitcase of excellent leather. Fearing to show myself in Jülicher-Strasse, I filled the suitcase with expensive but ill-fitting shirts, a pair of pale-green pajamas, toothbrush, toothpaste, and so on. Since there was no need to economize, I bought a first-class ticket, and soon found myself in a comfortable, upholstered first-class window seat, fleeing without physical effort. The cushions helped me to think. When the train pulled out, inaugurating my flight proper, Oskar began casting about for something to be frightened of; for not without reason I said to myself: you can't speak of a flight without fear. But what, Oskar, are you going to fear? What is worth running away from if all the police can wring from you is fresh, early-morning laughter?

Today I am thirty; flight and trial are behind me, but the fear I talked myself into during my flight is still with me.

Was it the rhythmic thrusts of the rails, the rattling of the train? Little by little the song took form, and a little before Aachen I was fully conscious of it. Monotonous words. They took possession of me as I sank back in the first-class upholstery. After Aachen – we crossed the border at half-past ten – they were still with me, more and more distinct and terrible, and I was glad when the customs inspectors changed the subject. They showed more interest in my hump than in my name or passport, and I said to myself: Oh, that Vittlar! That lazybones. Here it is almost eleven, and still he hasn't got to the police with that preserving jar under his arm, whereas I, for his sake, have been busy with this getaway since the crack of dawn, working myself up into a state of terror just to create a motive for my flight. Belgium. Oh, what a fright I was in when the rails sang: Where's the Witch, black as pitch? Here's the black, wicked Witch. Ha, ha, ha . . .

Today I am thirty, I shall be given a new trial and presumably be acquitted. I shall be thrown out in the street, and everywhere, in trains and streetcars, those words will ring in my ears: Where's the Witch, black as pitch? Here's the black, wicked Witch.

Still, apart from my dread of the Black Witch whom I expected to turn up at every station, the trip was pleasant enough. I had the whole compartment to myself – but maybe she was in the next one, right behind the partition – I made the acquaintance first of Belgian, then of French customs inspectors, dozed off from time to time, and woke up with a little cry. In an effort to ward off the Witch, I leafed through *Der Spiegel*, which I had bought on the platform in Düsseldorf; how they get around, how well informed they are, I kept saying to myself. I even found a piece about my manager, Dr. Dösch of the West Concert Bureau, confirming what I already knew, namely, that Oskar the Drummer was the mainstay and meal ticket of the Dösch agency – good picture of me too. And Oskar the Mainstay pictured to himself the inevitable collapse of the West Concert Bureau after my arrest.

Never in all my life had I feared the Black Witch. It was not until my flight, when I wanted to be afraid, that she crawled under my skin. And there she has remained to this day, my thirtieth birthday, though most of the time she sleeps. She takes a number of forms. Sometimes, for instance, it is the name 'Goethe' that sets me screaming and hiding under the bedclothes. From childhood on I have done my best to study the poet prince and still his Olympian calm gives me the creeps. Even now, when, no longer luminous and classical but disguised as a black witch more sinister by far than any Rasputin, he peers through the bars of my bed and asks me, on the occasion of my thirtieth birthday: 'Where's the Witch, black as pitch?' – I am scared stiff.

Ha, ha, ha! said the train carrying Oskar the fugitive to Paris. I was already expecting to see the International Police when we pulled in to the North Station, the Gare du Nord as the French call it. But there was no one waiting for me, only a porter, who smelled so reassuringly of red wine that with the best of intentions I couldn't mistake him for the Black Witch. I gave him my suitcase and let him carry it to within a few feet of the gate. The police and the Witch, I said to myself, probably don't feel like wasting money on a platform ticket, they will accost you and arrest you on the other side of the gate. So you'd better take back your suitcase before you go through. But the police weren't there to relieve me of my suitcase; I had to haul it to the Metro my very own self.

I won't go on about that famous Metro smell. I have recently read somewhere that it has been done into a perfume and that you can spray yourself with it. The Metro also asked about the whereabouts of the Black Witch, though in a rhythm rather different from that of the railroad. And another thing I noticed: the other passengers must have feared her as much as I did, for they were all a sweat with terror. My idea was to continue underground to the Porte d'Italie, where I would take a cab to Orly Airport. If I couldn't be arrested at the North Station, it seemed to me that Orly, the world-famous airport – with the Witch done up as an airline hostess – would do very nicely, that it was an interesting place to be arrested in. There was one change of trains, I was glad my suitcase was so light. The Metro carried me southward and I pondered: where, Oskar, are you going to get off? Goodness me, how many things can happen in one day, this morning a cow licked you not far from Gerresheim, you were fearless and gay, and now you are in Paris – where will you get off, where will she come, black and terrible, to meet you? At the Place d'Italie? Or not until the Porte?

I got off at Maison Blanche, the last station before the Porte, thinking: they must think I think they are waiting at the Porte. But She knows what I think and what they think. Besides, I was sick of it all. My getaway and the pains I had taken to keep up my fear had been very tiring. Oskar had lost all desire to go on to the airfield; Maison Blanche, at this point, struck him as more original than Orly. He was right too. Because this particular Metro station has an escalator. An escalator, I said to myself, can be counted on to inspire me with a lofty sentiment or two, and the clatter will be just right for the Witch. 'Here's the black, wicked Witch. Ha, ha, ha!'

Oskar is somewhat at a loss. His flight is drawing to an end and with it his story: Will the escalator in the Maison Blanche Metro station be high, steep, and symbolic enough to clank down the curtain suitably upon these recollections?

But there is also my thirtieth birthday. To all those who feel that an escalator makes too much noise and those who are not afraid of the Black Witch, I offer my thirtieth birthday as an alternate end. For of all birthdays, isn't the thirtieth the most significant? It has the Three in it, and it foreshadows the Sixty, which thus becomes superfluous. As the thirty candles were burning on my birthday cake this morning, I could have wept with joy and exaltation, but I was ashamed in front of Maria: at thirty, you've lost your right to cry.

The moment I trod the first step of the escalator – if an escalator can be said to have a first step – and it began to bear me upward, I burst out laughing. Despite or because of my fear, I laughed. Slowly it mounted the steep incline – and there they were. There was still time for half a cigarette. Two steps above me a couple of lovers were carrying on brazenly. A step below me an old woman, whom I at first, for no good reason, suspected of being the Witch. She had on a hat decorated with fruit. Smoking, I summoned up – I worked hard at it – the kind of thoughts that an escalator should suggest. Oskar was Dante on his way back from hell; up above, at the end of escalator, those dynamic reporters for *Der Spiegel* were waiting for him. 'Well, Dante,' they ask, 'how was it down there?' Then I was Goethe, the poet prince, and the reporters asked me how I had enjoyed my visit to the Mothers. But then I was sick of poets and I said to myself: it's not any reporters for *Der Spiegel* or detectives with badges in their pockets that are standing up there. It's She, the Witch. 'Here's the black, wicked Witch. Ha, ha, ha!'

Alongside the escalator there was a regular stairway, carrying people from the street down into the Metro station. It seemed to be raining outside. The people looked wet. That had me worried; I hadn't had time to buy a raincoat before leaving Düsseldorf. However, I took another look upward, and Oskar saw that the gentlemen with the faces had civilian umbrellas – but that cast no doubt on the existence of the Black Witch.

How shall I address them? I wondered, slowly savoring my cigarette as slowly the escalator aroused lofty feelings in me and enriched my knowledge: one is rejuvenated on an escalator, on an escalator one grows older and older. I had the choice of leaving that escalator as a three-year-old or as a man of sixty, of meeting the Interpol, not to mention the Black Witch, as an infant or as an old man.

It must be getting late. My iron bedstead looks so tired. And Bruno my keeper has twice showed an alarmed brown eye at the peephole. There beneath the water color of the anemones stands my uncut cake with its thirty candles. Perhaps Maria is already asleep. Someone, Maria's sister Guste, I think, wished me luck for the next thirty years. I envy Maria her sound sleep. What did Kurt, the schoolboy, the model pupil, always first in his class, what did my son Kurt wish me for my birthday? When Maria sleeps, the furniture round about her sleeps too. I have it: Kurt wished me a speedy recovery for my thirtieth birthday. But what I wish myself is a slice of Maria's sound sleep, for I am tired and words fail me. Klepp's young wife made up a silly but well-meant birthday poem addressed to my hump. Prince Eugene was also deformed, but that didn't prevent him from capturing the city and fortress of Belgrade. Prince Eugene also had two fathers. Now I am thirty, but my hump is younger. Louis XIV was Prince Eugene's presumptive father. In years past, beautiful women would touch my hump in the street, they thought it would bring them luck. Prince Eugene was deformed and that's why he died a natural death. If Jesus had had a hump, they would never have nailed him to the Cross. Must I really, just because I am thirty years of age, go out into the world and gather disciples round me?

But that's the kind of idea you get on an escalator. Higher and higher it bore me. Ahead of me and above me the brazen lovers. Behind and below me the woman with the hat. Outside it was raining, and up on top stood the detectives from the Interpol. The escalator steps had slats on them. An escalator ride is a good time to reconsider, to reconsider everything: Where are you from? Where are you going? Who are you? What is your real name? What are you after? Smells assailed me: Maria's youthful vanilla. The sardine oil that my mother warmed up in the can and drank hot until she grew cold and was laid under the earth. In spite of Jan Bronski's lavish use of cologne, the smell of early death had seeped through all his buttonholes. The storage cellar of Greff's vegetable store had smelled of winter potatoes. And once again the smell of the dry sponges that dangled from the slates of the first-graders. And my Roswitha who smelled of cinnamon and nutmeg. I had floated on a cloud of carbolic acid when Mr. Fajngold sprinkled disinfectant on my fever. Ah, and the Catholic smells of the Church of the Sacred Heart, all those vestments that were never aired, the cold dust, and I, at the left side-altar, lending my drum, to whom?

But that's the kind of idea you get on an escalator. Today they want to pin me down, to nail me to the Cross. They say: you are thirty. So you must gather disciples. Remember what you said when they arrested you. Count the candles on your birthday cake, get out of that bed and gather disciples. Yet so many possibilities are open to a man of thirty. I might, for example, should they really throw me out of the hospital, propose to Maria a second time. My chances would be much better today. Oskar has set her up in business, he is famous, he is still making good money with his records, and he has grown older, more mature. At thirty a man should marry. Or I could stay single and marry one of my professions, buy a good shell-lime quarry, hire stonecutters, and deliver directly to the builders. At thirty a man should start a career. Or – in case my business is ruined by prefabricated slabs – I could revive my partnership with the Muse Ulla, side by side we would dispense inspiration to artists. Some day I might even make an honest woman of the Muse, poor thing, with all those blitz engagements. At thirty a man should marry. Or should I grow weary of Europe, I could emigrate: America, Buffalo, my old dream: Off I go, in search of my grandfather, Joe Colchic, formerly Joseph Koljaiczek, the millionaire and sometime firebug. At thirty a man should settle down. Or I could give in and let them nail me to the Cross. Just because I happen to be thirty, I go out and play the Messiah they see in me; against my better judgment I make my drum stand for more than it can, I make a symbol out of it, found a sect, a party, or maybe only a lodge.

This escalator thought came over me in spite of the lovers above me and the woman with hat below me. Have I said that the lovers were two steps, not one, above me, that I put down my suitcase between myself and the lovers? The young people in France are very strange. As the escalator carried us all upward, she unbuttoned his leather jacket, then his shirt, and fondled his bare, eighteen-year-old skin. But so businesslike, so completely unerotic were her movements that a suspicion arose in me: these youngsters are being paid by the government to keep up the reputation of Paris, city of unabashed love. But when they kissed, my suspicion vanished, for he nearly choked on her tongue and was still in the midst of a coughing fit when I snuffed out my cigarette, preferring to meet the detectives as a non-smoker. The old woman below me and her hat – what I am trying to say is that her hat was on a level with my head because the two steps made up for my small stature – did nothing to attract attention, all she did was to mutter and protest a bit all by herself, but lots of old people do that in Paris. The rubber-covered bannister moved up along with us. You could put your hand on it and give your hand a free ride. I should have done so if I had brought gloves along. Each tile on the wall reflected a little drop of electric light. Cream-colored pipes and cables kept us company as we mounted. It should not be thought that this escalator made a fiendish din. Despite its mechanical character, it was a gentle, easygoing contrivance. In spite of the witch jingle, the Maison Blanche Metro station struck me as a pleasant place to be in, almost homelike. I felt quite at home on that escalator: despite my terror, despite the Witch, I should have esteemed myself happy if only the people round me on the escalator had not been total strangers but my friends and relatives, living and dead: my poor mama between Matzerath and Jan Bronski; Mother Truczinski, the grey-haired mouse, with her children Herbert, Guste, Fritz, Maria; Greff the greengrocer and his slovenly Lina; and of course Bebra the master and Roswitha so lithe and graceful – all those who had framed my questionable existence, those who had come to grief on the shoal of my existence. But at the top, where the escalator ended, I should have liked, in place of the Interpol men, to see the exact opposite of the Black Witch: my grandmother Anna Koljaiczek standing there like a mountain, ready to receive me and my retinue, our journey ended, under her skirts, into the heart of the mountain.

Instead there were two gentlemen, wearing not wide skirts, but American-style raincoats. And toward the end of my journey, I had to smile with all ten of my toes and admit to myself that the brazen lovers above me and the muttering woman below me were plain ordinary detectives.

What more shall I say: born under light bulbs, deliberately stopped growing at age of three, given drum, sang glass to pieces, smelled vanilla, coughed in churches, observed ants, decided to grow, buried drum, emigrated to the West, lost the East, learned stonecutter's trade, worked as model, started drumming again, visited concrete, made money, kept finger, gave finger away, fled laughing, rode up escalator, arrested, convicted, sent to mental hospital, soon to be acquitted, celebrating this day my thirtieth birthday and still afraid of the Black Witch.

I threw away my cigarette. It fell in one of the grooves in the escalator step. After riding upward for some distance at an angle of forty-five degrees, he traveled three more steps on the horizontal; then he let the brazen detective lovers and the detective grandmother push him off the escalator onto a stationary platform. When the gentlemen from the Interpol had introduced themselves and called him Matzerath, he replied, in obedience to his escalator idea, first in German: 'Ich bin Jesus,' then, aware that these were international agents, in French, and finally in English: 'I am Jesus.'

Nevertheless, I was arrested under the name of Oskar Matzerath. Offering no resistance, I put myself under the protection and, since it was raining on the Avenue d'Italie, the umbrellas, of the Interpol men. But I was still afraid. Several times I looked anxiously around and several times, here and there – yes, that is one of her talents – I saw the terribly placid countenance of the Black Witch among the passers-by on the avenue and then in the crowd that gathered round the paddy wagon.

I am running out of words, and still I cannot help wondering what Oskar is going to do after his inevitable discharge from the mental hospital. Marry? Stay single? Emigrate? Model? Buy a stone quarry? Gather disciples? Found a sect?

All the possibilities that are open nowadays to a man of thirty must be examined, but how examine them if not with my drum? And so I will drum out the little ditty which has become more and more real to me, more and more terrifying; I shall call in the Black Witch and consult her, and then tomorrow morning I shall be able to tell Bruno my keeper what mode of existence the thirty-year-old Oskar is planning to carry on in the shadow of a buggaboo which, though getting blacker and blacker, is the same old friend that used to frighten me on the cellar stairs, that said boo in the coal cellar, so I couldn't help laughing, but it was there just the same, talking with fingers, coughing through the keyhole, moaning in the stove, squeaking in tune with the door, smoking up from chimneys when the ships were blowing their foghorns, when a fly buzzed for hours as it died between the double windows, or when eels clamored for Mama and my poor mama for eels, and when the sun sank behind Tower Mountain but lived on as pure sunlit amber. Whom was Herbert after when he assaulted the wooden statue? And behind the high altar – what would Catholicism be without the Witch who blackens every confessional with her shadow? It was her shadow that fell when Sigismund Markus' toys were smashed to bits. The brats in the court of our building, Axel Mischke and Nuchi Eyke, Susi Kater and Hänschen Kollin, they knew: For what did they sing as they cooked their brick-meal soup: 'Where's the Witch, black as pitch? Here's the black wicked Witch. Ha, ha, ha! You're to blame. And you are too, You're most to blame, You! you! you! Where's the Witch, black as pitch? . . .' She had always been there, even in the woodruff fizz powder, bubbling so green and innocent; she was in clothes cupboards, in every clothes cupboard I ever sat in; later on, she borrowed Lucy Rennwand's triangular fox face, ate sausage sandwiches skins and all and sent the Dusters up on the diving tower: Oskar alone remained, he watched the ants, and he knew: it's *her* shadow that has multiplied and is following the sweetness. All words: blessed, sorrowful, full of grace, virgin of virgins . . . and all stones: basalt, tufa, diorite, nests in the shell lime, alabaster so soft . . . and all the shattered glass, glass transparent, glass blown to hair-thinness . . . and all the groceries, all the flour and sugar in blue pound and half-pound bags. Later on four tomcats, one of whom was called Bismarck, the wall that had to be freshly whitewashed, the Poles in the exaltation of death, the special communiqués, who sank what when, potatoes tumbling down from the scales, boxes tapered at the foot end, cemeteries I stood in, flags I knelt on, coconut fibers I lay on . . . the puppies mixed in the concrete, the onion juice that draws tears, the ring on the finger and the cow that licked me . . . Don't ask Oskar who she is! Words fail me. First she was behind me, later she kissed me hump, but now, now and forever, she is in front of me, coming closer.

> Always somewhere behind me, the Black Witch.
> Now ahead of me, too, facing me, Black.
> Black words, black coat, black money.
> But if children sing, they sing no longer:
> Where's the Witch, black as pitch?
> Here's the black, wicked Witch.
> Ha! ha! ha!

Glossary

Bollermann and Wullsutstki: popular characters, symbolizing German and Polish elements, frequent in Danzig jokes or stories.

Burckhardt, Carl Jacob: Swiss diplomat and historian who served as League of Nations High Commissioner of Danzig, 1937–39.

Cold Storage Medal: the colloquial name given to the medal for service in the German army on the arctic front.

Currency Reform: the West German monetary policy established in 1948. The introduction of the Deutsche mark to replace the inflated reichsmark had a highly beneficial psychological effect on German businessmen and is considered the turning point in the postwar reconstruction and economic development of West Germany.

Draussen vor der Tür: a drama by Wolfgang Borchert describing the hopeless situation of the returning prisoner of war after World War II.

Edelweiss Pirates of Cologne: the most notorious of the armed bands of youths which appeared in Germany toward the end of World War II.

Forster, Albert: Gauleiter, or Nazi district leader, of Danzig from 1930. On September 1, 1939, Forster declared the Free Treaty provisions null and void, suspended the constitution, and proclaimed the annexation of Danzig to the German Reich with himself as sole administrator.

Frings, Joseph Cardinal: Cardinal of Cologne, today the official leader of all German Catholics.

Greiser, Arthur: President of the Danzig Senate from 1934 who signed a treaty with the Nazis regularizing Polish-Danzig relations. After World War II he was condemned to death in Poland as a war criminal.

Hartmannsweilerkopf: Vosges Mountain peak fiercely contested by the French and the Germans in World War I.

Hitler Youth Quex and SA-Mann Brand: leading characters in popular books and propaganda films who represent ideal members of the Hitler Youth and the SA and who become martyrs for the Nazi cause. Quex, for example, is murdered by Communists. On his deathbed he converts his father, who is a Communist, to National Socialism.

Jan Wellem: popular name for the elector palatine Johann Wilhelm (1679–1716), whose monument still stands today in Düsseldorf.

July 20th conspirators: a group, led by high-ranking German generals, who made an attempt on Hitler's life in 1944.

Kashubes: a Germanized West Slavic people living in the northwestern part of the earlier province of West Prussia and in northeastern Pomerania. Until 1945, some 150,000 people spoke Kashubian as their mother tongue. The language forms a transitional dialect between Polish and West Pomeranian.

Kasperl: a popular puppet character, similar to Punch.

Käthe-Kruse dolls: individually designed, handmade cloth dolls from the workshop of Käthe Kruse, one-time actress.

Kyffhäuser Bund: a right-wing, monarchist, ex-serviceman's association of a paramilitary nature founded in 1900. Its merger with other servicemen's groups after World War I resulted in a combined membership of over four million.

Matka Boska Częstokowa: an icon representing the Virgin Mother which hangs in a monastery church in Częstokowa and is traditionally believed to have been painted by St. Luke. Its miraculous power is said to be responsible for the lifting of a Swedish siege in the seventeenth century. One of the most famous religious and national shrines in Poland; still visited annually by throngs of pilgrims.

Niemoller, Pastor Martin: a Protestant clergyman and the leading figure in the anti-Nazi Confessional Church who spent seven years in a concentration camp.

Organization Todt: the organization directed by engineer Fritz Todt which conscripted forced labor – often children – for construction work, notably on the fortification of the West Wall in 1938 and the Atlantic Wall in 1940.

Pan Kiehot: Polish for Don Quixote.

pay book: unlike American soldiers, who carry no identification but their dogtags, the German soldiers carried a booklet containing full information as to their vital statistics, military history, and pay.

Poland is not yet lost, etc.: in reference to the Polish national anthem (*Jeszcze Polska Nie Zginęla*).

Rauschning, Hermann: President of the Danzig Senate 1933–34. Rauschning ended his association with Hitler and the National Socialists in 1934 when he became opposed to the policies of the Danzig Gauleiter Forster. He fled from Germany in 1936 and subsequently wrote several books criticizing the Nazi regime

Rentenmark: the temporary currency established in 1923 to stabilize money during the inflationary period in Germany following World War 1.

Sauerbruch, Professor Ferdinand: a famous German surgeon (1875–1951).

Speicherinsel: an island formed by the Mottlau River in the middle of Danzig so called because of its famous half-timbered grain warehouses.

Strength through Joy (Kraft durch Freude): a Nazi organization which provided regimented leisure for members of the German working class. It provided theaters, sports, travel, and vacation opportunities at reduced prices. No organized social or recreational group was allowed to function in Germany except under the control of this official, all-embracing organization.

Sütterlin script: the standard German script developed by Ludwig Sütterlin and taught in schools from 1915 to 1945.

Winter Aid (Winterhilfe): the major Nazi charity set up under the slogan 'War on Hunger and Cold' to which the German people made compulsory contributions.

ZOB: Zydowska Organizacja Bojowa, or Jewish Combat Organization, an underground movement formed in the ghetto in 1942–43.